Praise for David Hai

'Promises to recall epic fantasy's finest'
Tor.com on *Mage's Blood*

'For anyone looking for a new sprawling fantasy epic to stick
their teeth into, *Empress of the Fall* is an ultimately satisfying
journey into a fascinating and chaotic landscape'
ScFiNow on *Empress of the Fall*

'Modern epic fantasy at its best'
Fantasy Book Critic on *Scarlet Tides*

'Hair is adept at building characters as well as worlds,
and his attention to his female players is welcome in
a genre that too often excludes them'
Kirkus

'Adult fantasy lovers who enjoy historical fiction and
intricate political plots will love this book . . . Epic'
Boho Mind on *Empress of the Fall*

'Vivid, dynamic characters and terrific worldbuilding . . . Readers
of epic fantasy should definitely check out this series'
Bibliosanctum on The Moontide Quartet

'Truly epic'
Fantasy Review Barn on The Moontide Quartet

'It has everything a fan could want'
A Bitter Draft

Also by David Hair

THE MOONTIDE QUARTET

Mage's Blood
Scarlet Tides
Unholy War
Ascendant's Rite

THE RETURN OF RAVANA

The Pyre
The Adversaries
The Exile
The King

THE SUNSURGE QUARTET

Empress of the Fall
Prince of the Spear

HEARTS OF ICE

THE SUNSURGE QUARTET BOOK III

DAVID HAIR

Jo Fletcher
BOOKS

First published in Great Britain in 2019
This edition published in 2019 by

Jo Fletcher Books
an imprint of Quercus Editions Ltd
Carmelite House
50 Victoria Embankment
London EC4Y 0DZ

An Hachette UK company

A CIP catalogue record for this book is available
from the British Library

PB ISBN 978 1 78429 091 7
EBOOK ISBN 978 1 78429 092 4

10 9 8 7 6 5 4 3

Typeset by Jouve (UK), Milton Keynes

Printed and bound in Great Britain by Clays Ltd, Elcograf S.p.A.

MIX
Paper from
responsible sources
FSC® C104740

Papers used by Quercus are from well-managed forests and other
responsible sources.

This book is dedicated to all working in mental health. They have the lives of our most vulnerable people in their hands, a burden they bear with sensitivity and selfless care. Thank you.

TABLE OF CONTENTS

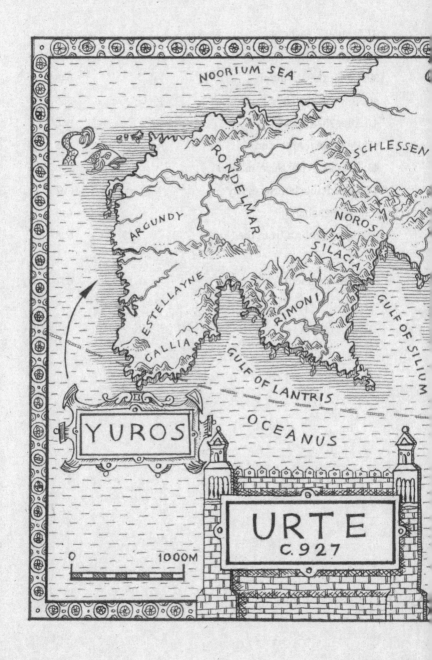

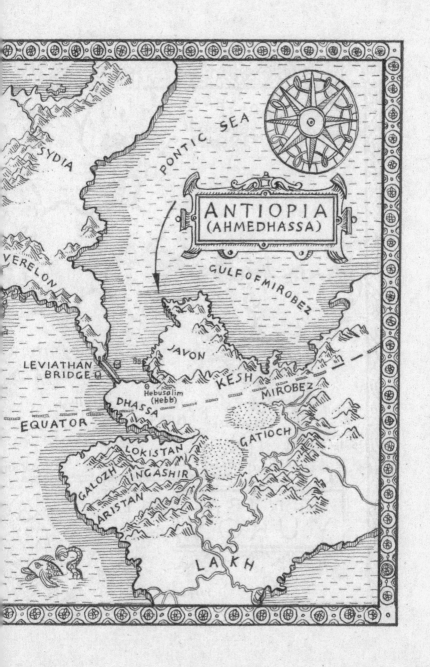

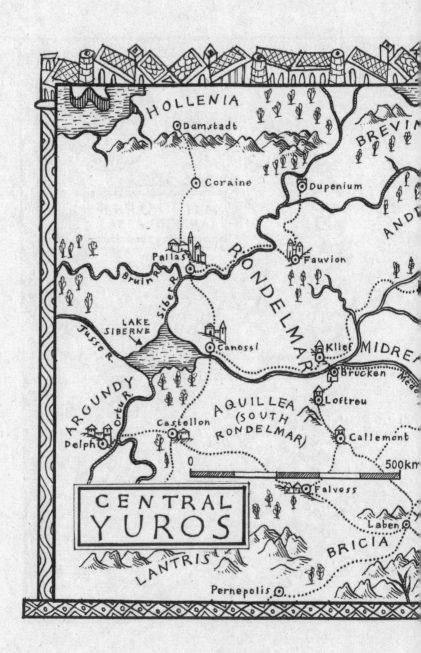

CENTRAL YUROS

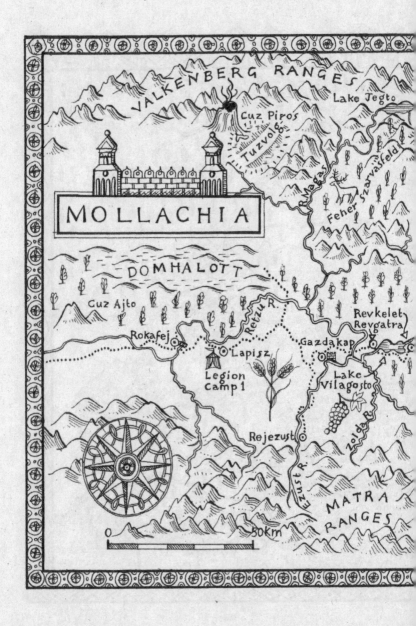

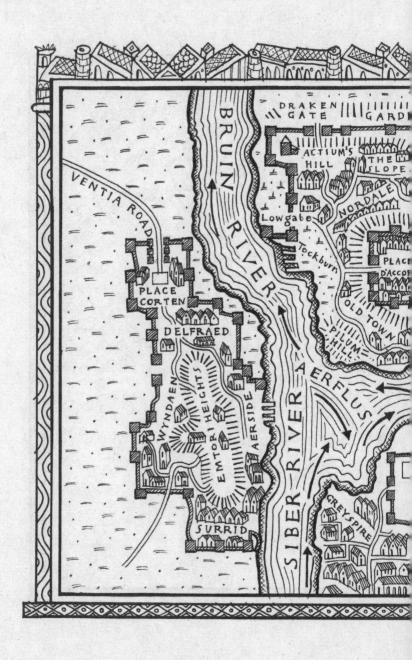

0   1   2km

6 km to Finostairre

NORTH WALL

SERTANUS PARADE

GRAVENHURST

Roidan Heights

OLD WALL

IMPERIAL BASTION

HIGHGRANGE

ESDALE

Roidan Heights

DAWNPORT

CLEAVE

Fisheart

KENSIDE

NORTHBANK

DELTA PIERS

BRUIN RIVER

CELESTIUM

SOUTHSIDE

Fenreach

Sharrod Fens

Lac Corin

PALLAS

WHAT HAS GONE BEFORE

The Events of 930–935
(*as related in* Empress of the Fall)

In Junesse 930, a newly formed mage order, the Merozain Bhaicara, save the Leviathan Bridge and use its gnostic energy to destroy the Imperial Windfleet circling above; the resultant deaths of Emperor Constant and Mater-Imperia Lucia create a power vacuum at the heart of the Rondian Empire.

The Church of Kore reacts quickest: Grand Prelate Dominius Wurther, entrusted with Prince Cordan and Princess Coramore, Constant's children, prepares to form a Regency Council to secure the continuation of the Sacrecour dynasty. But Wurther's confidante, Ostevan Jandreux, tips off his kinswoman, Duchess Radine of Coraine, who sends mage-knights to capture Cordan and Coramore from under the Church's nose – and discover the hitherto unknown Lyra Vereinen, daughter of the late Princess Natia – and a prime claimant for the throne.

With their rivals paralysed by the disasters of the Third Crusade, the Corani persuade Grand Prelate Wurther and Imperial Treasurer Calan Dubrayle to abandon the Sacrecours and join the Corani camp; Wurther's support is conditional on the banishment of Ostevan, in revenge for his betrayal.

Radine and Lyra are greeted by great rejoicing when the duchess marches her soldiers into Pallas, aided by the fairy-tale circumstances of Lyra's rescue and general fear of civil war.

But Lyra, a complex young woman with her own secrets, is no one's compliant tool. Her father is unknown and despite being a pure-blood mage, she's never been trained in the gnosis – when she does awaken to magic, it's not the gnosis, but the heretical arts of dwymancy. Even worse in Radine's eyes, she's fallen in love with her rescuer, Corani knight Ril Endarion, deemed by all a highly unsuitable partner, especially when Radine is insisting she take the formidable Corani hero Solon Takwyth as her husband.

On the eve of the coronation, Lyra blindsides the duchess by marrying Ril in a secret ceremony conducted by Ostevan, who, facing exile, is acting out of spite. After Lyra has been crowned the next day, she declares her marriage before the world, leaving Radine, Takwyth and spymaster Dirklan Setallius no choice but to accept her actions. After striking the new crown-prince, Takwyth goes into voluntary exile.

Despite this shaky start, the Corani are able to face down their rivals and the succession crisis appears to have been resolved. In relief, Pallas and the Rondian Empire settle into dealing with a new world and a new ruler.

Five uneasy years pass, during which the Rondian Empire struggles on. The people are increasingly unhappy as the Treasury has been forced to impose heavy taxes to rebuild Imperial finances. The vassal-states of Argundy, Estellayne and Noros are clamouring for greater autonomy while warlords and mercenaries are warring in the far south. Duchess Radine dies, still embittered by Lyra's betrayal. Lyra has two miscarriages and remains without an heir of her blood, but she and Ril continue to reign in Pallas, with Cordan and Coramore held as hostages.

In Ahmedhassa, Sultan Salim Kabarakhi I of Kesh is trying to rebuild his realm, with the aid of the mighty Eastern mage, Rashid Mubarak. His efforts are undermined by corruption and by the Shihadi faction, who are demanding revenge against the West.

In 935, as new crises develop in the East and West, a secret cabal rises. The members wear Lantric theatre masks, concealing their identities, even from each other, but they answer to Ervyn Naxius, a genius unconstrained by anything resembling morality. He offers the cabal members powers to match the Merozain Bhaicara – use of all sixteen facets of Ascendant-strength gnosis – through a link to an ancient super-daemon called Abraxas; they also have the ability to enslave others using the daemon's ichor. Once Naxius has proved that the daemon does not control the link, the 'Masks' join him, seeking to become rulers of a new era.

In the West, the cabal plots to supplant Empress Lyra with the pliant Prince Cordan. Ostevan, now a Mask, engineers a return to court as Lyra's confessor and begins infecting people with the daemon's ichor, masking the effects behind the seasonal outbreak of the riverreek illness, in readiness for kidnapping the royal children.

The climax of a jousting tournament intended to bolster Ril and Lyra's faltering rule is the joust between Ril and an 'Incognito Knight'. When the unknown victor is revealed to be Solon Takwyth, returned from exile, he begs a boon from Lyra before the adoring crowd: that he be forgiven and permitted to return to Corani service. His manipulative request forces Lyra to accept – just before she learns that Cordan and Coramore have been abducted. Setallius, her spymaster, must find the Sacrecour children before they can be used against her.

Meanwhile in the East, the Masks strike a savage blow: at the height of the Convocation, a religious and political event that shapes future policy, Sultan Salim is assassinated by the Masked Cabal. The only survivor of his household is Latif, his impersonator, who goes into hiding. Rashid Mubarak seizes control, and shifts policy towards war. His sons, brutal Attam and cunning Xoredh, advance his plans for a Shihad; the holy war against the vast and hostile nation of Lakh is intended to unify his new sultanate.

Rashid's nephew, Prince Waqar, is investigating Salim's murder and the related poisoning of his mother Sakita, Rashid's sister, when he meets Tarita Alhani, a Javon spy. They discover hints that Waqar and his sister Jehana may be able to wield a mysterious power – but before the mystery is solved, Rashid sends Waqar south to Lokistan on a secret mission.

In Dhassa, mage-brothers Kyrik and Valdyr Sarkany are reunited. The princes, heirs of the tiny Yurosi kingdom of Mollachia, have been captives in the dehumanising breeding-camps run by the Eastern magi; Kyrik was released into the care of a Godspeaker, an Eastern priest of Ahm, while

Valdyr, who has remained true to Kore, has been a slave-labourer for five years. He has been under a gnosis-suppressing Chain-rune since his capture as a child and has never gained the gnosis. Having secured the brothers' release, Paruq takes them by windship to Yuros, where he is conducting missionary work among a tribe of Sydian nomads. The brothers learn that the Sydians might be distant racial kin to their own people, but they go on alone to Mollachia, where they are captured by tax-farmers, a by-product of Empress Lyra's efforts to fund her reign. Their dead father owed a fortune in taxes and two Rondian legions, one led by siblings Robear and Sacrista Delestre, the other by Governor Ansel Inoxion, are now stripping the country of its wealth. The Sarkany brothers are imprisoned and left to die – but members of the Vitezai Sarkanum, legendary freedom fighters, discover and rescue them, and a resistance movement begins. Kyrik returns to the Sydian steppes to recruit aid, knowing the price will be marriage to Hajya, the fiery Sydian witch. Valdyr distinguishes himself against the Rondian occupiers, but is still unable to gain the gnosis, despite having his Chain-rune removed.

In Pallas, Naxius and his Masks are readying their coup. Ordinary citizens, apparently suffering a virulent outbreak of riverreek but in fact possessed minions of Abraxas, are used as shock troops in coordinated assaults on the Imperial Bastion and Celestium, the Church of Kore's holiest site. The attack is coordinated with a planned unveiling of Prince Cordan as the new emperor and the arrival of a Sacrecour army at the gates.

Meanwhile in the East, the new sultan's careful long-term planning reaches fulfilment: Rashid has assembled a vast Windfleet of ships and now reveals the Shihad's true target – the Rondian Empire. The only thing preventing invasion is the Leviathan Bridge itself – if the Ordo Costruo or the Merozain Bhaicara unleash the powers of the Bridge's towers, as they did against Emperor Constant's fleet in 930, Rashid's fleet would be destroyed.

At this stage, a new variable enters play: the heretical form of magic known as dwymancy has long been believed extinct – but now fate or coincidence has placed four dwymancers in the midst of these world-changing events, although two of them don't yet realise their own power.

In Pallas, the apparently indestructible Masks are on the brink of seizing power in both Bastion and Celestium – until Empress Lyra inadvertently uses dwyma to destroy one of them. In the Celestium, a burst of light from the shrine of Saint Eloy, a dwymancer who supposedly abjured his powers for love of Kore, fells another Mask.

In Mollachia, on a wild night on the sacred Watcher's Peak, Valdyr Sarkany uses the dwyma to freeze a legion of Rondian solders, killing Robear Delestre, just as they're about to defeat Kyrik and his Sydian riders. Only Robear's sister Sacrista, the better soldier of the siblings, survives.

In the East, the dark side of dwyma is revealed when Sakita Mubarak, a member of the Ordo Costruo, is slain, revived by necromancy and enslaved by the Masks, who compel her to use her devastating powers to destroy Midpoint Tower, obliterating herself in the process.

Waqar and Tarita are too late to stop her, but they find mysterious artefacts in the tower, as well as some clues, just as Rashid's windfleet appears on the southern horizon, heading for Yuros. Waqar at last accepts that his beloved and respected uncle is probably working with the masked assassins – and is therefore behind his mother's death.

It is Julsep 935, and for the first time in recorded history, the East is invading the West. The Ordo Costruo and Merozain Bhaicara cannot prevent the invasion – all their energies must go into repairing the Bridge before it's washed away completely. And for the first time in five centuries, dwymancers with unpredictable, devastating powers are walking the lands. What they do may damn East and West to aeons of suffering.

The Events of Autumn (Julsep-Octen) 935
(*as related in* Prince of the Spear)

The Rondian Empire has barely survived the attempts of the Masked Cabal to unseat Empress Lyra Vereinen and Grand-Prelate Dominius Wurther on Reeker Night; now it reels in shock at the tidings of an Eastern invasion.

The Masked Cabal are still at large: Jest, Tear and Angelstar launch another plot to bring Pallas under their power; while the Eastern conspirators known as Ironhelm, Heartface and Beak prepare for the next phase of their campaign to take control of the Shihad.

Crown Prince Ril Endarion is appointed to command the Imperial Army, a role he is grateful to take, not just to help safeguard the realm, but also to escape the breakdown of his marriage. A fateful kiss on Reeker Night with lifelong friend Basia de Sirou has burgeoned into an adulterous affair. Leaving his tangled personal life behind, he throws himself into the impossible task of knitting five rival groups into one Imperial Army, but as the Rondian soldiers trek south, they are increasingly divided and uncoordinated. Engaging in aerial reconnaissance of the Shihad advance, Ril comes into contact with a new form of enemy: Keshi magi riding rocs: giant eagles constructed by animagi. The roc-riders are led by Prince Waqar Mubarak, who has been given responsibility for protecting the skies above the Eastern advance.

In Pallas the heavily pregnant Lyra researches the dwyma, the heretical magic that saved her on Reeker Night. She's helped by Dirklan Setallius, Solon Takwyth and Basia de Sirou, but her progress is hampered by her blind spot: her affection for Ostevan Jandreux, her confessor and closest confidante – who is also Jest. Using drugs and religion, he manipulates her, seeking to escape his daemonic thraldom to Ervyn Naxius and the daemon Abraxas.

The beautiful Medelie Aventour lures Solon Takwyth into the latest conspiracy to unseat Lyra – then Medelie reveals herself to be Radine Jandreux, the late Duchess of Coraine, who is not as dead as everyone believed. Her youth has been restored and now Radine/Medelie is bent upon Lyra's fall; she and her conspirators believe they can succeed where Reeker Night failed.

Popular movements are also growing outside the court, including support for an ancient democratic system called suffragium, propounded by a radical named Ari Frankel. The Rondian Empire has already lost control of southern Yuros to the mysterious 'Lord of Rym'.

Ostevan almost succeeds in his attempt to seduce Lyra, playing on her insecurities over Ril's relationship with Basia, but his perfidy is exposed and in her fury Lyra unleashes the dwyma. Ostevan barely escapes; Naxius considers killing him, but instead accelerates his plans to seize both Bastion and Celestium. Initiating mystical contact with Lyra, he lures her to the Shrine of Saint Eloy, where he intends to capture her.

In Mollachia, Valdyr Sarkany is coming to terms with having slain so many using the dwyma, a power he barely understands. He is disturbed by the attitude of the Mollach people to their new Sydian allies, but it's more important he returns to Watcher's Peak to learn about his new power. Along the way he rescues an injured wolf, naming it Gricoama. Unknown to Valdyr, the man who tortured him in the breeding-houses, Asiv Fariddan ('Beak' of the Masked Cabal), has arrived to seek the source of dwyma-energy his master Naxius sensed. Asiv infects Governor Inoxion with daemon ichor as part of his plan to trap Valdyr, but the governor is slain by Sacrista when he attacks and infects her. Weakened, Sacrista is captured and interred alive by Dragan, head of the Vitezai Sarkanum, in a barbaric Mollach ritual called the Witch's Grave.

Meanwhile, Valdyr's brother Kyrik has brought the rest of Clan Vlpa into Mollachia, together with a group of Schlessen and Mantauri, minotaur-like constructs, led by Fridryk 'Kip' Kippenegger, a former Legion mage. Kyrik learns he is sterile; his inability to provide heirs with Hajya to the Mollach throne would destroy the vital alliance, so he keeps this secret.

Waqar is desperate to find his sister Jehana, but the invasion means he is forced to leave the hunt to Tarita Alhani, the Merozain mage from Javon, not knowing that Alyssa Dulayne, his uncle's former mistress – now Heartface of the Masked Cabal – is also seeking her. The trail leads to Sunset Tower, one of the five towers of the damaged Leviathan Bridge. Alyssa lays siege, but Tarita manages to get inside and finds Jehana.

Meanwhile the Shihad is advancing across southeastern Yuros, capturing cities in the sparsely populated region of Verelon. Sydian tribes are flocking to Rashid's banner. Latif, the assassinated sultan's impersonator, is part of an elephant unit enduring the horrors of war.

As autumn advances towards winter, matters come to a head. Ari Frankel finds men willing to advance the cause of suffragium, and in doing so, break up the empire, but before this relationship bears fruit, he is captured by the Inquisition, to be shipped north to stand trial.

At Sunset Tower, a traitor lets Alyssa in – but Jehana escapes, thanks to the heroism of Tarita and an intelligent construct known as Ogre, who was created by Naxius.

In Mollachia, Asiv Fariddan has infected Dragan with daemon ichor and turned the whole of the Vitezai Sarkanum to his will. He fatally wounds the guardian spirit of Watcher's Peak, the White Stag, trapping Valdyr on the mountain, and unleashes a horde of Reekers at Kyrik's coronation. Hajya is captured or killed, and Kyrik barely escapes.

In Pallas, the Masked Cabal strike again. Tear (Medelie) moves against the Bastion, and while Lyra is visiting the shrine of Saint Eloy in the Holy City, Jest (Ostevan) and Angelstar (the Inquisitor commander Dravis Ryburn) seize the Celestium. But Solon Takwyth has in fact turned spy, not traitor, and with Dirklan Setallius, kills Medelie/Tear. However, one conspirator escapes with Cordan and Coramore, which removes the only safeguard preventing Garod Sacrecour from rebelling. In the Celestium, Lyra and Wurther escape Naxius and the Masks, but the Winter Tree is destroyed, endangering the entire dwyma. Lyra goes into a labour, but despite Naxius' attack, safely delivers Rildan: her son and heir.

At Collistein Junction, the Imperial Army finally meets the Shihad in open battle, but they are badly outnumbered and disjointed. Waqar's windfleet and roc-riders win the air battle – and Ril is slain by Waqar in a desperate mid-air duel. It is thanks only to Brician general Seth Korion, a hero of the Third Crusade, that a rout is prevented.

It is now Noveleve 935 and winter is almost upon Yuros. Valdyr is on Watcher's Peak, fearing for Kyrik's life and dreading the return of Asiv. Jehana, Tarita and Ogre are in the ocean, seeking to escape Alyssa Dulayne. Rashid celebrates victory, but if his army doesn't find shelter before midwinter, a million men may freeze to death. And the widowed Lyra's only consolation in defeat is that her enemies are finally unmasked and staring at her from across the Bruin River in an Imperial city that is now the front line of a new civil war.

PROLOGUE

The Masquerade (Angelstar)

After Impact

Before two things collide, there is an orderly symmetry: the trajectory of the project-ile and the lines of the wall. The ranks of battle are laid out just as the generals command. The two jousters arc towards each other, lances set. All plans remain intact, all variables are calculable – but after impact comes chaos. No one can know exactly how the collision will play out, which units will hold and which fold, whether the lances will break and where the splinters will fly, but it's those details that decide everything.

JERVYS TAREWYND, MAGE-SCHOLAR, KLIEF 832

The Rymfort, Pallas, Rondelmar, Yuros
Noveleve 935

Dravis Ryburn, Knight-Princeps of the Holy Inquisition, strode along a vaulted corridor in the west wing of the Celestium, the massive domed edifice in Pallas-Sud, when he heard a shout, the crash of something falling and the clang of steel on steel. He paused, raising a hand.

The cohort of Inquisitorial Guard behind him halted and his body-guard, sleek and elegant Lef Yarle, looked at him enquiringly.

'It'll just be a skirmish,' Yarle said. 'The Pontifex's men are going room by room.'

'I would investigate.'

Yarle obeyed instantly, gesturing to the lead men.

They had the door open in seconds and with swords at the ready, stepped through – and then, hesitating, the serjant said, 'My Lord, I don't think–'

'We know that,' Yarle drawled. He entered, then sent a mental report into Ryburn's mind: <*It's safe enough.*>

Ryburn told the rest of the cohort to stay outside and walked into what turned out to be a records room. The shelving had been toppled, chairs and desks overturned and documents were strewn everywhere. Two headless corpses lay amidst the chaos, black blood flowing from neck-stumps and soaking into the paper; their heads were lying several feet away, the expressions of rage slackening. Both had been priests.

Three more black-eyed clergy were on the far side of the room, spinning to view the intruders. They snarled, dark drool running down their chins, but as they saw Ryburn, that sound became a subservient whimper.

Beyond them, barricaded into the corner by a toppled desk, a soldier of the Kirkegarde was at bay, black ichor on his blade and his expression horrified, counter-balanced by a fierce will to live. He'd done well to take down two of his assailants already: clearly a young man of promise.

'My Lord!' he cried, as he recognised Ryburn, 'Please, help us—'

Us? Then Ryburn caught sight of a flash of a nun's cowl and a glimpse of pale skin, cowering behind the makeshift barrier. Two frightened, pleading eyes peered out at him.

Ryburn signalled and Lef Yarle blurred into action: three sweeping blows, delivered with a dancer's grace and a blacksmith's power, and the remaining priests collapsed, their heads thudding wetly as they rolled against the desk.

The young nun gave a sobbing cry while her protector stared in awe. He lowered his blade and made the Sign of Corineus, fist to heart. 'My Lord,' he gasped, 'my life is yours.'

So it is.

'What's your name, soldier?' Ryburn asked, while Yarle pulled the barricade apart with kinesis so the pair could emerge.

'Tees Velan,' the young man replied, 'Fourth Century, Second Maniple of Kirkegarde IX.' He fell to one knee, pulling the woman down as well. 'My Lord,' he asked, bewilderment overcoming his fear, 'what's happening?'

What indeed!

'A cabal, led by Ostevan Jandreux, the queen's former confessor, has

2

seized power here in the Celestium. Grand Prelate Wurther has fled and Ostevan has taken the title "Pontifex", which signifies his desire to rule both sacred and secular empires. He's been aided by these Reekers.'

'They're everywhere,' Velan panted. 'I managed to rescue Sister Briolla, but we were discovered – everyone here has the Reeker disease, my Lord – they're like animals.'

'They're worse than animals,' Ryburn replied, gesturing for the young man and the terrified young nun to rise. 'Animals don't kill for pleasure, or likewise spread disease. These are highly infectious rabid beasts, Velan, possessed by a daemon. Any they bite will be similarly afflicted.'

The young nun – she was pretty enough, if one's tastes ran that way – gave a shocked wail, and Ryburn's eyes went to her rent sleeve. Blood was soaking into the pale blue cloth.

'Please, you're a mage,' she gabbled, 'please, heal me, Milord—'

Ryburn glanced at Yarle, who always knew precisely what he wanted, then locked his gaze on Velan, engaging mesmeric-gnosis to ensure the soldier couldn't look away. As he did, he allowed the black ichor in his veins to flow into his eyes.

'No . . .' the Kirkegarde man whimpered in despair.

'But yes,' Knight-Princeps Ryburn drawled maliciously.

Yarle gripped the nun's coif and tore it open, baring her throat as his teeth lengthened. He bit the girl, pumping ichor into her, while Ryburn kept Velan's eyes locked on his own.

'This thing you fear? It is not to be feared,' Ryburn told the young man. 'It is simply a communion of minds, united in purpose. It is a Church, a haven, a cause.' He licked his lips. 'Give me your wrist, Velan.'

'No, I cannot,' Velan choked out. He strained to move, to fight or flee, but mesmerism and kinesis held him bound. Beside him, Sister Briolla, clutching her torn throat, collapsed to the paper-strewn floor, choking on blood that was already turning black. Ryburn could hear Abraxas crowing as the daemon latched onto her mind, rending and conquering.

Yarle wiped her ruby blood from his mouth, purring.

'Did you know, I began my career as a torturer?' Ryburn remarked. 'Newly made a mage, commanded to inflict pain, to disfigure and disable, sometimes to extract a confession, other times simply to punish. Many found it hard, but I excelled, for I reconciled my conscience with my belief that nothing we do in this life matters – one is either destined for Paradise with Kore . . . or eternity in the pits of the Lord of Hel. I merely hastened the work of Destiny.'

'M . . . Mercy,' Velan stammered, staring at Briolla, convulsing on the floor.

'But of course,' Ryburn went on, ignoring the plea, 'eventually I concluded that this Church is a huge lie. There is no Kore. Corineus wasn't His son, just a dangerous lunatic. The Church is built on the sand of lies and all that awaits us when we die is eternity with the daemons.'

'No,' Velan whimpered, tears welling in his eyes. 'Kore be my hope,' he began, the opening words of the evening prayer, pausing as Briolla made a strangled sound and started gouging her own face as she struggled with some unseen terror.

'So the only hope one truly has is that when we die, we become a daemon ourselves,' Ryburn went on. 'That is the gift my Master, the man who opened my eyes, gave me.'

Master Naxius, in whose care my soul resides . . .

'But enough of that,' he concluded. 'Time is passing.' He gestured to Yarle, who gripped Velan and with an almost tender sigh, in stark contrast to the brutal way he'd taken the nun, bit the soldier, looking at Ryburn with the hint of a tease as he stroked the young man's cheek.

Women were soft, flabby dairy-cows, good for nothing but drudgery, but a man could be whatever you wished, hard or soft, giver or taker. It was a total mystery to Ryburn why most men failed to realise this. Something about the breeding instinct, he assumed – but who truly wanted a child anyway?

As Velan fell to floor beside the nun, his eyes beginning to bulge, Ryburn pulled Yarle to him, black hair against blond, coarse ruggedness against almost preternatural pallor and beauty, and kissed him hungrily.

'There's something about the biting that always makes me hard,' Yarle breathed.

Ryburn squeezed his forearm. 'Unfortunately, the Master awaits us now. But we have tonight – and the rest of eternity.'

They left the nun and the soldier to thrash their way through death into rebirth as Reeker slaves. By now there were few free humans left in either the Rymfort or the Celestium, but they had kept the attack carefully contained and the outside world remained oblivious, unaware that the Holy City had fallen.

But the bitch empress escaped, and so did Wurther . . .

'Come,' he said. 'Our new Pontifex awaits.'

They found Ostevan Jandreux in another overly ornate room in the next wing, his effete features aglow with satisfaction, his shoulder-length brown hair and goatee newly combed and oiled, a stark contrast to the bent, dithering man beside him. The Knight-Princeps wasn't fooled: Mazarin Beleskey, with his shock of pale hair all over the place might look foolish, but he was a genius, not just in the arts of arcane gnosis, but also in the physiology of murder.

I'd not trust him at my back, though: he might be Ostevan's bloodman now, but he's just betrayed his former master, and he was Wurther's for years.

Ryburn and Yarle left their cohort outside with the Pontifex's own Reeker-bound cohort and silently took their places at the round table. Ostevan, ignoring the elevated throne, took the seat to its right as the air above the throne started shimmering. A dark-robed figure appeared: an aetheric projection composed of light and the gnosis. 'Good afternoon, Brethren,' said Ervyn Naxius, his voice unusually strained as he flicked back his cowl to reveal a pale, wizened face with heavy circles beneath the eyes.

Ryburn was interested to see Naxius appearing in his true form, rather than the more youthful visage he often wore: altering one's appearance, even in an aetheric projection, was taxing, and the Master had disappeared during the attack on the Celestium.

Perhaps he's been wounded?

'Greetings, Master,' the four men started, but Naxius cut them off with an irritable gesture.

'Report,' he rasped, his breath laboured.

Ostevan got in first. 'The Celestium is ours – we've infected most of the surviving clergy – we've made them "Shepherds" so they'll have greater control of their bloodlust. The empress and her inner circle know what's happened, but most of Pallas remains unaware.'

'How has the empress reacted?' Naxius asked.

'She paraded Wurther through the Place d'Accord and he told the masses that the Celestium is in the grip of a Reeker infection and that I have usurped him. They've closed the river ferries and seek to isolate us, but with the army down south, her resources are limited.'

'And her state of mind?'

'In public, she is stoic and stalwart. By displaying her son, she's earned the commoners' sympathy – but she's just given birth, she's in widow's black, her husband just killed, and she is clearly vulnerable. The empire will begin to fragment.'

Naxius frowned. 'That would be unfortunate. I wish to seize one empire, not a dozen kingdoms. Pull the dukes into your sway.' He turned to Ryburn. 'Knight-Princeps, you command the Kirkegarde and the Inquisition: how many men have you?'

'I command ten thousand men in two legions; and twelve Inquisitorial Fists, being one hundred and forty-four mage-knights, but most are in the south, so the empress has more men than us. Sister Tear was supposed to deliver us the Bastion.' *And you were supposed to capture the empress*, he didn't add.

'Sister Tear failed us,' Naxius acknowledged. 'But the royal children's capture frees Garod Sacrecour to act. He'll march to your aid long before the empress can rally support.'

'What news from the south?' Ryburn asked.

Naxius gave a tight smile. 'Have you heard the rumours of defeat? They're true: the same day you captured the Celestium, the Imperial Army was defeated by the Shihad at Collistein Junction.'

The Master looked pleased, but Ryburn was troubled. After all, the Rondian Empire was the bulwark of the Church of Kore: it was supposed to be invincible. Naxius had Masks among the Shihad; Ryburn had believed the Eastern invasion was just a distraction, a means of dividing the empress' resources to enable their coup. But this news raised an uncomfortable question.

Who does Naxius wish to be victorious? Surely not these Eastern scum?

'The Rondian armies are falling back to Jastenberg,' Naxius went on. 'Prince-Consort Ril Endarion is dead and the survivors are splintering.

Duke Garod's forces never saw combat; they are already retreating north.'

'So who opposes the Shihad?' Ryburn asked.

'Those survivors who have not yet run, and the Argundians, who were late to the battle.' Naxius sniffed. 'I care not. What concerns me is that we have uncovered a secret nest of dwymancers. I require the capture, alive and unharmed, of one with the potential awakened but not fulfilled; such a person can be enslaved. Not Lyra Vereinen, though: she's bonded too deeply with her dwymancy. I need her dead.'

'As you command,' Ryburn said emphatically.

'The dwyma is a heresy,' Ostevan said. 'We can use that to ostracise Empress Lyra and break down her authority. She can become the author of her own demise if we're patient–'

'No,' Naxius snapped, 'I want her dead *now*! *I want her gone!*' His sudden flash of rage silenced the room.

The Master claimed her as his own, but she eluded him, Ryburn mused. *She really is a threat – but Ostevan still lusts for her. His time as her confessor has addled his judgement.*

When Ryburn joined the Master's cabal, three years ago, accepting the mask of Angelstar, the force of divine retribution, he'd quickly realised that his fellow conspirators were shifty and dangerous. Only he was truly loyal.

Tear and Twoface are dead. Here in the West, there's only Ostevan and me left. But when this is done, only I will remain, seated at the Master's right hand. And Lef will sit at mine.

'I'll destroy her myself,' Ryburn vowed.

'Do so, and you will have my favour.' Naxius' voice was filled with venom. 'Hold the Celestium until the Sacrecour army comes, then unleash war across the river. Any further questions?'

There was a brief silence, then Maz Beleskey asked, in his tortuous, exasperatingly roundabout way, 'Master I would ask, which is to say, I wish . . . no, I would even say, *need* . . . to know if these ranks – by which I mean this circle . . . will we be replenished? Will we be reinforced, renewed?'

He wants a Mask, Ryburn realised.

'That process is already underway,' Naxius replied, which was clearly news to them all.

Ostevan flinched, while Ryburn couldn't stop himself glancing at his lover. Lef already had a daemon-beast beside his heart, implanted from Ryburn's own chest.

Lef deserves to be elevated ahead of all others. He's one of us in all but name.

'Some may be permitted to join us when their prowess and loyalty are fully proven,' Naxius said, already fading from sight as he spoke. 'You have your instructions. Whomsoever brings Lyra Vereinen down will have my favour.'

When he was gone, Ryburn found himself staring at Ostevan and wondering what having the Master's favour might mean, for himself . . . and for his rivals.

1

Divided City

The Age of the Gods

To the ancients of Lantris, the age preceding theirs, the Age of the Gods, was when divinities walked Urte. They looked upon it as an ideal time, but truly, if real, it would have been nightmarish. Imagine immortal, all-powerful tyrants destroying cities, razing mountains and drying the seas on a whim; raping, thieving and murdering where they would, all the while expecting to be worshipped. Better such gods never existed. Though of course, we of Rondelmar have the magi to fill their sandals . . .

THE BLACK HISTORIES, ANONYMOUS, 776

Pallas, Rondelmar
Noveleve 935

Panic could strike at any moment: a paralysing terror that threatened to drive Empress Lyra Vereinen to her knees. When she was surrounded by others – in the midst of court, with her backbone locked rigid – she masked it stoically. Her counsellors gave her brave speeches to recite, and somehow she got through them.

But when she was alone, that dread, that the entire world was coming apart, would rip out her spine. The pillars she clung to – her infant son, and the few colleagues who had held true in these darkest days – were so fragile she feared they'd be swept away at any moment.

This morning, four days after the terrible events in the Celestium, she woke shaking from nightmares of being throttled by men in Lantric masks. Now she cradled her son with desperate adoration: her tiny Prince Rildan, heir to the thrones of Rondelmar and the Rondian

Empire. His hungry mouth latched onto her left nipple, taking sustenance, giving back need.

All I now do is for you, little one.

From the moment she'd realised she was pregnant, everything else, from ruling a fractious empire to learning the secret power of the dwyma, had been subordinated to bringing Rildan safely into the world. Now her focus must be his protection, and it would not be easy. From her bed she could see through the open curtains right across the river to the dome of the Celestium. After so long wondering who and where her enemies were, she now knew exactly: they were on her front doorstep. Proclamations declaring Grand Prelate Wurther a criminal and heretic had gone out, signed by both Ostevan Pontifex and Dravis Ryburn, Knight-Princeps of the Inquisition: her bitterest foes.

She couldn't touch them. The bulk of her armies were in the south and she still didn't know how many had survived the battle at Collistein Junction. Her paltry forces here might just outnumber those of Ostevan and Ryburn, but an assault across the mighty Bruin was impossible; there simply weren't bridges or boats enough to land men in sufficient force.

Silently, she named her foes: *The Masked Cabal: Ostevan, the new Pontifex, my former confessor – and Jest of the Masked Cabal. Knight-Princeps Dravis Ryburn, who was openly wearing the mask of Angelstar. Ervyn Naxius, the Puppeteer who controls them all.*

Duke Garod Sacrecour, reunited with his young kin, Cordan and Coramore, in whose name he has declared war. Everyone who hates me is rallying to his banner.

Edetta Keeper and all her fellow Keepers who have deserted me.

Sultan Rashid Mubarak, who defeated our army and killed my husband.

Tears were stinging her cheeks. Angrily, she blinked them away. *I can't afford weakness: I must be strong!*

So many people relied on her: all the Corani who'd come south when she'd ascended to the throne; those people who'd embraced her rule would be punished when the Sacrecours swept back into power. And all the Rondians spread far and wide across Yuros would suffer if the empire disintegrated into chaos. It would be a bloodbath, if she failed them.

She also knew many more would cheer if she fell, and laugh as she was dragged to the gallows. It had been almost six years since the Third Crusade had ended in chaos and left the Rondian Empire destitute and she knew many blamed her for their suffering, even though it had been the Sacrecours who'd plunged Yuros into that ruinous failed Crusade.

Rildan, oblivious to her misery, gave a contented gurgle. He gazed at her with wide-open gem-like eyes, milk dribbling down his chin, while Lyra stroked his face and marvelled at him. *I'll protect you, little one. No one will hurt you, ever.* She lost herself in the smooth, silky skin, the minute details of nails and wispy black hair, those extraordinary eyes . . .

. . . and then he was screwing up his face and grizzling and reality came crashing back in. Domara, the royal midwife, arrived at the bedroom door, holding out her hands imperiously. For a moment Lyra felt an irrational dread at parting from her child, but the day was calling and she must gird herself for another round of pretending to be brave in the face of disaster. So she surrendered Rildan.

Domara vanished with her prize and Lyra was left with her bodyguard.

Basia de Sirou was gazing out of the window, her hand resting on her well-worn sword-hilt. Those who didn't know her well might easily mistake her for a young man, with her lean frame clad in leathers and her auburn hair kept boyishly short. Her artificial lower legs were concealed by her leggings, and by her practised grace.

Lyra wondered how Basia was coping. *She was sleeping with my husband: she must be at least as distraught as I am. She deserves rest, but I need her. And I trust her; she's saved my life more than once. I even like her. But I have no idea how to comfort her.*

Hours before the Masks' attack, Lyra and Basia had forged a détente: the cuckolded wife and her rival reaching a private arrangement, for the sake of happiness. But Ril had been slain in battle before he ever knew that, and now awkward questions needed to be asked.

Buttoning up her gown, Lyra asked, 'Basia, what do you wish to do now?'

Basia didn't look at her. Her voice, normally cultured and knowing, cracked uncharacteristically. 'I don't know. Part of me wants to go south, as I should have before.'

She didn't need to remind Lyra that it was she who had forbidden Basia from joining Ril.

'But Ril's friends among the Corani knights all died,' she went on. 'Every damned one of them – the Joyce brothers, the Falquists, Jos, Malthus . . . everyone I grew up with. Now Lord Sulpeter's sycophants are running the show and they'd just tell me to rukk off.'

'Wherever you want to go–'

'I never said I wanted to go anywhere,' Basia snapped.

Silence fell between them again and stretched out until Basia's eyes went round and she clutched her heart. 'Oh, my God . . .' she choked, staring out of the window.

Alarmed, Lyra dragged herself from the bed and hobbled to join her. 'What is it?'

Sobbing, Basia just pointed, and as Lyra followed her gaze, the whinny of a horse carried on the breeze and a grey-white shape glided past her window and dipped into the garden below.

Then she realised what it was: Ril's pegasus.

'Dear Kore,' she breathed. 'Pearl's flown all the way home from the battle!'

Finally, they looked at each other, exchanging a fraught look, their eyes running over with tears, and took the balcony stairs into the Queen's Garden. They could hear Pearl snorting somewhere ahead as they passed through the Rose Bower and found the pegasus drinking heavily from the pool. Her coat was plastered with sweat and there was a massive patch of dried blood staining the saddle and her haunches. The scabbard and lance-holder were both empty.

Lyra, clutching at Basia's hand, heard herself make a whimpering sound.

Pearl raised her head in warning, snorting and pawing the ground – then she recognised them and went still. They approached carefully, then Lyra found herself grabbing at the saddle and sobbing into the bloodstained leather, while Basia cradled Pearl's head, moaning in pain.

'You're home,' Basia whispered at last, to the pegasus. 'You're home now, Pooty-girl.'

Pearl nickered softly, nuzzling the mage, as Lyra joined Basia at

Pearl's head. Stroking her soft nose, she murmured, 'She's yours, if you want her.'

Basia hesitated, then said, 'No, she came here, to your garden. She belongs to you.' She stroked the bloody mane and added, 'I have a flying beast of my own.'

'We'll see if she decides to stay.' Lyra heard the tramp of boots and saw the Volsai master, Dirklan Setallius, appear with a squad of Imperial Guard. 'It's all right, Dirklan,' she called, 'It's Pearl. She's come home.'

Dirklan dismissed the men with a wave of his gloved left hand. The old man was a forbidding figure, tall and thin, his long silver hair curtaining his patched left eye and scarred cheek, but Lyra had always found him a comfort.

'Do you wish her stabled, Majesty?' he asked.

Lyra and Basia shared a glance, then Lyra said, 'No, she can stay here. The grass is thick.'

'She'll eat the roses,' Dirklan warned, brandishing some papers. 'I have today's despatches.'

'One moment.' Lyra turned back to Basia and said softly, 'Anything you wish for, anything at all, it's yours.'

Basia wiped at her face awkwardly, then said, 'The only thing left of the man I loved is his child – your child. I want to stay here and help keep him safe. That's all that matters.'

Lyra's arms acted ahead of thought, reaching out and wrapping themselves around Basia's skinny shoulders, and Basia slowly returned the embrace. Finally, the Volsai woman pulled away and said in a thick voice, 'I'll wash Pearl down. She's a mess.'

It's Ril's blood . . .

'Let's do it together,' Lyra said.

They worked in silence, both weeping, unbuckling the saddle before scrubbing her down using water from the pool, the pure dwyma-blessed water that had cured daemonic possession. Lyra was conscious that Aradea, the genilocus of this magic place, was watching them through the eyes of the lizards and birds. Dirklan sat and waited for them, recognising this was necessary for both his queen and his protégé.

To Lyra, it felt like an omen. Her husband's beloved steed had returned – to her. Ril was still with them in spirit, watching over their child. It gave her strength to go on.

When they were done they hugged again, and though neither spoke, Lyra sensed that they'd created a deeper bond. 'We both loved him,' she whispered, for though her own love for Ril had withered over the past months, once he'd been her all. 'Thank you for staying. I do need you.'

Basia nodded mutely, then backed away and fled. Lyra watched her go, tears running down her own cheeks, wishing she could crawl away and hide. But Dirklan was waiting – the world was waiting.

She left Pearl to wander the cold, autumnal garden, and took a moment to touch the energy of the dwyma, a coil of light inside her chest that joined her to all creation. The web of light held – in the tumult of the attack on the Celestium, the ancient Winter Tree, planted by Saint Eloy to be the nexus of the dwyma, had been burned down – but she'd long been using this garden as the heart of her own dwymancy, and the dwyma itself had endured, the loss of even the Winter Tree absorbed.

Feeling comforted by Pearl's return, she sat beside Dirklan on the bench, clad only in her filthy, bloodstained nightgown and robes, and steeled herself to hear his news.

'Would you rather not change also, Majesty?' Dirklan asked in his dispassionate voice.

Lyra shook her head. 'What better garb for hearing the latest disasters?'

He flinched, but said, 'Oh, it's not all so bad, Lyra. The army was beaten, but not annihilated, and the generals are pulling it back together. And I spoke to Veritia, my agent with the army, this morning: she's bringing Ril's body home. You'll want a state funeral, I presume?'

'No,' Lyra replied, 'no state funeral. I'll not set my grief higher than anyone else's. I want a small funeral, no ostentation, no parades, nothing public.'

Dirklan frowned. 'As you wish.'

'I did love him,' she whispered, 'but we lost our way.' She put a hand over her belly, a protective gesture that had become habitual during her pregnancy. Now, instead of a hard lump, she found only a disorienting squishiness. The plump-faced woman with dark circles under her eyes who stared back at her from the mirror upstairs didn't look like her either.

Looking concerned, he asked, 'How are you bearing up?'

'In truth, I'm exhausted. Rildan wakes every few hours for feeding, there's an endless queue of courtiers wanting to pay respects and the council business just never ends, does it? Calan Dubrayle is constantly petitioning me over Treasury and Imperocracy measures, Dominius Wurther's complaining endlessly about Ostevan . . .'

'And your spymaster keeps taking up your time,' Dirklan concluded for her.

'And him,' she agreed, smiling tiredly. 'But he, at least, is never an imposition.'

'That's a relief. None of us wish to distress you, Majesty.' He glanced up at her balcony. 'There's no need for you to feed Rildan. Wet-nurses aren't hard to find – and most noblewomen don't feed their children at all.'

'I'm not having Rildan fed by another,' Lyra said firmly. 'He's my son and he'll drink his mother's milk. He's made from my body, so it'll be better for him.'

'That's one view,' Dirklan said, 'but the mage-healers are adamant that one woman's milk is the same as another's.'

'No, and that's final. I've told Domara this and I won't discuss it further.'

Dirklan smiled approvingly. 'Well, I've always held it to be the best thing too. How are you feeling in yourself? You said you gained something of the gnosis when you were in the Shrine of Saint Eloy?'

'It's gone again,' Lyra replied, 'or at least, I can't sense it, not the way I can the dwyma. You said sometimes that's all a pregnancy manifestation amounts to? I fear that's it for me. And as for the rest of me . . .' She winced. 'The healers never stop poking and prodding me. They tell me they've managed to seal the tears but they still hurt – the scabbing itches like mad. My stomach looks like a deflated pig's bladder, I have stretchmarks and I feel bloated and ugly. You're lucky you're not a woman, Dirklan. Nature has given us the worst of the transaction.'

'And yet you most commonly outlive us,' he replied.

'You must fight in wars,' Lyra replied. 'I suppose the birthing bed is our battlefield.' She glanced towards the door. 'What am I to do? A year of mourning is traditional, but the world will see a widow and therefore deem House Corani weak. They will expect me to at least become engaged.'

'Is that what you want?'

'No – Kore's Blood, Dirklan! I've just lost my husband. It might not have been love at the end, but it was at the start and I always esteemed Ril. I need time to grieve and heal.'

He sighed and admitted, 'I doubt you'll get it, Majesty. Your reign is precarious right now. Garod has declared war and most of our men are in the south. Everyone sees our weakness and they'll push us hard. Empires don't just fade away, Lyra, they collapse in blood and destruction. There are *centuries* of grievances out there, from Hollenia to Rym, Argundy to Noros. If they think we're dying, they'll try to bury us. It's not an exaggeration to say that millions will perish and no man or woman alive will be unscathed.'

' "The Empress of the Fall" – that's what people used to sing when I came to the throne,' Lyra remembered. ' "The Empress of the Fall, she won't last at all".'

'Give them a scent of blood and she won't,' Dirklan replied. 'It pains me to say it, but you're right: we need allies and that means a remarriage – to a strong man with many legions. A prince of Argundy or from the southern duchies, someone to counter Garod.'

'Yes, I know. Truly, the people liked Ril, but they never feared him. It's Solon Takwyth they always wanted.' She bit her lip. 'So should I just engage myself to Solon and have done with it?'

The fact she'd rejected Solon for Ril five years ago was a poisonous irony.

Dirklan considered, then shook his head. 'Solon has shown his loyalty – you can count on him already. And he doesn't bring us extra men. We need a fresh alliance with soldiers backing it. Garod Sacrecour's got at least eight legions sitting in Dupenium and Fauvion, which roughly matches our own manpower.'

'So will he march?' Lyra asked anxiously.

'Eventually, yes: Garod did send the bulk of his men south with Sir

Brylion Fasterius to fight the Shihad, but they never actually joined battle; I have no doubt he's ordered them home. He'll be readying for war, but he won't march until his men return.'

'So we have what? A month? Six weeks?'

'At best. It's almost winter; troop movement will soon become extremely difficult in the north. In terms of an alliance, only Argundy, Canossi or Aquillea could feasibly get soldiers onto riverboats and reach Pallas in time to make a difference. But the truth is, they won't help us now. If we're still standing in spring, they'll aid us then.'

'Then we're doomed . . .'

He took Lyra's hand. 'There's always hope. The other dukes will expect Garod to win, but they know it's not a done deal, so they'll stand back and watch one destroy the other, then back the winner.'

Lyra sagged. 'Dear Kore, do we have no *real* friends? Half the Pallacian nobility have left court, ostensibly to return to their own estates for the winter, but it's obvious it's to avoid being dragged down with us. Everyone who swore allegiance is backing away.'

'The Pallas mob rioted in our favour when the Sacrecours fled in 930. Garod's promised reprisals, so the citizens fear his return. That's no small thing. And the Corani *hate* the Sacrecours – you'll not be betrayed from within again. The sidewinders like Ostevan have already fled our cause.'

'So at least I'll be free to mourn until spring. You know everyone thought Ril and I had the perfect marriage, but neither of us were happy. It's the dream I miss more than the man. Does that sound terrible?'

'It's entirely understandable, Milady,' Dirklan said softly.

She wiped at her leaking eyes. 'All those miscarriages – I felt such a failure. And now our son will never know his father. But he *will* have a mother, and I'll do anything I have to for him. So if that means leading the princes of Yuros in a dance, I'll do it.'

'Playing the coquette isn't easy, Lyra,' Dirklan warned. 'Some of the princes of Rondelmar are buffoons, but you need an experienced, capable leader, and someone like that will see you as little more than a throne and a breeding heifer. Ril was content to let you rule, but they won't be: they'll want to be emperor in power, if not title.'

She set her jaw. 'Dirklan, I've exercised power for five years now. I read and understand every law I pass. I actively chair the Royal Council and make important decisions *by myself*. I preside over the Royal Assizes. I *will not* surrender my prerogatives. I'll marry a crown prince, not an emperor.'

'Potential allies may be put off by such terms.'

'I know, but that's my opening bargaining position.'

'So you see your next marriage as a hostile negotiation, rather than, say, a romance?' Dirklan sighed, a wry smile on his lips.

'I'd rather not marry at all, but Rildan must have a powerful new father.'

'Such a man will want his own son to rule after him, not Rildan.'

'I might be unable to bear another child,' Lyra countered. *I control my body.* 'Rildan will rule after me.'

Dirklan understood her. 'It makes you vulnerable. "An heir and a spare", they always say.'

'As long as the spare comes second, I'm perfectly happy, but Rildan comes first.' They fell silent a minute, then she admitted, 'I'm still reeling from all we've lost, but I don't have time to grieve. I have to freeze my heart and rule with my head – and anything else I can use.'

'I concede we are in desperate straits.' He paused, then added, 'The Rimoni philosopher Makelli teaches that rulers need a heart of ice, to do what's necessary without mercy or remorse.'

'So not the *right* thing, but the *necessary* thing?' She lifted her chin. 'A heart of ice. Very well.'

'You're asking a lot of yourself, Lyra,' Dirklan said, handing her a parchment. 'Here's something for your icy heart to consider. These are the men and women we know to have been part of Tear's conspiracy. Those struck through are dead. Those marked X are captured and awaiting trial.'

As Lyra scanned the list, names stood out: Edetta Keeper and Jean Benoit, Guildmaster of the Merchants' Guild, had escaped, but among the captured were Edreu Gestatium, head of the Grey Crows, the Imperial bureaucracy, and Chaplain Ennis, the Grand Prelate's secretary. But her eyes kept returning to the struck-through name of Medelie Aventour, revealed to be Tear of the Masked Cabal.

'How could such a young woman have led such a conspiracy?' she wondered aloud.

Dirklan gave her a sideways look and replied carefully, 'You yourself are a young woman. But she was more than she appeared. "Medelie Aventour" was an assumed identity.'

'Of who?'

'We've not discovered,' he replied.

Yes, you have, she thought irritably, *and you think it will hurt me to know*. She decided to leave it for the time being. 'I don't want a public trial,' she said. 'We can't afford to let people know how close they came to winning. Once you've extracted all the information you can, execute them. I don't want to see them.'

So this is the new me – but they didn't just try to murder me, they tried to kill Rildan too.

'How is Solon bearing up?' she asked. She couldn't imagine him as a spy. 'It can't have been easy, playing along with the cabal, getting intimately involved with Medelie Aventour.'

'He's taking it very hard. He's no conspirator and he did struggle with the duplicity. We found him unconscious the following day – he has a shattered right collarbone and leg injuries, but more worryingly, we had to empty his stomach of an almost fatal amount of liquor. The healer-magi have him in care at present, but they fear he'll never have the same strength or freedom of movement again.'

'But I thought gnostic healing could do anything?'

Dirklan laughed hollowly. 'If only. Superficial wounds and simple, clean cuts can be dealt with easily, but more complex injuries like his take time and energy. Without the mage-healers, he'd certainly have lost the arm. But, of course, there's the emotional strain . . .'

'We did ask an awful thing of him.'

'I asked it, and he agreed,' Dirklan replied. 'In one point he failed, because he didn't uncover who the mysterious "Selene" was until too late. Had we known, our preparations would have been very different and Edetta Keeper would not have got to Cordan and Coramore.'

'I'm sure he did all that could be done.'

'The woman he was bedding knew who Edetta was, so he should

19

have been able to find out,' Dirklan replied. Then he added, 'But I'm sure he did as well as any non-Volsai could have.'

'We're not all born intriguers, Dirklan,' Lyra said tartly.

'See you remember that, when you embark on your spring wooing,' the spymaster replied.

'I shall – but we have to survive winter first. What news from the south?'

'Rolven Sulpeter is leading the Corani retreat, but he's a broken man – Sanjan, his son and heir, died in the aerial affray. Prince Elvero Salinas got the bulk of the Canossi out, but they were savaged pretty badly by the Keshi light cavalry. Only the southerners – that's the Fifth Army, led by Seth Korion – acquitted themselves well. They're providing the rearguard as the army retreats to Jastenberg.'

'And the Argundians?'

'They never arrived, and are now retreating.'

Lyra closed her eyes, feeling her despair bone-deep. 'Can the Shihad be stopped?'

'Well, they fielded more than half a million men, which is four or five times our number at least. We need new defensive lines and a bad, bad winter to slow them down.' He set his jaw. 'It's a Sunsurge year, Lyra, which means extreme weather. That might be our greatest hope.'

It sounds more like our only *hope*, Lyra thought gloomily. She wished she knew how to express her deep gratitude to this forbidding-looking, but loyal and diligent man.

'Do I have the right to make you a full member of my Royal Council, Dirklan?'

He smiled appreciatively, but shook his head. 'Membership of the council is bound by centuries of legal tradition, Milady: Grand-Prelate, Lord Treasurer, Arch-Legate of the Imperocracy and Knight-Commander. No one else – oh, traditionally the father of an emperor can be made Chancellor, but you have no parents. But thank you for the thought.'

He departed, while she lay back and thought about poor Solon, and what he'd gone through. *Dominius said he'd call on him,* she remembered. *I hope that helps.*

*

The stench emanating from the whitewashed cell was the first clue that all was far from well, but Grand Prelate Dominius Wurther had been around enough seriously drunk men to be largely inured to the reek of alcohol and illness. It didn't even put him off the roasted chicken leg he was gnawing on.

His bodyguard, a young Estellan with the pretentious name of Exilium Excelsior, didn't fare so well. As the full force of vomit, spilled whiskey and urine struck them, Exilium reeled and turned an impressive shade of green.

Wurther walked in, waved his drumstick cheerily and said, 'Dear Solon, you're a mess.'

He wasn't exaggerating. The Knight-Commander of the Rondian Empire was lying on his side, heavily strapped about the left shoulder, with his arm bound up in a wine-stained sling. A strand of drool hung from one corner of his mouth; there was a pool of regurgitated food on the floor beside his cot. His sheets were spattered in vomit too, the piss bucket had been overturned and even from the doorway Wurther could see he'd soiled himself.

'Exilium, summon the chief healer – now.' Wurther tip-toed with surprising grace to the shutters and wrenched them open, letting a blast of cold, wet air into the cell.

The young Estellan looked doubtful – he hated letting his charge out of his sight – but after a moment he hurried off, returning shortly with a tired, harassed healer-mage.

'How dare you neglect the Knight-Commander in this way?' Wurther demanded.

The healer flinched. 'My lord, we're doing our best, but we can't be everywhere.'

'Clean and bathe him, then bring him to me,' Wurther commanded. 'In your office.' Then he stalked out, making a mental note to destroy the man's career at the first opportunity.

It was almost an hour before Exilium showed a freshly washed Solon Takwyth into the healer's office. He was wrapped in an oversized tunic which revealed his shoulder and neck bound tight in clean bandages; his arm was now strapped to his side.

Takwyth was in his fifties, but he'd never truly looked it until now, thanks to the gnosis. For two decades he had been accounted the greatest knight in Koredom, a man's man, proving himself many times over at the joust, never beaten in combat. His scars and uncompromising ruggedness gave him a charisma mere good looks couldn't match. But right now he looked like an abuse victim.

Wurther was working his way through the healer's brandy, but he didn't offer Takwyth a glass. 'Sit down, Solon,' he invited. 'You look like you need to Unburden.' As head of the Church of Kore, he didn't perform the confession and forgiveness of sins very often these days, but he'd always enjoyed hearing about other's people's; they were so instructive, and often entertaining.

The knight slumped into the armchair. 'Must I?'

'I think it would help.'

There was no great friendship between them and their alliance in service of Lyra Vereinen was of convenience, but Wurther generally found people grateful for a sympathetic ear usually said more than they should.

Solon proved no exception. 'Very well, Dominius,' he sighed. 'Let me tell you of my fall.'

His tale emerged slowly: the first unexpected approach from the beautiful Medelie Aventour and the even more unexpected discovery of a torrid passion. Solon's late wife had been uninterested in either Solon or the joys of the bedchamber, so until now, his sword had been the only love of his life.

'Dear Kore, how *that* changed!' Solon admitted now. 'She was young and old, innocent and wise – truly, a lover like I'd never even known *could* exist. She wanted to be ridden so often it made my flesh strain, despite all the gnosis can do. She desired acts I'd always thought sinful, but I revelled in them . . .' His voice trailed off.

'And then?' Dominius prompted gently.

'And then I found out the truth: that she wasn't "Medelie Aventour" at all. She stole that identity before I even returned to court. She was here to plot the downfall of the empress.'

'And you pretended to help?'

'She wanted me to succeed Lyra – her conspirators all did. I was to be their puppet, someone they could place on the throne and control. With Dirklan's encouragement, I played along.'

If you'd not betrayed Medelie's conspiracy, you'd be emperor now, Dominius mused. *And I'd be dead.* 'You went to Setallius when?'

'Immediately – I'm no traitor. Lyra is the head of House Corani and I am loyal to my House.'

'Even though many would sooner see you on the throne? Even though Lyra jilted you at the altar? That's remarkably forgiving, Solon.'

'I'm a man of honour and I swore on my life to Kore Himself to serve her.'

All praise chivalry, Dominius thought. *That complex code of honour prevents rampant bullies with swords – of which you, Solon, are a prime example – from stomping the rest of us beneath their boots.*

'Then you've more honour than any man I know,' he said.

'Have I?' Takwyth said. 'I don't *feel* honourable. I learned how to lie with every part of my being. I had to convince Medelie I was hers, body and soul – words, voice, eyes, the ways we made love, all of it. I tell you, I almost lost my way.'

'But you didn't,' Dominius reminded him.

Solon met his eyes. 'It was a very near thing.'

'And now she's dead?'

'Aye, she's dead: we set traps and she stepped into one that cut her apart.'

'At least you were spared having to take your own blade to her,' Dominius noted.

'That's what Dirklan says,' Solon said bitterly, 'but he doesn't understand: I spent virtually every hour of every day with her. I tasted every part of her, and I filled her so often my balls still ache. I can't hear a woman's voice without thinking it's her. She haunts me, day and night.'

'It was lust, Solon, that's all: an urgent emotion. It'll wither and die. What you felt for her wasn't love but the *pretence* of love. You fooled yourself as you fooled her. You'll find yourself again. Pray, to Kore Above.'

'Pray,' Solon snorted, looking away. 'With all due respect, Grand Prelate, I don't believe in Kore, but I do believe in *souls* – we magi know *they* exist. Mine now feels tainted.'

Dominius wasn't offended; he didn't believe in Kore as a divine entity either. But he did believe in the Church's place as the guide of society. 'Focus on Kore's message of salvation: that righteousness cleanses the soul. You walked a dark path, but you know where the light is.'

'I hope you're right.'

'I'm always right,' Dominius said blithely. 'I'm the Voice of Kore: it comes with my job.' He sipped at the brandy, which was too good for that useless healer. 'You're still the strong man of House Corani.'

'A strong man? Am I still that? I've neglected my swordsmanship in favour of intrigue and fornication and it's almost destroyed me. And now the healers say my shoulder bones and muscles will never regain full strength. For twenty years I've ruled the training yards and the jousts: it's the basis of my authority.'

'No, that's how you *earned* authority.'

'But I'm losing that strength,' Solon admitted. 'I'm a fifty-year-old man, Dominius. We magi might be spared the worst ravages of age, but my strength is waning and younger men are coming through: some I'm afraid to spar with, lest they beat me to my knees.'

'Strength at arms is just a fraction of your importance, Solon,' Dominius replied. 'You've commanded in battle, won victories. You're rooted in our country's traditions – you understand how things should be. Personally, I'd sooner you ruled the Rondian Empire than an unpredictable woman, especially as . . .' Realising he'd said too much, he fell silent, but Solon had looked up.

'You know too, don't you? Medelie said you did – that Lyra's not who she seems.'

He says who, not what . . . Dominius had been thinking about Lyra's heretical dwyma, but he put that aside to consider her unknown father. 'What did Medelie know?' he asked sharply. 'Who was she really?'

Solon was clearly reluctant to reveal her name, but at last he said, 'She was Radine Jandréux.'

'*Radine*?' Dominius yelped, his eyes widening. 'Dear Kore, that's . . .' He'd been going to say *impossible* – but of course it wasn't, not with the gnosis. *No wonder the man's a wreck.* 'I'm so sorry, Solon. That must have been Hel.'

24

'She was also Tear – she'd turned against *everything* she once believed in. It's better she's forgotten.' Solon gave him a sick look. 'And I never told you this.'

'Anything discussed in the rite of Unburdening is sacred and may not be revealed elsewhere.'

But what a titbit: that the old Corani Dowager, believed dead these last four years, had returned as their worst enemy – and now the Keepers had fled to Dupenium to support Duke Garod, and Brylion's Second Army was on its way home. Were he a betting man, he wouldn't be wagering on Lyra's survival.

But unfortunately I'll be second to the executioner's block. My bridges with Garod are well and truly burned. I'm as tied to Lyra's reign as this man, and that means protecting both the secret of Lyra's birth . . . and her heresy.

'It was I who first suspected Lyra's doubtful provenance,' Dominius told Takwyth. 'Ainar Borodium, for all his faults the rightful emperor, was already dead when someone got Princess Natia with child. Natia died without revealing who. I presume Lyra told Ostevan – she told that snake everything. We must hope he can't misuse that secret.'

'What of your own loyalty to her?' Takwyth asked shrewdly.

'Me? I'm the rightful Head of the Church of Kore, ousted by my worst enemy and forced to grovel to the empress for shelter,' he grumbled. 'Lyra and I are like oxen hitched to the same wagon. We pull together or we go nowhere. Although I admit to having little confidence in her.'

They looked at each other in silence for a time and Dominius was pleased to see that Solon was no longer steeped in misery. *If I give him a worthy purpose, he'll pull through.*

He finished the last of the brandy and slapped the table. 'Hear me, Lord Takwyth: this Unburdening is concluded, and here is your penance in remittance of your sins. Give up drinking for a month, at least. Practise your swordplay again, so that you may beat the young tyros down. Regain your confidence.'

Solon's face became haunted, then he set his jaw. 'I'll do it.'

'Good! And listen – get "Medelie" out of your system. Take another woman and use her hard. No one that resembles her, though! A pretty blonde perhaps,' he suggested slyly, 'one who looks like the queen.'

Solon shot him a hard look. 'Do not disrespect our sovereign.'

'I can disrespect whomsoever I please – that also comes with my job,' Dominius replied. 'And the prince-consort is dead, so someone needs to be filling our good queen: why not you?' He leaned forward. 'You can still be emperor the right way: take the throne by taking Lyra. Be her strong shoulder when the next crisis strikes and let nature take its course. You might knock some of that girlish innocence out of her.'

Solon contrived to look both offended and intrigued. 'Why would you say this?'

'Because though Medelie's coup was deplorable, the intention of putting you on the throne was the correct course.' *And right now, I'm beholden to a dwymancer and that could destroy me.*

'It's an unusual penance.'

'I'm out of practise,' Dominius said genially. 'Believe me, after all she's been through, she'll be grateful for someone to hold her at night. She's frightened, and with good reason.'

Solon grimaced, but he said slowly, 'I do admire our young queen, but her body is supposed to remain inviolate until she remarries. And she's no Medelie.'

Clearly Medelie Aventour – *Radine, by Kore!* – had been more than a lover: she'd been a drug, and Takwyth had over-indulged. 'Lyra's not a nun any more,' Dominius replied. 'She's ripe for a good plucking. If you don't, someone else will.'

Solon pointedly changed the subject. 'I've heard Ostevan's taken the title "Pontifex". What does that mean?'

'It means the greedy slime wants Lyra's job as well as mine – united Crown and Church, ruled by him. He'll fail. We've closed the river ferries and we're preparing a blockade of Pallas-South. You're needed, Knight-Commander: great matters are afoot.' He rose to his feet and said, 'Solon, if there's anything you need, ask and it's yours.'

The Knight-Commander shifted awkwardly. 'One thing only, Dominius: Edetta Keeper taunted me for not killing the Sacrecour heirs – I had Cordan and Coramore under my blade, but couldn't kill them: did I do right?'

No, Dominius thought, *you should have killed the little snits.* But he didn't say so. 'Why did you spare them?'

'I did it because I've seen them grow these last few months. They're not the nasty-minded versions of their father they used to be. The Reeker Night attacks changed them. Lyra won their affection and loyalty. Even I came to like Cordan. He has the makings of a decent man.'

Ten minutes with Garod will knock that out of him, Dominius thought, but Takwyth still looked so fragile. 'You did the honourable thing, Solon.'

And possibly damned us all.

Dupenium, Rondelmar

'Nephew, are you ready?' called Duke Garod, the lanky, dyspeptic lord of Dupenium.

Cordan Sacrecour glanced at his younger sister Coramore and they surreptitiously squeezed hands. Royal heirs were supposed to be brave and not need comforting, but he'd never needed reassurance more than now. He knew he didn't look regal; at fourteen years old he was a little pudgy, with his father's pallor and ginger hair. Even the coronet and made-to-measure armour they'd dressed him in made him feel foolish, not martial. But Uncle Garod was displaying him daily from the palace balcony, like a performing exhibit.

Take the salute, Cordan! Wave your sword, Cordan! Now go to your room again, Cordan!

'Come on, boy,' his uncle grumbled, 'we're going to war for you. The least you could do is look grateful!' He gripped Cordan's shoulder and marched him onto the balcony to the sound of blaring trumpets.

Dupenium was no Pallas. The square they overlooked was large, but not as massive as the Place d'Accord in Pallas. Dupenium Cathedral was a block away, and not half so grand as the Celestium. The palace from whose balcony he waved at the gathered populace was a pale shadow of the mighty Bastion. Cordan had never lived here, yet everyone kept saying 'welcome home' and expected him to be happy. He'd swiftly learned to hide his tears.

The square below was packed as usual, full of men in the scarlet and purple of imperial Dupenium, and when they saw Cordan and Garod they burst into cheers. Cordan hated the greedy hope he saw on their faces.

They all think that when Uncle Garod kills Lyra, they'll become rich as lords. They don't hear how Uncle Garod laughs at their pathetic dreams. And the fact was, Cordan didn't want Lyra to die. *Solon Takwyth fought to protect us. Lyra saved Coramore from the daemon inside her. Prince Ril saved me on Reeker Night.* That Ril was dead tore his heart – but Garod had laughed with gleeful malice when he'd heard, crowing as if he'd slain the prince-consort himself.

Cordan glanced back and gave Coramore a tremulous smile. Her cascade of ginger curls had been tamed with diamond-headed pins and she was dressed in green, her best colour. But then he felt the cold gaze of Jasper Vendroot, his uncle's spymaster, and flinching, he turned back to the crowd and waved again, wishing the earth would swallow him up.

After the parade, he was taken to the Great Hall. The duke, on his traditional high throne, had Cordan and Coramore seated on lower seats to his right – *because you're not emperor yet, boy* – and glowered at the coterie of priests, leaning on their crosiers as if ascending a mountain, as they approached the throne beneath the suspicious eyes of the courtiers.

'Helios Prelatus, ambassador for Ostevan Pontifex,' the herald boomed.

Cordan licked his lips nervously. Lyra and her people had discovered that Ostevan was one of the awful masked cabal who had unleashed the Reeker Night attacks – and poisoned Coramore. Beside him, his younger sister's face was white with fear.

Helios Prelatus was a southerner, judging by his olive skin and black-grey hair, and he spoke with a Lantric accent, which did nothing to quell Cordan's fears. Lantric masks now haunted his dreams.

'Greetings, Duke Garod, and Crown-Prince Cordan,' Helios wheezed. 'My master, Ostevan Pontifex, sends his felicitations.'

Cordan was half-convinced that the man's eyes would turn black and his mouth sprout fangs, but he knew that Vendroot was using gnostic detection spells – examining the mind and body of every supplicant to ensure they weren't one of the daemon-possessed Reekers. Presumably Helios had passed such a test.

'I return your greetings,' Garod replied. 'But tell me: what does "Pontifex" signify when Church and Crown have been legally separated for centuries?'

'Ostevan selected the title purely to differentiate his reign from that of Grand Prelate Wurther,' Helios replied smoothly. 'It doesn't imply more than that.' He gave Cordan a smarmy look and added, 'He most earnestly wishes to see you take the throne, my Prince – as do all people of goodwill.'

Do they? Cordan doubted it. Lyra believed the civil war Garod was intent on would be a bloodbath that would ruin the whole empire.

'Does Ostevan Jandreux have anything to offer us but solicitous words?' Garod enquired.

Cordan guessed that using Ostevan's *Corani* family name was an insult, but Helios immediately batted it aside.

'Ostevan Pontifex relinquished his family ties when he took the cloth, as do all we Anointed Sons of Kore. He offers the full weight of the Church in support of your endeavours.'

'*Half* the Church,' Garod corrected. 'In other words, he wishes me to ride to his rescue.'

Helios Prelatus ignored the sarcasm. 'Already our strength matches the Corani and their Pallacian adherents. With our forces united, the false empress cannot stand against us.'

Garod contemplated that, then said, 'We have heard that Ostevan Jandreux fornicated with the queen and is part of the so-called "Masked Cabal" behind Reeker Night. Why should House Sacrecour align with such a one?'

The court buzzed at the accusation and Cordan felt a flare of hope that perhaps his uncle had seen through these *evil* people. But Coramore whispered in his ear, 'Uncle Garod knows it's true; he's just pretending he cares.'

Cordan threw her an anxious look. Cora might be two years younger than him, but she'd always seen things more clearly. Even though he had the gnosis and was learning to be a mage, she could still get to the heart of things faster than him. 'How do you know?'

'I had that *daemon* in my brain for a month: believe me, Uncle knows.'

Helios Prelatus gave Garod a complacent smile. 'Dear Duke Garod, the lies the Corani have spread about my master could fill a tome. Reeker Night was nothing more a riot incited by poverty and rightful hatred of the empress. There were no "daemons". And my master is without sin, unlike our cuckolded queen and her unlamented consort.'

You bastard! thought Cordan. He'd have leaped up, but Coramore caught him just in time.

'Shush,' she hissed. 'Not here.'

You were one of those possessed, Cordan thought wildly. *Lyra and Ril saved us* – But fear throttled his words.

'Then we are reassured,' Garod drawled, publicly accepting Helios' lies. 'Join us, Celestial Ambassador, for tonight's feast. We have much to discuss.'

Only Coramore's hidden hand, wrapped around his, gave Cordan the strength to mask his disgust.

2

Vigil

The Missing Angelum

One of the puzzles of Wizardry, the summoning and control of spirits, is this: Why are there only daemons and ghosts in the aether? According to the Book of Kore, there should also be Angelum, benign spirits who serve Kore and guide the dead to salvation. In more than five hundred years of gnostic study, no verified encounter with an Angel has been substantiated.

FEODOR PRELATUS, THE CELESTIUM, PALLAS 853

Hegikaro Castle, Mollachia
Noveleve 935

The sewage of Hegikaro Castle was removed from the keep in three ways. Garderobes for the nobility's use had been carved into the outer walls, feeding the lush grass beneath, and night-carts collected everyone else's piss and excrement while the castle slept. There were also internal chutes for all manner of soft rubbish leading into subterranean drains that emptied into Lake Drozst, below the promontory where the castle sat. Over the years these drains had occasionally been renovated, leaving a maze of obsolete pipes below ground that certain princes had been known to explore in their adventurous youth.

It was one of these disused drains that saved Kyrik Sarkany's life. He burst up through the thin ice at the edge of the lake, hidden from his enemies a hundred feet above by the darkness for those crucial moments it took him to stagger ashore, find the drain and crawl up to it. He'd grown since he and Valdyr had played here as boys, but there was just enough room to slither through to where he knew he'd find a dry space.

Once there, he collapsed, shaking, and closed his eyes. He barely opened them in the next three days. The passing of time was marked only by a glimmer of daylight at the end of the pipe. He knew which pipes passed clean water, the gnosis gave him heat and light and he ignored his ravenous hunger, disciplined enough to lie low. As far as he knew, his enemies believed him dead, his body trapped beneath the ice.

Inside, that's what he felt like: a corpse, floating in frigid water. He could still scarcely comprehend that Dragan Zhagy, a man he trusted utterly, had turned on him – if he was still Dragan at all, because he'd fought more like a man possessed. All of the Vitezai Sarkanum men had, many of whom Kyrik had known since childhood.

Possessed . . . He remembered an instant in the battle when he'd tried an exorcism spell against Dragan and had felt the spell begin to work – until it was overwhelmed. He'd been on the right track, but his gnosis hadn't been strong enough. Now to all the world he was dead – in truth, he wasn't sure he wanted to live anyway, not when Hajya was gone. He'd seen his wife fall in that awful slaughter, along with Thraan, the Sydian chieftain, and all Clan Vlpa's most senior men.

Let me strike Dragan down and I'll go thankful to my grave . . . But to do that, he had to somehow escape and find his brother. Valdyr hadn't made it to the coronation, and when Kyrik recalled leaping from the tower of the keep, he was sure he'd heard Valdyr's voice on the winds. *And how else could the lake surface have frozen at that precise moment? No, Valdyr's alive somewhere and I need to find him.*

He was scared to move by night, when the hunters were most active, but the daylight hours were likely suicidal as well. He had no idea when his chance would come.

Then Mollachia lived up to her wild reputation: thunder cracked and Kyrik risked moving to the drain opening to watch the storm roll in across the frozen lake. Jagged lightning flashed in the gloom as visibility collapsed and he realised that this might be his only real chance.

His ruined coronation robes were hardly fit travel garb, and he was armed only with his dagger – but escape required stealth and luck, not a blade. He looked around before jumping to the gravel three feet beneath, where he was able to fully straighten for the first time in days. The rain slapped against his cheeks and the wind caught his clothing, making him stagger.

To his left, the docks of Hegikaro were dimly visible; a few fishing boats had been caught in the ice and were now stuck tight. To his right, the shoreline vanished into the oncoming storm. He was at the foot of the promontory, a rocky hill studded with sparse vegetation upon which the castle was built.

As he extended his gnostic senses, he sensed something and looked up to see four men on a ledge some thirty feet above him: Vitezai hunters. He knew them, and hope flared that they might have been absent from the coronation and un-afflicted. He almost called a greeting, but one peered down at him and he saw blank, dark eyes and bloodstained clothing and blackened, bloody drool running from their mouths.

'Kyrik,' they chorused, in low, fell voices.

He spun and ran out onto the ice, and with a collective snarl, they jumped effortlessly down and bounded after him.

He poured heat and raw gnostic energy into his limbs, putting on a burst of speed, but they kept pace as he stormed across the ice. The castle swiftly vanished as the storm struck and the baying of the hunters blended with the keening of the wind. The torrential rain made the ice treacherous and he fell twice, but his pursuers were also slipping as the shore vanished and they were surrounded by a world of murky grey and white.

He glanced back to see the Vitezai men pelting after him had teeth bared and were howling like beasts. Three days and nights of no food and freezing temperatures had drained his reserves; his strength began to fail and he realised they were going to catch him, so he turned, pulled out his dagger and knelt, muttering a prayer. The four Vitezai men roared triumphantly, surging towards him. Their faces loomed out of the rain and fog, contorted with hate, their weirdly soulless eyes black as oil.

Kyrik invoked the gnosis, calling raw light and heat to his dagger. As the four men closed in, he shouted aloud, drawing in all the energy he could, and plunged the dagger in the ice. With a loud cracking sound, heat and force radiated outwards, channelled into a cone before him, and the ice came apart, shattering in a wave that swept under the men's feet. Their faces contorted in sudden alarm – then they fell through, bellowing again and thrashing madly as their heavy clothing quickly became sodden and dragged them down into the depths of the water.

Kyrik closed his eyes, muttering a prayer to Kore, though he feared they were beyond their god's reach.

Then he rose, reeling from the exertion of the spell and feeling sick at the thought that he'd slain men he suspected had been trapped and used. He backed away, carefully feeling his way in case the spell had also weakened the ice where he stood, when suddenly the broken ice started shifting, the water churned and a dark hand, coated in rime, clawed at the solid edge.

Dear Kore, one of them is still alive.

Before he could react, the Vitezai man rose from the frigid water, his skin almost blue with cold, his eyes fixed on Kyrik. He recognised Arvi Pehac.

For Kore's sake! I played with Arvi as a child – must I do this? But he kindled blue gnostic fire in his hands, his heart thudding. *No, Arvi. Please, fall back and die . . .*

'We have your wife, Kyrik,' Arvi rasped. 'We've got your filthy animal wife.'

Hajya's still alive? Kyrik almost fell to his knees. *She's alive . . . Oh Kore . . .*

Arvi advanced, his fingers bent into claws. 'If you want her, come back to Hegikaro.'

He's lying . . . Kyrik intensified the fire in his hands. 'I don't want to have to do this, Arvi.'

'We're going to slaughter your Sydian pets, but we'll keep your bitch in a kennel and feed her your brother's carcase.'

Valdyr! The faces of those he loved filled his mind . . . and Arvi stalked closer. 'Stop, Arvi!'

Then Arvi's voice changed to Dragan's. 'If your father could see you now, Kyrik, he'd be ashamed. How could you bring those sub-humans to our beloved Mollachia?'

Kyrik's mind threw up the last image he had of the gazda: the man he'd loved like a father, changed to a snarling killer, wielding the gnosis and sneering threats.

It broke the spell and he lifted his hands just as Arvi charged. Blue fire erupted from his left hand and blasted into Arvi's chest, burning away clothing and blackening his skin as it punched a fist-sized hole and sent him flopping onto his back.

'I'm sorry, Arvi,' Kyrik panted to the man's soul.

Arvi Pehac sat up and looked down at his chest. He laughed. 'Is that all you have, weakling?' He rose again, and now Kyrik realised he was overmatched – just as a dark shape ghosted in and buried a sword in the man's flank. Before Kyrik could yell a warning that these men needed beheading, Arvi yowled piteously, black smoke bursting from his eye-sockets and mouth, and he fell to the ice, unmoving.

Kyrik looked at his rescuer, expecting to see some pure-blood Imperial battle-mage, but it was Rothgar Baredge, the resolute but completely human Stonefolk hunter, who stared back at him.

'Roth? What did you do?'

Rothgar prodded the body regretfully. 'I just killed my old friend Arvi.'

'Stay away from him,' Kyrik warned, edging forward, but Arvi was showing no sign of sitting up or otherwise coming back to life. Kyrik looked at Rothgar's sword. 'Kore's Blood! That blade's argenstael, isn't it?'

'Aye,' Rothgar said laconically.

Argenstael, Kyrik marvelled. The silver and steel alloy was notoriously brittle and difficult to keep from going blunt or corroding; it was mostly employed by travelling entertainers for stage use because it glittered so nicely. 'You inherited it, right?'

'Aye: my grandpa got duped into buying her. I'd sell her if I could, but we're married.'

'You're *what*?'

'Old Stonefolk custom – our first bride is a sword. Grandpa couldn't afford a decent blade so he gave me this thing. "Wulfang", he named her.' He sniffed. '"Knitting Needle" would've been a better name.'

Kyrik thought about the slaughter at the coronation, and how the black-eyed men had been all but un-killable. *A silver alloy*, he thought excitedly. *Perhaps we can stop them after all?*

'How did you find me, Roth?'

'I didn't, really. I was just looking out across the lake and saw someone running, just before the mist closed in. Didn't know it was you until I got closer.'

'You won't believe the tale I have to tell.'

'Save your breath: Fridryk Kippenegger's with me – he escaped the coronation and bumped into me a mile or so east of here. So I've heard the news – and I'm so sorry. Kore's Blood, Kyrik – has the world gone mad?'

Kyrik exhaled bitterly. 'It surely has.'

Watcher's Peak

Valdyr Sarkany stroked Luhti's cheek anxiously. Beside him, the fire crackled and the broth bubbled, filling the air with steam and warm, wholesome smells. At the edge of the camp, the wolf Gricoama paced, unable to rest. Around them, snow was banked up in waves, but the flames kept the cold at bay.

The old woman was slowly dying, and she was taking all of her precious knowledge into the dark; she who'd been Lanthea, one of the four great dwymancers of ancient times.

Why can't I help her? Why can't she pull through this?

Centuries ago Luhti had bonded with the dwyma-energies of this place. Watcher's Peak was home to a genilocus, a guardian spirit who intermediated between the dwyma and a human capable of wielding that power. The genilocus of Watcher's Peak had been the legendary White Stag of Mollachia, but Asiv Fariddan had torn out the White Stag's throat and in doing so, had mortally wounded Luhti and banished the ghosts of her fellow dwymancers, her son Eyrik and the shaman Sidorzi. Now her soul was bleeding out.

'Valdyr,' she whispered throatily, jolting him out of his reverie.

'Luhti! Can you eat broth? It's snow-rabbit and fennel.'

Her gentle, wizened face crinkled in a smile. 'That would nice,' she breathed.

He spooned some of the thick fluid into a metal bowl, then fed her, worrying that she looked weaker every moment. Her weathered skin was increasingly waxy and her breath was shallow. All Valdyr could do was tend her and pray.

Gricoama nuzzled the old woman, who broke off eating to make mewling noises, as if she and the beast spoke the same tongue. Perhaps they did. Valdyr had saved the wolf a few months ago, when he'd found the beast injured and near death. He remembered that moment with vivid clarity. Zlateyr had told him that though the dwyma was immense, big things were made of many small things. Without knowing how, he'd taken that insight and healed the wolf.

Could I do the same here? He laid a hand on her shoulder, trying to nerve himself.

She put a hand over his and shook her head. 'I'm not wounded, Valdyr. Losing the White Stag has merely hastened my time to die. There's nothing you can do.' She murmured something in Gricoama's ear and the wolf backed away and howled, the sound echoing down the peak.

Valdyr offered Luhti more broth, but she shook her head drowsily. 'That's enough,' she murmured.

He finished the spoonful himself, then helped her rise and pee behind a rock at the edge of the clearing, before settling her again. He'd seen death before, but little of old age; it was distressing to see someone who'd been very much alive declining so fast.

A dark shape strode out of the murk, carrying firewood. Zlateyr, Mollachian folk-hero and Luhti's partner beyond life and death, gave him a grim look, then knelt beside her. In the legends they were brother and sister, but Valdyr now knew that they were kindred only in a metaphoric sense, bonded by the dwyma. Like Eyrik and Sidorzi, Zlateyr was a ghost of the genilocus, and like Luhti, he was dying, although it wasn't obvious; there were no physical signs. But he had a strange kind of hollowness, his footfalls barely dented the snow and his clothing no longer rippled in the winds.

What will I do when I'm left alone? Valdyr worried. He went to the southern edge of the clearing, pulling his furs closer about him against the chill. Night was falling again and snowflakes were drifting down. From late Decore to the end of Febreux, when the rivers and lakes of Mollachia froze and the ground was buried in snow, there was naught to do but to wrap up by the fire. To be without shelter and warmth was death.

The wolf-pack that followed Gricoama kept leaving dead snow-rabbits and hares on the lower slopes for them, and somehow Zlateyr kept returning with dead wood from the forests below. Valdyr knew his job was to learn all he could from Luhti, before their precious time ran out.

Zlateyr joined him and asked, 'Do you know what transpires in the valley?' He was a lean, weathered man, with lank black hair and a rakish goatee. The founder of Mollachia wasn't Andressan as tales told but Sydian. *Just like the Vlpa tribe Kyrik has brought here*, Valdyr reflected.

'I've not seen or heard anything more,' Valdyr confessed. Four nights ago, looking out over the valley, he had somehow seen his brother Kyrik, trapped by some evil thing in Haklyn Tower, the highest point of Hegikaro Castle. Valdyr had been able to use the dwyma to ice over the lake just after Kyrik plunged in – the dwyma wasn't like the gnosis, it didn't do small magic as a mage could; it was more like a giant sledgehammer affecting entire regions. The ice had been the best he could do, to cut off predator from prey, but since that moment he'd sensed nothing further of his brother.

What if I killed Kyrik that night? What if there's nothing left to fight for?

'There's *always* something to fight for,' Zlateyr said, responding to his thoughts in that eerie way he and Luhti had. 'This valley is full of frightened people, both Mollach and Sydian. They need you.'

'But what is it we're fighting?' Valdyr asked. 'I knew those men with Asiv: they were decent people – but they weren't themselves any more: their eyes had turned black and the only way to keep them down was by beheading them. And when Asiv bit the White Stag, he infected it with that same kind of venom; it turned the Stag's veins black – so what are we dealing with?'

'I've not seen it before,' Zlateyr admitted, 'but right now, our first responsibility is to Luhti.'

'But I can't help her,' Valdyr blurted. 'We need a healer.'

'A healer would do no good,' Zlateyr replied. 'She's dying.'

'Then what can I do?'

'Sit with her and learn.' Zlateyr placed a strangely weightless hand on his shoulder. 'You are her heir, Valdyr, so you must learn from her while you can.'

'But I know *nothing*!'

'The dwyma isn't like the gnosis – you don't need books.' He tapped Valdyr's chest. 'You learn in here. Go, sit with her: I'll keep watch.'

He walked out into the snow, and was immediately swallowed up by the gloom.

With a heavy heart, Valdyr reached inside himself, where a coil of green-gold light slowly spun. Hesitantly, he touched it – and myriad sensations struck him. He saw a much younger Luhti: a gentle-faced girl with fine golden hair. Then her tresses led him further afield, to a blonde woman with a pale face, cradling a new-born child to her creamy breast. She looked right at him and he panicked . . .

. . . and then he was back here, on the hill-top. Gricoama had joined him and was pressing his warm flank to his leg and looking up as if to say, *Come back to the fire*.

He did so, lowering himself down beside the dying dwymancer, who woke with a shudder, smiled at him, then laid a hand on Gricoama's head. 'You did well to save him,' Luhti wheezed. 'He's your White Stag.'

Then she closed her eyes again and her breathing slowed. In moments, she was asleep again.

The next morning, Zlateyr still hadn't returned, but Luhti lingered on, so Valdyr had no choice but to stay and keep watch over the dying.

Can you hear me? Is anyone listening? The woman's voice quivered through the dwyma, calling in Rondian. It was the blonde lady with the new-born child, but Luhti was adamant that Valdyr not respond. *In the northern empire, they kill people like us*, she'd warned him. But Luhti was dying, and Valdyr could hear the stranger's voice straining through the web of the dwyma, sometimes fearful, sometimes pleading, on other nights almost hopeful. He worried that ignoring her was a mistake, that maybe she had the means to help Luhti, if only they asked.

With a heavy sigh, Valdyr shut her out, removed himself from the inner world of the dwyma and focused on what lay before him. Days were crawling past, each one exactly like the other. Zlateyr came and went, an increasingly spectral presence, leaving dead wood for the fire. Gricoama would hunt and return with prey for the pot, and at times he fell asleep beside Luhti. He felt almost as if the wolf and the ancient dwymancer were conversing; once, he even woke to see them limned in pale light.

But all the while Luhti was slowly deteriorating.

Has it been a week? Two, even? In the drifting slowness of featureless grey days and nights he'd begun to lose track of day and night. He worried that Kyrik was out there, needing his help, but there was no way of knowing.

He went to the fire again, ladled more rabbit stew into the bowl and fed the semi-conscious old woman the broth, as she couldn't chew any more.

Please, is someone there? the woman's voice called again.

'Don't listen,' Luhti croaked, her eyes opening. 'If it's not a trap, then she's a fool and a danger to us.' She grasped his wrist in her cold bony hand. 'I remember when I was new to this, I thought I had to save everyone. I banished storms and inadvertently caused droughts. I'd try to save one species and accidentally exterminate three others. I tried to find a balance between humanity and nature and left a trail of wreckage across both kingdoms. You have a power now, Valdyr Sarkany, but it's ponderous and unpredictable. Use it sparingly.'

Valdyr felt very unready. 'But I barely understand the dwyma.'

'Neither do I.' She smiled crookedly. 'I just *live* it. Listen, Valdyr – when I die, Watcher's Peak will die with me. Right now your connection is through me, so you'll need to create your own bond with the dwyma. You and Gricoama must create your own genilocus. Until you do so, you'll be weak and vulnerable.'

'But how–?'

'Hush.' She gripped his hand and a vision filled his senses: the Elétfa, the tree of light that embodied the dwyma. Energy from the sun streamed in and new life bloomed, flowing through everything that lived, from plants to the creatures that fed on them, to the animals that fed on those; and when something died it broke down to fuel more new life: a cycle from leaves to branches to stems to roots to waste and decay and moisture, evaporation, rain and new life. A vast, intricate circle.

'Nothing's perfect, not even this,' Luhti murmured. 'Look beyond the light.'

He dragged his gaze from the Tree and peered, blindly at first – until he saw, floating like clouds in a night sky, blobs of un-light, constantly shifting shape. There were thousands of them, each composed of un-guessable lesser forms, shreds of darkness that were mostly mouths, like comets of darkness, serpents of entropy that howled with dread and jealous hunger as they orbited the Tree of Light.

'What are they?' he gasped.

'Daemons,' Luhti replied. 'The Tree is formed of energy and they're too fragile to bear full exposure, but they subsist on the energy they leech from the system – by devouring souls. Their desire is to enter the cycle and claim it, make it theirs. Some men serve them, including the man you know as Asiv and the man who was once Dragan, and all those they've enslaved. Left unopposed, they will grow more numerous, become bloated with power and suck the Tree's sap until it withers and dies. They've been trying to do so since time began.'

Valdyr shuddered. 'Then what can we do?'

'Cut the tendrils through which they feed: their servants on Urte. Sever those, and we protect the Elétfa.'

'But the daemons are immense . . .'

'Yes, but how much mightier is the Elétfa?' She let go of his hand and the vision faded.

'Was the Elétfa always there?' he wondered, still overwhelmed.

'Ysh, since life began. Life sustains it, and it sustains life in a virtuous cycle. Listen, Valdyr: when we first dwymancers came to be, there were no genilocii and our powers were localised, until four of us realised that by building a link to the Elétfa, we could unify the dwyma. The magi didn't like that. They feared our purpose and we had to flee: to here, this little mountain kingdom. Eloy, Dameta, Amantius and I went to the volcanic mountain you call "Cuz Sarkan" – ysh, it's now named for your family – and we made a place there where the fruit of the Elétfa grows. Go there, when you're ready.'

He had dozens of questions still, but she was visibly failing and he realised in horror that they were out of time. So he asked the most urgent one: 'How will I know when I'm ready?'

'You'll know,' she said, as her face shed years and he saw her again as she must have been when the dwyma first touched her: a sunny-faced young woman with a snub nose, soft golden hair and a laughing mouth. 'Goodbye, Valdyr,' she murmured. 'Look after my garden.' Then she looked beyond him, to where Zlateyr waited. 'Give me my last moments with my love.'

Valdyr blinked away tears and rose. Gricoama whined and together, they backed away, leaving Zlateyr kneeling with Luhti, holding her and whispering urgently. Then the Archer tossed back his head and cried out, a wail that faded into a choked swallow of grief. He laid a hand on his heart before extending it towards Valdyr.

'Kore be with you, Valdyr Sarkany. Free your lands. Protect the Elétfa.'

The blanket that had once enveloped the old woman flopped to the ground, empty. And as it fell, the shadowy form of Zlateyr, founder and hero of Mollachia, faded into the mist and was gone, leaving Valdyr and Gricoama alone.

3

A Rolling Cage

The Lantric City-States

The Lantric city-states, centres of culture, learning and wealth, thrived for two hundred years before the Rimoni Empire conquered them – and promptly copied many of their institutions. Those included for a time suffragium, the practice of electing officials to govern society. But neither culture ever solved the problem of how to subjugate the wealthy elites. Nor have the Rondians.

JAPHET TORANIO, ORDO COSTRUO ARCANUM, HEBUSALIM 868

North of Jastenberg, Noros
Noveleve 935

The wagon lurched into motion, joining the hordes fleeing Jastenberg. The mounted men flanking it touched spurs to the flanks of their horses and the column began to rumble again. The populace of Jastenberg were no fools: the city had no outer walls, having long outgrown the original defences, and no one had ever considered they'd need more – after all, Noros was in the heart of the empire – who could touch them?

Sultan bloody Rashid, that's who, Ari Frankel thought morosely. *Not that it's my problem.*

He gripped the bars of his cage to keep himself from tumbling across the floor and straight into another beating from the brutes he was penned up with. Blood seeped from the sodden bandage round his head and his clothes dripped water. He was so cold he was constantly shaking; the broth they'd been fed during this latest break was already congealing in his guts and had done nothing to warm him.

He and his fellow inmates were prisoners of the Inquisition, accused of sedition and being shipped north, where they'd all be found guilty and executed. The outcome was a forgone conclusion, but the Church apparently wanted to make an example of him in particular: the full penalty of the law was to be applied, which meant he'd be eviscerated whilst being hanged.

It was a surreal feeling, knowing that he would die horribly without ever knowing if the damned empire would defeat the Shihad, or if Empress Lyra – whom he imagined to be a pampered, stupid innocent – would survive when the Sacrecours attacked. It was galling to think that the world would go on without him.

He made the mistake of remembering his dead parents, letting their faces fill his mind, but as they'd been when he found them, disembowelled, hanging from the rafters of their own house, alongside his friends Lothar and Bek. All of a sudden his stomach heaved and he threw up through the bars.

'Fuck you,' his neighbour snarled, 'you soft-gutted whimperer.'

'Sorry,' Ari choked out.

'Shut the fuck up,' the man scowled, and slammed Ari's face against the bars. Stars exploded, he slid to the floor and someone else kicked him in the ribs – then an Inquisitor rattled his lance against the bars.

'Cool down, you scum,' he shouted, and because he was a mage, they all stopped.

Neif Coldwell, his only remaining friend, grabbed Ari under the armpit and hauled him up. They clung to each other as Ari wheezed. *Now it's just Neif and me . . . we'll die together too.*

'I really thought we'd turned the corner,' Ari panted. 'All those crowds, getting bigger and bigger – and then . . . *and then* . . . Oh Kore, they're all dead.' A massive sob pushed up through his throat and he couldn't keep from convulsing as grief exploded from him.

'Kore's sake, someone shut this cunni up,' the man behind him snarled. 'Fucking blubberer.'

'It's going to be all right,' Neif told him, which was *stupid*, because *nothing* was going to be all right.

'They're going to pull out our fingernails,' Ari groaned, 'and they'll brand us a–'

'*Kore's Balls, someone kill this fucker!*' the thug roared. 'I can't stand his damned whining.'

'Yeah, shut it,' someone else gritted. 'We all know what we're in for.'

'Hey, Quizzies,' another yelled, 'kill this cunt right now – or let us do it–'

'Shut up,' Neif shouted. He'd never been a brave man, but suddenly he was roaring like a lion. 'All of you, *shut up*: my friend is a great man and he doesn't deserve to be locked up with you scum!'

Ari winced. *Now they really will kill us . . .* Though perhaps this would be a better way to die.

But all that Neif's outburst earned him was a cuff in the face and more derision.

'Why, who is he? Ril bloody Endarion? Get lost on the way to the battle, did you, darlin'?'

'Na, it's Elvero Salinas – got drunk at the jousts again?'

'Na, na, na,' the burly thug with the ready fists shouted, glee contorting his face as he grabbed Ari's collar and bunched his fist, 'this little lard-arse is Dominius Wurther hisself, on the run from the Celestium, en't ya?' He chortled, then punched Ari in the nose.

Stars burst in his eyes – *again* – and blood clogged his nostrils.

'Bastard!' Neif roared, lashing out with a punch that caught the man on the cheek.

The thug didn't even flinch, just spat and laughed. 'That all you got, fucking wimp? I'm gonna–'

'Wait, Gorn,' a low, cutting voice said. The thug froze and looked at the lean man with swarthy features and cruel eyes in the corner. 'C'mon then, skinny lad,' the man said. 'Tell us: who's yer "great man" then?'

Ari would have as soon Neif said nothing, but the words tumbled from his friend's mouth. 'I wouldn't expect illiterate imbeciles like you to know, but this is Ari Frankel, the champion of suffragium and the greatest–'

'He's *Frankel*?' the swarthy man said, his tones somewhere between curious and disbelieving.

'Who the fuck's Frankel?' Gorn asked, readying his fist again.

'I heard 'im speak last week,' someone said. 'Yeah, that's definitely 'im: chubby fella, big mouth.'

I'm not chubby, Ari thought blearily, really not sure if the swarthy man being interested was a good thing.

'You've been circulating pamphlets pointing out the failings of our betters,' the man drawled.

'That's right,' Gorn chortled. 'There was that one about the empress and her confessor – it was fuckin' hilarious – I loved the expression on 'er Maj's face: "Oh my goodness, Ostevan, is this pwoper?" That's what she was sayin' while the priest nailed her. Heh, heh. You remember that one, Lazar?'

It was Ari's turn to stare. 'You're *Lazar*?'

Their eyes met, Ari's frightened, the swarthy man's gaze ironic. 'Aye, I'm Lazar.'

Neif gulped and began to babble, 'I'm sorry, I never meant that *you're* illiterate or an imbecile–'

Lazar nodded to Gorn, who drove his fist into Neif's midriff. He went down in a choking heap, ignored by everyone else.

Ari was too scared to take his eyes off Lazar.

Every few years, in every region, an outlaw of the people arose and had their time of infamy, before inevitably being caught and hanged. Some had noble tales of injustice to fuel the legend; others were just vicious killers. Lazar of Midrea was something of both: the former legion centurion had retired to the customary plot of land, only to have it stolen by a rapacious mage-noble. His response had been to embark on a dramatic burning-and-killing spree.

'So they caught you here?'

'It got too hot in Midrea,' Lazar drawled. 'Crossing the river usually throws off pursuit, but this time the Quizzies were in town.' He looked Ari up and down. 'I've read your treatise on suffragium, Frankel. Nice ideas, if this were a nice world. But the only way the poor can ascend is by climbing a stairway built from the corpses of the rich.'

'I've never advocated violence,' Ari said firmly, despite his utter terror.

'And that was smart,' Lazar replied. 'Sedition gets a man hanged. But believe me, folks what listened to you knew that bloodletting would be a part of it. Men I knew joined us after hearing you speak and reading your work. Folk know you have to break the old to make room for the new.' He eyed Ari coolly. 'You understand that, right?'

Say no and he loses interest . . . and I maybe lose my life.

'I do understand.'

Lazar smiled, which was as chilling as his glare. 'Shame to meet you here, Frankel. Been a good haul for the Quizzies, this jaunt south: got you, got me, and they still managed to dodge the rukking battle.' He looked at Gorn. 'No one touches this man, or his friend. They're with us.'

Lazar shuffled forward as far as his chains allowed and offered his hand. His grip was cold and firm, his hands rough against Ari's smooth skin. 'I hope we share a gallows, Frankel. Would be an honour.'

East of Jastenberg, Yuros

An army marching to battle was like a horse on parade, its gait stiff and controlled. An army in flight was a spooked horse running headlong; it needed someone to grab the reins.

That'll have to be me, Seth Korion thought as he topped a rise and saw the mess before him. The plains to the north straddling the Imperial Road were choked with men and wagons, all trying to flee westwards, away from the enemy. The many vehicles that had lost wheels or been overturned in the panicked rush had been abandoned, leaving precious supplies for the enemy. There were no columns, but he could see amongst the rabble groups of men staggering along in some kind of formation behind a centurion, pilus or serjant who'd kept their wits and kept their unit together.

As if to press the point, the dark clouds overhead and intermittent squalls had left the fleeing men soaked to the skin and scared of their own shadows. Defeat could do that to even the bravest.

Fortunately, most of my military career has been spent retreating. And Seth had already worked out a plan, of sorts. *Right, time to see what we're made of.*

He turned to his officers. 'Delton,' he said to his chief aide, 'these men are Corani, but I don't see Lord Sulpeter's people here, so we'll take charge. Get our battle-magi down there and get those men into lines. I don't care which unit is which, just get them moving to a drum – marching pace, no faster. Herd everyone back to the road and flank the columns with cavalry.'

And so it started. He turned his attention to collating the scouts' reports and sending out more, then checking the casualty lists. There were dozens of status updates from his officers to be reviewed as well.

'Where are those damned Argundians?' he demanded during a lull. He looked at Chaplain Gerdhart: he was Argundian and he had kin in the Third Army, which had conspicuously failed to arrive in time for the battle three days ago.

'I just spoke to my cousin Jurdi,' Gerdhart replied. 'They're thirty miles ahead of us, also retreating.'

'*What?* I asked Prince Andreas to help us set the rearguard!'

'Jurdi says Prince Andreas refused – you'll get an official response soon enough, I expect.' Gerdhart was clearly embarrassed. 'They're seeking defensible positions west of here.'

'Kore's Balls!' Seth raised his gaze heavenwards. 'Apologies for the blasphemy, Chaplain, but honestly . . .' He turned to Culmather, his seer-mage and main liaison with the other commanders. 'Find Lord Sulpeter – we need to meet and coordinate. What of the Aquilleans?'

'They're away to the north,' another aide, Mortas, reported. 'They got their arses kicked.'

Seth permitted the levity, only asking, 'Do we have word of Prince Elvero?'

'There are rumours that he took a javelin in the back, sir, but nothing's been confirmed.'

The Aquilleans had been outflanked and carved up during the battle and hadn't responded cohesively since. If their commander was dead, that explained it.

'Then they'll need men to rein them in and get them to safety. Mortas, find out what you can.'

'Are we going to make a stand, Milord?' the remaining aides asked eagerly.

'Not this side of Jastenberg,' Seth replied. 'First we have to regain control of this army.'

'We will, sir,' the aides choroused. Seth's force had held their line, the only Yurosi units to do so, and they still believed in themselves, and him.

He had to hope that self-belief would hold up in the bad days to come.

Seth turned back to Gerdhart. 'What's happening with the prince's body?' He still had that ghostly image in his head, of Prince-Consort Ril Endarion's pegasus landing before him with the man dead in the saddle. After they'd cut the body free, the winged horse had flown away.

'That Volsai woman, Veritia? She has our fastest carriage. She's taking responsibility for seeing the prince home to Pallas. She was hoping to commission a windship in Jastenberg, but with half our fleet now firewood . . .' His voice tailed off and Seth grimaced at the reminder.

Since the surviving Rondian windships had fled west, the skies had been empty of anything except the triangular-sailed Eastern craft and construct riders.

Seth sagged, then chastised himself: his men needed to see *energy*, not exhaustion. He clapped his hands. 'To duties, gentlemen. I want to see order from chaos by sunset.'

Gradually, they did regain control. Seth rode down to the plains himself so he was visible, and when a trio of Keshi windships swept overhead, he directed the barrage, a storm of crossbow bolts and magebolts that forced the enemy to draw off before they lost their sails.

They've marked where we are, he thought with a sigh, but that was inevitable.

The weather had quickly worsened after the battle, just as it had after Shaliyah; the inevitable aftermath of all the weather-gnosis that had been expended in the conflict. The sun vanished and the wind blew the torrential rain sideways, drenching the suffering men yet again. Scouts and messengers streamed in and after reporting, joined the rest of the bedraggled army huddled around spluttering cooking fires, or sought solace in a bottle or jug.

Once Seth's guard cohort had erected his pavilion and their own tents, he settled in to read the evening despatches, but he'd barely

49

scanned the first when his tent flap opened and a tall black-robed woman with an unruly mop of grey hair strode in.

'As I never, Seth Korion,' she said in greeting.

Seth rose smiling, spilling his papers. 'Jelaska Lyndrethuse!'

The Third Crusade veteran and his fellow battle-mage swept him into a deeply unmilitary hug and kissed his forehead. 'By Kore, it's good to see you,' she exclaimed.

'And you,' he replied, finding himself blinking back tears, even though Jelaska was cranky, bad-tempered and the scariest necromancer he'd ever met. 'What are you doing here?'

'I've come to cover your arse,' she drawled. 'I understand the Noories keep trying to stick lances in it.'

'That's the truth. But where were you and yours four days ago?'

Jelaska scowled. 'Andreas insisted he'd not outstrip his baggage train, even after Ril Endarion ordered him to split his forces and get his cavalry to Collistein Junction. I suspect he was under orders to stall.'

Politics, Seth thought. *We lost a battle and good men died because of Imperial tabula.*

'How did you get permission to advance?' he asked.

'Permission?' Jelaska sniffed. 'It's my family legion so I'll do as I Kore-bedamned like.' She swept up Seth's goblet and drained it. 'I told Andreas that if he had any balls he'd ride with me.'

Seth laughed. 'That must've gone down well.'

'Like a bucket of swill, but he knows me well enough to take a slap every so often. My lads are the only battle-hardened legion he's got and I'm twice the mage he is, so he sings low when I'm around.'

That sounded about right. 'I thought you were going to retire after the Third Crusade? Didn't you come out of it with enough gold to bathe in rose-oil for the rest of your days?'

'Sure, but turns out, I love this shit.' Jelaska chuckled. 'And my sister's son's a right little smeerlap, so no way was I going to let him lead the family legion.' She plonked herself down onto a stool. 'So, what do I need to know?'

They ate while he updated her, agreed on her deployment and route of march, then set to gossiping of the old days and people they both knew. Seth thought Jelaska looked tired, and despite her occasional dark laugh, there was a gloom about her.

'Are you truly well?' he asked at last.

'In truth . . . well, you know I all but died back in 930. I only pulled through using the sort of necromancy the Gnostic Codes don't like. The hungers I have now? They aren't the ones I used to have. I resist, but it's a slippery slope. My time is coming soon and this campaign looked like a good way to go out.'

His good mood died. 'I'm sorry,' he muttered.

'Oh, don't be. I've had a fine old life – and I'm not dead yet. But *I'm* choosing my time.' She got to her feet and they hugged farewell, then she was gone again.

After that he badly needed another, stronger drink, but that wasn't a luxury he could afford. There were still dozens of papers to read and orders to draft before he could rest. *How much time have I got?* he wondered. Without the windfleet he was almost blind, and the one thing he didn't know was the thing he most needed to.

Where's the enemy?

Collistein Junction, Kedron Valley, Yuros

The truism that a fleeing army moved faster than a pursuing one was new to Waqar Mubarak, but the phrase was on everyone's lips in the sultan's court, and no wonder. Within a day, the Rondian army had vanished over the western horizon, but rather than pursue, the Shihad commanders were more inclined to drink the captured wine and slap each other on the backs, each man loudly proclaiming his own heroism or brilliant tactics. Meanwhile the ordinary soldiers licked their wounds and tried to sleep, a few miles from where wolves and crows picked over the battlefield.

'I don't understand why my uncle doesn't press the advantage,' Waqar muttered to Baneet, Tamir and Fatima, as they gathered in his pavilion. Even behind closed tent-flaps, it paid to keep your voice down and your opinions discreet, even if his uncle was Sultan Rashid Mubarak, ruler of Ahmedhassa.

Or perhaps *especially* because of that.

'We need to bury the dead,' Tamir replied. 'We need to tend the wounded and let the exhausted recover. We'll be moving again soon enough.'

'Soon,' big Baneet agreed, glancing every few seconds at the gnostic spear beside him. Usually Baneet was their calm rock, but tonight he looked drawn and feverish.

The death of Lukadin, who'd perished wielding that deadly spear, was on all their minds.

'We should be mourning,' Fatima said, sitting on the floor with her head in Baneet's lap. It was improper, but she and Baneet were lovers and this was a private space. 'We should be praying for our friend's soul.'

The great battle five days ago had been a stunning victory against the Rondian Empire, but there had been great losses too. The Rondian legions had superior equipment and training, while most of the Easterners were conscripts and barely equipped at all. Thousands had been cut down on the front lines, fighting toe-to-toe against heavily armoured men. But in the end, numbers had won the day – thanks to victory having been won in the air above the battlefield.

That victory belonged to Waqar, but he and his friends knew that truly, it belonged to Lukadin and the spear. 'Remember that moment?' Baneet said. 'The Rondian windships had us by the throat. We were becalmed, they were carving us up – and then Luka . . .'

As his voice trailed away into silence, they all looked at the spear again.

It was some sort of experimental weapon recovered from the Ordo Costruo. The solarus crystal behind the spearhead fed on sunlight and unleashed gnostic energy in deadly, unstoppable bursts. But it had a debilitating effect on its wielder – Lukadin had almost killed himself destroying a string of Rondian ships. He'd been left little more than a husk afterwards, and had been easily slain. But now Baneet had claimed the spear and even Prince Xoredh, the sultan's son, had been forbidden to take it off him.

Waqar would have been happier if the spear had burned out; he knew Tamir and especially Fatima felt the same. *Will we lose Baneet in the next battle?* he wondered, but there was nothing he could do; Baneet was determined.

'I spoke to Sultan Rashid last night,' he told them, knowing this wasn't going to be an easy discussion. 'Once we have found winter quarters, he wants me to leave the Shihad.'

His three friends stared, looking stunned. *'He wants what?'* Tamir asked.

'Is this Attam's doing? Or Xoredh's?' Fatima snarled. They all knew Rashid's sons despised Waqar and were always trying to diminish him in their father's eyes.

'No,' Waqar replied heavily, 'it's about my mother, and Jehana.'

'Is there news?' Tamir asked, for all of them; they'd heard nothing in the six months since Sultan Salim had been assassinated and Sakita Mubarak had been murdered by a mysterious masked cabal; those deaths had opened the path for Rashid, Sakita's brother, to become overlord of the East. At the same time Waqar's sister Jehana had been spirited away and hidden by the Ordo Costruo. Waqar had been permitted to hunt for Jehana, right up to the eve of the Shihad.

They all shuddered, remembering how they'd seen Sakita, reanimated by necromancy, destroy the Midpoint Tower of the Leviathan Bridge; her actions had allowed Rashid to send his massive windfleet across the ocean to invade Yuros. And now Waqar knew just how special Sakita had been, for she had been a wielder of a forbidden magic called the dwyma. He was still struggling with the knowledge that he and his sister had been *bred* to be dwymancers as well.

'Rashid wants me to find out more,' he told his friends. 'He says dwyma is superior to weather-gnosis. He thinks I'll be able to stop the winter.'

'That's impossible,' Fatima scoffed. 'It takes *dozens* of magi just to change the weather for a day, and then you get chaos for a week.' She indicated the world outside their tent where rain was lashing down, the after-effects of the weather-gnosis used during the battle.

'For magi, yes,' Waqar agreed, 'but apparently my mother was the greatest weather-mage ever because she was secretly using dwymancy, not the gnosis.'

'But how will you find someone to teach you?' asked Tamir, the most scholarly of them. 'Dwymancy is a heresy, according to the Church of Kore. And the Ordo Costruo will never help you – you're the sultan's nephew, after all.'

'I have no idea,' Waqar confessed, 'but Rashid says he knows people who can help.' He didn't need to hide his unwillingness amongst friends; they all knew how exhilarating, terrifying and utterly compelling being a wind-rider was. There was nothing like duelling for the skies against the cream of the Rondian knights, flying giant eagle-constructs, the rocs of legend. To put that aside to seek a power he wasn't sure he wanted was a maddening thought. But Rashid had never been someone you refused.

'So when do we go?' Tamir asked.

We, Waqar thought fondly. Where he went, his friends went; anything else was unthinkable to them. But he'd had to fight for the right to take his friends with him. They were all experienced roc-riders now and Rashid had wanted to put them in charge of the fliers while he was gone. But in the end the sultan had agreed that Waqar would need help.

He'd also had to fight for Baneet to be able to keep the spear.

'In the hands of one of our Shihadi magi, such a weapon would be decisive in any battle,' Rashid had argued, 'and we have many fanatics happy to sacrifice themselves for the cause.'

But when Waqar had pointed out that he might need just such a weapon on his mission, and that Rashid would likely lose more than a few magi trying to take the spear off Baneet, his uncle had reluctantly agreed.

'Anyway,' Waqar said, trying to sound upbeat, 'I'm to remain in command of the wind-riders until we reach our winter base – hopefully this place called Jastenberg. Rashid doesn't believe the enemy are capable of defending it and it's large enough to house the entire Shihad, provided the units sleep a dozen to each house.'

'What about Jehana?' Fatima asked. 'Did that Jhafi bint find her?'

Tarita Alhani, the mage-spy from Javon who'd helped them, had promised to keep looking when they'd parted after the destruction of Midpoint Tower.

'I've not heard anything,' he admitted, and Fatima looked at him with an expression of sour vindication. She didn't like Tarita – or any other female who she considered to have an unworthy interest in Waqar. They'd been lovers once, although in truth Fatima was happier with big-hearted Baneet, but that hadn't made her any less protective.

'It's time for bed,' the big man rumbled, pulling Fatima to her feet; the solarus spear was in his other hand.

When they'd gone, Waqar poured Tamir another glass and refilled his own. Seeing Baneet and Fatima together had reminded him forcibly that he'd lost his own lover in the battle. He and Bashara had only just begun to explore their feelings for each other; any chance of building a real relationship had been snatched away by a Rondian lance. He felt hollowed out by loss and missed her dreadfully, especially when the lamps were snuffed and the noise died down.

He refused to use a female captive, but thankfully they'd also captured lots of wine . . .

The Rondian soldiers had carried short shovels with proper steel heads and a decent haft, far better than anything the Easterners had. They turned out to be perfect for burying the dead.

Latif rammed his purloined shovel into the sodden ground, wrenched another wedge of muddy soil out and flung it over the lip of the trench. To the left and right, hundreds of men were doing the same, some singing hymns, albeit desultorily, while drunken officers barked the occasional order.

Beside the holes were piles of bloodied corpses, white, brown and near-black, all stripped to their small clothes and piled together. The piles dotted here and there were just separated limbs, but no one was bothering to match legs and arms and heads to bodies, not when they were all going into the ground together anyway.

This is wrong, Latif thought as he plunged his shovel in again. *A man should be burned, not put in a hole to rot. No wonder daemons haunt these lands.* But they couldn't waste fuel on funeral pyres, and if they didn't find shelter before winter began, they'd all be dead. *How will you shelter a million people, Rashid?*

Finally, it was time to fill in the holes. Latif clambered out first, then hauled up Sanjeep, a paunchy, balding Lakh man. It was Sanjeep's elephant Rani they both rode to war. Sanjeep was at least fifty, twenty years his senior, and he loved Rani as much as anyone he'd ever loved in his life. They'd both been worried about the beast when she'd been wounded in the battle, but praise Ahm, she was mending.

'Where's Ashmak?' Latif wondered aloud.

Sanjeep wagged his head, the ubiquitous Lakh gesture of many meanings; he'd not seen the battle-mage who commanded their tiny unit of three men and one elephant either. They'd lost a third of the forty beasts of Piru-Satabam III in the battle, trying to assail the enemy and never breaking through.

'I am hoping he is tending to Rani,' Sanjeep answered, as they shambled over to the nearest heap of bodies. 'Latif, remember that day we first saw rain in Yuros? Everyone danced like the first day of monsoon – and that was the last day I felt warm.' He put his hands on his hips and looked up at the thick clouds as rain splattered his face and soaked his already sodden clothing. 'I am *so sick* of this cold, stinking, muddy, wind-blasted place. I want to go home and see the sun. I want to be warm again. I don't care if I never see rain again.'

'Me too,' Latif sighed, bending over the bloated corpse of a skinny Dhassan with a gaping hole in his chest. 'Come on, you take this poor beggar's legs . . .'

It was more than a week after the battle before Piru-Satabam III finally loaded their howdahs and crews onto the backs of their elephants. The storms had finally petered out, but everything was wet through, from their clothes and bedding to the churned-up landscape. The men were slipping and sliding all over the place and the wagons were already bogging down, but the elephants ploughed inexorably forward through the mud.

'Rani can walk for all three of us,' Sanjeep said cheerfully.

'It's good to be moving,' Ashmak remarked. 'I'm sick of this place.' What Ashmak had to complain about, Latif wasn't sure – he'd mostly been drinking with his fellow low-blood magi, when he wasn't bedding the captive women.

'It's now a holy place,' Latif replied. He stood beside the scar-faced former Hadishah assassin in the top perch, amidst their sleeping gear and spare quivers of arrows. 'The Godspeakers have blessed it.'

'It's haunted,' Sanjeep called from the lower nest of the howdah. 'I'm glad to be leaving, and so is Rani. Elephants are very sensitive to the spirit world.'

Ashmak snorted, but he didn't contradict the old Lakh. 'The Rondians on our flank were tough,' he remarked, scowling at the remains of the earthworks where the Westerners had continually repulsed them.

That's because Seth Korion commanded them, Latif thought. That glimpse of his old friend galloping into the fray, gnosis-fire lancing from his hands, was etched into his memory. He wished he could just *talk* to Seth, just to find out how he was, to know if he still loved poetry and music. *Or were all those good things bled from you in the Crusade?* But he couldn't admit to knowing who the enemy commander was, so he just chewed some betel-leaf and dreamed of better times, while the Shihad lurched into motion again, to carry war deeper into Yuros.

4

Out of the Ocean

Construct Creatures

The creation of new forms of life was made possible by the gnosis: animagery thus stands at the very border of the known. The Gnostic Codes were swift to try to regulate its use, for in theory, an animage could create a lifeform that is inimical to us, and superior in every way.

LIVIA LAVIDIUS, KORE SCHOLAR, 823

Verelon Coast, Pontic Sea
Noveleve 935

The ocean was freezing, and no whale swam on the surface by nature, so for the three figures clinging to the beast's back, the journey was a brutal test of fortitude.

But Tarita Alhani was a Merozain Ascendant, able to use all facets of the gnosis, and though she wasn't equally proficient in all areas, Water and Air were primary affinities, so she was able to stick to the side of the whale and use animagery to prompt it to surface regularly for them all to gulp down fresh air.

Jehana Mubarak, clinging on to the left side of the whale's fin, was using a gnostic spell to breathe, Tarita assumed. The princess didn't look cold, although she was clearly exhausted.

It was Ogre who worried Tarita the most: the giant construct might be over seven feet tall and massively solid, but his skin, normally a khaki hue, had gone pale and his wide, brutish face looked terrified. He'd spent most of his life in the lower reaches of Sunset Tower and the open skies and vast ocean were overwhelming him. Most of Tarita's concentration was spent calming him, encouraging him to *just hold on*, and prompting him to breathe. Her mind, locked around his, could feel his fear.

<Hold tight, Ogre,> she repeated. <We're nearly there, just hold on . . . >

He was clinging to her as tightly as to the whale, arms as wide as her waist were clamped around her, his big eyes mostly squeezed shut, but sometimes they'd lock onto hers as he began to panic anew. She kept up a stream of reassurance – he was her *friend* and she would *never let him go*, that this was easy for a *big strong man* like him – and so far at least, it was working, his breathing becoming less frenzied.

Tarita had survived some scrapes, but this was without doubt the strangest night and morning of her life. She'd been caught unaware when Alyssa Dulayne and her Hadishah broke into Sunset Tower, but she'd managed to get Jehana and Ogre out – although in truth, it was Jehana who'd got them out, and summoned transport in the form of this whale too.

She presumed Alyssa and her cronies in the Masked Cabal wanted Jehana for her potential for *dwyma*. Dwyma was slow, unlike the gnosis, but it was *immense*, and Jehana might be the only dwymancer alive. The Ordo Costruo had tried to hide and protect her, but they'd failed.

So now it's up to me . . .

They'd been clinging to the whale's back for eight hours now; Jehana had summoned the great beast, but she hadn't been able to direct it. Once she'd admitted that, Tarita had taken over and put them on a northwesterly tack. Darkness had masked them from pursuit, but the sun was rising and unless Alyssa believed them dead – which was highly unlikely – she'd be hunting them.

<Up and stay up,> Tarita sent into the brain, and the whale, who was surprisingly intelligent, rose at once into a torrid seascape under slate-grey winter skies. Tarita looked behind her, fearing she'd see hunting windships, but the skies were empty of anything but clouds.

'*Acha!*' she shouted, because in spite of anything else, this was truly *exhilarating*. In eight hours they'd probably travelled three hundred miles. She rose to her feet and while Jehana and Ogre stared at her fearfully, she shouted, 'We're *alive!*' and gestured wildly towards the south. '*Rukka te*, Alyssa! *We're alive!*'

Jehana looked pained, but Ogre managed a smile, then rumbled, 'Others aren't.' His expressive face was mournful.

'I know, Ogre,' Tarita called, 'and I'm sorry.' The Ordo Costruo might have barely tolerated him, but they'd taken him in; they were his people. 'I'll get you to safety, I promise.' She scanned the northern horizon and this time she glimpsed a dark line behind the waves. 'Land – I see land–'

'How far?' Jehana gasped.

'Who knows?'

'I have read calculations by the Magisters,' Ogre put in unexpectedly. 'One can see sea-cliffs of a hundred yards from more than twelve miles. But sea-cliffs are often twice or three times higher,' he went on, curiosity mitigating his fear. He chanced kneeling, which made him taller than Tarita, and peered. 'We're about twenty miles from land.'

Tarita liked that about Ogre: his looks belied his fierce intelligence. 'We need to make landfall before Alyssa finds us,' she said, just as another huge wave reared up. They plunged into it and emerged spluttering, but they were both grinning madly. She slapped Ogre's shoulder and laughed. 'Good man, Ogre – now, breathe, both of you: we're going in again!'

Jehana, clinging on beside them, just looked miserable.

Less than an hour later, they reached a wet shelf of rock, carved over millennia by erosion. It was low tide and the surface of the water was about thirty feet below the shelf, which extended some eight hundred yards from the foot of the cliff. The waves breaking against the slick, treacherous rock surface had scoured it clean, even of barnacles.

'Don't go too close,' Jehana warned. 'If a wave picks us up, we'll be hurled against rocks.'

'I can see that, Princess,' Tarita snapped, then pointed. 'Look – there's a channel!'

The journey had required all Jehana's reserves. She felt drained to her very marrow, unable to take much more. She was in Tarita's hands, but she didn't entirely trust her. *She's a Jhafi spy*, she thought for the hundredth time. *What does she really want?*

Ogre worried her too. Although he was surprisingly intelligent and compliant, his massive body and sub-human face made her profoundly uncomfortable. *He can speak and use the gnosis – but such constructs are forbidden.* Perhaps the Ordo Costruo were right to let him live – but could he really be trusted?

However, Jehana's prime concern was what she should do now. Something had happened to her at Sunset Tower: she'd touched the power she sought, the *dwyma*, but she needed to do more. All her research spoke of guardian spirits, *genilocii*, bonding with dwymancers, so clearly she needed to find such a thing, so right now, she hadn't much choice but to stay with Tarita. So she let the Jhafi guide the whale along a channel winding towards the sea-cliffs. When they reached a dead-end, Tarita used kinesis to make a twelve-foot standing jump and landed gracefully on the rocks.

'Come on!' she shouted to Ogre.

She thinks of him first, when I am royalty? But Jehana also had the gnosis, so she leaped from the whale's back unaided, dried herself with a wave of gnostic-heat, although it left her dizzy with exhaustion, then she kissed the ground. *We've actually made it!*

Jehana severed her bond to the whale, which looked up at her with one giant eye, then rolled and quickly vanished beneath the water. For a few moments they lay there, taking stock. Tarita was the only one of them with a weapon, her curved sword, and a small leather satchel. At least they'd managed to hang on to their footwear, but they had no food, no water-bottles, no other clothing, and the wind was already beginning to cut through them.

'We need food and fire,' Tarita said after a moment, 'and fast.' She pointed to a notch in the sea-wall, about half a mile up the coast. 'See that low point? We'll make for it; we'll find a way up there.'

Jehana groaned, her body stiff from clinging to the whale so long, but Tarita was right, they had to move. She glanced doubtfully at Ogre, who was staring admiringly at the diminutive Jhafi. His crude leather tunic, his only clothing, fell to his knees. He and Tarita were a strange contrast: she was maybe five feet tall and slender; he towered at least two feet taller, with a barrel chest and arms and legs like tree trunks. His gnarled skin was peppered with rough body hair. He was probably thrice her bulk and weight. His sheer size was frightening.

What species went into breeding him? Jehana wondered. Knowing that she herself had been bred for the dwyma heightened her discomfort – but at least her parents had been human.

As if sensing her regard, Ogre rumbled, 'Is the Princess well enough to walk?'

'I'm fine,' she said tersely, 'but I'm hungry.'

'I have read that tidal flats often trap creatures in the pools,' he said, already looking around.

'So let's all keep our eyes open for trapped fish,' Tarita said. 'Come on.'

They found themselves traversing a strange, surreal landscape. The giant tides of Urte had eroded the land down to the bedrock; beneath most sea-cliffs the tidal flats were often several miles wide. Jehana had read that many coastal communities made their homes in places like this, where food could be plentiful. *I hope there are none here*, she thought. *The last thing we need is to be seen.*

They might have been called flats, but they were anything but, which made them hard to traverse. There were channels everywhere and they had to leap a lot of gaps, even swim some stretches. It took hours to reach the cutting Tarita had spied and by the time the cliffs were rising above them, the pallid sun was beating down.

Suddenly, with a big splash, Ogre plunged his arm into a pool. When he pulled out his fist, he was holding a fish, which he quickly gutted with his taloned fingers, then used the gnosis to a heat a piece of stone. In just a few minutes, he was offering it to Tarita, who grinned and gobbled it down, to Jehana's disgust. Ogre had already caught and prepared another, which he offered to Jehana, but she waved it away, so he ate it whole, bones and all. He burped loudly, making Tarita laugh and slap her thigh as if this were high comedy.

A dirt-caste and an illegal construct, Jehana thought sourly. *And my life's in their hands.*

But she'd been raised to be polite, so she hid her thoughts. Eastern culture was courtly and formal and the Ordo Costruo had prized civilised behaviour as well as learning. More than that: her life might depend on a harmonious relationship with these two, and she was hungry, so she graciously accepted some of the crabs and shellfish that Tarita and Ogre were making a game of catching, and thanked them.

Then she glanced out to sea. Her heart dropped into her stomach. 'What's that?' she called to the laughing Tarita, pointing at a large dot on the edge of vision.

The Jhafi stared, then swore. 'It's them – come on, we've got to get out of sight–'

Even as she spoke, Jehana felt something like a diamond-tipped shaft of energy strike her gnostic wards. She strengthened them instantly, rote learning overriding alarm, and the sense of being sought vanished. 'Someone just tried to scry me,' she told them and followed as Tarita picked up the pace, leaping across another channel and then storming through a small stream, kicking up spray.

The dot was now visibly closer, the triangular wedge of a mainsail clear.

'At least it's only one ship,' Tarita said, as they neared the cleft they sought. 'There were at least a dozen circling the tower, so I think it's probably just a random search.'

'Does she know how we escaped?' Ogre rumbled, sizing up the next channel, the widest so far.

'I'd be surprised,' Tarita remarked. 'Can you jump, Princess?'

Can she say 'Princess' without making it sound like an insult? Jehana grumbled to herself, but she asked, 'Wouldn't her main fear be that we went to Midpoint Tower? Or South or Northpoint?'

'She would fear that more,' Ogre agreed, again surprising Jehana with his intelligence. 'Why didn't we?'

'Talk later,' Tarita told him, slapping his big rump. 'You go first, Big Boy.'

He leaped, using kinesis to propel him across the channel, and when he landed heavily, Jehana noticed with a shudder that his toes were clawed.

Tarita turned to her the moment Ogre was out of earshot. 'He deserves to know why we're here.'

'No.' Jehana did not wish to speak of the dwyma in front of the construct. She turned to jump, but Tarita grabbed her.

'If you don't tell him, I will,' she said belligerently.

'I am a *Mubarak*,' Jehana snapped. 'Blood of Ahm, in any civilised place you'd be beheaded for touching me—'

'Well, luckily for me, we're *not* in any civilised place, are we?' Tarita retorted. 'We're in the Yuros wilds, *Princess*. Can you find your way? Do you know how to find food or make shelter?'

'No – so it's a good thing I brought a *servant* with me, and her beast of burden!' Jehana spun back and leaped the gap. She slapped away Ogre's attempt to catch her and strode on.

I'm being mean-spirited, she admitted to herself, but what was said was said. To be royal was to be right. So she put the matter behind her and hurried onwards without a backwards look. Another scrying attempt broke on her shields; it was definitely stronger this time, but she was fairly sure it wasn't Alyssa.

They found my room, she surmised. *Someone I don't know is using my possessions to find me.*

A small waterfall tumbled from the cutting looming above, spraying their faces. The windship was closer, although still miles to the south, but the tide had turned and waves were beginning to race across the flats. As yet they were breaking well short of the base of the cliffs, but the giant clouds of spray were alarming.

'Come on,' Tarita shouted, 'the waves can cover the flats in minutes! Ogre, can you climb?' When he nodded, she gently punched his big belly and said, 'Then lead the way, my friend, and we'll see you at the top.'

Ogre grinned, lighting up his ugly face. He kindled Earth-gnosis and clambered up the vertical stone, clinging like a fly.

Tarita turned to Jehana. 'Well, Princess?'

'My affinities are Water and Earth,' Jehana told her. 'I'll manage.' But having to climb was humiliating when Tarita, a Merozain-trained mage with all sixteen gnostic studies at her fingertips, just engaged Air-gnosis and soared upwards. She was sweating in rivulets by the time she made the top, and was grudgingly grateful when Ogre's big hand closed about her arm and he helped her over the edge.

'Thank you,' she said, using Rondian, his favoured tongue.

'Sal'Ahm alaykum,' he replied, and while hearing the Keshi words coming from his inhuman mouth was strange, she appreciated the effort and gave him a gracious nod of thanks. Although they could see no human traces, they instinctively kept their voices low.

There was no path, so they followed the stream up a steep slope, taking care on the wet, mossy rocks, until they climbed past the reach of the high tide and plunged into thick, untamed vegetation. Birds flitted from bush to bush and insects hummed.

'It's all so green,' Ogre said, wonderingly.

'How long were you on Sunset Isle?' Tarita asked him.

Ogre considered. 'The Master broke with the Ordo Costruo in 893 and I was rescued in 922, when I was eleven years old. I was born fully grown, with . . . not memories, but knowledge. I could already speak different languages and I knew how things worked, like fire and numbers. I used to dream of a life in open spaces . . .'

Jehana and Tarita stared at him, but there were no points of reference regarding age: no grey hairs, few wrinkles and while his teeth might have a yellowish cast, still he appeared timeless. 922 was thirteen years ago, so if he'd been seven then, that made him only twenty. That accounted for his strange naïveté at times.

'How long did your Master breed you to live?' Tarita asked.

It was an intrusive question, but he said, 'Master said Ogre would live as long as any man.'

Tarita's eyes widened. 'Then he was generous.'

Ogre considered, then rumbled, 'My Master was never generous.'

Who is this Master? Jehana wondered uneasily.

They left the cutting and entered a thick copse of pines. Jehana began to breathe easier, but Tarita was anxious. 'They'll pay special attention to anywhere it's easier to climb the cliffs, so best we keep moving. Where are we heading, Princess?'

'The Vantari Hills,' she replied, thinking of her research into the early dwymancers.

Tarita winced. 'I'm only guessing, but that could be as far as four hundred miles northwest.'

Ogre patted his big stomach ruefully. 'I'm going to fade away.'

'You've got plenty of meat on your bones,' said Tarita. 'I, on the other hand, could well starve.' Apart from an ample bosom, she was skinny as a stick.

Jehana wondered if she had used the gnosis to sculpt her body. She'd never been overly worried about her own looks, and sculpting flesh was hard and energy-sapping, so she'd never had the slightest inclination to try it. On the other hand, she'd also never walked more than a few miles in a single day before. 'A shame we can't make a skiff and fly,' she sighed.

Tarita snorted. 'If we had tools, a workshop, sail-cloth, rope and some nails – and three months up our sleeves, why, certainly we could, Princess. But you'll notice we have none of those things.'

Jehana scowled. 'I was just making a comment. Listen, you don't need to stay with me—'

'In case you've not noticed, we're being hunted from the skies,' Tarita interrupted. 'Once they've decided we're not in any of the other Ordo Costruo-held towers – and believe me, Alyssa Dulayne will have ways of learning that – then she'll concentrate on this coast. We've got to avoid clear skies, hide our fires and cover our tracks, not to mention work out where we are and how to get to where we're going. You can't handle that alone, so you're stuck with us, Princess. Get used to it.'

Jehana exhaled, but she was right. 'What about your Merozain friends?' she asked. 'Are you in contact with them? Do they know you're here?'

Tarita grimaced. 'If only. I'd need a damn good relay-stave to reach across the seas, and anyway, since Midpoint Tower crashed into the sea, the whole of the Leviathan Bridge is under threat. Everyone in the Merozain order, from Alaron and Ramita themselves down to the newest neophyte, are working on saving it. Only an Ascendant can stand the wild energies for any length of time, and they're working day and night. I am given to understand that if they fail, there could be an explosion that will crack the skin of the world.'

Jehana shuddered. 'Then we're on our own,' she concluded glumly.

Tarita patted her arm. 'For now,' she conceded. 'But we're not helpless.'

*

Ogre couldn't stop gazing around in wonder. For the first time, he was free – and outside! These were actual *trees* he was sheltering under, and that was real *earth* beneath his feet, with fallen *twigs and leaves*, and *birds* and *insects* flitting about. Each new glade showed him something he'd only ever seen in books. After years of just the pounding of the waves outside, there were so many sounds in the air – and of course the sea was still audible and comfortingly familiar, the waves like a heartbeat.

He felt utterly alive here. He wondered how he'd endured Sunset Tower for so long – it had been a haven for him and he was grateful, but even there some among the Ordo Costruo had wanted him put to death for what he was, and for who'd made him. Escaping that claustrophobic environment, despite the hardships of the journey, was a blessing.

He wondered if the Master knew he still lived, and as ever when he thought of Ervyn Naxius, he heard the Master's voice: *I am aware of all you do, Ogre. I gave you strength, for labour. I gave you intelligence, because fools have no place in my service. I gave you the gnosis, to ensure you are useful to me. Of course I know you live.*

The Master had a compelling voice: it could be cold, logical and dispassionate, but it could swell up too, with triumph, contempt or bitterness. The Master claimed that only Reason swayed him, but he held grudges for *years.*

When the Ordo Costruo finally discovered their renegade Magister's secret lair in Spinitius, Naxius was away; but they'd found Ogre, working as an enchanter-smith on the Master's designs. They'd almost killed him, assuming he was a monster – then they'd discussed executing him, because he was an abomination, a violation of the Gnostic Codes. In the end, they let him live, but they'd kept him out of human sight.

Ogre is not a weapon or a tool. Ogre is not a monster. He is a sentient being.

That was what Antonin Meiros, head of the Ordo Costruo, had said at Ogre's trial: those words were why Ogre was still alive, and now they were Ogre's mantra. He dreaded the day someone decided that Antonin Meiros had been wrong.

Tarita reappeared on the trail and Ogre's heart lifted just to see her: the first person to ever call him friend. She'd pulled him from the fight when his berserk rage would have seen him killed, and kept him calm in the ocean when he'd been beset by a terrifying rush of new sensations. She'd even breathed air into him, mouth to mouth, when he would have drowned.

That had reminded him of his only kiss . . .

'There's an old cottage just ahead,' Tarita announced, shaking him from his thoughts. 'It looks deserted.'

'Do you fear a trap?' Ogre asked.

'Always,' Tarita replied. 'Neither of you two are the stealthiest, so best you wait at the top of the ridge while I go on alone.'

That was fair enough, in Ogre's view, but Jehana looked vexed. 'I can be silent,' she complained.

'The flash of your jewellery will give you away,' Tarita quipped, and not waiting for a response, darted back down the trail. Jehana glanced at Ogre, shuddered, then hurried after her. The construct followed her.

Tarita had found a small hillock covered with tall pines and inches deep in rotting needles. She crouched behind a fallen tree-trunk and examined the tiny log cabin built into the lee of a low bank. No smoke rose from the chimney and the undergrowth had almost swallowed it up.

Jehana sank to the ground, keeping her distance from Ogre.

After a few minutes, he said in Keshi, 'I'm not a danger to you.'

She pursed her lips, then said, 'You risked your life for me. I trust that you mean no harm.'

Ogre's face swelled hopefully. Silence fell over them again, a little less fraught than before.

Then Tarita reappeared in front of the cottage and waved.

Ogre offered Jehana his hand to help her rise, but she disdained it. He followed her down the slope, a little hurt. Friendship was clearly a rare thing in the big world.

'No wards, no sign of life. No one's been here for years,' Tarita reported when they arrived. Jehana followed her inside, but the hut was so small that Ogre settled for going down on one knee and peering in.

There was only one tiny, cluttered room. A table and two chairs, crudely made, had been broken, as had the brick oven. Smashed crockery and seasons of debris covered the floor. It smelled of animals and birds.

'I found an old grave out the back,' Tarita told them. 'I guess someone buried their wife or husband, then abandoned this place.'

'You'll have to clean it before we can use it,' Jehana commented.

'Excuse me, Princess?' Tarita gave Ogre an amused look. 'Let's each do what we're good at, shall we? I'll hunt and Ogre can lift the big stuff. You did a nifty job with the brooms and mops in the tower, so maybe you can clean?'

Ogre was a little surprised that it was the highborn princess who backed down in the end. 'Very well,' she said, in a surly voice.

'Cheer up,' Tarita said perkily, 'we'll be sisters one day.'

'I think not,' Jehana retorted, stomping back into the hut. Finding an old broom, she set to work.

'Come on, Ogre,' Tarita said. 'I need a hand getting the water tank back in place.'

Ogre drained the water tank, set it back on its stone perch and repositioned the guttering pipes so that any rain would start refilling it.

'Why are you and Jehana not friends?' he asked after a moment.

'I'm dirt-caste, Ogre, and she's royalty. Normally I'm not allowed to talk to people like her.'

'But you're both magi?'

'Yes, but when she sees me she just sees sun-blackened skin and uncouth manners. And I just see a self-centred snob.' She winked and added, 'Of course, it doesn't help that I kissed her princely brother.'

Ogre frowned. 'What brother?'

'Waqar,' Tarita said, raising her voice to ensure Jehana heard. 'He's tall and very handsome, and he kissed me right on the mouth. I think it's love,' she added loudly, winking at Ogre.

Jehana hurled some broken crockery out the door with a loud harrumph of disgust.

Pretty girls fall in love with handsome princes, Ogre reflected: that was another of the themes of the *Fey Tales*. 'Ogre is too ugly to be loved,' he said morosely.

Tarita laughed. 'You're not ugly – you're the handsomest ogre I've met. I'm sure the lady ogres love you.'

'There was only one Lady Ogre,' Ogre replied sadly. 'Master made her. He named her Semakha. We were together for a time. We even kissed, once. But next day Master took her away and I never saw her again.'

Tarita looked hurt by that, to his surprise. 'I'm sorry, Ogre. That was cruel of him.'

'Ogre thinks of her often,' he admitted.

'I'm sure she's out there waiting for you, Ogre.' She raised her voice. 'Just as Waqar's pining for me!'

Jehana threw a broken chair out the door. 'Haven't you got some hunting to do?' she called in an acid voice.

Tarita grinned at Ogre; it was a moment unlike any other he'd had. Shared mirth. Not even the nicest of the Ordo Costruo had given him that. *This is,* he decided, *the best moment of my life.*

Except for that kiss. 'Do you really think Semakha is out there?' he asked.

'I do, Ogre.' Tarita looked up. 'I'll tell you what – you help me get the princess to her brother and I'll help you find Semakha. Tarita and Ogre, on a quest for love – agreed?'

He blinked, his heart swelling, then he dropped to one knee, seized her hand and kissed it. 'Agreed!'

Sunset Tower, Pontic Sea

Alyssa Dulayne sat in the senior magister's suite in Sunset Tower. On the bed, the young Keshi warrior she was currently bedding was locked in sleep by mesmeric-gnosis. The room smelled of wine and bodily juices.

She looked like a statuesque Yurosi woman with long, curling golden-blonde hair, but when she was too tired to sustain that body, her real form emerged: scalped and scarred, with a bent and flayed spine that still wept blood. But she was fully rested tonight and in command of all her beauty, to honour her Master.

She stared into the smoke pouring from the brazier, calling with all her strength. Incense filled the air and the aether reverberated to her call. Then a drawn, aged face appeared in the smoke.

'Alyssa,' Ervyn Naxius rasped. 'What is it?'

'I've captured Sunset Tower, but Jehana Mubarak escaped.'

Naxius' bloodshot, predatory eyes narrowed. 'How?'

Alyssa gave him a terse explanation: how she'd got inside, only to be thwarted at the last. 'There was a way out of the tower we weren't aware of: a window opening beneath the ocean. Somehow they broke it and got out.'

'You say "they"?'

Alyssa hung her head. 'Jehana . . . and the Jhafi spy, Tarita Alhani.'

'Her again? I thought you were going to deal with her?'

'And I will, but I couldn't be everywhere at once.'

Naxius pondered. 'So, just two young women, in the middle of the ocean. Surely you can find them?'

'They're both magi, and water hinders scrying. I've had to send wind-ships in every direction, but I'm concentrating on the other towers of the Leviathan Bridge, and the Pontic coast. There's been no sign of them yet.'

'*I want that girl.*'

'I'll find them, Master, I promise.' She hesitated, then asked, 'What shall I do about the Tower?'

Naxius considered. 'It concerns me that the Ordo Costruo and Mero-zains together might repair the Bridge too soon and be able to join the war. But if we destroy another tower, it might render the Bridge beyond repair, which will also free them . . .' He thought for a bit, then said, 'I think the Bridge can sustain the loss. Set the controls to overload the solarus crystals in the dome – you'll have about an hour to get to the horizon – and then . . . Goodbye, Sunset Tower.'

Three hours later, Sunset Tower had been ransacked of all valuables, including clothing belonging to Jehana Mubarak, and now it was just a scarlet dot on the southeast horizon, a red star against the night sky.

Then that entire quarter of the sky flashed the deepest crimson, like the most vivid sunset. A wave of force broke over Alyssa's windfleet and she feared it might tear her ships apart, but they weathered the battering and in a few seconds it was over.

Alyssa smiled as the men on her windships cheered wildly. *Another dagger to the ribs of the damned Ordo Costruo*, she thought. *What a beautiful evening.*

5

Hearts of Ice

Of Gods and Money

That gods cannot be taxed by worldly institutions seems a clear-cut principle, but it is in fact one of the murkiest set of statutes lurking in our law-books. However, even to point this out is to earn the opprobrium – nay, the downright hatred – of the godly class.

BLAYDEN MALCOTTO, IMPERIAL TREASURER 861–868, MEMOIRS 872

Pallas, Rondelmar
Noveleve 935

The streets of Pallas were choked with anxious burghers with soot-smeared clothing and skin. Smoke hung in the frigid air, rolling up from the docklands to lap at the slopes of Roidan Heights, as tangible as the fear.

As Solon Takwyth, heavily strapped up inside his armour and still in pain, led his force into Kenside, someone recognised his blazon and called, 'It's Lord Takwyth!'

Most of the echoing voices sounded relieved, but some faces hardened: the Corani were outsiders still, only tolerated by the Pallacians, as they had House Sacrecour – in their eyes the noble Houses were all as bad as each other.

'What's happenin', Lor' Takky?' a fishwife called fearfully.

'I'm on my way to find out,' he answered, scratching his chin; the beard he was growing in a belated attempt to conceal some of the scarring on his left cheek itched like Hel. He kept his voice calm, but the reports were alarming.

'There's bin burnings in't docks down Kenside 'nd Fish'art way,' a roper yelled from the doorway of his hole-in-the-wall shop. ''nd there be things in't water too!'

That's what his aides had told him in the early hours of the morning when they'd hammered on his door to wake and arm him: *The dockers say creatures in the river stormed the docks and set them alight*, they'd reported. *They torched the ferries and riverboats and now fires are spreading into the warehouses behind the riverfront.* They sounded like the same possessed construct-creatures that had aided Ostevan's seizure of the Celestium.

Solon listened, then waved his thanks and kicked his steed into motion again. In the crowd, a flash of auburn hair worn *just so* caught his eye and he spun to see, but it wasn't Medelie, *because Medelie is dead*. For a moment he couldn't breathe . . .

He shook away the thought and the moment passed.

It was just after dawn and a sullen glow hung above them in the smoke-thickened air. His aides gusted Air-gnosis to clear the smoke as they clattered into a square two hundred yards short of the docks. There were soldiers everywhere, and he could hear the crackle of burning timbers.

Stolid Oryn Levis came to greet him, his bland, balding features sweaty and worried. 'We're bucketing in water from the wells because we can't get to the river,' he reported, his voice shaky. 'The snake-beasts in there are attacking anyone who goes near the riverbank.'

'Steady, Oryn,' Solon said, in a low voice. 'Is the fire contained?'

Levis wiped his brow. 'Barely. The Fire-magi in the Imperial Guard are doing what they can, but granaries are exploding as the wheat-dust ignites, and Reekers are coming out of the smoke and attacking the bucket-gangs.'

Ostevan's trying our strength, Solon thought grimly. 'Right, get the civilians out, bring up the Imperial Guard and protect the remaining granaries with Fire- and Water-magi. This is the frontline and we *are* going to hold.'

Levis saluted, then paused and asked quietly, 'Are you well enough for this, Solon?'

Inside the steel plate, his left arm was tightly strapped, but the healers had warned him that any jarring and his shattered bones would come apart again. 'I'm just here to give the orders, Oryn,' he said gruffly.

He assigned sectors, then left Levis to it while he formed up his own guard cohort behind Delta Pier. The roads were choked with anxious-looking men and women passing buckets of water, shouting instructions and encouragement. Everyone knew that if the fire got away from them, they'd be engulfed in moments.

He gave a hearty wave of encouragement as people shouted his name, then someone shouted, 'Where's the rukking Empress?' and he spun his horse and demanded, 'Who said that?' No one owned up and he shouted angrily, 'Kore's Blood, man! She's barely given birth *and* she is preparing to bury her husband – show some damned respect!' He glared at the faces and bruised eyes stared back, cowed by his fury. He pressed on, doubly angry now.

They passed into a zone of feverish activity, those at the business ends of the bucket-chains scuttling forward and hurling water into the smouldering wreckage of what had been a row of shop-fronted houses just behind the docks. As he arrived, the cheers were interspersed with as many roaring, 'Abaht feckin' time!'

Solon had just ordered his men down a narrow alley choked by fallen bricks and charred beams when a shrieking black-eyed youth suddenly pelted out of the rubble and leaped on the back of a man who'd just emptied a bucket. Both attacker and victim screeched as the Reeker buried his teeth into the back of the man's neck like a feral dog. The Reeker's victim convulsed as black ichor spread over his skin.

Instantly Solon forgot all his healer's instructions, jumped off his mount and strode forward, blasting mage-fire at the Reeker. He readied his blade as more stormed from the alley, but his attacker was already up again, his blank-eyed ferocity familiar to those who'd fought on Reeker Night. Solon had the Reeker in a kinesis-grip, readying a blow – when a knight in a white tabard bearing the Crossed Keys, the Grand

Prelate's personal sigil, flashed into the mêlée, beheaded the Reeker with one massive blow, then took down the next two while Solon's men closed in.

Impressive, Solon admitted silently.

Once the immediate danger was past, the man lowered his hood and raised his visor, revealing a smooth, olive-complexioned, square-jawed face. 'Exilium Excelsior, Prelate's Guard,' he said formally. 'Grand Prelate Wurther sent me to aid you.'

So this is Wurther's young prodigy? From Estellayne, if I'm not mistaken. Fine, let's see what else he can do.

'You have to sever the heads or destroy the brain to bring these black-eyed bastards down,' Solon rasped. 'You hear about Reeker Night? Same thing.'

The young man said coolly, 'It limits the killing strokes, but I will manage.'

We'll see, Solon thought. 'Don't get bitten,' he warned, then he turned to his cohort and shouted, 'Cuts to the neck, thrusts to the eyes and mouth. Watch each other's backs, stay close and *stay alert.*'

They reached the end of the alley unopposed, then fanned out left and right into the dockland warehouses at the foot of Delta Pier, along Merchants Way, where the river freight was unloaded. Before them was a wall of fire burning out of control, sending heat rolling over them. The only thing preventing the blaze from spreading from the warehouses was Merchants Way itself, which was acting as a natural fire-block.

Solon turned to his aides. 'We need men here, to protect the bucket-lines – Halter, you take a cohort east; Jezeryn, go west. Find the edges of the attack, and get men right down to the water, protected by magi! The wells can't cope with this – we need to use the river.'

The two men took their commands and ran off, quickly vanishing into the smoke. A windskiff zipped overhead, spraying conjured water into the conflagration, and it too was gone. More men poured through and he picked out a runner, telling the lank-haired skinny youth, 'Boy, ask Sir Oryn to send another century to me.'

He only realised it was a girl when she saluted and said, 'Yessir.'

'Name?'

'Lexia, milord. Trainee Imperial Water-mage.'

There's women everywhere *these days*, he thought grumpily. He knew times were changing, but this didn't feel like any place for trainees. 'Find him fast, then get to safety,' he told her, ignoring the disdainful look she gave him as she turned to go. 'It's not because you're a woman,' he called, but it was too late, she'd already vanished.

Lexia quickly returned with Oryn Levis and his men, all wearing soaked scarves as meagre protection against the smoke.

'Battle-array, Oryn,' Solon instructed, 'along this road.'

They all turned as something howled amidst the flames and a renewed wave of heat washed over them from the wall of fire. Then the runner, Lexia, shrieked, 'Watch out!'

Flames gushed around a seven-foot-tall figure with a gigantic serpentine body and four arms, each holding a weapon, as it slithered out. The wave of mage-bolts that immediately targeted it were repulsed by shields that momentarily flared red and almost instantly returned to blue, barely touched. It reared up on its serpent body, lashing out in all directions, but mostly at Solon–

–but it didn't come close, for Exilium Excelsior had already interposed himself, blocking one thrust while cleaving through shields to strike through the wrist of another arm, then spinning athletically away. Oryn Levis, standing beside him, was lashed aside by the snake-tail and sent tumbling like a market-square skittle. Lexia, shrieking, plunged an ineffectual blade into the creature's coils, ducked under a blow from a lower arm, tripped and sprawled – as, *somehow*, Exilium hurled himself sideways into the air so the lashing tail passed under him, then he landed astride the tail, plunged his blade down and skewered it. He went cartwheeling away before the vicious counterblow could touch him.

'Bring it down!' Solon bellowed, shielding the fire gushing from the creature's mouth as the soldiers tried to lunge in with spears. The serpent-construct was female, he realised, judging by the small bare breasts on its torso, the feminine hips and face. Her eyes were jet-black and she had the half-dead look of a Reeker, but she moved with sinuous speed, perfectly coordinated despite that grotesque shape.

Her whiplashing tail smashed over half a dozen men, then she spewed flames over them, leaving them screaming.

Her eyes locked on his . . .

. . . and then she was Medelie, swaying towards him. '*Solon, darling, I'm here . . .*'

For a moment, he was transfixed—

—until something blurred at the corner of his eye and the creature snarled as a thrust meant to impale Solon met Lexia's chest instead – the girl had dived in front to save him. She jolted, clutching at the blade as she slid to the ground.

As if out of nowhere, Exilium appeared again and hammered his sword through the snake-woman's back and into her heart. The Estellan hadn't realised she was a Reeker: he blanched as the construct-woman turned, impervious to the blow, but swayed from her thrusting sword, then unleashed a massive blow, severing her head, which fell to the ground, spraying black blood everywhere. In seconds the creature was just a twitching pile of outsized flesh.

By the time Solon got to Lexia, she was already dead. He hammered the ground in frustration, then looked up at Excelsior and said, more grudgingly than he'd intended, 'Well done.' Being outshone, even under these circumstances, *hurt*.

He lurched to his feet as reinforcements poured into Merchants Way and strode towards a pale-faced Oryn Levis, meaning to berate him for his hesitancy – just as two more snake-creatures launched from the flames, bearing war-axes. Oryn met the first male head-on, ignored the axe-blow that left a great dent in his mail and, swinging his longsword, cleaved the construct in half.

All right, Lumpy, you got there in the end.

He turned to see Exilium evading a blow from the second creature. He dodged the lashing tail with another of his miraculous leaps that finished with a blade driven through the top of the construct's skull: it collapsed like a pole-axed oxen.

Holy Kore, that prick really is good . . .

'What are these things?' Oryn asked, dismayed. 'Where have they come from?'

'Blame the Keepers,' Solon snarled. 'They had oversight of the Imperial Beastariums. Edetta Keeper is behind this. But they're killable.' He patted Oryn's shoulder. 'Secure Merchants Way. I want them swept back into the river.' Then he turned to Exilium. 'You, stay with me.'

Frustrating though it was to not be able to fight, watching Exilium Excelsior in action was almost a privilege. He had the fearlessness of youth and an athleticism that Solon had lost years ago. If he lived and avoided serious injury, he'd eclipse any other knight Solon knew of.

Including me. I hate this growing old . . .

The morning wore on, a steady counter-attack in which their main weapons were buckets of water. The fires ran for two miles along the Kenside docklands, from Northbank in the east to Fisheart in the west, and it was well into the afternoon before the blazes were doused. Solon's cordon fought off hundreds of Reekers and dozens more constructs during the day, but by dusk he was able to leave the situation with his captains. He took the Estellan with him and went to seek Oryn Levis.

They found Lumpy at a crossroads, overseeing a pyre of enemy dead. After they'd brought each other up to date, Solon turned to Exilium. 'You did well today, sir. My thanks.'

'It was an honour to serve,' the Estellan said, without any expression, then with a bow he was off, striding away through the smoke.

Solon and Oryn stared after him.

'I never saw anything like an emotion on his face in the whole day's fighting,' Solon commented. 'Even when we had to deal with dead women and children. He's like a *galmi*: a piece of clay brought to life.'

'Damnably good with his sword, though,' Oryn commented. 'If all *galmi* fought like he did, we'd be unnecessary.'

'With young men like him coming through, we're going to be unnecessary soon anyway.'

He must have sounded bitter, because Lumpy immediately leaped to his defence. 'Milord, it was you who turned the tide here, not him. Thank Kore you got here when you did.'

'You'd have managed, Oryn,' Solon told him, clapping him on the back, although that probably wasn't true.

79

Having seen the ability of these constructs to erupt from beneath the surface of the water, they set up a perimeter well away from the river-bank. Those who'd been bitten and infected were escorted to the Bastion; at least they knew how to deal with the infection by using star-vation and sunlight. The burned-out warehouses were still smouldering, but at least the area behind Merchants Way was well-doused.

'We need the entire riverside watched,' Solon reminded Oryn. 'Post magi in pairs, every hundred yards, on four-hour shifts, from Dawnport to Tockburn. Use students if we don't have the numbers. And warn our people in Emtori this could happen to them.'

'I'll see to it,' Levis promised, surveying the wreckage bleakly. 'Milord, will you join me for a beer? I need to wash this from my palate.'

Dear Kore, I need more than one . . . But he remembered his penance. 'I've got reports to write, Oryn, so have one for me – in fact, I'll stand for all the lads.' He handed Lumpy his purse, slapped him on the shoulder and trudged wearily away.

All the way back to the Bastion, the pressure inside him twisted his gut, the knot of thwarted ambition and his need for Medelie, twisting round and round.

Dear Kore, just give me a bottle and a bed . . .

The silence was his god's reply.

Traditionally, the Imperial family were interred in a crypt beneath the Bastion. It wasn't large – Sertain's descendants were all pure-blooded magi, blessed with long lives but cursed with few children. The sarcophagi and tombs, lavish containers for the last remains of genera-tions of Sacrecours and their closest allies, were organised by clan: there were Fasterius, Mardius and Gerontius chambers, as well as a few memorials to briefer alliances. The Corani had only a tiny cell, housing Lyra's grandmother Alitia, who'd been married to Emperor Magnus.

This is where my mother should be buried, and her husband, Lyra thought, but of course, Natia and Ainar Borodium had been declared traitor by Mater-Imperia Lucia and their bodies burned. *But Mater-Imperia has no burial place at all*, she suddenly thought, some form of cosmic justice:

Lucia and her son Constant had been burned to cinders over the Leviathan Bridge in 930.

Ril would lie in the Corani cell. She'd demanded a private ceremony: the last thing she wanted was a bunch of courtiers pretending they'd respected a man they'd resented. Many families who'd lost sons at Collistein Junction were already using Ril as their scapegoat.

So it was a small gathering: Calan Dubrayle, Solon Takwyth, Oryn Levis, the young Estellan guard Exilium Excelsior, with Domara next to her cradling Rildan. Dominius Wurther presided while Dirklan Setallius haunted the catacombs like a wraith, trying to ensure their security.

Although how will we ever feel safe again? she wondered.

She clung to Oryn Levis' arm, because pudgy, gentle Lumpy was the most comforting presence there, listening to Wurther's sonorous voice. 'Brothers and Sisters in Kore, today we are gathered to remember our brother Ril Endarion and to commend his soul to the Most High.'

Wurther switched to High Rimoni, the language of ritual now spoken only by clergymen and scholars, and the strange words washed over her while she stared dry-eyed at the open casket; she'd spent that night in vigil, burning candles for him and shedding all the tears inside her. Ril's body had been preserved by healing-gnosis, but there was no mistaking his pallor and waxen skin for anything other than death.

Oh Ril, I'm so sorry. If I'd borne you a child years ago, all might have been well. Or maybe I should have done as Radine bid and married Solon: then none of this might have happened – or at least, Radine wouldn't have been involved and you wouldn't have had to lead an army who plotted against you from the first. I chose love, when I should have chosen obedience . . .

She bit her lip at the bleakness of that conclusion.

Is duty the only pure thing in this world? Is love a poison? No, I refuse to believe that.

She took Rildan from Domara's arms and hugged her sleeping son to her chest, letting his tiny heartbeat keep her own from faltering. Oryn Levis draped an arm awkwardly about her shoulders and she let him, because being strong was beyond her right now. But somehow she got through it, placing her own ritual gift for in the casket, watching Basia laying two knotted feathers from Pearl's wings over his heart, then she took her bodyguard's hand and they stood mute as Solon, Oryn, Calan and Exilium closed the coffin and lowered it into the sarcophagus. The stone lid had a relief-carving of Ril. When it shut, the hollow *boom* sucked the marrow from her bones.

'He will be missed,' Calan Dubrayle said soberly. Oryn mumbled something kindly and backed off, leaving Solon to claim her arm and steady her. He looked shattered from his labours at the docks.

'Convene the Royal Council,' she told the men.

'Milady, you are grieving,' Solon said. 'We can meet tomorrow.'

A heart of ice, she reminded herself. *I must be strong.*

'No, we'll meet this afternoon,' she said firmly.

An hour later, still in her funeral black, Lyra settled at the head of the table, unable to hold back a weary, uncomfortable sigh. She was stuffed into a corset to give her waist some sort of shape, which made breathing far from easy. It was only a week since she'd given birth and Domara was constantly nagging her to go back to bed. *But I have an empire to run . . .*

'Gentlemen,' Lyra said, 'we have much to discuss.'

Her council was small: Solon Takwyth, her Knight-Commander; Dominius Wurther as Grand Prelate and Calan Dubrayle, there both as Lord Treasurer and temporarily filling in for the deposed Imperocrator as well. Dirklan Setallius had an advisory role only, and no vote. She had a veto, but she rarely used it, preferring consensus where she could get it.

The afternoon sun lit the glass dome above, basting the ceiling murals in colour, but none of them were in any condition to enjoy it: her councillors looked as exhausted as she was.

Solon was dealing with the continuing dockland attacks. The last two nights, construct-creatures had risen from the waters of the Bruin River and the Aerflus to ravage Pallas-Nord and Emtori. He and Oryn Levis had been constantly rallying the senior knights and Imperial Guard, fighting in shifts, not just killing constructs and Reekers but dousing the blazes springing up everywhere. The damage had been horrendous – hundreds of families had lost everything and they'd had to house the survivors in tents in the larger city squares. The vast Place d'Accord now looked like the camp of an invading army.

His report was delivered in a weary, haunted voice and he never looked up, which was unlike him – the Knight-Commander was usually very direct.

Does he think I blame him for this? she wondered. *Because I most certainly don't.* When he was done she made a point of praising him, but he remained dour and silent.

'How are the people taking these attacks?' she asked.

Wurther answered first. 'My clergy are making it very clear that this is Ostevan and Ryburn's doing: illegal constructs assailing the common people? The mob know who is to blame.'

The mob? Lyra thought worriedly. 'I don't like that term.'

'When they're angry, they're a mob,' Dubrayle put in. 'They blame us for not protecting them: they want us to strike back.'

'Would that we could,' Solon said, 'but the cream of the Imperial and Corani legions are still in the south.'

Or in the ground, he could have added; Lyra was glad he didn't say the words, but they all knew he didn't have to.

'We don't have the manpower to cross the river, nor do we have the ships,' the spymaster said. 'Those on our side were burned out in the first attack and the nearest bridges are ten miles upriver, and more to the point, they're held by the Inquisition. Right now we're helpless.'

'Garod's men are returning from the south,' Solon added. 'He'll have the numbers to attack us soon.'

'Let's burn their ships, then,' Wurther rumbled.

'I wager they'll be ready if we try,' Dirklan pointed out.

'Can we feed the people who've lost their homes and businesses?' Lyra asked Dubrayle.

'We're doing our best.' The Treasurer rubbed his brow. 'But the Imperial granaries are dangerously low and lest we forget, this is a Sun-surge year so the harvest will be poor, count on it. And the Treasury is empty. We are – and this is now official – bankrupt.'

Lyra felt sick to her stomach but she tried to keep her voice steady as she asked, 'What does that mean in practical terms?'

'We have no money, not even to service debt. Come next month, we won't be able to pay our people, so they won't be able to buy food and essentials either. The tax money coming in from the vassal-states is insufficient for our liabilities and in any case, once word gets out, it'll stop altogether. Then our soldiers will desert, the vassal-states will rebel and so the bloodbath begins. All the money in the realm now lies with Garod or Ostevan – or with Jean Benoit's Merchants' Guild, which has always flouted our tax laws. They're all in this together: Garod, Ostevan and Benoit will buy support and promise the world, and then it's every man – or woman – for themselves.'

'It won't come to that,' Solon growled. 'The Corani will remain loyal.'

'But that won't matter, because the Imperial Guard won't, and the Pallas mob will rise with them. Your people won't get out of the city intact,' Dubrayle said.

Your people, Lyra noted. *He's distancing himself already.*

'Then why are you still here, Lord Treasurer?' Dirklan asked coolly.

Dubrayle looked up at Lyra. 'Because I still have one final plan, my Queen. An extreme one.'

Lyra looked from face to face. Wurther's usual bonhomie was buried beneath gloom, Dirklan looked fragile and Solon sullen. There was no energy in these men on whom her reign depended.

I'm doing this for Rildan, she reminded herself. *We can't let greedy dukes and masked cabals destroy us.* 'I will do whatever it takes, Lord Treasurer,' she said. 'I'll consider any plan, and if it's approved, I'll back it to the hilt.'

Dubrayle gave her a considered look. 'Then hear me out – and gentlemen, this means you too. Firstly, and this is the lesser of my two proposed actions, I said earlier that the Merchants' Guild has always flouted the tax laws. They hide their income in paper companies, smuggle goods past our toll stations and deliver us falsified documents. My people know this, but they cover their tracks well. Indeed, it's fair to say that every noble house – even many of your supporters – does the same. I've heard merchants and nobles boast of their cleverness in evading tax. "We are the ones who create wealth here," they say, "so let us be unfettered by tolls and taxes and we'll create more wealth." They make it sound so persuasive – and if you cave in to them, they do extract more wealth – for their own coffers. Only a fraction gets re-spent and meanwhile they gobble up the freedom of smallholders and weaker rivals, continually consolidating power in their own hands. They're as much an enemy of the empire as the Shihad is. Show me a wealthy man and I'll show you his true tax records: I guarantee they'll reveal him as a traitor.'

'But you've said you can't touch them?' Lyra asked.

'We need to try something else,' Dubrayle said. 'Call upon every noble house to deliver a Crusade Bond, a pledge of their patriotism towards the Rondian Empire, in its defence against the Shihad. The amount will be a *loan*, to be repaid when the crisis is over – which means when the Treasury is able. Those who donate will be named and honoured in court. Those who do not will be shamed.'

'But these men have already given men and equipment,' Solon said.

'Let them give more,' Dubrayle said hoarsely. 'Let them give until they bleed, because they're the ones with something to give! If they don't, this empire will collapse around their ears, and then where will they be? Empires don't just fade away amiably. They crash down in flames.'

'Approved?' Lyra said flatly, looking round the table. She really didn't want debate, but in any case, no one objected. 'All right. What else?'

Dubrayle glanced at Wurther before going on, 'Secondly, there is one entity whose immense wealth is within our reach, which has never been taxed. The Church of Kore.'

Everyone stared at him, then all eyes went to Dominius Wurther.

The Grand Prelate glared at his old rival. 'Dubrayle, you slimy little turd,' he rasped. 'I knew you'd try to turn this to your advantage. *Kore is God! Gods do not pay tax!* And I thank Kore Himself that our queen was once a nun and understands that.'

Dubrayle looked sidelong at Lyra, trying to see if Wurther's attempt to elicit her aid had succeeded, but she schooled herself to give no sign, although he was right: every part of her rebelled at the notion of earthly institutions, especially one so universally loathed as the Treasury, putting themselves above Kore Himself.

And yet . . .

'My Queen,' Dubrayle said tersely, his eyes full of passion now, as they always were when he spoke of money, 'please hear me out. Prelates and croziers boast of their personal wealth and the lavish lifestyles they enjoy in their country abbeys. The Church takes in thrice the income your Crown does and where does it go? Into roads or bridges or businesses? Into badly needed windships, or new equipment for the Imperial legions? Not at all: it goes into paintings of clergymen, gilded with haloes in anticipation of their sainthood. It goes into gold-plated roof tiles and lavish murals and sculptures and clothes and jewellery and houses. It goes into the best of wine and food that Yuros can offer. It goes into land purchases and bribery of officials—'

Wurther had been visibly trembling with anger, but now he rose to his feet, shouting in a spray of spittle, 'This is the Empire of Kore on Urte – Kore *is* the Empire!'

'Sounds like something a "Pontifex" might say,' Dubrayle retorted.

'How *dare* you? All the years I've put up with your carping and I've never heard such treasonous bile—I demand you withdraw this outrageous demand! If the Crown is bankrupt, look to your own failings, Worm!'

Solon and Dirklan were simply listening, not taking sides, Lyra noted. And for all her initial revulsion, she reminded herself that she was fighting for the survival of *everyone* tied to her reign, and all those who would suffer if civil war broke out. *I'm fighting for Rildan.*

But she was still appalled.

'Milady,' Dubrayle said, appealing to her directly, 'across the river, your enemies are calling upon the vast network of the Church to support them. While *we* know that Ostevan and Ryburn are members of the Masked Cabal, most people, and certainly most of the clergy, do *not* know that. Ostevan is presenting his deposing of Grand Prelate Wurther as a just action and promising a "new Era" in the Church with a raft of populist reforms that should have been implemented years ago. Dominius won't admit it, but he's lost control.'

'I have *not*,' Dominius shouted, pounding on the table, but the Treasurer ignored him.

'We have a few weeks at most before all the Church's wealth disappears into the Celestium. Take it now and you'll save the Treasury and weather this crisis: Majesty, you'll survive to fight another day.'

The Treasurer's voice was strident and his eyes were boring into her, pleading for her understanding, but Dominius' lugubrious face was also turned towards her and he was shaking his head in horror.

'Milady, *please*, don't let this secular nonsense tempt you,' the Grand Prelate begged. 'Your soul is being purchased by this gutless leech. You *cannot* listen – it is your soul at stake . . .'

Lyra could scarcely think past the clamour of condemnation in her head. Visions of her childhood in the convent returned, of the kindness – and cruelty – of the sisters. If she taxed the Church, could such places even continue to minister?

But where does all that money go? she thought, remembering the wealth that had poured into the convent on market days, the tithing in kind, the estates left by dead people trying to purchase their way into Paradise. Certainly none of it reached her Bastion, where whole galleries had been closed off now because it cost too much to clean them. And there were neighbourhoods of such squalor in the city even the Imperial Guard didn't enter except by the cohort.

Then she thought about the ornate, sumptuous splendour of the mighty marble domed palaces across the river. She'd always thought of it as the rightful splendour due to Kore, but how could it be, when Ostevan was now wallowing in that luxury and plotting her downfall?

Dear Kore, how can such a decision be placed in my hands?

She looked at Takwyth, but his gaze slid away, and that was so unlike his usual frankness that she wanted to stop everything and ask him *why*. But Dirklan gave her an encouraging nod that she couldn't read at all.

This is too much for me, she thought. *I need to think. I need to pray.* She wondered if that latter impulse meant her decision was already made. *Is that instinct my answer?* Or was it just rote-learned weakness, the evasion of responsibility – to pretend some higher power had made a decision that was really hers?

Gutless leech, Dominius had called the Treasurer because of this proposal – but how much courage did it take to challenge centuries of legal tradition at the potential cost of his entire career? Throughout the five years of her reign, she'd thought of Grand Prelate Wurther as an ally, primarily. He could be infuriatingly self-serving, but he was witty and affable and he had enough flexibility to tolerate her dwyma heresy. He was like a kindly uncle, wayward at times but fundamentally on her side.

Dubrayle, on the other hand, was dull, pedantic and reduced everything to a fiscal value. He was obsessed with money and contracts, things that bored her, and she'd never liked or wholly trusted him. *Has he been a truer ally all along?*

She badly wanted to postpone this decision, to take counsel with her conscience and her God, but if they were now penniless she couldn't . . .

'Lord Dubrayle,' she said, 'how would such a thing be implemented?'

'No!' Dominius gasped. 'My Queen–'

'*How?*' she said again, holding up a hand for silence, because asking *how* didn't imply a decision, in her mind at least.

Dubrayle's gaze locked on hers and she realised that he'd never expected her to even countenance the proposal. But he was seldom unprepared and responded swiftly, 'We'd enact sumptuary taxes and estate levies. Assessors would be sent into each Church property to confiscate wealth of an obviously *non*-religious nature – silver and gold platters, jewellery, ostentatious secular clothing and the like, armouries, stockpiles of commercial goods – anything we can convert to coin. And each bequest would be retrospectively taxed back to the beginning of your reign, with a requirement that one quarter of all land and property gifted to the Church be paid to the Crown as estate tax.'

Dominius' face had gone grey. 'This is an infamy,' he choked.

'Infamy, infamy, you've all got it in for me,' Dubrayle drawled.

'Please don't disrespect His Holiness,' Lyra chided the Treasurer.

'But you'll let him rob me?' Dominius thundered. 'I'll not stand for this–'

Somewhere along the way, Lyra realised that the decision was made. With Dubrayle's vote and her casting one, she could settle this. *This is survival*, she thought, *but somehow, I'll make it better – one day, when Garod is dead and the Shihad is broken.*

'No, Grand Prelate,' she said, 'the decisions of this Royal Council have always been made collectively, and however much we argue and debate behind these doors, we will present a united front to the world. I agree to Count Dubrayle's proposal and I wish to see the laws drafted. You will support them by word and deed.'

'I'll go into exile,' Dominius countered. 'I'll fight this, and you, if I must! The vassal-states will unite behind me–'

'The dukes want money as badly as us,' Dubrayle countered. 'I'm betting they'll follow suit.'

Dominius looked apoplectic now. 'Never! I am leaving–'

'No,' Lyra replied firmly, 'you are my guest, and I wish you to remain.'

The room feel silent as Dominius stared at her, his big hands clenching and unclenching. Even Takwyth was roused from his gloom, staring at her with unreadable eyes.

Dear Kore, I've just placed the Grand Prelate under house arrest . . . My soul will go straight to Hel.

Dominius visibly reined in his fury. 'Milady, don't make such a far-reaching decision when you are consumed with grief. You've just buried your husband – don't let your emotions blind you.'

Typical man, to blame my emotions, Lyra fumed. 'I'm not emotional, Grand Prelate. I have a heart of ice. You and your clergy will speak in favour of this measure. That is my will, and it shall be done.'

She saw Dominius glare at Solon, as if some point had been proved, but then he sagged and she knew she'd won.

'You have my approval,' she said, looking at Dubrayle. 'Draft the law and bring it to me.'

The Celestium, Pallas

The Hall of Leaven might have begun life as a huge bakery for the Kirkegarde barracks in the 600s before falling into disuse, but as it had the advantage of being halfway between the Celestium and the Rymfort and, more importantly, was entirely underground, with concealed access, it became a handy place for informal meetings as the Knight-Princeps and Supreme Grandmaster of the Kirkegarde became increasingly autonomous from the Celestium.

This time, the summons to the Hall of Leaven came from neither the Knight-Princeps nor the Pontifex, but their Master, Ervyn Naxius.

And he won't be happy, Ostevan worried as he paced the corridor, a single mage-knight behind him. The man had been infected by Abraxas and his identity crushed by the daemon; now Ostevan genuinely couldn't remember his name.

The regular thud of boots on stone echoed through unseen nooks and crannies until they entered a smallish space where two thrones faced each other across a circular table set with a dozen plain chairs. Ostevan took his place just a few seconds before Dravis Ryburn appeared and sat on the Rymfort throne opposite. His coarse, dark features were a stark contrast to the feminine beauty of his lover, Lef Yarle, who stood behind him.

Ostevan met Ryburn's gaze coolly, feeling the menace and malice radiating from his colleague and rival.

Then the sound of a woman's shoes clip-clopped on the stone floor and to his surprise, Edetta Keeper appeared. The haughty grey-haired woman made for a chair between the two thrones.

Before he could react, a silvery light appeared and the spectral image of a third throne manifested, with a robed figure hunched in the seat, his face cowled.

'Thank you for coming,' said the aetheric projection of Ervyn Naxius. Unusually, he looked all of his centuries of age, and his dry voice, projected through a relay-stave, crackled faintly. 'What is your status?'

He turned first to Ryburn, who gestured to Lef Yarle, which surprised Ostevan. *Is he giving Yarle a stage to prove his worth, or disassociating himself from bad news?* Yarle had a reputation as the best up-and-coming swordsman in the Church, if not the empire, and he had an almost preternatural beauty. Now he brushed away a lock of blond hair falling artfully over his perfect, so-pretty face. *If men attracted me, you'd be hard to resist*, Oste-van conceded. That Yarle shared the bed of his master was an open secret. Frocio men were seldom able to be so obvious, but Ryburn's fear-some reputation gave him a certain immunity.

Even Yarle's rich voice was melodic and alluring. 'We've raided across the river for three days and burned or stolen every vessel larger than a dinghy. We hold the river towns on the Bruin and we have cut off every way the empress can assail us by land or water. She has no sizable wind-fleet, so we're secure. Once the Sacrecour army arrives, we'll be ready to attack.'

It was a fair appraisal. A good many of the snake-men constructs had been lost, but they'd fulfilled their main purpose, and in any case, over-use of them ran the risk of frightening off potential allies.

'We now have a split clergy,' Ostevan put in, to prevent Yarle from taking all the glory. 'Wurther has taken shelter with the empress. But we need to be mindful that we don't alienate the common people.'

'Why?' Ryburn sniffed.

'Because there's lot of them. That's why they're "common".'

'Agreed,' Naxius said. 'Garod Sacrecour's army is now on its way back north. It will reach you before the month's end. You've destroyed the ability of the Corani to hurt you, so now abide and prepare for the decisive strike.'

Ryburn was irked to concede the point, Ostevan noted with pleasure.

Edetta spoke for the first time, her voice cool. 'I've been in Dupe-nium, ensuring Garod Sacrecour toes the line. He's buoyed by the return of Cordan and Coramore and prepared to commit men at our command.'

'Excellent,' Naxius purred, then stared at Edetta. 'Tell me of those children: Coramore was possessed and now she's not. Lyra forced Abraxas out of the girl and now he can't return. How did that happen?'

'We don't know, Master,' Edetta admitted.

Ostevan had felt it when the girl had vanished from the shared mind of the daemon, but he'd thought it some kind of suppression spell, not a permanent solution. *Can we actually be freed?*

'Find out,' Naxius told Edetta. He looked around the circle with malevolent eyes, clearly in a foul temper. 'The queen and her dwyma remain a threat. An untrained dwymancer is a potential asset, but she's passed that stage. Step up your efforts to kill her.'

'She's buried deep inside the Bastion, Master,' Ryburn said, his rough tones ill-suited to supplication. 'I sent a daemon-possessed snake-man into her dwyma-garden during the raids, but lost contact with it the moment it entered. I fear conventional assassins are required.'

'Then *use* them,' Naxius instructed shortly. 'Get inside the heads of those who surround her. Find places you know she will be and lie in wait. She's not even a mage – she can't shield! Just. Kill. Her!'

Ostevan didn't wait for the others but dropped to one knee and promised, 'Of course, Master. We will not fail you.' The others followed, parroting his words, but he'd been first.

When the Master was angry, that mattered.

Dupenium, Rondelmar

Princess Coramore Sacrecour took about a week to twist all the maids, servants and guardsmen who manned the royal suites around her fingers. She still shuddered at the memory of sharing her head with that horrible, vile Abraxas, but the insights he'd provided into the character of the people around her had left their mark. She could read people so much better now, almost as if she could see into their souls. She didn't like much of what she found, but she'd discovered the little levers she needed to pull to get her way.

That included being able to escape her minders when she wanted to, and today was just such a day. Cordan was locked up with his private gnosis tutor – she *so* envied him having the gnosis already – and Uncle Garod was overseeing the muster of his legions. It was bleak, with sporadic showers hammering down on the cold, mossy stone of Dupenium Castle, and the air was bitterly cold, so she swathed herself in a thick grey woollen cloak before slipping down the servants' staircase and out through a postern gate into the family cemetery.

Her ancestors had ruled Dupenium since before the Ascendancy of Corineus and the coming of the magi. There had been Dupeni among the Blessed Three Hundred and they'd quickly seized their old home city and married into the Sacrecours of Pallas. Dupenium had been the second city of the Rondian Empire for half a millennium.

The cemetery and crypts surrounding her marked that passage of time with increasingly grandiose mausoleums and marble statues and chapels dedicated to this or that august forebear. With her red-gold hair covered by a cowl and her pallid face shadowed, Coramore wafted through the old graves like a ghost.

She didn't know what she was doing here, only that she wanted to be alone to enjoy the silence in her head. No Abraxas; no wall of shrieking mouths and raking claws and beady, staring eyes. No cacophony of hate and fear and lust and misery reverberating through her subconscious; no running commentary on the faults and failings of all around her, no exhortations to violence or self-abuse.

Just this wonderful silence.

I'm sick of the parties celebrating Brylion Fasterius running away from the battle at Collistein Junction. I'm sick of Uncle Garod crowing about Ril's death and Lyra's grief. I hate them all.

Then a flash of colours caught her eye amidst all this miserable grey stone and mud: a gleam of rich scarlet and emerald. She went to look, making her way through a tumbledown gap in a low wall into the oldest part of the cemetery and clambering over graves with broken marble covers revealing yawning darkness beneath.

The red was a berry, a single bead like a bloody tear, hanging amidst a cluster of lush green leaves. A single tree was thriving while all the others around it withered in the winter cold. She sucked in her breath. She'd seen another like this.

It's like the sapling in Lyra's garden, the one beside the pond whose waters drove Abraxas out of my body.

She looked around her, but she was totally alone and the rain was beginning to sweep in again, so she plucked the berry, crawled into the doorway of the nearest crypt, where a lintel sheltered her from worst of the rain, and bit down.

A sharp, sour taste filled her mouth and for a moment she had an insight . . .

The rain feeds the soil, that feeds the roots, that causes the tree to grow . . . along with the sunlight that dries the rain and takes it up into the clouds . . . where it becomes rain. Life is like a tree of water and light . . .

6

Gazda and Kirol

Silver

It was discovered very early on that certain plants and minerals were either more pliant to the gnosis or resisted it. Both have their place. One of the more intriguing is silver, which has been found to hinder certain applications of wizardry and necromancy.

JOVAN TYR, HEALER, 783

Gazdakap, Mollachia
Noveleve 935

Dragan Zhagy paused his mount on a hillside overlooking the town of Gazdakap, which in the old language meant tollgate, but it was rooted in the same word that gave him his title: Gazda. There had been a gazda, a warden of the people, before there had been kings, and Gazdakap was the place where the levies were taken from traders for the gazda's upkeep.

A delegation from the Imperial Legion stationed in Lapisz had arrived in town that night. They'd heard rumours of the overthrow of Kyrik Sarkany and wanted to meet with the new power in the land: Dragan himself.

Except I'm not the supreme power here, Dragan mused grimly. *That's Asiv, who gave me this devil-choice: to die tamely, or to accept the curse of Abraxas.*

You'll have all the powers of the daemon, but you'll be the one who wields that power, Asiv had promised, and that much was true. *You'll become a mage-king, with all of the gnosis at your fingertips.* That was true too. But in other ways Asiv had played him false.

95

*He never told me what it would actually be like, to house a daemon in my skull
and a spawn in my chest. I've never revelled in killing as much as I do now. Any
anger I feel is magnified tenfold. I'm becoming a monster.*

But even worse was what had been done to his beautiful, innocent
daughter. Asiv had infected her too, when he'd promised he wouldn't –
that was bad enough. But Sezkia had been profoundly damaged by that
invasion and he could barely bring himself to look at her now, to see
the thing she'd become.

But he forced himself to face her as she pulled back her hood, freeing
blonde hair that tumbled over her shoulders, framing her pale, red-
lipped face. Her eyes were radiant blue, at least when the daemon inside
was quiescent. She wore a close-fitting red dress today, the low-cut bodice revealing a creamy cleavage.

She looks like the ghost of a harlot, Dragan thought miserably, but said
only, 'We're here.'

'Here,' Sezkia echoed blankly, a parody of his demure child, and
hearing the emptiness in her broke his heart all over again. She'd been
pious and he imagined that virtue had made her fight all the harder
against the daemon. *I succumbed to this evil willingly, but she fought.* That
shame ate at him.

When her eyes went black, when Abraxas was controlling her, she
radiated menace, but right now she just looked lost. 'It's Gazdakap,' he
reminded her.

'Gazdakap,' she echoed.

'We're here to meet with the Imperial Legate.'

'Legate . . . Oh.'

Father and daughter took the path down the slope and into the village. The few villagers out and about slunk away, when once they'd
have greeted him heartily.

A Rondian cohort was lined up in the well-square, led by two red-
uniformed magi. The Imperial seal on their tabards told him they were
a legate and secundus, the two most senior mage-officers of the legion.
The legate was a tall, soft-faced man of middling years with a fashionable haircut and a beard that failed to conceal an irresolute chin. His
secundus, an older man, had the flushed face of a drinker.

Dragan swung from the saddle and helped Sezkia down before addressing them. 'Legate Galrani? I am Dragan Zhagy, Gazda of Mollachia.'

'Cavan Galrani, Imperial Legate of the Impetrates XXV legion,' the legate replied. He sounded Midrean. 'This is Secundus Rian Trevalla.' They shook hands, then Galrani indicated the tavern. 'Shall we?'

Dragan knew this little scene was supposed to make him feel intimidated: he and his daughter were putting themselves into the power of the much-vaunted magi. But he had Abraxas inside him ... He suspected the Rondians were alarmed by the destruction of the Delestre legion and the mysterious death of Governor Inoxion. They needed reassurance, and to reach some kind of accommodation.

The tavernier touched his forelock; he knew Dragan, which meant the foaming mugs of ale he set before the three men were sure to be his best. The blood-red wine he handed to Sezkia made her eyes light up, then she sniffed it and pulled a disappointed face.

When do we kill them? she breathed into Dragan's mind, fixing her eyes hungrily on Galrani.

He quietened her, then raised his cup in toast. 'To a peaceful resolution.'

'I can drink to that,' Galrani said grandly, then launched straight in. 'I understand that a gazda and a king are not the same thing?'

'Ysh. A king – we call it "kirol" – is hereditary ruler of the people. A gazda is an elected guardian of the people.'

'Mostly against your own king, if my knowledge of your history is correct?' Galrani asked. 'Such a thing would not be tolerated in the empire.'

'Our kings have never much been pleased by it either, but the tradition is strong.'

The legate glanced at his secundus, then squirmed a little uncomfortably as he noticed that Sezkia's eyes were still fixed on him. 'Your daughter is very beautiful, gazda, but I don't understand her place here?'

'She's here to aid negotiations,' Dragan said stiffly, while inside him Abraxas snickered. 'Let me update you on events in Hegikaro. At the end of Octen, the people of Mollachia rose against Prince Kyrik Sarkany at his coronation, in rejection of his policy to give refuge to Sydian barbarians. I now control Hegikaro, and will continue to do so – as gazda. We will resolve the matter of the kingship in our own time.'

'What befell Sarkany? And what about the Sydians?'

'Sarkany is dead, although some are spreading a lie that he escaped into the wild. He did not, and his few remaining supporters are being hunted down. The Sydian scum he brought to the wedding are all dead: the chieftain, the whore he "married" and many others. The rest are in the Domhalott.' He leaned forward. 'My men could guide you to them.'

Galrani and Trevalla shared another look, cautious but clearly interested.

You've been left isolated, leaderless and scared since Inoxion died, but I'm offering you the chance to pretend you brought a rebellious kingdom back to the imperial bosom. Try not to bite my hand off.

The discussion proceeded apace as he explained where the Sydians were to be found and how they might be trapped and killed. The Imperial officers lapped his words up like the beer they swilled. Trevalla was quickly almost incoherent, downing three for every mug the others managed. Sezkia's wine was almost untouched.

Having agreed their plans for what remained of the Vlpa clan, they set about agreeing how they would divide their authority in Mollachia thereafter. Dragan let them have the better of the negotiations – he had no intention of fulfilling the terms, so the concessions meant nothing. Finally, the essentials agreed, he leaned towards Galrani. 'There is one more thing. As you know well, the prized mage blood is of great value and would enhance any line. I am anxious to bring it into my family.' He indicated Sezkia, who smiled and licked her lips slowly, letting her tongue play along the rim of her teeth as she eyed Galrani.

The legate's eyes bulged. 'You want me to . . . uh . . . *spend time* with your daughter?'

'She is fertile right now, and she is a virgin.'

Galrani's gaze shot back to Sezkia: a girl as lovely as a rosebud, ripe for the plucking – and *his* to pluck.

Dragan had heard that women were thrown at magi all the time, so Galrani would see nothing untoward in the offer; he'd already bedded dozens of the Lower Valley girls and at least two bastards had been implanted in their willing bellies.

The legate offered his hand to Sezkia and they rose, eyes locked hungrily on each other.

Dragan turned to Trevalla. 'Secundus, while we're waiting, let me show you the cellars here. Ale is all very well, but you look like a man who appreciates a *real* drink. I know I do.'

They left half an hour later, leaving two new allies behind them.

Or rather, slaves.

Osiapa River, Mollachia

It was a week or more since Kyrik had stumbled across the frozen Lake Droszt and into the path of Rothgar Baredge and Fridryk Kippenegger. They were still being hunted relentlessly, day and night, by the Vitezai. The daemon-possessed men could see in the dark, and during the day, someone was scouring the countryside using infected birds controlled with animagery. Every dusk they saw whole flocks of dying birds, for such lesser creatures couldn't sustain possession for long.

That left just dawn and twilight when the wilderness was largely empty of hostile eyes, but the terrain was challenging at the best of times, so they'd travelled little more than twenty miles in that week.

Now, as dusk fell and wolves started howling in the distance, Kyrik looked up at the giant moon, wondering where his brother was and if Hajya really was still alive, somewhere in Hegikaro's dungeons. And whether he'd live to find out.

They huddled into the wilderness camp, a small crawl-space formed by a rock-fall two seasons ago where they could shelter from the wind and snow. Even better, the light of a small fire would be concealed from enemy eyes. They had been subsisting on little more than snowmelt and Rothgar's meagre travel rations, supplemented by the occasional snow-hare, but tonight Rothgar passed around a flask to warm them.

Kyrik raised the flask. 'Friend Kip, in Mollachia there was once an old tradition, sadly lapsed of late, that I recall my grandfather performing:

the cup-wish. The first to drink at a gathering makes a wish for the future happiness of those present. My wish is that your folk find peace and safety here, despite this difficult beginning.'

They all drank to that, then Kip asked the Stonefolk ranger, 'May I see your sword?'

Rothgar stopped whetting his blade and handed it over with a rueful look. 'This is the Baredge sword. "Wulfang", her name is. My honour is in her.'

'Her? Your sword is a woman?' Kip guffawed. 'That's crazy!'

'To my people, a man's sword is his first wife. It's given the night you turn fifteen.'

Kip examined the blade with a frown. It had a crosspiece formed as a wolf's head and the steel had a lustrous, watery look. 'It looks expensive,' the big Schlessen said dubiously, handing it on to Kyrik.

'All women are expensive,' Rothgar chuckled. 'It's a silver and steel alloy called argenstael – it's brittle, and a beggar to keep sharp. The weight's all wrong, too. But my stupid grandfather said the sacred words over her, so she's ours for eternity.' Then he chuckled. 'And she might just be our secret weapon.' He described its deadly effect on the possessed men.

Kyrik was still thinking of Hajya – and about the *Sabie de Kiroli*, the royal sword of Mollachia, which he'd lost in Lake Drozst. *I have neither my wife nor my sword. I'm a king without a kingdom, a husband without a wife . . . But I'm still alive, Dragan.*

And so was Fridryk Kippenegger. The last time Kyrik had seen the big Schlessen, at the disastrous coronation, he'd been hurling himself through the stained-glass windows of Hegikaro Cathedral, a Clan Vlpa girl in his arms. Their defences had collapsed by then and it was every man for himself. Kip had told them the girl, Korznici, had immediately left to seek her own clan in the Domhalott. No one had heard from her since.

As they compared notes, they built a picture of exactly what they faced: good men infected by some kind of possession and turned into killers. But they could be killed by beheading and by argenstael – or even just by silver, perhaps; that was worth exploring.

But Dragan Zhagy had been something more. He'd become a mage, far more powerful than Kyrik's quarter-blood strength, and although ferocious, he'd been rational still, not crazed by blood like the Vitezai men.

Kyrik went to speak when something growled, out of sight, and they all went still. Kip gripped his big zweihandle, but Rothgar motioned him to stillness and readying his bow, crept down towards the opening.

As Kyrik moved silently to join him, the hunter, moving with painstaking slowness, drew and aimed. Six seconds passed like an eternity – then Rothgar let out a slow breath and loosed.

They heard a muffled thud as something fell.

Rothgar signed again for silence and readied another arrow. It was another full minute before he lowered his bow and clambered through the small hole and down the rock-fall. Kyrik followed, while Kip stayed by the fire, readying their gear. Rothgar was standing over a dark mound in the snow.

'It's Ferdi, one of our hunting dogs,' he said sadly, looking at the black fluid running around the arrow jutting from the right eye socket. It smelled like sewage.

'Good shooting,' Kyrik murmured.

'I had to get an instant kill, straight to the brain,' Rothgar said in explanation, then added, 'He's a bloodhound; he could smell us.'

'Then we need to move,' Kyrik said, even though it was freezing and would soon be snowing again. They'd all noted the strange way the infected men appeared to be aware of what was happening to each other, as if one intelligence controlled them all. 'Others may already have sensed his death, or been aware of what he'd found before you killed him.'

They were moving again inside ten minutes, creeping back to a stream that joined the Osiapa River as it danced down its course towards Lake Droszt. Moving at night was a risk; for all Kyrik and Kip were magi and Rothgar a seasoned hunter, their pursuers had better night-sight. For the first time in weeks the clouds were thin and Luna was full: Urte's giant moon made the night almost as clear as day. Their luck held, even when they almost ran into a patrol of black-eyed Vitezai men stumbling down the trail towards them.

'Did you see the way they walked?' Rothgar noted, when they were gone. 'Two of them tripped on tree roots – they were moving as they do in daylight.' He pointed up at the moon. 'I think Luna blinds them for us.'

'Mater Lune is the patron of crazy people,' Kip chuckled. 'Of course she's protecting us.'

The land Kyrik had gifted Kip's Schlessen tribe, thanks for getting the Vlpa clan into Mollachia, was still some twenty miles from where they stood, but at the next fork in the trail, Rothgar took an unexpected turn.

'Shouldn't we go that way?' Kyrik asked.

Rothgar tapped his nose. 'Kip's people have moved.'

Kyrik trusted him enough to just follow along and they camped that night in the mouth of an old silver mine, long since closed. His final thought as he fell asleep was of Valdyr, wondering where he was and if he was safe.

But his dreams were all of Hajya, as she had been, blended with nightmares of what she might now be.

Feher Szarvasfeld, Mollachia

Valdyr left Watcher's Peak on a bleak midmorning, two nights after Luhti and Zlateyr passed from the world. He spent a day grieving, Gricoama at his side, but the next morning, the beast made it clear they must go. Reluctantly, Valdyr agreed. The nature of Watcher's Peak had already started to change, just as Luhti had warned. The dwyma was fading and the peak no longer offered him protection, or a path to power.

Gricoama and I must forge our own genilocus by going to Cuz Sarkan. It wasn't far, but it wouldn't be an easy journey. Cuz Sarkan, or Dragon Mountain, lay to the east, in the mountains at the head of the valley-kingdom. The River Szajver, the Bloodmouth, which sprang from caves beneath the active volcano, was red with iron ore. It was a perilous place, not visited lightly.

Luhti said I'd know when I was ready. I surely don't feel ready yet.

He set out without a plan, intent only on finding somewhere safe from Asiv. Magi couldn't scry through stone, so he decided to seek one of the closed mines in the upper Osiapa and Reztu Valleys, hoping he might meet a hunter or trapper who knew what was happening in Hegikaro.

It was a frigid morning, with the wind howling through the peaks bearing flurries of snow. Winter came to Mollachia in Noveleve and never left before the end of Aprafor. Up here above the snowline, almost all life ceased for four to five months of the year. He rubbed the remaining fat from the night's meal on his exposed skin and piled on every fur he possessed before they left. He could still sense the dwyma, but not as intensely, and when he tried to touch it, it was like trying to grasp an eel in a vat of oil – frustrating, even frightening, like a foretaste of going blind. Luhti had been right, somehow he needed to re-bind himself to it.

But he pushed aside that worry and concentrated on the journey. They descended Watcher's Peak cautiously, and when they reached the trail-marker, a stag's skull nailed to a post, dark shapes closed around them, grey-brown and low-slung. They bobbed their heads as Gricoama passed, then followed. They were his pack, now.

Gricoama and his wolves led him east, a difficult descent along a track Valdyr didn't know, and by midday they were picking their way through pine forests that had never seen an axe, crossing tiny streams already beginning to freeze, skirting clearings, avoiding open skies.

Every so often he felt what he assumed was gnostic scrying; he could even smell Asiv's sickly opium sweat in the air, but the dwyma still hung like fog about them and the Eastern mage couldn't pierce it.

When they rested, he chewed the last of the previous night's meat – until he heard a single wolf cry from behind them. The whole pack – there were two dozen wolves shadowing him now – rose to their feet.

Our trail is found. Almost choking in his haste, he gulped down his mouthful, jumped to his feet and took off at a steady run. One beast after another started peeling off and dropping back, until he and Gricoama were alone.

As far as he could tell, they were heading east across the northern edges of White Stag Land. Gricoama was deliberately seeking out places known better by beast than man. All the while Valdyr tried to grasp the dwyma, but the further he was from Gricoama, the harder it got. He realised just how much Luhti had helped him, acting as their conduit; without her, he was feeling increasingly helpless.

But there were signs that the dwyma itself was aware of their passing: he heard whispers on the breeze and strange shapes would form in the fog, like watching eyes. The sense of being concealed intensified as snow flurries and mist enveloped them, covering their back-trail. Luhti had told him that without a dwymancer to articulate its will, the dwyma was quiescent. *Perhaps it's Gricoama's presence*, Valdyr thought – and the wolf looked back, eyes flashing. His heart thumping, Valdyr ruffled the beast's fur gratefully. *We're in this together.*

Gricoama trotted confidently forward, leading him into a crevice, where they found a tiny camping site, the sort hunters left for themselves in the wilds. 'Well done,' Valdyr praised the beast, 'you are a saver of lives.'

While Gricoama went hunting, he ate strips of dried meat moistened by snowmelt and warmed in the embers, letting his mind drift about the fringes of the dwyma, which was as deep as he could get into it at the moment.

The mysterious northern woman didn't call into the aether every night, but this time she did, very late in the evening, when Valdyr had almost given up.

<*Hello?*> he heard faintly. <*Is anyone there?*>

Valdyr hesitated: she was clearly Rondian and that meant the empire. *But dwyma is a heresy. Who is she?*

But he was at an impasse. He needed someone who knew what he was going through, someone to share experiences with, so he put aside a lifetime of trusting no one – and Luhti's explicit warning – and threw his voice into the web of energy, unsure if he could even make himself heard.

<*Allo? I hear you?*>

He felt the blonde woman recoil in shock and excitement, then she *reached* and his vision of her sharpened. She was pretty, but she looked tired, careworn, with the soft pallor of someone seldom subjected to sun or wind. Her blonde hair was tied up loosely. Her heavy blue velvet dress and shawl matched her lovely blue eyes.

<*My name is . . . Nara, of Misencourt,*> she sent, her mental voice courtly, to his ears at least.

<*I'm Valdyr,*> he replied, momentarily forgetting caution, then blurted, <* . . . of Midrea.*>

<*Midrea?*> She looked startled. <*Dear Kore, that's hundreds of miles away . . .* >

Her eyes focused on him intently and he realised that she could likely sense as much about him as he could about her . . . That alone almost made him snap the link, but no . . . he decided to remain, for now at least. For a long minute they just stared at each other, but weirdly, despite his harrowing memories of the breeding-houses and the over-whelming anxiety women always brought on, she felt *safe*. She was like him, someone the dwyma had accepted. And she was also hundreds of miles away.

<*I don't think distance matters much here, Lady Nara,*> he ventured, regaining his tongue. She didn't contradict his use of Lady. *A Rondian noblewoman . . . using the dwyma in a land ruled by magi . . .* He was stunned.

<*I'm somewhat new to this, I confess,*> she replied.

<*So am I,*> he admitted.

<*When I first sensed you, an old woman was with you,*> Nara said. <*Is she with you now?*>

He decided he needed to give a little if he were to gain anything, so he answered truthfully, <*She was part of the genilocus, but she's died now. Truly died, that is. Her spirit has gone. There's just me now.*>

<*I'm sorry,*> Nara replied, and she sounded genuine. <*But we do have each other.*>

Something like an embrace happened between them, as if she'd suddenly and impulsively wrapped unseen arms around him, and he almost recoiled in shock, especially as it came with new sensations – scent, and touch. She smelled of perfume and – to his mortification – of breast milk. He instinctively pushed her away, as gently as he was able.

<*I am pleased to meet you,*> he said formally, to reassure her that it wasn't a rejection but a need for distance. <*You know the word genilocus, then?*>

<*I do, and dwymancer. And Lanthea – the old woman was her, yes?*>

<*Ysh, Lanthea . . . 'Luhti', she preferred,*> he answered and impulsively, cautiously, opened up his mental defences. Some kind of river opened up between them, flowing with information in a rush of visions and memories. He learned that her people were beset by some kind of daemon that possessed people through a form of infection and his heart thudded.

<*They're here too,*> he told her. <*The lower valley is overrun. A man from the East brought the infection. My brother and I are trying to resist them.*>

<*In Midrea?*> she breathed. <*Why have I not heard of this?*>

Why should you have? Valdyr wondered. Then he processed the images she'd shared, of castles and knights. *Dear Kore, she's Pallacian nobility!*

She was clearly distressed at his news. <*I'm very sorry to hear that, Valdyr. I had no idea the Reeker infection had spread outside the north.*>

He understood Reeker from their wordless communion – and he glimpsed a memory of hers: of a masked man being destroyed by the dwyma itself. <*How did you defeat . . . Twoface?*>

She looked at him carefully and he could sense her weighing up what it was safe to share. <*The energy came from the genilocus. I really didn't touch it. It was like pure sunlight, pulled from the leaves of the trees and focused into a kind of beam.*>

He was surprised she would trust him with such information, considering they'd only just met, but he could offer her something in return: <*Lady Nara, with the dwyma I summoned a storm when we were attacked – or rather, the dwyma sensed my need and used me as its channel. I had no control, really, but we buried them under sixty feet of ice.*>

He thought it best not to mention that the people he'd killed weren't actually Reekers but men serving Imperially contracted tax-farmers. Who knew her connections in Pallas?

Her eyes widened. <*Dear Kore . . .* > she gasped. Her voice trailed away as she considered his revelation.

<*Since then I've learned how to direct lightning and freeze tracts of water,*> he

added. <*Some days I feel like a giant in a child's nursery, trying not to crush the toys.*>

He almost confessed his current dilemma – that all these feats had been with Luhti's help and now she was gone – then he decided that might be a step too far. But he felt safe with Nara: he sensed a good heart, a positive and caring person, like his brother.

But they were both tiring fast. <*I think I need to rest,*> he confessed.

<*Me too, I'm sorry.*> She looked genuinely disappointed. <*I'm so glad we've finally spoken. I'd almost given up believing anyone would reply.*> She hesitated, then added, <*Valdyr, this might sound crazy, but the dwyma chose us, so I believe we should help each other.*>

Her words made him glow inside. <*Ysh . . . I mean, yes, I think so too.*>

Something like a kiss brushed his cheek as she vanished.

He turned his head to find Gricoama licking his cheek, his eyes bright. He hugged the wolf, heartened after the days of doubt.

'I've found someone like me,' he whispered.

7

Salted Earth

The Sacrifice in Tabula

Tabula – the Game of Kings – includes a well-known gambit where a powerful piece is sacrificed, to lure the opponent into an unfavourable position. Emperor Sertain Sacrecour, whose love for and mastery of the game is legendary, claimed to have invented the strategy.

ORDO COSTRUO COLLEGIUM, PONTUS, 749

Jastenberg, Noros
Noveleve 935

Seth Korion walked his horse up the gentle slope to where a gaudy pavilion in Canossi red had been erected, looking 'like the nip on the empress' left titty!' as he'd heard his irreverent guard cohort chuckling. When he'd given them a stern look, they'd swiftly added, 'Kore bless 'er name.'

'An' bless her titties,' added the scrawny, loud-mouthed Bowe, not quite out of hearing.

Seth decided to let his men be little boys for a moment, if that's what it took to cheer them up. He gazed west at Jastenberg, a distant smear in the twilight gloom, then he confronted the pavilion: this would be the first time the generals had gathered since the débâcle at Collistein Junction and already recriminations were flying.

He swung from the saddle, handed his reins to a squire and saluted Pilus Lukaz, whose cohort came to a crisp halt. Like most veterans, they could turn on the moves when the knobs were watching. 'Stand them down and see about food, Pilus,' he told Lukaz.

Seth entered the pavilion, followed by Delton, to be met by the smoothly handsome Elvero Salinas, Prince of Canossi.

'Welcome, General,' the prince said distantly. 'I trust all is well.'

'As it can be,' Seth responded. 'Congratulations on your resurrection from the grave.'

'A small miracle,' Elvero smirked; the death of one of his impersonators had given rise to the rumours. Seth didn't believe in hiding behind impersonators, but the Canossi were delighted over the ruse.

While introductions were made, he scanned the room. Lord Rolven Sulpeter, the Corani commander, was back in control after being incommunicado for four crucial days, apparently mourning his son, who'd been lost in the air battle. Seth respected a man's right to grieve, but not the timing. Sulpeter might be commander-in-chief, but his was now the weakest force. Tab Faltros, his aide, a priestly looking man, hovered anxiously over his charge.

Prince Elvero introduced his own senior aide, a sleek, swarthy individual named Gui Detrosca, a rakish man who walked with a bad limp. 'Gui was the finest rider in Koredom, and he is a brilliant mind to boot,' Elvero enthused.

Delton had told him that the Canossi were still a rabble and that Detrosca's 'brilliant' mind was mostly devoted to pleasing Elvero. *A friend he takes pity on*, Seth thought. *Loyalty's a fine thing, but not when it detracts from efficiency.*

Then he was introduced to the Argundian contingent: Prince Andreas Borodium was a tall, muscular young man with a sour face, a sculpted blond moustache and disdainful blue eyes. There was no warmth in his greeting and he clearly felt introducing his aide was beneath his dignity, so the man beside him remained anonymous.

An awkward silence fell, then Sulpeter raised his goblet. 'A toast, gentlemen, in memory of Prince-Consort Ril Endarion. May Kore grant him peace.'

Seth raised his goblet, murmured, 'Grant him peace,' and took a sip. *A brave man who was given an impossible task and will now be scapegoated for the defeat.*

Andreas Borodium began the evisceration with the wine still wet in their mouths. 'We drink, but in truth he failed us, and his queen. If he'd been able to organise his forces, we wouldn't be in this position.'

'If your men had been at the battle, Prince Andreas, perhaps you might have the right to criticise,' Rolven Sulpeter retorted bitterly. 'Perhaps we might then have been victorious – and my son still alive.'

'Prince Endarion chose to march out of my reach,' Andreas snapped. 'It's no fault of mine.'

'If Argundians advanced as swiftly as they retreat, you'd have made it on time,' Elvero sniffed.

'I understand your flank collapsed,' Andreas replied haughtily. 'How appropriate that your impersonator was struck down from behind, eh? If your men faced their enemies, they would hold their lines.' He raised his goblet in Seth's direction. 'I praise our southern kin, who did their duty when others failed theirs.'

Argundy claimed Bricia and Noros as racial kin when it suited, though they'd notably failed to aid the Noros Revolt in 908. But Seth was in no mood to be used as a pawn on this tabula table.

'My men held better ground and had recent experience in the field,' he replied. 'The battle was in the balance until our warbirds began to fall from the skies. That was the turning point – how did the Keshi achieve it?'

His dispassionate answer, and the question he raised, quelled the burgeoning passions in the tent. 'I'm told there was some weapon wielded by the enemy's eagle-riders,' Sulpeter said, his voice pained. 'If that's a taste of what we face, what hope do we have?'

Faltros placed a consoling hand on Sulpeter's shoulder.

Is he ready to fight again? Seth wondered. He happened to meet Salinas' eyes and saw scorn.

Clearly no one knew anything about this secret Keshi weapon.

'What does the empress command?' Seth asked. 'Do we have any orders from Pallas?'

Faltros raised a parchment, showing them the Imperial Seal. 'Empress Lyra commands us to fight on, to deny the enemy winter shelter and bring them to battle when we are recovered. She's ordered the Second Army under Sir Brylion Fasterius to reinforce us, under our command.'

The non-arrival of the Sacrecours was a bigger scandal than that of the Argundians. 'I think we can all agree that Fasterius' dawdling cost us dear,' Elvero said. 'If that craven were here, I'd put his head on a block.'

There was a universal murmur of agreement to that sentiment, one that Seth shared entirely. He'd not met Brylion Fasterius, but his reputation did him no credit. 'Will Fasterius heed her command?' he asked.

Prince Elvero snorted. 'Brylion's men are already marching back home – via Pallas, no doubt. We'll have a new emperor by Martrois.'

It was a blow, but not a surprise. 'The empress is still our ruler,' Seth maintained. 'Let Fasterius face up to his treachery – we have a war to fight. Has she appointed a new overall commander in place of Prince Ril?'

'Lord Sulpeter has been made Lord Commander in the South,' Faltros replied.

'She's not sending Solon Takwyth?' Andreas asked sharply. 'Why would she not send her most renowned commander? Surely he's recovered from his wounds by now?'

'I believe Lord Takwyth is required in the north,' Sulpeter replied sourly.

'Aye, to fight Duke Garod and whoever sides with him,' Andreas grumbled. 'Here we are, milords, guarding the empire's gates, while those at the high table betray our liege.' He downed his goblet and held it out for a servant to refill. 'I for one would rather support the empress against that Dupeni brigand than be forgotten here in the south.'

Of course you would, Seth thought. *You're a northerner and you think the south a wasteland.* Aloud he said, 'I'm sure there are other places we'd all rather be, but here we are, with a task to perform.'

'I too would rather be in the north, preparing my son's tomb,' Lord Sulpeter said bleakly. 'But General Korion is right – here we must be.' He turned to his aide. 'Faltros, give us the butcher's bill, my friend.'

Faltros read from a sheet of parchment, 'The First Army, the Corani, have lost the equivalent of half our fighting strength: we now number only four legions, some twenty thousand men.'

'*We* are at full complement,' Prince Andreas boasted. 'Eight legions, forty thousand men, fresh and ready.'

Easy to say when you avoided battle, Seth thought sourly.

'I've reorganised my army into five legions,' Prince Elvero said. 'We took a pounding and lost valuable equipment during the retreat.'

Because running fast is easier with no shields and spears, Seth reflected, before giving his own summary. 'My men withdrew in good order. All of my units took casualties, but I've kept the units intact, pending reinforcements. I have seven legions, at about eighty per cent strength.'

'Then we have twenty-four legions in all – that's more than a hundred thousand men,' Tab Faltros announced. 'That's a massive army in normal circumstances, but our scouts estimate that the Shihad still numbers in the region of seven hundred thousand combatants, at least.'

'Their morale will be high, too,' the dispirited Sulpeter added. 'Ours is diminished.'

Yours is, certainly, Seth thought. 'At the moment they're strung out and unwary,' he noted. 'A swift counter with cavalry could dent that morale, buy us time and give our soldiers something to cheer.'

'A counter-attack?' Elvero said incredulously. 'Were you not listening? We're outnumbered seven to one at best! We need walls to defend.'

'But it's the last thing they'll expect,' he told them, then sighed inwardly, knowing he had no support. He moved on, tapping the map. 'Then we must stop Rashid right here, at Jastenberg. This is the last place where his route will be constrained by geography: if he takes Jastenberg, he can push northwest to Augenheim, west through Knebb into Aquillea, or south into Noros. This is our last chance to bottle him up.'

The tent fell silent, then Sulpeter said, 'Jastenberg isn't defendable. It has no walls. It outgrew them years ago and the Governor of Noros spent the money raised for new walls on building a country manor in Venderon.'

It was undoubtedly true, but it helped no one right now.

'One hundred thousand men can't fight from behind walls anyway,' Seth replied. 'What's wrong with these very heights we now occupy? They have elevation, they run north-south and but for the valley of the road, which we can fortify, it would constrain Rashid to fight on a narrow front. We could hold him, right here.'

He looked around the tent, hoping to see nodding heads and stiffening spines, but instead he saw excuses forming on claret-stained lips. 'It's too soon,' Sulpeter complained. 'Our men are in no condition to fight.'

'But Prince Andreas' men are fresh, and by his own account, eager to fight,' Seth replied.

'You misunderstand me in your enthusiasm, General,' Andreas put in, also reading the lack of energy in the command tent. 'My men have suffered on the march. We could hold our flank, of course – we are stout Argundian warriors – but we can't stiffen the whole line.'

'No,' Sulpeter said. 'I admire your spirit, but you're young, General Korion. Experience tells me that this is a battle we're not ready for. The empress has put me in command, and I *command* that we will not fight here.'

That left Seth no room to wriggle. He stepped away from the table in annoyance. *He's got less experience than I have in real fighting. I'm sick of hearing that I'm too young. My men held – his didn't.*

Faltros raised his weak voice. 'We must deny the enemy access to Midrea. That must be our priority.'

Sulpeter supported his man. 'We passed numerous points on the Augenheim Road where highlands dominate; there we can prevent the enemy advance. Do you agree, Prince Andreas?'

Clearly this was to Andreas' liking, as he swiftly bowed. 'I approve.'

'We can't just block that one route,' Elvero pointed out. 'The enemy could also advance west through the Knebb Valley and into Aquillea and Bricia. The lands are steep there, with many narrow passes and bridges. We must deny the enemy that route too.'

'But if you all retreat northwest or west, how will you protect Noros?' Seth asked.

They all turned to look at him coolly and he realised that this had already been decided behind his back. Sulpeter pretended to consider, then said, 'As we can't stop them here, we must deny the enemy access to the imperial heartland. If the enemy chooses to go south rather than north, it buys us more time to deal with them.'

'There are only Noromen to the south,' Elvero yawned. 'I don't see why the empire should expend valuable men to protect a kingdom that rebelled as recently as 908.'

'Three of my seven legions are Noromen,' Seth protested. 'They enlisted to protect their homeland.'

'They enlisted to take orders from their superiors,' Prince Andreas said loftily.

'They may not see it that way,' Seth retorted.

'Of what relevance is that?' Elvero demanded. 'Do you give only popular orders, Korion? A general who can't enforce his will on his subordinates is no commander at all.'

Seth faced him, his temper rising. 'My men can take orders, Prince. I'm here to debate strategy and I say that ceding Noros is to give the sultan the winter shelter he will be desperate to secure.'

'The only place large enough for him to shelter in winter is Norostein, three hundred miles south of here,' Sulpeter replied. 'He won't go there. He'll stay here in the north, and it's here we'll contain him.'

'Like you contained him at the Junction?' Seth snapped, probably unwisely, but he was angry now.

Elvero stepped forward and thrust a finger into Seth's chest. The Canossi was bigger than him and stared down from a nine-inch height advantage. 'Who do you think you are, Korion? Some kind of military genius, just because of your family name? You think you did well in the battle at Collistein Junction, but you only cowered behind ramparts instead of trying to seek advantage over the foe. It's only through good fortune that you came through smelling of roses. There are words for such conduct.'

Seth's heart thumped. They were now in duel-of-honour territory and Elvero was a renowned swordsman, one of the best in the empire. And one thing Seth *wasn't* was a swordsman.

But I'll be rukked before I take that sort of shit unanswered.

'How did *your* meeting with the foe go, Prince? Did charging an enemy ten times your strength across open ground work out? I have words for *your* actions too: reckless, arrogant, asinine stupidity.'

Elvero had probably never been addressed like that in his life, because his sleek face went livid. He cracked his gauntlet backhanded across Seth's face, making his head reel. 'You craven pig – I challenge you, and I'll gut you!'

'Go rukk yourself,' Seth replied, wiping blood from his nose. 'If you can't take the truth, you're not fit to be in command of a blasted tea-wagon.'

There would've been more blows, but Andwine Delton risked his career by seizing Elvero's right arm, then Prince Andreas stepped in, his face a mask of amused indifference. 'I believe the empress forbids duels, gentlemen.'

'I don't give a fuck what a *convent girl* says,' Elvero replied. 'My honour demands satisfaction.'

'Your "honour" got your men killed,' Seth told him. 'Rashid dandled you like a tavern-girl, then spanked your arse. It's just a shame your men died for your incompetence.'

<*Sir!*> Delton squawked into his head.

The duel would've taken place there and then, but Sulpeter was having none of it, especially after Elvero's sneering dismissal of the empress' will. 'Calm yourselves, gentlemen,' the old earl shouted, spittle flying. 'By Kore, the shades of our fallen must weep to see you both. You will not trade insults like common peasants.'

Elvero was still staring at Seth with murder in his eyes.

Time to take the moral high ground, Seth decided. *Kind of.* 'Of course, Lord Sulpeter.' He stuck out his hand towards Elvero. 'I withdraw my criticisms of the prince. I'm sure it's no fault of his that his position was overrun.'

Delton winced.

Elvero ignored the offered hand. <*At dawn, you gutless worm,*> he snarled into Seth's mind.

Seth lowered his hand, his face smarting. 'Suit yourself.'

'You should both be ashamed,' Sulpeter snapped. 'These are my orders: the First and Third Armies, that's the Corani and Argundian forces; will defend the Augenheim road. The Fourth and Fifth – the Canossi and the southern confederation, will defend the Knebb Valley.' He pointed at Seth and Elvero. 'Find a way to work together, or be replaced, gentlemen.'

The four generals bowed their heads in acceptance, though Elvero still bristled with menace.

'What of Jastenberg?' Prince Andreas asked.

Sulpeter scowled. 'It can't be defended, or left for Rashid to occupy. We'll burn it to the ground, and every other village he might conceivably shelter men in. Am I understood?'

That made Seth sick to the stomach, but if Sulpeter wasn't going to stand and fight, it made sense.

'Then you have your orders,' Sulpeter concluded, and abruptly he looked tired again. 'Gentlemen, our tempers are frayed; defeat is hard to take. But we're on the same side and we must stand together. Forget your grievances, for the empire.'

They all chorused something positive in response, then Sulpeter showed he wasn't born yesterday by saying, 'Prince Elvero, please stay a moment – the rest of you may go.'

He's making sure we don't leave at the same time and end up at drawn swords. Suits me. Seth saluted, made his farewells and hurried outside with Delton. 'Come on, let's get back to our camp,' he told the aide. 'Could you ask the squires to bring our horses?'

Delton turned to go, then said, 'Sir, that was brave, to stand up to Prince Elvero like that. People say he's one of the best swords in Koredom. But I suppose as a Korion you're in the same rank.'

Seth snorted. 'Me? Our Arcanum blade-master said I was the worst swordsman he'd ever seen, bar none.'

'I've seen you in battle, Milord. At the Junction, your counter-charge saved the line.'

'That's tactics, Delton, not sword-swinging. Believe me, I'm no danger to Elvero. Now, go and sort the horses – and get Lukaz and his men up and moving.'

Once they were out of the Canossi camp and on the road, his guard cohort marching along behind in loose order, he signalled to Delton to join him. 'Right Andwine, listen carefully. All our legions are stationed on the south flank, which is good, because we're going south, not west. Start signalling my legion commanders: tell them to break camp and march.'

Delton gulped. 'They'll invoke the courts-martial, Milord!'

'Only if they can reach me. They can try to arrest me after the war if they want, but I'm not going to let Rashid have Norostein without a fight. I grew up there.' He looked at Delton steadily. 'Are you with me?'

The aide looked horrified, but he asked, 'Can Elvero hold the Knebb Valley without you?'

'Of course – he's of ducal blood,' Seth said sarcastically, then he added, 'My mother could hold the Knebb Valley with her ladies-in-waiting. And once winter grips the heights, Rashid won't even try to force it.'

'Then what will the sultan do?'

'I rather imagine he'll send most of his army straight for Norostein,' Seth replied.

'The very place we're going?' Delton said weakly.

'The very same. Now, get those messages away. I want us on the road by midnight.'

Delton saluted, then shyly smiled. 'It's a Hel of a length to go to just to avoid a duel, sir.'

Seth grinned. 'I'd go further if I needed. I'm really that bad.'

As Delton drew aside and picked up a relay-stave to begin the task, Seth touched a family talisman beside his periapt and quickly told his wife what was happening, then instructed her to evacuate the manor at Bres and get to his more secure castle at Fanford. He had to assume there would be reprisals. Carmina was anxious, of course, but she was ex-legion: he knew she'd be underway at dawn.

After breaking contact, Seth's mind moved steadily down a mental list, ticking off items and thinking about the terrain they would traverse and the city they'd eventually defend. It was a giant task, to pull an army out of line and forge one's own path, but long journeys were made step by step.

It occurred him that this deed would either destroy his family name or immortalise it. Right then, he didn't really care which it was. Removing his periapt from where it nestled against his chest, he sent out a series of gnostic calls.

If we're going to march ourselves into a trap, I'm going to need people I know and trust . . .

His army was moving by midnight. There were no drums, and torches and lamps were kept to a minimum, but Seth's forces contained enough men who'd done similar manoeuvres during the Third Crusade, most notably to escape Ardijah and Riverdown, that they managed. And out of sight but only a few miles away, Jelaska's Argundian legion on his left flank was keeping pace as they travelled south. It'd taken all of about three minutes to convince her that the real action was to be had in Norostein.

You'd die of envy if you missed it, he'd told her.

I'm a necromancer, darling. I doubt Envy can kill me, she'd replied. *But let's not take the risk, eh?*

Seth trotted his horse forward to join his guard cohort. 'Are your men ready to march?' he called to the veterans arrayed in front of the cohort.

'We're always ready, sir,' big Vidran drawled. 'Day or night.'

'We fuckin' love marchin', beg pardon,' Bowe threw in. 'It's what we join't up for.'

'Sir,' Harmon called, 'I hear tell the whole Noorie army is like to up an' follow us – that right?'

'It's likely,' Seth admitted.

'Good,' Harmon said, before practising a graceful lunge. 'Hate to think we'd miss the main show.'

'Yeah, we thought we'd be stuck on some fuckin' hill watching our spit turn to icicles,' Bowe said. 'Instead we can canoodle w' Noros girls an' chuck spears from the best walls in the south.'

'I'm glad you lads approve,' Seth said drily. He signalled to tall, lean Pilus Lukaz, who faced his men, and gave the order.

'Guard Cohort, on the double . . . march!'

And with that, Seth thought, *this act of treason is underway.* But oddly, he felt a strange sensation of rightness, as if this was exactly where Creation wanted him to be.

*

It's good to be in the air, Waqar Mubarak thought as Ajniha surged into the west. *It's where we belong*. And escaping the poisonous fumes of the command tents was a gift. His cousins Attam and Xoredh had been throwing their weight around, seeking to cut Waqar down to size after his successes in the battle.

Behind him, his flight of twenty birds and riders soared in his wake with Baneet, Tamir and Fatima at the fore. Strange reports from the vanguard of the Shihad had sent his fliers forward. It was bitterly cold, so they were all swathed in wool and leathers, with scarfs wrapped around their faces and eye-glasses protecting their vision.

They quickly saw what had vexed the scouts: a sullen red glow on the western horizon, at exactly the wrong time to be sunset. In fact the sun was rising behind them, a crimson pastel smeared over bleak clouds. The *Kalistham* contained chapters on omens: the sun setting at dawn was a bad one.

By the time he and his flyers arrived, he'd already guessed what they'd see, but it was no less awe-inspiring and awful: perhaps twelve square miles of city on fire, flames streaming into the air, creating thermals that buffeted the rocs. Lesser fires burned outside the main city as well: all the farms and manor houses in the countryside were ablaze, while columns of refugees and soldiers poured north and west.

But not south, he noticed.

<They're running away,> Baneet sent. Fatima was making crowing sounds, as were most of the fliers behind them. <The cowards are afraid to stand and face us!>

Waqar took little encouragement from it. *If they're going to burn everything in our path, then where will we winter? What can we forage?* The more he thought of it, the less he saw it as a sign of their enemy's collapse and more as a sign of their resolve.

But he kept his misgivings to himself as they circled above the burning city. The skies had belonged to his roc-riders since the battle, although like the windfleet, their losses had been severe. Transport of supplies was now the priority, so the windship fleet had been dissipated in all directions. The sultan planned to bring to it back together once the enemy turned at bay.

<Come on,> he called to his flight. *<We've seen enough – let's try to get back before our wings freeze.>*

Two hours later, still shivering from the cold, Waqar entered Rashid's pavilion to report. Xoredh was with the sultan, but his elder brother, Crown-Prince Attam, wasn't present. That question was answered before Waqar could ask it.

'Attam has been given command of the force advancing through Trachen Pass,' Rashid said confidently. 'They will capture this city of Venderon while we occupy Jastenberg.' He turned to Waqar. 'What was this mysterious western dawn, Nephew?'

'They've burned Jastenberg and are retreating to the northwest.'

Rashid went still and Xoredh jerked his head up from his platter. 'Burned, you say?' the sinister younger prince said. 'Then we've taught them to fear us. They salt the earth and run.'

Rashid's expression was unusually troubled. 'They clearly had no confidence that they could defend it,' he mused, 'but I'd counted on that city for winter shelter.'

'It's only a little cold weather,' Xoredh drawled. 'Our men can take some discomfort.'

'The winters of Yuros bring more than discomfort,' Rashid said heavily. 'Snow can fall many yards thick. Birds drop dead on the wing. And this is a Sunsurge year, so the weather will be at its worst.'

Then why did we launch our invasion at such a time? Waqar wondered.

As if he'd read his nephew's thoughts, Rashid said cryptically, 'Other factors determined the invasion dates.' Something passed between him and Xoredh; father and son nodded in unison.

'Then why didn't we stay in Verelon?' Waqar asked, irked to be excluded. 'We could have wintered in Spinitius, then marched in spring.'

'Verelon is an under-populated wasteland and the cities are too small,' Rashid replied. 'And it would have allowed the enemy to hold the Silas River against us. We had to penetrate as deeply as possible in this first season of the campaign. Done is done. We must adapt.'

'So what's our new plan?' Xoredh asked.

Rashid gestured to the map table. 'Behold, Jastenberg is no more and the Yurosi are in retreat. North and west, you say?' he asked, looking at Waqar.

'We looked at the southern road, but saw no one,' Waqar replied. 'But the north and west roads were choked with civilians and soldiers.'

'Excellent,' Rashid said. 'Let enemy resources be soaked up dealing with the homeless.' He traced a line on the map towards Augenheim. 'They will fortify this pass, hoping to make us winter in the open.' He then tapped a place called Knebb Valley. 'They'll block this way also, to prevent an advance into Bricia. But we'll go south, into Noros.'

'Will the empress reinforce her armies?' Waqar asked.

'I doubt it, Nephew. The empress has problems enough, even without us. A civil war is about to break out in the north that will fracture opposition to us. By spring, the Rondian Empire won't exist; there will just be divided kingdoms ready and waiting for us to gobble up piecemeal.'

How would you know they're going to have a civil war? Waqar wondered.

'So,' Rashid went on, 'my brother Teileman will take one hundred thousand men to Knebb, to protect that flank. General Valphath will situate a further hundred thousand near Jastenberg, to face the main Yurosi army in Augenheim Pass. Both must weather the winter in the open, so will be given double rations and extra clothing. I myself will lead the main body of the Shihad south to link with Attam's force when it emerges from the Trachen Pass Road at Venderon. We will then march on and take Norostein by the end of Decore.'

'Winter will be upon us by Decore,' Waqar warned.

'We know that,' Rashid said tersely, 'but the weather will still be manageable. With Jastenberg razed, it's the nearest undefended city.'

Cutting it fine, Waqar worried. 'And my roc-riders?'

'Take them south with the advance guard. Scout the enemy and report to Attam.'

'We will be tireless, Great Sultan,' Waqar said. 'But what about my *other* mission?'

Rashid smiled gravely. 'You may speak plainly in front of Xoredh.'

Waqar gave Xoredh an uneasy look. 'If you wish me to seek the dwyma, should I not leave immediately, so that I have time for the task and can perhaps affect the winter weather?'

'Not when seizing Norostein unopposed could solve that issue for us,' Rashid replied. 'Concentrate on aiding the army, Nephew. That's your task for now.'

But others could lead the roc-riders, Waqar thought. Then he thought: *Perhaps you don't think you'll need me to learn the dwyma after all – because someone else will provide that power in my place?*

That could only mean Rashid was closing in on Jehana.

Where are you, Sister?

8

Shrine of a Dead God

The Coastal Communities

On Urte, the sea is impassable and most large settlements are far from the coast. However, many small communities live close to the sea. Yuros is ringed by tidal zones, often miles wide, where sea-life and debris are washed up every twelve hours, a cornucopia of riches for those with the courage and hardiness to collect them.

ORDO COSTRUO COLLEGIUM, PONTUS 593

Vantari Hills, Verelon
Noveleve 935

Where am I? Jehana wondered miserably. Geography had never been her strong point, and in any case, the southern coast of Yuros had been pretty much a blank space on the maps at the Arcanum where she'd been educated: just a giant cliff of no importance, where no one lived and nothing happened. In fairness, judging by the last two weeks, that was pretty much the truth, except there were more trees than she'd anticipated.

Thankfully, she thought, glaring unseen up at the distant silhouette of one of Alyssa's windships, which were overflying them every day now.

They'd managed to remain undetected so far – Alyssa might have many ships and men, but it was becoming clear she had no idea where Jehana actually was. They'd not encountered anyone on the ground and the scrying attempts had stopped.

But progress was slow. They were probably managing only five or six miles a day, so in the three weeks since they'd made landfall they'd come a hundred miles or so. Their goal, the village of Epineo somewhere in the Vantari Hills, had been mentioned in connection with the dwymancer Amantius. Without a map, some features to navigate by or someone to ask, they could only guess at where they were.

There were hopeful signs, though. Every so often as they moved through the stands of pine interspersed with scrub-covered slopes, they would stumble across stumps of pillars or broken walls, traces of long-ago attempts to civilise the wilds. More intriguingly still, they'd begun to find old relief carvings on some rocks. Just now, they'd been brought up short at the sight of an eerie visage somewhere between man and squid, with an extra eye in the centre of the forehead, carved into a grey cliff-face.

'Another one.' Tarita glanced at Jehana. 'What did you say it was again?'

'I didn't,' Jehana replied shortly, thinking, *The dwyma is my concern, not hers.*

Ogre crunched down the path to join them. When he saw the carving his ugly, childlike visage filled up with awe. 'Squidman again,' he rumbled.

'It's the biggest by far,' Tarita noted. 'And look – there's a cave beneath. I should go in first.'

'No, I will,' Jehana said quickly. 'If this is important, you might disturb it.'

'What if there are wolves or bears?' Tarita asked. 'We'll go in together.'

Jehana was irritated by the way Tarita constantly took charge, but her own gnosis was primarily Theurgy – mind-magic turned out to be not particularly helpful in the wilds, unlike Ogre's nature-based Hermetic gnosis, and Tarita was a Merozain, so she could do *everything*.

'All right,' she said grumpily, 'but don't touch anything until I've seen it.'

'Why, what are we looking for?'

'I'm not sure,' she admitted, 'but I'll know when I see it.'

Tarita and Ogre shared a doubtful look.

There was a disturbing familiarity between them. Jehana didn't understand their friendship at all: he was an illegal construct and she was a mage, and they were complete opposites. *What could they ever find to say to each other, for Ahm's sake?*

Once beneath the carved cliff, they edged through a tangle of vines and undergrowth until they reached the cave-mouth they'd glimpsed, but it was worth it. Close up, the carving was impressive, and moss around the eyes gave it a disturbing illusion of sentience. The third eye contained a strange symbol of a swirling hexagon.

Ogre put his face close to the soil and sniffed, his eyes glowing amber-brown as he engaged animagery. 'Nothing recent,' he rumbled. 'Animals don't come here.'

'That's odd, isn't it?' Tarita commented.

'Perhaps Squidman scares them away?' Ogre mused. 'I can't hear birds, either.'

'I think they flew off when you farted.'

They snorted in mutual amusement, while Jehana rolled her eyes. 'Children,' she said severely, which only made them laugh more.

He's right about the birds, though, she thought. *I can't hear any birdsong at all.*

Tarita sent a floating globe of gnosis-light into the cave. 'Look, there are old torches.'

She and Ogre went inside. After a moment's hesitation, Jehana followed. A rough antechamber lay within, with steps leading upwards. The air was cool and dank and the sound of running water was loud. As they climbed, the space opened out to a larger cavern, perhaps forty yards in diameter. Slimy moss streaked the rough-hewn walls and the floor was wet, which added to the chill. Beneath another relief-carving of the squid-headed man was a small pool lapping at the rear wall. This time he was of human height, with arms spread in welcome. There were crude letters slashed into the stone on either side of his head.

'Ugly brute, isn't he?' Tarita said. 'He even makes you look pretty, Ogre.'

The small Jhafi girl and the hulking construct were constantly doing this, Jehana thought irritably, back-slapping, exchanging crass jokes and insults, all very matey. She interrupted their bonhomie to say severely, 'He's some kind of sea-god.'

'Is it Seidopus?' Tarita asked.

'Probably. Seidopus was the dominant god of this region. The tidal communities would placate him with offerings to ensure a good catch and a safe return.'

'Look, over here,' Ogre said, stepping to the right where a smaller chamber was inset. His mage-light revealed a stone slab held up by two kneeling figures, one male and one female. The chunky nudes had snaky hair and squid-like faces, idols of a forgotten cult. 'There's a female?'

'Calascia,' Jehana told them. 'She was the mate of Seidopus.'

Ogre prodded the desiccated debris of ancient offerings before the altar. 'Perhaps there are old treasures here?' But the rotted mounds just crumbled under his touch.

'There's no insects in here, either,' Tarita noted.

Nothing living, Jehana thought. But despite this, she didn't feel unsafe.

Ogre returned to the main chamber and examined the letters etched into the wall. 'Look,' he said, 'Old Frandian runes.'

Jehana raised her eyebrows, surprised he knew such a thing. 'Can you read it?'

'I don't know much, but maybe,' Ogre rumbled. '"Doorstep" or "mouth" – the Frandians used the same word for both. They . . . um . . . *offer* or *give* . . . to . . .' He frowned. 'The next rune is the same swirled hexagon as outside.'

'That fits with an altar,' Tarita said, admiringly. 'You're not just a pretty face, Ogre.'

Jehana was unwillingly impressed, but she was pleased that this confirmed her suspicions. *We're definitely getting close.*

Tarita went to the pool at the carving's feet. 'I bet this rises from an underground spring.' Clear light blooming from her fingertips, she touched the water and studied what she read there. 'It's fresh enough to drink. We could spend the night here.'

'If I were a bear or a wolf, I'd den here,' Ogre said. 'Why is it empty?'

Put like that, Jehana felt a little doubt, but her legs were aching badly and she needed to rest. 'I'm tired, my knees hurt and I've got blisters,' she moaned. 'We should at least stay the night. And really, it's perfect:

there's water for washing, we can set a fire in the pit and Ogre gets a separate chamber.'

'I think we'll be okay for one night, Ogre,' Tarita agreed, before teasingly adding, 'And you *really* need to wash.'

The big construct's eyes twinkled and he said, 'I smell better than either of you, and if anything is driving the creatures away it's you, Little Bird. Make sure you wash last, so the rest of us have some clean water.'

Tarita poked her tongue out and Ogre did the same, only his was at least nine inches long, purple and disturbingly mobile. They both burst out laughing.

'Grow up, you two,' Jehana snapped. 'I'm washing first.'

The pool in the upper chamber was only a foot deep, but that was enough to strip off and immerse. As she crouched to get in, the carving's upside-down reflection overlaid her face, giving her tentacles for hair, just like the woman carved into the lesser altar. She shuddered and almost changed her mind about bathing.

The water was frigid, but she called gnostic energy to her body to stay warm. Being naked beneath the image of Seidopus was disturbing, but nothing untoward happened. She rinsed her frayed clothes then used the gnosis to dry them and herself, thinking ruefully of all the wonderful dresses she'd left behind in her rooms at the Ordo Costruo.

Dear Ahm, I'm so sick of all this running and hiding. It's been weeks now.

But surely this cave meant that Epineo had to be near, the place where Amantius had finally been trapped by Kore's Inquisition. *I'll find Epineo, I'll somehow gain the dwyma, and then …* She wasn't sure what would come after, but at least she'd be better equipped to deal with Alyssa . . . and Rashid.

Tarita and Ogre were making up a fire-pit, exchanging ribald banter in Rondian, but they fell silent when they saw her. 'I'll go next,' Tarita said. 'If Ogre jumps in the pool, he'll empty it.'

Ogre's laughter boomed around the chamber, but as Tarita disappeared, Jehana saw a deep sadness in his face, even dread, quite at odds with his laughter.

'Are you all right, Ogre?' she blurted.

He hung his head. 'Ogre is remembering a bad time ... with the Master.'

Ervyn Naxius, the Ordo Costruo renegade, Jehana thought with a shudder. His very name was a caution against the evils of knowledge untrammelled by morality. All of a sudden she felt a wave of pity for the creature, to have been the slave of such a master. *Of course he's seen terrible things.*

'I'm sorry I've been short with you,' she said suddenly.

'Ogre understands. This is hard for you. For us all. But it is good to be free, yes?'

His hopeful expression lifted her. 'Yes Ogre , it's good to be free.' She hesitated, then asked, 'Do you have a real name? Calling you Ogre is like calling someone "boy". It feels wrong.'

Ogre frowned, then he shook his head. 'No, Ogre is Ogre. He doesn't mind.'

'You should say "I don't", not "He doesn't",' she told him. 'You never say "I"?'

'Master said "I" was reserved for people,' Ogre said in a flat voice.

'You *are* a person,' Jehana told him.

The way his face brightened rewarded her efforts, and left her feeling better too.

Tarita reappeared, freshly washed, and while Ogre went to take his turn, the two of them prepared the meal. Tarita never said she'd overheard the conversation, but there was a definite mellowing in the air between them as well. They spitted the pair of rabbits Tarita had brought down earlier and by the time Ogre returned they were roasting above a small fire, filling the air with succulent smells, while roots boiled in the pot they'd scavenged from the old hunter's cabin.

That night was the most harmonious of their journey together so far. Tarita related amusing tales of misadventures as a scullery maid in Javon, and Ogre chilled them with some recollections of Naxius, carefully edited, Jehana suspected.

Finally, yawning, Ogre retired to the upper chamber, Jehana curled close to the fire and Tarita took the first watch.

In seconds the princess fell straight into a dream of clinging to the great whale as they escaped Sunset Tower – but then of *being* the whale, soaring through the depths, unfettered and free . . .

. . . but sometime in the night, her dreams turned menacing. The sea was full of dark shapes, toothy beasts that were hunting her, closing in. She woke, blinking in the darkness. There were sounds amidst the rhythmic crashing of the waves and the splash of rain outside the cavemouth – sounds distressingly like the slap of leather soles on wet stone.

She went and stared out into the night . . . to see figures stealing out of the darkness: Hadishah, their heads wrapped in scarves, blades gleaming in the moonlight. She opened her mouth to shriek a warning – then froze as the assassins unwrapped their scarves, revealing hairless, misshapen squid skulls instead of human heads . . .

. . . and Jehana jerked truly awake, still wrapped in her blanket, her breath short and heart thumping.

But Tarita was still at the cave entrance, studying something in her lap, the fire still glowed and the only sound was the rain outside. It was just a bad dream. She sagged in relief and in seconds was falling back into oblivion.

With Jehana asleep and Ogre in the other chamber, Tarita decided it was time she checked on her two most arcane possessions. First, she pulled her scimitar from its scabbard and examined the blade. It had been in a cabinet in Midpoint Tower – the Mask called Felix had used it to effortlessly break ordinary steel swords. She hadn't noted anything special about it beyond that high tensile strength, but she sensed the sword had some greater property. What it was, however, remained hidden, even from her inner eye.

She sighed and replaced it, then took out the book, carefully swaddled in layers of waxed and gnosis-enhanced cloth to protect against water damage. The book, *Daemonicon di Naxius*, was a record of the dealings of the infamous Ordo Costruo renegade with the daemon world.

But it was either encrypted or written in a language and alphabet she didn't know. She suddenly wondered if Ogre might be able to read it and decided she'd show him, once they reached a safe place.

She carefully rewrapped it before extinguishing the torch and settling into her watch. Jehana was muttering and twitching in some bad dream, but then she subsided.

Tarita roused Ogre sometime after midnight, then went to sleep herself, grateful to finally close her eyes.

Jehana woke the next morning feeling better rested than at any time since escaping Sunset Tower. They spent another day in the cave before moving on, this time following the path back towards the sea-cliffs.

'Epineo was a cliff-top dwelling,' she told Tarita. She was feeling more alive, this close to the pulse of the ocean.

Emerging from a gully carved by a small stream onto a rocky outcropping, they all stopped short. Before them stretched the coastline and the endlessly changing wonder of the ocean. As they watched the waves rolling in, Tarita announced, 'I could live by the sea.'

Jehana gave her a rare smile, while Ogre nodded his misshapen skull in agreement.

'The eternal sea,' Ogre intoned. 'I used to watch the waves from Sunset Tower. Sometimes I would even walk outside, on the island.'

'Do you want to go back there, when this war's is over?' Tarita asked.

He shook his head. 'I'm finished with small places. I want to see everywhere.'

'They won't let you,' Jehana said sharply. 'They hid you for your own protection.'

Ogre looked crestfallen and Tarita rounded on her. 'I don't think that's the only possible outcome, Princess – and I won't let my friend be shut away again.' She turned to face him. 'I mean that, Ogre – they won't shut you away again. I want you to see the world.'

He beamed gratefully, then pointed to the west. 'Look.'

They all stared at the outcropping he was pointing to – and sucked in their breath as they discerned straight lines among the tangled rocks and weatherworn scrub.

Is that Epineo? Jehana wondered.

The sun was westering, so they hurried on, stopping short when they found weathered stone steps winding into the pine trees – and unexpectedly, they were walking past dilapidated stone huts set either side of a bubbling stream. Tarita bade the other two stay while she scouted the area.

After quickly flitting in each direction, she returned and reported, 'There's two dozen huts at least, mostly just with one room, but they all have fire-pits and chimneys. There were maybe fifty, sixty people living here. We can pick out our own huts to use.'

'Where did they all go?' Jehana wondered. 'Was this Epineo?'

'I don't know.' Tarita's wave took in the bleak, windswept greys and dark greens and the bitter chill of impending rain in the air. 'It's a dismal kind of place, but it's got all we need. We can camp here, at least.'

Jehana examined an altar stone beside the stream sporting another carving of Seidopus. 'I know what you mean. I grew up in a desert. I thought water meant life. How can Yuros contain so much water yet be so cold and empty?'

'What did we expect, a Rimoni villa with thermal pools?' Tarita replied, with forced cheer. 'Let's stop here a few days and recover properly. Hey, Ogre, let's pick out our huts. Make sure yours is far enough away that I can't hear your snoring.'

'I will,' Ogre said in a moping voice, wandering off absently.

Tarita had clearly expected some kind of banter. 'He's very up and down just now,' she noted.

'When he thinks about Naxius, he becomes upset.'

'I've noticed that too. I think Naxius forced him to torture people sometimes. He needs a good mystic-mage to clean his memories out. I've tried, but I don't have the skill or experience.'

'Be careful,' Jehana told her. 'Minds are complex: you could do more damage than good.'

'I know,' Tarita admitted. 'I do think just being out of that tower is the best thing for him, though. I know the Ordo Costruo were protecting him, but we all need to be free.'

'You think the world will let him lead a normal life? Sunset Isle was the best place for him.'

'You heard him. He doesn't want to go back.'

Jehana wrinkled her nose. 'It won't be his choice. And you need to be careful: he thinks you're an angel of Ahm, Tarita. You can't just joke and laugh with him like that. Don't you see you're twisting him round your finger?'

'I'm just treating him like a normal person!' Tarita flared.

'That's probably the cruellest thing you could do,' Jehana retorted, 'because everyone else will treat him as he is: a monster. You're doing him no kindness by giving him false hope.'

With that the princess stalked off to choose her own hut, hoping she'd made Tarita realise that unequal friendships could be cruel.

Alyssa Dulayne stalked down the gangplank of the windship and stepped onto grasslands inland of the Vantari Hills. Another ship landed alongside and both Keshi crews watched her fearfully. They had quickly learned that to displease her could be fatal; they trembled on her every whim – which was just the way she liked her inferiors to behave.

'Well,' she demanded of the man awaiting her. 'What have we found?'

The tall Hadishah she'd addressed rose from where he knelt, his forehead pressed to the dirt. Nuqhemeel was scarred, with greying hair and an aloof manner, one of the few older Hadishah to survive the Third Crusade. He was diligent, if uninspired. 'One of the scouts found larger-than-human footprints beside a stream in the coastal hills,' he reported.

Magi in hiding were notoriously hard to find. They generally knew the tricks of the trade – how to use caves and running water as well as wards to prevent scrying – and could live off the land easily. Add in the fact that Alyssa didn't really know any of them well enough to scry them effectively and it was like hunting with a blindfold on. But those footprints must be the construct – if he'd escaped, he was surely still with Jehana.

'Why would she come here?' she wondered aloud.

Nuqhemeel shook his head. 'We don't know, Lady. Perhaps she's seeking the Shihad?'

By wandering into that tangle of gullies and cliffs? No . . . It's more than that. Abruptly she turned away and strode out on her own, conjuring and calling into the aether.

The Master responded almost immediately. *<Yes, Sister Heartface?>*

<Master, we have found traces of Jehana Mubarak.>

Naxius' mind caressed hers approvingly. <*Where?*>

<*In the Vantari Hills, on the Verelon coast,*> she replied. <*But she's proving elusive. I wonder if she's here for a purpose? Are these hills a place she is running to, or through?*>

<*The Vantari Hills do play a part in the history of the dwyma,*> Naxius answered. <*Amantius was one of the four most notorious dwymancers. He met his end there when a Fist of Inquisitors caught him. They claimed he was dangerously insane, so forewent a trial and put him to death.*>

<*Amantius?*> She didn't know the name. <*Thank you, Master. Was there a particular place associated with him?*>

<*Let me see . . .* > Naxius went silent, then his voice returned. <*Amantius was captured and killed in a place called Epineo.*> He showed her the location with his mind.

When he broke the contact, she opened her eyes, momentarily disoriented as her awareness rushed back to her normal senses. Then she felt a tingle of anticipation. *Jehana, I'm coming for you – and when I find you, I've a little surprise prepared . . .*

Not all research was beneath her, not when the reward was tangible and immediate. During her dark years before the Master saved her, when her body had been broken and she'd lived in constant pain, she'd tried every remedy she could find. She'd discovered a spell that mimicked the power of a Souldrinker: with it she could draw another's intellect, memories and power into herself. Of course it violated the Gnostic Codes, but she cared nothing for that.

I'm already a daemon-possessed magus – how much more powerful would I be if I were a dwymancer too? Powerful enough to eclipse the Master? And to devour him too?

It wasn't that she was ungrateful to Naxius – but in the end, the thought was intolerable that *anyone* could be her Master.

9

Church and Crown

An Eastern Concept of the Gnosis

In this new era, one of the great challenges facing the East is the gnosis. Now that we have young men and women bred with this Western magic, we must re-examine our attitude to it. We must ask ourselves whether this ferang evil must be reassessed morally and theologically. We must not simply replicate the Yurosi magi: our magi must be guided down a better path, leading not just to temporal power but spiritual enlightenment.

AHMED SULOM, JA'ARATHI SCHOLAR, PEROZ 933

Klief-Fauvion Road, Rondelmar
Decore 935

Another coughing spasm convulsed the man slumped beside Ari as the caged wagon shook and rattled through another poverty-stricken village. Every man in the wagon was ill – they were probably leaving a trail of slime through Rondelmar, so much phlegm was being expectorated.

'Anyone know where the fuck we are?' someone groaned, but no one answered.

Somewhere east of Canossi, Ari estimated blearily, looking around. Most of them were wrapped up in their own misery, but for a moment he met Lazar's chilling stare, before flinching and looking away.

Another mid-afternoon on yet another cold, dreary northern winter day, with rain threatening, the days shortening and the road a river of slush winding through bleak grey-green moors and scattered copses of bent, leafless trees. The wind was a sour exhalation bearing the reek of fens. This tiny village was just like all the rest, nothing more than a number of hovels for the wretched and indigent. Crows cawed malevolently as the wagons halted beside a well and the Inquisition Guardsmen dismounted.

'Neif,' he muttered, shaking his friend's shoulder. 'Wake up.'

'Mhh . . . ungh . . .' Neif murmured, jerking awake, then lapsing back into a doze.

'Neif,' Ari said again, 'we're stopping.'

'S'what?' Neif moaned.

'They might feed us.'

'Can' eat, Ari . . . Jus' wanna sleep . . .' Neif rolled over and coughed up green phlegm into the rotting straw on the cage floor. Ari shuddered at the sight of fashionable, worldly Neif looking like a dying scarecrow, but they all did.

'Hot food, Neif,' Ari murmured, though they'd had nothing but cold scraps since Klief.

'Jus' wanna die.'

You'll get your wish soon enough, Ari thought sadly, putting a hand on his friend's shoulder. 'Come on, we're nearly there. Just a few more days.'

Then the trial, if we get one. Then the noose.

In Klief, a city full of colonnades and marble plundered from Rimoni, the Inquisitors had handed over their small caravan of prison-wagons to the Inquisition Guard, ordinary soldiers in black uniforms with permanent scowls. Since then, the weather had worsened and several prisoners had died of the ague that now gripped them all.

'Lucky bastards,' the thuggish Gorn said, as each corpse was hauled out and dumped in a ditch.

This is the world you've made, Lyra Vereinen, you heartless bitch, Ari thought. As the journey progressed he'd grown to hate them all savagely; the Sacrecour-Fasterius-Borodium-Vereinen-Jandreux-Salinas and all their ilk. *The world would be better without them.*

The prisoners stared out at the peasants who watched the guards taking on water; the gaggle of terrified men who dared not let soldiers catch a glimpse of their women or children. The commander led his men swaggering into the hovel that passed for a tavern and without a word – or payment – they hauled out a few barrels of ale and loaded them behind one of the cages.

An eerie keening floated in the air, like a lonely hawk, and Lazar looked up, his cold eyes suddenly interested.

One of the guards went still, while his fellows, oblivious, cackled on . . .

. . . then a dark shape streaked over the small square and a torrent of fire raked the Inquisition Guardsmen, setting them ablaze. Within moments they were screaming and writhing in agony as smoke and flame engulfed them. More cries like birds of prey filled the air above and now Ari could hear the thud of giant wings. Blue bolts of light suddenly lit up the sky, cutting down those guards who had escaped the conflagration.

One of the attackers appeared right before their cage: an armoured man on the back of an impossible creature: a giant leonine body topped with an eagle's head and borne aloft on feathered wings. The beast caught the guard commander in its claws and tore him to bloody shreds, while the armoured man vaulted from its back and carved another man in half with a brutal double-handed swing of his blade. He hacked down three more in as many heartbeats.

Green and white: Corani men, Ari thought. *Is this a rescue? Are we saved?*

Perhaps they were, but first of all it was a slaughter: the Inquisition Guard detachment had no magi, while all of the raiders shimmered, protected by gnostic shields. In half a minute they'd cut down those few foolish enough to fight.

The prisoners cheered voraciously to see their gaolers cut down, but as the fighting stopped and the first man, the gryphon rider, strode from the smoke, they all fell silent, staring as he removed his helm. He was a big man, perhaps in his fifties, balding and blond of face.

He wasn't terribly impressed by the captives.

'I am Sir Oryn Levis,' the knight said. 'Who are you men?'

Knight-Commander Takwyth's second, Ari thought, straining to recall his admittedly sketchy knowledge of the nobility. He tried to think of a clever lie to get them freed, but some fool called, 'We're prisoners of the Inquisition.'

The Corani knight's face frosted over. 'On what charges?'

'Heresy, mostly. That's what the Church labels all crimes – so they can claim the right to judge.'

'Heresy? Seems a misuse of the term to me,' Levis sniffed, as more of his men appeared from the clearing smoke. They brought their giant winged beasts to heel with silent gestures, cooing over them like they were pets. One of the Corani, a rough-clad redhead, found a satchel in the guard commander's saddlebags and rifled through. Ari wondered if he might be a Volsai.

'Milord, here's a manifest of the prisoners' charges.'

Levis scanned the papers, then grunted. 'Which one of you is Lazar?'

Lazar stood slowly. He was in better condition than the rest, for those loyal to him – or still scared of him – had been slipping him half their meagre rations. 'I'm Lazar.'

'These charges say you're a diabolist, sworn to Lucian, Lord of Hel,' Levis read, his voice bemused. 'They say you've murdered, raped and pillaged your way through southern Rondelmar and Midrea.'

'Lucian is a child's tale,' Lazar sneered. 'I fight for freedom from tyranny.'

'What's "tyranny" to you?'

'Sacrecours,' Lazar replied.

A very smart answer, Ari realised.

Levis pulled a face, then turned to the redheaded man. 'Master Patcheart, what should we do with them?'

Patcheart looked them over, then called, 'Are these men yours, Master Lazar?'

'Aye, they're my crew,' Lazar replied.

Levis scowled at Patcheart, then said, 'We can't take you with us. If I let you go, and leave you the weapons of these dead Inquisitors, what would you do?'

'Kill Sacrecours,' Lazar replied smoothly.

Liar, Ari thought. *You'll butcher these villagers, take all you can carry and head for the hills.*

The redheaded man looked like he knew that, but maybe he thought any brigand loose in Sacrecour territory was a problem for his enemies.

'*Expediency rules in the Kingdom of Chaos,*' Ari muttered, a phrase from *Res Publica*.

'Free these men,' Levis said, scanning the charge sheets again.

Ari felt his knees given way as a wave of utter relief overwhelmed him – then Patcheart said, 'Wait – which one's Ari Frankel?'

'I am,' he squeaked, as fear gripped him again.

The man turned to the knight and said, 'Milord, this one I know: his name and words are all over pamphlets that've been cropping up in Pallas. He's a genuine seditionist. He needs to stand trial, him and his associate . . . Neif Coldwell.'

Levis looked Ari up and down, his amiable features turning cold. 'Our *beloved* queen doesn't deserve muckrakers like this spouting their poison. Bring them both.'

Minutes later, Ari and Neif, still in chains, were slung over the back of a terrifying winged lizard, right before it launched itself into the sky – and if he could've hurled himself into the void he would have. But instead those thudding, impossible wings sped him north, towards the executioner's block.

Gravenhurst, Pallas

'My Queen, when I said I'd really rather you were a hundred miles away, I meant it,' Dirklan said, as Lyra's unmarked carriage rattled down the steep road. 'The word's gone out that we're moving on the Church *right now* and people are pouring into the streets. Ostevan may have seeded the mob with assassins.'

'I must be present when this begins,' Lyra replied, wondering when this jolting was ever going to stop. 'To do less would be cowardice. I'm more worried that the Church has been forewarned – we're going to look foolish if the cathedral is empty.'

'Saint Baramitius has been watched from the moment we decided to act.' Then he admitted, 'Obviously, it's not certain the treasury's untouched . . .'

'If Dominius has tipped them off, I'll raid his city manor myself,' Lyra said tersely, which drew a chuckle from Basia, sitting bolt-upright beside her.

Lyra peered between the curtains but there was little to see in the pre-dawn gloom, just darkness broken by occasional street lamps that provided glimpses of brick houses and feed troughs, alley-mouths and closed windows. A handful of drunks were slumped against the walls but nobody was moving but them.

Dominius had been sulking for the last two weeks, but in the end, Dirklan had persuaded him to offer his support, using the currency of secrets, favours and influence, Dominius' favoured coin. Once he'd been given the right to claim any plunder that could be considered legitimate iconography, and promised certain exemptions when he was reinstated as Grand Prelate, he'd been an invaluable resource in identifying the churches, abbeys and monasteries throughout the north which shared that happy combination of large treasuries and corrupt clergymen.

'I'm not too worried about Dominius,' the spymaster commented. 'He now recognises this as a chance to oust certain rivals. I admit to being impressed at his own network: he has dossiers on *everyone*, listing their virtues and their *many* vices. Of course, most of them were lost when he fled the Celestium, but his memory on such matters is outstanding. I think it's his hobby.'

'It's a distasteful hobby,' Lyra said primly.

'Sorry you disapprove.' He smiled. 'It's a hobby of mine too.'

Lyra threw him a warning look, not in the mood for making light of the matter. *If the people rise over this, Pallas will become untenable.* 'Are Dominius' people in place?'

'Yes, and they'll go in with my Volsai,' Dirklan responded.

Lyra didn't envy Dominius' people; his inner circle of clergymen, who'd stood by him when the Celestium fell, convinced by the reports of Reekers and Masks and united in loathing of Ostevan, now probably thought they'd chosen the wrong side.

The driver rapped on the roof. They could hear a furious babble of voices outside. 'I wish you'd stay inside here, Milady,' Basia said tersely. 'This carriage is warded, but we can't protect you properly out there.'

Lyra was grateful that Basia had elected to stay, but there was no way she was going to hide from her actions. 'Thank you,' she said, 'but I must be seen taking responsibility for this.'

'Then *please*, stay behind me at all times.' She shared an uneasy look with Dirklan, who, wrapped in faint blue wards, was already dismounting. Basia shielded Lyra as she climbed down into of a corridor of soldiers facing outwards, shields locked. The only thing she could see other than the backs of her guard was Saint Baramitius' Cathedral towering above them, the largest church in Pallas-Nord. Its glowing spire speared the dark clouds hanging heavy in the sky, the moon just a hint of a shrunken crescent. It was bitingly cold, but Lyra was hit by the heat of anger emanating from the sea of faces and fists penning the soldiers in.

'It's the Queen,' someone shouted. *'It's the Queen!'* The wall of people in front of the cathedral slammed into the men protecting her, but they shoved back, shouting and swearing as their feet slipped on the wet slate.

'She's come to watch her thieves,' a woman shrieked, hurling herself at the shields. *'Thieving bitch – thieving Corani bitch!'*

Rotten fruit and vegetables pelted over the top of Lyra's protectors, splattering onto the gnostic shielding. Basia grabbed her arm, shouting, 'Please Majesty, *move!*'

'Thieves – Northern thieves!'

A kinesis-powered shove slammed into the mob and pushed them stumbling back, crushing those behind. She heard screams, more outrage than agony, then the crowd shoved back, hammering into the guardsmen again, fists and feet flailing.

'Kore hates you, Lyra,' someone bellowed, and the call was taken up. *'KORE HATES YOU!'*

For a moment Lyra was paralysed by horror, but Basia all but frogmarched her down the corridor of armed men as the garbage raining down turned the ground to a slippery pulp. Then a big armoured figure strode to meet her and with him shielding her other flank, they reached the cordoned space before the cathedral.

It was hard to ignore the insults pelting her: *'You're going to burn in Hel, Lyra Vereinen!'*

'The Church belongs to Kore – have you no shame?'

'Rukk off, you thieving whore!'

Lyra swayed dizzily, but the armoured man steadied her and she realised it was Solon Takwyth, his visor raised, his branded left cheek livid in the torchlight. She realised suddenly that she had never been so close to him before. She hadn't quite appreciated how imposing he was. Standing more than six feet tall, his already powerful build was accentuated by his armour and cloak. She wasn't too proud to cling to him.

'Thank you,' she tried to tell him, but her words were swallowed by the blaring crowd.

The spymaster ghosted up, his one good eye brightly intent. 'Come inside, Majesty; it's best you're out of sight until this subsides.'

If it ever will, Lyra thought, looking at the baying mob. The square before the cathedral was packed and every window was filled with equally angry faces.

She let the Knight-Commander draw her into the cathedral, then stepped away. 'Thank you, Solon, I can manage now,' she said, and looked around the interior of the church, beholding a scene of vandalism that made her shudder. Scores of men in Imperocracy livery were gathering up everything that gleamed or glistened.

'Have you found what you sought?' she asked anxiously.

'We have,' Dirklan replied. 'They clearly had some warning, because we were met by barricades at the doors and the neighbourhood had been roused, but they didn't have enough time to empty the strongroom.' He pointed grimly to a trio of mage-healers who were seeing to the injured, priests and citizens. 'It got bloody, I'm sorry, and there have been deaths. It's the same in every parish, I'm hearing.'

We've spilled blood in our own churches . . .

Lyra bowed her head, praying for forgiveness, then followed her spymaster deeper into the building. In the centre of the dagger-shaped cathedral – for the weapon that slew Corineus – in the space known as the *cruxgarde*, she found a growing pile of plunder.

'This is what you found?' she gasped. 'Dear Kore!'

The pile towered over her head and stretched for twenty yards at least in every direction. There were chests full of coin, golden candlestands and goblets, platters and cutlery, piles of weapons, both ceremonial and real. She'd never seen so much jewellery – what wasn't gold was silver or pearl or amber or jade. Some of it was priestly, but most of the gems were clearly intended to adorn women. There were paintings, not just of religious figures, but of mythic scenes, full of nude figures in the Lantric style, with plenty of naked nymphs and faeries. Tapestries gleamed with gold thread.

'There's as much again still below,' Dirklan said. 'Urbanius Crozier, the head of this cathedral, was deep in the trough. He's now on the way to the Bastion, under a Rune of Chain. We've set up cells behind the Imperocracy.'

'Is this typical?'

'It's the worst so far, but there's a lot of money in the rural abbeys too. Plenty of abbots live like feudal lords. The problem is, most of the monasteries could double as fortresses – I have no doubt we'll need to lay siege to some.'

'Dear Kore – are we just giving Garod an excuse to destroy us?' she wondered.

'He's already got his excuses,' Solon put in, re-joining them. 'Milady, it's really better you're not here. Let us take the blame.'

'I will *not* hide,' Lyra repeated firmly.

Solon, accepting her determination with suppressed frustration, touched his fist to his chest, then told a passing centurion, 'Start bringing the wagons through; we need to get this loaded.'

While he returned to the cordon outside, Dirklan took Lyra and Basia to the vestry, which was even more lavish than her own guest suites, the giant four-poster beds hung with rich brocades, the wardrobes stuffed full of priestly robes and women's clothing.

'In the cellars below are thousands of bottles of very fine wine,' Dirklan commented, then asked the Imperocracy officer currently tallying the loot, 'Any guess at the value?'

The man just shook his head, eyes wide in awe. 'It'll take a while, Milord,' he managed.

Lyra bit her lip, her anger simmering. 'Take me back to the square. I have to be seen. This is my policy.'

Dirklan and Basia bowed stiffly and led her back to the threshold, where the double doors had been thrown open. The sun was up now, revealing the dense crowd of angry men and woman crawling over each other like ants, hammering at the shield wall that protected her, howling abuse. It reached a new crescendo when they saw her again.

'*THERE'S THE DIRTY THIEF! CORANI BITCH!*' Worst of all, another chant could be heard, insidiously brewing below the main clamour: '*SACRECOUR! SACRECOUR!*' Stones and coins were pelting the shields around her, pinging away in tiny sparks.

What have we done?

Dominius' clergyman climbed onto a pulpit erected behind the cordon, but he was shouted down as a betrayer and struck by thrown missiles until he staggered away, bleeding.

For a moment she couldn't think past her sin. *Rildan will never live to be emperor. We're doomed* . . . but then anger rose, directed first at herself, and then at Ostevan, who'd toyed with her and now backed her into this corner. *I'm a Corani*, she told herself. *Our symbol is the badger, and she-badgers always come out fighting.*

'Dirklan,' she snapped, 'bring out the treasure. I want these people to see it.'

'They'll riot, Lyra – we're barely holding them as it is.'

'*Bring it out*,' she snapped, thinking for an instant he'd defy her, then he also thumped a fist to his chest and strode away. Basia was looking at her like she was insane. *Perhaps I am* . . .

In a few minutes, a line of men came trooping out, labouring under the weight of chests of gold and ornaments. At the sight, the entire crowd surged forward, only the kinesis of the mage-knights in the cordon holding them back.

'*They're trying to take it out*,' someone screeched. '*Hem them in, break that wall!*'

'Mark who said that,' Dirklan snapped to an officer. 'He's been planted by Ostevan.'

'*SAVE THE GOLD FOR KORE*,' the crowd shrieked, battering the shield-wall, now three men thick. '*SAVE THE GOLD – DON'T LET HER TAKE IT!*'

Lyra saw cudgels and knives thrusting through the gaps, and although the officers were ordering their men not to strike back, some would. *I must do something!*

She turned to Basia. 'Make sure everyone can hear me.' Then she shouted, '*Dump it here*,' to the men carrying the plunder and strode to the priest's pulpit.

Solon appeared and shouted in her ear. 'What's happening? The wagons are out the back.'

Lyra ignored him. '*Dump it here*,' she shouted again, then she climbed the pulpit. Basia's shields locked around her, sparking every time they were struck by stones or coins or rubbish.

'*PARISHIONERS, HERE IS YOUR CROZIER'S GOLD*,' she cried out. Her voice was cracking, but Basia enhanced it, making it cut through the deafening crowd until it bounced off the far walls.

As she shouted, she flung her arm behind her, showing them the ever-growing pile of treasure in all its glittering glory, and the spectacle struck those at the front dumb.

'THIS IS WHAT YOU GAVE TO KORE,' she shouted. 'ALL YOUR TITHING – ALL YOUR BEQUESTS – ALL YOUR TAPER MONEY, LIGHTING CANDLES TO THE DEAD! URBANIUS LOCKED IT IN A HOLE UNDERGROUND. LOOK AT IT – *LOOK AT IT!*'

There was near-silence now. Those unable to see started clambering for a view. The faces were still angry, but there was also awe, and finally, she could see the beginnings of doubt.

She certainly had their attention.

'*Give it back to Kore*,' a man shouted, deep in the crowd.

She'd seen the way to start. She called to a guard, pointing, 'That picture – hold it up!' Then she whirled to face the crowd, conscious that everyone – her own people and the crowd – were staring at her like she'd gone mad. But although she was terrified, she was riding a wave of fury.

'LOOK AT THIS: DOES URBANIUS CROZIER REALLY NEED A PICTURE OF THE QUEEN OF PERSEPOLIS IN THE NUDE? IS THAT *HOLY*? IS THAT *SACRED*?'

She got what she wanted: a little laughter and a whole lot of confusion. She snatched up a gold platter being held aloft by another guard, one who'd grasped what she was doing. 'I DON'T EAT OFF GOLD, BUT URBANIUS DOES!' She threw it aside and took the gem-encrusted goblet he was offering her. 'NICE WINE CUP – AND YOU SHOULD SEE HIS CELLAR! YOU WANT TO GET DRUNK? URBANIUS' TAVERN IS THE PLACE!'

A little more laughter greeted this and more importantly, the pressure against the shield-wall visibly eased. They were listening. She dropped her voice, no longer having to shout to be heard.

'You give your money to the Church on trust: it's a pledge: you give, so they can serve Kore, and by serving Kore, serve you. Urbanius and his ilk have broken that trust.'

That set off a murmuring and she had a moment of hope.

Then that same male voice called, 'It was your mate Wurther what corrupted the Church!'

'Red scarf, seven rows back,' she heard Dirklan mutter into the ear of a stocky, short-haired woman with a scar on her temple – Brigeda, if she recalled correctly.

'Grand Prelate Wurther *supports* our cleansing of the Church,' Lyra called back. 'Look – his men are here with us.' She pointed at the bloody-faced priest cowering behind his pulpit.

'Wurther's your prisoner,' the same man shouted. 'It's *Ostevan* will cleanse the Church!'

'Ostevan rose against Grand Prelate Wurther because of this matter!' Lyra called back, throwing all of her conviction and vehemence into what was an inspired fib. 'Ostevan seized power to try to *stop* this just and righteous action: it was *Ostevan* who *burned* the docklands – Ostevan was behind the Reeker attacks! *Ostevan is a Sacrecour puppet!*'

Take that, she thought furiously, looking to see who *dared* answer back next. She glimpsed Basia's face, strained with the effort of amplifying her voice while still shielding. Her bodyguard was gazing at her with visible admiration.

'I pledge you this,' Lyra shouted, trying to wrap this up, 'anything in this treasure that is truly religious will be returned to the cathedral.

Any damage caused will be repaired: on this, you have my word. But we *will* purify the Church of these excesses and return the Church to Kore!'

Unbelievably, after all the virulence and hatred, some of the people actually cheered.

The mob . . . it blows with the wind . . .

Lyra glanced sideways at the man with the ledger book. 'Can I give any of this back to the people, to placate them?' she asked quietly.

The Treasury man almost swooned at her suggestion. 'No, *please*, Majesty, we need it all – to just throw money to the mob is a bad precedent. And it's inflationary,' he rounded off, as if that was the clincher.

Solon said, 'Don't, Milady. Reward them for rioting and they'll just do it again.'

She hesitated, then sighed. *They're probably right.*

'You've done enough, Lyra,' Solon said, stepping in close. 'Now you shou–'

Then Basia grunted and staggered, blue lines shimmering as thin dark shapes, shrieking like angry wasps, punched holes through her shields. An arrow tipped in livid scarlet light flashed past Lyra's face and smashed into Basia's lower left leg, jerking off her feet and to the ground. Solon grabbed Lyra, holding her against his big frame as magefire burst around them.

'Basia!' Lyra shrieked, struggling to get her head free. The bodyguard was on the ground, not moving. Beside her was the Imperocrat who'd been tallying the treasure, on his knees, eyes closed and clutching the ledger to his chest, trembling violently as he prayed.

'*Basia!*' Lyra called again as armoured men had closed about them, then, with Solon carrying her at the heart of it, a moving phalanx formed and began bludgeoning its way along the cordoned lane to her carriage.

The next few moments flashed by in a series of snatched images: Solon's set, determined face; equally frightened soldiers and civilians, all flailing about; the horses rearing in terror as the carriage was mobbed; the knights in front of her roaring, 'Make way – *make way!*'

Then she was hurled head-first into the carriage. She scrambled to her knees as Solon pushed in behind her, making the suspension sag dramatically. He hammered on the roof as he slammed the door and warded it, roaring, 'Move, *move!*' He removed his helm so his orders would be better heard, revealing his sweat-soaked, close-cropped hair plastered to his skull and his new-grown beard dripping.

The carriage lurched into motion, the outriders clattering beside them, but they were moving at a crawl. 'What if they're lying in wait?' Lyra hated the tremble in her voice.

'The driver knows to vary the route,' Solon said. He enclosed her hands in his huge gauntlets. The space was small and damp heat flooded off him in waves – and Lyra found she was in the same condition.

For a time they just stared at each other, unable to speak, then the dam broke and she started babbling, 'Dear Kore, poor Basia – they shot her leg . . .' Then her brain belatedly caught up . . . 'They shot her leg: her *lower* leg . . . her *artefact* leg . . .' And she couldn't stop the hysterical giggles welling up. Then she clamped her fist into her mouth, because it truly *wasn't* funny. Her brain whirling, her heart pounding, she felt vividly, incredibly *alive*, despite the horror of the last few moments.

'The archer panicked,' she realised. 'They tried to start a riot but I turned the crowd and that made the archer panic – surely the people will see what we're up against now? They'll understand . . . *maybe* . . . But this is just the first morning . . . Oh Kore . . .'

Then it struck her, as if for the first time, that *nothing* was safe, that but for luck and her protectors, she'd have taken a shaft through her head or chest and come apart in a burst of gnostic fire. 'They *shot* at me . . . If you'd not–'

She began to shake uncontrollably.

Solon dropped to his knees and engulfed her in his strong, steel-clad arms. 'It's all right, Lyra,' he said soothingly. 'I'm here and you're safe. They can't reach you and never will, I swear.'

She clasped his steel casing, not quite crying, not quite hysterical, but on the very edge. *I'm in shock*, she told herself, remembering Ril telling her how even experienced warriors could become *unhinged* . . . *Your blood is up, you feel incredible, and then it hits you just what kind of knife-edge we all dance on* . . .

'I'm sorry,' she choked into Solon's right ear, 'I just . . . I just . . .'

'I know, I know,' he answered, and she realised that he was shaking too, but with a different, coiled-up kind of tension. With sweat carving rivulets down their faces, his beard chafing her cheek, all her pent-up dread blended with the adrenalin of her escape to rip her defences down.

Slowly, as if each motion was taking an era, their mouths met and she tasted him on her tongue, felt heat bleeding into her as she clung on, and for a moment she drowned in the sensation of being held, of being *wanted*, as his hands slid down her sodden dress.

His tongue pushed into her mouth and she was almost frantic to have something more of him inside her . . .

Then with a groan he pulled away, just enough that he could see into her eyes, and for a moment there was a very different man before her: not the dour, impregnable fortress he usually presented to the world, but a man like others, with fears, vulnerabilities and needs.

Someone *lost*, like her.

Then Ril's dead face flashed through her brain and she pushed him away, gasping, 'No, I can't – I don't . . .'

He was still clutching at her and she feared he *couldn't* stop . . . But then he did, jerking his whole body away, and gasping, 'Majesty – Lyra, I'm sorry, I'm so sorry–'

She pressed herself into the corner and looked away, trying to compose herself. 'No, I'm sorry,' she panted, wiping at her mouth, though she still craved his lips on hers. 'I was just so frightened for a moment. I'm all right now,' she lied.

He wiped his sweating face, hanging his head. 'Majesty, I overstepped. Please, be merciful.'

Merciful? 'Kore's Blood, Solon, you saved my life – you have my eternal gratitude.'

And you stopped when I asked, and I respect that even more . . .

They shared a look and she wasn't sure what she was trying to convey, except that to her own shock, this man she'd so feared was now inside her defences, and being held by him and shielded by him had felt both safe and dangerous at the same time.

When he spoke it was in hoarse tones, but with determined candour. 'Lyra, I've been widowed a long time, and then . . . well, you know about

Medelie Aventour. Being alone made me vulnerable and she used that. But now the loneliness is worse, utterly unbearable. Loneliness destroys our pride – it leads us to places we should never go. So if sometimes you're lonely, I want you to know that I'm beset by the same daemons.' He dropped his eyes, then lifted them again. 'Do I need to speak plainer?'

Dear Kore, he wants me . . . Me . . . !

The convent girl inside her was aghast, but the older, wiser Lyra who made decisions that changed lives was intrigued. She knew her own vulnerabilities, and if she was to flirt with powerful men in the months ahead, she needed to be more worldly than she was. And he was right, already the loneliness of her nights was dreadful.

But if we become . . . lovers . . . will that cost me whatever authority I have over him?

She couldn't deny that in the months since his return, Solon had been a courageous bulwark of House Corani. She didn't especially like him, but his behaviour towards her had been exemplary, at least until now – and she'd been as complicit in that as he. But his bulk and brusqueness, his arrogance and the repressed rage she'd sometimes sensed, all intimidated her.

Kore's Blood, I felt safe when he wrapped his arms around me . . . But to have him as my lover – do I really want that?

Love was a strange word; it meant too many things for four little letters to encompass. As queen and empress, needing to marry for state reasons, she might never know it again. Perhaps security and comfort might have to take its place. But this felt too soon, a reaction to fear, not a considered decision.

'Solon, I'm in mourning – Ril and I weren't perfect, but there was much between us.'

Though we were so far adrift of each other when he went away that I barely remember how it felt to be held by him . . . She realised with a jolt that she and Ril last shared a bed in Maicin, seven months gone. 'But Solon . . . you are *appreciated*.'

Whether he understood what she was trying to convey she wasn't sure, but at least they were able to look at each other again without cringing.

Finally the driver rapped on the ceiling to tell them they were passing through the Bastion Gates and they fell out of the intense, enclosed world of the carriage and back into step with the rest of the world. Solon hurried off to learn how the other church raids had progressed, while she went to her own rooms to wash, change and await those reports.

Before Solon left, he kissed her hand and she shivered at his touch.

Despite the tumult of the morning, as she lowered herself into a tub of warm water, she felt cautious satisfaction. Her campaign to secure the Crown's finances had begun, and the Pallas mob had hearkened to her. And Solon's kiss had felt significant, a milestone on her journey back from grief. Perhaps, just maybe, there was hope.

Dupenium, Rondelmar

Coramore sat next to Cordan, at Duke Garod's right hand in the Great Hall of Dupenium Castle, watching the Celestial Ambassador throw a tantrum before the entire court, and tried hard to not to giggle.

'It's the work of the Lord of Hel,' Helios Prelatus raged. 'Lyra Vereinen is Shaitan's Whore!'

'He's actually frothing at the mouth,' Coramore whispered in her brother's ear. 'He's been screaming for nearly half an hour now. I'm amazed he's still got a voice.'

Helios, who'd been so smugly urbane when he arrived, was indeed in a state: his hair was disarrayed, he was so red-faced he almost glowed and his robes were soaked under the armpits and down his back.

'Lord Duke, you *must* march,' he bellowed, 'you *must* restore sanity—'

Coramore glanced at Duke Garod, who'd been listening with stoic sympathy, occasionally interjecting with a 'Quite so' or an 'Indeed, yes' while not really agreeing to anything.

The court were agog, and why not? Empress Lyra had sent soldiers into every Church she could reach – although that was effectively just Pallas, Coraine and the rural lands around those two cities – and plundered them for treasure. Coramore, who'd disliked priests ever since getting her hands slapped for talking during catechisms, thought it was terribly funny. Her reading of her uncle suggested he thought the same, but he wasn't going to admit it.

The half-hour of ranting caught up with Helios, who fell into a bout of anguished coughing, and that gave Garod the opportunity to interject. He lifted his ducal sceptre and crashed it down on the table before him, compelling silence. 'Thank you, good Prelate,' he began, his voice resonant. 'We all share your shock at this outrage. Centuries of tradition, hurled in the face of Kore Himself – I wonder that He does not hurl thunderbolts down on the Bastion like the Lantric gods of old, eh?'

Helios went on wheezing, although he did manage to pull an annoyed face at the mention of pagan deities.

'Fear not,' Garod went on, 'for our muster proceeds apace. My kinsman, Sir Brylion Fasterius, has reached Klief on his long journey back north. Very soon, we will arrive together at the gates of Pallas, where no doubt the desperate populace will throw open the gates, eh?'

'The streets of Pallas are in ferment,' Helios spluttered, his face puce. 'You must–'

'I know what I *must* do, Helios,' Garod interrupted, his voice suddenly cold, 'and I certainly do not need to be berated about it.' He leaned forward and asked, 'How have the other duchies and vassal-states reacted?'

'Your Grace, the Kore-bedamned Midreans and Andressans have taken it as *carte blanche* to do the same. In Bricia they just stood by and watched the Imperial representatives march in and rob the churches and abbeys blind! Canossi and Aquillea likewise teeter on the edge of this heresy. And Argundy have closed their borders.'

Garod looked thoughtful, while Jasper Vendroot, his Volsai commander, murmured something in his ear. Coramore guessed her uncle was pondering how much advantage he could extract from this. After keeping Helios waiting a minute, he said, 'Of course, no such plundering of the Church's wealth will happen here, Ambassador.'

'It never crossed my mind that your Grace would sink so low as the Vereinen Witch,' Helios replied, although his expression suggested quite the opposite.

'Although we must not forget that waging this war to save your master will be expensive,' Garod added slyly.

Helios' face fell. *Give me half your money and I won't take the other half*, Coramore mentally translated. It was all she could do not to laugh out loud.

Cordan was mystified, until she explained it over dinner. She was getting used to being a lot smarter than her older brother, but that didn't matter. He was family and she loved him utterly.

One day I'll be his chief advisor . . . But what will he be?

10

Forest Haven

Cuz Sarkan

Hegikaro is the centre of our realm, the seat of power for our kings, but ask any Mollach and they will tell you that the heart of Mollachia is Cuz Sarkan, the Draken's Peak. The bones of draken can be seen embedded in the mountain's walls and Gerjamuth, the Father Draken, is said to dwell in the crater lake. His blood colours the Szajver River that flows from the mountain.

PATER KOSTYN, KORE PRIEST, MOLLACHIA 931

Upper Osiapa Valley, Mollachia
Noveleve 935

The morning after conversing with Nara of Misencourt – if that was her real name – Valdyr and Gricoama pushed eastwards through snow-covered high country into the headwaters of the Osiapa River.

But about mid-afternoon, after pulling himself up a slope hand over fist, his face frozen and snow caked in his furs and hair, he crested the rise to see Gricoama stop dead and look back, snarling. When he looked back, a dozen upright figures were emerging from the trees some two hundred yards below. They stared at him, then began to run in utter silence. Valdyr prepared to do the same when as many wolves burst from hiding places on the upper slope and went tearing towards the hunters, covering the snow-covered ground in leaps and bounds. The sound of snarling growls from both human and wolf throats floated up the slope.

A ghastly thought suddenly struck Valdyr: *What happens if a wolf bites an infected man?*

In moments every one of the hunters had been overborne and the wolves were worrying at their flesh; Valdyr fancied he could hear bones snapping. But then a sluggishness overtook the triumphant wolves . . . they started wobbling on their feet, and dread overtook him.

Gricoama snarled, his ears flattening, as the pack below wailed eerily – then they fell silent and began to drop to the snow, even as the men sat up . . .

Valdyr didn't wait to see what would happen next. He dropped his pack and pounded up the slope, Gricoama bounding at his side. They were at the edge of the autumn snow-line and the blackened trees were covered in rime, with crystalline shards hanging downwards like needles. As the snow piled higher, the steepening slope became ever more treacherous; any fall might be fatal.

Hearing panting behind him, he and Gricoama whirled to see the lead wolves were tearing up the steep slope, eyes now jet-black and jaws drooling noxious dark spittle.

For a moment Valdyr was paralysed, then the instincts that had got him through the chain-gangs of Dhassa took over. He stepped in front of the first beast, slammed one end of his seven-foot staff into its throat and hurled it backwards and off the drop, straight into the jaws of its oncoming fellows. The second snapped at his leg, but only snagged his robes. He twisted and crashed the staff down onto the beast's head, stunning it just long enough for his second blow to send it spinning down the mountain after the first beast.

He turned to see Gricoama evading the snapping jaws of the third wolf, then lunge in, jaws widening–

'No!' Valdyr shouted in despair as Gricoama's teeth punctured the smaller wolf's throat. Black blood spurted . . .

Valdyr backed away . . . as light flashed in Gricoama's mouth, the attacker's flesh rippled and a cloud of ash disgorged from the eye-sockets and mouth.

It dropped lifeless to the ground.

Dear Kore . . . What was that?

But this wasn't the time. The next wolves were already scrabbling onto their ledge and once again he was fighting for his life, kicking the first under the jaw to send it spinning, then driving the head of the staff into the eye-socket of the next beast, while Gricoama snapped the neck of another beast, white light flashed again and it too fell lifeless, its eyes blasted to ash.

The rest of the pack suddenly stopped in their tracks ... and the Vitezai huntsmen appeared at the rim of the ridge. '*Valdyr, now we have you,*' they chorused, and with a savage cry of lust and rage, men and beasts came at him.

Valdyr howled in defiance, followed an instant later by a sound like a giant sheet of glass shattering with a reverberating *snap* that made the air tremble – whether the concussion came from the world around him or from his own chest, he couldn't tell, but it left him gasping for air.

With an icy *crack*, the ground shook and Gricoama spun, grabbed the hem of Valdyr's robes and *yanked*. Valdyr, taken by surprise, sprawled backwards against the overhanging bank behind him—

—as a massive boulder hurtled down from above, smashed straight into the possessed hunters and wolves and snatched them away. Gricoama yowled and Valdyr scrambled backwards, scared beyond all reason as the light was ripped away by a wall of snow, rocks and uprooted trees pouring over the top of the bank above. With a deafening roar, the ridge where they'd fought was swept away.

Valdyr pressed himself against the rock, as far back as he could get, and clung to Gricoama, who was shaking as much as he.

I did that . . . I triggered an avalanche with my shout . . .

Or with the dwyma . . .

He hadn't intended any such thing, and even if it had occurred to him, he knew he'd likely have been too terrified to try it. Landslides were so dangerous, especially in winter. His shrill cry must have been just enough to set it off.

But he also couldn't deny the post-magic hollowness in his bones.

They were left partially buried themselves, but when the shaking earth stilled, the wolf scrabbled out first and Valdyr came after him, using his staff to sweep away the snow. They crawled to the edge to see if any foe survived, but other than the debris, there was nothing to see. The wolves and the hunters were buried somewhere beneath.

But Asiv knows where we are, Valdyr guessed.

He patted Gricoama's shoulder and said fervently, 'Well done.' He pondered those bursts of light; he thought it might be the same light he'd once seen outlining Gricoama and Luhti one night on Watcher's Peak. *She showed him something, or opened him to some power of the Elétfa . . . something that can defeat this evil infection.*

He wished he'd learned as much. But for now, they had to move, and fast.

For the remainder of the day they stayed off the ridgelines, keeping low and away from open ground, grateful for the fresh snow covering their tracks. Gricoama was quiet, mourning his pack, and Valdyr was in utter dread of Asiv ripping aside whatever veils were hiding them from his gnostic sight, but by dusk, no one had found them. They made camp, curling around each other, and slept, concealed in a thicket of twisted cedar. His last thought as he closed his eyes was a prayer to Kore that he be permitted to wake . . . and not see Asiv standing over him.

Asiv Fariddan took the skiff down a careful distance from the rock-fall, which was already covered in snow. Frustration was clouding his mind, because for the first time since his transfiguration, Abraxas wasn't enough. The malignant presence of the dwyma was resisting the daemon's powers.

Something burned the daemon from those wolves – could it do the same to me?

He walked to the edge of the rock-fall, opening up his senses until, through Abraxas, he could feel four survivors, human hunters, still alive beneath the ice despite their bodies being crushed and broken. He felt no pity: they'd failed him.

Let them suffer . . .

The rest of the hunters had been completely destroyed in the avalanche, their skulls crushed, and the wolves were all gone – unlike men, the daemon ichor consumed lesser creatures in a few days. But had the avalanche been triggered by the dwyma, or was it just ill-fortune? He couldn't tell – his powers were blind to the dwyma, and that was another troubling factor.

I can't find Valdyr – I can't even sense his power. How dare the universe conspire against me in this way?

He floated up to where Valdyr and his wolf had been cornered and tried to pick up their trail, but the snow – or perhaps the dwyma? – had covered their tracks. He raged for a bit, and then grew coldly calm as he reassured himself: half of the infected Vitezai Sarkanum hunters were patrolling the uplands, so it was surely only a matter of time before he found the Sarkany brothers again . . .

The infection is spreading, Kyrik thought, as he and Rothgar slithered to the edge of the clearing and studied the men below. They were dressed too lightly for the snow-covered ground and biting air and they moved feverishly, not with the hunters' normal relaxed, watchful gait. And with his inner eye, Kyrik could sense the use of raw magical energies that ordinary men had no access to.

Dragan was making more people into his slaves.

He and Rothgar didn't dare attack the four men below; all they could do was remain still and let them pass. Each day was a painstaking test in discipline, frustration and woodcraft, most of which had to be borne by Rothgar. While the gnosis was exceedingly useful in avoiding detection, just a puff of steam from a mouth or the trace of a footprint in the snow could uncover them. Luckily for him, Rothgar was Mollachia's most skilled woodsman.

A minute passed while the four men below sniffed at the snow, clearly sensing something. A short time earlier, Rothgar had smoothed away their tracks, but perhaps traces remained?

Don't come this way, Kyrik silently prayed. *I know who you were. I know your families.*

As if in answer to that prayer, the possessed hunters turned north-west and strode off up the opposite slope. They'd not exchanged a single word, gesture or look in the time Kyrik had watched them.

'Did something summon them?' Rothgar muttered in Kyrik's ear, once they'd gone.

'Not in any way I could hear. They went towards Watcher's Peak,' he added, worried.

Fridryk Kippenegger emerged from behind a giant pine, his two-handed sword drawn.

'Put that thing away before you accidentally cut down a tree,' Rothgar said with a grin.

Kip responded with a dramatic spin-and-swing, stopping the blow abruptly with the blade kissing the bark of the pine, before chuckling and sheathing the weapon. 'I'm sick of this creeping round,' he grumbled.

They'd been on the move for a week now, hiding below ground using a network of caves and disused mines Rothgar knew. They'd averaged only a few miles each day, not helped by constantly having to stop to erase their trail. They used gnosis to cross and re-cross the Osiapa River as they climbed into the hinterlands, but they were now hundreds of feet above the valley floor, where the land was locked in snow and ice.

That night Rothgar led them to a lean-to shelter beneath an immense boulder where an overhang kept away direct snowfall. There was an old fire-pit, dug in low and cunningly concealed. Kyrik fell asleep gazing into the embers, trying not think about Hajya; consequently, she was *all* he could think of: her dark curls, her earthy features and well-worn body, her wise eyes and hungry kiss. He bit his lip, trying not to cry, but it did no good, for tears pooled in his eyes then spilled down his face into the blanket as he lay and shook.

If Rothgar noticed, he gave no sign. Kip just snored on. Finally, Kyrik rose and gave Rothgar a helpless look. 'I'll take the next few hours. Can't bloody sleep.'

The ranger patted his shoulder and took his place beside the fire. He was asleep in seconds. Kyrik filled his mug and scanned the night, but neither moon nor stars could pierce the thick cloud and nothing moved. The snow came down in frozen, deadly silence. Not even wolves howled.

He felt his head nodding and shook himself awake – and a woman's voice whispered in his mind, *Kyrik, Kyrik . . . My love, help me!*

It was *her* voice, which was how he knew he was dreaming.

Kyrik's plan had been to re-equip – he was still wearing the ruins of his coronation robes and they were low on food – and try to find his brother, but as it happened, Valdyr, or rather, Gricoama, found them first.

They were traversing a forest glen two mornings after his dream when a grey wolf appeared atop a rise – then wuffled like a domesticated dog and pranced about. A few moments later Kyrik and Valdyr were pounding each other's backs, neither bothering to hide the tears in their eyes.

Once they'd let go of each other, Rothgar led them to one of his secret niches, tucked away out of sight and kept stocked with dry wood and some stores, so they could catch up on each other's tales.

'I'm so sorry,' Valdyr said, when Kyrik told him about Hajya. Although his younger brother had been suspicious of the Sydian witch when Kyrik first presented her, his remorse was clearly genuine. 'She would have made you a fine queen.'

That she would, Kyrik thought, his heart like a leaden lump inside him. Her loss still felt raw and immediate, but to be reunited with his brother was some consolation.

Lifted by Valdyr's return, Kyrik was able to think about the wider world for the first time, and especially of Clan Vlpa. By now, if she'd made it at all, Korznici, the seer's daughter, would be with them. That evening, when he took to his blanket, he used spiritualism, one of the Gnostic Studies he'd seldom invoked, and sent his spiratus streaming through the air. It was a risk – other magi with that affinity could detect such things – but it was necessary. He focused on Korznici, remembering her composed face and wise eyes. The Sfera had no Arcanum training, just the teachings of her fellow Sydian magi, but finding her wasn't hard. She was among her people on a snowbound plain in the Domhalott. She sat up when she sensed him and opened her inner eye.

'*Kirol?*' she said softly. To her, he knew, he'd be a gauzy thing, like a ghost. Anyone except another mage watching her would have thought she was talking to herself.

'Korznici,' he said, 'thank Kore and Ahm alike, you made it back to your people.

'Ysh,' she told him, 'but it was a hard journey.'

He could imagine the uproar when she told them of the massacre at the coronation. He asked who now led the tribe and learned that

Gershan, Thraan's youngest son, was to be made nacelnik, with a group of Elders forming a kind of regency council to advise him.

'I'm to be one of the elders,' Korznici – herself all of eighteen – said. 'I'm the highest blood of the Sfera remaining,' she added in a bleak voice.

'You have an old head on your shoulders,' Kyrik told her. 'You'll do well. But listen, there's much you need to do. You need to persuade the clan to move again, before the Rondians or Dragan attack. I know it'll be hard, but you must move north, into the mountains.'

'Into the mountains?' she said doubtfully.

'Ysh. The region north of you is volcanic – the Tuzvolg, it's called. The earth is thin there, and there are valleys where the snow doesn't linger. The pastures can sustain small herds for a few months. *Small herds*, Korznici – you must cull your beasts for food, and to preserve the pasture for the rest.' He knew the Sydian clans' herds were their lifeblood, and culling was a solemn and sacred thing, but this was survival.

'I'll tell the Elders,' she said, her voice reluctant. She bit her lip and added, 'Your name is not well-loved here right now, Kirol Kyrik. You promised us a new home, but led us into danger. Now Thraan and Hajya, those who trusted you most, are dead. Many say we should have stayed in Sydia.'

'I'm sorry,' he said. 'I truly had no idea what Fate would throw at us. But I will do all I can to make this right. For now, that means culling your herd and taking refuge in the Tuzvolg.'

After a few more words of encouragement, he sped back to his body, waking with a shudder as his awareness settled back into his skin. The camp was quiet, Rothgar on guard.

I'm sure I wasn't detected, he reassured himself. It had been tempting to scout his surroundings, but he'd resisted; until he knew more about what they faced, prudence was wise. But he felt he'd accomplished something, finally: a small step on the path of resistance. He silently vowed vengeance upon Asiv, Dragan and whoever else had gone willingly into the daemon's shadow.

Hegikaro, Mollachia

Dragan Zhagy sat on his throne, as the man before him bleated on and on.

'Gazda, this sickness among us,' Milosh Nirabhy, a self-appointed spokesman for the people, complained again. 'It's a *plague*, Gazda, like in the time of our grandfathers. We *must* send for help.'

Milosh was voicing the fears of the people with more courage than Dragan had ever thought he'd possessed, especially considering that many of the men he was complaining of were right here in the throne hall. His possessed men had been running amok, driving those unin-fected to cower in barricaded houses, eating their winter stores and praying for deliverance. Murder, theft and rape were rife and the daemon-infection was spreading.

It's my fault. I let this in and now the entire valley is falling under the daemon's sway . . .

The infected men were nominally under his control, but only when he was present. During the day they retreated into themselves, avoiding the light, allowing a semblance of normality to prevail, but at night, away from him, they prowled like hungry wolves. Nevertheless, he had to pretend authority.

'I'm aware of the sickness, Milosh,' Dragan replied. 'It comes from the legions in the lower valley. There are deserters on the loose, but we'll catch them. All will be well soon.'

Rip the bastard's throat out, Abraxas cackled into his brain.

He quieted the daemon with effort. 'Milosh, trust me. This will pass. The imperial legion will soon destroy the Sydian invaders, and then they'll leave.'

'But no one's seen a deserter east of Lapisz,' Milosh protested. 'They're our own—'

'*They are deserters*,' Dragan snarled, making his Vitezai men's hackles rise. '*Do not contradict me!*'

Milosh blanched and babbled an apology, fear coming off him like cheap perfume.

'Go now,' Dragan advised him. *Before I rip your head off.*

Milosh hurried out, almost tripping in his anxiety to be gone. Dragan was about to order one of his men to follow him out and bite him, then remembered that he'd arrived with others. *Too public. I'll deal with him later.*

'You should be more patient with him,' Asiv Fariddan purred, stepping from the shadows.

'In *my* throne hall I say what I like,' Dragan told the Keshi mage.

'Do you?' Asiv sniffed. 'For my part, I long to depart this frozen wasteland. As soon as I've found Valdyr.'

'This *wasteland* is my home,' Dragan replied, 'and I'm getting sick of your—'

Suddenly, his tongue twisted and rammed itself down his own throat. He gasped and fell choking onto the cold stone floor, oily drool bubbling from his lips.

'Remember who is the real Master here,' Asiv rasped.

Dragan's vision swam and his newly sighted inner eye showed him Abraxas' giant maw, opening around him in the aether. He shouted in dread as giant teeth gleamed.

Asiv clicked his fingers and suddenly Dragan was gasping down huge mouthfuls of air, his panic subsiding. 'Alert me the instant either Sarkany appears,' the Easterner drawled. 'In the meantime, send the Sydian witch to me. I wonder if Kyrik will be able to hear her scream through the aether?'

11

Healing of Body and Soul

Longevity of the Magi

Healing-gnosis, morphic gnosis, even necromancy, impart tangible benefits to longevity. But simply being a mage imparts the greatest benefits. All magi live longer, and the purer the bloodline, the greater the longevity. There are some Ascendants still living who were there in 329, at the Ascendancy of Corineus.

ANNALS OF PALLAS, 840

Lukhazan, Noros
Decore 935

Seth Korion's mount was uneasy and he pondered on animals' strange awareness when something unnatural was brewing. Some animagi believed it was the beasts' superior hearing and sensitivity to temperature, but no one actually knew.

'Yes, lovie,' Seth told the mare, 'something bad will happen, but I'll see you through.'

It was two weeks since he'd left the rest of the Rondian armies and marched his men south. One of Rolven Sulpeter's marshalls had politely delivered a formal arrest warrant, and he had equally politely torn it up in the man's face. He'd been impeccably courteous when he sent away the Earl of Kerno, who'd arrived intending to assume control of the Fifth Army; he'd never had much time for the Brician nobleman, who was known to be deep in the pockets of the Rondian Governor of Bricia. He'd started blocking the dozens of gnostic sendings, from Prince Elvero

Salinas in particular, accusing him of cowardice, dereliction of duty and other more personal insults.

And standing before him now was another coterie of noblemen who wanted his head, although for quite different reasons. The small delegation of provincial Noromen and their families had come to beg his forbearance.

He turned to his aides. 'Remember, these people are grieving and angry, and they have a right to those emotions. Be calm, hear them out and don't react if they overstep.' Then he turned to Pilus Lukaz's guard cohort. 'That goes for you men, too.'

Lukaz saluted stiffly and his men thumped their breastplates energetically.

The low rise on which they stood overlooked Lukhazan. The town, built on the slopes of a south-facing hill, was topped by a historic but largely indefensible castle, which was in any case not big enough to resist even a small army.

It was here that my father forced the surrender of the Noroman general Belonius Vult and turned the tide of the Noros Revolt, Seth thought. Or more likely, purchased Vult's surrender – the details were murky. The town had no fondness for the Korion family.

They'll be hating my name even more soon, he thought dourly, as he watched the streams of refugees heading southeast towards Venderon, knowing they'd get no refuge there either. Many families had had to be dragged shrieking and cursing from their homes.

Some of that despair and rage was visible on the faces of those now approaching him, a mix of men and women of all ages: the mage-nobles of Lukhazan, come to plead one last time. He climbed from his mount and went to face them.

The Earl of Lukhazan and his cousins and kin fell to their knees on the frozen ground, except for old Lady Hanna-Britt Fogell, who shuffled forth, her eyes so dark and skin so pale she looked like a corpse.

'Come to finish your father's work, have you, Korion?' she rasped.

'Milady, this is the very last thing I wish to do,' Seth told her.

'Then don't,' she choked out. 'Make a stand here, in these highlands where the great General Robler defeated the empire in the first year of the Revolt. A real man would fight here, and win.'

'Lady Fogell,' Seth said patiently, despite having had this same argument with every single one of the Lukhazan mage-nobles before him, 'we *cannot* make a stand here. The sultan would simply ride around us and seize Norostein, which is his real goal. What I must do here is deprive him of shelter, which is why the castle and the town must be broken, then burned. I'm *truly* sorry, you must believe me – and after this war, I'll help rebuild what's been lost. But I cannot allow it to fall into Rashid's hands intact.'

He hoped she could hear the very genuine pain in his voice, but instead she spat at his feet. 'You're craven scum, just like your father. We know how he defeated us: trickery, butchery and money. *We* remember. Good folk here pray daily for the death of his line.'

'I don't disagree with you over my father,' he told her, 'but if the empire is to survive – if our people are to survive – I have a job to do.'

'We're doing this to save Noros,' Andwine Delton put in unwisely.

Lady Fogell whirled on him. 'You godless Brician snit, what do you know? Would you burn Bres? Would you burn your own houses? My family have dwelt in these fair vales for three centuries. Our labour has gone into all you see around you. Our bones lie in the soil. A curse on all of you!'

Curses were impossible under the gnosis, but everyone flinched a little at her rage.

'Lady Fogell, may I escort you to your carriage?' Seth said, offering his hand. 'It's a long ride to Norostein.'

'Stay away from me, you *turd*,' the noblewoman snarled, tears rolling down her face.

'Either way, you don't need to see this.' Seth looked at the Earl of Lukhazan. Her son-in-law was a portly, uncertain man, currently fingering his thin beard. 'Lord Janses, please, the journey is long, and you should set out now.'

'We're watching,' the earl replied stiffly.

'If you must.' Seth touched his heart, in reverence to old Lady Fogell, because he truly did pity her, then turned back to his aides. 'Culmather, signal Mortas and tell them to begin.' Then he turned to Chaplain Gerdhart. 'Would you say a few words?'

Gerdhart looked from the distant castle and town to the cluster of mage-nobles before him, then bowed his head. 'Kore on High, watch down on us and see our struggle. In olden days pagans made sacrifice to their gods for aid, but we live in more enlightened times. Nevertheless, at times great sacrifice is required. Let this sacrifice aid our eventual victory. We mourn that which will be lost. Our hearts go out to those for whom this is home and we pray that one day we will build anew where these dwellings now stand.'

'Hear us, O Kore,' Seth called loudly, echoed by his aides.

Earl Janses and his people just stared sullenly out over the valley as the aether quivered, then came another quiver, and another, each stronger than the last, as the Earth-magi began their work.

Natural earthquakes could be small, localised events, or largescale and devastating. Earth-magi could do a little to alleviate them if they understood the local geology, but otherwise they were beyond magical control. But Earth-gnosis could also be used to *create* an earthquake – in which case the area was usually very specific, and the trigger-points could be nullified by any Earth-mage in the general region, even if they were a dozen miles away. That was why this had to be done now, before enemy Earth-magi could prevent it.

The energy pulses were growing and blooms of flame began to appear among the houses on Castle Hill as Fire-gnosis was triggered to aid the destruction. Some of Earl Janses' people started wailing. Seth wished he could make them understand how much he hated doing this – but to them he was lower than the Lord of Hel.

The tremors were getting stronger. The horses were visibly spooked, those animals left behind in the town – cats, dogs, foxes, vermin – were now streaming away from the walls and birds were rising in huge flocks into the air. And still the pressure built.

Then came a deep, chilling rumble, followed by a great *crack!* – and the earthquake was unleashed. For an alarming moment the ground rippled like waves on the sea, but the effect was much worse in the distant town. The castle was torn apart by the successive shakes, its collapsing walls spewing down the hillside. The central bailey imploded – then the hillside shifted and an avalanche of rock came smashing down in a wave, tearing up trees and engulfing houses. Moments later flames roared through the newly exposed broken timbers.

Lady Fogell fell screaming to her knees, weeping uncontrollably. The younger women of her House went to aid her, while the men braced each other's shoulders, looking at Seth with absolute hatred in their eyes.

Seth was walking slowly away, blinking back his own tears, when Earl Janses appeared behind him and placed a heavy hand on his shoulder. For a moment he thought the earl was going to punch him to the ground, but he just glared at him. The anger on his face was ill-suited to his genial features, but his voice sounded like the low snarl of a bear. 'Win this war, Korion,' he growled, 'or we will burn you and yours in turn.'

Seth placed his fist to his heart. He swallowed and managed to find his tongue. 'I swear I will gain the victory, or die trying.'

'Live or die, we care not: just win.' Then the earl turned to face his devastated home and fell to the ground, weeping.

A pillar of smoke in the southwest corner of the sky drew Waqar's attention. He turned Ajniha towards it, trusting his roc-riders to follow. Since Collistein Junction, the skies had been uncontested, the very few Rondian skiffs or fliers they'd spotted fleeing swiftly. But the empire had more warbirds, more windskiffs and more mage-knights on construct-beasts, so he expected the battle for supremacy in the skies would soon be renewed, although each day the skies grew colder. Perhaps aerial combat would cease during the dead of winter?

But for now his roc-riders were able to scout the enemy's troop movements with impunity. What he'd learned was slightly disturbing: not all the Rondians had retreated north and west. Some had headed south and were burning every building and unharvested field as they went. So Rashid's plan to seize Norostein would not go uncontested. But it was only a fragment of the Rondian force, no more than ten legions, surely not enough to stop the entire Shihad.

The masses of refugees were slowing the enemy retreat, too: the hundred-mile gap separating the Shihad advance guard from the Rondian rearguard was closing daily. There was every chance they'd bring them to battle before they even reached Norostein.

He turned his attention back to the smoke rising from below and swooped down to investigate, his roc-riders streaming down behind him. He found another large town newly destroyed by the retreating Rondians. A castle had been razed to the ground, probably by Earth-gnosis, and fire now ripped through the remaining buildings and the wheat fields outside. It had to be Lukhazan, which Rashid had hoped to seize intact.

Muttering curses under his breath, Waqar pulled Ajniha about and let Tamir, Baneet and Fatima draw up alongside, his eyes resting for a moment on the spear cradled in Baneet's big hands. The crystal pulsed dully beneath the spearhead.

<Let's circle lower and count the enemy,> he called to his flight of twenty, then more intimately, just to his friends, *<I want to try to capture an enemy commander and question him. You three take the eastward road from here, back towards Venderon. Find me a target, then guide us in.>*

His friends saluted and veered off, while he stayed with his less experienced fliers. These youngsters, replacements for those lost over Collistein Junction, were unblooded, new to winged combat and very much in awe of the veterans. It was an odd feeling, this reverence, but at least it meant instant obedience.

He spent the next forty minutes circling the town, watching some refugees taking to the hills instead of joining the flight south, which suggested the possibility of insurgency later in the campaign. Then Tamir called.

Waqar took his roc-riders back towards Venderon, where his friends were circling a column of Rondian wagons and citizens on foot, flanked by horsemen.

<There's a man holding a blue pennant down there,> Tamir called.

<We think he's the squire of a mage-knight,> Fatima added. *<His master is nearby.>*

Once he'd spotted the armoured rider, Waqar told his charges, *<Listen, my eagles: today you must be hard of heart. This is a war. When we attack, they are all the enemy. Go in fast, target enemy archers and knights first, then cause destruction and confusion. That means wagons and livestock. Always remember: the Shaitan-spawned Rondians did far worse to us in the Crusades, so be without pity.>*

The young ones were hungry for violence, but his veterans kept quiet, knowing how much he hated giving such commands. Fatima brushed his mind sympathetically, then they dived upon the column below, preparing bows and spells as the enemy wagons grew in size before they suddenly realised their danger.

An ineffectual flurry of scattered arrows rose to meet them, then he was over the column and streaming mage-bolts into the nearest archers. Behind him, those with Fire-gnosis blazed away at the canvas-covered wagons. By their third pass half the column were cowering behind rocks, hiding in ditches or just running, easy targets for his rocs, who swooped in, picked up men in their massive claws and ripped them apart. He felt the familiar sickness at the sight of women and children blasted in the backs by mage-fire: this was slaughter, not combat.

Then a wordless bellow of rage rose in the aether and he banked to see the knight they'd picked out earlier hurling mage-bolts into the sky, slamming fire into the shields of the nearest roc-rider. As livid blue light went ripping through the air, Tamir flew at the Rondian to draw his fire, while Waqar swung in behind him unnoticed.

He drew a javelin from the saddle-sheath and threw, using kinesis to slam it straight through the knight's shields and into his right calf, pinning him screaming to the ground.

<*You got him!*> he heard Fatima shriek and an instant later she was whooshing in, vaulting from the saddle and cutting down his young squire, the only man running to aid the stricken knight, before slamming mesmeric-gnosis into the knight's brain to bludgeon him unconscious. She yanked out the javelin and sent healing magic to his leg. In moments, with their captive slung over her roc's neck, they rose into the air.

<*Enough!*> Waqar called to his outlying birds. <*Up and north, rally on Fatima!*>

He worked Ajniha hard to catch her, drew alongside and sent a wordless burst of praise, echoed by Baneet as he too caught up. Flanked by her first lover and her current man, Fatima glowed, but Waqar could feel her warmest affection going Baneet's way, which made him ache a little.

Tamir joined them, bouncing in his saddle. <*Team work! We can beat these* matachods *with teamwork!*>

It was a good moment, but already Waqar could feel his mind tucking away images of the brief mêlée for his nightmares: screaming women and children caught in a fireball, horses panicked by the burning wagon behind them mowing down terrified civilians as they ran.` Somehow the ease of these victories was worse than the real battles. At least those felt like a contest, not murder.

The enemy prisoner was a middle-aged man, balding, jowly and be-whiskered, running to fat. He'd lost a lot of blood before Fatima got to him and was still groggy when Baneet manhandled him into Waqar's tent. They'd stripped him of his armour – decent quality, but overlarge for most Keshi – and he was wearing only a rust-stained under-tunic and leggings. Fatima had bandaged his right calf, but he couldn't put weight on it. She'd also Chained his gnosis; he was a half-blood, she estimated, same as her.

'I have rights,' he slurred, in accented Rondian. 'Respect the code.'

Waqar frowned and looked at Tamir, their best linguist. 'What did he say?'

'He thinks there's some kind of code governing this situation,' Tamir said, frowning. 'I think these people claim some "Code of Chivalry", whatever that is?'

At home, the harbadab, the Duel of Manners, would have dictated how this situation played out, but foreigners had no status within the harbadab except that allotted them by someone of sufficient rank. Where a mage fitted in was tricky: at home, theologically speaking, they were spawn of Shaitan, but in Yuros they were high nobility.

'Who are you?' Waqar asked politely.

'Respect the code!' the man barked again, but he was beginning to take in his surroundings and to notice that only Waqar in the tent was seated. 'I am of the Blessed and my house stands ransom for my return.'

It took a little back and forth until they understood that the mage-knight believed he could be exchanged for money from his family, a line with the ugly-sounding name of Vighan. 'I am Sir Torslo, kin to Earl Janses,' he said proudly.

Ransom was known in Keshi, but as magi had more value than gold, it was out of the question. A half-blood was priceless breeding-house stock.

'I pity the poor girls having to mate with you,' Fatima remarked, circling him. 'Who leads your armies?'

'Respect the code,' the man growled back, as if he were the one in power here.

Fatima drove a kinesis-enhanced fist into his gut and he folded to the floor. 'I said, who leads your armies?'

'Fati!' Baneet growled.

'I've been wanting to give a Rondian a good smack for a long time,' she said, nudging Sir Torslo with her foot. 'Come on, brave sir.'

Waqar was troubled by this, but he signed to the others not to intervene. 'Talk, Rondian,' Fatima jeered. 'Or do you only talk to Keshi girls when they're helpless, eh?'

'I – my name – I . . .' the man moaned.

Fatima raised her boot and the Rondian looked up at her, then at Waqar, eyes pleading.

'No, Fati,' Waqar told her and she pouted, but sullenly lowered her foot.

The Rondian gave him a grateful look, but Waqar ignored him. 'Baneet, your turn . . .'

Sir Torslo gaped at the giant Baneet, then babbled, '*Korion-Seth-Korion-Seth-Korion.*'

'Koreeyonsef?' Waqar asked Tamir. 'What does that mean?'

'Seth Korion,' Tamir corrected. 'He was the general at Riverdown – the one Rondian commander to get his men back across the Leviathan Bridge.'

The four friends exchanged a look. *Interesting enough*, Waqar decided. 'Ask him who burned his town?'

The threat of torture was enough to keep the knight's tongue loosened. He thought he was exchanging information for his freedom. The lowliest Keshi would have known better. An interesting picture emerged of division in the enemy command: this Seth Korion had turned renegade, retreating south in defiance of his peers. Unfortunately, the prisoner knew little of Korion's army, but he told them that Norostein was built on a plateau above the plains, watered by mountain streams behind the city – a formidable place, by his account.

When they were done, Waqar had the man taken away, to begin his journey to Kesh and the breeding-houses. There would be no ransom: the atrocities the Crusaders had perpetrated on their land were well known.

Once alone, he used a relay-stave and Sultan Rashid's secret sigil.

The sultan responded almost instantly and Waqar reported all he'd learned.

<*Well done, Nephew. I'll contact Attam and urge him to reach Venderon at all speed,*> Rashid replied. <*Unfortunately our windfleet is dispersed on re-supplying duties, so we can't send any units ahead of the march.*>

<*As long as Attam can reach Venderon before the enemy, we'll have enough men to defeat them,*> Waqar said confidently. <*The Yurosi general has fewer than eight legions.*>

<*I've not encountered this younger Korion,*> Rashid commented, <*but his deeds at Riverdown and Ardijah will make our men wary.*>

<*Should we keep his identity secret then?*>

Rashid thought for a moment, then shook his head. <*No, secrets like that are hard to keep – one glimpse of the enemy banners will betray his name. I'll have Godspeaker Ali Beyrami level atrocities against his name. Let our men hate him and that hatred will overcome any fear ascribed to his name.*>

Waqar wrinkled his nose. These were dishonourable tactics, and he disliked Beyrami intensely. Then again, it was likely this Korion deserved such treatment. <*Uncle, is there news of Jehana?*>

<*None,*> Rashid replied evenly, <*but I'm hopeful. Strong clues are being followed.*> He studied Waqar through the link, then added, <*You are fulfilling your role admirably, Nephew. I hear reports that you grow in decisiveness, ruthlessness and tactical awareness. I once observed that you lacked the killer instinct, an assessment I think you then agreed with. But you are maturing.*>

Waqar wasn't sure he liked the compliment. <*I do what's necessary, Uncle, but I try to remain honourable.*>

After their farewells, he didn't immediately signal to his friends that they could return. Instead, he sipped captured wine and thought morosely of this latest round of carnage.

Dear Ahm, if your Shihad is just, why does it leave me feeling like an evil-doer?

Latif, Ashmak and Sanjeep heard the Godsingers call for evening prayer and trudged through the muddy grass, leaving their elephant to chew mournfully on the green swathe. They joined the other elephant crews in a makeshift masjid, unrolling their prayer mats and giving thanks to Ahm for another day survived, offering prayers for their sultan and his victory before settling in to listen to the lesson given by a young wispy-bearded Scriptualist.

'Give praise to Ahm,' he read from his notes, 'for He has given his Believers the opportunity to strike down an Accursed Foe. We have learned that the Enemy before us are led by a dog named Seth Korion.'

A murmur filled the air as the Shihadi soldiers took in that information. The name Korion was known, of course: Kaltus Korion had been infamous as much for his brutality during the Second and Third Crusades as for his victories. But to Latif, the name conjured Seth, the son; a gentle, amiable young man with blond hair, a soft face and a gift for poetry, music and languages. The sound of his name came with the taste of fine wines and laughter.

'Ahm strike this animal down,' the Scriptualist shouted. 'This younger Korion is as great a monster as his father! Prisoners who fall into his hand are given the most excruciating dismemberments! He drinks blood each night, in preference to wine! One thousand rapes he has committed, of innocent Keshi women . . . girls . . . and *boys* . . . His crimes sicken even the daemons he prays to! His vile appetites are matched only by his craven cowardice, for he is too womanish to give open battle and is never seen in the fray.'

Latif had to fight not to laugh, but all round him he saw the soldiers lapping it all up and vowing revenge. *Ahm on High, I remember Ardijah and Riverdown – there was no murder of prisoners, no dismemberment or rape . . . But this is war . . .* So he kept silent as those around him blustered about how they'd wreak havoc upon the Devil Korion and bring him to his end.

'Korion sounds like an evil bastard,' Ashmak said darkly as they trooped back to Rani afterward. 'There's a thousand racheems on his head! I need that money for my son.' He'd got one of the Vereloni use-women pregnant – or at least Fara said it was his child.

'Let's just get on the road again,' Latif said dourly.

Since the burning of Jastenberg, when the Shihad had divided, Piru-Satabam III had been attached to the vanguard of the southern army, marching south. The latest name to be bandied about as a potential battleground was Venderon, a small city set in a fertile plain where they could maybe shelter for the winter. But Latif, who'd seen maps of Yuros in his former life, was doubtful.

'They burned Jastenberg, which is larger than Venderon,' he argued. 'They'll burn Venderon too. Only Norostein is large enough to contain their army, and it's defensible.'

'There's a limit to the burning a general can do before his own people turn on him,' Ashmak countered.

'Wishful thinking, my friend,' Latif said distractedly, his mind far away. *You're so clever, Rashid, with all your lies. History will remember you for ever as the man who defeated the mighty Rondian Empire. But you killed Salim with your Masked assassins and one day I'll see him avenged, even if it costs me all I have left.*

All afternoon as he rode south, he pondered how and when his chance might come.

12

From the Cliff

Souldrinkers

All peoples have their bogeymen, even the magi. Theirs are the Souldrinkers or Dokken (a name derived from the Yothic word for darkness). The Dokken can access the gnosis only by taking the lives of magi, and sustain it only by killing humans and consuming their souls. Many times the Church and Empire have moved against them, but still they lurk in the shadows.

LINDOREUS, THE HISTORY OF YUROS, 922

Vantari Hills, Verelon
Noveleve 935

Jehana lay shivering in the pre-dawn chill, missing her family. She and Waqar had been close as children, until family politics had driven them apart. *If only he'd joined the Ordo Costruo, he'd be here now.* But it was her mother she missed most of all. She'd always been there to comfort her, encourage, praise and guide her. *Alyssa Dulayne's people killed her. These Masked assassins must pay for that.*

Finally, the dawn chorus rose and light began to seep into her stone hut. She rose and went to the cliff, where she found a spot out of the wind. It was low tide – and she caught her breath as something metallic flashed in the rising sun, far to the west around the long crescent of the bay. She engaged clairvoyance and almost squealed with delight.

Some fifteen miles away at the most, a group of burly, tanned people in dun clothing were butchering fish trapped in a tidal pool. And as she moved her perspective, she caught a glimpse of straight lines and portals hewn into the cliff face above.

They're Tide People – perhaps it's even Epineo?

With a rising sense of destiny, Jehana watched them from afar as they fished, then retreated back to the cliffs as the tide turned and waves rolled inland. She let her scrying dissipate and thought about how she might approach them. Was it truly Epineo? Did they remember Amantius? Did they still revere Seidopus and his mate Calascia? How would they greet another dwymancer?

The roar and hiss of the waves were filling the air again as the sea reached the base of the cliff below and filled a small but deep lagoon at the head of a channel carved through the tidal flats.

It was time to head back and tell the others what she'd seen.

But even as she stood, two big wooden windships rose from behind the nearest inland ridge, only a few hundred yards away, their triangular sails billowing as they flowed through the air towards her.

'No,' she breathed.

'I'm afraid *yes*,' tinkled a voice and Jehana spun around to see Alyssa Dulayne emerging from behind a rocky outcropping, a vision of blonde perfection with her dancing ringlets and her gorgeous, cruel face aglow with triumph. 'Well, haven't you led us on a dance,' she crowed. 'But I fear it's time to stop the music.'

'*HELP!*' Jehana shrieked, aloud and into the aether, but her cry was cut off as light exploded behind her eyes, more powerful than anything in her limited experience, and she felt herself tumble.

A net of kinesis closed about her and scooped her up as the world ebbed away.

Tarita woke as a beam of sunlight pierced the overgrown window of her hut. There were mice scuttling around the remains of her meal, but she didn't mind. They hadn't woken her, but a perimeter ward had.

That wasn't a signal to panic – a rabbit might have innocently set off the hidden enchantment, which sent a warning pulse if something moved in their vicinity. But Tarita cast her senses wide as she drew her scimitar and dagger, then crept barefoot to the doorway.

<*Ogre,*> she sent quietly. His hut was across the small stream and she could hear him snoring, a sound like a drawbridge being lowered. She prodded his mind awake. <*Be aware – one of my wards was triggered.*> She sensed him mumbling his way back to awareness.

Then shadows began to move and she went still . . .

Ogre rolled over in his hut – it was the biggest, but he still filled it uncomfortably – and gripped the staff he was using as a weapon. With Tarita's voice echoing in his head, he saw her appear at her own doorway, across the stream, lissom in her worn shift, weapons in hand.

She cocked her head and gestured inland. He followed her gaze, but all he could see were a few ruined huts and the undulating tangle of trees and vines. Nevertheless he kindled shields and emerged, wishing he had something more damaging than the staff to hand.

Then a wave of robed figures came streaming in from all sides, crying to Ahm and kindling gnosis fire on their blades. *Hadishah!* And worse still, two windships appeared three hundred yards away, heading towards them.

Simultaneously, Jehana shouted, 'HELP–' but her cry cut off suddenly.

'*TARITA!*' Ogre roared, as he caught a mage-bolt in his shields, then another. He fired back, crashing a Hadishah over backwards, and smashed his staff one-handed into another man's chest.

'Ogre, get to Jehana,' Tarita shouted, as a dozen bursts of light came streaming in on her, but she was already moving, her shields crackling and her outline blurring behind illusory veils which frayed their aim. Her Ascendant strength did the rest, taking her through the storm unscathed, and she emerged ten yards to the right, dagger and scimitar extended and mage-bolts pouring from them, cutting down attackers as she came on. But her shields were scarlet and frayed: even an Ascendant could repel such assaults for only so long.

The Hadishah closed in, dozens of them, bursting from the undergrowth. Ogre bludgeoned another, his empowered staff crushing the Keshi's shields and then his ribs. Another man darted in and lunged, his blade slashing open Ogre's arm painfully.

'Ogre, find Jehana,' Tarita called again, using a pulse of kinesis to flatten two of her attackers. She rose into the air, her shields flashing incandescent red as they reached stretching point, and darted inland, back towards the oncoming windships, hoping to draw the bulk of the attackers away.

Ogre roared and struck at the man who'd wounded him, smashing his blade aside. His left fist hammered through shields and into the attacker's face, breaking his neck, but another mage-bolt pierced his shields, searing his left calf and sending a pulse of hot pain to his skull. Seeing red, he lashed out with the staff, which broke in two as it caved in another man's skull. He thrust the jagged stump through the next man's chest.

Suddenly there was a gap and he battered through it, hurling two man aside, barely noticing a slash to his lower back. He burst into open space and *ran*.

He wasn't built for grace, but with strength and length of stride he bullocked through the undergrowth, shielding behind him, ignoring the scatter of mage-bolts ripping past or dissipating on his protections as he zigzagged through the trees towards the coastal cliffs. He heard pursuit, but in moments he was bursting from the pines and almost overbalancing on the edge of the world. The incoming tide was roaring below.

'Jehana!' he roared, spotting her sprawled on a ledge fifty yards along the cliff-tops. A tall blonde woman was bending over her.

But the Hadishah had caught up with him and were wielding bared scimitars limned in gnostic energy.

He turned at bay, snarling in defiance as they closed in.

Tarita darted into the trees to avoid all the fire roiling over her; luckily, the foliage was too wet to ignite. She put her back to a tree and with her blades now incandescent violet with necromantic-gnosis, carved through the next pair of Hadishah to reach her, leaving only withered corpses, their life energy sucked into her blade to fuel the next blow. The next men wavered and she darted sideways into the maze of paths around the huts, seeking some way to draw the attackers away and then lose them.

Where's Jehana?

Ogre had headed for the cliff-top, but men had gone after him and there'd been nothing from Jehana since that one, choked cry. The realisation that she could already have failed made her feel sick, but she was alive and in motion. She shot into the air, but half a dozen mage-bolts pummelled her shields, throwing her down onto an ivy-covered roof. She hit hard, gashing her knees open. Yowling in pain, she dropped over the side, landing behind a man with a crossbow. She slashed open his throat as he spun, jerked the weapon from his grasp and kindling gnosis-fire on the iron head, she shot the man beyond him. He doubled over screaming as his innards fried.

The respite was momentary: more Hadishah poured around the hut from both sides; one daring fellow leaped to the roof, aiming another crossbow. Tarita blurred her image and sent an illusory form left while going right, but the crossbowman either wasn't fooled or got lucky, because his weapon followed her and the bolt grazed her shoulder before exploding in the ground. Rolling under a swinging blade, she came up and cut the attacker down as a fireball sizzled past and ignited a pine tree.

She rekindled wards before throwing herself right into the flames and wreathing smoke; when she came out the other side, her shift was on fire and her sight momentarily frazzled, clearing just as a shadow passed overhead. The deck of the windship barely a dozen feet above was crammed with archers.

Is the whole damned Shihad here?

She spun and with an almighty pull on her powers, using sylvan-gnosis and kinesis, she wrenched the burning pine out of the ground and sent it rocketing into the hull of the windship. Without even pausing for breath, she hurled herself away, just as the keel caught fire and the ship ploughed into the hut behind her, crushing the stone building and erupting in flames, the raw energy stored in the keel running wild.

A massive force-wave hurled her through air shredded by flying splinters. She crashed to the ground and rolled, then staggered upright, realised the windship was falling towards her and threw herself aside – straight into a swinging club that bludgeoned through her shields and struck her temple.

Black stars burst inside her skull and she spun away into nothingness.

The Hadishah closed in, brandishing blades glowing with mage-fire. Ogre saw no way through them and no hope beyond. The two windships were hovering above the ruined village, pouring arrows and fire down at where he guessed Tarita must be. Jehana was taken and he was trapped.

Most of the coppery faces before him were young, recent products of the breeding-houses, no doubt, but one was grey-bearded. It was he who stepped forward. 'Lay down your weapons and you'll not be harmed,' he said in Keshi.

'Why should I believe that?' Ogre rumbled in the same tongue.

'Because someone wants you alive,' the Hadishah replied, although he was clearly puzzled that anyone would want to spare such a degenerate brute. 'Some old master, I believe.'

No, not the Master . . . Ogre's mind conjured the ancient, evil visage of Ervyn Naxius and his whole being rebelled. 'Never!' he bellowed and before the Hadishah could move, he had hurled himself from the cliff and was plummeting towards the ground.

Something nudged Jehana's mind and she woke to find her wrists bound behind her back and her ankles roped tightly together. An oil-lamp lit the room. Judging by the cramped size and curved walls, she guessed she was in the cabin of a windship. The vibrating timbers suggested the ship was in the air.

She was lying on a narrow cot, her gnosis was Chained and Alyssa Dulayne was standing over her, her blonde ringlets cascading artfully over one shoulder. She could make out another shape on the cot opposite her, covered by blankets.

'Ah, the princess awakes,' Alyssa said merrily, speaking Keshi like a native. 'What a sweet reunion. I've always thought of you as family.'

Jehana struggled to right herself, cracked her head on the shelf above her head and sagged back onto the thin mattress. 'I'm *not* your family,' she snarled. 'Let me go.'

'Why on Urte would I do that?' Alyssa snickered. 'I've only just found you.'

'I'm Sultan Rashid's niece – let me go!'

'No, I'm afraid not, dear girl.' Alyssa swirled the wine in the goblet in her hand, then drank. 'But fortunately for you, my intentions are entirely benign. You see, I actually *want* you to succeed.'

Jehana looked at her in disbelief. 'You *what*?'

'My dear nearly-niece, I promise you: I want you to gain this dwyma. It sounds intriguing: vast powers over nature? I'm very excited.'

She wants me to gain the dwyma . . . and then *she'll take me to Rashid . . .*

'I thought you people wanted me dead?'

'We people?'

'The Masks,' Jehana said darkly. 'You murdered my mother.'

'Oh no, dear. Whatever you've been told, your mother *helped* us. Sakita destroyed Midpoint Tower voluntarily. I'm still distraught that striking such a mighty blow for the Shihad cost her life.'

'Tarita said Sakita was like a draug when she did it,' Jehana shot back.

'Tarita? You'd believe a dirt-caste Jhafi spy?' Alyssa waved her hand at the blankets on the opposite bunk and they slid off, revealing Tarita, unconscious, bloody and filthy, her ripped, burned clothes barely covering her.

'The little bitch brought down one of my ships,' Alyssa said malevolently. 'I'd as soon have gutted her, but a living Merozain for the breeding-houses would be *priceless*. This little slut's going to breed a whole army for us.' Then her face twisted and she added, 'But first I'm going to make her suffer for all the inconvenience she's caused me.'

Jehana stared at Tarita in mute horror, any hope of rescue completely obliterated. She shuddered, envisaging the living nightmare the girl's life would become. 'Please, don't hurt her. She's fighting for her people, as we all are.'

Alyssa's hooded eyes bored into her. 'What, sympathy for the gutter-bred trollop? Why should you care? At the very least, as soon as I can find a decent mage-healer I'll amputate her hands and feet so she'll never make a nuisance of herself again.'

She said it with such casual cruelty that Jehana almost vomited.

'You're a monster, a true jadugara,' Jehana whispered. 'You murdered all those Ordo Costruo who *raised* you.'

'Those hypocrites?' she scoffed. 'Bleating of peace while turning the Bridge over to the empire to permit three Crusades? Dear Ahm, killing Ordo Costruo is practically a religious duty.' She reached out and stroked Jehana's face in an almost lascivious way. 'Lovely Jehana, I *so* hope we can be friends again.'

You were never my friend, Jehana thought, pulling her head away. 'Don't touch me! I'll do as you ask, but if you hurt me – or Tarita – I'll tell my uncle that I want your heart ripped out. That's assuming you have one.'

Alyssa tittered mockingly. 'That's the spirit, darling. She tilted her lovely, evil face and said, 'Oh, by the way, the construct-creature's dead. He threw himself onto the rocks. The Master will be disappointed, but no one else cares. So you know: it was he who led us to you – the Master could always find his creatures. Another thing, this vessel is full of magi, so any attempt to escape would be futile, and as we're still on the ground, you can't even hurl yourself to your doom in some dramatic gesture. But really, my dear, I'm taking you where you want to go: Epineo, yes?'

Jehana's jaw dropped. 'How do you know?'

'Because I'm *awfully* clever,' Alyssa smirked. She gestured at a desk, where the silver-bladed scimitar Tarita had used lay beside a book wrapped in waxed paper. 'And these must be returned to the Master. You see, dearest, everything works out for the best in the end.' She laughed. 'Well, for me, anyway.'

13

Across the River

The Murder of Corineus

What are we to make of the testimony of Corinea in Hebusalim in 930 and her claims that Corineus was not the Son of Kore, you ask? My reply: nothing at all! Look at who sponsored her testimony: failed magi, Ordo Costruo heretics and atheists. I don't believe the woman who spoke was Corinea at all, or that a single word of what she said was true. Corineus is our Saviour, and we may only be restored to Paradise through Him!

GRAND PRELATE DOMINIUS WURTHER, THE CELESTIUM, PALLAS 931

Beckford, near Dupenium, Rondelmar
Decore 935

Despite all his misgivings, Cordan felt a dizzying rush of excitement as Duke Garod led him onto the platform overlooking the river and he saw all the barges choking the waterway, most already loaded with men in Sacrecour gold and purple.

'Behold, Nephew,' Garod said grandly, while his court cheered. 'The muster is almost complete. House Sacrecour are marching to restore you to your rightful place. Well, floating, at least,' he chuckled.

'How many legions?' Cordan asked, raising his voice against the martial music. As well as men everywhere, windships were constantly coming and going; it looked like the whole town of Beckford had lined the banks of the river to watch.

'I'm sending four,' Garod said, with relish. 'And Brylion is bringing seven north. I have it on good authority the Corani have only six, split across Coraine and Pallas.' He rubbed his hands together briskly. 'We'll crush them.'

And then I'll be crowned emperor, Cordan thought, and his blood couldn't help but quicken. *I like Lyra, but perhaps this is how life is: the strong take what the weak can't hold.*

Beckford, which lay south of Dupenium on the banks of the Bruin River, was the nearest port to the ducal capital and almost as large, but it hadn't been possible to fortify the place: the perpetually sodden ground flooded in an eye-blink and no walls encircling the town stood for long before subsidence brought them down. But every war the Dupeni had ever waged had been launched from here.

'But they have Solon Takwyth,' Cordan pointed out, remembering the Corani knight's kindness to him.

'One man,' Garod drawled. 'Don't fear, Nephew. House Corani's power was broken by the Shihad. Lyra's interregnum will soon be over and you'll be able to enjoy your birthright.'

'Will she fight, Uncle?'

Garod smiled coldly. 'I hope so. I really do.'

Lyra sat in her armchair, her mind in the hands of Aradea, who was currently inhabiting an owl on the railing of her balcony. Basia was tending the fire and ensuring she was protected, but Lyra was barely aware of her; instead, the whole of western Yuros filled her mind.

She sensed a shimmer a thousand miles away as Valdyr entered the web of energy: the Tree of Light, the Elétfa, as he called it. She smiled in anticipation. The Mollachian was a reserved, aloof person, but they'd conversed in this way several times over the past weeks and a kind of warmth was growing between them.

<*Valdyr*,> she called, <*it's me, Nara.*>

Lyra was coming to enjoy the role of Nara. She was winsome, supportive and gentle, a wise woman of the natural world, courageous in defending her mystic realm. She'd never been a convent girl and she believed in love and its healing powers. Lyra kept her real identity secret: it was clear the empire wasn't a welcome presence in Valdyr's life and he was coming to trust Nara, so . . .

<Nara?> he responded, and suddenly they were able to see each other inside their heads. With a little tug of the web of light she was with him in some nebulous *in-between* place. She wore the same clothes, although they were gauzy to the touch. He was tall and strongly built, as big as Solon Takwyth, although his moustache was a little outlandish, clad in rough hunting leathers. She could feel the ghostly presence of his wolf nearby.

She formally kissed his cheeks, although there was little physical sensation, more like a brushing of awareness that brought rushes of imagery, then stepped away. <It's good to see you.>

<And you,> he replied, always just that little bit wary. <What do you wish tonight?>

She smiled. <Let's just explore, shall we?>

For the next hour or two, she and Valdyr travelled hand in hand without leaving their respective homes, his a tent beside a lake and hers a palace. They ranged from fox lairs deep in the countryside to the giant, ice-encrusted cliffs of the Hollenian coast and on to mighty Lac Siberne in Argundy, which was so large it had dangerous tides. They found a storm in the hinterlands and sent it out over the Brevian Sea, just for practise. Valdyr was hindered by having lost the genilocus of his mentor, Luhti, and not yet having created a new one, so she was the one bearing the load, but he was her guide, having the greater knowledge and experience.

Finally, sitting talking beside Lac Siberne, an idea started forming, born of her mounting fears for the future. *Brylion Fasterius' army is nearing Pallas-Sud*, she thought anxiously. *Valdyr probably doesn't care, but this is part of the whole Masked Cabal's plans, and the Reekers are plaguing his homeland too . . .*

<What is it?> he asked, sensing her discomfort.

She framed the request carefully. <Valdyr, if I had great need of your help, to protect people from the daemon-possessed, would you help?>

<Of course,> he replied promptly.

No Pallacian would give their trust so blithely. She'd been surprised to learn that they were of an age: at times he had the grimness of an older man, one who'd seen too much, although occasionally he could be almost boyish.

<I'm frightened they'll strike again,> she said. <We think they're planning an attack and I've been wondering about making the winter come early, to prevent soldiers from marching.>

<Do some of the northern lords use these possessed men as soldiers?> he asked. <That's happening here too: they're resistant to cold, and hard to kill.> Then his eyes brightened. <Oh, there's something else. One of our men has an argenstael sword – that's a silver and steel alloy. We think the silver might have some kind of poisoning effect on the possessed men. We've not been able to properly research it yet, but we're hopeful.>

Lyra stared at him. <Silver?> she blurted, barely believing her ears. <Silver?>

Feeling her excitement, he launched into a description of what his people had learned and how.

Dear Kore, they have a weakness!

The moment she'd bade Valdyr farewell and disconnected from the dwyma, she summoned her spymaster.

Their plan frightened Lyra: the risks were enormous. But as she worked with Dirklan and Solon, she gradually began to believe it might just work. Seeing the two men working together gave her some insight into how, despite their differences in temperament and even mild dislike for each other, they'd been able to preserve House Corani after 909.

They also involved Torun Jandreux, the current Duke of Coraine, Radine's forty-year-old son, via relay-staves. He was an unimpressive, balding man who embodied the least qualities of his forebears, but he dutifully did as he was told, which was all that could be asked.

Thank goodness he's married! At least I won't have to find excuses not to marry him when my mourning is over, Lyra thought. But Torun had consented to secretly move all four of his remaining legions to Pallas, leaving Coraine only lightly garrisoned.

'Useless prick,' Solon muttered, wincing as he massaged his shoulder. He'd recently had to have the wound opened up again so a metal sheath could be fused to the weakened bone.

'Duke Torun does his best,' Dirklan said peaceably. 'That'll give us roughly the manpower we need – and we've got more news on Brylion Fasterius' army. They're on the Pallas-Canossi Road.'

'Aye,' Solon confirmed, 'most of them are still some twenty miles south of Pallas-Sud, in the Earldom of Paldermark. it's an easy march – two to three days – but he's still encamped.'

'Unsurprisingly, Brylion Fasterius is reluctant to get too near Pallas-Sud, because he knows about the Reekers,' Dirklan explained. 'But Ostevan's been smart: he's left the ordinary burghers of Southside and Fenreach alone. A lot of them have fled the city, despite the season and nowhere to go, but there are still more than a hundred thousand of the city's poorest in there. Human shields, one might call them.'

'We still don't yet know when Brylion will march,' Solon growled, 'or when Garod will strike in support – he'll send his men down the Bruin from Beckford on war-barges, so we must be ready to act at short notice.'

The kiss they'd shared still hung in the air between them, but Lyra hadn't spoken with him of it again, nor spent time with him alone. She didn't feel ready. She hoped he understood that nothing might ever come of it. And in any case, the impending attack had killed all thought of passion. She was consumed by the knowledge that no matter what she did, there would be suffering and death.

Don't do this, Garod. No matter how it turns out, so many will die if you do.

Solon Takwyth sipped his beer slowly, his mood bleak despite the slow haze of early intoxication that was settling on his shoulders like a warm mantle. The day's meetings were over and he'd decided enough time had gone by that he could risk alcohol again. With the weather miserable outside, this lunch had turned into a long, relaxed swilling session.

Oryn Levis was listening amiably while Roland de Farenbrette recounted a yarn from the dark years, the post-909 ordeal when the Corani had fought for their lives against countless raids into their lands from Dupeni-held Bruinland. They spoke of those times fondly now, but they'd buried a lot of good men. Nestor Sulpeter, Lord Sulpeter's third and now eldest son, listened with worshipful eyes.

The barracks hall of the Bastion had been the home of the Corani

DAVID HAIR

mage-knights for the past five years. Their banners hung on the walls now, northern beers were shipped down from Coraine to wet their tongues and Corani songs rang from the rafters. But Sacrecour relief-statues were carved into the stone walls and painted on the roof ceiling, a reminder that this sojourn could end as suddenly and bloodily as the last.

'You remember the Coraine road in 909, Solon?' Roland said suddenly. These days they were friends, but this rough-faced, belligerent man was a hard drinker with an iron fist he liked to throw around. Solon had had to beat him down many a time in the early years. Roland's nose was still crooked from one of those encounters, but he now regarded that as a badge of honour. 'You cut down three Sacrecour champions in as many blows. Some said those pricks were the finest knights alive.'

'They were posers,' Solon growled, as Nestor lapped his words up with the beer.

Solon flexed his shoulders, trying not to wince. The mage-healers had opened him up yet again when the flesh and bone around the metal rod they'd inserted had become infected. Now the whole wound was swollen and leaking pus, horribly painful to move. 'Rukk me, this damned shoulder's murder.'

'Will you be ready for the big day?' Nestor asked eagerly.

Only Solon, Dirklan and Lyra knew the full details, but the mage-knights were all aware that *something* was in the offing. Four legions were due in from Coraine any day now, and anyone with an ear to the ground could read the clues: rosters, supply build-ups, variations to routine. Some had worked out everything pointed towards a certain date in two weeks' time, the one he and Dirklan had settled on.

Unless the enemy acts first.

'I'll be ready,' Solon growled, though in truth he felt weak and fragile. Exercising for any real length of time was a struggle, and sparring was absolutely out of the question.

Truth is, these lads just need direction, and someone level-headed to guide them.

But his current state was still aggravating. Every moment of weakness was like the shadow of old age sinking claws into him. He felt like the wound symbolised his life ahead: side-lined and ineffectual.

'The Grand Prelate's bodyguard sparred with some of the lads today,' Roland noted darkly. 'Exilium Excrement, or whatever his name is. Heh . . . mind you, he kicked the shit out of our boys.'

'He moves like you did, when you were young,' Oryn Levis said to Solon.

'I was never that girl-pretty, Lumpy,' Solon sniffed. 'A few of the lads should rearrange his face.'

They laughed about other pretty-boy upstarts who'd been taken down in training-yard brawls over the years. The yards were the furnace that tempered a legion, the place where the hierarchy was established and maintained. Men were broken down and built up there. It was the only place Solon had ever felt truly comfortable.

He'd just raised his hand to order another round when one of the runners came in and spoke to the guards. Recognising the young man, he beckoned him over. 'Milord, sorry to interrupt,' he said, giving Solon a scrawled note.

Solon unfolded it. It was from Setallius, a terse fragment that made his heart thud.

Brylion is marching.

Shit, Solon thought, pushing his tankard away and rising. *It's happening now.* As the pain of moving hit him, he thought he'd never been so unprepared for action in his life.

'Oryn,' he commanded through gritted teeth, 'turn out the barracks. Brylion's coming.' His shoulder screamed but calling on all his resilience, he ignored it. Striding across the room, he shouted, 'Up, lads! Steel shirts and blades! The Sacrecours are on the move!'

Lyra had insisted that she be present, presiding from her throne as the mage-nobles and the legion commanders were briefed.

'The Sacrecour Army, the cowards who evaded fighting the Shihad, are marching on Pallas-Sud,' Solon told the assembled Corani commanders. 'They've got windships and they've got control of the bridges upriver. Garod Sacrecour launched flotillas of barges from Dupenium and Fauvion two nights ago: they've been spotted a hundred miles upriver. We're about to face overwhelming numbers. We have to act – we need to deal with our enemies piecemeal before they unite.'

'When will we march?' someone asked. 'And where to?'

'Within hours,' Solon replied. 'That's all you need to know. Tell your men to get kitted up, establish staging grounds inside the city, but keep them indoors so that anyone flying above has nothing to see.'

Lyra could see the commanders were perplexed. Wars were summer and autumn affairs, and men prepared for imminent combat outdoors, in the morning, not indoors at night.

'Gentlemen,' she said, above the rising babble, 'I know we ask a lot, but now is a time to trust your commanders. Remember Knight-Commander Solon Takwyth's record is exemplary: he has never been defeated. Believe in that, as I do.'

Except he's not even capable of fighting right now . . .

She rose. 'My prayers will be with you,' she said. 'Be ready at a moment's notice.'

She swept out, indicating Dirklan should follow. They paused outside the door and she asked, 'Solon looks like death warmed up. He mustn't take an active role.'

'He knows,' Dirklan replied. 'We've briefed Oryn. He'll take the active command.'

'I mean it,' Lyra said. 'Tell Solon that once we move, he's to share the vigil with me in the chapel. Tell him it's a *direct order*, and it's his *duty* to attend upon me. Those are terms he should understand.'

Dirklan smiled wryly. 'They are indeed his favoured words.'

'And you, Dirklan?' she asked. 'Are your people ready?'

'They are. Most are already in position and I'll be joining them soon.' He still hadn't actually revealed whatever vital task his Volsai would be fulfilling.

'We weren't planning to move for another two weeks,' she said nervously. 'Are you sure you're ready?'

'It's all in hand,' he told her. 'We'll be moving the instant you advise.'

She put her hand to her chest. *The instant I advise. It all depends on me.* 'Then I must go,' she said fearfully. 'Dear Kore, this is too soon – I don't even know if Valdyr will be able to help me tonight! It's an hour later where he is – he may even be asleep. I don't think I can–'

Dirklan took her hand. 'Lyra, deep breaths. Valdyr promised he'd talk to you tonight, remember. He'll be ready, and so will you.'

'I hope you're right.' She left him and hurried to her garden, Basia behind her. She trusted Solon and Dirklan to do what had to be done, to move their pieces into play. The plan was laid, only the date had changed. But if this failed, her enemies would be here before she could try again.

And the real heart of their plan rested with her, and her alone.

'Is this safe?' Basia demanded tersely as they reached the pond at the heart of the garden.

'I honestly don't know . . . If I lose control of it . . .' Lyra set her jaw. 'I won't.'

They shared a taut look, then Basia stepped away and conjured gnostic veils, closing them off from the outside world and ensuring no one could watch.

Lyra took a deep breath before falling to her knees. She scooped up the cold water and drank. 'Aradea, my Lady, I'm here.'

The garden fell still, the wind dropped and the birds went silent. An owl in the beech tree opened huge eyes to look at her, a cautious weasel peered out from behind a clump of dead lavender, then Pearl emerged from the trees, stared at her for a moment, then turned and vanished again. Her senses went deeper, to the toad sleeping beneath a rock beside the pool, the beetles and worms within the earth, until she could feel the slow drawing of moisture into the veins of the trees. Through it all energy flowed, circles within circles within circles of life, ever-changing, ever-cruel, ever-vibrant: animals feeding on each other, creatures mating and breeding and dying and decomposing to feed the soil, light striking leaves and feeding the plant that fed the insect that fed the eel. Water and energy, earth and air, and all hers.

'Lady Aradea, I need your strength.'

The leaves moved and the Leaf-man mask in the old fountain subtly altered. The moss in the eye sockets gleamed and she knew the genilocus, the place of power, was listening, that Aradea was *here*.

The dwyma opened to her, her veins became those of a leaf in the Tree of Light. She sent her awareness into that flow.

<*Valdyr? Valdyr? Please, this is Nara. Can you hear me?*>

Pallas-Canossi Road, Central Rondelmar

Sir Brylion Fasterius and his men had been marching all day, the drums hammering out time and a half, and they'd covered almost twenty miles despite the snow and mud. The hills to the north were thick with pine trees: Paldermark Forest, only four miles away and good shelter if a storm did strike.

Brylion slapped his stallion's rump and jolted up the slope to check out the terrain ahead. Behind him, the columns were stamping down a farmer's fields, erecting tents and preparing fires ready to light when the sun was down: skiffs didn't fly after dark, so it would be safe then.

Atop the rise, he reined in and surveyed the neatly tended farmland, with tamed hedgerows and streams channelled to irrigate the fields. He told his aide and permanent shadow, his nephew Macron, 'We'll camp in the lee of this hill tonight.'

'Yes, Uncle,' Macron replied promptly.

When he'd been first assigned, the lad had been a cheeky little snit. *Arcanums don't teach the little beggars the one thing they need to learn: obedience*, Brylion had thought, but a few beatings had quickly sorted that out.

His orders now were explicit: advance as swiftly as possible, get his men to Pallas-Sud by midday, ready to be hurled across the Bruin River. Cousin Garod was floating his own men down the river. Together, they'd trap the Corani inside the Bastion, and the end result would be inevitable: *Little Lyra's vapid head on a spike in Traitors' Cloister.*

Brylion stroked his thick dark beard, studying the road ahead, before shifting his gaze to the evening skies above. To the east was darkness, to the west a sullen glimmer – no red skies tonight. And to the north, the clouds were churning in a way he didn't like.

'There's a storm brewing,' he rumbled. He liked deploying his deep voice just so, to make a man's spine go watery. It certainly worked on his arse-wipe of a nephew, who squeaked inarticulately in agreement.

Is that storm natural? he wondered suddenly, but he couldn't feel anything wrong with the air, the way one could if Air-magi were rukking with the weather. But visually, it was all wrong, coiling in towers as if some giant unseen finger was stirring up the clouds. And the darkness spoke of snow. Any man of the north knew that when the sky turned black like that, you got yourself indoors, found a bottle and a fat-arsed tart and hunkered down to wait it out.

But I've got fifteen thousand men out here . . .

'Rukk this, we're not camping after all,' he growled at Macron. 'Send for runners – tell the drummers to beat double-time – we've got to reach Paldermark Forest before that storm hits us. *Move, I say!* That storm looks like a rukking killer!'

He spurred his stallion hard and they bounded down the slope, shouting at the rankers, 'Move, you laggards! Move, if you don't want to freeze to death!'

The men stared, then following his pointing arm, saw death in those roiling clouds tumbling in from the north. That woke them up, even as the drums quickened. He rousted his aides and sent them out to recommence the march.

'Move you, yapping dogs! Get 'em moving or die!'

Pallas, Rondelmar

To anyone watching, Lyra was simply kneeling beside a pool in her private garden as night fell, while thunder rumbled menacingly to the north. But in her mind's eye, she was standing on a mountain with one hand stretched to the heavens, her other gripped by the man beside her. Around them, the wind shrieked like the death-wails of a Brevian washer-wraith, a Caller of the Dead. Rain tore at them and hail scoured the rocky peak.

'More!' she shouted to Valdyr. 'We need more!'

Valdyr responded, guiding her hands to the clouds behind them and she strained, pulling them across the skies and hurling them towards a dark patch of land below. He was the mind and she the muscle in this strange place: their joined hands crackled with lightning and raw energies. She could feel his breath in her lungs, her heart beating his blood. It was exhilarating and terrifying.

She sensed bewildered weather-magi trying to prise away her grip on the skies, but they didn't know who they were up against, or how to fight her. Their ineffectual efforts fell away and she forgot them.

Inside her mind a panorama spread: she could see northeast all the way up the Bruin River to Dupenium, twinkling like a star – and the Sacrecour barges heaving on ice-crusted waves as they frantically sought the banks. The river was turning hard as crystal; she could feel the deaths of each fish as their bodies froze. To the east, Fauvion shuddered as a blizzard Valdyr had found over central Andressea rolled westwards and gales whipped across the land with vicious force.

Part of her was utterly dismayed, but this feeling of potency was terrifyingly glorious.

Pallas spread out around her feet. She could sense humankind everywhere, cowering under shelter, but for many, it wasn't going be enough. The poorest, those in Southside and Fenreach and outside the walls of Pallas-Nord, were screaming as roofs were ripped away, but still she didn't relent, for her son's life was one of the stakes. Instead, she roved south, following the dark line of the Canossi Road, until she found wave upon wave of running men, three legions of Sacrecour soldiers, staggering towards the only shelter in miles: a forested hill just a short distance ahead of them.

She gripped Valdyr's hand even harder and hurled the storm into their faces, but it wasn't enough. *'More! More!'*

If they reach the trees, they'll survive, and then Pallas will fall and all this is for nothing.

'MORE!'

Somewhere a wolf snarled and Aradea vented an owl's cry. Lyra's desperation rose, because this *wasn't enough* and it *had to be*: for Rildan, for all of the Corani.

'Together!' Valdyr shouted, pulling her to him, his dark hair streaming

and his face wrathful as an old god's. She laid her head against his chest, felt his heart thudding, and let him guide her hand to the north, where another storm was brewing, racing in to fill the void they'd created with their manipulations. *'There, yes, there—'*

It was a brutal thing, a hurricane exhaled from Death's own lips, and they needed it *here*.

She tore at it, screaming at the effort, wrenching and ripping – until it came free.

14

The Storm

The Sunsurge

The time of the Sunsurge falls between Moontides, and is the opposite. During the Moontide the ocean is at its lowest, rising to its height during the Sunsurge, making the coasts hazardous, and bringing wetter and colder weather to Yuros and northern Antiopia. In the latter, this is welcome, but in Yuros there are often devastating storms and the harvests are detrimentally affected.

ORDO COSTRUO COLLEGIATE, PONTUS

Pallas-Canossi Road, Rondelmar
Decore 935

At some point the forced march became a headlong, howling panic. Brylion Sacrecour rode among his men, flogging them along because the pricks were all going to freeze if they didn't shift their arses. They were already giving their all, but each moment he became more certain that it wasn't going to be enough.

'Move, damn you bastards, *move it!*'

Macron was with him, wrapped in his cloak, gnostic heat burning out like an oil-lamp. Brylion was doing the same, fighting the cold as the world froze around him. His magi should get through this, but the rankers would be rukked if they couldn't reach shelter and snow was already hammering them backwards. Debris ripped past them, lost gear and torn branches whirling though the storm like twigs. The sky was roaring: he felt as if he was trapped in the throat of a giant beast whose exhalations froze his very skin.

Suddenly he realised that he and Macron were the only ones still moving forward; everyone else was just standing, leaning into the wind or falling to the ground in the least patch of shelter, or being tossed backwards like thrown toys, victim of a child-god's tantrum.

He grabbed Macron's arm and blared: <Fuck it, we've got to get out of this.>

Macron nodded numbly, his face blue despite the energy he was burning. Brylion grabbed the lad's reins from his numbed fingers, slammed his spurs into his stallion's flanks and drove the beast into the daggers of sleet ripping at them in malice.

They passed a clump of men huddled together like baby mice. He'd likely be chipping them off the plains tomorrow. Other bodies were strewn about, already coated in snow, and then the wreckage of a wind-skiff hurtled by, sails torn and hull shattered, the pilot a broken thing lashed to the tiller.

Rukking fool, thinking he could out-fly this! He'd grabbed Macron because the little snit was family, after all, and his brother's heir. *Come on, lad, stay with me!*

Macron nodded gamely, but he was scared witless. Brylion lost feeling in his fingers and toes and his stallion's heartbeat laboured, but Macron's gelding was faring even worse, staggering on wobbling legs, so he pulled alongside and hauled the freezing boy across to his own saddle. A moment later a howling gust tore the gelding away.

<Hold on, lad,> Brylion sent grimly, spurring the stallion on. They crossed a field strewn with discarded equipment and dead men lying in clumped snow and ice, while wolf-calls yowled in the sky above. There were human voices up there too, male and female throats shouting words he couldn't quite catch.

Someone's doing this to us, he realised, and his fear deepened.

By now it was almost dark, but the near-constant lightning lit the landscape in staccato, jagged bursts. He saw a pine tree ahead, and beyond it, a wall of them, coated in ice. Legionaries were clumped together like snowdrifts, climbing over each other in their desperation for shelter and heat. A few men had somehow managed to light fires.

Hel will be like this.

He spurred towards the nearest copse . . . just as the pines exploded.

He'd heard of such a thing, where the sap freezes and the wood expands in a sudden, shattering burst, splintering the trunk and bringing the tree down, although he'd never seen it actually happen – but suddenly the nearest pine *cracked* and jagged splinters were flying at him. There was no time to shield, only to cower. Macron jerked in his arms as his mount staggered and collapsed.

Years of jousting, of knowing how to roll clear when your horse goes down, saved Brylion: using kinesis, he kicked free of the stirrups and with Macron still locked in his arms, landed clear of the horse, the breath knocked out of him by ground hard as stone.

Then in the flare of lightning he saw the thick foot-long splinter embedded in Macron's throat. If his nephew hadn't been sitting in front of him, it would have been in his own throat. The boy died two gurgled breaths later.

Brylion snarled, fighting the urge to stagger to his feet, draw his sword and *hack some rukker to pieces*, but the instinct for preservation won out and instead, he crawled to the fallen stallion, slashed the beast's belly open and as soon as the hot rush of intestines and blood trailed off, he burrowed in.

He didn't often pray, but that night he had no trouble.

Dear Kore, give me the chance to kill the murdering cowards who did this to my boys . . .

Pallas, Rondelmar

Sometime around midnight, Lyra realised that they'd done enough. More than that, they'd reached their limits. She and Valdyr were exhausted, and so too was the weather. The clouds, used up, were lifting. The wind was still howling, but it was a low moan, not a vengeful shriek.

She laid her face on Valdyr's chest, inhaled his wood-smoke smell and wondered who he really was.

A rebel in one of my kingdoms. An enemy, if he knew who I really was.

With a painful effort, because she felt like a part of him, she disengaged and let her hands drop, relinquishing the storms and the power. Gasping for breath, he did the same. Facing her, his eyes big, he smoothed his ridiculous drooping moustache, utterly unfashionable in Pallas for centuries, and looked at her enquiringly.

'Have we done enough?'

He did as I asked with barely a question . . .

'I think so,' she said. 'Valdyr, thank you for taking me on trust. We've taken lives, but we've saved many more.'

He flinched at the reminder. 'Who died? Who were you fighting?'

She looked away, wondering what to say – what could she say, without revealing who she was? Would knowing help him, or put him in danger? And the reality was, she wasn't sure she knew what they'd achieved anyway. Her vantage had been too high, too removed for her to know if they'd done more than give a few men frostbite.

Or whether we've wiped out half the north . . .

'I probably won't know until the morning despatches . . .'

'*Despatches?* Who are you really, Nara?'

She bit her lip, which was as painful in this imagined place inside both of their heads as in the flesh. 'Valdyr, I was protecting good people from bad people, using the only weapon I have. I have a son, newly born. I would do *anything* to protect him.'

They stared at each other silently and she could feel his inner struggle: trust wasn't easy for him and she'd used all his knowledge to do something he wasn't even sure was right.

I can scarcely blame him if he turns away. How would I feel if he'd done the same to me?

'As you said, the dwyma chose us both,' he said, finally. 'I'll trust you for now, Nara. I just hope you'll learn to do the same for me one day.'

She was so overcome by his faith in her that she lost their link, fell from their imagined place and went hurtling down a vortex . . .

. . . and into her body, which convulsed and would have pitched headlong into the pond if Basia hadn't caught her. Sometime during the night, Basia had wrapped her in several blankets and built a fire beside the pool to warm them both.

For a few minutes Lyra let herself be held, closing her eyes and clinging to consciousness, until she found the strength to ask, 'Did we succeed?'

Basia listened to the aether, then nodded. 'It's done. We're going in.'

'Then take me upstairs,' Lyra begged. 'I need to see my son . . .'

Greyspire, Pallas-Sud

Dirklan sensed the storm ease and was first to prise open a shutter and gaze outside.

His people had been infiltrating the south side of the city for days now, crossing upstream in dinghies at night and creeping into Fen-reach, Southside and Greyspire, in the very shadow of the Celestium and the Rymfort. The ordinary burghers were frightened, though few had seen a Reeker or had any idea what had really happened. They knew only that Ostevan's new regime frightened them, and Dirklan's people diligently fed those fears, telling them that the people behind Reeker Night had seized the Holy City – and that aid was coming. They'd receive all the help and shelter they needed after that.

He looked upwards first: the clouds, so full and heavy above them for weeks, were clearing as if some giant hand were sweeping them aside. Stars emerged in glittering splendour and the full moon beamed bright as a twilit summer's evening. But the scene it lit was of deepest winter. He whistled softly, despite himself. Lyra and her mysterious ally had done what it would have taken a hundred weather-magi weeks to do, if they could manage this sort of power at all. He was overawed.

His vantage overlooking the Aerflus had been carefully chosen, for it looked towards the western ramparts of the Rymfort. He gazed at the water, marvelling to see the giant confluence, where the two mighty rivers collided in a swirl of eddies and whirlpools, frozen solid, and so suddenly that the peaks and troughs and spirals of the surface had been captured in a wondrous ice sculpture.

<Are you seeing this, Dirk?> came Raven's mental voice; the Volsai was currently on the Kenside Docks with Oryn Levis and his command group. <The Bruin's iced up too – Tully says it's solid right to the bottom.>

<Tell Levis to move now,> he replied, turning to Patcheart, a stringy for-mer swindler with lank red hair and a bravo's swagger. 'It's time, Patch. You know what to do.'

He led his small group out into the newly frozen streets, wading through snowdrifts three feet deep and more, as all over Pallas-Sud other groups began to do the same.

Patcheart ensured he was last to leave the hut. As soon as he was alone he pulled a specific coin from his purse and conjured a faint gnostic link. Instantly, Edetta Keeper's formidable mind closed over his like a fist.

<Well?> the renegade Keeper demanded.

<Dirk fell for it,> Patcheart sent. *<We're going in now, right where I told you.>*

<Now? You mean, right now?> He sensed alarm, and that the Keeper was in a warm room, drinking wine. But then her vindictive, satisfied glee resonated through the link. *<Excellent. I'll be waiting,>* she replied. *<You won't regret this, Patcheart. Garod knows how to reward loyal friends, and so do I.>*

<I just want to be on the winning side,> Patcheart sent back. *<I've seen what happens to them who get that particular decision wrong. House Corani is doomed and I'm not going down with it.>*

The Rymfort, Pallas-Sud

Dravis Ryburn sat beneath a candle, pondering this riddle: if love is the opposite of evil, can an evil man love? *Because I am wholly evil – but I love Lef utterly.*

His eyes drifted every few minutes to his lover, sleeping partially uncovered, his perfect body an ivory carving of smooth muscle clothing finely chiselled bones.

The book in Ryburn's lap argued that an evil man's love was inher-ently selfish, but Ryburn was unconvinced. He'd never felt so selfless as when he was with Lef, through all the complicated movements that were required when two powerful men negotiated the dance of forbidden desire. The subtle hints, feeling out whether the other was *one of us*, the flirting disguised as competitive striving, the cautious, guarded conversations that might lead to intimacy, a revelation or a confession.

And then the surrender.

Our love is not predatory, it's not exploitive, nor demanding. It's transcendent. He smiled lazily and thought, *Perhaps I'm not really evil then?* It was a thought for pondering next time he couldn't sleep.

He put the book down, sensing the citadel around him settling into the deepest hours of the night, his possessed men quiescent at their posts, those asleep twisting and turning in Abraxas-dreams of hungers and needs. Outside, the storm had passed.

He turned his mind to the coming day. Brylion Fasterius was on his way with his legions; Garod Sacrecour's men were travelling on river-barges and the Celestium stood ready to welcome them. This impasse would be broken. They'd storm the Bastion and bring an end to Corani rule.

And then we'll deal with Ostevan and Edetta.

The Celestium, Pallas-Sud

Ostevan didn't really sleep any more. The daemon voices in his head gave him no rest. And anyway, the dead of night was the perfect time to think, even a night as bleak and stormy as this, with almost continuous thunder and lightning, the air so cold that all the shutters had to be warded shut and they were burning through fuel by the cartload just to prevent the entire city from turning to ice. But storms were storms; there was no hint of weather-gnosis in the air and he presumed dwyma would have a similar taint.

As long as it breaks by dawn, we're on course: Brylion's legions will march in, Garod's men will appear on the Bruin and the assault will begin. There was nothing the empress could do to match their numbers – her reinforcements were still several days away in the north and by the time they arrived, the Bastion would be back in Sacrecour hands. What concerned him was what happened afterwards.

And how we deal with Ryburn.

He wasn't alone tonight, for once; his companion lounged on the opposite sofa. Edetta Keeper, an androgynous woman who looked about forty but was thrice that age, sipped her wine. She was similarly afflicted by insomnia on this particular night, and appeared distracted. Someone had been gnostically communicating with her most of the evening.

'Relax, Edetta,' he told her, swinging a leg. 'We're in this together.'

'How can I be sure Ryburn doesn't know our plans? Abraxas could be telling him everything I do.'

'Keeping Abraxas out of your senses is as simple as maintaining a mental ward. Trust me, Ryburn's ignorant.'

'What of Naxius?' she asked.

'I'm certain we're locked doors to him too.'

'But isn't that in itself going to make the Master suspicious?'

'Of course. But he knows that if we let the daemon run free in our heads, we'll be eaten up from the inside. Giving us this autonomy was necessary. In the end, Edetta, everything comes down to trust.'

'I wouldn't trust me,' Edetta snorted.

'I said more or less the same thing – he said it was my treachery that he trusted *most* about me. I rather think he'd be disappointed if we weren't all trying to backstab him, and each other.'

Edetta raised her glass. 'You and I are working together, though.'

'We are,' he agreed.

He regarded Edetta as a vicious, malicious, jealous, manipulative and untrustworthy cow, and she likely had a similar opinion of him. But they had found common ground in the desire to rid themselves of rivals.

'So, tomorrow we'll rule Pallas,' he observed. 'The Pontifex and his Queen, the new rulers of Kore's Empire.'

She brightened. 'Indeed. Now remember, I want my own magi-knights and the Bastion. And the Volsai. Oh, and don't even *think* we're going to consummate our so-called union – we're immortal and we don't need heirs!'

'It never crossed my mind,' he replied, truthfully. 'But I want the Volsai.'

And so the haggling went, carving up the future . . .

. . . until the thunder outside suddenly stopped and the world went utterly still.

Edetta cocked her head. 'The storm's broken.' Then her periapt lit up and after a muttered conversation with someone through a gnostic link, she murmured, 'Interesting . . . A trap I've laid is in play . . .' She rose to her feet. 'I have to be there.'

Ostevan waved his hand amiably. 'Good luck.'

She gave an ironic curtsey and hurried away. He remained seated, sipping his wine and listening to the stillness, anticipating the day to come. *Garod and Brylion will be here tomorrow and we'll be carving the Corani turkey come dusk . . .*

Some ten minutes after Edetta's departure, he sensed something else: prickles of energy, little gnostic hums and discharges, akin to the first buzz of a swarm of wasps entering a garden. Despite the cold, he went to the north-facing windows and sent heat through the thick ice encrusting the outside of the shutters so he could force them open. He stared out over the inner walls of the Celestium compound to the river and Pallas-Nord rising beyond.

The night was now utterly clear, the moon hanging huge in the sky above, streaming light over a stark, glowing landscape. The Bruin was a ribbon of white, utterly unmoving, the ferries and boats on the southern bank locked in the grip of sheet-ice. Even the Aerflus was still, something he'd never heard of.

And advancing across the ice were thousands of men, moving in silent, disciplined ranks towards him.

He stared.

Then he opened his mind and blared a warning.

Dirklan, Mort, Patcheart and a dozen Volsai waited beside the grilled hole, just large enough that a man could slide through, one at a time. They checked weapons and made small talk and fretted . . .

They'd just sent Brigeda's team into the underground crawl-tunnel. According to Patcheart's information, it led into ventilation holes for an old repository beneath the Hall of Leaven, midway between the

Rymfort and the Celestium. The repository contained vital documents belonging to Edetta Keeper, research into daemon possession that could give them an edge. Brigeda, a tough, muscular woman with short auburn hair, had taken her sneak-thieves in five minutes ago and now they awaited her signal.

Mort Singolo slunk over to join him. The Axeman was anxious; he hated confined spaces. 'If I'd known how much sitting around doing rukk-all was involved in this job, I'd have told you to sod off,' he grumbled.

'No, you wouldn't.' Dirklan grinned. 'You love getting paid exorbitantly for doing next to nothing.'

'Oh, I've no complaints about the pay – just the bloody boredom. It's driving me to drink,' the Axeman replied. 'Speaking of which . . .' He unstopped a whiskey flask, took a slurp and offered it. 'Try this: Brevian Highlands.'

It was good: smooth and peaty, just as Dirklan liked. He took a second sip, then returned the flask. 'The latest dispatches from the south are in. Seth Korion's broken ranks and taken his army south towards Norostein. Rolven Sulpeter wants him arrested and strung up.'

'Damn right,' Mort grunted.

'Oh, I'm not so sure,' Dirklan said. 'Elvero Salinas was happy to let the Shihad ravage Noros, and so was Andreas Borodium. That would have given Sultan Rashid the winter base he needs. I think Korion's done the right thing – again. He was the only who had a realistic view of what we faced at Collistein Junction, and he was the only one who kept his head when the battle started.'

'If he's a Korion, he's a prick,' Mort sniffed.

'His father was, certainly. But I think we'll be grateful to Korion the Younger before the war's over.'

Mort stoppered the whiskey and pocketed it. 'I think we've got quite enough shit going on up here to keep us busy without worrying about Rashid. If we survive winter, we'll think about him then.'

Then Dirklan felt a mental nudge and Brigeda's voice whispered, <*I'm in, Dirk. Patch's info was good: I'm looking through a stone grille at an anteroom below the Hall of Leaven.*>

<Good work. Secure the room and await us.> He broke contact.

'That was Briggy: we're in, lads.' He nodded to Patcheart. 'Follow me, Patch. Stay close.'

He shed his cloak, revealing his usual black leathers beneath, tied his long silver hair in a ponytail and took off his eyepatch and left gauntlet. His silver eye and hand caught the moonlight briefly as he passed an upper grille, then he folded his frame into the tunnel. He might be old, but he was still lithe.

Mort followed, muttering exhortations to himself – he *really* didn't like being below ground – then came Patcheart and the rest. They had to crawl, but Dirklan had outgrown any claustrophobia long ago. He wriggled to a hole, swung out and round, dropped and then helped Mort down.

'Good thing old garbage needs ventilation,' Mort noted, his voice a little higher than usual as he tried to joke his way through the fear. 'Be a bugger getting in otherwise.'

'Shh,' Dirklan whispered. 'We're getting close.'

Two more narrow passages and he was dropping into a darkened, empty room to find a young woman they called Skidder waiting for them. 'Briggy took the lads into the chamber down the end of this passage,' she said, pointing to a large door on the left. 'The other way leads to stairs going up.'

'It's a bloody rabbit warren, innit?' Patcheart grinned, drawing his stiletto. 'Let's go.'

Dirklan led the way, striding along the corridor towards the door, which was unlocked and led to a large, darkened chamber with a pool of light in one corner. He could make out human forms in the shadows, but no one came forward.

'Boss,' Patcheart said from right behind him, 'don't go any further.'

Patcheart had sidled into Setallius' left flank as the small group of Volsai fanned out, facing the two dozen or more men who emerged from the shadows. The dim light indicated that they were at one end of a long, high-ceilinged room that contained racks upon racks of old parchments.

A drip of sweat ran down Patcheart's forehead as the crucial moment arrived.

'Boss, don't go any further,' he told Setallius, then gazed into the darkness and added, silently, <Now.>

Light erupted on all sides, a blinding flash that tore the darkness apart, revealing two dozen mage-knights in gleaming armour surrounding them, and behind those, Brigeda and her small team, gagged and chained to the walls. The knights wore tabards quartered in purple and white: House Sacrecour in exile; they'd worn purple and gold when ruling the empire but those were now Lyra's colours.

'Welcome to my little hideaway, Dirklan,' Edetta Keeper cackled, stepping forward. 'You thought it was your idea to come here, but I fear it was mine. There's nothing down here of value and never was, and now you're trapped in my lair. Tabula-mio,' she smirked, then she looked at Patcheart. 'Take him.'

Patcheart reversed the stiletto, slammed the hilt into Dirklan's skull and the Volsai commander crumbled at his feet. Beside him, his second, Scammel, placed a blade against Mort Singolo's throat.

'You bastard!' Skidder bellowed in fury.

'You'll get yours any minute,' Patcheart told her, turning to Edetta Keeper with a flourishing gesture. 'Milady, as you see, I always deliver.'

Mort turned his head, even though Scammel's knife carved a furrow in his throat. 'Patcheart, you piece of shit.'

'Move again and you die, Axeman,' Scammel rasped.

'Perfect,' Edetta Keeper purred, advancing with a girlish spring in her step. 'You've done wonderfully, Master Patcheart, and will certainly get the reward you so richly deserve.' She nudged the fallen Corani spymaster with her dainty shoe. 'I trust you haven't broken his skull – I need to pick apart what's inside it.'

As her mage-knights closed in around them, she dropped to one knee, conjuring a Chain-rune, and reached out. For a moment her shields overlapped Setallius' body.

Dirklan's right arm flopped sideways and a sliver of silvered steel erupted from his sleeve, glinting momentarily as it flew up under the Keeper's chin and vanished, except for the tip which punched through the top of her skull like a helmet spike. Edetta folded noiselessly, her expression going from triumphant to slack.

'Ha!' Patcheart roared, spinning and plunging his left-hand dagger into the eye socket of the nearest Sacrecour, while Scammel, Mort and the others – all primed for this instant – hammered into the possessed knights, their silvered blades disrupting their ability to shield. Fully a third went down in that first attack; the rest stepped backwards, and three of those were cut down from behind by Brigeda's team, who'd secreted lock-picks and their own argenstael stilettos on their bodies. In moments Edetta's guards lay dead, with blasted-out eyes and ash in their veins.

Brigeda shouldered through the press, grabbed Patcheart and gave him a massive bear-hug. 'You beauty!' she roared. 'If you were only a girl, I'd snog you senseless.'

'Pretend,' he suggested, puckering up.

'Rukk off!' Brigeda guffawed. She hauled Dirklan to his feet and hugged him too. 'You okay, boss? That dork didn't hit you too hard, did he?'

'Barely touched me,' Setallius said, giving Patcheart a sly smile. 'Well done. You played her perfectly.'

'Sometimes I surprise even meself,' Patcheart said, trying for modesty but likely failing. 'She even fell for the whole "let's use Briggy to lure the rest in" thing! Keepers, eh? All that power and still naïve as nuns.'

'Luckily for us,' Dirklan agreed. 'That was my biggest fear, that they'd just kill Briggy's team.'

'I expect my bonus payments to reflect that,' Brigeda remarked. She looked around the room. 'Well, we nailed her: what now? Do we just leave?'

Dirklan raised a hand. 'Lads, ladies, listen. We knew this was a trap and we put our heads in it not just to get at Edetta. We're *inside* their defences now – just as Oryn Levis is about to launch an assault across the Bruin.'

'*What? I thought*–' Patcheart exclaimed, his mind flip-flopping, then racing on. 'Huh!'

'That storm just froze the river solid,' Dirklan told them, 'and now Lumpy needs us to wreak a little havoc. You know the sort of thing: take down sentries, open gates . . .'

Patcheart watched his colleagues take this in with appreciative nods and low whistles; he was just as impressed. 'You're a genius, boss – but best we move. Right now, you can bet Ryburn and Ostevan know Edetta's gone, and maybe how and where.'

'You're right, Patch,' Dirklan said. 'To work, lads: let's make mischief.'

Ryburn came to his feet as the death of Edetta Keeper's guards transmitted itself through the interconnected mind of Abraxas. Lef Yarle, sensing it too, rose silently from their bed and bared his teeth, his eyes black.

If I have a regret, it's that I took Lef into this pact, Ryburn thought morbidly. *Although at least we will share eternity.*

He reached for his periapt and called, found Ostevan Pontifex fuming, told him to look to his Celestium and to seal the tunnels to the Hall of Leaven. <*If you're taken, I'll not have a back door opened into my fortress,*> he told the Pontifex, closing the contact before seeking Brylion Fasterius and Garod Sacrecour in the aether.

Minutes later, he was spitting ichor.

Black-eyed servants, summoned through the daemon-link, mechanically dressed and armoured them as he hurriedly told Lef what he'd learned. 'That damned storm – it can't have been natural! Brylion and Garod have been well and truly rukked – they may have lost everyone.'

He hadn't realised someone as pale as Lef could blanch. '*Everyone?*'

'The storm went beyond freezing. Most of their legions were caught in the open, even their relay-staves shattered in the cold so they couldn't report. All evening they've been dying and we've not even known! And now the Corani are attacking.'

'How?' Lef asked sharply.

'Across the river: it's frozen solid.'

Lef took a moment to take that in. 'But we've only got one legion inside the citadel!'

'Exactly. But we have walls and they'll not take *my* fortress!' Ryburn dropped his arms as the servants finished arming him. 'I'll take the walls – you take the Halls of Leaven, flush out Edetta's assassins, then lock it down.'

They seized one final kiss, then strode off in opposite directions as the Rymfort came to life around them.

This citadel can hold for ever, Ryburn told himself. *Let the bastards come!*

The Bastion, Pallas-Nord

Now Lyra had no ability to influence anything, her fears multiplied. Her anxiety affected Rildan, who was fractious as he fed and squalled as he was taken away by Domara. Lyra's hands shook as she wiped spilt milk from her breasts then buttoned the front of her nightdress. She rose and went to her window.

'You should try to sleep, Majesty,' Basia suggested. She looked as apprehensive as Lyra.

'*Sleep?* How can I sleep with all *this* going on?' She could see torches on the river, flickering orange tongues amid the black tide crossing the vivid white ice. 'They're fighting now – are there any reports yet?'

'It's too soon.'

Lyra threw up her hands in exasperation. Her heart was thudding, its rapid pulse matching her quick, shallow breathing. She couldn't remember feeling this afraid, even on Reeker Night, when fear had been overtaken by the need to act. But tonight, all she could do was wait.

'I'll pray,' she blurted, reverting to default despite her years outside the convent. 'I'll use the private chapel on the floor below. Check it while I make myself decent.'

Basia hurried out while Lyra pulled on the first gown she found, a white silk with fox-fur cuffs and collar, wrapping it round her nightdress. She ran fingers through her hair and when Basia returned, ordered, 'Find out what's happening.' When the bodyguard hesitated, she snapped, 'The royal suites are the safest place in Pallas – I'll be fine. Just get me some news!'

It was a relief to find the chapel empty. She collapsed onto a kneeler in a side-chapel where she'd mounted an Eastern statue of an angel ascending into the skies on pearly wings. They'd found it among Ostevan's possessions. It was a beautifully formed nude, more art than religious icon, but she liked it.

I should be giving it to Calan to sell, she thought wryly. *It's hardly a Kore piece.*

She'd barely settled when she heard slippered feet and a big shape knelt beside her, just in reach. 'Oh, Solon! I'd have thought you'd be following the assault.'

'My queen commanded me to join her in prayer,' he reminded her dourly.

'So I did.' She smiled apologetically. 'I was worried you'd damage yourself.'

He sighed heavily and stopped himself trying to flex his shoulder. 'I probably would,' he admitted. 'The healer offered me poppy-milk to sedate me, but I don't want to sleep.' He looked at her intently. 'You did it – you froze the river . . .' He shook his head in wonder. 'How do you feel?'

'I think I've wiped out Brylion's legions,' she said, in a faltering voice. *Dear Kore, what kind of monster am I?* She put a hand to her heart. 'If we're victorious, perhaps I'll be able to forgive myself . . .'

'We *will* win,' Solon said. 'Oryn's taking in four legions. We've rounded up every argenstael weapon in Pallas and silvered the rest of our blades. Our tests on the captive shepherds suggest the silvered weapons aren't as effective as the argenstael, but it still affects them. We could wipe those Reeker bastards out.'

'They were once good men,' Lyra reminded him.

He dropped his eyes. 'Aye, you're right. But the men leading them aren't.'

They fell silent for a while and she tried to pray, but the tension of waiting made concentrating impossible. She felt like she was going mad with anxiety.

Her mind drifted to *that kiss*, and how safe she'd felt when Solon had held her; for once, his stature and presence had not felt intimidating, more like a bulwark against the dark. It gave her the courage to voice her thoughts.

'You're right about the loneliness,' she admitted. 'It's intolerable.' Then she went scarlet.

'I've thought a lot about you,' he replied. 'It helped me to . . . *deal* with Medelie.'

Medelie the traitor, who gave him everything he wanted.

'I'm not her,' she said sharply. 'I don't have her . . . um . . . ?' *Willingness . . . ? Bravado . . . ? Is that all men want? Confidence, and enthusiasm?*

'I know you're not her,' Solon answered. 'I wouldn't want you to be.'

'I thought she was "all a man could want"?' Lyra said.

'All that a certain kind of man could want: ravenous in bed and out, ambitious and ruthless.'

'But you're not that sort of man?' she asked, then cursed herself at the bluntness.

He flinched. 'For a while I was. But I remembered myself in time.'

'I'm sorry. It must have been Hel for you.'

'It was a dark road, but I'm walking back along it now. Trying to let it go. Your example – your goodness, your caring nature – helps me through. But at night . . . I think about her still.' He shuddered involuntarily.

My 'goodness'? My 'caring nature'? 'Solon, I'm not "good" or "caring". Tonight I may have killed *ten legions* of Sacrecour men. *Fifty thousand people.* Civilians too, when that storm hit Southside and Fenreach. I'm a *mass murderer . . .*'

She choked at that, and like a dam bursting, she was shaking uncontrollably, torrents of tears gushing from her in painful bursts as she bent over and almost fell. Solon's big arms caught her and he pulled her to his chest, gave her something to cry into, something warm against the freezing of her heart.

I'm not an Iceheart, she tried to say. *I'm not, I'm not.* What came out, she had no idea, only that she was looking up at his scarred, bearded visage from inches away, half-blinded by tears with her lips drawn upwards like a new-born bird seeking food.

He kissed her forehead while she clung to him like the last rock in the hungry sea.

The Rymfort, Pallas-Sud

The enemy are already inside. Dravis felt his hackles rise as he stormed along the northern walls above the main gates to the Rymfort, only to see fire break out inside the main keep behind him. He knew what it meant: Setallius' men were already loose, in before Lef had been able to pen them.

He's violated the purity of Kore's Inquisition.

He looked over the battlements to the killing ground beneath and saw ranks of Imperial crossbowmen forming up. He didn't have to give the orders for his black-eyed soldiers to raise shields.

But the first strike came from above as dark shapes streamed out of the night and javelins sleeted down from winged jousting beasts. Before he could warn his mage-knights to shield, a storm of *silver-tipped* javelins struck, scything down a dozen of his best men. They yowled as the agony of the metal pierced their ichor-laced bodies, losing their grip on the mind of Abraxas and falling, writhing helplessly.

No! No! No! No!

He blazed Ascendant-strength mage-fire that enveloped a flying beast and its rider, tearing them both from the sky, but his men were now looking skywards, their shields all over the place. Suddenly hundreds of crossbows *cracked*, more silver-tipped shafts tore through the air and each hit took a man to the ground. They kicked at the earth in agony, most not dead yet, but helpless until they could find the strength to wrench out the shafts.

The defence was still in pieces as a dozen ladders hammered into the curtain wall and with a roar of '*CORANI!*' the first men began to climb. A silver-headed crossbow bolt lanced towards his face and he barely shielded in time, felt the fletching graze his cheeks. More Corani mage-knights flashed overhead, javelins striking all round him, and he could hear cheering all along the riverbanks as more Imperial and Corani men clambered from the iced-over river to join the fray.

This can't be, he thought wildly. *The Rymfort has* never *fallen.*

He saw a pair of Inquisition warbirds trying to rise from the southern side of the keep, the only two he had air-ready, but an Imperial ship appeared above and fire burst over the sails of his vessels. They veered and collided, struck the curtain wall and both were immolated as one of the keels exploded. As in a nightmare, the wall fell inwards.

Shouting in dismay, he seized his periapt. <*Ostevan? Where are you?*>

There was no answer.

<*Lef?*>

Again the aether was silent, and he shrieked inside his head.

He whirled, slammed fire along a ladder that had clanged against the wall beside him, then hurled it away, burning men falling, but it was no good: the cursed silver was ripping through his men and the attackers were sweeping along the battlements.

A knight clad in white and green dashed in from the right; Ryburn battered away a sword-thrust then took the man's face off with a burst of mage-fire that speared through his shields.

Then a white-clad knight appeared behind the dead man, his tabard bearing the Crossed Keys of Wurther's own guard. *Exilium Excelsior*, he realised as the man's blade flashed at him: he caught the blow and hurled kinesis that should have ripped the Estellan from the battlements, but somehow Exilium flashed aside into the crenulations on the wall, as his sword – *which reeked of silver* – raked out and almost speared through his visor. He threw his head aside just in time, hacked a cross-cut at the man's side, which was blocked, then traded pulverising blows, battering the Estellan with fire until his foe's tabard burst into flame, then lining up a killing thrust, utterly consumed with destroying this *traitor* who'd rejected his *beloved Inquisition*–

–when something stabbed into his back and his blood turned to fire.

He staggered, half-turned, his sword flailing, and saw some bulky, lumbering, *graceless* man, who bunched his big arms and battered his riposte aside, just as Exilium Excelsior drove his silvered sword into his chest and out the back of his breastplate.

Dravis Ryburn's sight filled with darkness and then his vision flashed red. He reached for Abraxas, shrieking for more power, more energy–

Then Exilium smashed a double-handed blow down and he felt his neck halve. His skull smashed against the stone while he glimpsed his body – eight feet away – crumple.

Then Abraxas swallowed him, and eternity began.

Exilium Excelsior saw the Knight-Princep's eyes fly open, his mouth an 'O' as his head bounced and rolled to a halt, while the torso collapsed. All round him, the nearest defenders yowled, staggered and dropped weapons to clutch their faces, moments before they each met a decapitating blow. He gasped for breath, still more than shocked to be alive, because he'd been certain he'd been about to die, beaten down by a power beyond anything he'd ever faced.

He looked gratefully at Oryn Levis, who was leaning on his silvered sword, breathing heavily. 'Grafia, amigo. Ryburn was . . .' *Too much for me? Not in technique*, he decided, *but in Ascendant strength*. 'He was strong.'

'Aye, that he was. Buy me a drink later,' Oryn offered. He clapped Exilium's shoulder, the first gesture of acceptance he'd had since arriving in Pallas. 'Come on, Estellan, let's go find that pig's boyfriend.'

Lef felt Dravis Ryburn die through the daemon link, but he'd have known it anyway. You didn't share a bond like they had and not feel it when it was torn asunder.

He'd been coordinating the men trying to find the Volsai assassins, but those had already dispersed and now he was rushing from disaster to disaster, always a step behind. But when Dravis went, everything changed.

Why fight, when there's nothing that matters left to defend?

Tears running down his cheeks, he backed away, and the daemon-possessed men at his command faltered, their purpose wavering as his did. He didn't care. Every one of them could perish, for all he cared.

What matters is who took my love away . . . He'd caught a glimpse through the daemon's mind. *Exilium Excelsior, you're mine.*

When he'd met Dravis Ryburn, Lef had been a Volsai. Dravis had turned him into an Inquisitor and given him a power beyond price. With his lover now gone, honour knew only one path: to find those who had killed him and feed them to his daemonic master.

He dashed into the shadows.

Ostevan sensed Edetta's death and then Ryburn's and did as any good tabula player would when the end is nigh: he flicked over his queen and conceded the game.

But not the war.

He gathered his most precious possessions – his periapt and the chain of the Pontifex – and hurried for the southern gallery. It was empty, but through Abraxas, he could feel every death, and those deaths were coming nearer and nearer.

He stripped, then faced the banks of windows and gestured. With a crash, the glass exploded outwards; he hurled himself into the air, webbed skin billowing beneath his arms and becoming membranes that caught the air as morphic-gnosis contorted his limbs and shoulders. Something like a man-sized, hairless bat went flapping out into the frozen sky, radiating heat and streaming Air-gnosis as it tore from the vast dome and out over the city.

Almost, he turned in the air and flapped towards the Bastion, wondering where that *damned dwymancer bitch* was, but sanity prevailed: there were knights in the air, too much silver to chance contact, and windships hovering in the skies over Pallas-Nord.

No, we don't throw it all away in a fit of hatred. We run, and plan a counterstrike . . .

So he soared away into the clearing skies, while Abraxas gibbered hatred and vengeance.

Lyra heard footsteps, then the double doors to the chapel opened as she and Solon tore themselves away from each other, the remembered touch of his lips on her brow burning like a brand.

'*Yes?*' she called, rising to her feet beside the Knight-Commander.

It was Basia, bursting down the middle of the aisle. '*Lyra!*' the bodyguard was shouting, her normal ironic posturing shattered, 'they're inside the Celestium *and* the Rymfort! Ryburn's dead! Edetta's dead!'

Lyra reached for Solon's hand and clung to it as her heart pummelled her ribs. 'Thank Kore! Thank Kore!' For a moment she thought she'd faint from sheer relief. 'And Ostevan? What of him?'

'We don't know. They're looking for him, Yarle too.'

'But what of—? Have we—?' Lyra stammered, trying to ask five things at once.

'What of casualties?' Solon asked gravely.

Basia noticed him for the first time – and the hands he'd clamped about Lyra's. Her eyes narrowed fractionally, but she made no comment. 'No one . . . well obviously, *some* casualties – but we caught them by surprise. No one warned them about the . . . uh . . .'

Murderous storm, Lyra finished for her. But guilt was swept away in her utter relief. She sagged dizzily. 'We won? I don't believe it . . . But Garod's still out there,' she added, trying to get some perspective on this giddy sense of triumph. 'Probably Ostevan too. This isn't over.'

'But it is tonight,' Solon said, his hand still clasping hers. 'Tonight is a victory. Whatever you had to do to earn it was worthwhile,' he told her firmly, and she was grateful for that.

But then they heard more footfalls and the three of them turned as a crowd of courtiers burst in, Corani in white and green, already broaching wine and ale kegs and shouting praise to Kore and their *Beloved Majesty*. They were minor nobility and court functionaries, people she barely knew, but in seconds she was swamped in well-wishers and being drawn to the feast hall as music and songs broke out. The sense of relief, that the weeks of living in a divided city with the threat of imminent violence was finally over, broke down barriers, and she found herself the centre of a swarm of kissed hands, bows, curtseys and even hugs from the boldest. She let it sweep her away.

Victory! Victory . . .

'To our victorious Majesty,' Solon boomed, his voice filling the room as faces turned his way, full of exultation and relief. 'May she reign a hundred years!'

It was well after midnight. Basia had gone to bed and Lyra was finally alone. She'd escaped her courtiers after three hours, leaving them to dance and drink, her face flushed with wine and dancing: her first dance in months, taking her place in the swirling circles and squares, clapping and laughing and getting more than a little tipsy. Now her legs ached as she sat in her favourite armchair, exhausted yet wide awake. She'd shed the dress she'd worn and was wrapped in just a nightgown, feeling slightly wicked to be so near to naked.

And remembering that kiss . . .

Reports had continued to be received from the Rymfort and Celestium as she celebrated. All the people she cared for most still lived, and indeed, casualties had been miraculously light. Dirklan and Lumpy were going floor to floor in the Celestium, hunting out surviving Reekers and trying to find Ostevan, if he still lived.

She looked up in alarm as she heard a clicking sound from the servants' door and half-rose as it swung open, then a big shadowy figure stepped through and her heart fluttered as she recognised Solon, clad in a knee-length nightgown and bare-footed. 'Majesty,' he said in a hoarse, resolute voice.

'Lord Takwyth,' she said, standing up and facing him. She remembered facing down old Radine Jandreux with the fact of her marriage to Ril, the defiance she'd felt and the sense of power. And she thought also about Medelie Aventour, a shadow presence here in this room. She could sense Solon measuring her against the other woman and felt a strange urge not to be found wanting in passion, even with a man she still feared more than desired.

I told Dirklan I wanted to grow up. Maybe that includes this.

She let her nightgown fall from her shoulders, her eyes challenging him.

He didn't bother with more words, just closed the door and gathered her in his arms. She felt her whole body flush with fever and her limbs felt hollow, but when he kissed her again, his beard prickling her cheeks as his tongue invaded her mouth, she felt a bolt of need go through her that made her spine tingle and her loins heavy with want.

She dragged him down onto the rug before the fire, finding herself making throaty noises as they kissed. Then he reared over her, pulling off his own nightgown off. His erection already jutted out, rigid and thick, but instead of impaling her then and there, he parted her thighs and lowered his head. She felt a sudden surge of alarm as old inhibitions rose up, but when she tried to catch his head and push, tried to protest, she couldn't form the words. He kissed her mound, which was a sin. *Forbidden*. *Dirty*. But as his tongue slid over her nub and into the top of her cleft, the sheer sensation froze her, a soft tingling so exquisite her protest became a moan and her thighs parted further, as if they had a will of their own. He licked again and again, each stroke shivering through her, calling something up from inside. She felt her cleft flood as he lapped her up, like a great cat.

I'm a sinner, she groaned inwardly. But she didn't – *couldn't* – make him stop. *Because this is what sinners do. They revel in their own fall.* The hands she'd intended to push him away instead grasped and cradled his head to keep him there as she descended into a kind of rapture. She forced her old self to look away while she permitted this forbidden, *glorious* thing . . .

As he feasted, languid bliss became urgent, mounting gushes of pleasure, until she felt the dam inside her burst and she climaxed harder than she would ever have thought possible, convulsing uncontrollably as explosive grunts burst from her and her vision swam.

Then he was upon her, pulling her legs around him and locking her in his big arms, kissing her again with her body's juices still wet on his lips. His erection filled her as his hands gripped her face.

'Look at me,' he told her, his eyes inches from hers. 'Don't look away.' Then he began to move again while his soul bled from his eyes. '*Lyra* . . . *Lyra* . . .' His hips rocked and he made her gasp again, then everything was aimed at *that spot*, and all she could do was cling to him, grasping his back, each thrust leaving her airless, drowning in a rising tide of pleasure like wine and mead and everything sweet and sticky – and then he groaned, '*Medelie!*' and, louder, '*Lyra*.' His hips bucked and he *ram-ram-rammed*, and emptied himself.

She realised he was crying and held him, pressing his face against her neck, and as he slipped from her, his mouth fastened on her left nipple, right over her thudding heart, and he suckled hard, his mouth pumping as her milk flowed.

Dear Kore . . . we've both gone mad . . .

About a minute later, he rolled off her, onto his side, facing away, his massive frame shaking. Despite some mortification at what they'd just done, she rolled over too and cradled his back. 'Solon? It's all right. I'm here.' Consoling him felt like the strangest act of all. But his shaking subsided and after a minute he twisted to face her.

'She's gone now,' he whispered hoarsely. 'Medelie's gone . . . That last moment, it was like an exorcism . . . Like casting a daemon from a host-body, naming it and sending it hence, and then there was just you.' He pressed his face to her and kissed her, her milk on his lips. 'Thank you.'

'My gratitude to you too,' she whispered. 'I needed that.' She glanced down at her bared left breast, still raw from his suckling. 'I hope you've left my son enough milk.'

He blushed. 'Milady—'

'Hush. I didn't mind, truly.' In fact it had been oddly soothing, and powerful.

But the enormity of what she'd just done intruded. *It's only two months since Ril died*, she thought, trying to feel guilty because surely she should be. *I've sinned. I'm faithless. I'm a slut. The nuns were right . . .*

But the guilt didn't come, and calling herself names didn't work either. Nor did it obviate the satisfaction that was radiating outwards from her pleasantly aching groin. She'd seldom climaxed with Ril, but somehow those shackles had melted away. And the last time she and Ril made love had been more than six months ago.

How can I have been so frigid with one I loved, yet taken such pleasure with someone I don't?

Clearly, the change was in herself. Whether she approved it, she wasn't sure. Images of Ril's body, olive-skinned, lean and almost hair-less, contrasted with the hairy, muscular bulk of Solon, but when Solon kissed her again, tasting her, she surrendered to it easily, feeling herself go wet again. 'Mmm,' she sighed.

'What time is it?' he murmured.

'The tenth bell just rang,' she replied as his hand slid down her side and stroked her hip. 'Rildan usually wakes just before the twelfth bell, an hour or so before dawn.

'Plenty of time,' he murmured. 'Do you wish to go to bed?'

'Let's just stay here.'

He smiled at that, and sitting up, reached to put more wood on the fire. She leaned against him, trying to get comfortable around his unfamiliar presence. He regarded her silently, then asked, 'You seemed unwilling at first to be tongued? Don't you like it?'

She looked away, colouring. 'Um . . . it was just that I've never had that before.'

He looked incredulous. 'With respect, Lyra, you were married for five years – surely you're not a complete innocent? Did you and Ril never . . . explore?'

She didn't want to think of her and Ril, but forced herself to reply. 'He wanted to, but I was too scared, too ashamed. To me, the things he suggested were dirty and sinful. The convent matrons taught the village women that a righteous woman must lie passively on her back. They insisted only "natural intercourse" was permitted in the eyes of Kore.'

'But no one actually listens to that shit, do they? Ril Endarion was certainly no prude – he cut a swathe through the court of Coraine before you came along.'

Lyra dropped her gaze, feeling mortified. 'I couldn't bring myself to do anything *unnatural* – all I saw was sin, sin and more sin. We quarrelled over it, and then came the first miscarriage and our love was broken thereafter. He stopped wanting me. It became nothing more than duty.'

Solon looked away. 'I'm sorry. I thought you were happy together.'

'We mostly were. Just . . . not in this room.'

The fact that she'd chosen Ril instead of him hung heavily in the air, but thankfully, he didn't voice it. Instead he said, 'I could teach you much, if you wished to learn?'

Could I? Lyra wondered. *Take a lover, solely for pleasure – and instruction?* She recalled what she'd said to Setallius, about needing to be more worldly, maturing into someone the princes wouldn't eat alive. And she also thought about how the lonely, fearful nights had been crushing her spirit.

We've just won a great victory. Finally, there's light ahead, a new dawn coming. So why not enjoy something for myself? It's not like I'm not a blushing virgin. She felt for the right words. 'Solon, I'm willing. I want to learn. I *need* to.'

He frowned, suddenly seeing where this could be going. 'Men are attracted to innocence, and—'

'It's not about attracting them, it's about *seeing through them*, don't you see? Politics, ceremony, even battle, I've been through, but love-making scares me. My marriage failed – *I* failed. Being courted again – as I must, if we're to gain allies – scares me witless, but I need to be worldly and confident. I need to be in control.'

Solon looked taken aback, but he said slowly, 'Very well. I'd never thought to be a . . . do you know the Rimoni word, "gigolo"? It's a male prostitute. It's not a role I'd envisaged this late in life.'

Lyra looked stricken. 'No! That's not what you are,' she said quickly, 'but I need to be clear: this is a season of pleasure, not a romance. I will have to re-marry for State reasons. You understand that. This affair lasts only so long as I say.'

He looked away and she feared she'd lost him, but then he said, in a formal voice, 'I agree your terms.'

He cupped her cheek and kissed her mouth again, then shifted his hand to her right breast, heavy with milk, and began to massage it. It hurt a little, but felt good too, and she found herself shifting, writhing back into him.

'Solon—'

'Hush,' he whispered. 'Listen . . . can you hear that? Silence – just you and me, and time on our hands to enjoy *this*.' His hand slid down her belly and into her and she felt more barriers crash as his big fingers slid inside. 'You have a kind of innocence,' he went on, his low voice rever-berating hypnotically through her, while his fingers had their way with her. 'We need to get rid of that.'

*

Some unknowable time later, they rolled apart. After all the intensity, it was more than awkward to speak, so she just stared up at the ceiling, catching her breath, feeling sweaty and battered and used . . . in a very good kind of way. Earthy. Fecund. Womanly.

I don't really even like you, Solon Takwyth, but I'll let you do this to me. Because I like it. And, Kore forgive me, it's what I need right now.

15

Freihaafen

The Rune of the Chain

The first thing Emperor Sertain commanded Baramitius to do was to seek a way to lock up the gnosis of anyone who disagreed with him. That was Sertain: Lord of Paranoia. Baramitius devised the insidiously evil Rune of the Chain – and within weeks Sertain founded the Volsai. Tyranny was upon us.

THE BLACK HISTORIES (ANONYMOUS), 776

Freihaafen, Upper Osiapa River, Mollachia
Decore 935

Kyrik sat beside the steaming lake, overcome with relief and more than a little awestruck as he looked around. *How did I not know about this place – and do I really want to give it away?*

After somehow evading Dragan's possessed hunters, Rothgar had led them to a narrow ravine filled with a clammy mist that swallowed them up, forcing them to navigate the maze by touch and the gnosis – until they'd emerged into a valley perhaps a mile wide and three deep. There was a steely-grey lake in the middle, from which rose thick plumes of steam. The pine woods carpeting the slopes gave way to thickly grassed shores. On one side of the lake was a hill surmounted with a partly complete wooden palisade. Within the enclosing fences they could see hide tents.

He turned to his companions. 'I'm a very generous man,' he chuckled, before fixing Rothgar with a mock reproving eye. 'Or rather, you are, with my possessions.'

'Perhaps I erred, Kirol,' Rothgar said, 'but Kip's people needed such a haven. It's well hidden, even from the air, the pastures and lake are rich, it has plentiful timber and other advantages—'

Kyrik held up a hand to stop him. 'Don't worry. I'd have rather known, but perhaps it's good that I didn't. Does Dragan know of this place?'

'I hadn't got round to telling him,' Rothgar said wryly, 'but that was sheer luck; it was just that our paths hadn't crossed.'

'Then Kore guided you,' Valdyr said fervently.

'And Ahm and Minaus,' Kip chuckled. 'They visit often.' He winked. 'After all, this place is Paradise.'

Kyrik glanced sideways at Valdyr, but his younger brother was brooding over something. Not being sure how safe they were, he'd followed Valdyr the previous night when he and Gricoama had left to commune with the dwyma, but his brother and the wolf had just sat down and gone into a trance for about four hours. Knowing better than to wake them, he instead built a fire and wrapped both man and beast in blankets, although neither had appeared to notice. When they'd reappeared next morning, Valdyr said only that it was dwyma matters.

Now they watched the distant figures swimming in the lake, this valley's great treasure. It was heated by hundreds of steam vents below the surface, so no matter how deep the winter snows, it was always hot, perfect for bathing after a day's hard labour.

'Come,' Kip said now, interrupting Kyrik's musing, 'let's eat.' He led them back to the main camp, to the central *langhausen*, or longhouse. The roof and walls had just been finished and Kip had ordered a celebratory meal.

The gathering was the strangest community Kyrik had ever seen: Mantauri, Schlessen and Rondian men, Ahmedhassan women, and children, both human and Mantauri. The latter were strangely winsome creatures with a slow patience, unlike the quicksilver human children. The mixed group really pleased him; it showed him it was possible for unity and goodwill to overcome prejudices. His cup-wish that night was for harmony among them.

He found himself sitting next to Kip's wife for the first time. 'Sal-Ahm, Kirol Kyrik, Prince Valdyr,' Sabina greeted him in Rondian, her voice a sultry, thickly accented Eastern purr. She was statuesque and voluptuous, with dark hair to her waist and an entrancing face, quite possibly the most beautiful woman he'd ever seen.

'Alaykum Sal-Ahm,' Kyrik replied in Keshi. 'A lovelier welcome one could not wish to see. You look like Hebb royalty.'

Sabina gave him a sideways look. 'And yet my husband courted me by abducting me during the Third Crusade,' she said, with a twinkle in her eye. 'He walked into my tent, threw me over his shoulder and stole me away.'

Kyrik blinked, somewhat appalled. 'Oh. I see . . .'

'Do you?' she said, her expression both amused, and a challenge. 'In Dhassa I was just a whore, forced to perform foul acts in alleys for pittance. Here I am the wife of a goodhearted man, I have two beautiful sons and I have seen wonders. And I can still speak my Mother Tongue with my fellow wives. I've been blessed.'

Well, that's me in my place, Kyrik thought. 'My apologies, Lady. I leaped to a conclusion.'

'Ai,' Sabina said, forgiving him. 'Ahm blessed me that day. The war was almost over, I was no longer of value to my owner and there was no transport home. I would have been dead in days, had not my husband claimed me.' She looked down, then lifted her chin. 'And I do love him.'

'The gods blessed us both,' Kip said, breaking in. 'Sabina was my first Eastern woman, and I never forgot her. When I saw her on the roadside, it was a sign from Minaus . . . and Ahm. And now see what we've made here.'

He gestured around the room, filled with people drawn from such diverse places.

Since arriving, Kyrik had been labouring alongside the rest of the men, felling trees or splitting logs for the palisade and buildings. The massive Mantauri bore huge yokes hung with many water-buckets, or carried whole pine trunks on their shoulders, while the wives gathered around banks of cooking fires to prepare the meals.

And all of them here at my invitation, Kyrik thought. *Dragan would have been appalled, even before the daemon took him.* Likely, most of his people would have been. But seeing the harmony and industry evident here gave him a strange feeling of rightness.

'Has this valley a name?' he asked Rothgar.

'The few who know of it call it Vizsforo, "Hot Water",' Rothgar replied.

'My folk are calling it *Freihaafen*,' Kip said, leaning in to be heard above the chatter in the hall. 'It means "the Refuge".'

'How is it our father never knew of this?' Valdyr wondered. He was feeding Gricoama scraps of meat. The huge wolf was completely gentle around the people.

'Those few of us who knew wanted to keep it from being spoiled by settlers,' Rothgar said. He gave Kip a wry look. 'I guess I've messed that up.'

Kyrik bit his lip, then said, 'Kip, let's formalise this: it's yours. Just leave me space for a royal retreat. Rothgar might have overstepped, but he's done well. I grant you and your people this place in perpetuity, but under certain conditions: it remains a part of Mollachia, and you may not bar fellow Mollachs unless I bar them too. Is that agreeable?'

'It is, and thank you,' Kip said. 'It's a kingly gift.'

Kyrik thought about the Vlpa, stranded in the Domhalott without leadership, not to mention his own people, who were likely cowering in their homes now, understanding neither the bloodbath of the coronation nor the change in their menfolk.

'I think more and more people will be taking to the forests in the coming months,' he said, thinking aloud. 'In times of troubles, Mollachs have always returned to the wild. We'll need to bring them here.'

'Freihaafen isn't large enough to support many more people than we have now,' Kip noted. 'And we'll have no crops until spring. But certainly we'll do what we can.'

'They'll not find this place easily,' Rothgar commented. 'We'd need to guide them, and that risks Dragan's men finding us. That's the biggest risk, right now.'

'Ysh,' Kyrik agreed. 'We need a plan.' He looked at Valdyr and added quietly, 'Sorry to ask, but we may also need your gifts, Brother.'

To his surprise, Valdyr didn't flinch, as he usually did when the dwyma was mentioned. 'I'm at your service, Brother,' he said, stroking Gricoama's ruff. 'I've made a kind of friend, who might be able to help.'

*

The work of creating a stronghold in Freihaafen took on a renewed sense of purpose. They knew they had to be ready for assault.

'At least we now have a fuller idea of what it is we fight,' Kyrik told Valdyr as they walked down to the lakeshore. 'It's daemonic possession, spread through daemon-blood: *ichor*. They share one intellect and can only be killed by damage to the brain or decapitation . . . but we now know they're vulnerable to argenstael and silver.'

'And to the dwyma,' Valdyr reminded him. 'There's something in Gricoama's bite – I don't yet know what – that's deadly to them.'

That was heartening. But Kyrik was haunted by the taunts of the men on the lake: could Hajya still be alive? The idea that his indomitable wife might be a prisoner of these monsters almost paralysed him with grief and anger.

If it's true, I'll free her, one way or the other. I have to.

The plight of his wife's people was his other urgent issue. He hoped they'd done as he'd asked and gone to the Tuzvolg, but that wouldn't put them out of Dragan's reach. And he'd not been able to reach Korznici to find out.

But his days weren't all anxiety, heartbreak and hard work: every evening the small community of humans and Mantauri collected at the lakeside.

'Embrace the strangeness,' Kyrik reminded his brother as he and Valdyr padded down the path. His back and limbs ached from the hard labour and he was already anticipating the power of the hot springs to relieve his aches and pains. 'This is a unique place – savour it.'

'I'm trying, Brother,' Valdyr murmured.

Valdyr was completely awestruck by the Mantauri, but his eyes still flinched if they happened to rest on an Eastern women; he was clearly still haunted by the Keshi breeding-houses. And he was self-conscious about his back, horribly scarred by floggings in the Dhassan chain-gangs.

Communal bathing wasn't a part of Mollach culture, but it was in the East and Kyrik felt liberated by the nudity – unlike his brother, who hunched awkwardly, one hand over his groin. Kyrik didn't tease him; Valdyr was too brittle for levity.

'This is Paradise, is it not?' Sabina called in Keshi, wading over to join them, a young boy pressed to her chest. She looked like a goddess of Motherhood.

Valdyr blushed and looked away.

'Isn't Yuros the first plane of Hel in Amteh lore?' Kyrik replied.

'It is, but Ahm has blessed little parts of it,' Sabina smiled. 'Your brother isn't comfortable?'

'He'll get used to it,' Kyrik said, hoping it would prove so. 'This must be very strange for you, Lady?'

Sabina sat on a boulder with her breasts matter-of-factly displayed, bouncing her baby as he chortled happily. 'On the contrary, Yuros is exactly as I was taught: freezing cold, peopled by men who are like beasts and full of heathens and danger. The Godspeakers spoke truly.'

'I suppose they did,' Kyrik laughed. He remembered what Kip had told him of their five years since the Crusades, how his small group of veterans and their wives had been ostracised by their forest tribe and forced to wander as mercenaries. It hadn't been easy, he was sure, despite Sabina's calm assessment. Close up, he could see the toll of time and two pregnancies on her body and face. But it only added wisdom to her beauty, he decided.

She reminded him painfully of Hajya, although they were nothing alike in looks.

Kip waded over to join them, his elder son on his massive shoulders squealing delightedly. He kissed his wife and murmured something, then handed her the child. She gave Kyrik a warm smile, then waded ashore, a child in either hand. The water cascading down her back made Kyrik's heart ache.

'You miss your wife,' Kip noted.

'Ysh,' Kyrik said. 'But the terrible thing is, I pray she's dead, not infected and alive.'

'No, pray otherwise,' Kip replied. 'What can be done can be undone.' He turned and followed his family from the lake.

But that's the hope that's killing me, Kyrik thought.

Valdyr said, 'What Kip said? About things that are done being undone? There's someone I could ask.'

Kyrik had been waiting to hear about this mysterious *someone*. 'Who?'

'When I was with Luhti, we sometimes heard a woman calling through the dwyma. After Luhti died, I responded. We speak often now: her name is Nara of Misencourt.'

The name meant nothing to Kyrik. 'What do you know about her?'

'Well, not that much. She's Rondian, from Pallas.' Valdyr hesitated then blurted, 'The other night, we pulled storms from all over the north. We froze the Bruin River and dumped a blizzard over Rondelmar.'

Kyrik stared. '*You did what?*'

Valdyr looked at him solemnly. 'It's true. She said Pallas was being assailed by the same creatures we face: "Reekers" is what she calls the possessed men. They are led by powerful conspirators who wear theatre masks.'

Kyrik sat back, utterly stunned. 'You helped another dwymancer you've never met to make storms in Pallas? Dear Kore, Valdyr ... dwymancy is *heretical* magic! The Inquisition could come here!'

'She needed my help. I've learned so much from her – and what Asiv has done here isn't an isolated thing; it's happening in other places. We can work with them.'

'I thought I was the trusting one,' Kyrik exclaimed. 'Kore's Heart, Valdyr, you're meddling with empire politics. Do you want the damned empress looking our way? Or the grand prelate? You mustn't talk to her again!'

Valdyr bowed his head. 'Is that a command?'

Kyrik almost barked out, *Ysh, of course it is!* But he bit his tongue, because Valdyr clearly had more to say.

'The thing is,' his brother said, 'with Luhti gone, I can't use the gnosis unaided. I need Nara's help.'

'Then speak to her if you must,' Kyrik conceded, 'but for Kore's sake, be careful!'

They fell silent for a time, looking around at the other bathers, turned to silhouettes by the thick steam. There was primal beauty in the scene, the snowy mountains and forested slopes, the stark severity of the winter sunset and the distant clamour of the evening birdsong. When a Mantauri male rose abruptly, water cascading from his winter pelt, it was like watching a primaeval leviathan rise from the sea to conquer the land.

'This is a special place,' Kyrik breathed.

'Ysh, it is very beautiful,' Valdyr agreed.

'No, it's more than that. Look at Kip's Schlessen and Rondians – white men, all married to Eastern women with half-breed children, mingling peacefully with illegal constructs made for war. It makes me believe that eventually my Mollachia will find a similar tolerance.'

'First we have to kill Asiv and Dragan,' Valdyr growled. 'If we can't do that, we'll not last the season.'

16

Not Worth Dying Over

Silacia

The badge of Silacia is the wolf, and that's what they are: pack animals who kill to live, produce nothing and steal all they can. They were the plague of the Rimoni and are no more contained by Rondelmar.

MYRON JEMSON, ARGUNDIAN, JOURNEYS SOUTH, 887

Venderon, Noros
Decore 935

Seth Korion cantered into the gaggle of aides and runners clustered below a hill a mile north of Venderon. The town was a grey-stone, red-tiled blotch amid burnt-out fields of corn and wheat, with a small river barely a foot deep winding lazily through. He found his junior aides, Rano Culmather and Frim Mortas, arguing with a battle-mage. He had to interrupt twice before they recognised him.

Tempers are short, he thought. Destroying Lukhazan had been trauma enough, but he'd had reports that the enemy were getting too close for comfort now. Another few hours and they'd be within range for Keshi spells to counter their large-scale Earth-gnosis. Suddenly the fate of his retreat south was coming down to fine margins, even though the enemy were still many miles away.

'Culmather, come with me. Mortas, deal with whatever the issue is.'

Mortas faltered. 'He says a scout is missing and—'

'Listen to what he says, then decide, Mortas. You have my trust.' Seth deliberately turned away, forcing his subordinate to take the decision. He focused on Culmather, who, even though only a year younger than Seth, was inclined to treat him like a father. 'What's happening, Rano? Is there a delay?'

'No, I think we're ready, sir,' Rano Culmather replied. 'The Earth-magi are just arguing over the magnitude of the earthquake required.'

'Tell them to err on the high side,' Seth said tersely. 'We only get one chance.'

'Yes, sir, but apparently the soil is porous and the water table is high, so they're worried the quake will shake water upwards through the soil and cause flooding that will bog down our retreat. Our wagon-train won't clear the valley for three hours – hence the delay.'

'Fine, three hours is acceptable.'

Culmather moped his brow. 'Yes, sir, but a Seer from Noros VIII – that's the Alpenfleur Legion – says she's tracking a group of Keshi Earth-magi and they're only an hour away from this valley – they'll be able to counter our earthquake when they get here.'

Countering a spell took a lot less energy and skill than casting one, and large-area spells like weather-gnosis, earthquakes and the like could be affected by someone inside the affected region, or even bordering it. Normally Seth found that reassuring, as it prevented lunatics from razing cities, but right now, *he* was that lunatic. 'What's in the wagon-train?'

'Supplies and refugees, sir. Three thousand people from here in Venderon.'

Seth considered. *If the seer is right, we have to act now . . .*

'Begin,' he said shortly. 'Warn the wagon-train, but get that quake started. I'd rather lose a few wagons than cede Venderon intact.'

Most days, command was just basic problem-solving, but even so, no solution was ever ideal and no one was ever entirely happy with him, no matter what he did. And *everyone* was happy to delegate matters upwards. In the end all he could do was make a choice and take responsibility for it.

He watched the mage-engineers as they created their protective circles, then linked hands, like ancient Sollan drui performing a pagan ritual. Minutes crawled by as ochre-coloured light glowed softly inside the circle, then sank into the earth. The birds went silent, the wind went still and all of Urte held its breath.

Then the ground shook and like everyone else, Seth dropped to one knee, releasing his reins and letting his mare, her eyes rolling, move away. Everyone staggered at another tremor, then another, and another, and suddenly they were all hanging onto the ground as it rippled in waves. He looked at Venderon and saw dust billowing upwards from the ground. Trees wavered, the ground rumbled, then a steeple crashed down, chimneys started smashing through the red-tiled roofs, the ground was torn apart like a ripped cloth and the straight road leading south shook into a squiggle.

The town vanished into a plume of dirty air.

Seth stood shakily, as Tadeus Tanderaum, head of his army's Ordus Artificio, approached. The mage-engineer's stout, rock-like form looked more solid than the ground he walked on.

'Success, I believe, sir,' the engineer boomed. 'Very soon, water will pour out of the ground throughout the plains, sir. *Liquefaction*, they call it: the water table being shaken upwards through the earth. Permission to inspect, sir?'

'Granted. Good work, Magister Tanderaum. Make sure the wheat fields on the south side of the town are burned behind us. The Alpenfleur Legion are currently our rearguard. Stay with them and accompany them south.'

They exchanged salutes then Seth took his aides and started riding south. 'Check on that wagon-train, Rano,' he told Culmather, 'but first, tell me about the terrain in front of us.'

'Once past Venderon, it's a slow, straight climb to Norostein,' Culmather replied. 'There's no more big towns – but no way to slow the enemy down, either.'

There are always ways to slow an enemy down, Seth thought grimly. *Most involve the sacrifice of men.*

Apart from the rearguard, his legions were now all south of Venderon, protecting a mass of refugees from Lukhazan, Venderon and dozens of smaller towns and villages, dots on maps that were now smouldering ruins among blackened fields. Venderon had grown up around a crossroads: the north-south road from Norostein to Jasten-berg, the western road to Lukhazan and the far less-travelled eastern road that wound through inhospitable country to Trachen Pass, which was closed through Decore to Febreux, buried under ice and snow. It troubled him that he really didn't know what might be out there, but the Shihad would have had to cross the highest part of the pass in late Noveleve and there was no evidence they'd done so. *But on the other hand, who's actually gone and looked?*

He turned to Frim Mortas. 'What was that about the missing scout?'

'Trachen Pass Road,' Mortas said. 'He's probably lost, but I told the tribune to find him.'

Seth nodded approval – he'd have done that whatever Mortas had done, provided he'd done *something*. It was indecision that paralysed an army. As it happened, he also agreed – and felt somewhat uneasy.

His senior aide, Andwine Delton, came riding back to join them from the valley floor. 'You should have seen it, sir,' he called. 'Water just rose up from the earth – the animals were terrified, and the people were on their knees praying.'

'What've we lost?'

'Four grain wagons tipped over. The grain's waterlogged, but we're trying to salvage what we can. I'm having the rankers take a bag each and getting the refugees to ditch anything unnecessary so they too can help carry the corn.'

'Good work,' Seth said, glancing left and right. They'd reached another crossroads where a burnt-out collection of houses still smoul-dered. 'What's this place?'

'Folks coming out of Trachen Pass who want to bypass Venderon and go south to Norostein come this way.'

Seth peered east, towards a deep green sea of trees, surmounted by the silhouettes of mountains among the clouds. 'So anyone traversing Trachen Pass could come *here*?'

'Yes, sir,' the aides chorused.

'Three guesses why that makes me nervous?' he asked rhetorically.

Before anyone answered, a low, shrill call echoed from above and they looked up to see dark shapes flitting through the clouds.

From the east, a trumpet sounded.

Venderon-Norostein Road, Noros

The lesson of Yuros, Waqar Mubarak decided, *is that weather matters: a lot.* In Ahmedhassa, he'd been oblivious to the climate; heat was heat and even the rainy season was really just a period of occasional rain. Winter, the wedding season, was a brief and mild drop in temperature, welcomed by all. Sometimes sandstorms blew in from the deep desert, but mostly the skies remained blue and the air still and hot.

But in Yuros every day brought change. Rain was always lurking and the winds were seldom still. Temperatures rarely soared – but they could sure as Hel plummet. *How do the Yurosi stand it?*

He was wrapped in oiled leathers, using the gnosis to stop both himself and Ajniha from freezing. Waqar tried to peer through the swirling clouds while the roc shrieked miserably. They were gliding at two thousand feet, mostly engulfed in murk, occasionally dipping into clear patches. Scared of colliding, he constantly pulsed warnings, and the others were doing the same.

Then they burst from a bank of murk and found themselves over Venderon. It must have rained recently, because the ground was flooded and the streets were like streams. Then he peered closer and swore when he saw the damaged buildings.

Dear Ahm, they've destroyed another city. We'll never house anyone there.

He'd sent Earth-magi with the advance guard to try to prevent further gnostically induced destruction, but evidently they'd failed. He took Ajniha into a slow turn northwards, buffeted by a crosswind and lashed by rain, and quickly found that advance guard, just north of the ruined town. They were led by a column of plodding elephants who were churning the main road to slush. *That's not going to help our men either.*

Baneet and Fatima were at his shoulder with the newer flyers ranged behind. Then Fatima spotted more rocs, returning from a patrol into the south.

<*Brother!*> Waqar called, spotting Tamir, who'd been leading the scouting party, <*What's happening?*>

<*We've caught up with the enemy rearguard!*> his friend replied excitedly. <*They're pinned down, five miles south of here. Attam's there and he's throwing everything at them.*>

Attam's men must've finally arrived from Trachen Pass, he thought, adrenalin beginning to pump. <*Any losses?*>

<*Three,*> Tamir's voice was pained. <*We ran out of javelins and it's too wet for the bows. You can hardly see when you go in and the arrows come out of nowhere.*>

<*We'll take it from here,*> Waqar called over his shoulder, as their birds crossed. <*See you tonight in camp – bring arak–*>

Then Tamir was gone and Waqar took his birds down, swooping through low clouds and bursting out over a chaotic scene. As Tamir had reported, Attam's vanguard had indeed caught the retreating Rondians, at a crossroads south of the wrecked city of Venderon. There were thousands of men below.

<*Finally!*> Fatima exclaimed.

<*Ai,*> Waqar replied calmly, though his throat was filling with bile at the thought of all the indiscriminate killing to come.

Most of the Rondian legionaries were lined up facing the southeast, where Attam's heavy Dhassan cavalry were arrayed; more were emerging all the time from the Trachen Pass road. The rain was intense, forcing the Keshi horse archers to go in close; they were paying a high price against the Rondian crossbowmen.

<*Listen,*> Waqar called to his flight, <*we'll go in on that easterly wind, fast and hard. Javelins for the first three passes, then mage-bolts. It's too wet for arrows.*>

He was buffeted with acknowledgements, eager and tense, then he sought Baneet on an intimate contact and reminded him, <*Don't use the spear. It's just a skirmish, not worth dying over.*>

<*Ai.*> Baneet sounded distracted and Waqar realised he was locked in a mental embrace with Fatima. For a moment he caught a waft of her

scent and broke the contact, embarrassed. For an aching moment he missed Bashara, then he angrily refocused on the fight to come. He allotted targets, then called, <*Now, now, now!*>

He touched Ajniha's right flank and the giant eagle banked and hurtled downwards, the tailwind speeding them along as he plucked a javelin from the saddle-sheath, kindling gnostic fire on its tip. Rain lashed his shielding, making the world a smear, but he picked out a wagon, hurled his javelin and saw his missile ignite – but the wagon was sodden and the flame didn't take. Then Ajniha was streaming upwards again, the rest rising in his wake.

He took them around again, seeking enemy magi, or any target of worth. *Someone who can make me feel like I'm fighting, not just killing.* A glimpse of gnosis-flame caught his eye and he spotted a black-robed woman with streaming grey hair. He was lining up the throw when suddenly the air round him concussed, Ajniha screamed and they went hurtling sideways. He hauled on his reins and took the roc upwards, but one of his birds went streaking straight into the turf, its body alight; the rider shrieked right up until impact.

<*Ballista!*> Baneet shouted, as a Rondian windship swam out of the mist and another eight-foot bolt streaked across the sky and speared a second bird. Then the big warrior shouted, <*It's mine!*>

<*Baneet, no!*> Waqar and Fatima shouted, but Baneet had already plucked the crystal-headed spear from his saddle-sheath and was setting it like a lance. Waqar called again, but Baneet's mental shields locked him out.

<*Chod! Get clear!*> Waqar howled, hauling Ajniha aside as a livid white bolt of energy burst from Baneet's weapon at close range, slamming into the enemy windship, smashing a hole in the hull–

–and with a massive blast, the keel exploded, sending lethal shards of wood hammering through the air in all directions, amidst a bubble of searing heat. Waqar hung on grimly, the straps straining, as Ajniha spun through the air, until at last she flattened out, awash with terror and relief. He hauled on the reins and brought her round, his eyes desperately seeking.

He was in time to see the warbird hit the ground, crushing a wagon and horse team. For fifty yards around it, men had been flung outwards in a circle and few were moving. Among them were torn and broken giant eagles, at least three who'd failed to get clear.

Roaring, 'BANEET!' Waqar sent Ajniha streaking back into the fray while faces stared upwards in terror. Fatima followed, crying her lover's name at the top of her voice.

<Fati–> came an agonised response.

<There!> Waqar shouted. Before Ajniha had even landed he was ripping at the straps and vaulting into the mud beside his friend. At first he didn't realise that Baneet, on his back, was lying among the shredded remains of his roc, so dismembered was it. Baneet was only a little better: his clothing was blackened and burning, and wood splinters were jutting from bloody wounds in his torso and right thigh.

'You were too close, you idiot,' Waqar shouted, while his brain screamed in denial, but Fatima pushed him to one side and hurled herself onto her lover, her hands already bleeding healing-gnosis.

Suddenly Waqar's senses screamed and his shields burst into life just in time to deflect a thrown javelin. He shoved the first of a trio of Rondian rankers aside, parried the second and blazed fire into the third's chest, blackening his armour and throwing him backwards.

'The raghead's a rukkin' mage!' one yelped, and the three of them took to their heels and ran. Rain sleeted down, killing visibility, but the roar of battle was all round.

'Waqar,' Fatima wailed, 'he's stopped breathing – Bani!'

He turned at the sheer despair in Fatima's voice to see her bunch her fist, then hammer it into Baneet's chest. White light exploded, Baneet convulsed, his whole body jerking, and his eyes flashed open.

Then they fell closed again and he went utterly still.

'Bani!' Fatima screamed. 'BANI, NO!'

Waqar felt his world lurch. Ajniha was squawking: the mist swirled and hooves thudded. From above, one of his fliers called, a warning, <Prince Waqar, watch out!>

My friend is dead . . . Baneet's dead . . .

He spun about him, seeking – and there was the deadly spear, its crystal dead, lying in the grass beside Baneet. He staggered towards it, all his ancestors booming out the need for vengeance, a chorus of fury. *It's my duty, I must take up—*

'No!' Fatima's hand closed on the spear. Her eyes blazed and the crystal shimmered back to life.

Dear Ahm, no . . .

'Waqar,' she said in a toneless voice, 'let's go.'

She called her roc and propelled herself with kinesis onto its back as it glided by. Waqar stared after her, then turned to look at his friend, but Baneet was scarcely recognisable. His big frame was shrunken in death, half his hair was missing and his face was blasted by fire and streaked in blood. Everything was *wrong*.

Ajniha called again, as if to summon him, and this time he obeyed. Almost before he had mounted, she was leaping into the air, wings spreading, and they shot upwards like an arrow. Oblivious to the battle, hating the war's very existence, he turned the roc's face north. Behind him he heard Fatima call his name, then he felt something like a mental shrug and she began barking orders, readying the flight for the next pass, her voice devoid of emotion.

Tears streaming down his rain-lashed face, Waqar took Ajniha home.

'Milord, please, we have to get you out,' Andwine Delton was saying, but yet again, Seth waved him away.

'We're not leaving,' he snapped back. 'This is where we *must* be.'

Around them, with the air reverberating to shouts, screams, hissing arrows and clanging steel, runners were rushing hither and thither, bringing him the pleadings of his legion commanders. Just picturing the battlefield, the shapes of the lines and who was where, was almost impossible.

'But Milord—' Delton tried again. Seth ignored him.

Turning to Culmather, he asked, 'Where're our warbirds?' He'd expected to see windships above, but could only see enemy skiffs and rocs.

'One got blasted and the other flew off,' the aide shouted above the clamour. 'It was the same weapon that destroyed the fleet at Collistein Junction, sir!'

Oh no, Seth thought, but he said calmly, 'Thank Kore they only used it once.'

'But what if they're targeting us now, sir?'

'Then there's nothing I can do about it. Are there any reserves left?'

'Just the emergencies, sir. Rionel Tyr's cavalry are trying to hit the enemy flanks, but there are more enemy horse coming.'

'Then bring him in. We can use his cavalry to counter-charge if they punch through.'

This was his worst fear: hordes of Keshi horsemen had emerged from the Trachen Pass road and while some attacked, pinning down his forces, the rest were trying to outflank him to the south, attempting to cut him off. The Waystar Legion, guarding the crossroad with Jelaska's Argundians, had been facing sustained attack for hours now, from both mounted archers and lancers. Bricia X was facing the enemy to the south. So far they'd managed to throw back three determined pushes, but the real concern was his northern flank, where his own Bricia II was fighting alongside Noros VI, the Silver Hawks. Enemy footmen supported by horsemen and elephants had caught them up, so any kind of breakthrough would hit the baggage train; thousands of women and children would likely be taken. Old men among the refugees were picking up weapons and joining the lines, for all they were unarmoured and often infirm – and there were even women fighting now – some had been dragged from the lines by the Keshi, screaming as they were borne off.

He was now behind the lines of Noros VI, the Silver Hawks, who were barely holding. They were spread too thin and badly outnumbered; even their commander, Legate Yarronis, had been fighting in the lines. One more big push by the enemy, who had more men flooding onto the battlefield every minute, and they'd give way.

Then another flight of giant eagles swooped by, raining down javelins again. Seth and his men shielded frantically, but the projectiles were too swift to block easily. Right before his eyes, the runner who'd just reported took a javelin in the midriff that exploded. Pilus Lukaz's rankers were battered yet again, with the loss of two more. The veterans were hunched together praying, all except Bowe, who was gesticulating furiously at the heavens and shouting, *'Kore, you fucker, save us!'*

Not sure that'll bring divine favour, Seth thought, turning back to Delton. *Project calm*, his father would have said. 'It's time to bring the reserves into the line.'

'Aye, sir.' Delton's face betrayed the import of the order: *Reserves In* was the last order before *Every Man for Himself*. 'Milord, you're too valuable to lose here. You really must be ready to escape.'

Kaltus Korion had never fled the battlefield, or abandoned his troops to die.

Nor will I.

Attam Mubarak sat on his warhorse, salivating. Rainclouds still covered the battlefield, but in his mind the sun was shining, because this had the taste of victory. In the valley below, strung out over a mile or so, twenty thousand Rondian rankers had been brought to heel, overtaken and were now being battered into submission. His cavalry held the high ground east of the enemy position, ready for the charge, while his infantry were now streaming into the fray, though they were exhausted from the march.

When we break these slugskins they will open the gates of Norostein to us.

The aether throbbed and he felt his father's presence. <*My son, you have found them?*>

<*Sal'Ahm, Great Sultan: I'm about to destroy them,*> Attam snarled back. <*Three legions at least, trapped south of Venderon with nowhere to run. The Korion is here, too.*>

Rashid's face filled his inner sight, his father's face looking uncharacteristically worried. <*Have a care: that one has escaped the noose before.*>

<*Not this time, Father. I'll mount his head on a spear as a trophy.*>

In response he felt a touch of concerned affection. <*My son, I have not said this enough: you are my eldest and my heir, and I am proud of you.*>

That was unexpected. Attam had always felt that Xoredh, the smarter one, the deeper thinker, was their father's favourite, even though Rashid had always told Attam that the throne would be his, and his alone.

He wondered what Xoredh had done to be discounted so emphatically.

<*Thank you, Father. I dedicate this victory to you,*> Attam sent back, unable to keep emotion from his mental voice. Then the link was broken and he was back in the present, with his prey finally at bay.

'Are the elephant units in position?' he asked young Hasif of Peroz, a royal bastard and mage who acted as his message-bearer. The relay-stave in Hasif's hand was turning the rain hitting it to steam.

'They are, Great Prince.'

'Then send them in: hit them where they're weakest and the lines will fold.'

Attam waited until that attack was launched, then turned to his cavalry commander. 'Are we ready, Efa?'

'We're ready, Great Prince,' Efarim Tulk rumbled.

Attam wiped the rain from his head and replaced his helm. 'Then let's go and kill Rondians.' He signalled to the trumpeters and a series of brazen blasts heralded his movement to the head of the serried ranks of Hisan-Thaqiil. The Dhassan riders had been trained in the Rondian ways of mounted fighting; they might not be knights by title, but they were mounted, armed and armoured the same way.

'Hisan-Thaqiil, forward!' the cry rang out, and as one, the first heavy hoof-fall slammed down and like a wave, they flowed into motion, trotting down the slope towards the enemy and making the ground shake . . .

'Piru-Satabam III, advance!' Hazarapati Selmir shouted from the rearmost rank as rain began to pelt down again. Sanjeep nudged Rani into motion and the front rank of ten great beasts began to plod forward across the battlefield to the low rise where the enemy now stood at bay. Latif and Ashmak shared an ironic look.

'Will our brave commander *ever* lead us from the front?' Ashmak wondered.

'When the enemy are already running,' Latif answered, checking his bow-string was waxed and that his quivers were properly covered. The cramped turret of the howdah swayed rhythmically as Rani picked up speed.

Ashmak was peering ahead. 'At least we're not going up against those bastards,' he said, pointing at the Rondian centre, where thick lines of grey-cloaked men with tear-shaped shields were arrayed, bristling with spears.

'Argundians?' Latif muttered. 'See that black-robed jadugara behind them? She was at Riverdown. They say she can rip a man's soul from his body from a hundred paces.' *Jelaska*, he remembered: an old woman with a husky laugh who'd visited him in his prison-suite at Ardijah to play tabula – to understand the Eastern mind, so she'd said.

'Riverdown,' Ashmak echoed. 'This victory will erase it, Brother. We'll take the witch's head for you.'

Nothing will erase Riverdown, Latif thought. *All my nightmares were of that time – until the Masked Cabal murdered Salim and my family and gave me new ones.*

The elephants began to jog, splashing through puddles and mud, eating up the distance to the front line. Soldiers parted before them, shouting blessings and encouragement, while above, the roc-riders wheeled and dived, blazing gnosis-fire. The clamour rose as they surged through a retreating group of Lakh spearmen, one of them carrying a screaming white woman over his shoulder. Latif readied his bow beneath his blanket, trying to keep the string dry until the last moment, then Ashmak shouted, conjuring shields as enemy arrows flew at them. Sanjeep wailed a prayer for Rani's well-being and Latif's hands blurred into motion.

Nock-draw-aim-loose, nock-draw-aim-loose, nock-draw-aim-loose: three arrows flew in quick succession, then Rani slammed into the shield-wall, trunk lashing and tusk-spikes flailing. The brutal collision made the howdah sway wildly, but below them the thin line was buckling. Three men were crushed as Rani staggered through, lurching as a spear pierced her flank, but it was a shallow gouge only and the Rondian spearman was knocked aside, then crushed. On either side of them, other elephants burst through.

Latif shot the next spearman he saw below, only realising as he died that he'd been a woman. Ashmak blazed fire into the reserve lines and then they were overrunning the old men and women and wounded rankers who'd been trying to stem the tide; those reserves were effortlessly swept away by Lakh and Keshi spearmen rampaging through the gaps the elephants had made. They butchered the wounded men, but contented themselves with clubbing to the ground those women who couldn't fight well enough to need killing.

Ashmak slammed a heavy hand onto Latif's back, the wordless relief of survival, as they reached clear space behind the broken lines. All but one of the elephants had made it through. Latif saw Selmir – still in front of the old enemy position, standing in his howdah, arms raised to the heavens as if he alone had won this moment.

Then a cold blast of energy gusted in from the left and they turned as one to see a new mist rising from the ground, this one violet in hue. The temperature dropped dramatically.

Then someone gasped, '*Ahm most High*–'

A pale smoke emanated from the mouth of a corpse and taking man-shape as it rose, becoming part of the mist, from whence came an inhuman wailing, not from human throats but from the fog itself: a daemonic shrieking of grief and horror. To Latif it sounded like the newly dead, despairing at the eternity laid before them.

Jelaska is a necromancer, he remembered.

A wave of terror struck the Shihadi men, an unreasoning need to flee that bypassed the head and went straight to the heart – and the feet. They stumbled backwards a few steps, then even the animals succumbed, blundering about until suddenly they were all running, men, horses, elephants, unseeing and uncaring, bowling over anyone in their path, screaming for mercy as they pounded along . . .

It didn't last, of course: Ashmak and his fellow magi roared out counter-spells and shortly thereafter, most of the men and elephants pulled up sheepishly, west of the enemy lines, no one quite looking at each other. Even Selmir didn't have the nerve to berate them – he too had been at Riverdown and Latif could see that he too remembered the Argundian jadugara. No one was in any hurry to return to the fray.

The place where they'd fetched up was a small rise affording a view of the battlefield. Selmir decreed he was awaiting new orders, a fine excuse for standing round doing nothing. The terrifying mist was gone now, but the Argundians and Rondians had used it to pull back another two hundred yards and reform into shorter lines. But they were far fewer, and hundreds of refugees had been killed or taken; already the screams of the captured women were mingling with the howl and clatter of the battlefield.

War makes savages of us all. Latif closed his eyes, praying for Ahm's forgiveness.

Just then, the ground quivered; they could feel it even high up in the howdah on Rani's back, and he opened his eyes just as the wind lifted and the rain eased. As if a curtain had been pulled aside, they could now see the slopes to the southeast, where the massed ranks of the Dhassan heavy horse, Prince Attam's much-vaunted Hisan-Thaqiil, were trotting forward, towards the enemy centre.

'Holy Fire,' Sanjeep blurted, 'look at them all.'

They stared as the charge began to pick up momentum, rank after rank of horsemen plunging down the half-mile slope, spears held high, trumpets braying.

'Dear Ahm, who can stand against that?' Ashmak breathed.

'Sir, we'll never stand,' Delton was pleading. 'Sir, please come out of the lines. You need to direct the fight—'

I'd love to, Seth thought, *but there's no need for tactics now. There's only this.*

He could take seeing battle up close and giving the hard orders; it was the actual fighting that sickened him, paralysing him. There was something about having a sharp point stabbed at him that turned his legs to jelly and befuddled his mind so badly he could barely remember how to shield or parry.

Dear Kore, make death quick . . .

The charge of the enemy heavy cavalry, a solid mass of steel-encased lance-bearing knights, was making the ground shake. And behind them, another mass had appeared, lighter horses bearing maroon- and grey-cloaked riders who were galloping hard; they'd caught up with the rearmost lines of cavalry and were set to follow them through.

Seth could hear the serjants bawling, 'Long spears! Crouch, brace and hold! Aim for the horse, not the rider!'

They were the right tactics, but unless they stopped the first rank dead, the second would go right through them, and then it would be every man for himself, fighting until he fell. Seth thought of Carmina and his daughters. *Did I tell them I love them enough? Do they know?*

'Thank you, Andwine,' he said, shaking his hand. 'Let's give our best.'

'Yes sir,' Delton said thickly.

Then someone said, '*What in Hel . . . ?*'

The maroon-clad light horse, careering down the slope at twice the pace of those in front of them, had hit the rearmost heavy horse – and slammed their lances into the Dhassan knights' backs. Then out came swords – *straight swords* – and they began carving into the next rank, while those in front, their vision constrained by visored helms, their hearing non-existent, ploughed on oblivious.

'Someone's fucking them in the arse!' Serjant Bowe roared, as all along the line the Bricians began to notice. 'Give it to them, you bastards – right up the jacksy!'

How appropriate, Seth thought, staring as another rank of Dhassan heavy horse went down, then another. Then finally *someone* – a mage, probably – managed to get a warning to the front Dhassans and they began to wheel – but the maroon-clad newcomers were right amongst them now and butchering the enemy pitilessly. Some of the Dhassans tried to turn and fight, while others tried to plough through Seth's shield-wall, where the long boar-spears were braced and waiting. He winced as dozens of horses ran themselves onto three or four spear-heads at a time before collapsing, their thrown riders swiftly engulfed and pinned down while spears and swords were rammed through their bodies.

Seth noted with shaky appreciation the professionalism of their mystery deliverers, the way two or three of them would target a single Dhassan, blindside him and bring him down, and the accurate, if brutal, killing strokes that followed. The grey-and-maroon-clad horsemen were using their now superior numbers, momentum and the higher ground to deadly effect – and suddenly there were no enemies between them.

His Bricians were shouting and crowing, jumping up and down in sheer relief.

Seth took a moment to survey the battlefield: to his left, the remnants of the enemy cavalry were now pelting back down the slope, towards the north, but a few drew off and he glimpsed the Mubarak's personal lion banner and saw a shaven-skulled Keshi staring back at him; he could feel hatred rolling off the Mubarak prince, until he turned his mount and galloped away.

A shrieking sound came from above and he looked up at a wedge of giant eagles swooping in. The rider of the lead bird was carrying a spear with a glowing head which was levelled, more or less, at where he stood. He bellowed a warning, but even as he did a storm of mage-bolts rose from different points around him, lancing into the eagles and turning the enemy shielding scarlet, then a ballista shaft ripped through the air and the enemy birds scattered – and the glowing spear never spoke.

Seth stared after the birds as they swooped away down the valley and only then realised he'd forgotten to breathe. *That was a close thing*, he thought shakily. *He was aiming for me*.

He muttered a quick prayer, then asked no one in particular, 'Well, how're we all doing?'

A glance down the valley told him the answer was, not so badly any more. All the enemy units were now falling back. The left was still intact – just, maybe, but Jelaska was already busy reinforcing it. The centre was still strong, and the lethal enemy cavalry had been smashed by the newcomers, whoever they were. Most importantly, their road south was still clear. Dusk would be soon upon them, and with it, the chance to slip away.

Another chance to master the art of retreating, he thought wryly as he walked through his men, projecting nonchalant calm.

The grey-and-maroon-clad riders were very well equipped and oozed that cool competence that only came with experience. They had reformed in front of his lines as if on parade. They were a right mix: olive-skinned Rimoni, lean, swarthy Silacians and Estellani, blond Argundians and other Northerners, bearded Bricians and dour Noromen. So, mercenaries, with the badge of a gold coin.

A lean rider in a velvet cloak trotting down to greet him removed his helm to reveal a well-remembered visage: a ferret-clever Silacian sporting a black goatee.

'Anyone here know the way to Norostein?' the Silacian drawled.

'Ramon Sensini!' Seth exclaimed, unable to stop a huge grin breaking out over his own face. 'Have you never heard of "communication"?'

'Si,' Ramon said airily, as he dismounted, 'but surprises are more fun. Forgiven, *amici*?'

'Forgiven, and forgiven!' Seth threw his arms around his old friend and pounded his back, hugging him for what was probably an embarrassing amount of time, then held him at arm's length, barely holding back tears of joy.

Suddenly, anything seemed possible again. Even victory.

Waqar was still awake when Fatima returned, but he was nowhere near sober. Tamir was passed out beside him, surrounded by empty arak flasks. The pavilion was scorched and the cushions shredded. He couldn't remember how or why.

'Fati?' he slurred, looking up dazedly.

Fatima was cradling that *Ahm-bedamned* spear, its crystal pulsing in time to her heart. She stopped at the flap, shaking her head slowly. 'Poor Waqar.'

He tried to stand, lurched, almost fell then grabbed a tent pool and clung to it, swaying. 'Fati, I'm sorry. You were . . . in love. Baneet *loved* you . . .'

'I know,' she said. She leaned the spear against a pole before walking to him and hugging him. She looked utterly composed, as if entirely at peace with the world.

'I can't imagine . . . what you're going through,' he said, trying to empathise through the swirl in his head.

She stroked his face with her right hand, which was utterly freezing. 'I'll be fine, Waqar. I'll see him Paradise soon. It's you I worry about, when we've all left you behind.' Gently, she pushed him away.

'Fati,' he pleaded, trying to embrace her again, 'stay – have a drink.'

She planted her hand in the middle of his chest and shoved gently, sending him sprawling in the mess. 'Leave, Waqar. Go and find Jehana. Learn what you need. If you stay here, this war will kill you.'

She turned to go and he shouted back, 'It'll kill you too!'

He didn't need to see the look on her face to know she didn't care any more.

'No – *Fatima!*' He tried to stand again, but ended up just grovelling at her feet. *Remember?* he wanted to scream, *we were lovers too—*

But that was already ancient history.

'Go to sleep,' she said sadly.

Then she was gone, and a few moments later the alcohol struck him like a cobra-bite. He fell sideways as Creation went mercifully black.

17

Not Broken, Not Dead

Constructs

The Beastarium of the Pallas Animagi is vast, covering acres of ground north of the city, and is heavily fortified, primarily to keep things inside. Within, all normal morality is shed; only the rigorous pursuit of knowledge matters. The animages build new creatures from the parts of others, recreating the bestiary of legend: pegasi, griffins, basilisks and all the creatures of Lantric myth, and others yet unnamed.

BAEL FORZYN, RENEGADE ANIMAGE, HEBUSALIM 867

Vantari Hills, Pontic Peninsula
Noveleve 935

Tarita, clad in only her burnt, frayed shift, knelt shivering in the icy slush. The rain and hail lashing her skin traced the welts and gashes left by the whips. Her left eye was puffed up and sightless; she tried not to probe the fresh gaps in her teeth with her tongue. The Chain-runes had been bound into joined iron manacles which confined her to the lashing post set in a clearing.

Tarita's body had been the lever Alyssa had pulled to get her way with Jehana; despite the initial contest of wills, the outcome had always been inevitable.

She fantasised about escape, but there were always two Hadishah tormentors on guard while the remaining windship crews salvaged whatever could be recovered from the wreckage of the crashed vessel.

The one I brought down, she thought vengefully.

But Jehana was a captive and Ogre was dead, plunged into the deadly tide. She was only alive because she had value. She wondered if she should be grateful for Alyssa not wanting some low-blood getting her valuable Ascendant womb with child; at least that had prevented rape.

'You're for Rashid himself, I wouldn't doubt,' the jadugara had crowed over her, 'or better yet, his sons.'

'Do they prefer their women beaten?' she'd managed to sneer through her split lips and broken teeth.

Alyssa had just laughed and let the men beat her up again, although nothing made her burn more than their pissing on her.

Jehana capitulated, of course. Yes, she would do as Alyssa said. Yes, she would go to Epineo. And yes, she would place herself at Rashid's command.

I've failed, Tarita thought miserably, *and I'll pay the price for decades to come.*

If she could have killed herself, she would have. She'd tried not eating, but a Hadishah mesmerist quickly forced her to capitulate – and they'd beaten her again, just for the fun of it. Not all the Hadishah were cruel – the tall, gloomy man they called Nuqhemeel restrained the very worst of them – but most of them took an unbridled delight in victimising her that spoke of cruelty bred or trained into them.

The rain finally blew over, leaving her freezing cold and trying to blow bloody snot from her nose. One of the guards emerged, bearing a platter of food. 'Ho, Merozain, you hungry?' he snickered. 'Or are you starving yourself again?'

She'd realised, belatedly, that she should harbour her strength, lest some opportunity miraculously arise, so she grovelled before the platter, eating by dint of burying her face in the mound of slush and trying to lap it up. The guard watched, utter contempt on his face.

'Ahm on High, look at her: just like an animal,' he tittered. 'The dirt-caste bitch is reverting to type, eh. I bet she fucks like a she-goat.'

'Don't touch her,' his comrade called. 'She's destined for the prince's harem.'

'Which one?' the first one asked.

'Xoredh, I heard.'

Tarita shuddered at the thought of the sultan's cruel second son, but even that didn't stop her gobbling frantically; then she was forced to endure the guards' gaze as she passed urine and defecated where she was chained.

'Dirty little bitch,' he sneered.

'Shut up and chuck her waste away,' the other man called. 'It's your turn.'

Tarita had been here for three days. From overheard conversation, she'd worked out that Alyssa Dulayne had already left for Epineo with Jehana.

You're not broken, she told herself for the hundredth time, glowering silently at the back of the retreating guard. *You're not dead.*

I'm not dead.

Luck had played a part, but Ogre's survival mostly came down to his will to live.

When he fell, it was straight into a small lagoon hollowed out by the powerful tides right at the foot of the cliff. No sooner had he smashed into the water than another wave came gushing into the pool, battering him against the rocks until he was bloody and almost unconscious – until he'd managed to grab a boulder and using Earth-gnosis, created a handhold. Once secure, he pulled himself above the surface of the water and frantically gasped in fresh air – then the next wave struck and rather than lose his fingers, he let go and was swept into the torrent again, tumbling helplessly as the wave receded, sucking him down a jagged channel towards the ocean half a mile away.

The next wave hurled him back into the base of the cliffs again, but through the spray and roar he saw robed men gliding down on Air-gnosis, presumably to make sure he was dead.

As the wave surged towards the sea-wall, he saw a dark opening. Knowing he was about to die, he used every ounce of strength left in him to flail blindly through the spume, clinging to barnacle-covered boulders that ripped his hands to shreds, to that crack in the rock. In his last-ditch attempt to survive, he exerted his gnosis and *changed*.

Master Naxius had never told Ogre what manner of beast had been merged with his human forebears to create him, but Ogre had an affinity for animagery and the easiest shape to assume was a shaggy thing with immense digging claws, which is what he became now. Using Earth-gnosis, he scrabbled to the upper surface of the crack and clung there as voices called outside, 'I thought I saw something—'

He felt a questing mind brush against his.

'No, wait . . . You feel that?' Then a light shone below him and two magi waded into the narrow cave. Standing waist-deep in the water below him, shielding and with mage-fire running down their blades, they peered around. It was inevitable that they would look up, so Ogre didn't give them the chance. He let go and dropped like a falling boulder, his raking claws plunging through shields that flashed scarlet then imploded. For three or four furious seconds there was just steel, flesh and gore. He caught flashes of terrified faces and heard himself roaring as another wave crashed into the cave . . . The new wall of water hurled him to the back of the cave, where he clung to a rock just above the flood and gulped in air, until most of the water was sucked out again in a terrifying rush, bearing the two dead Keshi away and leaving him gasping.

Others will find the bodies . . . must move . . .

With hands and feet gripping the stone, he started seeking . . . *seeking —*

—there! He sent a blast of destructive Earth-energy upwards into the crack he'd spotted and it widened, sending stone crashing down into the swirling water below. This was a softer seam, perfect for his needs, and he launched himself into it, using his beast-claws and drawing air with him as he burrowed up and away from the seawater churning below . . .

And then he burst up into the place he'd detected: a narrow tunnel bearing a small underground stream that now emptied into the hole he'd made. He was naked, his skin torn, his talons bleeding, barely able to breathe, but he heaved himself onwards until he found a perch just large enough to house him, only a foot above the surface of the stream.

He lay there, panting and shuddering, utterly spent.

Only then did he have the chance to grieve for Tarita and Jehana, taken, or already dead.

That horrifying knowledge crushed him, leaving him numb, until exhaustion claimed him and he fell into darkness.

*

Ogre woke some unknowable period of time later to find himself shouting. He'd been dreaming of Tarita: she was engulfed by enemy and he couldn't reach her, no matter how he fought. It was a mercy to escape the dream's sticky threads.

He lit a gnosis-light and peered about. His body had reverted to its natural form, but the wounds remained and every inch of him hurt. He was in a dark, relatively smooth tunnel of stone, somewhere inside the sea-cliffs, but he could hear and feel the waves, crashing so hard the stone quivered; even here, perhaps a hundred feet deep, the reverberating noise was deafening.

For a long time, he was unable to think past his despair.

But when he did start to function again, he could sense someone scrying for him, trying to penetrate the stone, and calls echoed in the aether: Keshi magi in communication. Fear impelled him to stir again.

Someone must've seen those bodies: they'll guess I'm in that cave . . . and if they find the hole I made, they'll know where I went. I have to move, and cover my traces.

The Master had taught him the art of moving through stone. He'd naïvely believed that Earth-gnosis would enable him to pass through the ground as easily as walking, but the reality had turned out to be quite different – and quite terrifying. Not only did he have to open up the way in front, he also had to push the debris behind him, creating a kind of mobile hole which needed constant maintenance; a badly formed space could collapse at any time. That took time, an immense amount of energy, and air, and as few Earth-magi had any affinity with Air-gnosis, suffocation was a constant risk. Wasting energy on gnostic light would have been crazy, which left him reliant on his own senses in the total darkness.

And then there were all the natural perils of the subterranean world: snake burrows, fox dens and poisonous millipedes, pockets of poisonous gases and, worst of all, trapped water that could fill your hole and drown you. The dangers were myriad.

And none of that took into account claustrophobia, which could destroy all training; even pure-blood Earth-magi could suddenly develop that petrifying fear of confinement.

But I've done it before . . . And perhaps Tarita or Jehana yet lived – perhaps they needed him? *If either lives, I'll free them, or die trying. I owe them that* . . .

So Ogre took on his clawed beast-body again. Summoning all he'd learned in the Master's painful, terrifying lessons, he started burrowing.

He progressed worryingly slowly, filling in behind him to obscure his passage, and the quality of the air was worsening, but he sensed another space ahead . . . He struck a curved chunk of bedrock first, though: the incredibly solid volcanic stone was the hardest to meld, but the soil around it was almost saturated, he could hear running water again and worse, his body was now coated in mud. Only then did he realise that the space he'd been making for was mostly water as well . . .

Do I enter this space and risk finding no more air? Or shall I push upwards, hoping I can reach the surface before I suffocate, knowing I will be exhausted and helpless . . . ?

He was so tired, he could barely think straight, but the wrong choice would be fatal.

He made his decision, conjured more Earth-gnosis, then summoning his last strength, went on digging his way towards the subterranean chamber below, drilling a cylinder as wide as his shoulders. The brownish light of the gnosis-energy was dazzling his light-starved eyes and although he was working as fast as he dared, he knew he was coming to the end of his endurance. If he didn't reach the opening he'd sensed soon, he'd collapse and drift into asphyxia. Head down, with blood rushing to his head and his breath running out, dizziness almost pushed him over into unconsciousness . . .

. . . when the ground beneath him gave way and he plummeted headfirst in a rush of debris, straight into bitterly cold water only a few feet below.

Thrashing like an eel, somehow he found the surface, conjured light and spotting a chunk of rock projecting above the water, scrambled onto it, out of breath, exhausted and dangerously cold. He collapsed, gratefully gulping down the surprisingly fresh air, onto the flattish surface and released his animagery shape as slowly as he could manage. He felt his body *shifting*, bones and soft tissues reverting to his true form, and lying there naked on the stone, the world faded away . . .

Ogre woke, his belly agonisingly empty, his lips cracked and throat parched, his entire body throbbing in pain. He had absolutely nothing – no food, no clothing, no weaponry . . . *But I'm alive*.

He crawled back down to the underground stream, drank heavily and then sat, shivering, taking stock. It wasn't a large stream, just a few feet wide, emerging into this subterranean cavern and then plunging into a tunnel and disappearing from sight. The walls were smooth, as if carved out over a very long time and often filled completely. There was nothing living in this space, not even fish or insects.

Soil was trickling from the hole he'd made; over time it might widen and collapse into this small space, but that wasn't an imminent danger; cold and hunger were the immediate threats. Trying not to think of what might await him, he lowered himself back into the water, called Air-gnosis and ducked into the tunnel, which quickly emerged into a wider cave open to the air where he could hear the roar of the sea below him. He hauled himself out of the stream just before it became a water-fall tumbling down the cliff-face and peered out cautiously at the sun. He judged it around midday, but how long it had been since the attack, he couldn't guess.

Best of all, gulls were nesting on a ledge right beside the hole. Before they realised he was there, Ogre had caught one by the neck, broken it and devoured the fishy flesh, then ate the screeching young as well; his ravenous need for sustenance completely overpowered any squeamishness.

Only when the nest was empty did he crawl back along the stream, drinking heavily to rinse the taste from his mouth. Animal instincts still warped his perceptions – too much time in beast-form and you became one, the Master had warned him.

But for now, maybe, he was safe, and that was enough. So he blanked his mind to anger, grief and the dark longings of the beast inside, rolled over and slept again.

*

When Ogre woke again, the rosy glow at the end of the tunnel told him it was near dawn. The aether was silent and he was starving, but peering out, he could see no one below and no windskiffs above. The tide had gone out again, no doubt soon to turn again.

Perhaps they'd given him up as dead? Perhaps the bodies of those he'd killed had been swept out to sea too fast to be noticed? Perhaps they'd moved on? He dared to hope. But in any case, he needed more food.

Using Earth-gnosis, he began to crawl, painfully slowly, up the cliff, until he hauled himself over the stony edge and collapsed, panting on the clifftop, and looked around. Far to the west, a line of lamps was bobbing along on the tidal flats. *Scavenger-folk? Perhaps it's even Epineo?* He pondered that for a moment. *If Alyssa has Jehana, would she take her straight to the sultan? Or would she take her to the place where she could open up her powers?*

The sun would soon be rising, and Ogre needed to hide. He clambered wearily up to the treeline before using animagery again; it didn't alter his bulk, but the lower-slung, more nimble form was better for burrowing through the undergrowth. He moved warily, sniffing and tasting the air on his tongue. Then he caught the scent of man and shivered in hungry excitement. The Keshi were still here . . .

18

A Season of Pleasure

Thaumaturgic Magic

The first magi were, with a few exceptions, practitioners of elemental gnosis, what we now call Thaumaturgy. These raw energies are regarded somewhat snootily today by the Pallas elites, as they have fewer of the subtle uses other crafts have, but elemental magic remains the cornerstone of Rondian military domination.

ORDO COSTRUO COLLEGIATE, PONTUS, 776

Pallas, Rondelmar
Decore 935

After the capture of the Rymfort and the Celestium, Imperial and Corani soldiers and magi laboured together, collecting the bodies and preparing them for burial, rounding up directionless Reekers and placing them into healing facilities, while dousing fires, organising food, blankets and coal for the refugees pouring back into Fenreach and Southside, as well as myriad other tasks. In Lac Corin, dozens of dead snake-men constructs had been trapped in the ice, their reptile bodies unable to deal with the sudden freeze.

There was a period of warmer, dryer weather as nature rebalanced and gradually the waters of the Siber melted the Aerflus; although the Bruin remained frozen, the ice began to retreat steadily upstream. In the streets, a wary sense of carnival prevailed. Pallas was wholly in the hands of the empire again and the citizens felt a renewed sense of security.

Four days after the attack, Lyra convened her Royal Council. As sunlight streamed through the large window at the end of the room, on a rare day when life felt glorious, she formally opened the meeting.

It was purely psychological, she knew: the benefits of waking to a bright morning, rested for once because Rildan had finally slept through a night, and rejoicing at having struck a telling blow at her enemies. And being *royally* ridden every night since. Her eyes trailed to Solon's face then shifted before she betrayed them both.

It wasn't love; at least, not what she thought love should be. There was little levity between them, just an immersion in carnality. She was still a little appalled at some of the things he expected of her, but surrendering to desire had become addictive. The *intensity*, the sweaty intimacy, filled her senses, while her body responded to him like a yearling to a master horseman.

I wish I could have been this way for Ril. He deserved a better wife. Then she thought about that and amended her thinking. *No, he deserved a lover more aligned to his needs.*

'Milady?'

She realised they were all waiting for her to begin, while her mind was still in the bedroom. 'Gentlemen,' she exclaimed, 'I know you're all hugely busy, but with so much happening, we need to stay *abreast* of matters.'

She hadn't intended to use the word; it just came out, with lots of unwanted imagery. She pushed it aside and soldiered on. 'First of all, thank you all so much! I see light behind the clouds now, and that's entirely down to your efforts.'

Dominius Wurther was still sullen – he hadn't yet forgiven the Church raids – but Calan Dubrayle, Solon and Dirklan were all visibly tired yet energised.

'Please, your reports, gentlemen,' Lyra went on. She knew they all wanted to talk about the military success, but she didn't want that to dominate. 'Treasury first.'

'Milady, the Church confiscations proceed apace, but the returns are lessening,' Dubrayle reported. 'Those remaining have had a chance to conceal their wealth or send it on to the Celestium – but of course, now that Her Majesty holds the Celestium, there is opportunity–'

'Dear Kore,' Dominius exclaimed, 'your enemies within the Church are defeated – surely you can't mean to let this *thief* rampage through *my* demesne?'

'But the legislation wasn't just aimed at Ostevan,' Dubrayle observed. 'Think how much gold has been piled up under that dratted dome for all these years–'

'Calan,' Lyra reproved, 'it's the house of our Lord Kore, not a "dratted dome".' She bit her lip, her gaze going from one man to the other. 'However, I do require a full accounting. Apply the law and submit me the books.'

The grand prelate made disgusted noises, but Dubrayle just frowned. 'That could take months.'

'But the Treasury is now solvent, correct? And the bankers will see that our enemies have suffered a massive setback, so you should be able to secure loans again to tide us over until the next harvest?'

Dubrayle said reluctantly, 'Well, yes, although the Merchants' Guilds have hidden their money effectively and the Crown Bond issue is still lagging. But if I do have your permission fully investigate the Celestium . . . ?'

'You have it. Take your time – and get it right.' She looked at Dominius. 'In the meantime, nothing is to leave your treasury, Grand Prelate. I want full cooperation with the Treasury. Normal business may be enacted, but anything unusual requires our joint approval.'

'This is your hour of triumph, Milady,' Dominius observed sourly. A note of pleading entered his voice. 'For Kore's sake, let the policy end soon. *Please*, before you lose the love of every subject in your realm.'

'Our Queen doesn't want for love,' Solon put in, making her pulse thud at the double meaning; she realised he too was momentarily tongue-tied. 'What I mean to say is, we're seeing far less resistance to this policy now,' the Knight-Commander said, recovering quickly. 'The tale of her speech on that first morning and her near-assassination has grown in the telling. Many are saying that Kore saved her and blesses her – and you, too, Grand Prelate, for your wise return to the frugal Church of the past.'

'There never was a frugal Church in the past,' Dominius fumed.

'But now you're being given credit for one anyway,' Dirklan observed. 'Well done, Holiness.'

He glowered. 'You really are a piece of work, One-Eye.'

Poor Dominius, Lyra thought. 'You're our friend, Grand Prelate,' she reminded him, 'and your fellow counsellors shouldn't tease you. Your restoration is vital to the empire.'

'Then we will work towards that,' Dominius said, eyeing Dubrayle malevolently. 'At the moment the Celestium's still not safe, so I will remain in my Pallas-Nord residence. Please visit me soon, Majesty, where we can talk without interruptions.'

'I always think of you two as secretly the best of friends,' Lyra commented, somewhat optimistically. 'You've served together for so long that I can't imagine life without you.' She turned to Dubrayle again. 'Tell me, Lord Treasurer, what of the Imperocracy? It troubles me that you have to deal with two such important roles.'

Dubrayle blinked. 'Oh, it's no trouble, Majesty, I assure you–'

'He has too much power as Treasurer,' Dominius rumbled. 'Appoint a new Imperocrator before his megalomania grows beyond control.'

'Megalomania?' Dubrayle sniffed. 'Says the man who thinks himself "the Voice of Kore".'

'I *am* the Voice of Kore – it says so in his holy book. You're just a jumped-up clerk.'

'There is no precedent for one man holding two such powerful seats at Council,' Dirklan put in, heading off the altercation. 'It can only ever be an emergency measure.'

'But the emergency isn't over,' Dubrayle protested.

'You *are* the bloody emergency,' Dominius grumbled.

'I want candidates from within the Imperocracy by the end of the week,' Lyra announced decisively – she felt somewhat invincible this morning. *Eight hours' sleep and a good tumble – it's like medicine.* 'I'll interview them.'

'Let the Imperocrats apply directly,' Dirklan suggested. 'Otherwise the list might omit some good candidates.'

Dubrayle cast the spymaster a sour look. 'I resent the implication, Wraith.'

'Solon,' Lyra put in, to head off any more bickering, 'what's the military situation?'

The Knight-Commander sat up. 'What's left of Brylion Fasterius' main army – we estimate around three legions – has withdrawn to Essenbrook, forty miles north of Canossi, and I can tell you they are *petrified*. The deserters we captured are saying Brylion can't even convince them to march home to Fauvion until summer.'

'What are they attributing the storm to?' Dirklan asked.

'Weather-gnosis, at least to their men, but they surely know different.' Then Solon stopped, blushing bright red, and looked at Dubrayle. 'Erm, I . . .'

Oh Kore, Lyra thought. *He's just revealed my heretical power to the only man in the room who didn't know . . .*

The Treasurer arched his eyebrows. 'I'm not actually blind or stupid,' he remarked, 'and I do notice more than what's in my ledgers. Can we just assume I know and move on?'

Dirklan pulled a wry face, Dominius harrumphed and Lyra stammered, 'M-my Lord Dubrayle–'

He held up a dismissive hand. 'Milady, don't worry. It's a little hurtful not to have been formally told, but Dominius regards me as a heretic too, so welcome to the club.'

Dirklan burst out laughing, while Dominius muttered, 'Damned right you are.'

Lyra decided she really was invincible. 'Thank you, Calan. I appreciate your trust. I'm truly a loyal daughter of Kore, who loves the Church. My "heresy" is something I try to use only for the greater good.'

'I'm sure the Sacrecours might contest that, Milady, but frankly we here are so deeply in each other's pockets that we stand and fall together. Preserve your reign in whatever way you can and we all gain.'

'You're surely deep in *my* pockets,' Dominius grumbled. 'I've not noticed it the other way.'

'The Church avoided tax for centuries,' Dubrayle responded. 'I'll never catch you up.'

Lyra raised a hand to forestall another bout of sparring. 'Calan, there is no lack of trust in you. It's just that such a damaging secret was best kept to those who absolutely needed to know.' When he nodded his understanding, she turned back to Solon. 'Knight-Commander, please go on – and try not to spill any other of my dark secrets.'

'Yes, Majesty,' Solon said humbly. 'As I said, Brylion is out of the game for now. Likewise, Garod – the rivers and roads around Dupenium are empty and they've not even sent men to recover the bodies. He didn't suffer the losses Brylion did, but his barges and rafts were trapped on the Bruin about sixty miles upstream and the locals have reported hundreds of frozen bodies. There's already talk of the river being haunted.'

'We should arrange burials – they're on our land,' Dirklan put in, to which they all agreed.

'And as for the Celestium, our haul of enemies was impressive,' Solon said with a touch a satisfaction. 'Dravis Ryburn and Sister Pettara are dead and Maz Beleskey's captured. Only Lef Yarle and Ostevan escaped. So until spring, we may be secure.'

'But as I understand it,' Dirklan said, 'such storms cannot be conjured so easily in spring and summer.' When Lyra nodded, he went on, 'So we've only bought a reprieve. Garod's forces still outnumber ours and should they gain allies, our situation remains precarious.'

The table fell silent.

'That's why, come spring, I will formally end my mourning and remarry,' Lyra said, trying to sound calm. She wasn't sure how well she'd succeeded. 'What is the shortest possible mourning period in the eyes of the Church, Grand Prelate?'

'The standard is a year, to deter reckless entanglements,' Dominius replied, 'but that's just custom. The Church scriptures stipulate no less than three months: by Martrois, you will be free to remarry. And in any case, betrothal vows may be exchanged before then. You may consider yourself open for business right now,' he added, drolly.

'I still grieve my husband,' she replied, her eyes on Solon, 'but duty demands this of me. I am readying myself for that day. In the mean-time, what news of the Shihad?'

Solon shifted uncomfortably. 'Korion the Younger was right: the Shi-had have deployed only a holding force in defensive lines in the Augenheim Valley. The bulk of their armies march south to assail Norostein. The Noromen are burning their own towns and fields as they retreat. "We have scorched the earth and leave the enemy nothing" is what Korion's latest despatches say. He's gambling everything on his ability to hold Norostein.'

'If Rashid can't get his army into Norostein, they're going to freeze to death when the worst of the snows fall, certainly by Febreux,' Dirklan commented.

'Seth Korion,' Lyra said, tasting the ugly name on her tongue: House Korion had been a bastion of the Sacrecour cause for centuries. 'Where does he stand on the empire?'

'Disinterest,' Dirklan replied.

'Really?' Lyra asked. 'Doesn't Korion know that what happens *here* matters *everywhere*?'

'He's the Earl of Bres, nominally subject to the Governor of Bricia,' Solon said. 'Though in practical terms, that relationship works the other way round, as Bres is the only large city in Bricia, and Korion is *filthy* rich. He probably feels secure even from us.'

'He'll be a dangerous young man if he's the one to defeat the Shihad,' Dominius observed.

'Certainly secession is a risk, if he's victorious,' Dirklan answered. 'Rolven Sulpeter has issued warrants for his arrest for desertion, but no one's managed to have those enforced.'

'Is he married?' Lyra asked, wondering if this Korion might come a-courting in spring.

'He is,' Solon replied sharply, 'to a half-blood healer-woman he met on Crusade, a love-match, it's said. People claim his only concern is his family name and his duty to the empire.'

'*Family* name?' Dominius snorted. 'I knew his father, as evil a bastard as ever drew breath.'

'Oddly enough, I believe Seth Korion would agree,' Dirklan replied. 'I spoke to him when the generals were appointed a few months ago. He's level-headed and he believes in the *ideal* of the mage-noble. I can respect that.'

The other counsellors clearly thought this Seth Korion odd.

'Then the best place for him is *exactly* where he is,' Lyra decided. 'Should we rescind the arrest warrants?'

'I wouldn't,' Dirklan advised. 'They give us a hold over him, if we need one.'

'Very well,' Lyra decided. 'If he saves the empire, well and good: I'll give him a nice-sounding title.' *But if he then threatens my son's position, we'll crush him.*

The meeting moved on to more mundane matters after that, the usual round of accounts and court reports. As an hour slipped by, Lyra became increasingly distracted, watching Solon's hands and remembering the tunes they'd played on her body these past nights.

Finally, almost breathless with sudden need, she clapped, and announced, 'Gentlemen, we all have matters to be about. The next scheduled Council meeting is in three days' time.' She waited until they'd gone before she hurried from the room, feeling hot and constricted in her clothing, wanting to be naked, *wanting . . .*

Basia rose and moved to her side. 'Ask the Knight-Commander to attend upon me,' Lyra breathed in her ear, ignoring the way Basia's face stiffened. Of course she knew what was going on, and approval wasn't her prerogative.

You were making love to my husband behind my back. You don't have the right to criticise, Lyra thought defiantly, though rationalising was irrelevant, because this was about desire.

She was half-undressed when Solon entered and barely had time to turn before he seized her wordlessly and bore her down to the fur rug, turning her onto her back. It was almost frightening, but breathlessly exciting as well, to be *this kind of woman*. 'Dear Kore,' she breathed, 'my brain stopped functioning about an hour ago and I've been wet ever since . . .'

He gripped her hips, pushed himself into her, knocking the breath from her lungs, then rocked forward and began to thrust, bringing the simmering liquid heat inside her closer and closer toward boiling. She tossed back her head, grasping at his buttocks as they clenched, pulling him into her as he rode them both to a furious, grunting climax.

As they regained breath, looking at each other from inches away, she found time to wonder at herself. 'I've never been like this,' she whispered. 'I feel like I have a hungry beast between my thighs.' *Kore's Blood, that sounds crass . . .*

'A beast with two backs?' Solon said wryly, a conqueror's look on his face. He stayed inside her, clearly enjoying having her pinned beneath him.

She didn't mind too much either, but his weight became overwhelming. She slapped his buttocks. 'Out! Off!'

They got back to their feet, Lyra's legs wobbling at the pounding she'd just taken. She was still somewhat aghast at herself, though not regretful at all, nevertheless, a slightly awkward silence fell as they dressed. Their bodies spoke more fluently than their words, despite the intimacies.

'When will your courses begin again?' he asked, finally. 'I understand you'll be weaning Rildan soon.'

'Domara says probably in the week of the full moon. We'll have to be careful . . . I am *absolutely not* going to bear a child out of wedlock.' She bit her lip, because she felt like she'd just lost ground in her battle to maintain emotional distance. 'Solon, you know I enjoy what we're doing, but what I said still stands: this ends when I say so. If we make it to spring, I must be courted. I won't even look at you in public. They'll bring spies with them and the merest whisper could wreck our plans for an alliance.'

'But surely with your dwyma, you don't need allies, Lyra. You and I are sufficient.'

'No, you're wrong,' she said tersely. 'And it's not up for discussion.'

It's strange, she thought, *I still don't really like him, but I'll do this in a trice.* To which her darker side replied, *It's the rukking you want, not him.*

He didn't look happy, but he flexed his big shoulders carelessly. 'I don't need reminding.'

Perhaps love will come? she thought suddenly. *Perhaps this will forge it?*

Whether that was so or not, she still needed his loyalty, so she tried to offer him something. 'Solon, I'm asking for patience . . . Who knows, no one may want such a danger-beset wife. And I like how you feed my beast.'

'Then we'll feed it when we can,' he replied. 'See you tonight.'

He strode out, while she put a hand to her heart, which was still skittish. *If this is a mistake,* she thought, *so far it's a pleasurable one . . . But if it goes wrong, I'm going to be cringing at memories like these until I die.*

Dupenium, Rondelmar

The court at Dupenium gathered before their duke and Coramore saw that the courtiers weren't just shocked but *terrified*. Some power had reached across the miles to destroy not just one army but two. The reports were awful: half the men in Brylion Fasterius' command had died a dozen or so miles south of Pallas and thousands more perished on the frozen Bruin. Somehow, the mighty Sacrecour armies had been shattered without ever striking a blow, and their allies in the Celestium were also dead, or missing. The dream of regaining the empire was in tatters.

Everyone thought Coramore and her brother should be distraught, and in truth, Cordan was: he'd been watching the barges launch at Beckford and he'd been horrified at the things he'd seen when the storm broke – and the wagons full of frozen bodies afterwards.

But I'm laughing inside, Coramore thought coldly. *That's what Abraxas did to me: I have no compassion left.*

That wasn't to say she hadn't been powerfully affected: during that Hel-storm, each crack of lightning had blazed through her mind: she'd felt the thunder in her bones and heard the voice of Empress Lyra on the wind.

She did this . . .

Everyone here was talking about weather-gnosis, but she knew it was more. Every day, cloaked against the snow, she'd been creeping out to sit beneath the spindly, green-leafed brackenberry tree in the cemetery. It produced a new berry a day, which she diligently ate, and each time her sense of belonging deepened. And every night she dreamed of a much larger tree, one made of light.

The storm had come from that tree. She had no evidence of this, she just *knew*.

The much reduced court – whole families had left, grieving or too frightened to be seen with Garod any more – were listening to Helios Prelatus ranting about heresy: *dwymancy*, he said, was at the root of this abomination. Coramore, sitting beside Cordan, was listening dutifully while watching the clergyman balefully.

Then the sound of boots on stone came clipping towards the throne, Helios paused mid-flow, turned and then knelt as a man clad in scarlet and gold robes strode up.

Everyone went silent at the sight of Ostevan Pontifex.

The composure of the man, who had surely fled here through harrowing weather from the destruction of his own ambitions, was remarkable. A murmur rose around him as the courtiers recognised him, shooting sideways glances at Garod, who looked like he'd rather crawl beneath a rock than face his erstwhile ally now.

Coramore shivered and ducked her head, sensing something *more*. For the first time since she'd been purged of ichor in the queen's garden in the Bastion, she felt the appalling presence of Abraxas at the edge of hearing. It was all she could do not to flee the Great Hall. But no one else was reacting.

Can't they see it? she wondered. *Ostevan reeks of the daemon . . .*

'Ostevan Pontifex,' the herald belatedly announced, by which time Ostevan was already standing before Garod, bowing his head in cursory greeting: the senior man to his host.

Garod opened his mouth, then closed it again, lost for words, then settled for kissing the Pontifical Ring. Ceding leadership wordlessly.

'Greetings, Garod of House Dupeni, champion of the Sacrecours,' Ostevan said, his voice resolute. 'I come to you to confirm the tidings: the empress is unmasked! She stands revealed as the heretic and tyrant that we knew her to be: a pandaemancer, a creature of supreme evil, sits upon the sacred throne of Rondelmar – all who stand for the Light of Kore must unite to destroy her!'

His words rang through the silent hall, but if he'd thought to be greeted with loud cheers and vows of support, he was sadly disappointed. Silence reigned as the Dupeni mage-nobles looked from their duke to their self-crowned religious leader and back, visibly frightened.

'If you know what has befallen, you will know that House Sacrecour has been dealt a dreadful blow,' Garod replied at last. 'We're crippled, Pontifex. If the empress has such might at her fingertips, then we're powerless to act.'

A murmur of agreement greeted Garod's admission, while Coramore marvelled that Ostevan had the temerity to denounce another as evil when he himself stank of the daemon.

Ostevan drew himself up and raised his voice. 'Do not despair! I tell you as the Voice of Kore that hope is not lost: the power of dwymancy – *of pandaemancy* – is by its nature self-destructive and it *will* rip her apart: the ancient pandaemancers went insane and so too will she. And I tell you this: we will denounce her in every court from Argundy to Estellan, Hollenia to Brevis and throughout the south. She will be made known as the whore of the Lord of Hel that she is and the entire empire will rise against her!' Ostevan held out a hand of entreaty to Garod. 'Be the first to pledge her destruction, Duke Garod – become the natural ruler of the uprising against her tyranny. Destiny has marked you out as Kingmaker: lead, and all Yuros will follow!'

Coramore could hear the tide of whispers behind the words, the mesmeric exhortations that filled the aether, but no one remarked upon it, and all succumbed. Even before Ostevan had finished, courtiers were cheering; those around Garod were stomping and shouting their support as if none had ever doubted their power. She was distressed to see even Cordan swept up in the tide of emotion, joining the calls to *Burn the Heretic-Queen!*

Coramore felt it wise to join in, but even as she did, she felt Ostevan's eyes crawl from Garod to Cordan to herself and she shrank inside as the Pontifex's eyes narrowed in recognition.

But all he did was to join his voice to the clamour: 'Death to all tyrants!'

The Bastion, Pallas

After their transfer into Corani custody, Ari Frankel and Neif Coldwell were roped behind a mage-knight's warhorse. They were given rough boots, fed more or less adequately, but made to tramp twelve miles a day along country roads thick with snow. By nightfall they were exhausted, but their dreams were increasingly filled with what was to come: dungeon cells, torture, public condemnation and the noose.

After a week, they were loaded onto a ferry on the Siber River and chained to the railing, where they spent hours watching the shore float by. Eventually the ferry entered the swirling waters of the Aerflus.

'Aye,' the ferryman said to the knight guarding them, 'tellin' ye, nigh a week ago, 'twas: the whole Aerflus froze an' the Corani crossed on foot and rukked up old Ostevan an' 'is Reeker mates. It's meltin' now, but floes keep comin' down the Bruin, so the crossin' 'as become a game o' dodge the ice, tellin' ye.'

Ari stared, his gaze shifting from the Celestium to the Bastion, both coated in frost and overnight snow.

'Any news of that prick Ostevan?' the knight asked.

'Word is that he's fetched up in Dupenium,' the ferryman replied. 'We're at war, no mistakin' – Queen against Pontifex, and in our time? Half o' Kenside is burnt-out rubble, thanks to that bastard. We'll be dockin' at Tockburn today.'

'Just so long as we make the Bastion before sundown, I'll be grateful,' the knight replied, indicating Ari and Neif. 'I've got to get these two locked up and ready for trial.'

'What're they up fer?' the ferryman asked.

Neif roused, for the first time in days, and announced in a brittle voice, 'My friend is Ari Frankel, the man who speaks the truth rulers fear. His words make Kore Himself tremble.'

'There you have it,' the knight said amiably. 'Rabble-rousers, railing against the queen.'

'Well,' the ferryman drawled, 'we're abaht 'alfway 'cross – why not dump 'em 'ere an' save on rope?'

'Tempting,' the knight growled, 'but I'll not be the one to deny Her Majesty the pleasure of a good hanging.'

Ari felt his heart-blood chill, but he raised his chin, staring up at the Bastion across the icy waters, and said loudly, defiantly, 'Death to all tyrants.'

19

Epineo

Daemons and Ichor

It was Ervyn Naxius, Ordo Costruo researcher-turned-renegade, who discovered that daemons of the aether are composed primarily of an aetheric substance, which he blended with human blood to enable a daemon to be translated temporarily into our world. He called it 'ichor', and it's the basis of wizardry.

COVIS BALDYN, HOLLENIAN MAGE-SCHOLAR, DAMSTADT 811

The Vantari Hills, Verelon
Decore 935

Still in beast-form, Ogre slithered through the undergrowth, his senses alive to the wakening world. The sun rising over the eastern end of the Vantari Hills sent light streaking from the heart of the crimson and orange glow of dawn. Birdsong filled the air and smoke rose from three chimneys in the ruined village where they had been captured.

Now it was the Hadishah's demesne. From the bushes, he saw a wind-ship propped on wooden landing struts, guarded by at least two sentries. The only other Easterner currently awake was the wind-pilot, a Keshi woman in a bekira-shroud, who was recharging the vessel's keel.

Then he shifted to a better perspective and saw Tarita – and it took all his strength not to bellow in rage and burst from cover.

She was kneeling in the mud, her wrists chained above her head to a great wooden cross like an X set into the ground. Her head was hanging down, her matted hair covering her face. The skin visible through rents in her shift was cross-hatched with welts and open wounds. Her breath carried across the clearing, slow and thick with phlegm and despair.

He stared, his beast-mind seething as his claws flexed. But the Master had been a cruel, harsh tutor and he'd had no use for a mage-servant without discipline. That training enabled Ogre to suppress his anger and instead open his gnostic sight. He swiftly realised that Tarita was bound by a Rune of Chain, locking away her gnosis.

Tarita is Merozain, so the only one who could Chain her is Alyssa . . . It's beyond me to counter the spell . . . But then he saw Alyssa had chosen to bind the spell to the manacles, so they'd not wane in strength over time, or drain her reserves. That made the spell only as strong as the manacles.

There's a chance, then. But I'll only have moments . . .

The Hadishah camp was coming alive, so he backed into the brush and burrowed quietly into rotting leaves in the lee of a vine-covered boulder. With Tarita and the windship in view, he could see what he was facing. Another Keshi appeared, a tall, grey-haired man with a world-weary air, who bent over Tarita, lifted her chin, wrinkled his nose and called out, 'Feed and clean her.'

'Let the woman do it,' one of the sentries replied in a grumpy voice.

The grey-haired man straightened and looked set to vent anger upon the sentry, but the Keshi wind-pilot called, 'I'll do it.' She appeared at the side of the vessel, a small, bent young woman with exhausted eyes. 'I don't mind.'

The Keshi woman took a bucket to the stream, then returned and kneeling by Tarita, rinsed her with gentle hands.

The grey-haired Hadishah passed Ogre's hiding place. Scowling, he ordered the recalcitrant sentry, 'Get the fires stoked up – and if you tell me "Let the woman do it", I'll flog you myself.'

He stamped off, leaving the younger sentry muttering, 'That *matachod* Nuqhemeel's going to get what's coming to him one of these days.'

The camp was coming alive, revealing just eleven men and the female wind-pilot. Ogre wondered where the rest had gone; a dhou of this size would carry a crew of six and at least a dozen archers. The other vessel had crashed in flames, so he guessed most aboard would have been killed, but that still left at least seven men unaccounted for.

Did Alyssa take them up the coast? And is it Epineo?

He wondered where the rest of Alyssa's ships were, for she'd had dozens searching for them. Maybe now that Jehana was taken, they'd been sent away? That suggested there were things she didn't want the sultan to know about, which made Ogre even more anxious. Jehana was facing something awful . . . and he was out of his depth.

I need Tarita; she can unravel this. His eyes went back to his battered friend, so close, yet so hard to reach. He studied the Hadishah, trying to measure what he faced.

The wind-pilot was clearly a mage, and so too the grey-haired man, Nuqhemeel the *matachod*. There might be others. The Master had made Ogre a half-blood, so potentially he was stronger than anyone here, since most Keshi magi, products of the breeding-houses, were low-bloods.

I have a chance, but I'll have to do this right the first time.

He watched the men eat, then the crew loaded the windship, suggesting they'd be leaving soon. If he was going to rescue Tarita, it had to be in the next few minutes. Fortunately, all this activity meant their attention wasn't on the Merozain, and the pre-dawn gloom offered many shadows. He began to edge forward, still listening hard.

Then Nuqhemeel ordered the fighting men to collect their possessions and for a few moments Ogre could see no one. He let his animagery gnosis dissipate and the beast-shape bled away, leaving him in his half-healed normal body shape. He'd not have the giant claws and teeth, but his plan needed human fingers; and he had to suppress the animal rage simmering inside at the sight of his battered friend, or blood rage would engulf him.

I'll free her or die. Fuelled by that thought, he rose and broke cautiously from the undergrowth, flexing his fingers while trying to look every way at once. His luck held; he saw no one. He didn't go directly to the oblivious Tarita, but clambered through the open side-hatch of the windship. The hold was tiny for one of his stature, but he found what he sought: the windship's armoury and tools. He took a scimitar for

Tarita, then hefted the largest axe and returned to the hatch . . . as a crewman poked his head through the hatch, calling in Keshi, 'Who's there?'

Ogre abandoned stealth and burst from the darkened hold. The axe hammered into the man's rib-cage with a sickening wet thud. When he was hurled aside, another crewman was revealed behind him, and a Hadishah beyond. Their eyes went wide as they realised their danger, but Ogre was already blasting gnosis-fire at the distant Hadishah while his purloined axe crunched down on the skull of the second crewman, smashing it open like a pumpkin. Both dropped, already dead. Ogre leaped to the ground and hurtled up the small rise to where Tarita was chained to the cross-piece. He saw her battered face lift and twist his way–

–then the trap closed.

Light flared around him, sigils and lines burning as the air around him congealed so it was like wading in treacle. Tree-roots burst from the ground, lashing at his legs, stinging as they scored skin and wrapped round his big calves and ankles. He had a glimpse in the aether of Alyssa Dulayne's perfect face whirling in his direction, her eyes flashing in alarm.

He bellowed in rage, almost overbalancing as he tried to haul his limbs free, but blue fire was burning around him and Tarita. The entire clearing had been rendered into a giant holding circle, cleverly concealed from his gnostic sight by Alyssa herself. The roots wrenched at his legs and only his massive strength enabled him to take one final, futile step–

–which he used to steady himself, rip back his arm and hurl the axe.

An instant later he crashed to the ground – as the axe flew head-over-handle towards the nexus point where the manacle-chain binding Tarita's wrists was nailed to the cross-piece.

He threw true, and his strength was aided by kinesis. The well-honed axe-head struck deeply, smashing through the chain, and as light burst from the impact point, the links parted and the Chain-rune binding Tarita's wrists – and her gnosis – came apart.

Then the tree-roots dragged Ogre down. His eyes were dazzled by the flashing lights. Still not sure if he'd done enough, he sent the scimitar spinning through the air . . .

Tarita's manacles fell away and power surged back into her body like lightning, boiling in her blood as stars lit up in her brain. She saw Ogre go down and her heart almost tore, but there were men coming in from all sides, limned in shields, steel bared – and a scimitar was whirling straight at her.

She rose, blanking the agony of movement and the ripe stench of blood and sweat and piss in her nostrils, and caught the blade by the hilt. Utter hatred for what had been done to her fired her soul.

Right, you matachods, *let's see what you're made of . . .*

She flashed to Ogre's side, her shields battering away the first mage-bolts, and blazed back, punching arrows of light through the wards of the men converging on her and making them crumple. All the while she drew energy in, healing-gnosis to mask the pain – she could repair herself properly later – and raw power to *burn*, quite literally.

She seared the face off the first man, then carved the second, her worst abuser, almost in half. She threw a countering spell into the mess of strangling roots holding Ogre – *Bless him on High!* – and then she advanced, cutting down two men coming at her in a dazzling burst of light and steel. Circling back, she stood over her rescuer as he roused, so they could face those left together.

The young wind-pilot had been gentle with her . . . she could live. The greybeard had told his men not to mistreat her: maybe she could be merciful to him also? But he'd done nothing when they'd done so anyway . . .

Beside her, Ogre rose to his feet. He was battered, naked and radiating power. She was still stunned at his miraculous axe-throw and if they weren't still facing half a dozen foes, she'd have been kissing his feet in gratitude.

You came back for me, you wonderful, wonderful man!

But they weren't free yet, and Jehana was gone. She faced the grey-bearded Hadishah, the pilot and the remaining human crew and jabbed a finger at the older man. 'You,' she rasped, 'Nuqhemeel, yes?'

His face was ashen, but he nodded mutely.

'Where's Jehana Mubarak?' She'd got the impression he didn't like much of what he'd seen in Alyssa's service, but he was a veteran to a cause he likely believed in. 'I'm quite prepared to rip it out of you,' she told him, and she meant it, 'but maybe you'd rather live and let that *chotia* bitch Alyssa Dulayne face up to her own problems?'

Nuqhemeel shook his head, saying sadly, 'Our purpose is holy. I cannot betray it.'

Tarita sighed. 'Then let's pretend I'm sorry for what I'm going to do to you.'

'I know where she is,' Ogre rumbled, bringing her up short. 'I saw, when I was hiding. There's a scavenger village along the coast from here: Epineo, perhaps?'

Nuqhemeel flinched, which told her what she needed to know.

Tarita flashed Ogre a grateful look, struck again at his perception, even under stress. 'Ogre, you're my hero,' she told him fervently, and the big lummox blushed like a little boy. But he also pulled the massive axe from the wooden cross and snarled his defiance at the Hadishah, making them all take another step back.

'So, you know where we're going,' she said to Nuqhemeel. 'And Alyssa knows we're coming, as I just broke out of her Chain-rune. Do you want to die for her? I can think of more deserving causes for martyrdom.'

'She is a servant of our sultan,' Nuqhemeel said stonily.

'She's the Masked Assassin who killed Sultan Salim,' Tarita retorted. 'And now here's you, trying to help her secure Jehana – maybe you're a Mask too?'

Nuqhemeel looked troubled. 'We were assigned to her command. I've seen no Mask.'

'Obey and not think?' she sneered. 'Alyssa's working for herself, Hadishah. She's never given a shit about anyone else. You must surely have seen what she's like?'

The repressed disgust on the Hadishah's face said he had.

She had an idea. 'Ogre, go to her cabin and see what you find. We can wait.' Then she flashed him a grin and added, 'And find us some clothes, for decency's sake. Your overwhelming manliness is making these poor men feel small.'

Ogre laughed, although his thick body hair had kept his private parts mostly concealed. Her own modesty was in worse shape; her maamehs were all but hanging out of her ruined shift. Hopefully, her overwhelming womanliness was making these men feel even more inadequate.

Ogre clambered into the ship through the hold-hatch, while she kept watch on Nuqhemeel. Like a good soldier, he was weighing the odds of taking her on, now that Ogre was out of sight. 'You know I'm a Merozain,' she reminded him, 'so let's keep it peaceful, eh?'

He's an older man . . . He must have some retirement plans . . . Hopefully he wants to live through this . . .

Thankfully, Nuqhemeel settled back into watchfulness, as did his fellows.

Ogre clambered from the ship again, now with sack-cloth belted about his waist, carrying a bundle of rolled-up possessions. Some of those were Tarita's – her pack and the silver scimitar and book from Midpoint – but there was also a finely wrought carpet bag which he tossed at Nuqhemeel's feet.

The Hadishah reached down and opened it. His face dropped as he pulled out a copper Lantric mask, the exquisite lacquer-work depicting a heart-faced woman's beautiful visage. He stared at it, then shuddered. 'I was in Sagostabad the night Sultan Salim was murdered,' he said in a dour, sorrowful voice. 'The assassins all wore such masks. I saw what they did. Afterwards I was part of the investigating group, but the men in charge were fools who wanted to please Rashid, not learn the truth. Prince Waqar tried to look deeper, but he was obstructed. The "official investigation" concluded that the Ordo Costruo were to blame.'

Ogre growled. 'My order are scholars, not murderers, Assassin.'

Nuqhemeel met Tarita's gaze. 'Yes, Merozain, I've seen what Alyssa is. And more, perhaps: before she left for Epineo, she took four of my brother Hadishah aside. When they emerged from her chambers, their eyes were black as midnight. This is not . . . *right*.'

Tarita remembered how Sakita Mubarak had been. 'Was it necromancy?'

Nuqhemeel shook his head. 'No, something worse.'

Worse? Tarita glanced at Ogre. *What are we facing?*

But at least here they'd found a détente. 'Two of you are magi,' she told Nuqhemeel. 'You have a wind-pilot. You can survive the wilds. I suggest you stay away. This is now between Alyssa and me.'

It was a risk, but she was now certain that Nuqhemeel had been outraged by Sultan Salim's murder and would stay out of the equation. She sent them eastwards, along the cliff-tops, and genuinely hoped for their safety.

Once they were gone though, her composure dissolved. She dropped her blade, choked out, '*Ogre, Ogre*–' and hurled herself against his chest, where she burst into tears. For a while all she could do was sob, thinking of how close she'd come to the breeding-house nightmare. Ogre wrapped his massive arms round her and she burrowed into his grasp, shaking and utterly undone.

When her vision finally cleared and she could think again, she realised he was crying too, rivulets running down his cheeks. She pawed at his big, ugly-wonderful face, his heart painted across his lumpen features, kissed his cheeks and whispered, 'Ogre, you are a miracle. I owe you everything.'

'Look what they did to you,' he choked out, staring at her face, her broken lips and teeth.

'Don't worry, my dear friend,' she told him, moved by his concern and his tears. 'I'm the mistress of magic, remember. I'll heal, good as new.'

That probably wasn't true: gnostic healing wasn't easy, but she'd manage somehow.

But they had more urgent matters to deal with. Ogre put her down and broke the now-powerless manacles from her wrists with a chisel. Once she'd washed and found some clothing, there was food to wolf down and spring water to guzzle.

At last she got up and asked, 'Are you ready, Ogre?'

He straightened to his full seven feet and squared his massive shoulders. 'Ogre is ready.'

'*Shukran, effendi.* Let's go and kill that blonde bitch.'

She torched the dhou – it was too large for two people – and they took the auxiliary windskiff, which was soon rising into the dawn air, the sails billowing as she set the nose west towards the promontory where Ogre had seen the lights.

Dear Ahm, she prayed, *please let us be on time.*

Epineo, Vantari Hills, Verelon

The ocean boomed right beneath Jehana's feet, the gigantic waves surging in and striking the sea-cliffs only a few hundred feet below. The air was full of spray, visibility reduced to a few hundred yards of windswept, salt-encrusted stone. Bushes wedged into every crevice had been twisted sideways by the wind.

Jehana shouted above the deafening waves and shrieking seagulls, 'Is this Epineo?'

Alyssa was standing on the promontory beside her, her four Hadishah minions hovering silently behind her. They'd left Tarita chained to a post; Jehana was still appalled at how much her one flash of dissent had cost the Merozain.

And it was all for nothing, because I capitulated anyway.

Alyssa pointed inland, along the stream. 'The village is half a mile upstream. You'd hate it: it's a dismal hovel full of primitives clinging to a pathetic existence, preserving ancient traditions, blah-blah, who gives a shit? What matters is *down there.*'

She gestured down at a pool fed by a waterfall falling from the stream beside them. Jehana had to squint to make out an opening with a squidface carved above.

Seidopus, Jehana thought. She gave a hungry shiver: she could *feel* the dwyma here, despite the Chain-rune confining her gnosis: clearly the two powers truly were separate. But it still felt distant to her, even more remote than when she'd cracked the glass window beneath Sunset Tower and escaped, or when she'd called the whale to save them. Of course, she'd just eaten the specially marked fish then, and something had been freshly lit inside her. That flame was now just embers, and she knew that somehow, it needed to be permanently rekindled. That, she sensed, was why she needed to be here.

'I still don't see why you're helping me,' she muttered.

The jadugara turned to her, her face intent. 'Jehana, isn't it obvious? I want to present you to Rashid as a fully-fledged dwymancer. I want his favour again – and what better way than to present him with someone who can hold off winter and give him victory in battle? I want you, to win *him* back.'

Jehana studied Alyssa's face. For once, she didn't appear to be speaking with her usual barbed irony; she looked open, almost vulnerable. *But it's Alyssa*, she reminded herself. When she had been Rashid's concubine in Halli'kut, she'd always been deceitful. Though even as a young girl, Jehana had known that Rashid was *everything* to Alyssa . . .

Perhaps I can trust this, at least. 'Then what must I do?' she asked.

Alyssa smiled maliciously, more like her usual self. 'Heathen priests come here every day at dawn to sacrifice to their sea-god, but once a month a *special* rite takes place.'

'How do you know?'

'How do you think?' she leered. 'I asked one of these primitives. *Nicely.*'

Jehana shuddered, but Alyssa was still talking. 'This is the very place the dwymancer Amantius was high priest.' She pointed to the giant carving of Seidopus below. 'They took his dwymancy for divinity and they still worship him, in conjunction with Seidopus. And *today* it's their weekly holy day: in just a few minutes they're going to summon the genilocus.'

Jehana felt her heart thud. 'What are you going to do?'

'Why, I'm going to present you to their sea-god. Seidopus will claim you and you'll awaken to your true powers – then you and I will join the war and save the Shihad and Rashid will be so grateful, he'll be mine for ever.'

Can it be that simple? Jehana wondered.

20

Lord of Oceans

A Clay Puppet: the Brician Galmi

A galmi is a Brician gnostic invention, a construct made not of flesh and bone but of clay, which can be animated and made to perform certain tasks of limited sophistication. Its creation raised many ethical questions, which only intensified when galmi research intersected with animagery and produced the first intelligent constructs.

ORDO COSTRUO COLLEGIATE, HEBUSALIM 849

Epineo, Vantari Hills, Verelon
Decore 935

The morning sun broke through, scarlet fires streaking the sullen grey clouds and dramatically illuminating the coast and the eastern Vantari Hills. Clouds of sea-spray hung glistening in the air and the jagged cliffs were cast into stark silhouette: a sight of majestic, brooding beauty. The pounding of waves on rock was gradually replaced by the hissing of receding seawater as the tide turned.

Jehana's gnosis was still Chained, but Alyssa left her lightly guarded, content that their purposes were aligned, at least temporarily. *Which they are, for I want this too. What happens afterwards is where we differ*, Jehana thought, praying the dwyma would help her break free of Alyssa's control.

'How do we get inside?' she asked, looking down at the pool below, where the cave was now fully uncovered. 'Is that the only way in?'

'It's the only one I know of,' Alyssa replied, sounding unusually edgy. 'There are stairs to the base of the cliffs, and a path beside the stream that runs into the cave. The priests – you're going to laugh when you see them – hold public rites in the village, but the cave is only for the initiated. I'm expecting them any moment.'

'How do we get down?'

'My my, aren't you eager?' Alyssa tittered. 'Don't worry, there are stairs on the other side of this little headland.'

'Have you seen inside the cave?' Jehana asked irritably.

'I have. See that channel below, running into the cave-mouth? That feeds a large underground pool. I didn't sense any kind of power. Truly, my prime worry is that there's nothing preserved here but superstition.' Alyssa spoke with her usual smooth sarcasm, but her voice betrayed real anxiety.

She's worried, Jehana thought, *and she's right to be, for I have no intention of being her prize.* 'So what's the plan?' she asked, trying to portray willingness.

They caught a flash of orange light on the other side of the stream, a few dozen yards below them. Alyssa pulled her into the shade of the trees and they watched six white-robed figures holding torches pass by singing a hymn, although the words were indiscernible. In a few moments they'd vanished around the headland, only to reappear at the base of the waterfall, beside the sacred cave. They vanished inside as the east began to glow.

'We'll follow them in. It's going to be one big surprise party, for us all,' Alyssa said. 'Let's join the ceremony.'

I'm going to truly savour the taste of your soul, Alyssa thought, watching Rashid's niece hungrily. *I'm already an Ascendant mage – think how powerful I'll be when I'm a dwymancer too!*

She led the way, collecting her four shepherds en route. They'd been ordered to quiet the daemon inside them so that Jehana wouldn't see. She'd just opened a gnostic channel to Nuqhemeel, to order him to rouse his men and bring the windship here, when she felt the first tremor of her wards being triggered. She gained a glimpse of a big, brutish face, contorted in alarm. *Ahh – so the Ogre-creature is alive after all . . . and he's blundered into my wards.*

That would be an extra treat for later.

She had no doubt of the outcome: she was an Ascendant, while the construct was a mere half-blood: she'd staked the Merozain out in the open in case of just such an eventuality, as Master Naxius wanted his pet construct back.

I'll return with your petty prize, Master, then while you're purring, I'll be freeing my—

—but before she could even finish her thought, the unbelievable occurred: the Chain-rune supressing Tarita Alhani's gnosis shattered.

Alyssa's heart momentarily stilled. *How?*

Surely no one but another Ascendant could destroy her Chain-rune so swiftly – had the Merozains come to the rescue? But then she realised there was a simpler explanation: sheer brute strength. *I should have cast the spell directly onto the bint herself, despite the energy drain . . .*

And now Tarita was free.

She clapped her hands. 'Move,' she told Jehana sharply. 'Let's get this underway. Every second may count if we're to aid the Shihad,' she added grandly, feeling somewhat noble at the thought of being the saviour of a million men.

If I do that, Rashid will have no choice but to take me back – he'll forget Jehana ever existed.

Taking Jehana's hand as if they were the best of friends, she murmured, 'Well my dear, in the best Ordo Costruo tradition, let's go and study the heathen savages in their primitive rituals. I do love a field trip.'

Jehana trailed Alyssa into the cave-mouth, the eerily silent Hadishah moving behind them. Inside was a path beside the stream, which had carved a channel into the rock.

Jehana let Alyssa keep hold of her hand so the jadugara would think her compliant. *We'll see just how passive I feel afterwards*, she thought defiantly, but she was genuinely excited now. The moment she'd stepped into the cave she sensed an intangible presence; it spoke to whatever had been awakened inside her and whispered promises of more.

This really is where I'm meant to be, she thought, *despite the circumstances.*

There were burning oil-lamps every few yards, and echoes of singing drifted back along the tunnel.

'I'll be with you all the way,' Alyssa reminded her, somewhere between reassurance and threat, before telling her silent shadows, 'Conceal yourselves along this path. Kill anyone who comes.' Then she told Jehana, 'Come, dearest. Destiny awaits.'

They followed the stream along the tunnel until it abruptly disappeared into the rock. The path widened, though, and they ascended wet steps to a dry tunnel that Jehana thought must be above the high-tide mark. Ahead was a dim light, and the singing became louder. When Jehana glanced back, she could no longer see the cave-mouth. They rounded a bend to see a lit chamber beyond, at least sixty feet across and just as high.

Alyssa hesitated as Jehana went to enter. *Not so brazen now, Jadugara?* she thought – then she heard a silent call from the pool and walked in boldly. From the roof and floor extended giant pillars, white and pink stalactites and stalagmites. Before her, gathered around an altar, were the white-robed priests and priestesses of Epineo, each holding a torch.

Their faces were Yurosi, but deeply tanned; the women's sun-bleached waist-length hair in various shades of brown and blonde was twisted so that it resembled tentacles; the men had shaven skulls and long beards hanging in rope-like strands. When she stepped into the light they all gave a low moan, more anticipation than surprise, that echoed about the cavern.

She gathered her courage, then called in Rondian, 'My name is Jehana. I've been touched by the sea-god.'

Intriguingly, the tallest of the women called, 'Welcome, Promised Child. I am Rowan. You have been expected.'

Promised Child? Jehana felt a thrill ripple through her body.

'Come, join us,' Rowan called, 'but the one with you must keep her distance.'

Alyssa stepped into the torch-light and snarled, 'I come and go as I wish. But you carry on; I'll just make myself comfortable and watch.'

'The god sees you,' the priestess told Alyssa. 'You would be wise to avoid his wrath.'

'Your god has no idea what he's facing,' Alyssa said mockingly. 'My own wrath is pretty damned scary, too. But see, I come in peace, with a gift – this girl. Your "Promised Child". Make of her what you will.'

Rowan stepped forward. She must have been beautiful in her youth, but now her face was lined and weathered, her frame bony, her ropey red-gold hair faded. She radiated authority. 'Jehana,' she said. 'A lovely name for a special young woman. Will you join us?'

Jehana could feel the presence of the genilocus like a second heart-beat in her chest. Without a word, she took Rowan's leathery hand and allowed herself to be led to the altar.

Tarita took the skiff high, whooshing across the sky, calling the winds so miles were crossed in minutes. She was risking being seen, but Alyssa had to know she was free by now, and she needed the elevation to get the lay of the land and find her quarry.

She'd tied her hair back and used healing-gnosis on the worst of her wounds. Ogre, huddling against the wind in front of her, was battered too; they might not be fighting fit, but they were damned well ready for a scrap.

At last she caught sight of torches, right down at the base of the cliffs. The tide was going out and she could see a cave mouth where a stream had carved through the rock, below a tall, thin waterfall.

There . . . I warrant they're down there . . .

She took the windskiff down, and they went skimming across the tidal flats. 'See those falls? That's the place,' she told Ogre. 'When we land, be ready for anything.'

He grunted in acknowledgement and rolled his massive shoulders to loosen the muscles. Tarita took his cue and started limbering as best she could while keeping control of sail, tiller and keel. It was good to have the silver scimitar back; she was used to its weight and balance now, and in battle that mattered.

As they flew nearer, detail emerged: a giant Seidopus head was carved into the rock over the cave-mouth; it looked as if anyone going in would be walking into the sea-god's mouth.

'In there?' Ogre called, and Tarita nodded and spotting a flat area near the cave-mouth but in the shadow of the cliffs, still wet from the receding tide, landed there, hoping the ebbing sea wouldn't throw up a sudden rogue wave.

They climbed out, shields and weapons ready, encouraged that no one had yet tried to kill them; she hoped that meant Alyssa wasn't watching her back. But Alyssa on her own would be formidable: she really wished she had a dozen of the Merozain Brotherhood with her, but she and Ogre would have to suffice.

'Ogre, you know you don't have to go in with me,' she reminded him, knowing what he'd say, and he didn't disappoint.

'Ogre must stay with friend Tarita.'

I had to try. If I get him killed, I'll never forgive myself.

But she was grateful. 'Okay then, let's go. Just remember that I can look after myself – if things get rough, keep yourself alive.'

They waded across the channel, which was only thigh deep – or knee-deep on Ogre – to the torch-lit cave-mouth, then looked round and winked up at him. 'Watch out, it's Tarita and Ogre: saving Urte – princess by princess.'

Ogre gave her a toothy, goofy smile, then settled back into his hard battle-face.

Together, they entered the cave.

Alyssa watched the unfolding ritual, knowing her shepherds would give warning if they were assailed – having them present would be risky if this truly was a dwyma place, and in any case, she didn't want Abraxas to see what she did here. She had her own mind on lockdown so Abraxas couldn't see through her eyes; the silence was a blessing.

I'll be more than enough on my own, she thought, *I'm an Ascendant, and these six may be acolytes of Seidopus but they have* nothing. *It's going to be a marvellous day.*

She did have some anxieties, though. She'd contemplated taking firm control from the outset, but she doubted the sea-god would come if the invocations weren't genuine, so certain things had to be left to chance.

As soon as Jehana was awakened, she'd kill these fools, then using her Souldrinker spell, she'd ingest Jehana's very being, dwymancy and all. Just thinking about all that power was giddying. *I'll be the closest thing to a real goddess there's ever been.*

A murmur ran through the heathens gathered around the altar and her nerves tingled in anticipation. *Soon.* Something big had just swum up the channel and into the large pool, a dark shape that made the surface ripple as it circled. She caught her breath: it was the size of a whale, but it was moving in rhythmic bursts, like one of the tentacled horrors that sometimes washed up in tidal pools.

That must be it! The genilocus is here!

She drew on her gnosis, quivering with excitement. After so many years of suffering, her time had come. But when Rowan took Jehana to the altar and drew a stone knife from her belt, Alyssa was suddenly alarmed.

'What are you doing?' she demanded.

Rowan turned, a challenge in her eyes. 'She's safe with us, Spawn.'

Spawn? Alyssa felt sudden doubt. *She really does know what I have inside me . . .* How that could be, she didn't know, but her anxiety grew. 'Any tricks and you die first,' she warned Rowan.

The priestess didn't even blink.

That's the trouble with fanatics, Alyssa thought. *They think they're going to Paradise – let's see how she likes Abraxas instead . . .*

Jehana had been waiting for this moment all her life. Her mother had once told her, 'You'll feel yourself in the palm of a giant's hand, with strands of energy at the edge of perception, linking you to everything. When they touch you, there's a sense of infinite potential. You'll be able to count the stars, the fish in the sea, the droplets of rain. You'll feel the breath of insects on your skin and taste the colour of light.'

Now I understand, Mother, Jehana thought. *It's so close . . .*

The acolytes watched her with awed, reverent faces. Their stone knives didn't trouble her; she knew she was safe. *To them, dwyma isn't a heresy, it's religion. Seidopus is their god, and I'm His daughter.*

She watched with bated breath as Rowan raised the stone knife to her own arm. The skin was ridged with scars, a few obviously recent, still scabbed. The woman gasped a little as she made the blade bite deep, but she caught the welling blood in a clam shell, which she handed to the man beside her. One by one the acolytes added their own blood, all the while chanting their hymn.

'*Lord of the Ocean, Caller of Storms,*' they repeated, '*break the Land and consume its bones . . .*'

Jehana was handed the knife last. She took a deep breath, then calmed her nerves and sliced her forearm, adding drops of her own blood, feeling slightly dizzy from the cut.

'*Lady of Oceans, Queen of the Waves, give us your blessing, feed our young.*'

'Come,' Rowan murmured, holding the blood-filled clamshell and taking Jehana's hand in the other. She led the way down to the pool's edge and now Jehana could see something immense lurking below the surface, larger even than the whale that had borne her from Sunset Tower, and differently shaped. She felt a sudden tremor of fear. 'I don't—'

'Hush, don't be afraid,' Rowan said. 'We've all done this.'

Jehana looked at her in surprise. 'Are you—?'

'What you are? No,' Rowan said sadly. 'The sacred blood grew too thin, centuries ago. But we keep the faith and pray for renewal: for a saviour, like you.'

The sacred blood . . . Dear Ahm, she's a descendant of Amantius – they all are!

Horribly conscious of Alyssa's predatory gaze, Jehana stopped right at the edge of the water and watched as Rowan raised the clamshell and tipped the blood into the water.

The hymn abruptly ended and Alyssa's voice cut through the silence. 'What are you?'

'Be silent!' Rowan snapped. 'You are in the presence of the Lord of Oceans.' She stepped back and raised her voice so that it rang through the chamber. 'Master of Tides, I invoke thee. Here is thy daughter!'

No sooner had Jehana realised that the water at her feet was churning than tubes of flesh lined with suckers and thick as tree-trunks suddenly erupted from below. They grasped her, tossing her into the air as a beaked maw and saucer eyes appeared in the threshing water below. Before she could even cry out, she was torn from the world of air into the realm of water, the tentacles wrapped firmly about her legs and arms and waist, easily containing her ineffectual thrashing and drawing her inexorably towards that huge, toothy beak.

Jehana had to fight to stop herself blacking out in terror, but her last mouthful of air was expended in a scream that dissipated in bubbles, unheard.

Then a fleshy length of something exploded from the creature's maw, slithered irresistibly into her own mouth and down her throat and after that, her mind refused to see and her body to feel.

A woman's shriek echoed down the long tunnel and Tarita turned to look up at Ogre. 'Are we too late?' she whispered.

Ogre's eyes were like saucers in the darkness and he was so tense he was quivering – but so was she, she realised. She extended her senses with all the wily strength she'd been taught at the Merozain monastery . . .

. . . and shouting a warning, stepped in front of him, her shields blazing, just in time to catch a hurled dagger, which hammered into her wards and sparking, ricocheted away. Behind her Ogre grunted in alarm as shadows detached from the walls both in front and behind them. Pale light glinted on metal as they closed in.

'Light!' she bellowed, speaking in Rondian to warn Ogre but not their foes, and blazed a comet of vivid gnostic light into the air above them, which made the attackers recoil, clutching their faces. Combat reflexes took over and she launched herself at the first of the half-blinded men, kicking him into the rushing water, then clashing blades with the man behind him.

Ogre positioned himself back to back with her, sending his massive axe crunching into the skull of one attacker, while his left fist punched the next so hard bones cracked, and the man was thrown off the path and into the water.

Then her own fight took all her attention, for she was facing a trained killer of the Shihad who clearly had far more experience than she did. However, she had overwhelming gnostic power on her side, and she used that to deadly effect, obliterating her foe's shielding with a single devastating blast of energy before driving her blade through the man's chest – which should have been the end of the matter, but instead, his eyes flashed black, he spat a black gobbet of blood at her face and his sword-arm blurred back into action.

Swaying away from the dark fluids he was disgorging, her eyes closing by reflex, Tarita desperately shielded, which did deflect the slash aimed at her throat, although the blade instead sliced into her shoulder. Then something crunched wetly and she saw the man who'd refused to die collapse with Ogre's axe in his skull.

But it still wasn't over: the two men they'd hurled into the stream were climbing out and even in the dim light of the tunnel she could see their eyes were black and oily. She hurled lightning into the water, making it crackle and them dance, but they just grinned evilly, when they should have been dead.

'Ogre,' they said, their voices echoing in chilling chorus, 'the Master wants you back.'

Ogre visibly blanched.

Chod! she thought, *what monsters are we facing?* But she had noted that the pair with caved-in skulls had stayed down. 'Go for their heads!' she shrieked at Ogre as the dance began again: *parry-thrust-riposte and repeat*, while Ogre unleashed pulverising blows at his foe.

The end came simultaneously: engaging kinesis and using all her Ascendant strength, she lifted up her attacker and hurled him head-first into the rock wall, striking with a wet crunch; while Ogre's axe cleaved through first his foe's scimitar and then his neck, severing his head from his body.

This time neither man rose.

'*Rukka mio*,' Tarita swore. 'There's something going on here . . .' But this wasn't the time; it had been thirty seconds or more since they heard that scream. She grabbed Ogre's arm. 'My friend, we have to hurry.' And forsaking caution for speed, she broke into a run, Ogre lumbering after her, as a distant gleam of pale light emanated from deeper in the cave.

As the huge creature receded back into the churning water, taking Jehana with her, Alyssa shouted, '*What in Hel?*' and kindled gnosis-fire.

Rowan held up a hand to stop her. 'I've been down there – we all have. We're all servants of Seidopus and we have received his sacrament. The girl will be returned.'

Alyssa tried to read the other woman. *True . . . maybe.* She withheld her fury, for now at least. 'So she's safe?'

Rowan hesitated. 'Unless she is found wanting.'

Now you bloody tell me . . . Alyssa glared at her. *But if Jehana's found wanting, she's probably no use to me anyway.* She'd heard every whispered word exchanged by these pagan peasants: *So the bloods too thin now, is it? Then only Jehana will do.*

'Very well,' she scowled. 'How long?'

'Not long,' Rowan replied. 'What are your intentions for her?'

As if I'd rukking tell you . . .

'Entirely amicable,' Alyssa drawled, fooling no one. They glared at each other. *Whatever else happens, none of you are leaving this chamber alive,* Alyssa decided.

Jehana floated back to consciousness and her eyes flew open. She was on her back, in the gentle grasp of the genilocus, wrapped in massive tentacles and gazing up towards the dimly lit surface. Tiny bubbles were streaming from her mouth and she could feel gills in her throat, just as she had when she'd escaped Sunset Tower. She raised fingers and found them webbed; if she'd willed it, her legs would have fused into a tail, but she didn't, because she was lost in the sensation of being colonised from within.

Whatever it was the genilocus had put inside her – his tongue or other appendage – had now been withdrawn, but it had left *something* spreading through her body and into her veins. It was a gentle sensation, a benign conquest, as if it contained some kind of opiate to obliterate any pain or resistance. Instead she felt a warm, floating afterglow with hints of salt and blood, as if inside her a twisted rope of blue-green light was slowly rotating and she could reach through it to feel *everything.* The beast itself was a part of her.

My genilocus . . .

The sea filled her senses. It was a wonderland, one she could explore for ever, but it was a hungry place too, teeming with lifeforms, some so small they couldn't be seen, right up to the behemoths feeding on them. Predator and prey were locked together and every moment seethed with menace. The taste of salty blood tingled on her tongue and her whole being shivered in delight.

For five hundred years, my worshippers have been offering me blood, she thought. *What else would I crave?*

It was almost with regret that she felt herself being borne upwards, rising through the water towards the light with a silent cry, the genilocus' tender grasp all around her as she broke the surface . . .

. . . and then she was gasping, drowning on dry land, her heart hammering, until something gripped her lungs and squeezed them, expelling water which came gushing from her nose and throat in a salty rush. Her gills fused to her neck and suddenly she was a creature of air again . . .

. . . and a dark shape was looming over her.

When the water started churning again, Alyssa almost jumped out of her skin, but all the sea-beast – *god, genilocus, whatever* – did was deposit Jehana back at the side of the pool. As it sank into the depths again, Alyssa strode forward, gripped the girl with kinesis and pulled her from the edge.

What's happened to her? She stared, noting strange lines on her neck and an odd pallor to her skin, but to gnostic sight she was no different.

Rowan's face hardened and she opened her mouth to speak, but Alyssa kindled gnosis-fire in her hands, jabbed her finger at the red-headed priestess and her ropey-haired acolytes and snarled, 'Move and you die.'

Of course, they were too damned *religious* to listen.

They tried to rush her, but she blazed away with mage-bolts, sending six at once that cut them down until there was nothing left but burning robes and screaming fanaticism. Rowan was first to die, but her face was serene, as if her god would protect her. *Typical damned fanatic.* She screamed pleasingly enough, though, and her blood was the usual red.

Then, feeling a series of mental blows as her own servants died, she glanced behind her to the chamber's entrance. *That rukking Merozain is coming . . . Dear Darkness, I should have just gutted her!*

She had to keep one eye on the pool – if that *thing* was down there still, she couldn't risk being too close, but she engaged kinesis and floated Jehana's supine body to the altar, which looked safely out of reach of those obscene tentacles. The girl was soaking wet, but she was breathing steadily. Alyssa went to the stone slab and caressed her face, smiling in anticipation. *Adorable girl, really,* she thought, *but she has to go.*

She set wards about her, although there was no time for anything that would last more than a few moments, completing them just as, in a rush of panting, heaving chests and wide eyes, that *damned* Merozain and the Master's *rukking* pet burst into the chamber. They went stock-still as they caught sight of their precious princess – and the dagger Alyssa was holding against Jehana's throat.

'Oh goody,' she drawled. 'I do love an audience. Stay there, or our sweet princess will have a new mouth.'

Tarita and Ogre exchanged wide-eyed glances, but gratifyingly, they didn't move.

Fools . . . you'll be next, never fear. But first, it's time for this . . .

She kindled light in her periapt and began her special spell: the *Soul-Devourer*. Using a touch of wizardry, a smidge of necromancy and some mesmerism and mysticism to ease the passage, she conjured her own version of soul-drinking.

The Merozain must have realised what she was doing, for she gave a strangled cry, but it was too late; the protective wards Alyssa had just cast threw out gnostic spider-webs that turned their rush into slow motion . . .

All that power, but she knows nothing, she thought, eyeing Tarita malevolently. *I'll eat her next . . .*

She bent over Jehana. For a moment when she touched the girl's brain she worried that the princess had grown into something too large to swallow. She felt another presence, vast as an ocean and bearing down on her like a wave, and wavered. But she slapped her doubts away, clamped her mouth over Jehana's in a deathly kiss and drawing on that deadly combination of necromancy, wizardry, spiritualism and mesmerism, she sucked out her soul.

When I have every power, what will I be? Why, I shall be a goddess, and the world will bow before me.

Jehana's dream changed and Sakita's voice rang out in the darkness. *You'll feel yourself in the palm of a giant's hand, with strands of energy at the edge of perception, linking you to everything.*

She could feel it and touch it and name it. The genilocus was *here* and the entirety of the dwyma was opening up to her. A vision of water filled her: the rivers that fed the ocean were her veins, the streams and pools, the rain-puddles that seeped into the underground, the steam that rose to join the clouds above. All was water, and all was hers–

Then Alyssa Dulayne's face appeared in the sky like a risen moon and behind it, the sky filled with a vast mess of tangled body parts, shrieking voices, black eyes and reaching hands, blotting out the sky.

The dwyma rose to meet the threat and as it locked horns with Alyssa, she tasted the other woman's essence: a life of privilege turned to corruption, of appetites unchecked, forbidden things wantonly sampled and discarded. But behind that rampant selfish want lay a hungry ego, towering in its greed and utterly lacking in empathy.

'*Fight her – fight back,*' a male voice shouted – Amantius? '*You must fight!*'

But she had no idea how, and Alyssa saw that immediately.

Fight? the jadugara cackled. *What have you ever done other than bend to the wind, you spineless, pampered slip of nothing?*

Jehana tried, though, flailing and shrieking and biting and clawing as two immense waves, one vividly verdant, the other dark and crawling with parasite souls, collided inside her . . .

At first, there was only wonder. Alyssa's mouth fizzed at the taste of Jehana's soul, a bundle of memories and wants and fears and attachments wrapped around a core of puissant energy, like a giant ocean of light, cycling to massive currents – or was it the veins of a god, aglow with the blood of power; or a massive sea-creature with tentacles made of stars? Or even a giant tree of light?

Then it turned. It saw her and its arms or branches or veins rippled towards her through time and space and distance and she saw herself as its dark mirror, a spiderweb of unlight: a dark goddess, new-born.

'Try me,' she challenged, 'for I am your doom!'

Then it loomed closer and at last she realised that this place didn't belong to her and she wasn't even close to its equal. When a coil of light picked her up, she felt like a beetle in the palm of a giant – until it squeezed and *everything* came apart. She felt a cage of energy crush inwards and shrieked in panic, trying to get away, lashing out, biting and ripping, screaming for Abraxas and feeling the daemon respond, filling her with power – and yet still she was dwarfed.

Then that ocean-heart-tree of *Life* sent a spear of energy through her, lancing the daemon-spawn in her chest.

All life is alchemy, Naxius had once told her. *We're all made of elements, some mutable and some immutable. Some can be recombined, others remain in opposition. But crucially: that which is utterly inimical can never be brought unto sympathy.*

Inside Alyssa's mind, body and soul, two inimical things had been brought together: the Living world of the dwyma and the hungry Death of the daemonic. They collided . . . and then exploded . . .

. . . and suddenly she was back in the real world, reeling drunkenly, sprawling at the edge of the pool as her intellect reformed and she realised what she'd done – and how she'd *failed*. Abraxas was gone, the spawn in her chest was dead and all she'd lost left her bereft and flailing.

Then something massive gripped her and lifted. Her eyes flew open to see she was caught up by a roiling mass of giant tentacles and being drawn towards a massive bulk. She struck the water in a great splash and went under, choking as she tried to conjure, but shorn of Abraxas, she had only her own gnostic power, unused in too long. She was *too slow* – the tentacles parted to reveal a beak-like maw that opened as she was thrust head-first between banks of jagged teeth.

Her final shriek ended abruptly as the jaw slammed shut, at the exact instant that she threw all she had left of her own gnosis, pure-blooded and potent, in one final refusal of her end . . .

*

Tarita was struggling through the gnostic mesh-spell – something she *had* to learn if she survived this – when a massive, slimy bulk engulfed Alyssa, then slid off the stone floor and back into the pool. The spell impeding her came apart a moment before an explosive burst of energy ripped through the water. She and Ogre cowered as water and blood fountained and unidentifiable body pieces, human and inhuman, rained down on them.

The silence afterward was terrifying. The iron stench of blood filled the air. The pool was a slaughterhouse waste bucket.

She's dead . . . the bitch is finally truly dead, Tarita realised in awe.

But so is the dwyma beast . . .

Ogre put a protective arm over her. 'What happened?' he asked in a stunned voice.

'I have no rukking idea, Ogre. None at all.'

Then her eyes flashed back to Jehana. She bounded to the altar and examined the princess. She couldn't find a pulse, couldn't detect breath, so she gathered her mystic and healing-gnosis and plunged inside the girl's head. To her immense relief, she found Jehana's core intact and sparked life through it . . .

Jehana coughed, convulsing, and was momentarily panic-stricken to see someone standing over her – then she realised it wasn't Alyssa and recognition followed. 'Tarita?' she croaked.

'It's me – dear Ahm, I thought you were dead!'

Jehana turned her head towards the bloody pool, then curled into a ball. 'I may as well be,' she moaned. 'The dwyma's gone.'

The Masquerade (Ironhelm)

The Inquisition and the Kirkegarde

Holy Father, I implore you to reconsider, even at this late stage. The Kirkegarde has served the Sacred Throne faithfully for more than a century – what need is there to institute a new military arm of Mother Church when my knights could perform the duties of this Inquisition just as well?

GRANDMASTER BRACYN, KIRKEGARDE COMMANDER, PALLAS, 452

The Grandmaster is mistaken. The rooting out of heresy is not a soldier's task: it requires a different type of mind, one which can look beyond what seems to what is.

GRAND PRELATE ACRONIUS, PALLAS 452

Near Venderon, Noros
Decore 935

A dark-haired Keshi man opened a walnut box and took out a Lantric Mask, remembering the day he accepted it. Then with a small sigh that contained both satisfaction and regret, he placed it over his face and once more became Ironhelm of the Masked Cabal.

Then he made his way through the night to the back of the country mansion south of Venderon, which had been sufficiently restored to make an acceptable headquarters for the Sultan of Kesh. The guards averted their eyes, as they'd been commanded to do whenever a man in this guise appeared, and he entered the room where Rashid Mubarak, Sultan of Kesh and leader of the Shihad awaited with his eldest son, Prince Attam.

The two most powerful men in Kesh remained seated when

Ironhelm entered, but he didn't feel any need to give more than minor obeisance, despite the complexities of the harbadab, the Duel of Manners. He bowed his masked head and touched his heart, then took his seat at the table. A mute servant – he'd had his tongue cut out at the age of fourteen – poured wine, then withdrew.

The mask had special properties, moving as if it were skin, so Ironhelm was able to drink without removing it. 'A Brician red,' he commented, savouring the mouthful. 'It's good to be able to sup on a fine vintage without having to sell one's limbs to a Rondian trader, as we must at home.'

Rashid appreciated the remark; Attam did not – he drank arak, not wine. But then, Attam always had been just a barking dog in silks, in Ironhelm's eyes.

'We've captured little enough of it,' the sultan remarked. 'The enemy burn everything as they retreat.'

'I understand they were unexpectedly reinforced?' Ironhelm asked.

'It wasn't *my* fault,' Attam said, glowering. 'My brother should have warned us!'

'The reinforcements came out of the southeast, where no enemy were supposed to be,' Ironhelm replied. 'In war, these things happen. Blame the aerial scouts.'

'Ai, let's speak of Waqar,' Attam growled. 'He's all broken up over losing his fat friend and sulking because his girl has come running to me for shelter.'

Ironhelm's eyes narrowed. 'The girl with the gnostic spear?'

'Fatima.' Attam chuckled. 'She came to my tent that same night, offering to kill Rondians for me. "Waqar is broken and doesn't want to fight any more. Let me avenge my friends and I'll do anything you want," she told me. She's no beauty, mind, but what's a man to do?'

'Waqar is refusing to fight?' Ironhelm clarified.

'He's like a snowflake – he melts in the heat.'

'My nephew is sensitive, but he's not without backbone,' Rashid said sharply. 'Grief affects us all in different ways. In any case, I have another task for him.'

'The sister? Jehana?' Ironhelm asked. Attam also looked interested; he'd clearly already been briefed.

Rashid gestured in the affirmative. 'Why hasn't she been found? We need her, or someone else with those gifts.'

Control the dwyma, control the weather – that's Rashid's plan for Waqar, Ironhelm thought, knowing Master Naxius had other ideas. He wanted these dwymancers dead or under his control. They knew of only three: Lyra Vereinen, Valdyr Sarkany and Jehana.

Ironhelm was inclined to support the sultan on this. If Waqar had the potential, by all means let him explore it. *If he emerges with the dwyma, perhaps I can bend him to my will – and if he's a threat, I'll kill him myself.*

'Do you have any idea at all where Waqar needs to go, or what he needs to do?' Rashid asked Ironhelm.

Ironhelm considered. 'One of my brethren traced Jehana to a place in Verelon. That would be the place to start.'

He could have said more, but in truth, he was troubled. If he could have been spared, he'd already be winging his way to that place, where Sister Heartface had last been observed, before she'd blocked the link and fallen silent. Nothing had been sensed since.

Something went wrong. The bitch was supposed to kill Jehana, but no doubt she wanted more. That was Heartface, always scheming too much. But she hadn't been the only one; from what Ironhelm understood, others of the cabal had been trying to find a way to break the old magus' hold over them, despite being gifted this immense power by Naxius. And now Angelstar was gone too.

We're a dying breed . . . There were eight – now who's left? Jest, Beak and me.

'Send some good men with Waqar,' Attam growled. 'Men we can trust.'

The sultan shook his head. 'No, I wish to remain supportive so that he'll confide in me. I'm content that he select his own companions. His friend Tamir will be with him. They already have my leave to depart.'

Attam snorted at the mention of the diminutive Tamir, but Ironhelm believed him to be both clever and resourceful. 'I think he and Tamir are sufficient, Great Sultan,' he said, then changing the subject, asked, 'What of the war?'

Rashid leaned forward. 'It comes down to this: it's nearly Janune and Yuros has begun to freeze. I have almost a million men in thin cotton robes and sandals and the only major city near us is Norostein, sixty miles south. Sometimes life is complicated, but this is simple: we must get inside Norostein, or we will perish.'

Attam and Ironhelm considered that sourly. 'What of our stores?' Ironhelm asked.

'Three weeks before we must go to half-rations; three weeks after that we starve.'

'*Six weeks?*' Attam barked. 'Chod, is it that bad?'

'We can prolong it by going to half-rations immediately,' Rashid admitted. 'It will damage morale, but we may have no alternative.'

'I'm told this Helish region is buried in snow for weeks on end,' Ironhelm said. 'Rivers stop flowing and the temperature seldom lifts above freezing.'

'Then we must take Norostein, and we must do it fast,' Attam declared. 'I'll get my new bitch to break their gates with that spear and we'll be inside within days of arrival, Father – I promise you that.'

'I hope you're right,' Ironhelm commented. 'By the way, I learned something interesting from a prisoner. The enemy commander is Seth Korion – who led the so-called "Lost Legions" during the Third Crusade. His most devious advisor was one Ramon Sensini; he was the mastermind at Riverdown.'

'And?' Attam barked.

'It was Sensini's cavalry who crushed yours at Venderon. He and Korion will be leading the defence of Norostein.'

Attam bunched a fist. 'Is that supposed to intimidate me? No, I rejoice: the whole of the East has been longing to avenge Riverdown. I will decorate the gatehouse of Norostein with their heads.'

Rashid made an approving sign, then said to Attam, 'I charge you to make good your boasts: get to Norostein as fast as you can, break the gates and get us inside. Now I must speak alone with our visitor.'

Attam didn't look best pleased, but he downed his arak and strode out.

That Attam would take Norostein, Ironhelm had no doubt. Even without the girl's gnostic spear and despite leaving three hundred thousand men in northern Noros, they had overwhelming numeric advantage. Rashid had six hundred thousand men currently streaming south: twelve times the number of Yurosi who'd be defending the city.

'What do you think?' Rashid asked, when Attam was gone.

'Norostein has strong walls, the defenders' strength is in formation fighting and defence, they know the conditions and they'll be defending their homes. But numbers will tell.'

Rashid changed the subject without comment. 'What news from Pallas? You've spoken recently of civil war and the likely fall of the empress?'

There was news, but it wasn't good. 'The empress continues to defy her enemies,' Ironhelm admitted. 'She passed laws to enable her people to plunder the churches, which should have triggered revolt, but such was the wealth uncovered that many turned against the corrupt Church instead. On that wave of support, she marched men into the Celestium and reclaimed it in the name of her puppet, the Grand Prelate.'

'Surely that provoked her enemies?'

'There was no effective response because she buried two Sacrecour armies under a blizzard of such severity that almost every man died.'

Rashid's eyes widened. '*Dwyma*? Are you telling me the Empress of Yuros is a dwymancer herself?'

'Without doubt.'

For the first time, Sultan Rashid Mubarak's famed composure cracked. 'Ahm on High, if that's what she can do, we'll be wiped out! Jehana *must* be found – and Waqar *must* gain the dwyma! And the heathen empress must die – tell your Master that *she must die*–'

'He knows, Great Sultan,' Ironhelm promised. 'You must believe it's his highest priority.'

Ironhelm returned to his secluded pavilion guarded by dark-eyed Reekers and prowled through the surrounding woods, circling his camp twice as he contemplated his own next moves. Then he entered the pavilion, sumptuously decorated with a four-post bed and velvet curtaining, lit a brazier and in the smoke of various powders, focusing on a particular secret sigil, called into the aether, '*Master?*'

When Ervyn Naxius responded almost immediately, he reported, 'I've just spoken with the sultan, who is sending his nephew Waqar to seek Jehana. He now knows of the empress' secret power and her victories in the north. He's afraid the same will happen to him.'

'Allay his fears,' Naxius rasped. 'Brother Jest will deal with her.'

Ironhelm bowed his head. 'Is there news of Heartface?'

Naxius' lined face contorted with annoyance. 'None,' he growled. 'I suspect she has succumbed to temptation and paid the price.'

'Should I send men to the region?'

'No, I have a windship already en route. I am sending Plague and Famine.'

Ironhelm felt his skin prickle. 'Plague and Famine?'

'I have servants other than you,' Naxius told him, smiling coldly. 'Also Masks, Brother Ironhelm, but *higher* servants.'

Ironhelm had studied the *Book of Kore* to better know his enemies; it claimed there were four Angels of Destruction who would remake the world on the Last Day: Macharo, the Angel of War; Cadearvo, or Famine; Scaramu, who would bring Plague, and Glamortha, the Angel of Death. The pretentious names didn't trouble him, but this revelation of "higher servants" most certainly did. 'I understood that I would be given control of this theatre of war, Master?'

'Your brethren have proven unreliable, Ironhelm. Demonstrate your fidelity to me.'

Ironhelm bowed his head, biting his lip behind his mask.

'I mean it,' Naxius grated. 'I'm tired of the treachery, Ironhelm. Heartface thought to outwit me, and so have others, so *obedience* is now my watchword. The smallest hint of betrayal and you will scream for eternity.'

Ironhelm dropped to both knees and prostrated himself. 'I hear, Master. I obey.'

He was speaking to an empty room. Smoke curled lazily about him, but the Master's words still echoed inside his head.

Ironhelm knelt for a long time and *seethed*. 'I am an Angel too,' he snarled at last. '*I am the Angel of Pain.*'

He rose and summoned a black-eyed servant. 'Bring me a prisoner and my flaying knives. No, two. The night is young.'

21

Siblings

Heretical Magic

The first magi faced two deadly magical heresies: the Souldrinkers, an insidious parasitic form of the gnosis, and dwyma, a vast channelling of natural energies that drove its practitioners insane and threatened widespread destruction. Both were defeated. But some whisper of a third magical heresy that the Pallas Magi are unaware of, even today.

GREMUS POLL, FAILED MAGE, BREVIS 790

Verelon, Yuros
Decore 935

Tarita Alhani moved cautiously through the bushland. Her long black hair was severely tied back from her narrow coppery face and she was wrapped in close-fitting dun-coloured clothing so as not to stand out or snag on the undergrowth. Her face was mottled by bruising, her gums ached from the teeth she was regrowing and the skin on her back itched abominably, especially in the rain that soaked her clothes and made them chafe.

But right now, she had greater worries. She'd just discovered that the latest campsite she and her companions had set up was much closer to a Keshi supply-camp than she'd realised, and there were patrols nearby. Not that they were very alert. She crept to a small rise and looked down on a line of grumbling Eastern soldiers hauling a mule-train along a path and cursing loudly.

Keshi swearing is so much more colourful than Rondian, she mused. It was more inventive, more eviscerating. *Rondians just say fuck a lot.*

She slipped back into the undergrowth and crept along a deer path, leaving the invaders behind. It began to rain harder, the new constant as winter set in on the south coast of Yuros, and the noise and lessened visibility encouraged her to jog, especially as the birdsong told her the men were far away. Inside twenty minutes she found their latest camp and gave a low whistle to let the others know she was back.

As she entered the clearing beside the stream, Ogre rose from beneath a tree, his thin black hair plastered to his skull. Stitched-together furs barely covering his massive shoulders and torso were all soaked through and matted.

'There are Keshi nearby,' she called. 'We need to move – let's ready the skiff.'

Ogre's lugubrious features lit up at her voice; his seven-foot-tall, massively muscular frame and flat-nosed, wide, thick-lipped mouth with tusk-like jutting broken incisors made him look brutish, but his eyes were filled with intelligence, humour and perception.

'I'll pull it out,' he said, then he called, 'Jehana, time to go.'

Princess Jehana Mubarak emerged from the shelter of the forest, wrapped in a travelling cloak over Keshi robes, effortlessly beautiful despite her lack of make-up or finery. 'So soon?' she asked tiredly. 'We just got here.'

Jehana was still exhausted after her partial awakening to the dwyma at Epineo a week ago. She was probably the world's only living dwymancer, but the guardian spirit she had bonded with had been slain, interrupting the awakening and leaving her powers still unreachable. Their next steps were now uncertain.

'Any luck contacting Waqar?' Tarita asked. Jehana's brother was a potential dwymancer too, and finding him was now becoming urgent.

'No, but that's not surprising. Even with a relay-stave, I need to keep the gnostic sendings intimate so they can't be intercepted: that diminishes the range, and the lands west of us are mountainous, which doesn't help,' she replied. 'The chances will improve as we travel west.'

It's possible Waqar's dead, Tarita worried, but she kept that thought to herself; Jehana was fragile. She'd been uprooted from her pampered life as a princess of Kesh and was now a fugitive with a heretical power, adrift in foreign lands. That was quite enough to worry about.

Her mind churned over her options as she watched Ogre haul the skiff out of its hiding place in the undergrowth. Her mission, to spy on the Keshi royal family, had twisted and turned until now she was helping one of those royals survive against a cabal of Masked assassins.

I promised Waqar I'd find his sister and get her to safety – I'll keep my word.

'I'll help Ogre set up the skiff, if you can pack up the camp,' she told Jehana, and went to help her giant friend. She might be diminutive, but with her Ascendant-strength gnosis and his muscles, they soon had the mast up and the sales rigged.

They'd kept the keel fully powered and ready to fly, so a short time later they were clambering aboard. Tarita took the tiller, Jehana sat before the mast and Ogre behind it. Tarita energised the keel and called wind for the sails, they rose gently into the air and she turned their prow northwest and continued their journey towards the Rondian Empire.

Venderon, Noros

'Waqar? Are you really leaving?' Fatima called.

Prince Waqar Mubarak glanced over his shoulder and was relieved to see his ex-lover was alone. She might be more pugnacious than pretty, but she was still capable of lighting a spark in his heart, except grief and loss lay between them – and now she'd insisted on taking up the accursed gnostic spear that had killed Baneet, his friend and her lover.

'Ai, we're leaving now,' he said at last.

He ducked beneath the canvas shelter that was keeping the rain from their rocs, the giant eagle-constructs the sultan had ordered created, and strapped down the saddle-bags on Ajniha, his personal mount. It had been pouring for days on end, but today the clouds were thinning and he was ready to go.

Fatima grimaced. 'Attam says the sultan gave you a choice: stay and fight, or run off on some mysterious errand. "Naturally, Prince Softcock chose to run off," Attam said.'

'And you believe him?'

'Of course not. I've fought with you: you don't lack for courage,' Fatima replied. 'I just hope you understand why I have to stay. I need to gain vengeance for Baneet.' She hefted the spear in her hands. Its gnostic crystal was pulsing in time to her heartbeat. 'At least someone will be giving the enemy a taste of this.'

'It'll kill you,' Waqar said bleakly. *And when it does, my heart will break.*

'Then I'll be with Baneet,' she replied.

Waqar stroked Ajniha's flank. 'So you're with Attam now? He treats his women like shit.'

'I'm not "with" him, but I'm pledged to him so he looks after me, gets me what I want. I'll be there when we shatter the gates of Norostein and win undying glory.'

'"Undying glory"? I pray it's so.' He turned back to his task, wishing she'd go.

Fatima came up behind him and put a hand on his shoulder. 'You're off to find Jehana, aren't you?'

He turned, drinking in her determined face, remembering when it had lit up for him alone. 'I can't tell you,' he replied. 'Rashid swore me to secrecy.'

'Then it is Jehana. Good luck, Waqar. I'll pray for you.' She rose to her tiptoes, pecked at his lips, then went, leaving him silenced by her taste and the waft of her scent.

Tamir peered from behind his own roc. 'Are you going to stand there all day?'

No doubt he'd heard everything. Waqar forced a grin. 'Let's go, my friend.'

'Sure . . . but, erm, where? You've still not said.'

'Rashid told me about a place in Verelon: it's a starting point.'

'Verelon? That's *thousands* of miles away–'

'Then it's a good thing we can fly.'

They led their birds out of the pens into the slushy gloom of a Yuros morning. The air was bitter, but at least it was clear, and his heart lifted at the thought of finally soaring into the sky and leaving his cares earthbound.

I'm coming, Jehana. Ahm keep you safe.

Verelon coast, Yuros

<Waqar?> Jehana Mubarak whispered tremulously, holding aloft the relay-stave they'd retrieved from Alyssa Dulayne's windship. Projecting her voice into the aether, keeping the sending very tight to her brother's unique gnostic essence, she repeated, <Waqar?>

She'd tried every evening since they left behind the bloody carnage at Seidopus' shrine in Epineo. They were camped somewhere on the Verelon coast now, far enough inland that the massive tides didn't deafen them. Tarita and Ogre were chatting quietly around the fire as they cooked supper. The pair still made her nervous – Ogre was an illegal construct and Tarita was Jhafi, an enemy of Kesh – but her life was in their hands and so far they'd been true. She tossed more twigs into her own little conjuring fire and called again.

For the first time, quite without warning, she felt a response. <Jehana?>

She fed the link and conjured her brother's face in the smoke: black-haired, bronze-skinned, with a light beard: a handsome man, with the family look. She was struck at how stressed he looked, but that didn't diminish the joy of just seeing him.

'Sal'Ahm, Brother! Sal'Ahm – thanks and praise,' she tried to say, but what came out was a teary burble of love and sheer relief. He was speaking too, the same rush of emotion to know that the other lived and that perhaps very soon they could be together.

It was some time before they could exchange any kind of news: he was somewhere to the west – *Noros*, wherever that was – but he'd left the army to seek her. He'd lost two of his dearest friends. The war sounded awful.

Then he asked, <*But Sister, what of you?*>

<*So much has happened,*> she told him, <*but it can wait until we meet. We're flying west, from Verelon.*>

<*We?*> he said sharply.

<*I'm with someone who claims to know you: Tarita Alhani.*>

Waqar's face lit up. <*Tarita! She found you? That's magnificent – tell her she has my eternal gratitude.*>

This was the first time Jehana had heard the Jhafi spy's story corroborated, so his reaction was something of a relief – although he sounded a little too enthusiastic about the dirt-caste bint for her liking. *She claims he kissed her*, she remembered.

<*She'll be pleased to hear that, but I'm sure she'd prefer something more tangible,*> she responded. It was probably unfair, but why encourage her honourable brother into some foolish sense of obligation to a Jhafi?

<*How will we meet?*> he asked.

Jehana went to reply, then realised she knew little about Yurosi geography. <*I really don't know . . .* > She wished she had a map.

Then Tarita's bony hand gripped the relay-stave and she said, <*Sal'Ahm, Prince Waqar.*>

Waqar looked surprised, then he smiled. <*Thank you for finding my sister. You are an Angel of Ahm.*>

<*People say that all the time,*> Tarita replied airily. <*We're in central Verelon, east of Spinitius. We have a skiff, but the winds and the weather are bad. Where are you?*>

<*On a lump of ice in Noros, near the ruins of Venderon. The weather's been atrocious, so it's been slow progress. We're aiming to fly along the Kedron, down the Brekaellen, then east, but there are storms ahead.*>

<*Then you should fly due east and take Trachen Pass. It's much quicker. We can come to meet you.*> She paused, then added, <*There are three of us.*>

Waqar frowned. <*Who's the third?*>

Tarita laughed and said, <*I have a comrade so mighty he is known only as the Ogre.*>

At the fireside, Ogre blushed and chortled.

<*The O-gah?*> Waqar sniffed. <*Strange name. Can we trust him?*>

Tarita looked at Ogre. <*With our lives.*>

Jehana might still be uncomfortable around the construct, but she felt compelled to speak up. <*Ogre has proved his loyalty,*> she put in, winning a grateful look from Tarita.

The relay-stave was beginning to show signs of imminent burn-out so they broke off the contact and Tarita and Ogre returned to their teasing banter, while Jehana sat apart, to think. There were too many unresolved matters for her liking. She could now sense the dwyma flowing through her alongside the gnosis, but she had no idea how to grasp and use that power. If she *listened* to it, she thought she could sense others, too – not many, just a few ghostly presences, far away. Perhaps she could reach out to them, but that didn't seem wise.

Then there was Tarita: the Jhafi spy had surely fulfilled her mission, but she insisted on getting Jehana safely back to her brother. Why this was now her business, Jehana didn't know, but she suspected the girl wanted rewarding, perhaps even to seduce her brother.

I need to protect him: he's too nice.

And as for Ogre: only the Ordo Costruo would give shelter to such a creature: a gnosis-using, intelligent construct was utterly illegal under the gnostic codes. The sooner he was given back to the order, the better, for his own safety.

But it was too soon to broach all this, so she silently joined the others and they huddled in their blankets around the fire to eat. 'Who's on watch first?' Jehana asked. Tarita and Ogre wouldn't let her take a watch, regarding a palace-bred princess as incompetent in the wild. Gallingly, they were right.

'I am,' Ogre rumbled.

'I don't think there'll be much action tonight,' Tarita commented. 'Most of the windships are hiding from the weather.'

All the armies were west of here, fighting the great war: East against

West, Shihad against Crusade, Ahm against Kore. *A stupid war*, Jehana thought. *An utter waste of lives.*

They fell into a companionable silence. Ogre washed their platters and pots – despite his brutish appearance, he was fastidious – then Tarita brewed coffee before the two of them settled back down to watch the fire, pressed into each other's sides to share warmth. Seeing them together made Jehana oddly uncomfortable, but it prompted her to ask, 'So, what happens to Ogre after this?'

Tarita gave her an amused look, then announced, 'Ogre is seeking his Lady Ogre and I'm helping. Oh, and of course I'm looking forward to seeing your brother again.'

Jehana's temper rose to this challenge. 'You might have kissed my brother – you might even bed him, who knows? But you will *never* marry him. We're all grateful, but that goes only so far.' Then her eyes trailed queasily to Ogre. 'Did your maker create a female?'

To her surprise and slight horror, Ogre nodded wistfully. 'Semakha, her name was. Ogre does want to see her again. But does Semakha even remember Ogre?'

Tarita stroked his forearm and said, 'We'll find her – you'll see.'

'Tell me about Semakha,' Jehana said, interested despite herself.

Ogre sighed. 'Another being like Ogre, made by the Master. She was taken away before the Ordo Costruo found and rescued me. Ogre doesn't know whether she still lives.'

Jehana tried to picture a female Ogre, and a world that would allow two forbidden creatures to coexist. *It's impossible.* But she'd been raised to be gracious. 'Then I hope you find one of your own kind.' She rose stiffly to her feet, pulling her blanket with her. 'I'm tired,' she told them. 'We should all get some rest.'

Jehana fell swiftly asleep, but Tarita lingered by the fire, feeling restless. After the traumas of being captured, rescued and finally seeing Alyssa dead and Jehana safe, she was exhausted, not helped by having to repair herself from the abuse meted out on her when in captivity.

But Jehana's slightly pricklish attitude had left her irritably wakeful. Beside her, Ogre sat gloomily. 'What're you thinking, Big Man?'

He exhaled heavily and admitted, 'I was wondering if Semakha is still alive. The Master has been a fugitive for a long time. She may have died years ago.'

'It's possible,' Tarita admitted, 'but we'll find out.'

'If she's dead, then there's no one in the world for Ogre.'

'Why do you say that?'

'Because I've talked to Ordo Costruo and I read books: people only want those who are like them: the same race, cast, wealth, the same beauty. People pretend, they say "opposites attract", but that's not true, is it? A blonde marrying a brunette is not "opposites". And who in the world is like me? Only Semakha, who I kissed once and who may be dead.'

Tarita took a deep breath; this was tricky ground. 'It's way more complex than that, Ogre. I've heard it said that women seek men for their status because women have no status, while men seek women for their looks, because a beautiful woman enhances their status further.' She wrinkled her nose. 'But that's not love, that's partnership. I've kissed Waqar only once, too, and we're as opposite as can be, but I still have hope.'

'You are beautiful and a Merozain: many men would want such a wife,' Ogre replied.

'Beautiful? Ha! Bony with a face like a horse, more like! And I was born a dirt-caste maid, don't forget; in our world, that matters more than almost anything else. I curse, I have no manners, I drink and make dirty jokes and sleep with too many men.'

Ogre chortled. 'I knew I liked you for some reason.'

She laughed and slapped his arm, but her own melancholy returned swiftly. 'The real issue is this: when I broke my back, I suffered other internal injuries. This is my biggest and worst secret: *I'm barren*. So all I bring to a marriage is my wit, my dirt-caste manners and my admittedly magnificent maamehs.' She flicked a twig into the fire and watched it burn. 'It won't be enough for a Mubarak prince, Ogre.'

'I'm sorry you can't be a mother,' Ogre mumbled, 'but you're still a mage. That is desirable for a prince.'

She shook her head. 'Let's face it, Waqar is – what, fifth in line for the throne? The girl who gets him will be royalty through and through, and she'll come with land and alliances and a dowry so immense I couldn't even imagine it.' She added, 'He kissed me, but he'll have more beautiful girls by far in his bed every night. Noblemen marry princesses. I know my place.' She looked up at him and added, 'But Ogre, we'll find your Semakha for you. You will find happiness.'

'Broken teeth, undershot jaw, rough hide, shaggy, all muscle, ugly face – just like me, she was, but a woman,' Ogre told her, his voice unusually bitter. 'Only a freak can make another freak happy, yes? Only birds of same kind nest together.'

'Semakha will see what I see, Ogre. You're a good man: both a *man*, and *good*.' She patted his arm. 'And I'll still be your friend, no matter what.' She yawned pointedly. 'I'm going to get some sleep now. And Ogre, I think we're alone out here: trust in the wards and get some sleep as well.'

For want of a warmer place to be, she laid her head on his thigh and in seconds was floating into darkness.

Ogre piled another log onto the fire, then huddled deeper into the furs he'd stitched together from the clothing purloined from the Hadishah. He kept still so Tarita could sleep: she'd been doing all the flying and was plainly exhausted. The wind whistled past, carrying flurries of snow so cold his breath plumed from his nose and mouth.

It would be good if Tarita won the heart of her prince, he decided. The world was a brutal, unjust place where only wealth and power gave security. *Why shouldn't she have that?* If Waqar didn't appreciate her, more fool him.

And who knows, perhaps Semakha really is out there?

He cast his mind back to Naxius' hidden laboratory in Dhassa, a place of cruel, clinical research. He'd been bred to serve, given gnosis and speech and conditioned to be loyal. When the Master bred Semakha, they'd spent every waking moment together and Ogre had fallen in love, or what a lonely construct with no real life-experience imagined was love.

She was like me: repulsive, by human standards, but I didn't know that. To me she was beauty incarnate . . .

Tarita was snoring now, her black hair cascading into his lap. He gently laid his arm around her and did as she advised, trusting the wards to wake him if intruders came. With Semakha's face floating before his eyes, he drifted into a dream of that one solitary kiss and how wonderful it would be to love and be loved.

22

Making Love and Treason

On Gold and Trust

Men kill for gold and yet they cannot eat it, or hammer it into a useful tool. All they can do is exchange it for something else, so its value is only what you get in exchange. The sweat, time and blood to acquire it is only worthwhile if we can have confidence that the gold will yield the value we expect. Maintaining that confidence is the prime – some would say only – function of the Treasurer.

CALAN DUBRAYLE, IMPERIAL TREASURER, PALLAS 918

Pallas, Rondelmar
Decore 935

Lyra Vereinen, Queen of Rondelmar and Empress of the Rondian Empire, clutched the sheets, her back against the chest of her Knight-Commander Solon Takwyth, gasping at each movement as his loins slapped her buttocks rhythmically, his shaft swollen and intense inside her.

'Get there . . .' she panted as Solon heaved, 'get there, get there–'

He reached his trigger-point, his big hands grasping her breasts as he thrust deep and pinned her on her front, his full weight crushing her as she lay spread-eagled, his sweat and heat basting her back. She fought for air as he rode out a heaving climax, then he groaned and sagged onto her with a weary, pleased sigh.

'Out, out,' she panted, jerking her hips and gasping in blessed relief as he pulled out and rolled away. 'Unghhh . . . Dear Kore, Solon . . .' She gave up, breathless and utterly spent.

She'd woken as the first roosters crowed outside to find his hands teasing and his body poised, her weary moan taken as assent. That was an hour ago. Magi could energise themselves beyond the capacity of normal men – Solon boasted of it – but she wasn't a mage and couldn't always rise to the moment as he did, especially not for the fourth or fifth time in one night.

'Don't wake me next time,' she complained, then her addled brain realised what she'd said. 'That's not permission to take me in my sleep. It's a plea for rest.'

I think we've only had three hours' sleep – for about the tenth night running.

Solon grunted a little sourly and tried to embrace her, but she pulled away, her thighs and stomach aching, her nethers feeling raw and pounded. She sniffed her body and wished she hadn't, yawned and closed her eyes, craving a little more sleep . . .

. . . and the nursery bell rang.

No, no, let me sleep . . .

But her son needed her, so she groaned and rose, while Solon climbed out of the other side, looking mighty pleased with his efforts. He looked good in the half-light with his cropped hair and beard that went some way to hiding the scars marring the left side of his face, powerfully built, deep-chested and bulky: a manly frame. But she wasn't feeling wholly appreciative just now.

'Honestly, hadn't we done it enough already for one night?' she complained.

'You didn't seem to be having a totally miserable time.'

She was past blushing over such matters, and that of course had been half the point of this liaison. 'Last night was *wonderful* . . . This morning was . . . not so much. Please: more quality, less quantity.'

He looked somewhat hurt and confused. 'Quantity *is* quality.'

'Really? Honestly, I think you just like to boast of your tally with your drinking mates.'

'Not so,' he flared, and for a moment their strange combination of truce and liaison wobbled. They were disagreeing more as the novelty of their coupling wore off and truer feelings surfaced. It'd been only two weeks, and the good moments still felt gloriously decadent . . . but there had been fewer of them these last few days.

Am I so faithless that I'm tired of him already? Then she realised what she'd admitted to herself. *Tired of him* . . . Perhaps, a little: or maybe just tired. But she still craved what he could do to her when the mood was right.

She wrapped herself in a nightgown, went to the fire and stirred it with a poker. Solon pulled a tunic over his head and joined her, clicked a finger and it lit instantly: another advantage of being a mage.

She'd not really meant it to happen, but in the rush of emotions on the night her soldiers had retaken Pallas-Sud, she'd let him into her body. Her excuse to herself was he was helping her to become worldly, but it was more complicated than that. Solon, her most senior military man, was likely the only lover she *could* take safely. She only wished she loved him, or even liked him, but he was dour and controlling and she was constantly having to assert herself to keep control of the parts of her life he didn't belong in.

But the sex, despite this morning's uncomfortable encounter, could be utterly overwhelming.

Predictably, he raised the one matter she didn't want to discuss with him. 'Lyra, perhaps you don't need to marry outside House Corani. I think–'

She cut him off. 'Come spring, if we're still standing, I *will* re-marry, to get us the allies we need. We're not having that discussion again.'

He scowled, clearly wanting to command her obedience. But he also wanted her affection, so he usually shied away from pressing the matter.

He was also becoming more persistent, though. *Is he falling in love?* she wondered, squirming inside because that wasn't supposed to happen.

'If you'd married me in 930–' he began, trying again.

She cut him off. She knew that route only too well. 'If I'd married you in 930, I'd have still been in love with Ril, so I'd have hated you. There would've been affairs and executions and you'd never have allowed me the latitude to explore the dwyma – in fact, it would have been your excuse to be rid of me, if the adultery with Ril hadn't been enough. So when the Masked Cabal struck, there would've been no miracles to save us.'

'Also no Ostevan and no . . . Medelie,' he replied.

'So Medelie was bitter about me, personally?' she probed. 'About my *not* marrying you?'

'Who knows?' he replied, merely confirming that he did know. 'Still, you and I together feels *right* to me. We'd have found an understanding.'

'No, we wouldn't,' she said firmly. 'I was a naïve convent girl in love with the handsome knight who'd just saved my life. There would've been no "you and I", just simmering misery until it all broke apart. Forget it. What happened, happened and can't be undone.'

'Perhaps you're right.' He took her chin and kissed her mouth, whiskers and morning sourness and all, but she let him. 'There could be love between us,' he murmured. 'I'm certain of that. We just need time.'

But with Ril it was instant . . . Isn't that how love's meant to be?

'Go,' she said, pushing him away gently. 'You've work to do and I need to see my son.'

He left reluctantly and Lyra settled into her armchair. Moments later, Domara, the Royal Midwife, a severe woman with tightly bound grey hair and a hawkish face, brought in three-month-old Rildan Endarion-Vereinen, Crown Prince of Rondelmar, followed by a maid bringing her morning tea.

Rildan gurgled in recognition as he was settled onto Lyra's lap. The midwife and maid left and Lyra settled in for the most blissful, undemanding and utterly necessary thing in her life. While she fed him, her bodyguard, Basia de Sirou, joined her. She sniffed the air and wrinkled her nose.

'Yes, I know,' Lyra said; the room did smell of sweat and sex.

Basia didn't approve of her relationship – or whatever it was – with Solon; the knight-commander despised the Volsai and he had told Lyra several times that he couldn't see what use a wooden-legged woman would be in a crisis. It was just one of the increasing list of things they were disagreeing on lately.

That Solon had replaced Ril, Basia's own lover, in the royal bed was yet another tangle in the knotty warp and weft of their lives, but somehow the two women had found reconciliation in their mutual loss. They were friends, and Basia had become Lyra's only female confidante now the ladies of the court were afraid to ally themselves too closely with a queen they believed to be doomed.

So Lyra felt able to raise her uncertainties. 'Basia, you know more about men than I do,' she began, softening the blunt words with a smile. 'Does lovemaking get better over time?' She yawned and shifted Rildan to the other nipple. 'Honestly, I'm so tired right now that most nights I reach a point where I'd rather sleep than . . . you know.'

Basia pulled a reflective face. 'In my experience – and yes, I do have some – it gets better with a very few men, but with most there's a natural point where you just don't want them any more. You've tasted the meat – so to speak – and the garnish doesn't interest you. Especially if the main course never changes.'

'Oh, it changes,' Lyra replied. 'There's always some new act or position. But it doesn't get any *better*. Solon is wearing me out. No doubt Medelie could keep up with him, but I'm not a mage.'

Basia gave her a sympathetic look. 'Have you told him that?'

'I wouldn't know how. I'm sure he keeps a tally.' She sighed morosely. 'I want to know him better, but the more layers I peel away, the less of him I find.'

'Well, you know I've never seen him as anything more than a particularly successful bully,' Basia sniffed. 'He's a hollow man, a suit of armour with nothing in it.'

'No, he's more than that, I'm sure,' Lyra protested. 'But I can't reach whatever's inside. Perhaps the problem is me?'

Basia laid a hand on her arm. 'No, never think that. What we're all looking for is love. Sex enhances love, but it can't replace it, or create what's not there. Solon's not that man for you. You'll find someone else, if you're open to it.'

'Will I? People think I can choose any man in the world, but the truth is, come spring – *if* we're still in power – I'll have maybe four or five princes to choose from. What if I loathe all of them?'

Basia gave her a sympathetic look. 'I do understand, Majesty – even the lowliest tavern girl has more choices than you. But you know why it has to be.'

Lyra knew. She stroked her son's hair as he suckled happily, falling in love with him all over again. 'Yes, everything I do is for Rildan, and for House Corani. I know my duty.'

'Then you should focus on that. You need to make sure Takwyth knows his place. He already thinks he owns you – if you let him get emotionally involved, it'll be worse. Play with hearts and you break them.'

'I know,' Lyra said. 'Soon . . .'

But she thought of how good it was to have someone in her bed when she woke from a bad dream, or lay awake terrified her world was collapsing around her. The sheer physical comfort of another's protective arms still felt worth the sacrifice; it gave her the strength she needed. And she'd need that strength today, because among her duties was the sentencing to death of two men she'd never met.

Domara watched the queen depart for her morning at court, ensured the maid was busy, then descended by a back stair to the temporary chapel, where Father Germane, the new royal confessor, was hearing Unburdenings. She ignored the smattering of worshippers as she waited her turn, musing sourly that when a *fit and decent ruler* had sat the Imperial throne, the royal chapel had always thronged with courtiers.

It was the heart of the Bastion – and that girl wrecked it!

It was written in the *Book of Kore* that at some point, every man and woman must choose: are they living for themselves, or for something larger? Do they chose an animal life of feeding, breeding and dying, or do they take up arms in the Eternal Struggle between Kore and his despicable enemy, Lucian, the Lord of Hel?

Domara's family had always been neutral in the power-struggles of court, and her skills had won her the post of Royal Midwife through the reigns of four different rulers. But she wasn't neutral in the Eternal Struggle: she was a warrior of Kore – and she could feel Lyra becoming one of the enemy.

Finally it was her turn to Unburden. She swept into the curtained box, knelt and intoned the ritual words while her eyes pierced the curtain to ensure it was *him*. 'Father Germane, thank you for seeing this wretched sinner.'

'Dear Sister Domara,' Germane said, his voice melodic, soothing. 'What troubles you?'

'Father,' she told him, 'it's become *awful* here. That girl is getting worse.'

He didn't need to ask who that girl was. 'It must be hard for you,' he murmured.

'It's horrible to see her go bad, like watching an apple rot, and worse still to see a good man rot with her. I despair for him, the things I've seen the two of them do.' She looked up. 'Do you know of Lucian's Trident, Father?'

'I keep my eyes on the Light. I do not make study of the Darkness.'

'Nor do I,' she replied fervently, 'but there are things you learn when dealing with birthing.' She dropped her voice. 'The old tales say that the Lord of Hel has three cocks, two between his legs and one in his mouth, instead of a tongue. When he takes a woman, he penetrates her thrice at once, in each orifice. That's how witches are made.'

'Folk tales, Sister.'

'Oh, I know, but she *is* a witch: how else could she persuade the greatest knight of the realm to lay with her when her husband is but two months in the ground?'

She didn't tell Germane how she knew, and he didn't ask. Lyra was oblivious to the fact that the venting grilles could be used to spy, or that the linked balconies meant a crack in the curtains could easily be looked through. Perhaps that was wrong, but the girl's sins were worse.

'She's only a woman,' Germane commented. 'Surely it's Takwyth who is master of their sinful bed?'

'No, I've seen and heard her, directing him to do this or that. She's become a wanton. I sometimes wonder if there's a daemon in her.'

'They say daemons were behind Reeker Night,' Germane conceded.

'Exactly! What if we have a creature of evil on our throne? Did you know that the night the Aerflus froze, she was *conjuring* in her garden?'

'But that was the night the traitor Ostevan was made to flee the Celestium,' Germane pointed out.

'The word "traitor" is swiftly attached to any who oppose her,' Domara pointed out.

'Domara, she can't possibly be possessed. Others would know. Lord Setallius—'

'I don't trust that warmed-up corpse,' she interrupted. 'I never have. He's likely possessed too. My darling Constant never needed a spymaster at his side.'

People had tried to tell her that Constant had been a bad emperor, but she knew better: she'd brought him into this world. His son Cordan was the one who should be ruling now, that dear boy.

'Domara,' Father Germane said, 'your duty is to little Rildan: his body and his soul. His mother must be traumatised by what she's been through. Be patient and I'm sure she'll rediscover the Light.'

'How, when she refuses to see a confessor? They say she took your predecessor to her bed. I never trusted Ostevan.' Then she sighed and tried to let go her anger. 'I try to forgive her, Father. Kore knows I try.'

They prayed together, that Rildan might retain his native innocence and that the queen might rediscover virtue, though Domara's heart wasn't really in that sentiment. In her mind, *that girl* was past redemption.

'The next case is Frankel and Coldwell,' the court bailiff intoned. 'Incitement to High Treason.'

This is it, Ari Frankel thought. *This is the moment I've dreaded.*

Neif broke down again – he'd never had the courage to match his passion – but Ari felt only a glassy sense of unreality, as if this were all happening to someone else. Heavy-handed guards marched them down the corridor, chains clanking. The sound of the crowd grew as they approached, sounding like angry wasps.

They entered the chamber and the noise trebled as all heads turned their way: piercing eyes, gossiping mouths, the heat and sweat and perfume and piss-stink of close-packed bodies, all come to see *justice* served. It reminded Ari of his speeches in the south, the upturned faces, the hunger for something out of reach . . .

One last crowd . . . No, there'll be another, when they hang us.

He and Neif were standing before the judge, his friend barely managing to stifle his sobs. Ari just wanted it over and done. He scanned the faces below, then glanced up, behind the judge, and gulped.

Dear Kore, it's really her.

The queen herself was here, for *his* case, seated on the balcony above with a small group of immaculately attired men and women. Ari was momentarily bewildered, until he remembered that the Inquisitors had vindictively added the word 'High' to his charge of 'Treason' to ensure the worst possible punishment. High Treason required a royal witness, and currently the only royal person in the court of age was Lyra herself.

Watching the condemned is probably her idea of fun, Ari thought in sullen anger, but her presence had served to reawaken some of his fire. He took the chance to stare up at her, this one chance to see the person whose reign he'd dedicated his life to ending, along with all her so-called nobles.

You're all as noble as a plague of locusts.

The empress was pale from lack of sun. Blue eyes, and her hair was a honey-blonde hue: pretty enough, but of course she was – these mage-nobles could be whatever they liked. A full bosom encased in an embroidered dress of deep Corani green. Pursed, anxious lips and tired, dark-smudged eyes.

Yes, be worried, Ari thought. *They're going to lop your head off too, soon enough.*

She met his gaze, then tilted her head to the bearded man beside her murmuring in her ear – from his scarred visage, he had to be Solon Takwyth. Ari was good with body language: he knew at once that they were lovers.

I curse their damned fornication. May they take no pleasure in it, and die of the pox.

The bailiff hammered his mace down. 'The court will resume, Justiciar Corves presiding. The prisoners are charged with Incitement to High Treason, for which the penalty is death by hanging, increased to evisceration if active intent to commit High Treason is proven.'

Neif's legs almost gave way as the extent of the punishment sunk home. Ari didn't feel a whole lot better; evisceration was a horribly slow and agonising death.

'The arraigned are Ari Bergholt Frankel and Neif Carrick Coldwell, both of Jastenberg,' the bailiff announced. 'We have recovered testimonies taken by the Holy Inquisition documenting their infamous deeds.

The Church of Kore, as represented by the Grand Prelate's office, have agreed that this testimony is fair and unbiased, its provenance being the south, away from the current situation.'

That situation being that the empress and the Church are at war, Ari thought sourly. He wondered if any efforts had been made to verify the charges. *None, I'm guessing.*

'Do they have representation?' the justiciar asked.

'They do not, having no patron to stand for them,' the bailiff answered.

'Then they will be afforded the opportunity to testify for themselves,' the justiciar said, in a pained voice. Defendant testimonies were notoriously babbled, incoherent and seldom amounted to more than begging.

One last speech, Ari thought. He'd had little else to think of in the prison, barring the foetid cells, foul food, the cold and the incessant sobbing of his friend in the next cell.

The next forty minutes were a blur. He tried to follow the charges precisely, but he was too dazed from lack of food and water and sleep, and now the heat of the court chamber, to do much more than just remain standing without fainting.

Towns were listed, quotes from speeches cited . . . *Did I really say we should 'lop the bitch's head off' that many times? I thought I'd been more careful than that . . . though of course my dear former mentor, Assessor Hanzi Albroch, wrote the charges, so it'll be whatever he wanted and truth be damned.*

'. . . and all testimonies are cited and vouchsafed,' the bailiff concluded. He then produced a pile of papers. 'This man is notorious for the distribution of pamphlets containing libellous and lewd images of important and, ahem, royal personages.'

The pamphlets had little to do with Ari; men he'd never met stole his words and attached them to crude pictures – but denying them was likely futile. The justiciar examined them, his scowl deepening, then he said, 'I attest that these documents conform to the legal definition of High Treason. They are not suitable for display.'

There was a salacious murmur at that, and many glances at the queen, whose face was now quite pink.

There were more than a few depictions of you and your confessor, as I recall,

325

Ari thought vengefully. *You should have been more discreet, your Royal Majesty.*

'You've heard the charges, viewed the evidence and heard the testimonials, Milord,' the bailiff summarised. 'The question of guilt, extent of guilt, verdict and sentencing are now yours. At this point, the defendants may make plea.'

'Guilty,' blubbed Neif.

It was well-known that a guilty plea usually meant the sentence was more lenient, and anything more lenient than evisceration would be priceless. But a guilty plea eschewed the right to speak.

'Not guilty,' Ari countered, and Neif shot him a horrified look.

The crowd babbled until the bailiff crashed down his mace again and shouted, 'Silence!'

'You can hardly be not guilty if your associate is guilty,' Justiciar Corves told Ari. 'Don't waste our time.'

The implicit threat of evisceration hung heavy in the air.

'My friend is afraid,' Ari said, looking up at Queen Lyra. 'We are *not* guilty, and I would speak.'

'Then do so, defendant Frankel,' Justiciar Corves said in a chilly voice.

Ari stepped to the front of his tiny platform, began to strike his oratory pose and found his manacled wrists and ankles impeded the movement, momentarily throwing off his composure and balance. Some of the colder-hearted tittered.

Recovering, he surveyed the chamber. His dilemma was that the crowd, his natural audience, was facing the queen and the justiciar, so he had to choose to either look the people in the eye, or address those judging him. Habit would have him facing the people, but here, only one person truly mattered.

And I want to see the bitch squirm.

He turned again and looked up at Her Majesty. 'I was once a priest,' he began, 'an Inquisition Bookburner charged to seek out heretical texts and destroy them. My superior was Assessor Hanzi Albroch, whose name you've already heard today, being the author of the charges against me. I loved Kore and served him with all my being.'

The court chamber was silent as the people realised that this wasn't going to be some gibbering bore but someone who actually knew how to speak. And best of all, the eyes of the queen were locked on him.

'But I found another love than Kore,' he told her. 'Not a greater love, but *another*. Its name is "the People", and strangely, I found that love in a book written in Lantris a thousand years ago: the *Res Publica*, by an unknown Lantric philosopher. It tells of the death of a childless king and how "Suffragium" – the right of every citizen to vote for their leader – resolved the succession and led to centuries of wise and prosperous rule. Suffragium wasn't just a means of leadership, but a philosophy: that every person has worth and the purpose of society is to harness that worth by sharing wealth and knowledge. The Lantric City-States were, compared to the tyranny of the Rimoni that followed them, a pinnacle for humanity. That pinnacle is what I wish to see restored.'

'The Lantric City-States failed,' Justiciar Corves said, in a bored voice. 'Get to the point – if you have one.'

'Two centuries of just rule doesn't sound like failure to me,' Ari countered. 'Some rulers would love to achieve as much "failure",' he added, looking straight at Lyra. He raised his manacled hands. 'It is appropriate that I stand in chains before Her Majesty, because so many of us are in chains in her empire. Our voices are chained, because she fears dissent. Suffragium thrived on discourse, but she would gag us all – you all know what I risk by speaking today: to have my belly opened on a platform in a city square and my intestines cut out piece by piece until I expire. But I will not be silenced.'

By the way Lyra blanched, he guessed she didn't like to think terribly hard about evisceration either.

But only one of us is going to endure it, in the near future, at least . . .

'Some of us have our chains forged for us by poverty,' he declared. 'Tithing to the Church is mandatory, and taxes are paid not by those who can afford them, but those who *can't* avoid them – but what is a society for, if it's not for its people? Do we the people exist only to serve the elite?'

The crowd murmured again and he recognised the sound from countless town and village squares: the interest in a point made, warring with the uncomfortable thought that perhaps things really weren't as they were meant to be.

But he was also aware that in the Bastion, few of this crowd were really of *his* people.

'Did I incite people to kill the queen? No! I categorically deny that charge, in its many, vindictively repeated instances. Think of who wrote them: my bitter ex-supervisor. But did I exhort a change in the way this empire is organised and run? *Absolutely!* Let Suffragium enter it and purify it – let our rulers *serve* the people, not exploit them. Tithing, tax-farming, oppression: these are the marks of a tyranny. We're told the monarch is the parent of the people, but what parent butchers her own? What parent gags them and robs them and exploits them?'

Belatedly Ari realised that he was now red-faced and roaring at the queen, but a fist to the face from the bailiff swiftly reminded him. His nose exploded, blood filled his nostrils and he staggered backwards against the back of his box.

Neif stared, mouth agape, then he rounded on the bailiff and shrieked, 'You gutless fucker – try that again–'

The bailiff did exactly that, sending Neif's head rocking backwards and knocking him out cold. He fell beside Ari and for a moment it was hard to discern whether he was breathing.

'Order!' Justiciar Corves bellowed.

The bailiff went puce as he realised he'd overstepped – and in front of the queen.

Ari glanced up to see how Her Majesty was taking all this, a little surprised to see her face was tight-lipped, her eyes surprisingly intense for someone reputed to be an insipid milksop. She was actually *listening*. Ari exhaled sharply through his nostrils, blowing out blood and mucus. He wiped his face on his sleeve, then faced her again. He noticed she was wincing at the sight of his blood.

He found his voice again. 'One of my followers, a simple but good man, mistook the word Suffragium for "Suffering": *the Sufferers*, that's what he named us, we who live in the shadow of your throne, Majesty. I have no doubt you'll do your worst to me, because that is the nature of your kind: to repress those you pretend to care for and stamp down any who threaten your position of power. We the Sufferers know what you are, Tyrant – and we also know a better way. One day the people will rise to claim it. Until then, you can feast on my entrails and I wish you pleasure of it.'

For what felt like the longest eternity, his eyes were locked with the queen's. At last she looked away, and he felt an incredible sense of worth and vindication.

That was what all this was for! That moment!

Beside her, Takwyth was glaring at him murderously, as if his tirade had been directed at him personally. *So what? I'm dead anyway.*

It was amazing how brave you could be when you had no hope.

The bailiff picked up his mace and slammed it down. 'The verdict is now awaited.'

Ari didn't care: he'd spoken, the verdict was obvious, but he didn't regret a word.

The justiciar mumbled under his breath, then said: 'The defendant Coldwell has admitted guilt and is sentenced to hang in next week's Assizes.' Ari was glad Neif was still unconscious and unable to hear that. 'The defendant Frankel has failed to prove inadequate testimony and committed further slanders in his speech. His guilt is clear and his greater crimes warrant the full penalty of law. Death by evisceration, in next week's Assizes.'

So be it, Ari thought. *You can kill me now, my queen, and I won't feel a thing.*

Unfortunately he knew that in one week's time he'd feel absolutely *everything*.

Then a clear female voice lifted above the noise of the court's reaction: the queen, interceding in her justiciar's court, as she had the right to do. 'The Crown will permit clemency appeals on the eve of the execution.'

Ari jolted, his eyes shooting to the queen's face. It was intent and, perhaps, compassionate. Beside her, Solon Takwyth was still spouting furiously in her ear, but she didn't look cowed at all.

The knight-commander raised his voice. 'Majesty, I don't–'

'It's decided,' the queen said crisply. 'Am I a tyrant who can't deal

329

with criticism? I heard an angry man voicing issues we ourselves have raised in council. I did not hear sedition.'

Takwyth grimaced. 'But—'

'*I have said I will hear his appeal. I do not have to justify myself, sir!*'

Takwyth abruptly went red and shut his mouth.

Ari stared. *So the mighty Knight-Commander Solon Takwyth can be overruled by that slip of a girl? Who knew?* He wasn't overly impressed, though. *I've excused half her crimes on the basis that her counsellors were the ones really running things, but perhaps all this incompetence is truly hers alone?*

What was suddenly, crushingly clear, was that he was going to have a mind-numbingly fearful week. Because whilst courage had been easy to find when he thought himself dead, now he was going to have to endure hope.

Lyra hurried from the court, seething. She let Basia guide her footsteps. Solon strode alongside her. It wasn't that fanatic's words which had set her temper on edge – *although how* dare *he call me a tyrant?* – but having Solon contradict her in front of everyone. She spied an empty office and marched in. 'Solon, just you,' she said, waving Basia away.

Solon strode in, jaw set. 'Majesty?' he said shortly.

His authority's been undermined. I spoke over him in public, when he thinks his standing is more important than mine in maintaining perception of Corani rule. He thinks people need to see him giving the orders.

He thinks by bedding me, he rules me.

'I *will not* have it,' she snapped. 'I am Queen of Rondelmar and even were we to wed, I would *always* be Empress to your Crown Prince. There is no permutation in which you outrank me, Solon. *Know your place!*'

'But Lyra, you've just given license to every man in Pallas to slander you – you're tolerating sedition—'

'I did not hear sedition – I am *not* a tyrant—'

'Don't you see? He laid a trap: calling you "tyrant" so that you'd have to pardon him to disprove it—'

'You think me so foolish?' she retorted. 'Why? Because I'm a woman? I am not soft on treason, but I'm no tyrant either – and in any case, *I will have my way on this.*'

Momentarily, she saw anger boil up in Solon's eyes, but he quelled it. 'I'm sorry. We shouldn't quarrel.'

She swallowed, pulling herself back from the brink of doing something she wasn't ready for. Maybe Basia was right and she needed to end their affair, but the hunger was still there. 'You don't possess me, Solon,' she reminded him, softening her voice. 'You know our arrangement: do you want it to end?'

'No,' he said hoarsely.

There, I am the stronger one. But I'm not yet finished with you, Sir Knight.

She held out her hands. 'Then come to me tonight and I'll let you apologise properly.'

'Another beer, my Lord?' Roland de Farenbrette asked and Solon looked around the table a little blearily. Since that pointless tiff four days ago, he'd ridden Lyra a dozen times to make it up, but tonight she was meeting an ambassador from Hollenia, so he'd gathered his inner circle at a tavern in Highgrange.

'Why not?' he said genially. 'My round.' That brought a hearty cheer; he'd never stinted when it came to keeping his mates in ale. Oryn Levis patted his belly and Nestor Sulpeter, youngest of the line, hiccoughed while the dozen or so men around the table thumped their empty tankards, bringing the tap-girls scuttling.

'To the queen,' he toasted, once the mugs were full.

'The queen,' they blared, clanking cups and swilling.

He took just a sip – he didn't want to have too much tonight. He wanted to knock the breath from Lyra's lungs again later. *And knock her up too, if that's an option.* She was weaning her child and could be fertile already.

Take the queen, win the table.

'And how is our dear queen?' Roland asked slyly. Nestor Sulpeter and Oryn Levis leaned in to listen, but the rest of the table had broken into a favourite Corani drinking song.

Solon hadn't been one to boast as a younger man, but bravado was part of being a fighting man and as age crept up, he'd become more verbose, part of reminding them who was the biggest dog in the pack. 'You know what they say, Roland: keep a woman moaning in your arms and she'll not moan about you behind your back.'

'Like a good tupping, does she?' Roland sniggered.

Nestor chuckled, but Oryn pulled a face. 'Respect is due,' he said dutifully.

'Oh aye,' Solon put in firmly, 'I'll not have *my* woman disrespected.' He winked at Roland with his left eye, on Oryn's blind side, and surreptitiously drew a trident with spilled beer. Roland went goggle-eyed and almost lost his mouthful in a spluttering guffaw. 'Or should I say, my future wife.'

Oryn, who'd not seen the trident, looked up, startled. 'Is it formalised?'

'Soon,' Solon replied. 'She has to go through the motions with the southern princes but the fact is, no one will touch her. They fear Garod too much. And me.'

At least, I pray that's what happens.

'Then are our hopes of allies doomed?' Oryn wondered.

'We don't need them. They know what happened to Garod's armies.'

The three knights leaned in even closer and Roland asked, 'What did happen?'

Obviously he couldn't tell them about the dwyma, but Setallius had devised a good lie for such questions. 'That was the work of Lyra and a few loyal Keepers,' he told them. 'Weather-magic of a new and potent kind. Garod's magi couldn't detect it. She's probably the greatest weather-mage of our age.'

Nestor looked at him wide-eyed. 'So between you and her, Milord, we'll be unbeatable.'

Exactly, Solon thought. *Even a slow-pate like Nestor can see it. So why can't you, Lyra?*

Dupenium, Rondelmar

Coramore snuggled beneath the covers, watching the ice-encrusted window panes. The wind whistled through the draughty castle while outside, the snow swirled in flurries. She snorted into a handkerchief and pinched her cheeks to make sure she looked just that little bit sicker. Her ginger curls were matted and flat and when she sniffled every few seconds her servants and ladies-in-waiting tutted sympathetically.

She was in fact perfectly fine, but Ostevan Pontifex was here and she dreaded being caught alone with him. She'd decided being sick was the best way to ensure she was surrounded by people and well out of his way.

On her lap lay a copy of the *Fey Tales*. She'd been reading one of the more obscure legends from Ventia: 'Pensa and the Crowitch'. Beautiful *redheaded* Princess Pensa was kidnapped by a wicked woman known as the Crowitch, who could turn into a giant black crow, summon storms and ate human eyeballs. Pensa was rescued, of course – it was a fey story, after all – but not before the Crowitch ate Pensa's right eye, a loss that had turned Pensa into a prophetess.

She'd been reminded of the tale because a black crow had been tapping on her window every night for the past week, always after her ladies were asleep.

She looked up anxiously at the door opening, and smiled to see Cordan, fresh from his gnosis lessons; sometimes he entertained her by showing off what he'd learned. But her face froze as Ostevan Pontifex followed her brother into the bedroom.

Cordan looked at her worriedly as the clergyman bowed, although his rank meant he didn't need to do that. He stroked his elegant goatee. 'My dear Princess Coramore, I was worried when I heard you were unwell.'

Coramore saw the way her *stupid* ladies gazed at Ostevan in awe and rather more prurient interest, and that irritation counteracted some of her fear. *Can't they see what he is?*

'I'm dreadfully ill,' she replied. 'Horribly infectious. It's best people stay away.'

'Perhaps the healing touch of Kore can soothe you?' Ostevan suggested, making half the women sigh.

Coramore might be only twelve, but she heard the innuendo in his words; being possessed by a daemon had left her aware of such undercurrents. 'My healers are aiding me,' she said defiantly, 'and I need to rest.'

Ostevan's smile almost concealed the way his predatory eyes fixed on her. He glided to her bedside and laid a palm on her forehead. 'Hmm, quite cool,' he noted. 'I rather think you're almost better, Princess. You've recovered from worse, I'm sure.'

He knows I was possessed by Abraxas and that the daemon was cast out of me . . . He knows because Abraxas is inside him, right now. It was all Coramore could do not to scream.

But Cordan, all unknowing, came to her rescue. 'My sister needs to rest,' he said firmly. 'Her room is her kingdom.'

Ostevan's smile twisted. 'Of course.' He stroked Coramore's cheek, but his stare was poisonous. 'You and I can enjoy a nice long talk when you're better, Princess.'

When he was gone, Coramore rushed to the privy and vomited. *So much for your healing touch*, she snarled inwardly. *But then, you're nothing to do with Kore.*

That night, when she was woken by a tapping at the window, she crept to the casement and unlocked it. The crow was waiting, a red berry in its mouth. When she ate it, she dreamed of *Pensa and the Crowitch.*

But this time, she was the witch . . .

23

Silver Quest

Kesh

O Kesh, forge of mankind! Where impurities are burned from us by the pitiless sun, where heat pummels us until we are ready to be moulded to Ahm's design, on His anvil, where we are made anew as the blades of the Amteh. O Kesh, fiery sword, raised against Shaitan's icy hand: in you lies our salvation! You are in us, wherever we go.

GODSPEAKER MEHRANT, SAGOSTABAD 890

Freihaafen, Mollachia
Janune 936

Valdyr Sarkany swung his axe into the trunk of a tall but slender pine, making the whole tree shudder. He was bare to the waist and the sweat streaming down his scarred back made it itch all the worse. He tugged the axe out and wiped his brow.

'Three more blows,' the giant creature beside him challenged.

Hearing words come out of a nine-foot-tall beast with the head, horns and fur of a rufine bull was at best unsettling, but Valdyr was getting used to it, as he'd had to get used to so many things of late.

'Two blows, Maegogh,' he replied in Rondian, the Mantauri chief's preferred tongue, and laid into the tree again, using a little of his dwyma-insights, limited though they were, to show him where the tree-trunk was weakest. *Crunch! Crunch!*

Clear!' he shouted; the men with the ropes tugged and the pine crashed down.

Maegogh's face wasn't made for smiling, but his guffaw filled the clearing. 'Not bad . . . for a human.'

Logging was the prime task in Freihaafen right now: for the palisade and the Schlessen longhouses. The first was now complete and more were going up fast.

'Tell me, where did your people come from?' Valdyr asked, as he and Maegogh stopped for water.

'An Imperial Beastarium in Brevin,' Maegogh replied. 'We were bred for war, along with several other breeds, but some animagi took pity and freed us. As making constructs with speech, human intelligence and the gnosis is *highly* illegal, we were hunted down. They slaughtered those they found, but we managed to hide in Schlessen Forest, where we met Fridryk Kippenegger. And here we are.'

All the Mantauri could shield and use gnosis and Valdyr had seen them alter their bodies from four legs to two. 'The empire would've been mad to breed more of you,' he said, then he blushed. 'I mean, with respect . . .'

The giant bull-headed construct boomed with laughter. 'Given our clear superiority to humans, you mean?'

'Well . . .'

Maegogh ruminated on that, then said, 'Truly, they were mad, the Sacrecour animagi. The emperor ordered it, we were told, but most likely it was his mother, Mater-Imperia Lucia.'

Nara of Misencourt's enemies, Valdyr thought. *Perhaps the very people we unleashed the storm upon last month.* Guilt still plagued him over that, but perhaps she really was in the right. *It's time we spoke again.*

His interactions with Nara through the dwyma had been a strange mixture of distance and intimacy. Mostly it felt safe: they could see each other's spiratus, channelled through the web of life that was the dwyma, but still maintain separation. But being close, even in that way, was hard for him. His childhood imprisoned in a Keshi breeding-house and the abuse suffered at the hands of Asiv Fariddan had left scars both visible and hidden.

Nara had sensed some of that, but they hadn't discussed it. He dreaded her contempt, that she might regard him as less than he was – especially as he'd begun to dream that perhaps she could be his salvation: a gentle soul with whom he shared the dwyma.

At least I can endure the semblance of closeness with her and that's no small thing.

He was suddenly aware that, as he often did, he'd gone silent in the middle of a conversation. Maegogh was watching him curiously.

'You're thinking of a woman,' the Mantaur rumbled.

'I suppose I am,' Valdyr admitted. 'She's pretty, with blonde hair.'

'I prefer heifers myself,' Maegogh said, adding with a chuckle, 'Mantauri, of course: the cattle are safe from us.' He gave a droll smile.

'That's good to know. It'd be awkward if I found myself milking your wife,' Valdyr replied.

Maegogh raised a shaggy eyebrow. 'You made a joke! Miraculous.'

I suppose it is.

Maegogh patted his shoulder with one of his massive hands. 'It's good to see you smile, Valdyr. Now, how many blows for the next tree, eh?'

Later that night they gathered in the first longhouse: it was sturdy, with hide sheets covering the windows to keep the freezing night air out and a thickly thatched roof which muffled the sound of the rain beating down outside. Smoke from the fire in the big central hearth exited through a pipe in the roof.

The entire populace of the small valley was squeezed inside: sixty Schlessen and Rondian men and an equivalent number of wives, and forty Mantauri of both genders, not to mention four dozen human babies and a dozen Mantauri calves. Kyrik was pleased to see there was little segregation, even between the humans and the constructs. If they were to survive, absolute cooperation was essential. Nevertheless, tonight he was apprehensive, unsure how much he could ask of these people. He'd offered them a haven in his land in return for their help in getting past the Rondian garrison at Collistein, which they'd done. He'd never in his worst nightmares envisaged that they'd become his last hope of saving the kingdom.

'Greetings,' he said loudly, speaking Rondian, the one tongue everyone here understood to some degree. 'Firstly, I want to thank you all for your labours. This longhouse is well-made – Freihaafen has a good heart.'

Everyone clapped each other on the back and applauded themselves.

'My cup-wish tonight is that this place will be the haven from which spring our labours to free all of Mollachia.' He raised his goblet and drank, and watched them all do likewise, then went on, 'It's important that you all understand what's happening in the wider kingdom. You know already that at my coronation ceremony in Hegikaro, men led by Dragan Zhagy set upon me, my wife Hajya and the seniors of Clan Vlpa, as well as your Thane, Kip, who was my guest. You also know my belief that Dragan's men were possessed by a daemon, inflicted on them by a man named Asiv Fariddan.'

It sounded more like a story from the *Fey Tales*, but magic was real and no one batted an eyelid.

'You should also know that Clan Vlpa, the Sydian tribe who came with you to Mollachia, are now in the Tuzvolg, well away from the reach of our enemies. I've spoken to Korznici, their senior mage, and they are safe, for now, at least.'

There was more applause at this, but that was the only good news he had. After a moment he sighed and said, 'However, we are still in a dire position: Asiv controls not only Dragan's men, but he may also have agents among the Imperial Legion in Lapisz as well. Somehow, we must find a way to defeat them.'

'How?' one of Kip's Schlessens asked bluntly.

'We think we have a way,' Kyrik replied. 'Rothgar Baredge, a ranger of the Stonefolk, has made a discovery.'

Rothgar stood, drew his sword and held it high. 'This is Wulfang, my ancestral sword: the weapon my great-grandfather was conned into buying. It's made of *argenstael*, an alloy of silver and steel which is too brittle to make a decent blade. I've cursed it most of my life – until the day it took down a possessed man with a single thrust. I stopped complaining then. We think the silver is the key.'

Kyrik broke in, 'Silver is often used by magi to inscribe protective circles that trap summoned daemons.'

Corley, a burly Rondian blacksmith with a beard halfway down his chest, called, 'I've worked argenstael. It's not just silver and steel; it's lead as well. It's a bastard to get right.'

'The possessed men can endure pretty much anything but brain damage or beheading,' Kyrik replied, 'but Rothgar stabbed one in the chest and he went down instantly.'

'Oh, I'm not saying it ain't worth doing,' Corley said, 'just don't be thinking it's easy.'

'Noted, thank you,' Kyrik said. 'It might be that just a dip in liquid silver will suffice. In any event, we mean to find out.'

The men and Mantauri murmured eagerly at that and Kyrik had to raise his voice to be heard. 'Silver is a priority now – and fortunately, silver mines are the lifeblood of Mollachia. I myself will lead an expedition to Banezust – the mine is closed, but I believe that between me and the Mantauri, we can get in and recover smithying equipment and as many ingots as we need.'

A Mantauri named Brom displayed biceps like tree trunks and boasted, 'I'll bring home a wagon on my back.'

'Problem solved,' Rothgar chuckled, and the whole room fell to boasting until Kyrik held up a hand for silence.

'Even having argenstael and silvered weapons won't make victory easy,' he warned. 'The bite of these possessed men bite is dangerously infectious. But at least we'll have a chance.'

'This is good, yar,' Maegogh growled, 'but we cannot win from here. Hiding only buys time, it doesn't bring victory. At some point, we must go out and fight.'

'My friend speaks truly,' said Fridryk Kippenegger. 'Cowering doesn't weaken our enemies: Minaus knows this! We must gather those who are free, arm them and fight.'

'Yar, bruda,' the Schlessen Bullheads agreed, 'Gather the free—'

'Gather the free,' a cluster of Mantauri echoed, and the room filled with vows of intent.

Kyrik glanced at Valdyr, who was sitting with his arm around his wolf, Gricoama, who was following the talk as attentively as anyone present. Kyrik wordlessly invited his younger brother to speak, but Valdyr shook his head, so Kyrik instead turned to the Schlessen thane.

'What about supplies, Kip?'

Kip always knew his people's situation. 'We're in for a tough winter and we'll need to butcher some of the rufines,' he said, looking at Maegogh apologetically. 'The herd is precious, but we must live.'

The Mantauri owned the rufine herd; at times in dangerous territory they'd concealed themselves among the cattle. Maegogh wrinkled his muzzle, but he made a gesture of assent. 'It should be a last resort, but I accept the necessity. We must preserve our grazing, so long as the valley remains free. Should our enemies find us, that's the first thing we lose.'

'If they find us, we're all dead,' Rothgar put in. 'This is a fine hideaway, but there's only one way in or out.'

'We are the Bullheads,' Kip replied, 'and we don't die easily, man or Mantaur.' His people growled in agreement.

The rest was just housekeeping and soon after, the meeting broke up. Those adults who were still wakeful went down to the lake, walking barefoot through the snow and plunging into the hot pools, while Kyrik, Valdyr, Kip, Rothgar and Maegogh adjourned to one end of the longhouse to sip a brew that some of the women had made from fermented grain.

'The fact is, they'll find us soon,' Maegogh warned. 'We must be ready.'

'We need that silver, urgently,' Rothgar added.

'Will you come to Banezust?' Kyrik asked Valdyr.

'Perhaps . . . Gricoama and I need to find a certain place, but it's not a journey lightly made. I don't feel ready . . . but Banezust is on the way . . .'

'Where do you need to go, Brother?'

Valdyr bit his lip, then made an apologetic gesture. 'Honestly, if aught goes wrong at Banezust, it's best no one knows. I mean no offence to anyone, I swear. And . . . I think I'm going to need Nara's help.'

Kyrik had been thinking about that. 'You've had to somehow gain the consent of the dwyma to use its power, yes? Then so did this Nara, I presume?'

'I suppose so.'

'How does the dwyma judge your worthiness, then? Can it discern good and evil?'

'I don't think it sees in those terms,' Valdyr replied. 'Luhti taught me that the dwyma is the power of life, formed by living energy: its wish, so far as it has any, is to preserve itself. There's a part of the dwyma that sees humanity as a blight, one that destroys forests and kills animals. That's what drove the early dwymancers insane.'

'Comforting,' Rothgar remarked to Kip. 'I hunt for a living and you lot spend your days chopping down trees.'

Kyrik threw them a warning look, then said, 'Valdyr, I trust you. I know I said earlier that you shouldn't contact Nara again, but perhaps I misspoke. If you think you need her, then try. What is there to lose?'

Valdyr gave him a troubled look. 'I don't know, but there'll be something.'

Valdyr decided he would join Kyrik's expedition to Banezust. They took four days to finish the palisade and prepare and on the final evening he took Gricoama to his favourite spot on the far side of the lake where he'd made a little lean-to. Now he settled down to listen to the aether.

He'd been building up his courage. Physical peril had never held him back, but the world of the dwyma was murky and so was that of empire politics, and Nara represented both. But he took comfort from their previous interactions: he liked and respected her.

But she's also capable of using the dwyma to take thousands of lives. Does power of any sort warp us?

It wasn't an easy notion, but his need remained, so he lit a fire, stared into the embers and listened. When he finally felt her presence, he pushed his reluctance aside. <Nara?>

Instantly, they were together: she wrapped in furs in her wintry northern garden and he beside his steaming lake. Gricoama gave a soft grunt, as if he saw her too. She looked tired, but her blue eyes twinkled as she greeted him. 'Valdyr, I'm glad to see you.'

So was he, but he didn't want to say so, not when so much between them was unresolved. For a moment they floundered, then he blurted, 'How did you find your genilocus?'

She looked relieved to have a neutral topic. 'I didn't have to look: it found me. There are dwyma sites all over the north. Eloy, one of the first dwymancers, used dwyma-blessed brackenberry seeds to unite the dwyma. Saplings were planted all over the place. Was there such a tree at your old dwyma place?'

'There were old trees on Watcher's Peak,' Valdyr remembered, 'but that place was Luhti's, and it died with her.'

'So you need to find another?'

'Ysh: I've been told of a place, but she said I'd know when I was ready – and truthfully, I'm not sure I am.'

Nara frowned, lines creasing her serious forehead, then said, 'I'd send you a sapling or a seed if I could, but the original Winter Tree was poisoned and burned.'

'What do you mean, poisoned?'

'With daemon ichor, while there was no dwymancer to protect and guide the power.'

That a genilocus could be poisoned was alarming, but he was glad to know of the possibility. 'What did you do?'

'I've replaced the old Winter Tree with a sapling propagated from it, but luckily I've an older sapling already, in my garden. Thankfully, the dwyma network has remained intact and united here.' She looked up at him. 'What about you? How did you find the dwyma?'

He decided he could reveal this. 'For me, ghosts in the genilocus gave me a stag's heart to eat . . . I suppose the stag had been blessed by it somehow. But I'm struggling to learn how to properly gain and use it. My brother has the gnosis and he says that it's consistent and explainable – but dwyma doesn't seem to be.'

'But it's bigger, and it makes things right,' Lyra said, with certainty.

'Does it? Who were those men I helped you kill?'

She'd evaded that question before, but this time she answered. 'They were Sacrecour soldiers who were coming to destroy my people. I'm of House Corani.'

Aligned to the empress, then . . . Valdyr bit his lip. *Her people sent the tax-farmers here* . . . But Nara couldn't have been party to that . . . 'Thank you for telling me.'

Her spiratus drifted closer and her hand closed on his. 'It's so good to have someone I can talk to about this,' she said. 'I wish you weren't so far away. I'd love to see your land: it looks very beautiful.'

Her closeness, even though this meeting wasn't physical and she was a thousand miles away, felt claustrophobic and he pulled his hand free. She looked momentarily offended, then she backed away, giving him space.

'Can I ask where you live?' she said tentatively.

He swallowed. 'I don't think I should say.'

She looked at him squarely. 'Valdyr, if you would trust me with the name of your region, I might be able to aid you.' She bit her lip and said, colouring, 'I'm a powerful man's mistress. He could help you.'

Of course she's someone's woman, he thought dully. *Beautiful women are never unattached.* 'What sort of influence does he have?' he asked, his voice coming out more distant and judgmental than he'd intended.

She didn't look away. 'Enough to cancel debt . . . including tax-debt. To send more legions, or even recall the one that's there. What do you need?'

Dear Kore, he thought, *who on Urte does she sleep with?*

His tongue decided for the rest of him. 'Mollachia,' he admitted. 'I live in Mollachia.'

24

Walls

Be Prepared

Preparing the ground for battle is of immense value, as much for a mage as a soldier. Defensive wards are stronger when anchored. Traps can be laid and spirit allies summoned. But most important is to know your enemy.

XANN FERROGAN, VOLSAI HELM (COMMANDER), PALLAS 718

Norostein, Noros
Janune 936

Latif half-dozed, watching the patterns in the steam rising from their column, as Rani and the other elephants trudged along the iced-over muddy road that extended for a hundred miles from wrecked Venderon to here in the foothills of the Veronese Alps. Ashmak was snoring beside him in the top tier of the howdah, his head lolling against the wicker walls of their mobile tower. Wedged into his shoulder was a pale Vereloni woman with curly brown hair and a naturally cheeky face. She'd been someone's wife in Spinitius, but now she was a camp-woman, pregnant to Ashmak. War touched everyone, often ruinously.

'Ahm on High, it's cold,' Sanjeep was muttering from the driver's seat. The Lakh was suffering badly – they all were. The frigid air made their chests labour, exposed skin went numb, lips chapped, bones ached and muscles stiffened until they all moved like old folk.

They'd been climbing steadily all day and the milestones on the side of the road were finally counting down into single figures. Then Rani clambered up over a low ridge and the snow-covered trees parted to reveal the sight Latif had been waiting for. He nudged Ashmak. 'Brother, we've arrived.'

Ashmak jolted awake, disturbing Fara, the Vereloni woman. He joined Latif at the front wall of the howdah and they stared. The view filled Latif with dread.

Norostein, capital of Noros, was built in three tiers on the knees of the mountains. The slate-grey walls looked like they'd been excavated from the bedrock. A torrential river ran alongside the eastern flank and poured down the valley, where it was channelled into aqueducts and a moat that ran around the northern and western outer walls. Towers dotted the battlements. Atop the whole pile was a great castle.

'How in Shaitan's name are we supposed to get into that place?'

Ashmak just whistled. 'Hey, Fara, you see city before?' he asked in passable Rondian; he'd been spurred into learning once he'd found he was the father of Fara's child. Fara wasn't her real name, that was some awkward Vereloni word, but Ashmak called her that because Fara was Keshi for joy.

Fara shuffled on her knees to join them. 'Oh, Norostein,' she said. 'Very big. You not get in.' Her Rondian wasn't a lot better than Ashmak's – Verelon had its own tongue.

'You better hope we do,' Latif told her, 'otherwise we're all in trouble.'

'Oh,' she said miserably. 'Not good.'

It was as good an assessment as Latif could think of.

The elephants of Piru-Satabam III were diverted into one of the dozens of staging camps set up several miles from the city. The snow-covered landscape was bleak; the Rondians had burned everything on their retreat south, denying the invaders any forage at all. But they expected a few days' rest, at least: assault plans had to be drawn up and equipment readied.

It was a relief to enter the familiar chaos of the camp, with tents going up, feed-stands readied for the animals, cooking pits and latrines being dug and thousands of voices vying to be heard amidst the clamour. Ashmak took Fara off towards the whores' tent and didn't come back, leaving Sanjeep and Latif to settle Rani down and organise their own little camp beside her stall. Around them the usual fights were breaking out over missing gear and perceived slights, just as the Godsingers started wailing to signal the approach of prayers.

Dear Ahm, there're so many of us, Latif thought, taking in the expanse of tents, men and beasts that stretched as far as he could see across the plains. And above it all brooded the city.

They're up there; men and women I knew in Ardijah. Seth Korion, Jelaska Lyndrethuse. Ramon Sensini too, maybe, and his woman – what was her name? What about the priest Gerdhart, who thought he could convert me to Kore? Or those nice healers, Lanna and Carmina? Or the mad Schlessen giant, Kippenegger? What would they all think if they knew I was down here? Do they even remember me?

He had to fight the urge to stride up and knock on those massive gates and demand to see Seth. 'Let's stop this war, my friend,' he'd say, and Seth would open a cask of Brician wine and they'd solve everything. For a lovely moment, he held to that dream.

Then thunder cracked, lightning flashed in the Alps and he was back in reality, where Rashid's army was going to batter itself against that formidable pile of stone until one or other broke.

It began to rain again.

Seth and Ramon walked the walls of Ringwald, the highest tier of the city, which contained the old Royal Castle and the Governor's Palace. From their vantage they looked out across the lower tiers to the plains, which were covered in men, tents and wagons. There were campfires – too many to count – and the fug of smoke and steam caught the ruddy glow of the flickering flames, lending the scene an eerie, Hel-ish atmosphere.

Droplets began splattering down. 'It's Noros, so it's raining,' Ramon noted. 'I hate rain.'

'Better to be indoors, then,' Seth replied, 'rather than in a tent out there.'

'True: I've changed my mind – I hope it *really* pisses down: a complete deluge.'

Somewhat ironically, it was in this city that Seth and Ramon had first met, more than a decade ago, at the exclusive Turm Zauberin Arcanum. Seth had been enrolled there because his father had been overseeing the occupation of Noros; at the time, Seth could now see, he'd been an insufferable, gutless snob. Ramon had been a lowly part-Silacian student with doubtful parentage, his place funded by money of dubious provenance. Seth and his friends had bullied him mercilessly.

Somehow, being thrown together on the Third Crusade had turned them into friends.

'How's your daughter?' Seth asked.

Ramon got an uncharacteristically distant look in his eyes. 'My little Julia is a ray of light. Beautiful, and clever, too: of course, how couldn't she be?' he added with a wink. 'But I couldn't raise her,' he went on in a more subdued manner. 'She's with Lanna – you remember her?'

'Lanna Jureigh, the legion healer? Yes, of course. I thought you and she were, um . . . you know?'

'My life isn't one I'd ask of Lanna either,' Ramon said darkly. 'I sleep better knowing she and Julia are safe.'

Seth pressed his luck and asked, 'What about your father?' He was one of very few people who knew that Ramon was the by-blow of Calan Dubrayle, the Imperial Treasurer.

Ramon's clever face closed up; he'd never liked talking about that relationship, but he admitted, 'Surprisingly, we're in sort-of regular contact. He's got no other family, you see. He quite often calls me by relay-stave – and Julia too, I gather. He even sends her money – not that I let her go without – but we still have to keep it secret.'

The mercenary and the royal counsellor, Seth thought: *I bet you do.*

'I wish Alaron was here,' Ramon said, pointedly changing the subject. Alaron Mercer, Ramon's only friend at the Arcanum, had gone on to great things. He was now head of the Merozain monks, a magi order of unprecedented power, and living in Ahmedhassa with his Lakh wife and their children.

'Aye, that would be a blessing,' Seth agreed. 'I haven't seen him since the Crusade. But the Merozains and the Ordo Costruo are trying to save the Bridge; knowing Alaron, he's probably in the thick of that.'

'His father's still here, I think,' Ramon said. 'Vann's a good man.'

'Then we should look him up.' Seth gazed about, seeing the city of his youth with new eyes, noting the thick walls, the mighty aqueducts that supplied plenty of fresh water, the well-positioned towers. It was by far the strongest place he'd ever had to defend. And the coldest and wettest. He looked up at the heavens and groaned. 'Come on, let's find shelter.'

They could have used gnostic shields to deflect the rain, but that was showy; instead they had an impromptu race and Ramon blazed into an early lead, skimming down the steps at a mad pace and through an arch, just as Seth resorted to a kinesis leap to keep up–

–and Ramon careered headlong into a knot of well-dressed older men, crashing up against a startled lord whose gnostic shields softened the impact.

'Stop here!' the Noroman noble bellowed, planting his palm in Ramon's chest, just as Seth caught up. 'What are you two bravos doing in the palace grounds?'

'Kick his arse to Lowertown, Milord,' one of the lord's friends snickered, eying Ramon menacingly. 'He's likely crawled out of that gutter anyway.'

The largest of the man's entourage stepped in, flexing a fist. 'He looks like a damned Rimoni.'

'It's worse than that, I fear: I'm Silacian,' Ramon said mockingly, sweeping his Lordship's hand away from his chest. That was enough to bring half a dozen blades out.

Seth hurriedly broke in, before someone got hurt, 'Gentlemen, he's with me.'

The nobleman drew himself up, looking at Seth disdainfully. 'And who might you be, young man?'

'I'm–'

'My capitano,' Ramon blurted, cutting Seth off. 'We're just lowly mercenary commanders, looking for the throne hall.' To stop Seth contradicting him, he stood on his toes. 'We've answered the call to arms.'

Seth shut up, examining the other man's coat of arms, but didn't recognise it. 'Whom do we have the honour of addressing?' he asked, in his best courtly voice.

'I am Sir Tonald Grace, hireling,' the mage-noble announced.

Never heard of you. 'Your renown speaks for itself, Milord. And the throne hall?'

'The governor doesn't receive hirelings,' Sir Tonald sneered.

'We'll put you merc-scum on the Lowertown walls, over Gash Lane where the wall's crumbling, so you die first,' the larger man rasped. 'Now rukk off.'

Seth balled his fist. *Even I have a temper*, he thought, but Ramon was plucking his sleeve.

'A thousand apologies,' he said, pulling Seth away. 'We're just leaving.'

Seth allowed himself to be led off and once out of sight, they shrugged off the incident and scampered through the maze of alleys and manors, small gardens and cemeteries that comprised well-to-do Ringwald until they found the Governor's Palace.

'So, we're going to meet the Governor of Norostein,' Seth said, pausing before the gates. 'Imperial appointee, obviously. There's some chance he might want to arrest me.'

Ramon pulled a face. 'Should I have brought some of my lads?'

'No, protocol wouldn't permit them to be allowed inside anyway. But I need to risk it.'

'Fine . . . Is the king a factor?' Ramon asked.

'I doubt it,' Seth replied. 'Ever since the Revolt, the king's been nothing but a figurehead. Poor man: remember how they used to bring him out on feast days and display him, chains on his wrists and ankles? No wonder Noros hates the empire.'

At the gates, Seth showed his ring and crest and vouched for Ramon. Passing inside, they bypassed groups of older noblemen with their wives, who peered at them curiously, nudging each other as they recognised Seth. Most of the looks weren't friendly.

'The Korion name, eh?' Ramon smirked. 'It's refreshing to be in places where people hate you more than me.'

'There can't be many of those,' Seth laughed.

They were shown into the main hall where they almost immediately bumped into Sir Tonald Grace and his men.

'I thought I told you to be off,' the lord snapped, and turning to the herald, started, 'Here, these men are—'

'I know who they are, Milord,' the herald said mildly, before turning and booming out, 'Norostein welcomes General Seth Korion, Earl of Bres, and Capitano Ramon Sensini!'

Seth nodded at the startled Sir Tonald and strode into the room.

The governor's throne – once the king's – was set at the far end of the hall. The crowds parted as Seth and Ramon walked the central carpet towards a distant figure robed in Imperial purple and white, wearing a heavy chain of office and frowning.

But they were only halfway there when they heard a strangled cry and turned to see Phyllios III, the King of Noros, shuffling towards them, tears running down his cheeks. His robes were threadbare and the chains on his ankles and wrists clanked as he moved. The thin, stooped figure with a pasty complexion and thinning brown hair looked overcome. A few courtiers tried to intervene, but they were elbowed aside by the quartet of Royal Guard flanking him.

'Majesty?' Seth said uncertainly.

King Phyllios tripped, Seth stepped forward and caught the monarch as he fell to his knees and was then mortified when the king seized his hand and kissed it.

'I remember you, Milord,' Phyllios babbled. 'You and your student friends, bringing the Noros banners out before the Third Crusade? We lost so many, but only you brought our men home. *Only you*. And now you've brought your army south!' The king kissed Seth's signet, then raised his voice and shouted, '*Noros rejoices! General Korion has come to save us from the Shihad!*'

Seth felt himself go pink as King Phyllios rose and clasped his hands around Seth's, tears still pouring down his face.

Someone shouted, '*Three cheers for General Korion!*' and the throne room resounded with his name.

'Don't get big-headed,' Ramon murmured in Seth's ear. 'This is a power-play: if the Imperial army abandons Noros, then who should lead her defence? The governor?'

Seth was still digesting that when one of the Royal Guards stepped in and slipped his arm under the king's. 'Sire,' he said, 'please, you should be seated on your throne.'

King Phyllios cast a longing, loathing look at the end of the hall, where the governor waited. '*That's* my throne,' he breathed, for a moment not a chained dog but a wolf. 'Set us free, General. I beg you.'

Seth tried not to react, because the king had once led the Revolt against the empire Seth served, but it was impossible not to feel empathy for the down-beaten monarch, and something in his gaze must have reassured Phyllios, because he smiled and allowed himself to be led away.

No man should be treated like that.

Seth gathered his self-possession, then walked towards the governor, Ramon behind him. He gave the imperial salute, fist to heart, and said, 'Seth Korion, Fifth Army, reporting.'

The governor's major-domo spoke. 'Governor Rhys Myron welcomes you to *his* court.'

Governor Myron was a hirsute, dark-haired man with a calculating demeanour. His eyes trailed from Seth to Ramon to a clergyman lurking nearby. 'Welcome, General Korion,' he said, his voice guarded. 'Noros is indeed pleased to see you and your men. But we have much to discuss concerning the defence of the city.' He glanced at the major-domo and barked, 'Clear the court!'

This took time, mostly because Phyllios III could only shuffle and many in the court knelt and kissed his hand as he passed. Seth realised this was an act of defiance to the empire; as anticipated he'd walked into a complicated situation with many hidden pitfalls.

Noros revolted in 908 and it was crushed, but if we don't stop Rashid, there won't be a Noros left at all.

Eventually there were just a few men left in the long hall, clustered around the throne and looking at Seth and Ramon thoughtfully. Myron looked around the room, then frowned at a burly grey-haired man in his fifties at the back. 'Who are you?'

The grey-haired man cleared his throat. 'Justiciar Vorn Detabrey of Jastenberg, Milord. General Korion has taken me on as his legal advisor.'

I have? Seth thought, glancing at Ramon, who nodded faintly.

'That's correct,' Seth broke in smoothly. 'I'm, ah, not familiar with Noros law, so I asked for help.'

Governor Myron scowled but said, 'Of course. Well, here's the situation, Korion. I've got Lord Sulpeter demanding your arrest. I've got Treasurer Dubrayle demanding that I evacuate all our wealth by windship. I have enough food for four months in the emergency stores up here in the Ringwald – well, if the population was as normal – but there are almost three hundred thousand refugees in Lowertown. And I have only four legions – six if the two Noros legions in your army revert to me – which is far too few to defend the city. But my place is here.'

You would have already run if you could, Seth guessed, *but then you'd for ever be the governor who deserted his post . . .*

'As Governor of Noros,' Myron went on, 'I command that you return the Noros legions to me and surrender your commission as general. It's nothing personal, Korion, but I need my people in charge here. I could arrange that instead of you being taken to Sulpeter, you might escape to Bres . . . ?'

And become a fugitive. Seth quickly did the numbers. He had eight legions, forty thousand men, including Jelaska's. And Ramon's two mercenary legions, of course. If he gave back two legions, then he and Myron would have six each. But he needed eight to ten to defend the outer walls effectively. He turned to Ramon and found his friend had been pulled aside by the shrewish clergyman Myron had been glancing at – a prelate who appeared to be laying down the law to an unusually subservient Ramon.

What's going on? Seth found himself floundering, not knowing the terrain, but Justiciar Detabrey had stepped forward.

Speaking in that mock-puzzled voice lawyers often used to make a point, he asked, 'Lord Governor, doesn't an Imperial general in the field have authority over a local governor?'

'Only on the battlefield,' Myron retorted, in a surly voice.

'Yet Norostein herself is to be the battlefield,' Detabrey replied.

Myron glared. 'It isn't yet.'

'The enemy are encamped outside and readying their assault. By any legal definition, this is now a battlefield.'

Myron harrumphed, but he stopped to listen as a tall, austere-looking man murmured in his ear, then turned back to Detabrey. 'Even in such circumstances, the Imperial general only commands troop dispositions, supplies and discipline – but the point remains that Sulpeter has issued a warrant for General Korion's arrest.'

'The four Brician legions I've brought south were raised by me, and they'd just as soon be at home,' Seth replied, sickened to have to use the threat of mutiny with this *damned politician*. 'Magister Jelaska Lyndrethuse has brought her Argundian legion here, because of me. Capitano Sensini's two mercenary legions are here, because of me. Arrest me and you might find you've immediately halved your defences.'

Myron began to retort, then hesitated. 'This city can't hold with divided leadership.'

'Then don't divide it,' Ramon put in suddenly. He still looked somewhat pale and Seth sensed that he was absolutely furious about something, but his voice sounded defeated. 'Declare Lowertown the battlefield and place the city's defences in our hands. You'll control the food supply and the inner walls. If and when the city is saved, we'll depart and leave Noros in your hands.'

Seth frowned. That sounded a lot like surrender; that wasn't the Ramon he remembered. But when he tried to catch his eye, Ramon wouldn't look at him. Behind the Silacian, Seth saw the prelate was looking pleased.

What on Urte could a priest have over Ramon?

It wasn't a good compromise, but Seth realised he had little choice. It would mean letting down King Phyllios, and probably the bulk of the soldiers and citizenry too, but Noros politics weren't his concern. Of course, it also meant propping up Myron and leaving him free either to prepare for flight if the fighting went badly, or take the glory if it went well.

'What would you tell Sulpeter?'

Myron smiled tersely. 'That you have given your pledge to surrender when the city is safe and that I've accepted that noble offer in light of your value to the empire. I'm sure it would go down well at your trial . . . though of course we both know it won't come to that.'

We both know it will, Seth thought sourly. 'Very well, Governor, let it be so.'

There was a little more haggling, then Seth and Ramon were finally able to leave, their tails between their legs. Vorn Detabrey followed them and Seth turned and offered his hand to the justiciar. 'Thank you, sir, although I fear you're unwise to pit yourself against the governor.'

'The governor has legal authority, but my years in the Justiciary have taught me the limits of such things,' he said. 'I'm coming to believe that true power resides in the people.'

Seth raised his eyebrows. 'That's an unusual sentiment for a man of office.'

Detabrey smiled wryly. 'Perhaps I've prosecuted too many rebels of late. Anyway, General, I'll be available if you need me again.' He gave an address in Copperleaf in the second tier, then departed.

Seth turned to Ramon. 'What did that prelate say? I was set to defy that prick.'

Ramon shook his head. 'Too soon. Better to look beaten and lull them.' He cast a malevolent look over his shoulder. 'That priest knows who my father is and he's been using it to – well, let us say, "further his career".'

Seth bit his lip. That was a very close-guarded secret. 'Why should that matter right now?'

'Because when those pricks heard I'd shown up, they picked up my daughter Julia. Who is, of course, Dubrayle's granddaughter. Right now, I'm that prelate's bitch, and so is Dubrayle.'

Seth felt his spine sag. 'What's the prelate's name?'

'Pavius Prelatus,' Ramon growled. 'And he's a dead man.'

25

Legal Precedent

The Volsai

It is often said that knowledge is power, and the grandmasters of knowledge are those whose business it is to learn and exploit the secrets of others. Imperial spies – the Volsai – were created by Emperor Sertain and are the first signpost of his descent into tyranny.

ORDO COSTRUO ARCANUM, HEBUSALIM 793

Pallas, Rondelmar
Janune 936

'Justiciar Relantine, outline this case for me,' Lyra whispered to the portly man beside her, shifting on her hard, uncomfortable throne.

Every week it was her duty – one she could delegate but chose not to – to preside over the Court of Royal Appeal, which existed to adjudicate on potential miscarriages of justice. She was no legal expert and always had a justiciar with her, but she hoped she brought some humanity to what could be a cold process.

It was also harrowing. Only those condemned to die, or of noble or mage blood, could appeal to her, and the cases were always complex and often distressing. The punishments could be dreadful and she sought to mitigate those where she could.

The impressive Justiciary Halls had carved wood panelling and a high, curved ceiling painted with scenes of the Rimoni gods, especially featuring Criosa, Patroness of Justice.

'Majesty, this is an unusual case,' Rael Relantine replied. The senior justiciar was the primary candidate to be the next Imperocrator on her Royal Council. 'The defendant has signalled that if this goes badly for her, she'll appeal directly to you, but as it requires a decision today, we've moved the hearing directly to this court.'

'It sounds intriguing,' Lyra admitted, looking Relantine over. He had a mop of greying, curly hair, ridiculously long sideburns and a shaven chin which made him look like a plump rodent, but reports suggested a fair and open mind.

A tall, imposing man, the crown's legalus, rose. 'Your Majesty, peers of the realm, gentlemen of the court, the defendant is Lady Orsa Besham, titled possessor of Besham Castle in Siberland, on the Jusse River.'

'It's a large tract of rich farming land which commands the only safe ford on the Jusse, our border with Argundy,' Justiciar Relantine whispered. 'Highly strategic, in other words.'

'Argundy is our ally,' Lyra noted.

'Argundy claims all of Siberland and wars have been fought over it in my lifetime,' Relantine replied.

Lady Orsa, a widow, was being wooed by an Argundian knight from over the Jusse River. Her own kin, subordinate to her by law, were frightened such a union would pave the way for a fresh invasion of Siberland.

'Argundy is becoming increasingly bold,' the legalus said, 'The knight visits her frequently, with a retinue far beyond what is required. He seeks to intimidate as well as to charm. And the Lady herself is *indiscreet*.'

Lady Orsa was pinch-faced, and arrogant in her responses, and Lyra felt her sympathies waver. 'What's being decided here?' she whispered to Relantine. 'She's not married and she's free to be wooed – I don't hear a crime.'

'It's not a criminal case nor a moral issue but a property matter, Majesty.'

'Is her title in dispute?'

'In a manner of speaking.'

'Lady Orsa,' the legalus went on, 'I regret that I must be distressingly direct. Is the Argundian knight, Sir Baen var Pedan, paying court to you? And is he your favoured?'

'Yes,' Lady Orsa admitted, 'None of the bog-trotting fools my family place under my nose are worthy.'

The legalus turned to the justiciar. 'It is contended that Besham Castle is a strategic holding of Rondelmar and the Earl of Farris, the defendant's brother-in-law, wishes to choose her next husband.'

'He has no right to do so,' the defendant's legalus retorted.

'Not at present,' the legalus conceded, 'but legal precedents build future laws. As recently as 910, Argundy and Rondelmar fought over Siberland. If Besham Castle had fallen, Siberland might even now be Argundian. Yet this woman would hand the keys to one of the men who besieged her own keep.'

Lyra shifted uncomfortably in her seat. *Argundy see me as one of them, through my late father.* Last time she'd seen the Argundian ambassador, he'd hinted that she should be giving *her* people more.

Of course, Ainar wasn't actually my father . . .

So she paid close attention as the Crown case took shape swiftly and logically, arguing Besham Castle wasn't just a piece of titular property but a keystone in the defences of the empire. Lady Orsa had sworn oaths on inheriting it to uphold the sovereignty of her land. Marrying a potential enemy endangered the border.

Other damaging revelations came out: Lady Orsa was deeply in debt, perhaps a reason why the Argundian knight's wooing gifts were so gratefully accepted. 'So the heiress of Besham, keystone of the border, can be purchased,' the legalus declared. 'Debt leads to bondage – and here, to the altar!'

The defence rallied, reminding everyone that Lady Orsa's union to an Argundian wasn't illegal, while forcing a woman to marry against her will was. 'This court case is premature,' the defending legalus said. 'How do we know Sir Baen var Pedan will betray the empire? If he does, let it be contended then–'

'–by which time it will be too late,' the Crown legalus sneered. 'Has Sir Baen proposed?'

The defence legalus and Lady Orsa exchanged glances and the lady nodded sullenly.

'Then this matter *is* urgent,' the Crown legalus declared. 'Of course, normally the head of a family may *veto* a marriage, but Lady Orsa is her own guardian under law. Her wilful neglect of her duties endangers her lands and those around them, but she cannot be disinherited for those failings and we're not contending that she should be. If Lady Orsa were mad, we could depose her, but she's merely unfit to rule. She cannot currently be made to marry a more suitable man, or to accept supervision. Yet the empire requires a solution.'

'Is this risk real, Relantine?' Lyra murmured.

'I believe so: if Orsa was a steadier woman, perhaps it wouldn't have come so far. Not all noblewomen take their duties as seriously as you.'

'Nor all noblemen,' Lyra retorted, making Relantine smile in agreement.

The legalus reached his conclusion. 'The Crown proposes this: if – *and only if* – the realm's security is threatened by a titular ruler's neglect of duties, then they must consent to either supervision or subordination. Supervision would entail a governor being given control of the titular authorities of the titled person. Subordination would require that another be given precedence over them, from within their family. That person would be given the titular powers, but not the title. Or, in the case of a woman, at her discretion she may choose a husband approved by her family or legal guardians and that man would become titular lord.'

The defence's counter-proposal was simply that the Lady Orsa be trusted as titular head of a loyal family. He said she would always remember who she was, and delivered his speech movingly – but unfortunately, even Lyra didn't believe that.

The rest followed as predicted: the justiciar adjudicated in favour of the Crown and the Lady appealed to Lyra. The court went immediately into recess and Lyra went with Justiciar Relantine to a private lounge, to sip tea beside the fire and talk it over.

'I *really* don't like this,' Lyra told him. 'Any law that forces a woman to marry is reprehensible.'

'I agree, Majesty, but let's start at the beginning: should the Crown have the right to appoint a governor over a landed nobleman where our border is threatened by their incompetence or disloyalty?'

'I can dismiss an incompetent servant, right up to a Royal Councillor,' Lyra said, 'but I cannot touch the succession of hereditary land without proving treachery.' She thought about Garod Sacrecour. 'In some cases I can't even do that without sparking a war.'

'But would it be desirable to put your own person in, where someone titled is proving a dangerous liability?'

'I have prayed for such a right at times.'

'Well, this could be a way of securing it,' Relantine suggested.

She thought on that. 'If I accept that, the next question is this question of "supervision or subordination". We appoint governors in our vassal-states, so we have precedents. I'm not against it. But forcing a woman to marry . . . ?'

'It would give the family the chance to get its house in order. Remember that the proposal is that the *woman* has the right to choose this option, and to select a husband for her family's consideration. They might not approve her choices, but she wouldn't be made to marry someone she didn't select herself.'

'But couldn't such a thing be misused?'

'Most things can, unfortunately. Perhaps consider your own situation, Majesty. Let's say someone wanted to use it to depose you, or even force you to marry: they must go through the Royal Council, where you have a veto.'

'Fine, Justiciar, but Lady Orsa isn't me. What if she wasn't dislikeable, incompetent and broke? Just a woman who doesn't wish to let her jealous cousins steal her birthright?'

'An unmarried woman is always vulnerable, as I'm sure you're painfully aware, Majesty. Families are best left to resolve their own matters, if possible. This legal precedent would only affect strategic lands – of course, we'll need to define "strategic" very carefully. Most widows have children, or more senior men in their family; Lady Orsa is very unusual, being a titled widow with no close male blood relatives. This law would seldom be invoked. And don't forget, if the "incompetent" woman refuses to marry, a *Crown official* will be given management of their lands. No titled family desires that; it opens them up to all manner of risks.'

'I'll say,' Lyra admitted. 'Some of my governors are like foxes in hen-houses – and I don't mean that as a compliment to them.'

'Then do you see virtue in this solution, Majesty – and perhaps opportunity?'

Lyra sagged back in her armchair. These deliberations were always fascinating, but wearying, especially for a recently widowed woman recovering from childbirth who wasn't getting enough sleep, however self-inflicted that last was. But the Crown proposal appeared reasonable, and not too vulnerable to misuse. 'I will find in favour of the Crown, Justiciar,' she decided. 'Let it be so.'

Lady Orsa looked daggers at Lyra when the judgment was read, but Lyra was used to that sort of look by now. Laws would now be drafted for her approval, based on the legal precedent. She sent a little prayer upwards, hoping she'd done right, then focused on the next case: *Oh yes, Frankel and Coldwell.*

Frankel had *challenged* her and made her doubt herself, and although she'd been offended, she'd been intrigued by his ideas. *But is Solon right? Am I too tolerant of sedition?*

The prisoners were led in, both still chained hand and foot, shuffling along with heads down. Coldwell, the taller, skinner one, was shaking, but Frankel was watching her.

Judging me.

The skinny one fell on his face. 'Mercy, Majesty! We never spoke ill of you – *mercy*–'

He's nothing without his friend, she decided. She turned her gaze back to Frankel and said, 'Suffragium: the principle that all men are equal, yes?'

Frankel's eyes narrowed. 'Yes, Majesty, all equal–'

'All *men* equal, Master Frankel. There were no female characters in your book, *Res Publica*, I noted.' She'd skimmed it yesterday. 'Even the *Book of Kore* acknowledges that we of the "weaker, unclean gender" have the right to serve you menfolk.'

She rather liked the way his eyes lit up at her sarcasm.

'Majesty, the presence of women in *Res Publica* is clearly implied, and one has to remember the different periods. Female magi like yourself have advanced the cause of the feminine greatly by deed and example.'

Nice recovery, Master Frankel. 'But hasn't the existence of magi rather overthrown the whole concept that all men are equal? Clearly, a mage can perform the miraculous, but an ordinary man cannot.'

He perked up further. 'Ah, but you misunderstand what that actually means, Majesty.'

'Do I? Explain how: I *love* being corrected.'

He winced at her tone, but he had the gumption to carry on, 'What the phrase means is "All men must be treated equally by the laws and customs of society", Majesty. That murder is murder, for example, regardless of whether it is committed by a noble or a pauper.'

'All "men", again.'

'It's "men" as in mankind, Majesty. Women and men, together, equal before the law.'

'Did they achieve this in Lantris?'

He ducked his head. 'Er, no. Well, not properly. The right to vote and fully participate was only extended so far . . .' He trailed off.

'Let me guess? To males of wealth?'

He pulled a face. 'Yes, Majesty.'

She considered his words while studying a sheath of papers – the same pamphlets the justiciar had examined in court. They contained woodcut prints of various misdemeanours of the Crown and the Church, from tax-farming to warmongering, injustices perpetrated by the magi and clergy, and not a few personal slanders involving her in which she was portrayed as a vapid, promiscuous imbecile.

Some were quite funny. Others weren't. 'What was your involvement in these?'

Frankel was now bleakly dour again, as if he could again feel the disembowelling knives being readied. 'Some of the slogans are mine, garnered second-hand. I wasn't involved in their production or distribution, nor the pictures.'

'Your name is on all of them.'

'I asked them not to do that.'

'I'm sure you did.'

He raised his chin. 'Not out of fear, or even disagreement with the message, but because I had no control over them. I didn't like it, but my name gave it credence.'

'Did you exhort people to kill me?'

'No.'

She decided that she believed him. 'Do you wish to kill me?'

'No. I want the institution of royalty torn down. It's nothing personal.'

She showed him the most offensive pamphlet: an obscene depiction of her fornicating with Ostevan. 'This looks personal to me.'

He flushed, but remained composed. 'I had nothing to do with it.'

She nibbled her knuckles, a bad habit she was falling into of late. 'Very well, Master Frankel. I find you and your friend Master Coldwell *not guilty* of High Treason, or inciting it. I revoke the death order upon you both. But I do find you guilty of whatever crime covers calling me . . .' She picked up a random pamphlet and quoted; 'a *tyrannical sow in a pig-sty*. Defamation, yes? You are sentenced to . . .' She turned to Relantine. 'Do we still cut people's tongues out?'

Frankel almost collapsed in horror as Relantine said, 'Not usually, but you're Queen, Majesty.'

'Mmm. What would a Lantric ruler have done, Frankel? Didn't they throw people off cliffs?'

'That's so,' he squeaked.

Abruptly, she tired of the game. 'Master Frankel, I will not be called a tyrant. I permit far more be said in the streets about me than my predecessors ever have. But the world does not have room for your crusade. Magi and nobles rule it, for good or ill. Find ways to make us better; don't waste energy trying to tear us down. Now get out.'

Frankel and Coldwell stared. 'Uh ... jus' leave?' Coldwell said disbelievingly.

'Yes, *leave*. Find something else to do with your lives that won't get you hung.'

As Coldwell spluttered incoherent thanks, Frankel just stared. She gestured for the guards to get rid of them, which they did forcibly.

'He won't change,' Relantine noted, as the doors closed.

'Did I adjudicate wrongly, Justiciar?'

'No, you just gave him some rope. Don't be surprised when he hangs himself with it.'

She smiled sadly at that, then faced Relantine fully. 'I've made up my mind about who should take the vacant seat on my Royal Council . . . *Imperocrator* Relantine.'

She let him kiss her signet ring, hoping she'd found a new ally.

Ari and Neif stumbled on numb legs towards freedom, through a long arched walkway leading to the main gates of the Bastion and the vast expanse of the Place d'Accord beyond.

'She let us go,' Neif kept babbling. 'She let us go. Kore save the queen.'

Says my friend the revolutionary, Ari thought wryly.

They hurried into the light – *like babies passing through the birth canal into life*, Ari thought rather luridly. But at the darkest section of the gate-tunnel, right beneath a menacing-looking portcullis, a cloaked figure with lank silver hair stepped in front of them. A giant bearded man sporting twinned axes on his back loomed at his side.

'Master Frankel of Jastenberg,' the first man said. His voice had the timbre of age, although his pale countenance was difficult to judge. One eye was hidden behind an eyepatch; the other gleamed palely in the gloom. 'Leaving us, I trust?'

Ari stopped, suddenly afraid again. 'Of course we're leaving. Although I've been dragged halfway across Yuros from my home on trumped-up charges and left penniless,' he dared to fire back.

The silver-haired man smiled at that. 'You weren't *acquitted*, Frankel, you were *reprieved*.' He stroked his smooth chin then asked, 'Do you know who I am?'

'I know *what* you are: Volsai,' Ari spat.

The big axeman frowned, but One-Eye didn't react. 'Passage south won't be easy, Noroman. Jastenberg has been razed to the ground and the lands around it are occupied by the Shihad.'

Ari had heard that whilst in gaol. He was still grieving, for all he'd hated the place when he was younger. 'I have kin in Norostein, but that's under siege. I think I'm going to have to live here awhile – I've done it before.'

'Mmm, as a Bookburner,' the Volsai said coolly. 'Listen, Frankel, Queen Lyra meant what she said: she can take a little dissent, but you come up on sedition charges again and you'll go down.' Then he stepped closer and Ari tensed himself for violence. But the man only murmured, 'I can help you. Make friends among the rabble-rousers and tell me what they're saying and I'll see you've coin to get you through winter.'

To spy on my own . . . ?

Ari had no money, nowhere to shelter, nothing for food.

But I still have my pride.

'I'd rather eat shit in the dungeons again,' he snapped, grabbing Neif's arm and dragging him past the Volsai, not looking back, while the space between his shoulders itched like mad. But nothing struck him down and he emerged into the light, reborn. He limped with Neif across the Place d'Accord, still in a state of utter disbelief, not entirely sure these weren't the deluded fancies of a condemned man still locked in the death-cells.

They followed the main road into Tockburn with no idea what they'd do for food or shelter. Ari was steeling himself for more hungry days and freezing nights until he could find work; he could always scribe, he supposed.

But at the first crossroads, another cold-eyed man with lank hair stepped into their path.

'Frankel,' said Lazar. 'We heard you'd been reprieved.'

'Lazar? What are you doing here?'

The cold-eyed Midrean laughed drily. 'We ran out of Sacrecours to kill and thought "Fuck freezing to death in the wilds". When the Sacrecours got hammered by that storm we came here.' He looked Ari up and down. 'Down in Midrea, we're just outlaws. But here . . . I tell you, Brother, if you thought the south was ripe for rebellion, wait until you get the taste of this place. I know names, people who'll arrange for you to give speeches in secret. There's a strong urge to rebellion here, my friend. With your oratory and the right muscle, we'll be barricading the streets inside a month. Maybe even bring down the queen.'

'Why would you care about her?' Ari asked.

'Because once I had something, Frankel. I had a life – but I'll never have it again. There's nothing left for me now, but to drag down the sort of people who wrecked my life and take them with me to Hel.'

Dear Kore, he means it.

Ari's life as a dissident had always meant working with men he'd as soon not; among the disaffected, virtue and honour were not universal. But right now he saw little choice: it was either work with Lazar or go home. Embracing the man was like hugging a lizard and Ari's heart thudded as other men closed in: the prisoners he'd been carted north with, until the rebel and his henchmen had been freed to kill Sacrecours.

'I've got my whole crew here,' Lazar told him. 'We're going to burn this rukking city to the ground.'

Solon Takwyth strode through the practise yard where burly men with big shoulders hammered away with blunted swords at static targets or each other. He felt like an old lion watching the younger beasts circle, knowing the end would be soon.

'Milord?' someone called.

He thumped his chest in response, not looking, all his thoughts inward. *I've fought for House Corani all my life. I deserve to rule it – and yet my future rests on her approval . . .*

He could feel the mood between them changing. Just a few short weeks after laying Lyra for the first time, and despite having her every which way, he could feel her slipping through his fingers. The first two weeks she'd been insatiable; she'd wanted *everything*, but this week she'd been making excuses every other night, and those parts of the game she'd liked less were no longer on offer.

She should be wanting more, not less. Medelie did . . . It was galling, because he was growing more dependent on her, not less. He couldn't get the taste of her out of his mouth, or her enraptured face out of his eyes . . . *This is what I returned to Pallas for: to take down Ril Endarion and claim her. Ril's gone, so she should be mine.*

'Milord Takwyth?' That persistent voice came again.

'What?' he snarled, turning his head.

Grand Prelate Wurther's bodyguard, Exilium Excelsior, was about the last person Solon needed to see right now, especially as everyone had stopped to watch the exchange. Solon knew why: the practise yard was a bullpen where dominance was established, slights settled and the tallest stalks hewn down – you're too pretty, we'll rough you up; you're a bit timid, we'll break you; you looked at the girl I fancy, I'll smash your testicles; you talk too clever, I'll break your jaw – and all in the name of martial prowess, the only real measure of a man.

Except how his woman moans under him.

'Well?' he demanded, aware that Excelsior had beaten every man of note in the short time he'd been in Pallas. Men spoke of his speed, precision and preternatural technique with awe. But this was the first time he'd dared come to the Corani yards when Takwyth was here, and that was a direct challenge.

And his copper-skinned Estellan face really was far too pretty – it badly needed breaking.

'I would be honoured if you sparred with me,' Excelsior said, with a smooth bow. 'It's an ambition of mine to serve the queen as you do.'

Is it just? You're not getting near her, you cunt.

In truth, Solon had been avoiding this moment, scanning the yard to ensure the Estellan wasn't there before going down, although he'd been having him watched to spot weaknesses. But he'd not been able to resist a drink or two . . .

And that's bloody Lyra's fault. The nights I don't have her, there's only the bottle . . .

Beating this southern shit-smear would do much to restore his mood, though. Word would get round that the old lion had roared. And he knew how to ensure things went his way.

'Of course,' he growled, and strode into the middle arena as his men formed the circle, already nudging each other and placing bets. He took a practise blade, rejected it and picked up another, aware he reeked of wine and his guts were churning. 'Pure fencing or gnostic?' he asked as he flexed and limbered in a perfunctory manner, his mind still on women who got above themselves.

The Estellan executed a perfect set of thrusts and shrugged. 'As Milord prefers.'

'Pure, then,' Solon decided. 'No gnosis.'

Excelsior made a fancy bowing move that ended with his hilt pressed to his lips, the blade pointing skywards. 'Whenever Milord wishes to begin.'

As he drank some water, Solon glanced around the circle, noting the faces. Men he knew, all of whom he'd flattened at some time, then picked up and shook their hands, earning their loyalty. Good Corani men, wanting to see their lord knock this upstart down a peg or two – but also interested to see if he still had what it took.

He caught the eye of Sir Roland de Farenbrette. They called Rolly 'the blacksmith' because he fixed things, hammering those who needed a beating. Roland acknowledged slyly; he knew what was required.

Solon turned back to Excelsior. *Right, you greasy choirboy, let's see what you've got.*

The old lion and the young pretender: a dance older than mankind.

He launched himself at the Estellan, hammering in a flurry of blows until their blades locked at the hilt. He ignored the painful creaking in his damaged collarbone and dashed his foe's blade sideways, then lunged, fully expecting to see his wooden blade punch into his foe's gut.

But Excelsior somehow arced aside and cuffed at his face with his left fist, disengaged and danced sideways. Solon grunted angrily, belched last night's wine and turned, raining in blows from left and right to keep the Estellan penned, driving him to the edge of the circle, then kicking at Excelsior's front foot to tip him up and thrusting at his midriff—

—except that Exilium blocked it all, his planted foot withstood the kick, he lashed out with a kick of his own to Solon's midriff, then his blade slashed sideways. Only a frantic parry prevented Solon from being hit – but Excelsior was still moving, flowing into a lunge that Solon had no hope of blocking while off-balance . . .

Just as Roland de Farenbrette, behind the Estellan, slammed his gauntleted fist into the man's kidneys.

Excelsior staggered, his guard dropped and Solon charged, crunching his blade into the Estellan's ribs and probably breaking a few. He lashed his boot sideways into the young man's knee and saw it buckle sideways, ligaments likely torn, then drove a left uppercut into his face as he doubled over. Excelsior's whole body splayed in the air as his nose broke and blood sprayed. He dropped his blade as he went over on his back and his head smacked into the ground; his body twitched, then he lay in a limp heap.

Solon bent over him, making a show of asking, 'You all right, lad?' before breathing wine fumes into his face, and when the Estellan's mind responded, he grated <*That's how we rukk a cunni like you.*>

The Estellan groaned. <*Dishonour . . .* >

<*The only honour to be had is in winning, boy. You want to serve the queen? She doesn't need a weakling like you. She needs real men who know how to give her what she needs.*>

Excelsior's eyes blearily tried to focus. <*Queen . . . virtue . . .* >

<*Virtue? I've ridden her more times than you've had hot breakfasts. She likes it up the arse, like one of your Estellan whores, so you've got that in common, frocio. Now piss off and don't come here again.*>

Then he stood and said aloud, 'Well fought, boy. You've got promise.'

He strode away, rejoicing behind a stoic mask: *What a glorious bloody day!*

Behind him, Sir Roland rallied the lads to give the little snit the beating they'd all been dying to hand out.

Lyra paced back and forth, furious, and yet strangely relieved. *The truth is, I've been wanting something like this to happen, some firm reason to end it.*

She'd chosen a gallery on the north wall to meet with Solon, a semi-private space, but one where Basia, at the far end of the hall, would be in sight but not hearing.

He had a man beaten almost to death!

She'd chosen her most prim dress, high-necked and formless, and tied her hair back severely, because he preferred it loose. She wanted to appear untouchable. But when he appeared, walking blithely into the gallery, pausing, then spying her, she felt her belly warm: her traitorous body still craved him.

No, she told herself. *It has to end.*

'Lyra,' he said, breaking into long strides and sweeping into a bow, a smile touching his grim features as he went to embrace her, clearly thinking this was an assignation, a new venue for their games. Then he saw Basia in the distance and hesitated.

'Solon,' she said coldly, 'we need to talk.'

He flinched with what she hoped was guilt. 'What about?' he asked, straightening so that he towered over her.

'About what you and your men did to the Grand Prelate's bodyguard.'

He snorted dismissively, which angered her further. 'What of it? He tried to make a point, but I made one instead.'

'He nearly *died*, Solon. Healers had to drain blood from his lungs – a fine young warrior, Dominius' own bodyguard, the man who killed Dravis Ryburn, may be crippled for life. Is that what you are so proud of? The Grand Prelate and I agree that restitution is due.'

'Priests are like women,' he sneered, then he realised his misstep too late. 'I mean . . . I don't mean . . . Lyra–'

'Like women?' she echoed. 'How so? Because we're weak? Only useful when we're kneeling?'

His colour deepened. 'Lyra, I don't–'

'I cannot condone acts of senseless violence.'

'It wasn't senseless–'

'*What?*' she shouted, not caring now if Basia heard. 'How was it not senseless? *I expect better of you!*'

His face contorted, somewhere between fear and anger. 'You know *nothing* about the world of men, Lyra. We *compete*: it's what we do – and Excelsior came into the yards expressly to beat me down, *to break my authority*. He knew what he was doing and he knew the price of failure. So rukk him! He got what he deserved.'

'No,' she retorted, '*not* good enough. Would you like to talk about Roland de Farenbrette's role in this? Should I let the Grand Prelate drag you all into the courts?'

'The courts?' Solon sneered. 'Real men don't take their grievances to court–'

'Yes, I see that now: only *priests* and *women* do.' Lyra was absolutely seething now, and that gave her the strength to put her hands on her hips and say, 'That's it, Solon. I've had enough. We had an arrangement and I'm ending it, *now*.'

He'd been about to launch into some kind of tirade, but as her words sunk in, his expression went from anger to shock, then *hurt*. 'Lyra, I don't understand . . .' He tried to reach for her. 'This is *nothing* to do with us.'

Sweet Kore, how does he not understand? She stepped away. 'No, that's just it: it *is* about us. It reveals what you are when you're at your worst: a violent bully. I don't want such a man in my bed.'

'But I've *never* hurt you. I never would.'

'You think as long as you don't direct your violence at me, it's fine? Solon, this shows me that violence and bullying is part of you – I don't want to have to fear the man I sleep with.'

He looked bewildered. 'But I'm a fighting man.'

'Then fight for me,' she told him. 'But Solon, it's time to end our liaison. It was something we both needed, but we have to move beyond it. Both of us.'

'But I'm not ready . . . Lyra, please . . . I love you.'

She flinched. 'No, you don't: it's not love. We hardly talk. We never laugh. We have sex and we part.'

'I know what I feel,' he said, reaching for her.

She retreated. 'And so do I, and it's not love.'

'How would you know?'

'Because I loved Ril and I don't love you,' she shouted. 'I've told you it's over and that's all you damned well need to know.' She whirled and stormed away, ignoring his calls, shouting for Basia, who hurried towards her.

'Milady?' she said sharply. 'Are you–'

'None of your damned business,' she blazed. Her legs felt hollow, her chest too tight to breathe properly and her eyes were stinging, but she was damned well *not* going to cry.

Behind her something crashed, the floor shook and she almost shrieked.

'I hope that means it's over between you,' Basia remarked, as they both hurried onwards. 'And I pray you don't regret it further.'

Solon stared after her, his entire world lurching. *You can't do that to me*, he thought numbly. *Bugger 'arrangements', you're mine–*

He turned and then turned again, went to follow her, then stopped and stared at nothing, because *nothing* was suddenly *everywhere*.

She doesn't understand. Exilium Excelsior got what he deserved. I'm under siege and she's tearing down my walls.

Images tumbled through his brain: Lyra beneath him, Lyra kneeling with his rod sliding in and out of her. Lyra lying across his thigh and sucking him . . . And Lyra on the throne, and all his plans to be up there with her – above her. *Lyra. Lyra. Lyra. This is not over – she can't just back out . . .*

In the back of his head, Medelie snickered mercilessly. He clenched his fists as he opened his eyes and found himself looking up at the smug face of Emperor Sertain. Kinesis and Earth-gnosis fuelled his sudden rage and he punched the *Sacrecour bastard* in the face, ripping off the marble head and sending the whole statue crashing to the wooden floor, splintering the floorboards.

I will be emperor and I will rule her!

Domara found Father Germane in the old royal chapel, in the shadow of the Bastion's main citadel. The basic repairs had been done, but the niceties would have to wait until spring, when craftsmen could be brought in to beautify Kore's house. For all that, it had an austere quality she liked.

The comfateri was kneeling before the altar and she felt her heart lift as she saw him. 'Domara. Dear Sister, join me,' he offered.

They prayed together, then sat side by side on the front pew. 'Lyra destroyed this holy place, you know,' Domara commented. 'Ostevan, that slime, had tainted her, then she realised she'd been played with and went mad. Earth-gnosis, I suppose. A centuries-old house of Kore and she destroyed it. Lives were almost lost.'

'At least she resisted his advances,' Germane commented.

'Or grew tired of them,' Domara muttered. 'We all know Ril Endarion was screwing other women, so likely she took consolation with her confessor. Not all your brothers are as holy as you, Father.'

'Regrettably so,' Germane said. 'Still, I am given to understand that she has put Lord Takwyth aside.'

Domara scowled. In truth, she'd actually preferred Lyra's vice to be openly displayed. She now worried she was missing some greater evil. 'I know it's harsh to say so, Father, but everything about her rings false to me.'

Germane looked over her shoulder, dropping his voice. 'It's strange you should say that, dear Domara, because it has come to my knowledge that there is perhaps a great falsehood being perpetrated upon us all. Surely you have noticed that she looks younger than her age? Recently I heard a strangely *possible* explanation.'

Domara suddenly remembered they were outside the confessional cubicles: this wasn't an Unburdening and not under that rite's sacrament of silence. But longing to hear something that truly condemned Lyra Vereinen, she put aside her misgivings. 'What did you hear?'

'I heard that Ainar, her supposed father, was executed *two years* before she was born.'

Domara's jaw dropped. But when she thought of the girl's youthful skin and her guileless manner when she'd first come to Pallas, it made sense. 'Then who's her father?'

'No one knows,' Germane said. 'But when Magnus died, he bequeathed the throne to Ainar and Natia. When Lyra was presented to the world as Ainar and Natia's child, clear precedence was established over Constant and his issue, Cordan and Coramore.'

'But if she's not Ainar's, that ruins her claim,' Domara exclaimed. 'We must tell—'

Germane laid a warning hand on her arm. 'We must tell no one, for now. Believe me, there are many who would love to act on this information, but Lyra's royal council remains loyal to her – even my master, the Grand Prelate. But then,' he murmured, 'he's as steeped in vice as she is.'

She shivered to hear such a thing, though it gelled precisely with her own thinking. 'We are kindred souls, Father,' she said. 'Dear Kore, is there no one we can trust?'

'Don't worry, Sister,' Germane said, his voice soothing. 'Plans are afoot to bring her down. It won't be easy, but we'll bind her in chains and drop her down a deep well . . . metaphorically speaking, of course. There's a place for you amongst us, if you're willing?'

Domara thrilled to his voice, to his closeness. 'I'll do anything you ask.'

'Thank you for your trust, Sister,' Germane said. 'Now, here's what we intend to do . . .'

Once Domara had left, Germane closed the chapel and went to his vestry, where he could be sure no one would overhear. He filled a bowl of water and conjured with clairvoyance-gnosis. A dapper, dark-haired man wearing a glittering peaked cap of white and gold appeared.

<Lord Pontifex,> Germane sent, <it's begun. She swallowed the first hook.>

Ostevan, in Dupenium Cathedral, gave him an approving smile. <Well done, Germane. But be careful how you plant the second hook. Her reaction could either make her wholly ours, or break the trust you've built up.>

<Don't worry, Holiness, she's eating out of my hand.> Germane paused then asked, <What of Lef Yarle? I've heard rumours he's returned to Pallas?>

<Don't worry about Yarle. Your business is Domara. Make her your puppet.>

Germane hesitated, then daringly asked, <Master, I could better do so if you anointed me.> He knew what he was asking, but he doubted he'd be permitted the grace of a daemon-spawn inside him until his mission inside the Bastion was complete: Setallius was using silver to check everyone who came near the queen.

Predictably, Ostevan confirmed his suspicion. <You know why we can't . . . yet. But soon, my friend. Soon. The pieces are moving into position.>

26

Winter's Veins

Hard Winters

Gather any pair of old men around a fire and their talk will turn to winters past. And they'll always say this: the Sunsurge winters are the worst, a deadly potion of high waters, unsettled weather and fatal cold. I remember the Siber's rapids freezing in the 'White Bear Winter' of 893, cascades of water snap-frozen one dreadful night when every living thing abroad died where they stood.

GLASSYN BYNE, RONDIAN MAGE-HISTORIAN, 912

Trachen Pass, Norostein
Janune 936

A fortress stood above the Trachen Pass that led from the Brekaellen Valley westwards into Noros via a precipitous climb into jagged mountains and then a slow, twisting journey into the thick forests of eastern Noros. It wasn't heavily used, except by legions marching on Crusade during the last three Moontides. When it wasn't a Moontide year, it sometimes closed entirely.

This was a Sunsurge year, as far from a dry, warm Moontide as you could get, and the fortress stood empty and covered in thick snow. Tarita had been circling for some time, but she'd seen no signs of life, no wood-smoke, no footprints and no movement.

The weather had finally broken, allowing her to make the rendezvous, and Waqar Mubarak had sent a gnostic communication saying that he too was on his way. The skies weren't clear, but the winds had eased and the clouds weren't as thick with snow as usual. It was as good as it was likely to get.

'When we land, we'll need to get under cover as fast as possible,' Tarita told Jehana and Ogre, huddled miserably around the mast, wrapped in every blanket they had. They were all turning blue, despite channelling gnostic heat.

'I hope there'll be firewood, or we won't be able to stay long,' Ogre replied.

'We won't stay long anyway,' Jehana called. 'Why did my stupid brother choose a place above the snowline?'

'The snows are all the way down to sea-level now,' Tarita called back. 'There are no warm places in Yuros in winter, but this place will almost certainly be empty, and it'll have a roof. That will have to suffice.'

She landed on the open space in front of the small keep and was out of the craft immediately, weapons ready – but nothing moved. She scanned the aether as Ogre followed, brandishing the axe he'd taken from the Keshi. 'I'm not sensing any life,' she reported.

Ogre strode to the stable doors and hauled them open, shielding himself, but no one attacked. Jehana rose, graceful as always, and walked in, as usual forgetting that she wasn't surrounded by servants. Tarita and Ogre rolled eyes at each other and dragged the skiff inside. The stables were a mess and there was Keshi graffiti on the walls. 'Shihadi have been here,' Jehana noted, 'so we'll need to watch out for deserters.'

The three of them slipped into their usual routines: Jehana busied herself with lighting a fire and laying out possessions – mostly her own – while Ogre and Tarita went to hunt for fuel. The fortress wasn't large, just a keep with a curtain wall, and it was cold and draughty. The upper levels had been burned out, but there were several sleeping cells on the lower levels that were still habitable. Ogre took his axe to an ironwood beam and began to chop it up for the fire.

Just then, Tarita felt a cautious call through the aether. She responded, then said aloud, 'My handsome prince is coming.'

Ogre grimaced. 'Good luck. You'll need it.'

She poked her tongue at him. 'He'll be eating from my hand. You should wait inside, though, my friend. I need to get him used to the idea of you.'

Ogre looked doubtful. 'No one gets used to me.' She knew that he was afraid Waqar would take her away, and that her promises to help him find Semakha would come to nothing. It showed in his face as he waved his hand dismissively. 'Go, greet your prince.'

Whenever he felt their friendship was threatened, he became defensive and pricklish. It felt possessive, and she'd never liked that. But she composed herself and went out to the snow-covered courtyard, painfully aware that she was clad in an unwashed, travel-stained tunic and her already coppery skin had darkened even more from the glare of sun on snow. She hadn't washed in days and her hair was greasy and tangled. Her prince was unlikely to look at her and lick his lips.

Then Jehana joined her and somehow she'd contrived to look elegant simply by dint of hair-ties and kohl eyeliner and tying her robes *just so*. *Royalty*, Tarita thought. *No damned use, but always the best dressed in the room.*

Then she heard a shrill cry and two giant winged shapes came streaking out of the low cloud that wrapped itself around the high pass: eagles with bodies bigger than horses. She watched with interest as they landed; apart from a harrowing few minutes at Sunset Tower, where Keshi magi riding these creatures had tried to kill her, she'd not seen them up close. They were like rocs, the giant eagles of Keshi myth.

Then she looked at the two young men dismounting and she realised that although she'd tried to downplay this moment, she really did have hopes and ambitions tied up in Waqar.

I'm a mage, but I still have to work damned hard for status and luxury and comfort . . . royalty are just given such things. And he is a good-looking boy . . . More than a boy now, she sensed; she could see it in his thicker beard, his war-weary demeanour and the ingrained wariness of the fighting man. Youth had fled, but he was maturing into someone *kingly*.

Impulsively, she popped a button to show a little more cleavage – her best asset – and stepped into the light, flicking her hair over her left shoulder to show her best side and her most come-and-get-me smile. 'Sal'Ahm, Prince Waqar,' she called, with what she hoped was the right mix of allure and pep.

He looked at her . . . and then went right past her to Jehana, who bleated 'Waqar!' and hurled herself at him.

The siblings just clung to each other and sobbed for what felt like for ever.

Tarita met Waqar's friend's gaze . . . *Tamir?* The small, clever-looking Keshi gave her a knowing look and she felt utterly foolish, like the butt of a joke. *Which I am . . . Of course he's going to go to his sister first. It doesn't mean he won't look at me afterwards.*

She took a hesitant step towards Waqar's giant eagle, trying to pretend that had been her intention all along, but the bird gave a warning shriek and fixed its eye on her. Its beak was larger than her head.

'Sal'Ahm, Tarita,' Waqar called, still holding Jehana tightly. 'Ajniha doesn't know you – she's nervous.'

'*She's* nervous?' Tarita echoed. 'Try being morsel-sized and in front of her!'

Ajniha lunged and Tarita dodged, slipped and went over on her arse, rolling away from the roc's raking claw and propelling herself from reach. 'Holy Ahm!' she exclaimed, while the royals snickered.

Tamir grabbed Ajniha's reins. 'Best you keep your distance,' he told Tarita.

Tarita decided that she'd got the message. 'Control that damned thing!' she snapped, and stalked away, feeling like an idiot.

'Ignore her,' Jehana told Waqar. She felt positively luminous to be with family again. 'You're here, that's all that matters,' she exclaimed. *Mother's dead, I've been hunted and imprisoned and faced death, and now there's this power inside me I don't know how to reach or use. But you're here . . .*

'How are you?' she added anxiously.

'Much the same,' he said softly.

He didn't look the same, though. There was a new weight and maturity to him, a solemnity behind his old sparkle, and sadness too. His eyes had a haunted cast that she attributed to the friends he'd lost.

'Come inside,' she told him. 'We don't have much, but there's food and I've lit a fire.'

They left Tamir to stable the rocs and she led him to the hall, but she remembered just in time what was inside and stopped him. 'Before we go in, I need to tell you about Ogre.'

Waqar's hand went to his sword-hilt, a reflex she'd not seen in him before. 'Ai?'

Jehana let her own doubts show. 'He isn't human.'

'What do you mean?'

'He's a construct,' she explained, 'bred with intelligence, and the gnosis.'

'That's illegal!' Waqar exclaimed. The Gnostic Codes might be Yurosi, but Eastern magi adhered to them because they were mostly common sense. 'How did you come to be travelling with it?'

'It's a long story,' she sighed, 'but the short version is that the Ordo Costruo packed me off to Sunset Tower when the invasion began. We were attacked there by Heartface, one of the Masked cabal who killed Mother – she turned out to be Alyssa Dulayne. Tarita and this Ogre helped me escape. I'd be dead without them.'

'*Alyssa* was Heartface? Dear Ahm . . .' Waqar looked at her grimly, but with less surprise than she'd expected.

'She's dead,' Jehana reassured him.

'Ahm be praised!' Then he looked at her uneasily. 'But this "Ogre": did the Ordo Costruo make him?'

'No, someone called Naxius made him. The order freed him, but they kept him hidden at Sunset Tower.'

'Naxius? *That* Naxius?'

'Ai . . . but Ogre has been brave and loyal – well, mostly to Tarita rather than me – but he's risked his life. He deserves our help.'

Waqar took that in, then asked, 'And Tarita?'

'She's been brave too,' Jehana admitted, then added as if it was a joke, 'She thinks you're going to marry her.'

Waqar's eyebrows shot up. Then he sighed. 'It was just a kiss, a thank-you. It meant nothing.'

'Good. It would be cruel to lead her on.' Jehana took his arm and said, 'Let's go in.'

They entered the wrecked hall and Waqar peered around carefully, then settled his gaze on the bulky shape beside the cooking fire where two snow-hares were now turning on a spit. Ogre stood, then made a complicated gesture from the harbadab, of a lowly servant to a master. 'Sal'Ahm, Prince Waqar,' he rumbled in Keshi. 'Ahm smile on thee.'

Waqar was clearly taken aback, but he responded as a prince would to a favoured inferior. 'You are the Ogre?'

'Just "Ogre", Great One.'

Waqar's expression went through some complex changes, then he simply said, 'Shukran, Ogre. Thank you for all you've done for my sister.'

Ogre looked flummoxed in the presence of royalty, but pleased. Waqar led Jehana to the fire, where they sat, shutting everyone else out. 'Sister, tell me everything.'

The tale took some telling, especially when Tamir and Tarita arrived separately partway through and began adding their own accounts. Jehana heard properly for the first time about the murder of their mother and the hunt for the killers that led to Midpoint Tower and into the West. She told him about Sunset Tower and the journey to Epineo and the death of Alyssa Dulayne, though she was sketchy about the details, having been unconscious. 'And now we're here . . .' She peered at him and added, 'I have gained the dwyma, Brother – well, I have been awakened to it, but the genilocus, the guardian spirit, was slain. I must find a new one to fully gain the power.'

'You will,' Waqar replied. 'Uncle Rashid will be pleased. He wants me to possess it also.'

Uncle Rashid, who possibly ordered Sultan Salim's death . . . and Mother's, Jehana reminded herself.

Waqar told them his tale. Jehana, who knew his friends well, was saddened by the deaths of Luka and Baneet and Fatima's self-destructive state of mind; she'd been unsuitable, but she'd been important to Waqar. It stirred her heart to learn that he'd been instrumental in defeating an Imperial army, but she had mixed feelings over Uncle Rashid's unstoppable march.

Everything pointed to Rashid and the Masked Cabal moving as one, which raised a vital question in Jehana's mind. 'Will you tell Uncle Rashid that you've found me?'

Waqar hesitated, then said, 'No, not yet. Not until we know just what he's done. I'll need to lie to him – he's expecting direct reports from me, but I can keep him off the scent for a while, which might give us the time we need to find out where he really stands.'

Tamir broke the ensuing silence. 'The real question,' he said, 'is what do we do next?'

Waqar felt the weight of Tamir's observation like a yoke across his shoulders. *Ai, what do we do?* He studied Jehana – she'd grown more serious but no less protective of him since they last parted. *We're all each other has: the last of the Gentroi-Mubaraks.*

He let his eyes drift to Tarita. She had some of the spunk and dynamism of his most recent lover, Bashara, and he had noticed the way she preened earlier. But inside he felt hollow, empty of any inclination to admit someone else into his life. *And she's a Merozain Jhafi – that's too many hostile influences.*

He moved his gaze to Ogre. Obviously they couldn't take him anywhere public – he'd be put down, and perhaps rightly so. But a debt was owed.

'Tarita, Ogre,' he began, 'the Royal Family of Mubarak is deeply grateful for your service. My only regret is that I do not have the wherewithal here to honour that debt. Nor can I invite you to the court of my uncle for recognition – a Merozain from Ja'afar and a construct would not be safe. But I promise, you will be rewarded.'

Tarita and Ogre bowed their heads in thanks, though neither looked overly impressed.

'But Tamir's right,' he went on, 'what do we do next? Sultan Rashid wants us to return to him and serve the Shihad. Half a million men and more are outside Norostein, with little shelter. Jehana, he wants you to control the weather so that regardless of the battlefield, his men don't perish in a blizzard.'

Jehana gave him a troubled look. 'But Uncle Rashid probably had Mother killed.'

'I know, and I too crave vengeance for that. But those soldiers weren't involved; they just want justice for three Crusades.'

They shared a torn look, then Jehana said heavily, 'I don't know how anyway. I've got this thing inside me, but I don't know how to use it.

And the sea-genilocus that awakened me is dead.' She hesitated, then went on, 'Sometimes I hear and see others inside the dwyma – other dwymancers, I suppose. I think that maybe, if I tried, I could speak with them.' She looked at him. 'Should I try?'

He thought about that. If other dwymancers were here, they were Yurosi, enemies of the Shihad. *But perhaps I can put a blade to their throats and make them give us what we need?* 'I think we should try. But you need to be cautious. We can't trust them.' He hesitated, then asked, 'Do you think I might have this power too?'

'Definitely. Mother wanted to tell you of the potential, but she feared you'd place it at Rashid's service. She wanted you to join the Ordo Costruo of your own free will, then she'd have told you.' Jehana gave him a regretful look. 'If only you had, Brother.'

'Who knows what would have happened?' he replied tersely. 'I wish she'd told me.'

'Perhaps another dwymancer can guide us both: awaken you and teach us both.'

'It sounds like a lot to expect of a potentially hostile stranger.'

Jehana looked up at him. 'Mother told me that the dwyma isn't a cold tool like the gnosis: it's a oneness with the energies of nature. It *changes* you. She said she felt that at heart, all dwymancers would be brethren. She never met one, but she told that if she had, she'd have felt as close to them as to a sister or brother.'

'Mother was an idealist. Where there's power, there's conflict, Sister. Contact these people, certainly, but treat them as you would a potential enemy.'

Exhaustion overcame them all soon after, and they went to their blankets. The wind was howling outside and the draughty keep kept little heat in and little snow or rain out, but cells on the bottom level were usable. Waqar kissed his sister's cheeks and wished her goodnight, then took a lit timber to his own room and started a fire in a small cooking pit in one corner. He laid out his blankets and was about to set his wards when Tarita slipped inside.

He wasn't surprised, but he wasn't impressed either. 'Come for your reward?' he asked brusquely.

In answer she began unbuttoning her shift and for a moment he was simply stunned at her temerity . . . and she did have a voluptuous bosom for one so skinny, shapely and high, and she knew how to hold herself for maximum effect. But his grief for Bashara, his anguish over Fatima and the loss of his friends snuffed any spark of desire.

He stopped her hands with his and re-buttoned her shift, while she stared up at him with an expression that went from hope to stony anger.

'Suddenly I'm not good enough for you again, I see,' she said resignedly. 'I didn't have to, but I thought I meant more to you than some promise of reward.' Their parting kiss at Midpoint Tower hung in the air.

He faced her down impassively. 'I was kissing you goodbye.'

She give him a disgusted look. 'I haven't been laid in a year,' she complained. 'It's like I've got a disease.'

'I'm sorry. Talk to Tamir. Although he's lost his dearest friends too.'

'I don't want Tamir,' she retorted, from under lowered brows. 'I want you. Not as a wife or concubine or whatever – I'm not stupid! Just to light up the dark for a while.'

'I don't really know you.' The girl he'd kissed at Midpoint Tower had been lively and carefree, but this Tarita was jaded and adrift. *Or is that just me?*

She pulled a face. 'I'm not complicated. Some people collect coins or trophies, I prefer *moments*. Especially after the year I've had. Remember when we met? I was posing as a maid in the royal palace. To blend in I wore filthy cloth, bathed in a dirty river and put up with skin diseases and bad food. I had no possessions and no life – all so I could keep a watch on the enemies of my people. I've not been intimate with anyone just for pleasure for so long I'd almost forgotten how.' She turned to go. 'Don't worry, I won't plague you any more.'

He couldn't imagine living like that, but niggling doubts remained. Spies lied: it was part of who they are. 'Maybe you should try another type of work?'

She snorted softly. 'Ai, maybe.'

'After this mission, take time away. Find a friend, give them your love,' he advised.

'I thought that's what I was doing,' she retorted, then she snorted at herself. 'Actually, that's a lie: I don't screw my friends. It ruins the relationship.'

He shook his head. 'You see, that's just wrong. You have to be friends with your lovers for it to matter.'

'No, you're the one that's wrong. Sex feels just the same with whoever, but the ending doesn't hurt if you never cared. I like friendship – it's safe and comfortable – but getting naked with them burns the barriers and hurts everyone. It's best to keep the two apart.'

Waqar thought of Fatima and Bashara – losing them was still like having knives in his chest. But he'd not have wanted to forego those moments of intimacy. 'I couldn't live like that. Sex with strangers doesn't come near love. It ruins it.' He met her eyes and asked, 'Who did you lose?'

Abruptly she closed up. 'None of your business.'

He suddenly realised that Tarita, for all her pricklish cockiness and bravado, was a lonely soul. But he couldn't help that: right now, so was he.

He saw her out, went to his blanket and snuffed out his gnosis-light, but it was a long time before he slept.

Jehana sat in her cell, huddled over a fire, listening to the night. She heard Waqar's door open and close; followed by a brief, muffled conversation, then the door opened and closed again and soft footsteps passed by. She could guess some of it and was pleased Tarita hadn't inveigled her way into his bed.

She's not right for you, Brother.

She turned her attention to deeper things; to the coil of green light inside her, letting it grow in her mind. With it came warmth and a sense of floating through darkness as crystalline stars wheeled by like snowflakes. Then they took on a shape: a tree of light, vast and impregnable – until you saw the immensity of the darkness that surrounded it. She huddled towards it, fearing the emptiness.

A node of light where the snowflakes swirled like dancers drew her eye: there was a sense of presence there, so she tentatively, fearfully, called in Rondian: <*Hello?*>

Amber eyes like some kind of beast turned her way. 'Ysh?' a man replied in a strange Yurosi accent.

Her heart thudded as the dwyma shifted her perception and she was staring across a fire at a man and a wolf beside a steamy lake, beneath a waxing moon. The man was both young and old, with a weathered, grim visage, and long black hair and drooping moustaches. He looked as apprehensive as her.

'I am Jehana,' she called, remembering her brother's warnings about caution too late.

'I'm Valdyr. You're the sea-woman,' he added unexpectedly. 'We've sensed you before.'

She bit her lip, a little alarmed, but she pressed on, 'I'm new to this. I don't really know what I'm doing.'

'Then do nothing,' he advised. 'You can do much damage unknowing.'

'But there's so much I need to do,' she blurted. 'I need help.'

He gave her a troubled look.

'Please,' she said, her fears loosening her tongue, 'I'm lost and scared and people are looking for me and I don't know what to do. I need someone to show me.' She realised as she spoke that all that was entirely true. 'Please Valdyr, I am begging you. The dwyma chose me – I mean you no harm.'

He hesitated, glancing left and right as if seeking someone else to make the decision, but then he released a heavy sigh of assent. 'Ysh, ysh,' he breathed. 'Very well, Jehana. Come to Mollachia and I will help you. Come to Banezust – it's small, but it's safe. I will find you.'

A moment later he dropped from the web of light and so did she, the names Valdyr, Mollachia and Banezust echoing in her brain. She was still frightened, but she clenched a small fist in triumph. *I did it. I reached out and found someone like me. I'm not alone in this any more.*

27

The Silver Mine

Periapt

*A gnosis working can be aided by using the right tools. A correctly attuned periapt
can hugely improve the effects of a 'spell'. Even wooden periapts can aid the gnosis,
while amber or crystal is even more efficacious. But beware: a periapt is, like most
tools, also a crutch.*

LEPHANIUM, THE TOOLS OF MAGIC, PALLAS 834

Banezust, Mollachia
Janune 936

The landscape was starkly monochrome, deathly cold and utterly still.
No birds sang or flitted above, the sky was a sullen mass of snow-heavy
clouds and even the river was silent, frozen solid by the last blizzard.

Kyrik slithered forward, joining the Stonefolk ranger at the edge of a
gully, where the overnight winds had formed a rooster's comb of ice on
the ridge. They peered through the delicately formed crest to where a
snow-covered road wound up the side of a steep drop to a dark cave-
mouth.

'There's a man inside the opening, see?' Rothgar whispered.

Kyrik saw the man's outline and gnostic sight revealed the dark aura
characteristic of Dragan's daemon-possessed men. 'They're guarding
the silver mines: they've anticipated us.'

'That doesn't mean they know we're here,' Rothgar replied. 'They're
probably guarding all the mines.'

'I hope you're right. Is this the only way in?'

'I'm afraid so: the seam here was a devil to reach, and only one shaft struck silver.'

Kyrik grimaced and went back to studying the lay of the land. The village of Banezust was a mile below the mine, in hills near the Upper Reztu river, about sixty miles from Hegikaro. On a good day Asiv's wind-skiff could get here in an hour, but good days weren't common in winter. The question was, how many enemy were inside, and was there any silver to claim? Normally there were stockpiles of ingots already smelted, to make transporting them down the treacherous mountain roads easier. As the roads usually closed before the mines, there were always stockpiles left inside during the winter, usually protected by the Kirol's Household Guard.

We can deal with these possessed men, provided there aren't too many, but if Dragan or Asiv are here, it could be a death-trap.

'What do you think?' he asked Rothgar.

'We won't know until we get in.'

They sidled backwards from the ridge, staying low until they made the trees, where the rest of their party awaited; his brother Valdyr and the wolf Gricoama, Fridryk Kippenegger, with the two Schlessen brothers, Tens and Oskar Brosklein, and Maegogh, who'd brought four hulking Mantauri.

A lot of our biggest eggs in one small basket, Kyrik worried, as he joined the group.

'Is it guarded?' Oskar Brosklein asked. He and his brother were typical of Kip's Bullhead legionaries: veterans who'd taken Eastern wives; they'd been living in the Schlessen forests since the Third Crusade.

'Aye, there's at least one possessed man inside the mine,' Rothgar replied, and as the answer got diffused through Schlessen and Mollach, faces grew a little more tense.

'Two possibilities,' Kyrik said. 'One: There's just a few of Dragan's people, keeping watch. Two, it's a trap and there's lots of them, with Dragan or Asiv near at hand.'

'If they're vulnerable to silver, why don't they close the mine completely?' Tens Brosklein asked. 'It's not hard to close a mine shaft – a controlled fall and we'd never reach the silver.'

'Perhaps they can't close it?' Valdyr suggested. 'Perhaps even the presence of it makes the mine poisonous to them?'

'Or it's a trap,' Rothgar repeated.

'Yar, or maybe this, maybe that,' Kip shrugged. 'We go in, we find out.'

'Yar,' Maegogh rumbled. 'Let's go and see.'

'Tonight,' Kyrik decided, 'when it snows, to conceal our approach.'

They moved in after dark amid gently falling snowflakes floating down in a soft but bitterly cold breeze, gleaming in the faint moonlight that lit the skies behind the cloud: Mollachia in winter, at its most beautiful.

Kyrik had used Air-gnosis to reach his precarious perch above the mine entrance, where he commanded the approach, but was out of sight to those in the cave-mouth. In front, the open space where the wagons were loaded was currently buried in thick snow.

Movement at the bend caught his eye: two figures wrapped in furs and walking with staves had appeared, trudging up the road. He lifted his bow and ran heat into it to warm it, drew one of the few silver-tipped arrows they'd been able to make from their tiny stock of coins and nocked it to his bow.

'Hallo,' one of the two newcomers called. Rothgar. 'Is anyone there?'

'Who are you?' someone answered from within the cave.

'Just two travellers,' the other man, Kip, replied.

The possessed guards moved just as Kyrik had hoped, stepping from the cave-mouth and into his line of sight. The four of them fanned out, weapons drawn. 'We don't know you, "travellers",' the guard man rasped.

Well, it's working . . . Kyrik sighted on the spokesman's back, trying not to think of him as a countryman. He drew back on the string, breathing slowly, and took aim . . .

Kip reached over his shoulder for the hilt of his zweihandle. 'That's close enough,' he warned the oncoming men, whose faces were pale as corpses.

They didn't stop – and their shadowed eyes took on a dark liquid sheen.

Then an arrow thudded into the middle Reeker's shoulder from above – and he choked, staggered and collapsed, writhing and howling in a way that suggested the silver was doing just as they'd hoped.

With a roar, two Mantauri erupted over the ridge from the lower slopes, having used Earth-gnosis to climb, while the remainder of their band charged around the last bend. Kip shielded, drew his blade and blasted the nearest man with a mage-bolt. He dropped, but the second steamed past, raising his blade. Kip parried and hurled him away with kinesis, then hacked the next man in half with one blow. More arrows whipped past his shoulder and took the remaining Reekers down. While they were paralysed by the silver-tipped arrows, the Mantauri decapitated them, staining the snow with blackened blood.

'Right,' Rothgar said, looking up as Kyrik floated down, 'now Dragan knows we're here, so we need to move fast.'

Kip and Maegogh took the lead, wreathed in pale shielding and zweihandles at the ready. They kindled gnostic light in the palms of their left hands and Kip signalled to the Brosklein brothers to guard the entrance. Gricoama went back down the trail to scout for danger. Kyrik flanked his brother protectively as they edged into the dark opening.

The first tunnel was wide and high enough to permit horse-teams. It led to a large cavern with a big hole in the middle of the floor, surrounded by the wreckage of the rope-pulleys that worked the platform the miners used to descend into the shaft.

'Father brought us here when we were young,' Kyrik reminded Valdyr. 'The miners brought up the raw stone and did the smelting up there.' He pointed to an opening on the right. 'That's also where they stacked the smelted ingots.'

'It's empty,' Kip called, after peering in. 'And the smelters have been smashed up too.'

'It's not been a regular season,' Rothgar commented. 'The tax-farmers were here, and most mines were trying to conceal their finds . . .' He pointed to the pulleys. 'But look, this was done recently – the splintering is fresh.'

Kip joined Maegogh in peering down the shaft. Neither of them felt comfortable below ground, and shining his gnosis-light into the hole only emphasised that it was a long way down to the bottom.

The Mantauri chief sniffed. 'There's silver down there. I can smell it.'

'They must have thrown it in,' Kip guessed. 'They knew we'd come.'

Kyrik joined them and peered downwards thoughtfully. 'Then our problem is getting whatever silver we can find out. I'll use Air-gnosis to go down and have a look.'

'Maegogh and I can use Earth-gnosis,' Kip said. 'We can help—'

Then Valdyr went rigid. '*Gricoama?*'

They all heard a choked cry from the cave entrance and spun to hear boots thumping down the entrance tunnel, followed by a throaty snarl that echoed through the chamber. They all heard a man's death cry – and Oskar Brosklein burst from the tunnel, pale-faced and running madly, a crowd of dark shapes behind him.

Then a mage-bolt struck Oskar from behind, he went down shrieking and the next instant he was engulfed by a dozen snarling, bestial men. Kyrik sent a silver-topped shaft into their midst, but the men kept savaging the scout's body.

Kip swore: two of his people down already. Two new widows.

Then a blonde woman in a low-cut red dress prowled into the chamber, fire playing at her fingertips, her dead-eyed face glowing in the flames. Kip recognised Sezkia Zhagy from the slaughter at Kyrik's coronation. Surrounding her were the Mollach miners and their families, their eyes as black as the pits they worked, brandishing picks or just baring teeth.

'You're *so* predictable,' Sezkia jeered. 'Once you discovered the properties of silver, we knew you'd come here. Lay down your weapons and you'll serve us as hosts. Resist, and you'll die.' Then she saw the Mantauri and in an avid voice asked, '*What are they?*'

Kyrik counted the odds as men and women with ichor-black eyes continued to pour into the central chamber of the mines. *Rothgar has no gnosis. The four Mantauri do, and so do Kip and I.* He glanced at Valdyr, severed from his powers and with Gricoama outside somewhere. *Eight of us, six with the gnosis, against how many – sixty . . . eighty . . . ?*

Magi could do much, and he doubted Sezkia fully realised what she faced, but these were his own people. Killing a few in necessity was one thing, but so many? That was another thing entirely – especially as Valdyr said his friend Nara knew how to cure the possessed.

We need to buy time . . .

'Kip,' he breathed, 'the mineshaft – can we get us all down there?'

The Schlessen looked at him doubtfully. 'How deep is it?'

'Two hundred feet at least,' Rothgar murmured. 'Straight down.'

Kip scowled. 'Not good. We must fight.'

'I don't want us to go down slaughtering our own people,' Kyrik replied. 'We need a better way. I'll help Val; someone help Rothgar – the rest of you are on your own. Kinesis, Earth-gnosis, whatever you've got, use it.'

Kip looked at him doubtfully, then he nodded and his eyes momentarily went blank as he mentally instructed the others. A silent countdown ran through them as they tensed, ready to throw themselves backwards.

Sezkia spoke again, in Keshi, perhaps thinking only Kyrik would understand. 'Kyrik,' she called, 'it's your brother we want. The rest of you don't matter. Give him to us and the rest of you can go free . . . and uninfected.'

I doubt that.

'What do you want with Valdyr?' he asked, in case there was anything to be learned.

'We want to *research* him,' Sezkia said, in a most un-Sezkia voice.

That's Asiv talking, Kyrik realised. 'What do you hope to find?'

'Why he can reach the dwyma and how to propagate that. There's *so much* to discover–'

'No, I don't think so,' Kyrik said. '*Go!*'

He spun, grabbed Valdyr and engaging Air-gnosis and kinesis, he propelled them both backwards. The rest of his party flared with light as they shielded, then plunged into the darkness beside him. Rothgar was hollering in fright as Kip gripped him one-handed and bounded down the side of the shaft. Kyrik sent a light ahead of them, a floating globe that revealed a jagged rock cylinder some fifty feet in diameter falling beyond sight. Around him he could feel bursts of gnostic energy as one of the Mantauri dropped with Air-gnosis and others used Earth-gnosis to cling to the rock-face as they descended.

The dimly lit, wreckage-covered floor hurtled towards them, but Kyrik landed first and immediately pushed Valdyr to one side as the first of the Mantauri, Burzo, a big-horned Air-mage, landed beside him. Between them they used their powers to catch the others.

'As soon as we're—' Kyrik began, but his words were cut off as Mollach miners began to rain down on them, falling in absolute silence.

'Get back!' Kyrik shouted, appalled to see body after body smashed into the stone among them. Some struck head-first; they were never going to get up again, but most of them ignored their shattered bones and crawled towards them, snarling and drooling, until an axe or sword-blade cleaved their skulls and they went still.

After a dozen or so miners had been summarily despatched, the rain of death ceased and they heard an unholy screeching from above. Then it subsided into one voice: Sezkia. 'You've bought nothing but time and a slow death, Sarkany: there's no way out.'

Valdyr touched the dwyma. He could sense Gricoama outside, untouched, but helpless against so many enemies. Sezkia had stopped sending people down the shaft and they'd shifted the dead into a side-cavern, leaving just bloodstained patches in the dirt. Now the Mantauri were busy stacking hundreds of silver ingots that had been tossed down the shaft, in case they got the chance to move them.

Valdyr joined Kyrik, Rothgar and Kip, asking, 'Is she right? Are we trapped?'

'Well, the magi can probably get out,' Rothgar said drily. 'That just leaves you and me.'

'No one will be left behind,' Kyrik said firmly. 'Should we have stood and fought? Did I get this wrong?'

Kip shrugged his big shoulders. 'Done is done.'

'I can't even use the gnosis to call for help through this stone,' Kyrik groaned. 'And if we try to climb up, they'll hammer us as we reach the top. I'm sorry, I've botched this.'

'Yar,' Kip grunted. 'Live and learn, eh? Or not . . .'

Could Nara help? Valdyr wondered . . . and then he thought, *No: not Nara* . . . 'I've got an idea,' he said quietly.

He didn't bother trying to explain. Asiv was definitely on his way, so there was no time to lose. Without a genilocus all he could do was communicate, and the dwyma couldn't aid them here anyway – storms wouldn't reach them and an earthquake would be deadly. They needed *human* allies.

He strode away down one of the side-tunnels to find a quiet place where he could concentrate. He sat and leaned against a wall, closed his eyes and let the Elétfa fill his awareness. Once he could sense the web of light, he called, <*Jehana?*>

I barely know her, but she's our only chance.

It took a while, but suddenly there she was and he followed her presence . . . his awareness went streaming up the shaft and into the upper chamber where Sezkia's Reekers waited patiently, then he went streaking out into the night skies . . .

. . . and a moment later he was sitting in the prow of a windskiff, weightless and impervious to the rush of air. Jehana, facing him, was wrapped in a blanket and headscarf. 'Valdyr!' she exclaimed.

Of course, she was an Easterner: he'd been trying not to think about that, or the breeding-house years. 'Jehana,' he said, fighting the rush of bad memories, 'I'm sorry to startle you, but I need your help.'

'*My* help? But how?'

He wasn't even sure of that himself. *But if there's even a faint chance, it's worth it.* 'You said you were coming to Mollachia?' he said. 'You have magi companions, ysh?' Not that he needed to ask; the windskiff was proof of that.

'Ai, of course,' Jehana confirmed. She pointed to the right and he gaped to see two giant eagles soaring nearby, each with a man astride.

His heart thudded. *Perhaps they really can help!* 'Where are you?'

'Tarita, where are we?' Jehana called to the pilot in Keshi.

'Over Registein,' another voice replied – another woman, to Valdyr's surprise, but that could wait.

He switched languages. 'Registein Pass is the southeast approach to Mollachia, so you're even closer than I'd expected,' he told Jehana. She was visibly surprised to hear him speaking her tongue. 'We're trapped in a mine and you're our only hope – although I know what I'm asking might be impossible. But will you try?'

'You'll need to tell me everything,' Jehana told him.

He did, as swiftly and concisely as he could: where they were and what they faced. As she listened, he could see her eyes growing wider. *Well, it is a wild tale*, he conceded. *Possessed men, silver blades – and that's not the half of it.*

When he'd finished, she turned away and started hurriedly conversing with the pilot. His heart was in his mouth, for the wait felt like for ever, but at last she told Valdyr, 'Ai, we will come. Hold on. We'll be as fast as we can.'

28

To the Rescue

Religion: Zainism

Zainism is the founding doctrine of the new mage order, the Merozain Brotherhood. We need to understand it if we are to unlock the Merozains' unique gnostic powers.

REGIS SACRECOUR, DUKE OF PONTUS, 931

Duke Regis has spent too much time in the Eastern sun and his brains have cooked. There is nothing the East can teach us about the gnosis. The truth lies in Kore.

GRAND PRELATE DOMINIUS WURTHER, PALLAS, 932

Registein Pass, Mollachia
Janune 936

Tarita had been flying almost non-stop and she was utterly exhausted. They'd left Trachen Pass in abysmal weather and flown east into the Brekaellen Valley before turning north, propelled by all the wind she could summon. A few roc patrols had intercepted them, but Waqar had pulled rank and sent them on their way. Otherwise, the skies had been empty, and brutally cold.

Her tired eyes strayed to the prince, gliding on Ajniha away to her left. *I guess you're stuck with me a few more days*, she thought ruefully. It was embarrassing to be near him when he'd scorned her so decisively, but she'd agreed to help them in this one thing. Then she and Ogre would leave, no doubt to the relief of everyone.

Don't worry, darling Jehana. I'll never be your sister-in-law.

She went back to concentrating ferociously on managing wind and sails, watching the shape of the land as they sped down valleys and over escarpments until they were descending over the Collistein Pass road into Mollachia. She had only a hazy idea of what they were flying into, but whichever way you looked at it, a war-party trapped in silver mines by daemon-possessed men sounded potentially deadly.

<*A few degrees north,*> Jehana sent from the prow. <*It's not far now – less than an hour, I think.*>

Tarita's gnostic sight picked out the rocs glowing with heat to combat the crippling cold. She worried for them: these punishing conditions were far beyond their natural capacity to withstand and their riders' expenditure of energy would be a beacon to anyone with a sensitive mind. But time passed and miles flashed by and she sensed no one else around. They soared along a narrow river-valley filled with snow-covered pines and up a jagged gorge – and then Jehana pointed excitedly towards a small plateau in front of a square hole in the rock-face. <*There,*> the princess announced.

Tamir gave her a wave, then he and Waqar sped ahead while Tarita brought the skiff in behind.

'What's the plan?' Ogre rumbled.

'We go in fast and hard and if anything attacks, kill it,' Tarita shouted, so that Jehana could hear too. 'You have to decapitate, I'm told, or damage the brain: remember those four we killed at Epineo?'

Ogre's eyes widened. 'Does this mean the Masks are here already?'

'Ai. That's the way our luck goes these days.'

As Waqar and Tamir's birds landed, she took the skiff in and lowered the landing struts before drawing her scimitar. No one appeared to confront them, though.

'Ogre, sails!' she hissed, jumping out, and he obeyed instantly. Jehana alighted too, but she stayed with Ogre; Tarita was a far deadlier fighter than either of them.

Waqar turned to Tamir. 'Stay with Jehana,' he ordered him.

'Ogre can look after her,' Tarita replied.

'I don't know Ogre,' Waqar retorted. 'Tamir stays here – now come on.'

His presumption annoyed her, but she waved assent to Ogre, who was already busy furling the sails – the last thing they needed was for the skiff to be picked up by the winds and hurled into the ravine. The rocs were huddling against the rock-face – they'd need shelter too, or they'd freeze to death.

'Stay with the precious princess,' she muttered to Ogre. 'I'll call you if I need you.'

She caught up to Waqar at the mine entrance, which was empty. As they pressed into the shadows, Waqar grabbed her arm. 'Tarita,' he began, 'about us–'

'There is no "us",' she snapped. 'I've got your back, don't worry.' She glanced back at the skiff. 'Ogre could be a big help here, you know. And both Jehana and I know him–'

Waqar shook his head, saying mulishly, 'I don't know him.' He let her go and took the lead in what turned out to be a tunnel leading to a dimly lit chamber *filled* with Yurosi people, at least fifty of them – but they were standing absolutely still, facing the central mineshaft. Their silence was as disturbing as anything else.

<*I hope your swordsmanship's improved since we last met,*> she murmured into his mind, ignoring his scowl and reminding him what Jehana had learned from Valdyr. <*This daemon, Abraxas, possesses people by infection through biting. The infected share one mind. There are higher and lower forms: the lower are almost mindless, but the higher ones have enough intelligence to use the gnosis. We have to decapitate or destroy the brain to kill them . . . >*

If there was one of the Masked Cabal here, they were in for Hel.

<*Weaknesses?*> Waqar asked.

<*Valdyr says he's heard – ai, it's third-hand information – that killing the higher ones has a disorienting effect on the lessers.*>

They surveyed the chamber again: the daemon-possessed were mostly villagers, but there were a dozen who looked like hunters standing right at the edge of the mineshaft, beside a beautiful, pale woman in a long red dress.

<*See Red Dress?*> Tarita said, <*She's in charge – leave her to me. You take my back – and make sure to let those below know we're here. They'll come straight up the shaft to help us.*>

<*But–*>

<*Red Dress will be like Felix at Midpoint: remember him? I'll do her, you keep*

the rest off me.> She drew on the gnosis, tapping the count, *one, two, three* on his arm. Then she slapped his shoulder. *<Go!>*

She took a running leap and propelled herself into the air, arcing over heads that looked up too late, slamming kinesis into unprotected backs and sending four men tumbling into the hole. *That'll wake up the men down there!*

When Red Dress turned her way, she blazed mage-fire at her; it slammed into strong shields but still sent her flying against the wall. She swatted away a spear and landed, Waqar crunching to the ground behind her a moment later.

'We're here!' she heard Waqar bellow in Rondian as he pulsed kinesis into the crowd, hurling another half-dozen into the hole. Tarita kinesis-shoved three out of her way, anxious to close with Red Dress, as Waqar shouted again, 'Valdyr, we're here!'

Then as they'd planned, she and Waqar placed their backs to each other to fight the possessed villagers growling with one voice and surging towards them.

Red Dress rose, her face a livid smear of white skin, blood-red lips and black eyes. *'Kill them,'* she growled, as a big pick-axe flew to her hands.

Help was on the way, according to Valdyr, although what anyone could do with less than a century of legionaries, Kyrik didn't know – but a man's voice rang out from in the upper chamber, shouting 'Valdyr, we're here!' just as dozen or more possessed men and women plummeted into the mineshaft. Most perished on impact, but there were four men of the Vitezai Sarkanum among them and they landed on their feet.

Maegogh blazed mage-fire into the skull of the first, Kyrik and Kip followed suit, then they all closed in with silvered blades and it was just butchery. But they'd no sooner finished them off when a few more fell, crushing their skulls, and above a mass of snarling above, Sezkia's voice shouted, 'Kill them!'

Jagged light flashed, followed by the clanging of steel.

'Help's arrived,' Kyrik shouted, 'so let's get up there, any who can!'

While Kip and the Mantauri took running leaps at the walls and began to climb, Kyrik and the Mantaur Burzo summoned Air-gnosis and rose, shielding against more bodies tumbling down. They were his own Mollach people and all he could do was pray for their souls – and avenge their loss.

The mass of possessed villagers howled and came at Waqar and Tarita, but for every one they hurled aside, three took their place, so he shouted, '*Up!*' and leaped for one of the dangling chains hanging from the ceiling, some kind of pulley system.

The leap took them from reach just in time. Waqar grasped the chain in one hand, but Tarita hovered on Air-gnosis, blasting mage-fire at Red Dress.

Waqar fired off his own mage-bolts into the crowd, but with a roar, two black-eyed men came out of the darkness, each swinging by one hand from a chain while brandishing a sword in the other. Jerking his own chain into motion, Waqar frantically parried one while twisting away from the other. Using kinesis, he made his chain swing around the chamber, seeking these two new foes who could clearly reason and think for themselves, and as they came careening back at him, he slashed out, taking one man's arm off at the elbow and sending him spinning away – but he wasn't fast enough to avoid the other man's blade, which plunged into his calf. Pain shot through him, his grip failed and with no time to react, he crashed into the ground, only saved from serious injury by his shields. He'd landed at the very edge of the pit and now a sea of corpse-like faces with dead eyes surged forward to engulf him—

Tarita heard Waqar's cry, and that distraction was deadly: an arrow took her in the lower back, just as her shields wavered; it punched in just above her hip and she lost all control, pitching to the ground as the air burst from her lungs. She only just managed to shield enough to prevent being dashed against the rock, but she clung onto her scimitar—

—as her world turned to flames, barely repelled by her frayed shields. The heat was agonising and the shaft in her back hideously painful.

Then Red Dress burst through the sparks, and brought her pick-axe down with a blow strong enough to crack Tarita's skull like a palm-nut—

—but Tarita twisted like a cobra, yowling as the arrowhead tore sideways through her lower back muscles . . . and the pick-head splintered the rock beside her face.

Then she arched upwards, her vision glazed by pain, and plunged her scimitar blade straight through Red Dress's shields and into her belly.

The woman screeched, spitting ichor-laced blood . . . and raised the pick-axe again . . .

Tarita hadn't forgotten the incredible resilience of the possessed, though. She sent a paralysing burst of wizardry-gnosis along the blade, trying to stun the woman's possessing daemon – it didn't fully work, but it bought her another instant, enough that she could regroup. While the daemon was stunned, she flipped Red Dress with kinesis and tried the same spell again, this time with focus and far more intensity: and the woman flopped limply, unconscious.

''ware below!' Tarita shouted and kicked the pick-axe into the hole. She yanked her blade out of Red Dress's belly and threw a healing spell into the stomach wound, kicked her in the head to make absolutely sure she was out and spun to face the chamber and the next challenge—

—only to find that the daemon-possessed men and women were all reeling. Waqar was on the ground, shielding desperately and wounded in the leg, but the villagers were staggering about blindly.

So they were right. Harming a leader among these possessed does stun the rest.

Then a blond man and an immense giant in a horned helmet burst from the mineshaft and stood over Waqar to keep his attackers at bay. As more of the horned giants clambered out of the mine-shaft brandishing weapons, Tarita realised they weren't human. But no one was attacking them now and the blond man took charge, shouting, 'Don't hurt them any more – just herd them into the second chamber.'

Tarita gasped with relief, but she needed to finish dealing with Red Dress. She bound her with a Rune-of-Chain, but the woman gurgled weakly and her opened eyes were still black.

The daemon rasped, 'It won't hold, Merozain. She's still mine.'

Tarita used mesmeric-gnosis to knock the girl out, then straightened painfully. The arrow in her back was too damned close to her spine, reawakening hideous memories of paralysis, that awful numbness she'd never forget. She was almost fainting with the agony – until Ogre's voice roared through her skull and without another thought, she ripped out the arrow, seared the wound with a burst of healing-gnosis and hobbled for the cave-mouth.

Ogre was far from happy, and the young Keshi, Tamir, was equally apprehensive: night-time in a land neither knew, with the weather worsening, but they were commanded to remain here. He felt torn: should he stay here with Jehana and Tamir, or go to help Tarita?

Tarita is my friend. She needs me.

She'd gone to her prince last night on her own quest for love, but she'd emerged soon after and Ogre guessed that things hadn't worked out as she'd wanted. He didn't understand why Waqar would kiss her once, then reject her: that was unprincely behaviour in his eyes. And now Tarita was locked up in herself and he didn't know how to console her.

It's all so complicated. If I ever find Semakha, will it also be so distressing?

Then the aether shivered as gnosis energy was discharged in torrents inside the cave. He glanced sideways at Tamir, saw the young Keshi's mouth open and spoke first. 'I'm going.'

He hefted his axe, conjured light and strode forward, but before he'd got even halfway, he heard a choked sound behind him and turned, dreading what he might see . . .

With endless energy and every aspect of the gnosis at his disposal, Asiv Fariddan was spoiled for choice. He adopted a half-human, half-bat form, mostly for its hideous appearance, and hadn't yet been spotted by the trio beside the skiff.

Who are these intruders? he wondered, gliding in silently. He smoothly shapeshifted into human form, still naked and winged; with his inhumanly lovely face he was a dark angel, one of the Fallen Devi lifted from the pages of the *Kalistham*. His favoured blade was slung over his back and he drew it, as wrapped in illusion and concealed by their own skiff, he approached his unwitting prey.

Two of the Shihad's rocs were sheltering beside the cliff-face, also oblivious to his hidden presence as he rounded the skiff, right behind the backs of two young Easterners. A third person, a strangely large, misshapen figure, was walking towards the cave. When it conjured light he glimpsed its face in profile . . .

It's an ogre, surely the handiwork of the Master himself. He doubted the creature knew him, but when Asiv had visited one of Naxius' hidden bases in Ahmedhassa, he'd seen a creature just like this. *The Master would like him back, I'm sure . . .*

So Asiv glided in behind the young man, potentially the greatest threat here: he was protecting a particularly beautiful Keshi girl, if a little mature for his tastes. And perhaps she had value?

Some sport for later, he promised himself, driving his blade through the young man's back and skewering his heart. His victim gave a choked little cry and folded.

Asiv wrenched out the blade in a spray of blood and turned to the young woman, wondering who she was. He'd expected gnostic counters, but either she was too stunned to resist as he knifed her mind with mesmeric-gnosis, or she wasn't a mage at all.

Just some worthless whore after all, he smirked, as the ogre-construct turned, its lumpen face contorted with alarm. *Now for you . . .*

'No!' Ogre roared with voice and mind as he stared at the inhumanly beautiful, sinister winged man standing over Tamir's bloody form and reaching for Jehana and then, *'Tarita!'*

The princess' legs were wobbling like a new-born foal, then she too collapsed.

Ogre hurled a bolt of mage-fire at the winged man and charged, but his attack was effortlessly swatted away. The space between them closed, he swung the axe and surely the man couldn't block in time–

– but somehow the Keshi twisted out of reach, the axe-head whipping harmlessly past his face – then his expression contorted in glee as he jabbed a finger and purplish light exploded behind Ogre's eyes. He tried to recover, but the ground tilted and smashed into his forehead and everything went black.

Too easy, Asiv thought cheerfully as the big construct slumped beside the stricken woman and her dead protector. And fascinatingly, the

Ogre-creature had called 'Tarita' into the aether: he looked at the fallen girl again. Was this the Merozain that Heartface had warned of before she herself vanished?

Then Abraxas howled in his mind and he realised that the daemon's presence had just been ripped from Sezkia Zhagy's mind while others were also going down in there . . . It occurred to him that the Merozain might be inside the mine right now.

Asiv was many things, but he was not a warrior, despite his new powers. Going toe-to-toe with a Merozain didn't appeal at all. *Perhaps I should just take these prizes and leave.* Getting the skiff moving would take too long, though, and the girl was too large to carry, let alone the monster construct.

Then he realised the answer was in front of him. Engaging animagery, he examined the minds of the rocs and chose the one whose master was dead as it would be easier to control. It flapped to his side, shrieking at him, but didn't resist as he hurled the construct across its back, then turned back for the stricken Keshi girl.

Perhaps she's worth something – but can this bird bear us all?

Deciding not, he raised a hand to blast her with fire and finish the job.

Frantic with fear, Tarita limped from the cave-mouth, her injury a knot of brilliant pain despite her healing-gnosis. '*OGRE!*' she shouted as she sent a burst of gnostic light into the air to light the scene.

Her heart froze at the sight of Tamir's motionless bloody body, facedown in the snow, Jehana limp beside him and Ogre flung across the back of Tamir's roc. The bird's reins were being held by a naked, winged Ahmedhassan man: a black-haired, bronze-skinned, stunningly beautiful man. The braided hair meant he was most likely a Gatti. She wasn't surprised to see his eyes were tar-pit black, or that he snarled when he saw her.

So you're Asiv Fariddan, she presumed. He blasted mage-fire at her and she had to leap aside at the sheer force of the energy, but she kept advancing, propelling herself with kinesis, all the while hollering, '*OGRE!*'

The Gatti sprang onto the roc's back and targeted her again, his bolt searing the air between them, but she dodged and shielded, still tearing towards him – only to see the bird's great wings flap, lifting it away out of reach. Feeling energy flare, she shielded a mage-bolt aimed at the fallen Jehana, but the Gatti just laughed aloud and sent another blast, this time at her windskiff. Howling in alarm, Tarita fought her way to the vessel and grabbed her satchel containing Naxius' *Daemonicon* – the wards were keeping it safe – but then the keel caught alight and she propelled herself away as the skiff went up in an explosive burst of fire.

By the time she looked up again, the roc was gone, taking Asiv and Ogre into the darkness. Then the agonising pain in her lower back caught up with her. She gave a faint gasp and pitched over into the snow next to Jehana.

29

The Voice of the Rising

Rivers of Urte

Much is made of windships and indeed, they're a boon. But the rivers of Urte, which are far less affected by tides than the sea, carry hundreds of times more commerce than the windfleets. They are the veins of the empire. That's why Pallas and Delph, the greatest cities of the Rondian Age, are situated beside the greatest watercourses of Yuros.

JEAN BENOIT, MERCHANT GUILDMASTER, BRES 925

Pallas, Rondelmar
Janune 936

As they hurried down yet another faceless alley, Ari wondered whether this was the day grey-cloaked Volsai would appear and his fragile existence collapsed again. Since being picked up by Lazar, he'd spoken every night in old warehouses in Tockburn, Fisheart and Oldtown, even a burnt-out chapel in Kenside. He and Neif travelled with cowls raised and slept under guard, never twice in the same place. He was *so tired.*

And every night, another Pallas landmark burned: a guildhall, two chapels, a Watch-house, mansions of the rich. In Pallas, people feared fire more than the plague and Lazar's men employed it as a weapon, trusting the Imperial Fire-magi would arrive in time to protect the surrounding properties.

This can't go on, Ari thought every day, but every night, his words also caught fire. Tonight he was in Oldtown, near Pilum's Hill, and the men in the room – always just men, because of the threat of violence – were packed in like kippers in a net. They smelled that way too: these were rivermen, dockers and harbour hands, and they were rowdy and angry.

'*And here he is*,' someone was shouting above the din, '*the Voice of the Rising: Ari Frankel—*'

He leaped onto the stage and once again, all his pent-up fear and wanting and desire and hate came bursting out. 'Brother Sufferers,' he greeted them, straight into his stride. 'Here we are again, gathered in secret, fearing for our lives, because the empress will not hear *Truth*. We are hiding when we should be tearing down the sycophants and courtiers who adhere to her like leeches and making her see our reality! But would she hear us, do you think?'

'*The Hel she will*,' the crowd roared back, already well and truly in ferment.

'Aye,' he agreed, 'she'll not hear a thing because she's deaf to us and blind to us – Kore's Balls, she can't even smell us, and that's a rukking miracle—'

That one always got them laughing. But to be honest, the jibes and barbs he spat tasted a little sour in his mouth, given that he was only alive through the queen's mercy. Unfortunately, *"I've spoken with Her Majesty and she's both understanding and compassionate"* didn't cut it in the rabble-rousing trade.

'She's too busy with her intrigues and her power-plays to care about *us*,' he told them.

'Too busy fucking Solon Takwyth!' someone roared and the room rocked with laughter again. All Pallas was speaking of the alleged royal affair.

'When will we have a ruler who hearkens to us – or *is* one of us?' Ari shouted. 'Never, that's when, not when rulers are chosen by sword and gnosis and ordained by venal clergymen.' He showed them that old poster of Ostevan Comfateri, as he was then, screwing Empress Lyra. 'Never was there an image wrought that better showed our plight: Crown and Church, tangled around each other like serpents, their duties to Kore and their People forgotten: do they even remember we exist? But we'll not be forgotten any more: we will make them take notice—'

'How?' someone asked; the question had been primed.

'By making them see that the People don't want them: that there's a better way than tyranny – as the ancient Lantrics knew, and early Rimoni too – and we will never stop demanding *Suffragium*, rule by the People, for the People . . . we will burn their houses and their businesses and their barracks and their abbeys – we will tear down the edifice of empire until they concede this truth: *that they are no better than us!*'

And they lapped it up, shouting and hollering, roaring out his slogans until he caught the sign from cold-eyed Lazar and he finished, 'And let me leave you with this: I have a new pamphlet in the making: the *Marks of Damnation.* I will hammer it to the doors of the Bastion and Celestium if I must, to lay bare the sin and folly of these tyrants–'

Then it was time to grab outstretched hands and pump them, to let strangers bear-hug him and pummel his back, until he was out again, warded by thuggish Gorn and Lazar's other lieutenants. In moments they were hurrying through the alleys, dodging patrols until they reached that night's tavern.

Somehow, Lazar was already there.

'Good work,' he told them as pints were poured, then the serving staff vanished, leaving them alone in their corner of the inn. 'But what's this new pamphlet?'

Ari had been thinking of this one for some time. 'We need something that lays out everything that's wrong in one clear, concise manifesto.' He tapped his skull. 'It's all in here. I just need to hone it so that strikes to the bone.'

Lazar considered. 'How long do you need?'

'Just a few days.'

'Then take a break and get it done. No more speeches until you're ready.'

'I can do that,' Ari told him. *I might even get some sleep.*

Lazar clapped his shoulder, then rose. He'd barely touched his drink, as usual. To Ari, this latest drive was an emotional outpouring, an intellectual explosion, but to Lazar it was a military campaign against the class of people who'd destroyed his life. He wanted them all to die and he wouldn't relax until it was done.

When the rebel leader was gone, Ari sat sipping his drink, while Neif prattled on about the audience. 'Smelled like the hold of fishing boat, didn't they? Thought I'd faint! But—'

'Neif, quiet,' Ari murmured, and his friend shut his mouth instantly.

Things were different between them now. Neif had always been the reckless, loud, unquashable one, but the harrowing deaths of their closest friends in Jastenberg, the dreadful journey north and the trial had broken him. He rarely spoke in public now, not even to introduce Ari. He just followed him around, passive and mumbling.

'It really doesn't feel right to denigrate Queen Lyra,' Ari admitted aloud. 'She *listened*, and she actually understood what I was saying. And when she could've had us eviscerated – well, it all feels kind of . . . ungrateful, don't you think? To keep putting out that shit about her and Ostevan? And even if there was anything, that's long over, I reckon.'

'Dunno,' Neif said awkwardly.

When have you ever 'not known'? Ari wondered. *You used to have uninformed opinions on everything.*

'But nothing will change if we just give her a free pass out of gratitude,' Ari argued with himself. 'We can't be distracted from our mission just because she was nice to us once. The fact we have a queen is part of the problem, so she has to go.'

'True, that,' Neif put in dully.

The debate won, Ari took another swig of alcohol and clapped Neif on the shoulder. 'Tomorrow, my friend, we're going to write words that will set the empire ablaze.'

Highgrange, Pallas

The carriage rattled along a cobbled street in fashionable old Highgrange, east of the Bastion on Roidan Heights. Lyra had been told many times over that only Highgrange people *mattered*. Of course, the people telling her that were the ones who lived in Highgrange, where pureblood mage dynasties dwelt in centuries-old buildings, crammed with relics like living mausoleums.

Basia was peering warily out past the curtains.

'Surely we're safe here?' Lyra asked. 'We're barely outside the Bastion.'

'Nowhere's safe,' Basia replied, 'Assassins can be anywhere, and there's been more arson in Gravenhurst and Esdale overnight.'

The past few weeks had seen escalating numbers of burnings and food riots: perhaps driven by the rising price of basics. The Imperocracy was responsible for getting food from rural granaries to city warehouses, but the bad winter, exacerbated by Lyra's own dwyma-storm and the conflict with the Sacrecours, had created shortages, which was driving up prices. Many in the Merchants' Guild had sided with Duke Garod and fled to Dupenium, including the Guildmaster, Jean Benoit. Unrest on the street was now a constant, and Dirklan had advised her not to leave Roidan Heights. But Highgrange felt safe and it was her turn to visit Dominius Wurther in his mansion there.

'You look tired, Basia,' Lyra remarked. The skinny Volsai was pale and hollow-eyed as a corpse. 'Do you need someone else to take some of your duties?'

Basia sighed wearily. 'I drank too much and then I couldn't sleep,' she admitted. Lyra knew the feeling – she'd been guilty of the same weakness since exiling Solon Takwyth from her bed. The vast expanse of sheets now felt unbearable and only wine gave her the fortitude to face the empty darkness.

'It's unfair of Kore to take love away from you,' she told Basia. *That love being my husband* . . . But she felt no rancour any more, just regret.

'I've never thought Kore to be an overly fair god,' Basia observed drily.

'I pray for you,' Lyra blurted, 'that another might win your heart.'

Basia snorted softly. 'Oddly enough, I've had more men offering me a shoulder to cry on than ever. They must think grieving women are easy. But I'm being very picky.'

'I wish I'd been as careful,' Lyra admitted, 'but for a while it did feel good.'

They shared their *Men, what're they for?* look, and smiled.

Then the driver tapped the roof. 'We're here,' Basia remarked, 'Wurther's little home away from home.'

The grand prelate's city home, an elegant eighth-century mansion with Rimoni pillars and Northern-style arches, was set in an acre of priceless hilltop, but it was fully walled and solid as a fortress. Lyra and Basia hurried into the warm atrium and the doors were closed swiftly behind them, both to keep out winter's chill and any potential assassins.

'Majesty,' Dominius greeted them. As well as his guards, he had Lann Wilfort, the Kirkegarde Grandmaster, with him. 'You know Lann, of course?'

'Good morning, Dominius,' Lyra said, as they went through the complex dance of simultaneously kissing each other's signet rings, then she turned to Wilfort. 'Grandmaster, I've not had the chance to thank you properly for your defence, the day the Celestium fell. We're in your debt.'

The grizzled warrior bowed. 'No debt, Milady. A man does his duty.' He bowed again, and added, 'I regret I cannot remain; these insurrectionists have torched another chapel in Nordale and I must inspect the scene.'

As the grandmaster left, Lyra wondered about this latest campaign of burnings. *Surely Frankel isn't behind this, after I gave him clemency? I must ask Dirklan to investigate.*

'I hope you have a less destructive fire going, Dominius. It's bitterly cold today.'

'Of course, Milady,' Dominius replied, 'and some good mulled wine to warm the insides.'

'In the morning?'

'Hit the cold early, I say, and you'll be warm all day,' he rumbled, ushering Lyra into the main drawing room. They sat in big armchairs half-facing each other, half-turned towards the fireplace and welcome heat radiated into Lyra's face as she signed to a secretary to bring her papers and prepared to dismiss Basia.

Then Lyra noticed that the clergyman's usual bodyguard wasn't here; instead, a rather grim-looking Kirkegarde man was hovering at Wurther's shoulder. 'Is young Exilium still unwell?' she asked.

'You could say that,' Dominius answered, his normally jovial face looked grave. 'His injuries were far worse than initially thought and the healers are now worried he'll never fight again, and maybe never walk without sticks.'

Lyra put her hand to her mouth, momentarily sickened.

Dominius looked at her sideways and said, 'I gather you've already punished Takwyth.' She floundered at that and he chuckled. 'You should always just assume I know everything – I am Kore's representative, after all.'

She coloured, then decided embarrassment was undignified for a queen. 'I've ended the liaison. Do you wish to take legal action against him on Exilium's behalf?'

'No, Milady. Unfortunately, what goes on in the practise yards is best left well alone. In my experience, courtly behaviour is only possible because the knights have a place where they can blow off steam.'

'"Blow off steam"? This was a savage beating!'

'Aye, but a legal solution will earn Exilium nothing but contempt. Leave it well alone, Lyra.' Then he sighed, and added, 'To be honest, I was rather comforted that you and Solon had found each other. Such a union would hearten the Corani, in my view.'

She looked at him irritably. 'It would reinforce our insularity, Dominius. We need allies and I'm the most valuable bauble we have to offer. Solon and I were just two people licking each other's wounds.' Then she went scarlet as he roared with laughter.

'Sorry,' she said, in a small voice. 'That didn't come out well.'

'Ah, Majesty, you've just made my day. But regarding Solon, don't write him off. He's a flawed man, but we all are. You may yet need him.'

'I do need him – to do his duty. We had an arrangement, but it's over. He destroyed a priceless statue when I told him and I understand he's been like a petulant boy ever since.'

'All men are boys at heart, Lyra. We like to pretend wisdom and maturity, but the fact is, it's a rare man who doesn't revert to type when things don't go his way, especially in matters of the heart. And he feels wronged.'

'How do you know?' she asked sharply.

'I'm his confessor, at times.' His expression hinted that there was much he could tell her.

'Unburdenings are private,' she reminded him, completely unnecessarily.

'Of course.' He took a sip of mulled wine.

They looked at each other, then she winced and said, 'Oh, very well – what is he thinking? I'm worried for him.' Deciding she might need a drink to hear this, she took a heady mouthful and let it warm her.

He tutted amiably. 'Well, Solon, like most men, believes that when a woman gives her body, she also gives her heart. You might think he agreed to a temporary liaison, but to him, you were in love.'

'But he heard me lay down the rules and he agreed them.'

'I imagine he heard *blah-blah-blah*, then you undressed. Believe me, he thought you were in love with him.'

'He's telling you what he wants you to hear – Kore's Blood, aside from coupling, we barely spoke.'

'That's more or less normal in most highborn marriages. Solon's former wife seldom conversed with him and I gather Medelie Aventour only ever spoke of politics. Highborn marriages are arranged and couples often lead quite separate lives. Most men's sole criteria regarding the success of a relationship is the frequency of coupling and the woman's fidelity.'

'Wonderful . . . You make re-marriage sound so attractive,' she snarked. 'I suppose you think him in the right?'

'Well, it was a union out of wedlock and I'm the Grand Prelate of Kore, so it's my job to condemn all promiscuity. But I'm aware of what motivated you and I'm a tolerant man. I see you as an errant sinner, but not irredeemable.'

She snorted. 'How comforting. I don't regret it, by the way.' *Although I might easily come to.*

'I was sensing that. Lyra, we're all human animals who need shelter, food and company. If you believe you gained something from the liaison that has strengthened you, well and good, but you must accept that you left him a damaged man.'

'I can assure you I came out of it as battered and bruised as he did. Anyway, the affair is over. I need external allies: a prince of Argundy or Aquillea or Midrea, powerful men with big armies . . .'

'Oh, I understand your reasoning. I just don't agree with it. *A caged bird's worth more than a flock on the wing*: what you *have* is worth more than what you may *never have*. You're viewing Solon's loyalty as a given, and it may not be. He's ambitious, and he's crucial. You *must* secure him before you think about securing other allies.'

'Putting aside the fact that right now, I'm furious with him,' Lyra replied, 'my hand in marriage is our *only* bargaining chip. On our own, House Corani can't survive, or keep the empire intact.'

'But *whoever* you choose will destabilise the empire,' Dominius argued. 'There was a reason the Sacrecours only ever married from within their closest allies: to keep power unified. If you were to marry, say, Elvero Salinas, Canossi will suddenly be drawn directly into Pallas politics. Their Southern rivals will feel threatened and look to your enemies for aid. Whereas they would see House Corani, small but fiercely united around Empress Lyra and Lord Takwyth, as stable, effective leadership.'

Lyra nibbled at her knuckles, then sat on her hand irritably, trying to think this through. Dominius Wurther didn't make idle suggestions. She didn't know whether his reading of the situation was better than hers or not, but his opinion mattered. 'What do you get out of speaking for him?' she wondered.

'The joy of reuniting lovers, and stability to the realm.'

'Rubbish – you're worried that if the Corani fall, Ostevan will take back your throne.'

He lifted his glass. 'That's the stability I'm referring to.'

Lyra thought hard, but still she couldn't see her way to his view. 'No, Dominius, I not only don't love Solon, but right now I actively dislike him – and I'm extremely angry with him. I'll not say never, but right now is exactly the wrong time to speak to me about him. Ask again in autumn, if I'm still unwed.'

Dominius gave her rueful look. 'Well, don't forget that I asked, Majesty.'

'I won't, and I thank you for your advice, which I know was well-meant. And I appreciate your insights into the male mind – which is a little underwhelming, to tell the truth.'

'We're all of us just children, Majesty – men *and* women.' He looked up as a secretary tapped on the door and nodded. 'Ah, our other guest is here.'

They remained seated as the door opened and an attractive blonde woman wearing the insignia of the Kirkegarde mage-knights ushered in a black-haired, olive-skinned nun with deep, dusky eyes. The nun curtseyed and kissed Lyra's signet as the Kirkegarde woman withdrew silently.

'You remember Sister Valetta, of course?'

'Of course!' Lyra said, pleasantly surprised. 'Welcome – although I'm somewhat surprised to see you here – I rather supposed you and Dominius wouldn't get on.'

The Estellan nun's campaign for equality for women in the Church had resulted in a camp in the main square of the Celestium to try to make the grand prelate back down, but her sisters had been caught up in the violence when Ostevan and Ryburn seized the Celestium. Dirklan had estimated that more than a thousand women had died that day, although many more had managed to escape across the river or into the countryside and were now in refugee camps in the main squares – and continuing their protests. Between them and the food riots, it was difficult for anyone in Pallas to avoid getting an earful these days.

'We might not get on *theologically*,' Dominius replied smoothly, 'but politically, Valetta and I are seeking common ground.'

'It is as the Grand Prelate says,' Sister Valetta confirmed, her voice heavily accented and rather entrancing. 'He's been much more amenable of late.'

Dominius is trying to strengthen his hand against Ostevan, Lyra guessed, but whatever the reason, she was pleased: the Sisters' Crusade was something she believed in. 'I'm delighted to see you again, Sister.'

In moments they were exploring ways they could cooperate and Lyra dared to hope they were doing some good.

Security is passive, Lef Yarle reflected: *it cannot act, but only react – which gives an assassin the edge.* This was especially so because bodyguards saw so little. They made assumptions, their vigilance was dulled by repetition and boredom and they came to rely on others for things they should always check themselves. Queen Lyra's Volsai relied on Grand Prelate Wurther's security arrangements, which relied on the arrangements of others, which made each tier of security weaker than the one above.

Given that he was now within a few yards of Wurther and Lyra, he was living proof of that. But Setallius' Volsai were looking for a *him*; they weren't looking for a *her*.

Lef Yarle had always been an effeminate-looking man, his delicate bone structure and beauty easily enough for him to pass as a woman when he needed; indeed, the adventure of exchanging manly clothes for skirts, augmented by make-up and some subtle morphic-gnosis, had fuelled his sexual awakening. He called his female persona *Librea*, which in Lantric meant *free*. Librea was an itinerant Kirkegarde woman, a knight-errant, her history carefully fostered by him and Ryburn.

A week ago, Librea had volunteered to be Virago Valetta's personal bodyguard; he'd outwitted the silver-coin test by using mesmerism and sleight-of-hand to replace the testing coin with one he'd made of zinc and pewter. One test, easily fooled, and now 'she' was inside. He'd also added a false silver medallion to Librea's wardrobe; no one would suspect daemonic possession when they saw it around her neck.

Having delivered Valetta to her meeting, Librea was expected to help keep watch. The mage-knight guarding the door was already eyeing 'her' admiringly as they chatted.

Yarle knew Wurther boasted that his private lounge was among the best warded rooms in Pallas. *And yet here I am, the keys within a foot of me, dangling from this fool's belt.*

Yarle had refused Ostevan Pontifex's demands that he go with him to Dupenium to plot against the empress from afar; he had his own plans. *I began my career as a Volsai, I never closed my network and I never forgot how to kill with stealth. And I don't care about survival, only the death of my beloved's enemies . . .*

Most assassinations, in his experience, failed because the killer was more worried about getting away than striking the killing blow, but he had only revenge to live for. Eternity in the Hel that was Abraxas' mind wouldn't be Hel at all if Ryburn was there too.

He'd spent the past two weeks reintroducing Librea to Church society after *unfortunately* arriving back in Pallas just too late for the fall of the Rymfort and Celestium; Librea was eager to aid the Sisters' Crusade. Infiltration had been so easy, so far.

'So you're *the* Librea?' the mage-knight beside her asked. He was a clean-cut young man with typical Northern pallor and a steady countenance.

Yarle smiled demurely, with just enough twinkle to encourage him. 'You have the advantage of me, sir?'

'Anders Treach,' the young man responded. 'You won't recall, but I met you in Siberland last year.'

Siberland? Oh yes . . . One of the little missions Librea undertook every so often to maintain the persona. 'Argundian bandits? An unpleasant business.'

'Aye. We got them, though,' Treach replied. 'You killed three magi that day, and all before our party arrived.'

'Oh, they were just neophytes.' The self-deprecating tone was spot-on.

'They were Arcanum trained,' Treach replied, sounding very respectful. 'People I spoke to said that if you were a man – begging your pardon – you'd be a match for anyone.'

'Oh, to be a man,' Yarle responded drolly, adding, 'But believe me, I'm grateful to be a woman.' He flirted some more with his eyes, though his mind was elsewhere. His group of daemon-possessed men were now outside the walls of the compound. It was time to act.

He looked fully at Treach, and gave him a seductive look, full and frank, that was *all* Librea. 'So, Anders Treach, how long do you think this meeting will take?'

Treach coloured a little, licking his lips. 'Midday, I think.'

'Why, we have hours to fill . . .' Librea sashayed towards the young man, planted rouged lips against his ear and murmured, 'Are you standing to attention?' and grasping Treach's crotch firmly, felt it thicken. 'Oh, I see that you are. I'll see to your comfort, shall I?'

Treach stared in disbelief as the gorgeous woman slid down his body, freeing his member with practised ease, and then knelt and all but swallowed him, stroking and sighing justifiable compliments. Yarle felt the man's initial shock dissipate as pleasure overrode propriety . . .

You're a nice boy so I'll make your final moments enjoyable, Anders, and then I'll have Wurther and the empress in one room, without bodyguards . . . and that will be truly orgasmic . . .

Basia de Sirou had never been in the military, so she couldn't see the point in all this standing to attention at pre-designated posts. It just made you an easier target. So when Lyra dismissed her, she asked the grim-looking Kirkegarde called Falkerman, Wurther's duty bodyguard, where to find Exilium Excelsior.

'I'll look in on the poor beggar if you're okay here,' she said, and at his nod, raided the fruit bowl in the hall for some grapes, and headed for the stairs.

She found the small dormitory where Exilium lay, heavily bandaged, in a narrow bed. He peered at her through his one uncovered eye, puffy and half-closed.

'*Rukka mio*,' she whistled. 'They really put the bash on you, didn't they?'

He mumbled agreement. 'My . . . fault . . . sin of pride.'

Basia had always been damned careful who she trained with, and where. There were too many stories of young women fresh out of the Arcanums, dreaming of being accepted as equals among the knights of the Great Houses, being beaten and gang-raped to teach them their place. Her Volsai experience had been more accepting – and more underhand; Volsai men used lies, drugs and ambush to get their way with female trainees.

Or got knifed trying, she recalled grimly.

'So, are you going to get even?' she asked.

Exilium met her gaze. '*Si*.'

'Good for you.' She dangled the grapes. 'Hungry?'

She sat on the edge of his bed, amused by the Estellan's visible consternation, plucked a grape from the bunch and poked it between his lips. 'What're the healers saying?'

'My knee-cap's broken so I may never walk properly again.' Exilium gave her a sickly look. 'A swordsman who can't use his legs is useless.'

Basia pointedly lifted one leg and pulling down the short stockings, showed him her stump, socket and artificial shinbone and foot. 'The other one's the same,' she informed him coolly.

He went a pleasingly mortified hue of purple. 'I didn't mean . . . I'm just . . . I'm sorry.'

'That's okay,' she told him, patting one arm gently. 'After the amputations I considered taking my own life . . . But I got through it, and I'm glad. The life I'd thought to live was gone, but I dreamed new dreams.'

She went to get up and he surprised her by seizing her hand, holding her there. 'Grafia,' he said, his voice heartfelt. 'I needed to hear that. I think Falkerman thinks I'm gone already.'

'You'll show them,' she told him; she was sure of his fanatical dedication, if nothing else. For a moment she lost herself in his lovely dark eyes – but with his olive skin and black hair, he looked too much like Ril for her right now, and in any case, she suspected his stolid conservative primness would drive her mad.

They say it takes a year to truly mourn a lost love before you're ready to move on . . .

She squeezed his hand and let go, feeling some of her own weight lighten. 'The healer-magi really can perform miracles,' she told him. 'Dominius will have the very best working on you, I'm sure. I'm confident that you'll be back, and sooner than you know.'

Then suddenly the whole building shook and a spearhead crashed into the window – although it caught in the warded glass, it still sprayed fragments throughout the room. She flinched, her shields flaring, but not in time to prevent a couple of shards embedding in her forearm as she covered her face. More impacts sounded all over the front of the mansion.

Then something hit the wall outside their now-opaque window, the ballista-spear jerked out, and a man hurled himself into the room, rolling and coming up with the spear poised to slam down into Exilium's chest.

Basia had conjured mage-fire, already too late . . .

. . . as Exilium's right hand blurred, he pulled a naked blade from beneath his blanket and plunged it through the shielded attacker's defences and right into his chest. It must have been silvered, because

417

the attacker gave a choking cry, his black eyes glazed and the second blow, delivered from a sitting position, took his head.

'Holy Hell!' Basia gasped, truly impressed despite her shock. Then she heard shouts of fury and fear from below. 'The queen!' She threw a sickened look at Exilium and barrelled through the door, calling Lyra's name.

30

Lightning from a Clear Sky

The Angels of the Last Day: Glamortha (Death)

Death is a woman who rides a white horse, the same hue as her skin and hair, but she's robed in black, the colour of her eyes and lips. On the Last Day her scythe sweeps across the skies and the living fall, their souls laid bare for Kore's Judgement. She strikes without warning, lightning from a clear sky.

BOOK OF KORE

Pallas, Rondelmar
Janune 936

Lyra was surprised how calm she was when the spears struck and were caught in the fractured glass. She rose as Dominius pulled his crosier to his hands and encased himself in an opaque blue mesh of light.

'Don't fear, Majesty,' he said, 'this room has been warded to the hilt.'

Valetta had also shielded and now, rising to her feet, was shouting, 'Librea!' while the sound of more spears smashing windows echoed along the front of the manor.

Aradea, Lyra called, and felt something distant respond. In her mind's eye the pegasus Pearl whinnied and reared, wings unfurling, while the Leaf-man carvings in her garden all opened their eyes.

Then two more ballista bolts struck the windows and they shattered in a spray of broken glass, striking the magi's shields and turning the air to scarlet sparks. Moments later, four men burst through the shattered windows, rolling and coming up with drawn swords, their eyes oil-black and their mouths shrieking in hate.

419

Lyra would have been cut down in an instant had Dominius not shielded her, covering the few feet between them in a blur despite his bulk. The nearest man hacked at her and he blocked with his crosier, the thin twist of wood taking the blow without breaking. Then he sent a burst of blue light into the Reeker's face that blasted the front of his skull inwards and he dropped instantly.

But Valetta wasn't faring so well; her mage-bolt had taken the nearest attacker in the chest and caved in his ribcage, but she'd overcommitted to one foe and before she could focus on the rest, another had outflanked her and slashed her side. She collapsed, crying out in agony.

Lyra shrieked in fear and fury, '*ARADEA!*'

Verdant light bloomed in her mind, but she had no idea what to do with that power and once again it was Dominius who kept her alive, bellowing a spell that caused a deep blue light to surge from his right hand into the two remaining possessed men. Both were hurled backwards as something like smoke was wrenched from their mouths and their bodies collapsed.

Dear Kore, he tore their souls out!

'Milady, are you unharmed?' Wurther asked, bending over Valetta and pouring white light into her wound, sealing it. 'The good sister lives – can you help her?'

Lyra dropped to Valetta's side to find the nun alive, although in pain and groggy; the healing had merely stopped the bleeding. Pressing her hand to the woman's side, Lyra pulled her to an armchair.

'Grafia,' Valetta murmured and Lyra patted her arm, then gave her attention over to the dwyma: she could feel something coursing into her but it was sluggish. The histories all said the dwymancers' powers were immense, but when ambushed, they'd been nigh on helpless. The energy inside her was building, but too slowly, and she still didn't know what to do with it. *Blizzards and earthquakes can't save us here . . .*

With a shaking hand she drew her dagger, a beautiful argenstael stiletto she and Basia had dubbed *Papercut*, as it was mostly used as a letter-opener. Dirklan had given it to her after she told him about her conversation with Valdyr. She wished she knew how to use it.

Then three of the attackers jerked back to life, sitting up and snarling, and Dominius went as pale as Valetta.

'Queen and Grand Prelate in one room?' they said in unison. 'How convenient.'

He tore out their daemon, Lyra realised, *but it came straight back.*

As one the possessed men charged, while more climbed through the broken windows.

Basia didn't bother with stairs but dropped straight down the stairwell shaft, landing with feet planted and hacking down the man attacking Falkerman. She cut at the back of his thighs and was about to dash on . . . until she realised he was still standing. Then another man smashed through the shattered windows and she saw his eyes were black.

She and Falkerman shouted '*Reekers*–' at the same time; she blocked an overhead blow and aimed for her foe's neck, but a strong parry stopped her, even as the front door shook and she heard shouting from the grand prelate's drawing room. '*Lyra!*' she yelled as she launched another attack, this time almost losing her blade–

–until a mage-bolt flashed from above, locking the Reeker's shields over his right shoulder at the precise instant her blade beat his parry, chopped into his neck and lodged in his spine. Thanks to the silver the blade had been dipped in, his eyes lost their ebony hue momentarily and while he floundered, she hacked sideways, severing the spinal cord.

She glanced up, saw Exilium clutching the banister on the landing above and waved thanks. Beside her, Falkerman crunched a double-handed blow through his foe's helm and into his brain and he too went down.

Two more Kirkegarde pounded in, shouldering her aside and following Falkerman into the grand prelate's lounge. Falkerman took down the nearest attacker from behind as his men fanned out. Lyra was crouching before a stricken nun in a chair, while Dominius Wurther stood at bay, indigo light pouring from his hands and forming a wall of translucent blue; the wizardry barrier was keeping half a dozen Reekers at bay – for now, at least. Basia and Falkerman's men were on the wrong side of that barrier.

She dashed in and drove her silvered blade into the nearest downed Reeker's eyeball. The effect of the silver was less obvious this time – perhaps the silver was being consumed by the ichor? But the man still jerked and went still as the blade entered his brain. *Dirklan needs to know that*, she thought as she and the Kirkegarde rallied to Lyra and Wurther.

'Lyra!' she called, 'are you all right?'

The queen nodded distractedly. *Her head's inside the dwyma*, Basia realised, so at Wurther's gesture, she eased carefully through his warding and positioned herself in front of Lyra, while the remaining Reekers snarled on the other side of the barrier, hacking at it with blades limned with black light. It was beginning to come apart.

'You got anything better, Holiness?' she called to Wurther. 'A warding circle, perhaps?'

'This is my drawing room, dear girl,' Wurther called, cool as you like. 'Protective circles do tend to dull the ambience.'

Falkerman pointed to the door at the back of the room. 'Can we get out this way?'

As if in answer, the door opened and Valetta's bodyguard, an almost preternaturally beautiful Kirkegarde woman Basia knew, by reputation at least, as Librea, stepped through, wiping her mouth. 'Sorry I'm late,' she drawled. 'Sometimes distractions can be most distracting.'

Behind her, they saw a man twitching in a pool of blood, a dagger in his chest. Librea raised a sword and as illusions fell from her face, she became Lef Yarle. Six more armoured men, every one of them an Inquisitor using gnostic shields, followed him through. They were all black-eyed and grinning savagely.

'I dedicate this morning's carnage to Dravis Ryburn,' Yarle announced. 'He awaits me at the right hand of Abraxas.'

The tales told of omens and death-signs and the distant wail of the washer-wraith on the day you were fated to die. But Basia knew the *Book of Kore* said the Angel of Death was *lightning from a clear sky.*

She reinforced her shields as mage-bolts flew, then an Inquisitor loomed over her and a big battle-axe cleaved the air. Somehow she parried, but his sheer size and power were too much for her and forced her to one knee. Needing an edge to beat him, she jerked the argenstael dagger from Lyra's hand with kinesis and rammed it into the Inquisitor's groin, she forced it through shields and chainmail in a burst of mage-fire. The man crashed to the ground, black smoke boiling from his eyes and mouth.

Hail the mighty Papercut, Basia thought wildly, pulling the weapon free and simultaneously blocking a second man's thrust with her sword and shoving with kinesis . . .

But Falkerman was being driven back with brutal virtuosity by Yarle and the other two Kirkegarde knights were being overborne by the possessed Inquisitors. Wurther and Sister Valetta were frantically spraying mage-bolts into the fray, even risking striking their own defenders, but they were penned in a corner and fast running out of room.

<Help us!> she shouted into the aether. *<Anyone? Help us!>*

Exilium hobbled on in agony, his broken leg strapped rigid and useless, down to the next landing, drawn by the crash of steel and prickling of the gnosis in the rooms below.

Don't get up, the healers had told him. *Don't risk it, or you'll never walk again.*

But the fight was down there, and he was up here . . .

With a despairing half-sob, he used kinesis to propel himself to the railing and sent a mage-bolt into Basia's foe below. Then she and the Kirkegarde piled into the grand prelate's drawing room, which was where he needed to be.

Holy Kore, aid me! Clutching his blade and using kinesis to swing himself over the railing, he dropped down the stairwell, trying to shield his bad leg and control his fall, but he struck hard, jarring something inside the bad knee. The burst of white-hot pain almost broke him and he slumped to the floor, howling silently with eyes bulging.

But steel was belling on steel in the next room and he couldn't ignore it. He clawed himself upright, grabbed a ballista-spear lying amid the shattered glass, jammed it under his left armpit as a crutch and staggered into the drawing room to see Dominius Wurther blazing indigo light from his crosier into an Inquisitor, while Basia battled another black-eyed attacker, all the while shielding Lyra and the bloodied nun, Valetta.

On the far side of the room he saw Falkerman fighting Lef Yarle, who for some reason was powdered and rouged and dressed in woman's armour. But Yarle still moved with dreadful grace, spitting the Kirkegarde knight under his arm and into his chest. Black light exploded in Falkerman's torso as he crashed down.

'Hold on,' Wurther roared, *'hold!* Help's coming—'

Maybe, but it's not coming fast enough, Exilium thought. *We're all going to die.*

He lunged in and spitted one of the Reeker-Inquisitors, but without a silvered blade the blow was ineffectual – it did allow the Kirkegarde man a chance to behead the attacker, but the next possessed man had spotted him and launched a savage cut that required a full-blooded parry. Exilium instantly forgot his limitations: the spear butt slipped on the pooled blood, his right leg buckled and he crashed to the floor, contorting sideways just as the attacker's blade came at his face but instead of impaling him, it grazed his cheek and plunged into the floor . . . and stuck.

Exilium jammed the spear upwards into the man's groin, but the Reeker didn't flinch, just roared and yanked his sword free. Exilium raised his blade to block, but one of the Kirkegarde took the man on, so he slithered clear, wondering if he could even stand again . . .

'Rukka—' Basia grimaced as the Inquisitor's blade raked her left arm. Her vision swam as the pain jolted through her, she dropped Papercut, which clattered at her feet.

The Reeker-Inquisitor hurled a mage-bolt at her face; it splattered harmlessly on her shields but he was already on her, snarling with savage ferocity. She locked her hand around his wrist, fighting to hold off his blade as he crushed her backwards onto the table. His teeth filled her vision.

Then his eyes bulged and she twisted her head away as they exploded, spouting black smoke. She hurled the dead Reeker away and found

Exilium on the floor, staring at the bloodstained argenstael stiletto in his hand.

'Nifty, huh?' she told him. 'You can't keep it.'

Then Lef Yarle loomed out of the fray, his blood-streaked face mad with hate . . .

Somehow, Basia found the speed to turn his first thrust aside and even riposte, driving her sword through Yarle's guard and almost taking his right eye, but moving with balletic grace, the Inquisitor swayed away – and then the onslaught began. His blade was lightning-fast, breaking open her guard, slashing her left cheek, her right thigh, sending her backwards. She tripped over a chair and crashed to the ground.

She saw Exilium attack with the queen's stiletto, but Yarle viciously backhanded him, sending the weapon spinning across the room. The last of the possessed men went down, his skull blown apart by Wurther's pure-blood gnostic fire, but it was too late, because Yarle was standing right in front of Lyra, gnostic fire gathering on his blade . . .

Unarmed, injured and out-matched, Basia did the only thing she could think of. She threw herself into the space between the killer and his prey as he thrust his sword, and time stopped as every inch of the blade plunged through her right shoulder until the tip punched out of her back.

Her body blazed in pain, her fingers loosened and her blade dropped, and she was falling to the floor, which opened up as she spun into the stars, Ril's name on her lips . . .

Lef Yarle snarled in frustration and pushed the queen's *cripple* from his blade. He went for the queen again, but yet another of Wurther's insidious wizardry spells blazed, another attempt to rip Abraxas out of him, if even for a moment. He swung to counter it, his blade met the Grand Prelate's staff – and this time he shattered it, the concussive blast hurling Wurther backwards. He shook off the blast and lunged – but another blade just turned aside his killing thrust.

The dark-haired man wielded a sword in his right hand and a Rimoni-styled stiletto that *stank* of silver in his left. Yarle paused, then recognised the bandaged, battered figure before him: Exilium Excelsior.

The bastard who killed Dravis . . .

'I was planning on visiting you, Estellan,' he snarled. 'I've been wondering who's best . . . though I think we both know.' He battered aside Exilium's dazed attempt to parry, opening up his guard so he could slash at his throat.

Aradea, I need *you*, Lyra begged, reaching with all that she was.

There was a response, but it was trickling into her when she needed a flood. Her wide-open senses were connecting to the greater world: she could feel the sunlight outside, the ground and water below, but it was all blurred by the vengeful shrieking of Abraxas. There was no storm here to tap, no living wood or running water, no wind or fire: she was trapped indoors, away from anything she might use . . .

But right in front of her, Basia hurled herself in front of Lef Yarle . . . only to be spitted. She fell, her body going limp. '*No*–' Lyra shrieked as her bodyguard – her *friend* – slumped to the floor. '*Basia!*'

But Yarle swept on, now hacking at Exilium Excelsior, who could barely stand, while Wurther, plainly spent, reeled helplessly . . .

Then something smashed through the largest of the shuttered windows: a gleaming winged silhouette around which sunlight gathered – and poured straight into her, filling her in a torrent she couldn't contain . . .

. . . so she didn't try.

Exilium saw his duty clearly: to buy those he served a few extra seconds to ask Kore's forgiveness. It was a sacrifice he'd prepared for every day since his vocation was made clear: to die for Corineus, his Saviour.

The glowing blade carved the air and he could see the three moves Yarle would take to end it: he threw up too weak a parry and the counter knocked his blade askew. The next blow crunched down on his hilt, energy flared and the weapon was torn from his fingers. Yarle levelled his blade at Exilium's heart, saying something, doubtless mocking – but they were wasted words, for Exilium was barely conscious.

And at that moment, the windows burst open and he saw something large and glowing white with the wings of an angel. The pale figure of Queen Lyra went incandescent and a shockwave of light burst from her eyes as she looked at Yarle. The Inquisitor screamed as her gaze cut a luminous hole though the gloom, transfixing him, then he was collapsing, black smoke pouring from his eyes and mouth.

A moment later Lyra pitched forward and lay unmoving. In the midst of the broken glass was a white pegasus filling the room, stamping its hooves and neighing.

Exilium shook off the torpor of shock and crawled to Lyra's bodyguard as the grand prelate also slumped to the ground, his big frame shaking uncontrollably. He checked Basia, who was unconscious, but still breathing. He had no healing-gnosis, so all he could do was cauterise the vicious wound, then he crawled on to Falkerman, but he was dead. Sister Valetta was lying motionless on the table still, but she too was still breathing.

Then he dragged himself to the queen, sprawled on the carpet. 'Majesty,' Exilium called, still trying to make sense of what he'd seen.

An Angel came, in the shape of a pegasus. The Holy Light of Kore entered her and the daemon was blasted away. I've seen a miracle. He scarcely dared to touch her, for she was a sacred being, that was clear. It was all he could do to take her hand as he stared at her in adoration. *So beautiful, so pure. A living saint.*

'My Queen,' he whispered. 'I am your servant.'

Lyra opened her eyes and for an instant they *glowed* – then they softened, but her perfect face contorted. 'Where are you?' she asked in a panicked voice. '*I can't see . . .*'

31

The Lowertown Walls

The Edge of Morality

The question asked by everyone from street brigands to mage-lords is: how far should I go to achieve my aims? The line I draw is this: does your intended action require you to become the thing you must not? That is my limit, but some cross that line without remorse. That's why I hope there really is a Hel.

ESTABO DEL'ANIZ, ESTELLAYNE PLAYWRIGHT, RIOPORTA 870

Norostein, Noros
Janune 936

Deep, sonorous horns sounded as the open-topped palanquin bearing Sultan Rashid Mubarak was carried to the raised dais where he would watch the assault. White-clad warriors knelt in waves as he passed. In a gold-chased breastplate and a white turban wrapped about a spiked golden helm, with his scabbarded ceremonial sword gripped in his hand in a classical pose, he looked every inch the prophet-king at war.

Would that I really were a prophet, the sultan thought, gazing at the walls of Norostein a mile off across the muddy plains, but divination dealt in likely outcomes, not certainties.

The Great Prophet Aluq-Ahmed, founder of the Amteh faith, was said to have known the future in exact detail, but Rashid doubted that was true. He'd seen the Secret Scrolls, Aluq-Ahmed's so-called prophecies: mostly gibberish about snake moons and seas running dry, open to any interpretation you wanted. They could be useful occasionally, though. Ali Beyrami's Godspeakers had been picking out random phrases like 'seas of sand bury the ice mountain' and reinterpreting them as omens of victory, and the faithful soldiers *believed*. The hymns today were being sung with all the fervour he could have wished for.

He walked to his throne and genuflected to it, symbolically reminding all that Ahm was above every throne. Then he turned to each corner of the compass and lifted his sword-hilt to his men, an invitation to draw the blade of war, then facing forward, he swept it from the scabbard, as a ruler must be always first to draw steel and last to sheath it, every day of battle.

The men cheered, the Godspeakers wailed prayers, drums hammered. When they fell silent, he pointed the blade at the city and projecting his voice through the gnosis, cried, 'Men of the Shihad, holy warriors of Ahm: there is your enemy, the servants of Shaitan the Unholy. Behold his dark citadel: bring it down, for Ahm is your Light, Ahm your Victory! There is no defeat, no turning back: Martyrdom or Glory awaits!'

'*AIEEE*,' they wailed back, '*SUBHANNA-AHM – TABARAK-AHM!*'

The plans were laid, the orders issued, the troops arrayed. All that was left was for him to speak the words.

'*HUJUM TAKADAM*,' he shouted: *Go forth and attack!*

His sons joined him on the dais as the army lurched into motion. With a massive cheer, the drums boomed out, trumpets blared and the first waves advanced upon the walls. Elephant units trudged in behind the archers and in the skies above, more than a hundred windships and as many rocs circled.

There wasn't an enemy windship in view. *We have the skies, for once in our lives!*

Attam was a ferocious sight with his shaven skull and burly frame armoured for battle. Beside him Xoredh glided like a serpent, more lightly armoured, but always elegant. His two sons: his sword and his dagger.

Pride, as always, mixed with regret. Although they were utterly dedicated to him, in some ways he'd already lost them both. To rule was to utilise every tool at hand; one's own blood could not be spared. *I sacrificed the men they could have been to make them the men I needed.*

'Father,' said Attam, who would lead the assault, 'we're ready.'

'And with a few surprises for the Yurosi scum,' Xoredh added.

'Do you think the Enemy will realise our intent?' Rashid asked.

Xoredh answered, 'The Enemy know nothing of us. To them we're just a Noorie horde. They believe we know only one way to fight. They'll learn their error too late.'

For three Crusades, the opening skirmishes had always involved the Eastern generals sending in its chaff, the worst armed, least trained and most expendable, which generally meant disgraced men and criminals on punishment duty. It also eased the burden on stores. They followed up with arrow-storms and massed assaults, still throwing blade-fodder at the enemy to overwhelm and exhaust them. They would use their best only as the enemy tired.

But this time they were facing *Seth Korion* – not just a Crusade veteran, but a man who'd defied an army ten times the size of his own at Riverdown. Korion would know what to expect. Rashid had heard everything their Riverdown veterans could tell him of that battle, which had all come down to discipline, closely held formations, narrow fronts, and rapid responses to breakthroughs. Tenacity and superiority in close mêlée had counted – and that was in defending a mere sandbank beside a river. This time Seth Korion held the highest walls in southern Yuros.

To smash into Norostein quickly, we have to do something different. But there are risks.

Rashid hadn't broken the Ordo Costruo, defeated the Third Crusade, seized power in Ahmedhassa and launched an 'impossible' invasion of Yuros without risk. Only those who dared to strive for glory could ever grasp it. Even to reach for the stars was glorious.

'Be victorious, my son,' he told Attam. 'The weather-magi have promised us clear skies. You command the greatest army in history. Write your name in the firmament for ever.'

The weather is the biggest gamble of all. Without clear skies we can't bring our air superiority into play . . . But that means a few dozen Air-magi trying to wrest control of the weather from more experienced Yurosi Air-magi and from Nature itself. So far, the gamble held, but when weather manipulation failed, the backlash could be devastating. I've given us a few days of perfect conditions to take Norostein . . . but what if we fail?

Attam bared his teeth, knelt for his sultan's blessing, then rose and strode to his mount. For all his bulk he leaped athletically into the saddle and galloped down the ranks of ululating men to take his position in the vanguard.

Today, our best go in first, Rashid mused. *Are you ready for that, Seth Korion?*

'Are we ready?' Seth asked his aides for the hundredth time.

Andwine Delton and Rano Culmather looked at each other, then chorused, 'Yes sir.'

'Expect the worst and hope for the best, lad,' Jelaska Lyndrethuse murmured. Her long grey hair was tied back severely and she wore her loose black battle-magi robes over chainmail, a rare concession to the realities of battle. Her legion was away to the right, where the conical helms of the grey-cloaked Argundian pikemen gleamed in the dull light.

The battlemented clock-tower behind the main gatehouse of Lowertown had views over the entire north-facing wall, but it wasn't large, so he'd left his guard cohort below. Overhead, the skies were unseasonably clear: the Shihadi weather-magi were doing their best to aid the attack.

Such control can only last a few days, Seth mused, *and once they lose control, the counter-storm will be deadly. But can we hold long enough?* He'd had a few of his own weather-magi contest the weather, but they'd failed to break the Ahmedhassans' control.

A raucous fanfare below was followed by cheering and applause. The governor had given King Phyllios of Noros permission to fight, and he had just arrived. Phyllios climbed the tower, accompanied by Era Hyson, his serious-faced captain. The thin, stoop-shouldered monarch managed to make even the royal armour less than martial, but he looked energised, and no wonder: his chains had been struck off and his gnosis freed.

Governor Myron hopes he'll either disgrace himself or die.

'Ah, General Korion,' Phyllios said, with nervous good cheer. 'Have they begun?'

'You'll know when they begin,' Jelaska muttered.

'It's imminent, Majesty,' Seth interrupted. 'This isn't the best place – perhaps the view up in Ringwald might–?'

'Nonsense. I've lived up there all my life. I wouldn't swap this for a Royal Box at the Lantric Masques.'

'They'll come at us hard, Majesty, and we'll get the worst right here at the gatehouse.'

'I'm pretty sure Governor Myron freed me so I'd get myself killed,' Phyllios said, 'but to die in defence of my city is a better fate than any I could have imagined these past twenty years.' He leaned forward and, squinting into the distance, blanched at the vast ranks arrayed before the walls.

Their vantage gave them a view of the enemy until they got to within two hundred yards of the outer bastion; after that Seth had to rely on seer-magi positioned on the battlements. As well as men stationed on the walls, he had two legions in the streets behind. There were ballistae in every watchtower – and on many roofs inside the city as well, in case the Keshi got windships inside the walls. Logisticalus maniples with water-chains were at Lowertown Lake, in case of fire. Children, elderly and infirm had been evacuated to Copperleaf, the second tier, but every able-bodied man – and more than a few women – stood ready.

'They'll come at us with everything,' Ramon had predicted. 'Rashid doesn't have time to go through the usual build-up.'

Once again, Seth was staking his credibility on his friend's judgement.

The enemy drums rolled, trumpets brayed and the ground shook as more than two hundred thousand men advanced in unison, sweeping forward under the circling windships riding the northerly wind towards Norostein. The snap of coordinated movement sent a thrill through him as the days of frenzied preparation coalesced into the vital first moments of contact.

The aether began to crackle with gnostic calls from magi from Corby Tower in the west to the Aqueduct Gates in the east. The enemy were attacking every part of the defences – but not with the ragtag levies who usually formed the initial assault. This time they were facing fully armoured and trained Keshi spearmen and massed archers.

Ramon was right, Seth thought with a shiver. *They're going straight for the jugular.*

·

Attam's guard snapped to attention as the prince cantered into the midst of his coterie, young noblemen drawn to the sultan's heir by the air of violence and licentiousness he exuded. His entourage wasn't for the faint-hearted: bravado had to be matched by brutality. The weak were quickly unmasked and broken.

Fatima loathed them all, but she dared not be less than them. She knew that without Attam's explicit protection, she'd already have had her throat cut, gnostic spear or not.

All I ask is the chance to kill this Korion, she repeated to herself.

When Attam appeared, she bawled out her lungs like the rest, punching the spear into the air and shouting, '*Attam fi aman'Ahm!*' to invoke Ahm's protection on their prince, while their horses danced and the nearby soldiers ululated savagely. Impulsively she pulsed a ball of light into the sullen skies and there was a sucking-in of breath, then renewed cheering.

'An omen,' a Godspeaker shrieked, 'it's an omen of victory!'

Fatima felt a sudden crippling hollowing of the bones at the rush of energy from her body.

Attam gave her an annoyed look. 'Contain yourself,' he growled. 'Don't let them mark you until we reach the gates.'

Then he raised a hand and they all fell silent, straining to hear him. 'My father commands the advance!' he bellowed. 'Before us is the Enemy and behind us marches Winter. We must take the fortress, gut the Yurosi and take their homes. We will use their women and convert their children to the True Faith! This day will end with our army inside the walls!'

Then he pointed the way forward and gripping the spear tighter, Fatima put aside her worries for Waqar and Tamir and allowed herself to be swept along with them.

Only revenge matters. This is my moment.

The *Kalistham* taught that martyrs could expect a bed full of virgins as their reward, but she was pretty sure those virgins were supposed to be girls. How women martyrs were rewarded, she wasn't sure: maybe she got to be one of the virgins? *Some reward . . .*

Though I'd be a virgin again for you, Baneet, my love, she thought, blinking away sudden tears.

The first volleys of arrows rose into the air, mighty swathes of flying wood and steel, and sleeted down on the enemy's fortifications. All the world was brighter than normal, every sound more beautiful and more precious. They said your last moments were your most wonderful, because you got a foretaste of Ahm's Paradise. She could feel it calling. Feeling unstoppable, she shouted her thanks to Ahm on High for the gift of battle.

Dear Ahm, I hate war, Latif thought as Rani lumbered forward, a tower of flesh ploughing through the churned-up mud, following the Keshi spearmen into the assault.

'We're doomed,' Ashmak was moaning. 'What idiot sends elephants forward when there's no breach? We've not even bridged the moat. We're all going to die.'

'That's not your most inspiring speech,' Sanjeep called from the mahout's nest at the front of the howdah.

'What're we supposed to do, have Rani head-butt the walls?' Ashmak snarled back. 'Or just parade in front to give the Yurosi some target-practise?'

Latif glanced back at their commander's elephant, in a field half a mile back. *Pour your divine retribution upon Shaitan's minions and support the breakthrough*: those were the orders Selmir had delivered. He clearly intended to admire their work from afar.

'I'm sure Selmir's just following orders,' Latif commented.

'A good commander knows when to tell the idiot giving the orders to piss off,' Ashmak retorted.

'You're right. But we're still going in, aren't we?'

Ashmak pursed his lips and drawled, 'Aiiee, we are.'

'Then stop complaining and concentrate on shielding us,' Sanjeep called.

Ashmak's hackles rose, but Latif interjected, 'I'll do the shooting; you just keep us alive.'

He grimaced acceptance. Nominally, Ashmak commanded their three-man, one-elephant unit, but they'd been together so long that the lines were blurred.

The clamour grew: arrows were flying from the massed Dhassan and Keshi archers standing dozens of ranks deep, each man with huge bundles of shafts at his feet. The Yurosi bowmen wouldn't have the numbers to compete.

The walls ahead looked empty, but there would be men pressed low behind the stones, waiting to rise when the barrage ceased. The Shihad had not had time to construct siege-towers, but they had thousands of ladders.

Movement above caught their eyes: waves of giant eagles sweeping over their heads towards the walls, followed by lines of windships, sweeping in at low altitude. That gave him hope that Rashid might have some new miracle up his sleeve. *Because if he hasn't, we're going to be slaughtered.*

The first kills belonged to the Keshi archers as always, releasing their torrential downpour of steel and feathered wood and death.

Even though they'd prepared, there just weren't enough places for the defenders to hide when the air filled with lethally sharp arrows lancing down from above at an almost vertical angle. Barely exposed flesh was impaled and too many who dared a look fell with shafts through an eye-socket. The noise and thudding impacts panicked some into running; the few who did were cut down in seconds.

But Seth's veterans barely flinched. *At Riverdown we had nothing but trenches and dismantled wagons to hide behind*, Seth recalled.

Then the first wave of giant eagles came shrieking in, lancing magebolts and fireballs at the watch-towers, seeking to blast the ballistae crews and incinerate their weapons. They were protected, though, with wooden shields around the massive crossbows and gnostic wards, and each crew had magi empowering the shafts as they launched their fire-tipped six-foot bolts up and into the bellies of the birds flashing overhead, bringing several down.

Then came the low-flying windships, sailing into the barrage of ballista shafts. Some pierced the hulls, others set sails ablaze, but still they kept coming, except for two whose poorly warded keels exploded and crashed in flames onto their own soldiers.

<*They're coming in too low – they're too low* . . .> someone was squawking into the aether, then a Keshi windship slammed into the gatehouse tower and came apart. Burning oil gushed through the hulk as it lurched sideways and fell with a roar into the killing zone behind the tower. A moment later three more ships smashed into towers along the curtain wall and engulfed them in flames.

'Dear Kore, fire-ships?' King Phyllios wailed in shock.

Seth gripped the king's shoulder to steady him, then begun rapping out orders to bring the water-wagons forward and exhorting the ballistae crews to *bring those damned things down!*

'I'll go to my men,' Jelaska told him laconically, before floating from the clock-tower using kinesis. Her sudden absence made Seth feel a lot more exposed.

'Dear Kore,' said Phyllios, shaken. 'This is dreadful.'

'Majesty,' Seth replied gently, 'it's barely begun.'

He gripped the edge of the stonework as windships hammered into the outer walls, bringing down the outer gatehouse towers and cracking and breaking the tops of the walls.

Then the biggest vessel yet swept across the walls and headed straight for where he and the king stood.

Fatima saw flames erupt around the gatehouse as Attam's party advanced through the soldiers, the crown prince riding tall in his saddle, his cronies shouting eagerly as the walls loomed. More windships were ploughing into the walls, often ineffectually, but in two sections the battlements had been destroyed, leaving walls halved in height. She gripped the spear, saw the way its pulsing increased as her heart thudded faster, and remembered that awful feeling of being eaten from the inside as she discharged it.

I have to do this when it's exactly the right time . . . I'll not get many chances . . .

'Look,' exclaimed an emir's son from Peroz, pointing to an already burning windship that had hammered into the main gatehouse. The crew were just now bailing out, straight into the waiting blades of the enemy. The windship crews abandoned their vessels only when collision was upon them, even though they'd fall into Yurosi hands.

That's why we'll win, Fatima exulted. *Because we be believe enough to sacrifice everything.*

With a scream, the first wave of attackers reached the bottom of the walls and as the archers paused, ladders rose and slammed into the walls. At last the Rondian magi unleashed their gnosis and the enemy defenders came from under cover to hurl their javelins.

The real battle had begun.

'To the gatehouse,' Attam roared. '*Take the gatehouse!*'

Seth grabbed Phyllios while bellowing a warning to his aides, hurling himself off, the stunned king wrapped in his arms, an instant before the Keshi windship slammed into the tower. Bricks and timber rained down, bouncing off Seth's shields to strike the ground in a slew of blue sparks. He rolled onto the king and covered him against the burning timbers crashing down around them.

He glanced up to see the whole clock-tower wobbling in an alarming manner. He lifted Phyllios in kinesis-strengthened arms and ran, bursting from a billowing cloud of dust and smoke an eye-blink before the tower crashed down. White-robed Easterners hurled themselves from the windship, which had erupted in flames. Most landed badly, breaking ankles and arms and crashing to the ground wailing, but others rose like cats and started cutting down anyone in their way. Seth saw Culmather take a scimitar in the back as he staggered out of the wreckage, already concussed and virtually defenceless. Seth blazed mage-fire at the nearest enemy, then Phyllios remembered he too was a mage and did the same; his weaker blasts were not terribly accurate, but they bought a moment . . .

. . . then with a belligerent shout, Seth's guard cohort burst from inside the stricken building – clearly the lowest floor hadn't collapsed – and struck the Keshi from behind. Serjant Vidran's burly front-rankers carved through the Easterners, then Harmon's flankers danced in, flashing blades cutting down the rest, before they swarmed around Seth and the king, shields raised.

'Tol' you it were a stupid place to stand,' Bowe remarked. 'Top of a feckin' tower? I ask you!'

'Ye right, sir?' Lukaz asked coolly.

'All well, Pilus,' Seth replied, checking on Phyllios, who was moving easily despite the rough landing. But poor Culmather was gone, he saw, grimacing. 'Have you seen Delton?'

Andwine Delton, appearing a moment later, gave a choked cry when he saw Culmather's body, but immediately snapped into a salute when Seth turned his way.

Calm, always calm, Seth's father had told him once, when they were still talking. *All men want to know the man leading them is in full control.* 'Andwine, come with me. Pilus Lukaz, have someone take Culmather to the infirmary.' He turned to King Phyllios. 'Majesty, I implore you to return to the palace. The time hasn't yet come for you to be risked in battle.'

Phyllios straightened. 'A king must be seen to lead: he is the most powerful piece on the tabula board.'

Right now the king is more of a liability . . . 'A good player will *harbour* his power,' Seth retorted as the king's guards came running up, led by Captain Hysen. 'Majesty, please? I'll report to you this evening.'

Phyllios' pale, studious face looked pained, but he found a compromise that salvaged pride. 'I'll wait with my guards in Charterhouse Square, General, for when I'm needed.'

If you're needed, we're truly doomed, Seth thought grimly, but he smiled and bowed before striding away with Delton. 'Andwine, I must know how we're faring elsewhere. Relay-staves!'

At the inner stone towers of the gatehouse, the key to any keep, he found the immense steel-bound wooden doors still firm, but the outer towers were burning. It was here, more than any other point, that this day would be decided. He was looking about for the Shihad's way in when the whole edifice shook . . .

'Hang back,' Ashmak called to Sanjeep, as loudly as he dared. 'There are no breaches yet – we can't get in.' The ex-Hadishah was keeping up a strong shield and so far Rani had only minor wounds. Latif had been largely free to pick his targets. When they reached that great wall, the entire elephant formation wheeled left and started tramping slowly along it, the archers exchanging shafts with Yurosi crossbowmen on the ramparts.

Then a ballista in a half-wrecked tower came to life again, sending a steel shaft longer than Latif's body into the flank of the elephant before them in the line. The beast wobbled sideways and collapsed, crushing the spearmen sheltering behind it; its howdah and crew were hurled to the ground.

'Holy Ahm,' Latif shouted, 'we'll be next – Ashmak?'

'Ai, I see them.' He blazed a mage-bolt at the big crossbow, but their shields easily deflected. Latif tried to help, sending a torrent of arrows at the crew, but the mage up there knew his business, fending off both his arrows and Ashmak's mage-fire, while behind his translucent wards, the ballista crew cranked and loaded.

'Bring them down!' Sanjeep shouted, while hurling prayers at every Lakh god he knew. But with deadly inevitability the ballista swivelled, trained on Rani and spat its deadly load–

–and missed.

Latif, flinching away, glimpsed the shaft as it shrieked past Sanjeep's head and cut a path through the archers fifty yards behind them. For a moment, the universe paused for breath.

Then Ashmak leapt to his feet, lifted his tunic and waggled his cock at the enemy, screaming, 'Ha, you *chotias* – can't hit an elephant at fifty paces, you yoni-licking turds–'

He's not shielding . . .

Latif dragged him down an instant before a vivid mage-bolt carved the air where Ashmak's groin had been, while Sanjeep took the rare recourse of jamming a hooked metal rod into Rani's shoulder, forcing her out of the line and sending her running back towards their own lines before every other Rondian in reach sought redress for the insult. Archers and spearmen scattered before them.

Ashmak threw Latif off him, bellowing with laughter. 'Ahm Above, I love this – I *love* it!'

They jolted back through the lines until Sanjeep slowed Rani to a walk. Latif pulled himself back to a kneeling position, then thoughtfully tipped his remaining arrows over the back of the howdah, just beyond Rani's massive behind. 'Oh look,' he said. 'We ran out of arrows. Best we return to camp for more.'

'Excellent thinking,' Sanjeep called. 'Next time shoot faster, so we can retreat sooner.'

Latif looked back in time to see another elephant in the line take a ballista shaft through the skull. *That's us, next time we go back in*, he thought with a shudder.

Even so, twenty minutes later, their arrows replenished, they were trundling back into the fray.

Fatima bridled with impatience as Attam's men waited beneath the outer gatehouse, milling about on horseback and boasting of the feats they'd achieve when they broke inside. Meanwhile low-blood magi did the actual work, striving to undo probably *centuries* of enchantments to break the gates.

To the nobles, that's what these lowbloods were for – breeding-house fodder born not of carefully planned unions, but to the endless procession of Keshi villagers dragged from their villages to be impregnated by enslaved Yurosi magi. Low-blood menials had only basic training, but Attam's high-bloods wouldn't lower themselves to aid them.

Fortunately, the towers above the outer gatehouse had been broken, so there was no one to rain fire and arrows down on them. There was just this damned waiting. Fatima used it on divination, and her heart quickened: the man she sought was very near . . .

. . . so close she lost patience.

She urged her mount through the crowds, pushing aside Attam's bully-boys and just *daring* them to do something about it, shouting, 'Get out of the way–' to the low-bloods; when she brandished the spear, they scattered. *Good: word's got around.* She blanked the uproar on all sides and thought only of the nexus of the spells she sought to destroy. They were twinkling in her gnostic sight . . . *There.*

She levelled the weapon . . . just as Attam grabbed her arm.

'What are you doing?' he growled.

'I'm going to open these rukking doors,' she rasped. 'I've just divined that Seth Korion is in the gatehouse and I'm going to send the Shaitan-loving prick back to his Master's realm.'

'But I'm not–'

She shook her arm free and unleashed an incandescent bolt of energy that slammed into the huge enchanted doors, blasting them apart in a rain of splinters. As it did, a withering shockwave gripped her, making her reel in the saddle. Attam grabbed her arm again, this time to keep her upright.

Then with a ragged cry, Attam's friends went surging through the gates, ignoring his roars to wait . . .

. . . and a moment later, the air was filled with a hideous cacophony: the crack of crossbows discharging, the whoosh of fire blasting down from the walls on both sides of the narrow race beyond and the screams of those burned and impaled who could still draw breath. The next wave milled between the outer gates, their ardour dampened by the carnage before them, but a moment later, they too were mown down.

The prince was roaring for his friends to pull back, *pull back* – but someone else was screaming out orders to advance, and Fatima, who was swaying, barely conscious, while her horse capered fearfully – saw another wave cut down and then another, the space inside the gatehouse filling with torn, bloodied bodies. Somehow the open gate had its own gravity, pulling in men to the deadly breach.

Attam was looking at her like she was Shaitan's Whore. '*My friends*,' he snarled, 'those are *my friends* you've sent into Death's jaws–'

Then he backhanded her in the face and sent her into the mud.

32

The Breach

Religion: Amteh

The faith of the Amteh is a curious thing: an obscure oasis god made into a universal deity by the warlord and 'prophet' Aluq-Ahmed of Hebusalim. Though he was Dhassan by birth, it was in Kesh that his brand of militaristic preaching whipped up a zeal in his soldiers that carried them to conquest, and him to immortality.

ORDO COSTRUO ARCANUM, HEBUSALIM

Ahm is eternal, and the Prophet was the first to spread his Truth.

THE KALISTHAM, HOLY BOOK OF AMTEH

Norostein, Noros
Janune 936

That dreadful weapon is here, Seth thought, a chill gripping his heart. The aether still reverberated to that unmistakable, sickening energy surge. *We have to do something.*

He turned to Lukaz and ordered, 'Pilus, three men, with me.'

Lukaz, Vidran and Harmon immediately followed him up the back stairs of the inner gatehouse to a dark chamber with long, narrow slots facing inwards that overlooked the entrance to the city. The slots were lined with crossbowmen, firing swiftly as men behind reloaded and handed new weapons forward. There were battle-magi too, taking a little more time to aim, picking out special targets for their gnostically bolstered shafts. Opposite them was another such chamber; the crossfire was devastating their attackers, leaving bloodied corpses piling up in the race below, but more and more enemy were charging in.

A tall young battle-mage saw him and hurried over, almost dashing his own head against the low roof. 'General sir, welcome, we're holding, sir,' he rattled breathlessly.

'Are you commanding here?' Seth asked.

'Aye sir, Secundus Marvikus, sir.'

'Secundus?'

The young man faltered. 'Legate Baxhill was in the front tower when a windship crashed in, General.' He squared his jaw. 'The Noories have blasted open the front gates, but the inner portcullis and gates are intact.'

He paused as someone roared, 'Oil!' and a large flaming metal cauldron in the far corner was lifted and emptied into the killing space below. The screaming intensified.

Kore, this is a Hel of a business we're in.

'Our main worry, sir,' Marvikus went on, 'is that they'll scale the outer towers and force us to sacrifice this vantage.' He led them to another chamber overlooking the length of the race. When Seth peered through a firing slot he saw pierced and charred bodies piled three- and four-deep. A river of blood ran through the portcullis bars two-thirds of the way along, which was preventing further advance.

'You're doing a fine job,' Seth commented, trying not to think of those bodies as men.

'All the emperor's men couldn't take Norostein in 910,' Marvikus said proudly.

He doubted the young man had been alive then. 'And all the sultan's men will likewise fail,' Seth told him. 'What brought down the main gates?'

'We don't know, sir – once we lost the outer towers, we lost our vantage. It wasn't from the air, though; the fellows swear it was launched from the ground outside.'

'We'll find out,' Seth said. 'Well done, *Legate* Marvikus, you're doing a fine job.'

The young man's eyes widened at his battlefield promotion, but Seth was glad to see he wasn't overawed. 'We'll hold for you, sir.' He hesitated, then added, 'Thank you for being here, General. We all know you were ordered to stay in the north.'

'And miss this?' Seth replied, forcing a smile. 'No way. Carry on, Tribune.'

He took Lukaz and his escort up to the rear towers, where they could see along the race, now six bodies deep and still filling. The shattered outer gates were wrecked beyond repair: the blackened timbers and twisted metal looked as if a hundred magi had blasted it with mage-bolts all at once, but even that should have done only surface damage.

'It's like a draken breathed fire on it,' Serjant Vidran remarked casually, as if draken were no big deal.

Seth contacted Delton, a hundred yards below, and asked after the other lesser gates a mile east and west, but they were still intact as yet, although under heavy assault. Seth broke off the contact and thought about the air-battle over Collistein Junction.

This weapon that blasted windships apart: if they had a lot, we'd really know about it . . . so maybe there's just one?

He called to Delton, <*Andwine, ask the king if I can borrow his most disposable banner, please.*> He turned to Vidran. 'Let's see if we can tease our draken into sticking its neck out.'

He'd just turned back to face the gates when Delton blurted into his mind, <*Kore's Blood, sir, we have a breach at Gash Lane.*>

Ramon Sensini led a handful of his battle-magi down through Lowertown. He'd been leading the elimination of Keshi windships that had landed inside the Lowertown walls, but now there was news of a breach in the outer wall.

'Report!' he snapped to the commander of his mounted crossbowmen. Vania de Aelno had intercepted him beside a well he remembered vomiting into as a drunken youth, back in 926, at the edge of the Gash, the most notorious district in Lowertown.

Vania, a Rimoni woman in her thirties, was weathered but attractive in a black-haired and dark-skinned way; in truth, she could have passed for Keshi. She was also the best crossbowman in his legions. Ramon was rather fond of his mounted crossbow maniple; few legions had any, so they generally provided the enemy with a nasty surprise.

'It's target-practise,' Vania chirruped as she swung in beside him and they cantered down the winding street to Gash Lane. 'Our lads can shoot, for one thing. Really, it's not hard to think that you have to aim in front of those *gorgeous* eagles if you want to shaft the fuckers!'

'How many have we downed?'

'Seventeen, sir,' Vania beamed. 'It's been fun . . . well, in a "War is Hel" kind of way.'

'You enjoy your work too much, Vania.'

At *The Carpenter's Daughter*, a popular tavern on a small square, he found Lex Jarlson, a tribune in his Legion Prima. 'Lex, the streets beyond are too narrow for horses, so form your maniple up on foot, and we'll walk inwards and link up with the locals. Make sure they know we're on their side. Vania, bring your best; let's go and find whoever's in charge.'

Ramon took his command group in ahead, past ramshackle houses and down lanes barely three feet wide, full of refuse and discarded wine casks. The roar of battle grew until they rounded a corner and found a small square where stretcher-bearers were lowering a knight to the ground beside dozens of other men. He had a spear through his gut, but was still writhing in slow, desperate agony. Healer-nuns in pale blue robes moved from man to man, gnosis light gleaming as they did what they could.

'They're all screwed,' Vania assessed, earning dagger-looks from every healer in earshot.

'Tact, Vania,' Ramon reminded her. 'Come on, let's see who's in charge.'

To his grim amusement, it was Sir Tonald Grace. His boorishness had annoyed even Governor Myron, so he'd been sent to Lowertown to aid Seth's men. Seth, who did understand irony, had placed him at Gash Lane.

The knight, surrounded by his usual retinue, was shouting at underlings while lounging in front of a wine-shop whose door had been smashed in, despite looting being a hanging crime. The Noroman and his cronies looked up and Ramon caught phrases like 'merc-scum' and 'filthy Silacian' as he approached.

'Sir Tonald,' Ramon called, 'why are you here? The wall's that way.'

The nobleman scowled, then looked askance at Vania. 'Who's she? Your personal healer? Or just your tart?'

'Vania's the best archer in both of my legions and certainly all of yours.'

'Command is for men in a real legion,' Sir Tonald sniffed.

'I can do man-talk,' Vania drawled. 'Farting, beer and tits are my favourite things.'

<Not helpful,> Ramon told her silently before turning to the affronted knight. 'What's your situation?'

'The enemy have taken the wall above the lane,' Sir Tonald said, his tone suggesting it most certainly wasn't *his* fault. 'I'm creating a fall-back position.'

'We'll worry about fall-back positions if we've not re-taken that sector inside the hour,' Ramon told him. 'We must counter-attack, now.'

'My men aren't in any condition to counter. You ask the impossible.'

'I don't *ask*, sir, I *order* a counter-attack. Where are your reserves?'

Sir Tonald looked at the ground. 'They, er, withdrew when the wall fell.' He looked up plaintively. 'Four windships struck the walls, one after the other, only yards apart. It was Hel up there – fire, falling debris, hand-to-hand action – Hel on Urte!'

His report would have been more convincing if he'd not been spotlessly clean.

'Is this the spirit of the Noros Revolt?' grunted Jarlson, a dour-faced blond Argundan festooned with icons of every religion, for luck. 'I thought Noros bred *men*.'

'Si, these are just whining girls,' Vania tittered, with absolutely no sense of irony.

Sir Tonald's big, bruising shadow, a knight named Sir Mion Banance, squared up to Vania. 'Who're you calling a girl?'

Vania's left hand flashed with gnosis-fire concentrated on the tip of her index finger. It was inside Sir Mion's shields before he could raise them. With her twinkling fingertip an inch from his left eyeball, she said, 'I'd never compliment you so highly, good sir.'

Sir Mion eyed her fingertips warily. 'You wouldn't dare.'

'Wouldn't I?' Vania asked, shifting her finger to his left eye, then while he was distracted, kicked him in the groin with a *lot* of kinesis behind the blow. The knight gasped explosively and collapsed, his friends scrambled to draw blades and Vania's men raised crossbows.

'Good to see your men have some bloodlust after all,' Ramon

remarked to Sir Tonald. 'Let's channel it at the enemy. Follow me.' He strode past Vania, murmuring, 'Watch your back,' and led them towards the walls, leaving Sir Mion moaning noisily on the ground.

Within fifty yards, they'd found the front line: officers trying to rally the Noromen defenders reeling backwards with arrows in their shields. Ramon turned to Vania. 'Your lads onto the roofs, Vania, and pick your targets: magi, officers and anyone who looks competent. Tribune Jarlson, Sir Tonald, with me.

He drew his legion-issue shortsword and strode forward, moving with Lex Jarlson's skirmish line, but they ran into the enemy before they struck the walls: a line of dark faces, pale robes over leather armour, circular shields and curved blades, facing a thin line of Noromen. His maroon-clad mercenaries joined the defenders, who murmured greetings gratefully. Just a few yards away hundreds of Keshi spearmen were swarming over the broken wall, attacking along the battlements to widen the breach and to take the towers on either side.

Ramon raised his left hand and sent the most devilish brew of gnosis he could conjure into the enemy ranks.

In 930, at the end of the Third Crusade, Ramon Sensini, a half-blood Arcanum-trained mage, had been given a singular, incredibly rare gift: Ambrosia. The potion could turn even an ordinary man into an Ascendant mage, with raw power at least four times that of a pure-blood – if he survived it. Not everyone did. Ramon was one of a tiny elite of living Ascendants.

Except for those present at the time, he'd told no one and seldom displayed his full strength, but this was not a day for holding back. His affinities in Theurgy, the mental spectrum, and Fire, made his primary affinity illusion, but he could project mental assaults through mesmerism and even liquefy metal if given long enough.

He sent a torrent of fire, blended with projections of even more fire and the illusion of heat and pain. As the front ranks went up like candles, those behind were convinced that they too were in the same straits. With a devastating howl, most of the Keshi went down, screaming and burning; those behind shrieking and throwing themselves about were trying to douse *imagined flames*, but the effect was the same.

Lex Jarlson and his men, used to their capitano's way, didn't hesitate but ploughed straight into the wailing throng, butchering the enemy with brutal efficiency. Crossbows sang over their heads, cutting down any of the Keshi able to react. Ramon could hear Vania's sing-song voice directing fire, as well as the occasional, 'Hee, hee, got you!'

He leaped the tangle of blackened corpses, blasted at the next line and strode on, his men struggling to keep pace. Fire was a hideous weapon, one which seldom killed quickly, but there was nothing like it to spread fear. Sir Tonald and his Noromen stumbled up the slope, blanching at the blackened, blistered bodies as they expired.

'Who *are* you, sir?' Sir Tonald gasped, his face aghast, finally aware he was dealing with someone *way* beyond his power.

'I'm your commander,' Ramon said crisply, eyeing the hundreds of Keshi still filling the breach. 'Get your men forward: let's take those damned walls back.'

As gnosis-lit arrows lanced towards them he raised his arm. His shields flared, augmented by Air-gnosis to sweep the shafts away, then he sent his fire-illusion back at the enemy, taking out both magi and the archers shielding them. Vania's crossbowmen tore into the rest.

At last Sir Tonald's men were pouring forward as well, in a determined push to retake the wall. While the battle-magi led the way forward on the ground, Ramon and his men turned their attention to the wrecked windships that had effected the breach, using kinesis to shove the burning vessels off the battlements onto their own men below, until the enemy finally recoiled and retreated to the far side of the moat, shouting in rage and despair.

Jarlson joined Ramon in the breach, gazing out at the sea of dark faces below, then he pointed. 'Look, sir.'

Giant shapes were ploughing through the confused mass of Keshi and their allies: an elephant phalanx with wicker towers on their backs encased in shielding.

'Now what do we do?' Jarlson wondered.

Ramon set his jaw grimly. 'We hold.' He turned, saw something through the smoke and shouted, <*Vania!*> as a figure loomed behind her on the roof where she was standing . . .

. . . and she spun, slammed the bolt she was holding into the right eye of an armoured shape raising his sword.

The big man fell away.

<*Oh, poor Sir Mion: screwed in Gash Lane,*> she chirped happily, the bolt in her hand dripping blood. <*I was just praying he'd try that. Love and kisses, boss.*> She waved merrily, then turned back to directing her archers as the Keshi counter-attack began.

'It's a breach,' Ashmak crowed. 'An actual breach!'

Latif stared through the haze of smoke and steam. The skies above were still slate-grey and the cloud high, but there was a quality to the air that reminded him of the day Sultan Salim had taken all his impersonators to a demonstration of weather-gnosis. Rashid's new breeding-house magi had actually managed to create rain from a few sparse clouds, which was a minor miracle. But then the backlash had struck, the price for tampering with weather: a sandstorm had ripped in, razing a nearby village, and there'd been a horrific drought the next summer.

The air had the same taste, like sour citrus . . . someone's holding off bad weather for the attack. What are we in for afterwards?

But that was tomorrow's problem; today's was vastly more immediate. Where the wall had been broken by the ram-ships, a torrid to-and-fro battle had developed. Piru-Satabam III was being sent in to try to turn the tide, but as Rani trudged closer, Latif could see the Keshi had been driven from the wall and the so-called 'breach' consisted of the top twelve feet being knocked off the ramparts. The pile of debris in front of the walls – ship-wreckage, Keshi bodies and fallen masonry – was still burning, while Yurosi in maroon tabards and green-cloaked Noromen were busy erecting barricades along the damaged wall.

'Can we climb that?' Ashmak shouted to Sanjeep.

'Rani is good climber!' Sanjeep answered cheerily.

'Do we want to?' Latif murmured, but the advance had been sounded and all three elephant satabams were forming up. A hundred beasts was a solid wall of animal weight and muscle: once the beasts had battered through the defences, the spearmen forming up behind would swarm in under cover of the archers already trying to sweep the walls clear.

Trumpets blared and they went from walk to trot, the howdah lurching from side to side as they clung on. Latif cast his eyes along the walls, seeing ladders rising – and falling – everywhere, fire and lightning flashes, huge clouds of arrows, giant eagles diving and swooping, everything in motion like a wave breaking against a sea-wall . . . but the only breach he could see was in front of them and they were moving inexorably towards it.

The moment they were in range, the lead elephant was spiked through the skull by a fire-tipped ballista shaft. More bolts flew; two more beasts fell.

'Are you going to wave your danglies again, Ashmak-sahib?' Sanjeep called. 'Excellent tactic, I am thinking.'

'Shut up, you *matachod*,' Ashmak retorted amicably.

Sanjeep guffawed, then shouted, 'How about you, friend Latif?'

'If I got my lingum out, Ashmak would mistake it for a spear and try to throw it,' Latif told him, and the mahout erupted in laughter. The old Lakh had become increasingly hysterical as the day progressed, as if the only way he could deal with the terror of losing his beloved Rani was to pretend this was some vast entertainment.

Latif nocked and drew as the walls came in range. Ashmak pushed more energy into his shields. Ballistae cracked, bolts shrieked down, more beasts fell and Keshi volleys whooshed over their heads to try to strike down the enemy archers. The spearmen were in front of them now; the oblivious elephants thundering forward were crushing some underfoot and knocking others aside as the first wave ascended the slope of debris beneath the breach.

Suddenly a dazzling sheet of flame erupted from the middle of the lines, tearing through the heart of the first ranks. As the wave of heat and light engulfed them all, they heard the most hideous screaming from the lead elephants; with howdahs aflame, the crews flaring like lit tapers, the beasts, blinded and stricken, staggered, then rolled backwards, crushing injured and dying men beneath them. Volleys of crossbows met their next wave, tearing through the spearmen and hammering into shields and armour.

And now Rani began to take fire, arrows striking Ashmak's wards and the leather and mail that covered the elephant's head and flanks. Latif shot back at unidentifiable shapes on the walls above, his hands and the bowstring a blur, trying to empty his sheaths as swiftly as he could.

'*Selmir sends us to say, "To the Death",*' Ashmak shrieked, 'so we should go back and kill hi–'

Suddenly his shields flashed red and ripped apart and Rani staggered as a crossbow bolt struck her left shoulder and blasted a crater of seared flesh. She almost went down as Sanjeep, furiously shouting prayers, hauled on her reins. Two more beasts beside her rolled and thudded to the turf, both transfixed by ballista shafts.

Then a second wave of that awful fire washed down the slope and engulfed them, a dreadful heat and sizzling that bypassed Latif's flesh and went straight to his brain. Ashmak and Sanjeep howled, clutching their heads and shrieking as they dropped writhing to the wicker floor, while Rani stumbled in a circle, then thundered back down the slope and into their own ranks.

It took a moment for Latif to realise the howdah *wasn't* burning. Through the haze of panic, all the sultan's training on how to deal with enemy gnosis took over – his normal senses regained control and the feeling that he was being burned alive vanished. 'It's illusory,' he shouted at Ashmak. 'We're not on fire!'

But it hadn't *all* been illusion: his left sleeve had been completely burned away and the full length of his left arm was blistered and weeping and exceedingly painful. But they were alive, and that was a miracle.

Finally, he was able to look up. Rani had fled the fire, wise animal that she was, and now they stood among a cluster of Lakh spearmen who were showing little inclination to advance. Latif looked back at the 'breach' and saw that the Yurosi still held. At the bottom of the slope of rubble were at least thirty elephants, their bodies charred and twisted, and how many spearmen were crushed beneath and around them, he couldn't begin to say. Another two dozen of the great animals were lying dead or dying in the approach. Of the hundred great beasts, only about thirty were still standing.

Blearily, Ashmak pulled himself from the grip of the fire illusion or mesmerism or whatever it had been and gave Latif a shaky look. They peered down from the howdah and saw Sanjeep sprawled unconscious, twitching fearfully. Latif swore softly to himself, clambered down and eased the old man into a more comfortable position, then grabbed Rani's reins and headed for the camp.

If we're getting inside, someone else is going to have to do it . . .

Fatima was still wobbling from unleashing the spear, and from Attam's powerful blow, which had blackened her eye, but after yet another suicidal charge through the outer gatehouse had succeeded only in adding more bodies to the mountain of corpses in the killing zone, she still stormed through the remaining noblemen around Attam, shouting, 'Let me do it!' She pointed at the inner gatehouse, which now displayed the prize they'd all bragged of seizing: the Royal Banner of Noros. 'Look, the enemy banner is there!'

She was dimly aware that the Air-gnosis taint was growing stronger; Rashid's weather-magi must be fighting to maintain control of the skies. *Someone's holding back a storm*, she thought with a shiver. *We have to get inside, now—*

Attam glowered at her. 'Can you reach it?'

'I'm a mage – we all are here.' She glared around the group. 'Come on, Shaneef, Ali, Mizran, Doni – I thought you were big men? You talk like you are, but who was it who brought that gate down?'

'You did half the job and got everyone killed, *Almawt-Ramah*,' Doni growled.

'Death-spear', Fatima thought. *Ai, that's who I am.* 'So what happened to Death or Glory?' she sneered. 'Shield me long enough and I'll have the inner gates down too.'

Attam's eyes narrowed, then he turned to Shaneef. 'Summon every battle-mage we can find: I want massed magi protecting our *Almawt-Ramah*.'

As Shaneef hurried off, Attam told Fatima, 'If you're determined to die, girl, get us inside and make it a death to sing of.' Then he surprised her by kissing the palm of her right hand; in the harbadab that meant not just respect but also attraction.

I don't think so, she thought. *The only man I love is dead and I race to join him.*

They launched their assault mid-afternoon, sending volleys of arrows followed by a mass of men swarming towards the walls, but this time every man who went through the main gates was a mage, shielding with all his strength, with Fatima huddled in their midst. Attam sent others with Air-gnosis to the tops of the walls, where the Rondians were trying to clear the wrecked windships and regain control of the towers.

As they clambered over the piled corpses into the gatehouse Fatima could see only the men around her, their shields of hide and gnosis interlocked, their bodily smells mingling with the stench of death, of blood and voided bladders and bowels. Crossbow- and mage-bolts began slamming into them; she heard and felt the impacts, the red flash of stressed shields, the crunch of steel tearing into wood and hide and flesh and bone, the plaintive grunts and wails of men who folded and fell, but there were always others there to close the gaps, shouting encouragement and instructions.

We're only ten yards in . . . it's perhaps twenty-five to the portcullis.

With a ghastly roaring splash, oil cascaded over them and fire erupted. Several men shrieked and two more fell away, their clothing ablaze, but the Keshi magi countered the blaze and they shuffled onwards.

After the next volley, she shouted, 'Now!' and rose up, holding the spear high. The crystal blazed violently and she aimed it at the portcullis, carving a circle through the metal and wood, then falling to her knees as the gnostic recoil racked her body. Bolts and spells carved the air, cutting down more of her protectors, but it was too late: she'd done her job.

With a great rending and cracking, the heavy portcullis crashed down and those still alive roused themselves and with a ragged cheer, staggered forward, shields high and mage-bolts blazing, a mass of soldiers came piling in behind, singing to Ahm's glory. Looking up the rear gatehouse, she saw armoured men beneath the enemy banner.

'There,' she shrieked, 'he's *there*–'

She raised her spear for the second time in a few moments, ignoring the cost . . .

'Your Majesty,' Seth Korion was saying, 'I only wanted the banner brought forth, not your august self.'

'I must be a symbol of resistance,' King Phyllios replied earnestly. He looked up at his personal banner, flapping above. 'To do less would be poor form.'

'Dying is *very* poor form, symbolically,' Seth replied. 'Please, you could be just as symbolic somewhere else.'

The king gave him a peeved look, then brightened. 'If the enemy break through here, my Royal Guard are the best positioned unit for the counter-charge, are they not?'

Seth winced. 'Yes, and about that: pull back, Majesty, *please*. Let Ramon's cavalry take that position—'

'Oh no,' Phyllios said. 'The texts all agree that mercenaries can't be relied on, General. I'll see to it.'

The king left with a spring in his step, but at least he left. Seth rolled his eyes at his aide, then surveyed the carnage below. They'd just repulsed yet another mad charge into the race below while the men forward were still trying to clear the wrecked windships above the outer towers. The loss of the outer gates was luring the enemy into the death-trap that was the inner race, but another blast of the enemy's secret weapon and the gates could fall, which would expose the main road through the city and potentially trap and divide all his forces.

'The mage-engineers want to know whether to drop the wrecked ships above the outer gates outside the wall or inside the race,' Delton murmured in his ear.

'Outside,' Seth replied, then he hesitated. 'No, wait, if we choke it up completely . . .'

He'd not made up his mind when the next assault began: an attempt at a tortoise formation came edging round the outer gates and clambered onto the carpet of dead bodies as bolts rained down. But for the first time, strong shielding flared, far more than just one or two magi, making the barrage largely ineffectual. Keshi Air-magi flew into view and hovering in mid-air over the walls, began to target the mage-engineers around the wreckage and worst of all, one soared into the killing zone, spraying fire through the crossbow slots and into the gallery where the crossbow teams knelt. Seth heard shrieks of agony an instant before three bolts slammed into the man's back from the opposite side and he fell onto the bodies below.

And still that damned tortoise formation edged closer.

'Open them up, open them up!' he shouted, and a torrent of flaming oil struck the tortoise, but the blaze was swiftly countered, then the tortoise parted, a figure in a headscarf rose up, holding a spear topped with a glittering crystal – and an incandescent beam of light carved through the portcullis and the stone walls below him like a knife through butter. The portcullis crashed to the ground and the enemy started howling triumphantly.

That was the weapon! It's right here! Seth dived for cover, pulling Delton with him.

Then he felt the enemy weapon speak again, the aetheric blast chilling as it struck the gates below his feet and burst them open with a boom that must have been heard across the entire city.

With a roar, a wave of Keshi came tearing through the killing space and into the square behind him.

33

Martyrdom

Lessons from Akrersh

The Rondian Empire sent four legions to relieve Akrersh when Andressea's principle city was assailed by a Schlessen horde in 732. It sent twenty-four legions when Andressea sought to cede from the empire in 787. The lesson: the empire might claim it's protecting you, but Kore help you if you don't want its protection!

THE BLACK HISTORIES (ANONYMOUS) 776

Norostein, Noros
Janune 936

Newly promoted Legate Bastian Marvikus was conferring with Chief Engineer Tanderaum of the Ordo Artificio about how best to remove the two wrecked windships lodged atop the towers. He'd been up on the gatehouse roof near the outer towers for what felt like an eternity, although it was probably only fifteen minutes, when the engineers had been up here for hours. It felt *horribly* exposed, although the enemy kept charging into the killing race below and getting slaughtered. They couldn't resist the open gates.

War is mad, he reflected, turning back to the engineer. *And so's this man – or a genius . . .*

'It's all about leverage, Tribune,' Tanderaum said, rubbing his hands together as if this were an intriguing puzzle, not a danger to all Norostein. 'We're ready – but should we tip it outside the walls, or into the race?'

But before he could answer, another tortoise formation had entered the death-trap, but this one was shielding properly. A more immediate danger appeared when Air-magi erupted over the walls – and suddenly Marvikus found himself battling for survival. He was principally a Fire-mage, facing four hovering Air-magi, but after an instant of panic, realising he was more powerful by blood than any of them, he blasted them out of the air – just as a dazzling beam erupted from the tortoise formation below and brought the portcullis crashing down – and now this was a full-blown crisis.

As he shielded Tanderaum, they saw another bolt of that terrifyingly bright light blast open the inner gates with a horrifying *boom*. Almost instantly the race was choked with living Keshi, pushing forward over their own dead, roaring in triumph like madmen.

Marvikus whirled. 'Now!' he shouted to Tanderaum, '*NOW!*'

'But inside or out?' Tanderaum asked in a puzzled voice.

'*INTO THE RACE, YOU RUKKING IDIOT!*'

King Phyllios III of Noros had just reached his Royal Guardsmen, stand-ing to attention in the square, when he heard the *boom* behind him. He'd heard that sound every dawn and dusk, when the great gates were opened and closed, and he knew instantly what it meant. This was the heartbeat of destiny. He drew his sword and shouted, 'Royal Guard, fol-low thy king!'

Then he turned and spurred his horse into the fray. To his relief, the men came too. Most weren't magi and his own gnosis had been Chained since the Rebellion, which meant he barely was either, but shields kin-dled as he willed them and light blazed along his drawn sword as he galloped to the gates.

'*KORION!*' Fatima shouted, clambering over the squishy pile of corpses, clutching at those around her. The second blaze had left her reeling and dazed, but she could sense more potential inside her; she wasn't done yet. *I can still kill.* To emphasise the point she disintegrated a ballista on the inner tower, while roaring her challenge again. '*KORION!*'

Around her, those magi left were still sheltering her and fewer bolts came their way, giving them the opportunity to target the narrow stone slits that commanded the race and stall the blazing oil cauldron so that its deadly load splattered mostly harmlessly against the walls. A full hazarabam was moving in behind them and ahead she could see a big square where they could properly form up. They picked up pace, leading the army through to their destiny.

But where was her enemy? '*KORION*,' she yelled, '*KORION!*'

'So what's she got 'gainst you, boss?' Kel Harmon wondered. 'You knock 'er up then run out on her durin' the Crusades?' The flaxen-haired swordsman was sheltering with Lukaz and Vidran, yards from the blazing ballista.

'I swear I've never seen her before,' Seth muttered. *But that weapon . . .*

'Must say, wavin' that banner to provoke her worked a treat,' Vidran drawled. 'Must remember that fer the nex' time I want my arse kicked.'

Seth gathered his courage. The enemy were now streaming in, the gatehouse defenders were largely nullified and the defence of the city was failing. *If I'm going to do something, it needs to be now.* He rose to his feet, ready to respond to her challenge.

Fatima staggered as her small force of magi entered the big square. Shihadi soldiers poured in behind, dozens more with every passing second, and her heart pounded with joy. *I did this: I broke the defences: I saved the Shihad! Did you see me, Baneet?*

And then the dream twisted nightmarishly as the wrecked windships on the outer gatehouse tipped and fell with a sickening crunch into the race. She spun to see smouldering timbers crushing dozens of men beneath and choking the entrance to the city before erupting into flames, an intense heat that drove her and her men backwards into the square.

And suddenly those men were very few.

But defiance rose in her breast as she saw the richly caparisoned riders galloping for them across the flagstones, shouting some Yurosi gibberish. The one at their head might even be *Korion*, because he sure as Hel dressed like a blasted general.

She bared the spear again, shouted her enemy's name and called on the fires in her heart once more.

The race was completely choked, the breach temporarily filled and barely a hundred men had got inside the gates. Seth rose from shelter, wondering if the enemy below could be compelled to yield.

If that spear requires recovery time, perhaps we can take it?

But then Phyllios and his men entered the square and the accursed weapon was levelled towards the king, who was galloping like a madman towards the invaders, his sword raised.

'*I'm* Korion–' Seth shouted, desperate to try to avert the awful thing that was suddenly happening in front of him. He stood up, waved a hand, projecting his voice at the knot of Keshi – he saw one spin toward him, wielding that glowing spearhead: the weapon flared.

'*Kore's Balls,*' yelped Vidran, dragging Seth behind the battlements, Harmon hurling himself to the ground beside them. Delton stared, forgetting to shield, but Lukaz shoved him down, an instant before a bolt of light screamed upwards, striking the place where they'd all been standing a heart-beat before. Stone melted or shattered, glowing fragments flying and striking off Seth and Delton's shields.

'Come on!' Seth shouted, leaping up and hurling himself off the battlements. The light beam tried to follow him as he corkscrewed through the air on gnostic wings, soaring over the ground–

–as the king and his guard lowered lances and smashed into the Keshi magi at a full gallop.

The principles of chivalry – to strive for excellence, piety and humility and to be a protector of the weak – had been indelibly ingrained into Phyllios all his life. That was part of why he'd sanctioned the Revolt against the empire, why he'd led his oppressed kingdom against the mighty but corrupt Sacrecours. Those principles had sustained him through his long years of humiliation after the Noros Revolt failed.

It would never have occurred to him to hang back and let his guardsmen lead the way, for this was what he was born to do – but it wasn't something he'd ever excelled in, and he'd had no practise for a great many years. None of that mattered. He sent mage-bolts pulsing along the blade of his sword and into the crowd, and then suddenly he was among the enemy. He saw dark, hard faces and bared teeth, curved steel and gnosis tearing at his shields as his horse battered its way into the press of bodies, staggering as steel bit. Then the crowd shifted as more of his men came crashing in. Sound reverberated weirdly in his helm and everything about him was moving oddly slowly as he burst through a cordon of magi. His blade dipped, impaled a man through the throat and all but ripped his head off – and a shining figure spun to face him: a Keshi woman, momentarily helpless beneath his blade.

A knight must honour all women and be a champion of their virtue.

He froze, sword held high, her battered face etching itself on his soul as he stared down at her. She looked shattered, but her face was so radiant with purpose she looked almost holy.

Then she buried a spear he hadn't even noticed in his chest, the gem behind the spearhead pulsed and he felt his insides convulse. Smoking blood erupted from the massive wound as his back arched and his limbs spasmed, then he fell forward over the spear and expired.

Fatima stared into the face of the rather ordinary man, weak-chinned and irresolute but shining with some kind of inner vision, as his eyes faded and his shattered body failed him.

He had me . . . and yet he didn't strike. She peered at his helm and at last noticed the crown. *Who did I just kill?*

All round her his horsemen were mostly dying, ill-equipped to face magi, but it wouldn't last: more Yurosi were pouring in on all sides, driving the Keshi around her back up against the shattered gatehouse. The race was now choked with burning timbers. There was nowhere to run, and no support coming.

And Korion is still here, somewhere.

She wrenched the spear from the dead man's chest and checked her own guard: Shaneef and Doni were still warded, but the others were being cut down, and she knew that she had only one bolt left in her. She looked again for *Korion*, her eyes flashing to an armoured man hovering above the square, raining down mage-bolts at the men around her. She wavered, knowing she absolutely couldn't let the spear fall into Yurosi hands.

She raised the spear.

As she tried to kindle it, it barely flickered. Her heart clenched in her chest. She screamed silently in frustration and sudden fear. *I must get out*, she thought suddenly. *They mustn't get the spear.* She was ashamed to be seen running, but she knew her duty. Gathering her Air-gnosis, she prepared to take to the skies–

–when two men came bursting from an unnoticed stairwell door right beside her: a big, dark-haired Yurosi and a slighter man with pale hair. The former went left and the latter right, but neither had gnostic shields, so she wasn't overly concerned. She blasted at both with mage-bolts, expecting easy kills – but the big man sidestepped her bolts, moving like a panther, then swept into a low blow that jarred into her shields, while the other man actually used his *blade* to reflect her mage-bolt away. She'd never seen that done and it confounded her. She staggered to a halt, trying to follow the movement of the big man as he circled . . .

. . . and the yellow-haired man slashed the back of her thigh, slicing through flesh into bone. She howled and staggered, losing her grip on the Air-gnosis, then the armoured mage – the *Korion*? – appeared in the archway and she forsook vengeance and focused on her most vital task: swinging the spearhead at the stone wall–

–a blade punched through her ribs and she pitched sideways, utterly spent. But the spearhead struck the stone and the crystal cracked, ripping apart her heart as she called her lover's name.

Baneet's big, smiling face filled her eyes and she fell into his arms to shelter from the oncoming darkness.

Seth looked around, but the Keshi were all dead or disabled now, the square emptied of enemy. He watched Harmon pull his blade from the girl's chest, caught between relief and guilt at seeing such a deadly enemy fall. Then he picked up the spear and its crystal broke apart.

'What in 'el was that, sir?' Harmon asked, wiping his blade.

Seth scooped up the crystal and examined the pieces. There were dark metallic veins in it, and some kind of liquid seeping through them, but its light was fading fast. He pocketed it as the last glimmers winked out. 'One for the scholars, I think,' he told them. 'Bravely done, lads.

Not many ordinary men would duel a mage, let alone one with such a weapon.'

'Nuffink ordinary 'bout us, sir,' Harmon replied. 'Anyways, magi are easy.'

Seth raised his eyebrows. 'According to the *Book of Kore* we are the Lords Of War.'

'Seriously, most magi only learn how t' fight using the gnosis, which covers over a lot of poor technique,' Vidran put in. 'Kel and me? We could out-fence most I've seen, if'n they weren't using gnosis.'

Seth reflected on that; his own swordsmanship had always been pathetic. 'You may be right. Well done, regardless.' He checked the Keshi woman's body – she wasn't a necromancer, so she wouldn't be getting up again. She was painfully young, with a pugnaciously pretty face, which was oddly beatific in death, as if she'd found peace in release. He closed her eyes, arranged her limbs into repose, then stood, oddly perturbed.

Was it her, or the weapon? Do they have others?

He turned to the gatehouse, which was now roaring with fire from the burning windships. Any question of further assaults would be out of the question until the blaze had been contained. *<Legate Marvikus, my compliments,>* he sent, spotting the young battle-mage above on the inner tower, standing beside Engineer Tanderaum. *<You too, Master Tanderaum. But are those flames a danger to us?>*

<There are strong fire-wards built in here,> Tanderaum replied. *<The heat's a problem, but we'll manage.>*

<Then feed the fires, gentlemen. I want them to burn until evening.> Seth spotted Delton, standing shakily beside Pilus Lukaz. *<Andwine,>* he sent, *<tell Capitano Sensini we've no time left to lose. Two breaches, and likely more to come. The time has come to change the weather.>*

Weather-gnosis wasn't a precise thing, and it was much easier to disrupt than manipulate. As it required both Air-gnosis and divination, to manipulate air and to foresee the consequences, having both affinities made Ramon ideally suited to the task.

Nature *always* exacted revenge for tampering; for a day or two of whatever weather you'd contrived, you'd suffer the opposite for a week or so, but at a far greater intensity. Ramon had given Rashid's magi just enough rope to hang themselves by.

A lull had fallen over the battlefield as the assaults on Gash Lane and the gatehouse stalled. The time was right, and Seth's orders only reinforced his own instincts: it was time to strike back. *The Keshi started tampering four days ago. That's a lot of pent-up tension. Now we just need to blow their control apart.*

So he took Vania, his most accomplished Air-mage, to a deserted tavern with an upstairs taproom and big windows. They shed their armour, stripping down to rust- and sweat-stained undershirts and cleared their minds. Vania took up position opposite him, outside the protective circle they'd marked out to contain their spell. If they'd had more Air-magi to hand, they'd have considered wresting control, but as they didn't, they'd settled on a much nastier plan. Inside their protective circle, a frightened crow pecked at the invisible dome of energy imprisoning it. It had very good reason to be scared.

'Are you ready?' he asked.

'Sure, unless Sir Tonald's idiots are about to burst in and avenge their stupid friend.'

'Don't worry. I had someone stick a Keshi arrow through Sir Mion's eye so it looked like he'd copped it during the barrage,' Ramon replied. 'Tragic loss. So?'

'Let's do it, boss.'

Ramon started with mystic-gnosis to link their minds for the coordination this task required, then drew upon Air-gnosis and linked to divination. Vania engaged clairvoyance and created an image inside the circle, a cloud map of the skies for a hundred or so miles around them.

Time fell away as they concentrated, putting aside concerns about how their legions might be faring, or worries that enemies might burst in, and instead studied cloud patterns, seeking signs of where the interference emanated from.

They found the enemy weather-magi some ten miles north, shrouded in wards to prevent scrying; their position was betrayed only by the way the clouds above them moved.

'Got 'em,' Ramon said. 'Let's have a look.'

Vania wove clairvoyance and he empowered it, a subtle spear to pierce the Keshi veils unseen. He smiled quietly as their vision clarified, descending through misty swirls until thirty Keshi magi appeared, men and women, few of them terribly old. They were chanting together, holding hands and standing *inside* a much larger circle, but their wards would have disgraced an Arcanum graduate.

'They're just kids,' Vania commented. 'Aw, I could just lick them like cream.' Then she shrugged indifferently. 'They should have stayed in the desert.'

Ramon nodded acknowledgment, then sent a call into the aether.

<Arbendesai.>

The crow inside the circle before them jolted, flapped wings and then looked up at him. 'Sensini,' it cawed.

Ramon looked down at the daemon in the crow. 'You were quick, Arbendesai.'

'I like to stay close, in case you take a mortal wound.'

'Kore loves an optimist,' Ramon commented. He showed the daemon the Shihadi weather-magi. 'See this lot? Can you follow them back through the aetheric currents and do something about them?'

The crow-daemon peered, interpreting the images easily. 'As you command,' he replied. 'Name your strictures.'

'Get in and kill them. No delays, no side-tours, and if you succeed, you return immediately to the aether.'

Arbendesai cawed cheerily; this was an invitation to a banquet. 'As you command, master.'

The crow collapsed dead and the circle emptied of the daemon's presence. Ramon and Vania remained focused on the images before them, watching and waiting.

Ten minutes passed . . .

. . . and then something exploded into the circle of Keshi magi, a black blur that hung in the air as they gasped in terror, then burst apart in thirty lances of darkness, each with a black crow at the tip. The beaks stabbed deep into the right eye of every mage, piercing right through to the brain – and as one, the magi collapsed. There was a hoarse cawing, then flapping gleefully, the spectral crows began to feast, ignoring the people outside the circle hammering at the opaque shielding, trying to get in.

They'd succeed, Ramon knew, but it was already too late. He ended the conjuring and the vision faded.

Vania was looking at him with awe. 'That was chillingly effective, boss. Remind me not to piss you off.'

'Relax – you piss me off all the time, but you're still here,' Ramon told her. 'Actually, it wasn't all that impressive, just a set of circumstances that played into my hands. They were trying to maximise their power, so rather than stand *outside* their protective circle, they were *inside* it, and because their minds were locked into the spell, they could barely see anything except the clouds and winds and thermals they were manipulating. They were basically helpless, penned inside their own protective circle, but where something can get out – their spells – something can also get in.'

'So they shouldn't have worked inside the circle,' Vania mused.

'They probably didn't even know they were vulnerable.'

'Arcanum training, eh? You know, we could make a fortune teaching young Keshi magi.'

Ramon laughed. 'You have the soul of a mercenary, Van.' He looked around the taproom. 'Fancy a wine?'

'Looting is punishable by whatever,' she reminded him. 'Shouldn't we be getting back to the walls?'

'Nope. Poor Rashid's assault is about to run into a rukking big problem–'

As if to punctuate his words, a massive burst of thunder exploded across the skies.

Sultan Rashid Mubarak climbed down from his throne, buffeted by howling winds as the banners cracked and tore. Stinging rain sleeted in from roiling black clouds. Norostein was fading into the grey, illuminated only by the lightning jagging above. There was a malicious glee in the shrieking gales.

We failed, he thought numbly. *No, I failed.*

Defeat was a bitter drink, one he'd seldom tasted. *All* his precious weather-magi had somehow been slain and his few remaining Air-magi, none of whom were specialists in weather-magic, were telling him the next few days would be atrocious.

And we're trapped outside with no protection and that's my fault . . . and that of the man who told me this invasion must *happen in a Sunsurge year . . .*

With that thought to sustain his rage, he allowed himself to be bundled into his palanquin. A few units cheered as he passed, but their voices were swiftly ripped away. All over the plain he could see men battling the gales to reach camp. Fires had to be lit and kept alight, tents had to be secured, gear had to be lashed down, livestock had to be secured.

We were inside, he reflected bitterly. *Just for a moment, we were inside . . .*

As he dismounted before his rain-lashed pavilion, he saw Ali Beyrami, the Shihadi fanatic, standing in the rain, pleading to Ahm on High to forbear. As their eyes met, the cleric's dark eyes were unreadable.

I wonder who you blame?

Rashid hurried to his pavilion as the rain turned to hail the size of sling-stones.

34

The Decisive Move

The Kaden Rats

Throughout history the gnosis has been used for many things, including larceny, which is particularly embarrassing to those who claim the power comes from Kore. Criminal magi have been a fact of life ever since the gnosis was discovered – indeed, some would call Sertain's seizure of the Rimoni Empire and making it his own personal fiefdom the greatest theft in history. But the most celebrated mage-criminals are the Kaden Rats, who, like ordinary rats, appear to be impervious to extermination.

ORDO COSTRUO COLLEGIATE, PONTUS 863

Pallas, Rondelmar
Late-Janune 936

Ari Frankel had selected the venue for the unveiling of his *Marks of Damnation* carefully: the Cathedral of Saint Baramitius, in the district of Gravenhurst. Two months before, Empress Lyra Vereinen had begun taxing the Church here, so it was a deeply symbolic place to begin the new campaign. Lazar agreed, for more pragmatic reasons.

'Gravenhurst is a rabbit warren,' Lazar said in his quietly menacing voice. 'We can choke the streets with upturned carts and wagons at a moment's notice, which gives us time to get out the back. Saint Baramitius has that square in front too, a good space for oratory.' He eyed Ari thoughtfully. Even after all this time together, his gaze could chill Ari's blood. 'Are you ready for big crowds again? Are you prepared to risk all?'

'I'm ready,' Ari said firmly, almost quivering with excitement.

'You have to be,' Lazar replied, 'because the time is *now*. Come spring, the Shihad will be broken, the armies will return and Lyra Vereinen will be swept away. Whoever takes down the empress will be sure to stamp out dissenters like never before: the voice of the common man will be muzzled for decades. But if we can rise up while she's still clinging on, we can take and fortify the city *now*. We'll make this a true city-state, like your ancient Lantris.' He leaned forward. 'Are you ready for this to turn deadly?'

Ari thought of his murdered family and friends in Jastenberg. 'It turned deadly months ago,' he replied.

Lazar gave him a rare nod of empathy. 'It surely did.'

They finished their drinks and parted, Ari to the woodcut printers and Lazar to whatever Lazar did. Ari had been shown etchings carved into doors and lintels around the city, secret symbols serving as notices of clandestine meetings. He knew Lazar was bringing in men and weapons, but his own rebellion was different. His was a war of ideas. He honed his message endlessly, using screeds of parchment and ink, pacing his room, with only snatched moments of repose. The *Marks of Damnation* consumed all his thoughts now.

At the printer's workshop the wood-blocks were inked and pressed at a staggering pace. He wasn't entirely satisfied with the final draft, but time had run out. When he finally staggered to a cot at midnight, he slipped into unconsciousness within moments.

In no time at all Lazar's brutal enforcer was jostling his shoulder. 'Oi, Wordsmith, time to rise an' shine,' Gorn growled, nudging Neif in the ribs with his boot. 'You too, Coldwell. Boss says, "Get in, speak an' get out". Gottit?'

'The boss?' sniffed Neif, a flash of his old self. 'Who rukkin' started this movement?'

Ari touched Neif's arm warningly; arguing with Gorn was futile and painful. He staggered to the noisome bucket in the corner, although he barely registered the stench, squatted and purged; his bowels had been liquid for weeks now. After cleaning himself as best he could, grateful for the scrap of soap Neif had secreted from somewhere, he finger-combed his hair. He'd not shaved in days, he stank, he now realised, and he was dazed from lack of sleep.

But inside, he was burning with righteous fury. *My time has come!*

A bowl of gruel and they were off, smuggled down narrow alleys in the pre-dawn darkness, out of fishy-aired Tockburn and into cold, damp Gravenhurst, where the streets were quietly filling up. On the steps of Saint Baramitius he lowered his cowl and looked out over the square, but the moon had gone down half an hour ago and all was black. He could hear the susurration of a mass of people, but could pick out only a few faces. Then someone lit a taper and a moment later, as if at some unseen signal, everyone else in the square did.

Ari stared: the square had become the cosmos, a sea of stars, galaxies swimming before his eyes, and thousands of faces, lit by the orange flames, shone before him with desire and dread. In that moment, he realised that what was for him a personal crusade was *hope* to these people: for freedom, for release, for a decent wage, for escape from drudgery. The hope of a life well-lived and salvation beyond. It struck him dumb, because he realised that no system of government could ever fulfil the dreams of all these people.

Dear Kore, I'm going to let so many people down . . .

But he'd once told a justiciar that when the plumbing was broken, you didn't wait for the perfect solution, you found the best imperfect tool you had and set to work.

He looked at Neif, who was trembling, tears spilling from his eyes as he stared out at the sea of faces. They clasped hands wordlessly. His friend had lost his own voice in the past months, numbed by terror, but suddenly Neif found his tongue again: he stepped forward and shouted across the mass of luminous faces, 'His name is Hope; his words are Truth: he is *my* voice, *your* voice, the voice of Freedom – the Voice of the People . . . *Ari Frankel!*'

Ari had expected the usual mix of cheers and jeers, support and scepticism, but this was more powerful by far: *dead silence*, fraught with expectation and repressed fervour.

Here was the impact of Lazar's work. There were no dissenters here; everyone knew who he was. They weren't here to be persuaded, but to be *unleashed*. It was almost enough to freeze his tongue, but then the first words tumbled out and the rest just followed.

'My friends, my brethren, my fellow Sufferers, welcome. Today, at every church in Pallas and across the north; in Corani lands and Sacrecour lands and into Argundy, Canossi, Aquillea, Ventia, Hollenia and Brevis, brave men and women are greeting the dawn with hammers and nails to nail up this proclamation' – he brandished his pamphlet – '*Marks of Damnation*. There are seven grievous wrongs written in the *Book of Kore* that those who rule us perpetrate *every* day: systematic wrongs propagated by Crown and Church to oppress us. These seven cancers on the soul of our great people must be cut out and cauterised.'

He thrust out a hand, palm upwards. 'Hear me, Throne of Empire; hear me, Voice of Kore!'

Finally, the crowd spoke. Lifting their own hands, they echoed, 'Hear us–' as if this were a religious rally. '*Hear us!*'

'One: I accuse thee, Throne of Empire and Voice of Kore, of *Tyranny*: every day you torture, imprison and slaughter those who dare speak against you. Free us from Tyrants!'

'*Free us–*'

'Two: I accuse thee, Throne of Empire and Voice of Kore, of *Corruption*: every day you pervert justice, enshrining cronyism, nepotism and bribery above our rights to redress for your crimes. You rob us with tax and tithe. You tell us salvation can be purchased – from you. Who are you to extort coins at the Gates of Paradise? Free us from Corruption!'

'*Free us–*'

'Three: I accuse thee, Throne of Empire and Voice of Kore, of *Gluttony*: every day you fill your plates while we starve; every day you enrich yourself on others' toil. Why should the man with the sword reap the harvest of the farmer? Free us from Gluttons!'

As they chanted, he looked around, trying to gauge the crowd. Was he being too wordy? Was he succeeding? The responses were emphatic though, so he ploughed on with *Slavery* – but now, terrifyingly, he did hear a reaction: shod hooves clattering nearby, and shouting of orders, and a frantic hammering sound behind him which sounded like people inside the closed doors of the cathedral trying to get out.

Urgency seized him and he rushed through *Hubris*, suggesting that royal power was not Kore-given but stolen—

—and now windskiffs were appearing overhead, silhouetted against the rapidly paling sky. Dawn was coming and the authorities were closing in, faster than he'd imagined even in the most vivid nightmares. But he was nearly there . . .

Fornication got a big cheer, but the soldiers were hammering at the edges of the crowd now and the earlier solemnity was turning to fear and violence. Fists were pumping and the responses were fervent, but they were becoming ragged as people dealt with crushing pressure from all sides.

With the seventh, *Idleness*, he made the seething crowd wait, before culminating with, 'These Seven Marks of Damnation, my friends, seven accusations: I have to ask you: are they guilty or innocent—'

He barely finished the word before the crowd started screeching, 'Guilty – GUILTY – *GUILTY!*'

'Tear them down,' someone shrieked, but before everyone took up that call, Ari interrupted, calling at the top of his voice his most important sentiment: 'Suffragium: one man, one vote – Power for the People—'

But Neif was suddenly plucking at his sleeve as another windship appeared – a much larger vessel, and if he squinted, he could make out bowmen – and were those *ballistae*? Yes, it was time to run. But he had one last thing to do.

He strode to the cathedral doors and as the first shaft of daylight hit them, he took the hammer and nail Neif thrust into his hands and nailed his pamphlet to the wood. It listed the Sins, and finished, *These are your Marks of Damnation. Face your Accusers!*

He stared at it as he would have a new-born son. *There: the first blow—*

But voices were shrilling in warning and he spun, heart in mouth, as men limned in blue light dropped from the windship above. As the crowd panicked, he heard the shrieks of terror and cries of pain as men and women were pushed over; he heard limbs snapping and saw bodies trampled by their own . . .

He turned to run, but the air hardened around him. Gorn pulled out a crossbow – and collapsed howling as a bolt of light struck him in the chest.

A red-haired man in leathers landed on the steps, blue light gleaming on the edge of his drawn sword. Another man landed behind him, shielding his back. Ari looked around, but all Lazar's men had vanished; only Neif was left.

'Frankel, eh?' the redhead – surely a Volsai – said with almost contempt. 'You're coming with me, you mouthy turd.'

'Nooo!' Neif's scream echoed with everything they'd suffered on the road and in the cells and before Ari could grab him, he'd launched himself at the mage.

'*Neif*–'

But the mage had already stunned Neif with a massive kinesis blow in the face. Neif's not-very-concealed concealed knife fell from trembling fingers . . . as the Volsai's blade slid with hideous ease into his breast.

Neif staggered, stared down at the length of steel, murmured, 'Fuck . . .' and collapsed.

The Volsai scowled at his bloodied knife as Ari weighed the alternatives: he could grab Neif's weapon and die fighting, or live to be hanged and disembowelled.

He was about to go for the knife when the Volsai said, 'No. You're wanted alive.'

He took a step towards Ari – when a masked man in a wide-brimmed hat exploded from the crowd and lanced a mage-bolt at the Volsai, sending him staggering backwards as a second figure, a masked woman with bushy black hair, swept in and slashed the Volsai's throat. He went down choking on his own blood, wide-eyed and disbelieving, as a knot of men and women, rough-dressed but armed to the teeth, came to his aid.

The masked woman grabbed Ari's arm as he wobbled, on the edge of fainting. 'Come on, Wordsmith, let's get you out of here.'

Shielding as they exchanged mage-bolts with the windship above, the masked couple pulled Ari into the cathedral. His vision was blurred by shock at the sudden violence and hideous death, but the two magi – dressed, he now saw, in fashionable velvet doublets with small embroidered masks over the eyes and nose – dragged him through the cathedral, past outraged priests and nuns and into the catacombs below, where a wall-panel opened, revealing a dark tunnel. Gnosis-light flared, revealing a dirty but dry stone-lined corridor.

Neif is dead. Neif is dead. Neif is dead. He knew he should be crying, but his mind was too scrambled. All he could think of was that pamphlet, flapping in the breeze on its nail, and how it had felt to strike that hammer-blow. Then he recalled the arrows striking the crowd and his head swam. *Dear Kore, what have we done?*

'Come along,' the woman said, her voice hard but not unsympathetic.

'Who are you?' he asked weakly.

The man pulled off his mask, revealing a rakishly aristocratic face set off by a small moustache and dark hair in a ponytail. He doffed his hat. 'I'm Tad Kaden, and this is my sister Braeda.'

Ari's jaw dropped. 'You're the Kaden Rats?'

Tad Kaden made a flowing hand-gesture and bowed. 'At your service. Which at the moment, means getting you out of Gravenhurst alive. Shall we?'

'But I despise *everything* you stand for,' Ari stammered, probably unwisely.

'Told you,' Braeda commented to her brother, 'but do you ever listen?'

'Oh, I know he deplores us,' Tad said airily. 'Abuse of Kore-given powers, using gnosis to rob hard-working merchants, imperocrats and clergymen. Awful, really. But my dear Master Frankel – or may I call you Ari? – we're your *biggest* supporters.'

'He is, anyway,' Braeda grumbled, while Ari struggled to keep his legs from folding.

'And right now,' Tad went on, 'we're the ones who can keep you out of Volsai hands. Are you with us?'

Ari stared, too shaken to begin to weigh up the hypocrisy of this rescue, weighed against his terror of being disembowelled publicly. Terror won. 'I'm c-coming.'

'Excellent,' Tad approved. 'Welcome to the movement.'

'I've been in it longer than you,' Ari sniffed.

'Oh, I'm afraid not. My family have been funding sedition for centuries. Who do you think's been hiding you from Setallius? Who knows your name and face? Who's been paying for all the illegal printing presses, the hidden weapon caches and all the rest? You're taking on the magi-elite, Frankel. You need us if you're to stand any chance.'

By the time the Volsai found the tunnel beneath the cathedral, Ari was a mile away, breakfasting with his new friends.

On the streets, people were beginning to march.

Exilium Excelsior leaned heavily on the sticks as he hobbled into the queen's garden, a long, narrow slice of thick foliage beneath the Bastion walls. His body was still horribly battered from the deadly fight at the grand prelate's mansion on top of the near-fatal beating he'd taken in the Corani yards, and gnostic healing could do only so much, but he was, he'd been told several times, *exceedingly* lucky: somehow he hadn't ruined *all* the healers' efforts when he'd joined the fight to save the empress at Highgrange.

Even here the air was smoky. Zealots and fanatics had been crawling out from whatever rocks they hid under to burn and desecrate holy places with their seditious, evil words for the past two days as huge crowds marched through streets and gathered in the squares, chanting their Kore-bedamned slogans. Had the Lord of Hel claimed all their souls?

He negotiated a tangled maze of rose bushes, following the instructions he'd been given, and froze as a white pegasus with wings folded over its back trotted towards him. It had a shaggy, unkempt mane and a half-wild look to its eyes, but he recognised it as the beast he'd seen at Highgrange and was momentarily awestruck.

Kore sent it to Her . . .

The pegasus dipped its head once – *an acknowledgement or a warning?* – before dropping its head and grazing on the lush grass. He hobbled carefully past and came to an arch covered in red briar-roses. Through it was a small circular lawn beside a pool fed by a dribbling fountain with a Leaf-man carving on the base. On a bench was a black-clad woman, her blonde hair caught in a rough ponytail. She had a veil draped over her up-tilted face. It took him a moment to realise it was Queen Lyra.

'Majesty?' he asked anxiously.

'Ah, Sir Exilium,' Lyra called, her head jerking blindly in his direction. 'Sit, please.'

You destroyed a Beast of the Pit, he thought dazedly. *You're an Angel of Kore.*

There was nowhere to sit except beside her, which would have felt profoundly awkward. 'Er, I will stand, thank you,' he replied. He looked at her covered face and dared to ask, 'Will you recover?'

Her voice caught. 'I don't know . . . but they think so . . .'

His heart went out to her. Blindness had always been one of his greatest dreads. 'Majesty, you summoned me?'

'Just "Milady" suffices after the initial greeting,' she said. 'I'm told you wish to leave the grand prelate's service to be my bodyguard while Basia recovers – is that so?'

'Yes, Maj – um, Milady. Your sanctity has been a revelation to me. I *must* serve you.'

'Must?'

'Yes, Milady,' he said fervently. 'You are sent to us by Kore.'

'I'm not sure that's a universally held view, Sir Exilium. The people of Pallas are currently marching through the streets shouting for my downfall.'

'They are fools misled by daemons,' Exilium replied. 'They must be compelled to desist.'

'But marching isn't illegal,' Lyra replied, 'and nor is chanting "Suffragium", or even "I accuse". It's the arson and looting I can't condone, or the violence against loyalists. I'm having to deploy men I can ill spare to protect businesses which have earned the Royal Seal. These are our people – we're fighting ourselves.'

Exilium hadn't really paid attention before now, but if Queen Lyra believed it so, it was likely true. 'My wish is to serve you as bodyguard,' he repeated.

'Basia will recover, you know,' Lyra told him. 'The assassin's blade pierced her through, but he missed her lung and she's recovering speedily. And it's traditional that a queen is protected by a woman, Exilium,' she added neutrally.

'Your honour would be safe with me,' he told her. 'I have taken a vow of chastity, to strengthen my sword-arm.'

Lyra studied him with a composed, neutral face: 'Does that work?'

'Yes, Milady. I have aligned my natural talent to utmost dedication, with the goal of being the greatest swordsman on Urte, devoted to the service of Kore Above.'

'But shouldn't you therefore remain with Grand Prelate Wurther?'

Exilium paused awkwardly, for it pained him to choose one over the other, but he had no choice. 'Your Majesty, Grand Prelate Wurther is most certainly the chosen Voice of Kore. But he has not been touched by Kore as you have. I wish to aid Basia's recovery, and to work alongside her thereafter, in your service.'

'I'm glad to hear that you esteem Basia so much,' the queen said, somewhat wryly. 'Some men don't.'

Esteem Basia? Exilium floundered. 'I, erm . . . respect her skill, but I find her views . . . um . . . challenging,' he stammered.

'It often starts that way,' Lyra replied, confusing him even more. 'I'll consider your request, Sir Exilium, but I would not wish to give offence to my friend Dominius, nor to the Volsai whose duty it is to protect me.' She pursed her lips, then surprised him by saying, 'Dominius once told me that you defied the Inquisitors to protect him. What happened?'

Exilium straightened as much as he could. 'Knight-Princeps Dravis Ryburn told me that if I didn't betray the Grand Prelate, he would have my father and sister executed.'

'But when the time came, you remained true to Dominius?'

'I did, Milady.'

'And your family?'

He had to fight to keep his voice neutral. 'They were found dead in my home village.'

Lyra's hand gripped the bench. 'I'm so sorry.'

'They were pure souls and they rest with Kore,' he said, blinking away tears for his kin. 'I could not warn them, for fear of giving away my intent, but Kore has gifted me with being present at the demise of Dravis Ryburn and Lef Yarle, the two men who instigated their deaths. Kore is merciful.'

'Belief is such a comfort,' Lyra said, which was an odd thing to say, Exilium thought.

'Kore is our staff and comfort,' he quoted reflexively. 'Please Milady, accept my offer. I will service you with unswerving devotion.'

As she turned her head, the veil slipped, giving him a glimpse of her eyes, which had turned wholly white. He shuddered, and was glad she couldn't see his reaction.

But she gave him the words he hoped for. 'If Dirklan Setallius approves, I will accept your service. Go and see him when you leave me. But first . . .' She handed him a roll of paper. 'You can read, I trust? No one has actually told me what's on this.'

He frowned, his scowl deepening as he unrolled the scroll. 'Milady . . .' He hesitated. 'You don't need to hear—'

'Actually, I do,' she replied. 'A ruler must not be deaf to criticism. Read.'

'Yes, Milady,' he said dutifully. 'Er, it says: *"Throne of Empire and Voice of Kore, the* Book of Kore *proscribes Seven Marks of Damnation. We the People accuse thee of each: Tyranny, Corruption, Gluttony, Slaving, Hubris, Fornication and Idleness. Only through Suffragium may you be redeemed. These are your Marks of Damnation. Face your Accusers".*' Exilium looked up. 'Milady, it burns the tongue to speak such blasphemy.'

She shook her head. 'No, the empire *has* done all these things, in so many ways.' She rubbed at her sightless eyes, then asked, 'Is it signed?'

'No, Milady. Cowards never claim their work.'

She snorted softly. 'He knew he didn't need to. Ari Frankel wrote those words and hammered them to the door of Saint Baramitius' Cathedral.'

Exilium committed the name to memory. 'I will see him silenced,' he vowed.

'He's a good speaker,' Lyra commented. 'He's fluent and argues well. He would tell me that silencing dissent is the act of a tyrant. He believes he's saying what must be said, to make a better world.'

'The mob aren't capable of differentiating lies from truth, Milady. He must be brought to trial and the people disabused of his lies.'

She smiled, her expression oddly rueful. 'I believe that's the intention. My council is meeting this afternoon to discuss it. I wish I could attend, but legally a blind monarch is considered incapacitated and unfit to rule, so I'll have to trust them to play nicely until I'm well again.'

'Then Kore speed your recovery, Milady,' Exilium said fervently. 'You are needed by us all.'

Solon entered the Royal Council chambers and took his seat. Grand Prelate Wurther was already there, as was Calan Dubrayle, now just Lord Treasurer again, with the new Imperocrator, Rael Relantine, whom Solon didn't yet know yet. But it was Dirklan Setallius who'd been asked to chair the meeting.

'The queen sends her apologies,' the spymaster said. His voice was worried.

She won't even let me visit her, Solon thought bitterly. *I was her lover – has she forgotten that?* Though he knew she hadn't; it was why she was punishing him.

'How does she fare?' Dubrayle asked.

'The healers remain optimistic,' Setallius said. 'She's still tired, but that's normal: every mage experiences something of the sort after significant gnosis-use.'

Except it wasn't the gnosis, Solon thought sourly. *It was dwyma. Heresy.*

'I pray to Kore for her recovery,' the old scoundrel, Wurther, intoned piously.

'I take it you've secured her rooms?' Solon asked Setallius.

'Of course. She's never alone, day or night.' The spymaster's one-eyed gaze trailed to Wurther, then Solon. 'Exilium Excelsior is to join Basia de Sirou in guarding her.'

Solon felt his fist clench beneath the table. *That Estellan slime . . .*

'Apparently I'm a sinner, despite my rank,' Wurther chuckled, 'whereas Exilium believes our queen to be embodied with the soul of Celestia, the Sacred Mother of Corineus. He now wishes to serve only her.'

'The queen can't have a male bodyguard,' Dubrayle said, in a prissy voice.

'Exilium could be left to guard the Sacred Virgins of Castellon and not a girl would be deflowered,' Wurther laughed. 'Once he's recovered, Lyra will be in good hands.'

'I'm satisfied he's loyal and reliable,' Dirklan told them. 'He's still badly injured, but he'll recover, I'm told. I'm happy for him to take up the post, but in the meantime my Volsai are sharing the protection duty.'

'Exilium fought beyond the endurance of most men during that infamous attack on my city residence,' Wurther rumbled, sending Solon a disgruntled look. 'Had he not been already crippled, he might have saved more lives.'

I'll not be blamed for that, Solon thought sullenly. In truth, he was struggling to follow the discussion through the throbbing in his head. Wine was curdling in his stomach, but he craved another goblet. 'He should have known better than to enter my training yards. I went through similar in my youth.'

'So you believe such violence is a tradition to hand down to the next generation?'

'You know *nothing*,' Solon snarled. 'You're not a knight, you're a fat priest who needs others to shield him. Don't talk about things you damned well don't understand.'

'That's enough, gentlemen,' Setallius snapped. 'It happened, and we must learn from it. Dominius lost many good men. Let's ensure we're not so badly caught out again.'

The table fell silent and Solon thought about how acrimonious this meeting was without Lyra present. Probably without realising they were doing so, the men behaved better for her. She set a tone of compromise and conciliation. *She really is a queen now*, he thought. Then an image of her face in rapture beneath him struck and he flinched. Gallingly, this kept happening.

'How did Ryburn's assassin get so close?' asked the new man, Relantine.

Setallius rubbed his good eye tiredly. 'Because he picked his moment and prepared well. And because there are plenty of people in Pallas who are as hostile to Lyra as those enemies already in the open. Yarle had help.'

'Then we must further proscribe where and when she goes and who she sees,' Wurther rumbled.

They moved on to the next matter: the war in the south, where the Shihad was still battering fruitlessly at the walls of Norostein. 'There's now a feeling that the Shihad may be approaching a crisis,' Setallius reported. 'Their supply lines are closing, their windfleet is grounded and they face a Sunsurge Winter in the open.'

'Will Sulpeter attack the Shihadi force in northern Noros?' Wurther asked.

'He'd be foolish to,' Solon replied. 'The weather will do our job for us.'

'Then will no one relieve the siege of Norostein?' Dubrayle asked sharply.

'Why should we?' Solon grunted. 'They're only Noromen.'

Wurther went to protest, then admitted, 'I've known a few Noromen and they were nothing but trouble.'

'It's Rolven Sulpeter's decision. He's closer to the action than we are,' Setallius said. 'I too would like to think we could aid the city, but the fact is, we can't.'

'Can we talk about the *real* issue of the day?' Wurther said impatiently. He pointed angrily at the window. They could hear the angry rumble of the crowds in the Place d'Accord. 'Pallas is a city of a million souls and most of them are on the bloody streets calling for Lyra and me to be deposed. Tell me Ostevan and Garod aren't behind this. Tell me how four Corani legions and two Imperial ones are going to quell them?

Tell me what we're doing to round up the ringleaders and make an example of them. Tell me when the Corani cavalry will clear the Place d'Accord–'

'The queen will not sanction violence against our own people,' Setallius replied. 'It's not a crime to chant a few slogans or march around squares. The only thing that suffers is their own incomes. Let it burn itself out. They'll return to work when their purses are empty.'

'That's naïve, One-Eye,' Wurther fumed, and Solon was inclined to agree. 'This isn't a wheat riot; it's a revolt, and our enemies are behind it.'

'We must act,' Solon added. 'If I were in charge of security–'

'Which you're not,' Setallius interrupted. 'Listen, I've lost Gil Mannis and three other good Volsai: believe me, I'm angry. But we've got no evidence that Garod or Ostevan are behind this. Eyewitnesses saw *Tad Kaden* at the cathedral with this man Frankel. And there are similar riots breaking out all over the north, *including* in Sacrecour lands. Garod sent troops into a peaceful march in Fauvion yesterday and left thirty citizens dead and hundreds injured, which not only didn't solve the problem but escalated the violence overnight. We need to be patient and show restraint.'

'No,' Solon shouted, hammering the table, 'we need *decisive* action – a strong hand–'

'Hear, hear,' Wurther said, but neither Relantine nor Dubrayle added their support.

'Killing your own citizens doesn't deal with these matters,' said Dubrayle. 'Give them a little of what they want, undermine them, then discredit and ruin the ringleaders. It's been done before.'

'We know the people behind this,' Relantine added. 'Kaden, Frankel, Lazar – embarrassingly enough, we've had both the latter in our hands in the past few months and let them go. But that's bygones. I agree we need to act decisively, but not violently. Let's us unite around a plan and present it to the queen.'

'If our proposal includes using troops to break up assembled citizens, the queen will veto it,' Setallius warned. 'But certainly, let's see what we can agree on.'

The answer, predictably, was *not much*. The arguments swirled round in circles and two hours of heated debate and angry words later, the meeting broke up without agreement. Setallius and Dubrayle stone-walled everything Solon and Wurther threw at them, sometimes aided by Relantine, and although the recalcitrants were in the minority, they all knew the queen would back them.

Damn you, Lyra. You're no kind of ruler if you're too soft to make the hard calls.

But thinking of the queen only made *those* images rise in his mind again and for a moment he was with her on one of those torrid nights when he'd felt that the throne was within touching distance. He had to force away the vision and stamped furiously from the council chambers, resolving to go to the practise yards.

Kore help anyone who spars with me today . . .

When someone plucked at his sleeve, he whirled, his fists raised – but punching priests was apparently a bad thing, although right now he didn't see why. 'What?'

'I am Father Germane,' the middle-aged, pleasant-looking man replied. There was a calm solidity to his gaze. 'The grand prelate asked me to say this: he shares your frustration and invites you to meet him privately.'

Solon considered. *I thought the old hog backed down too easily in there . . . What's he got in mind?*

'All right,' he told the priest. 'Where?'

Saint Sava Church in Highgrange was only a few hundred yards from the eastern gates of the Bastion, but Solon had never been there before. It was primarily a funeral chapel for servants of the magi houses, small, but ostentatious – this was Highgrange, after all – with two-thirds of the space taken up with crypts and sarcophagi. Saint Sava had been some kind of menial in Estellayne who'd saved her mistress from a fire.

Solon shuffled in, trying to look anonymous in a plain cloak, and waited, brooding. Soaking in the silence, he watched the dust dance through the solid shafts of coloured light from the rose windows above the altar.

For twenty-seven years I've fought for Coraine, from the despair of 909 to our return in triumph in 930. Everyone knows I'm the force behind our resurrection. There's not a man in the Great Houses who would dare cross blades with me. I am acknowledged as the Knight of the Age.

But my shoulder can't take the punishment it used to: I'm a waning moon . . . I need to capitalise on who I am while I still can. So why should my fate rest on the whim of a fickle woman? And why can't I get her out of my head?

Every day was like a walking nightmare now as he vacillated between hate and love, wondering why he should *serve* her when he was her *master.* He'd proved that with his body so many times.

And this latest crisis, the madness in the street, had to stop. Lyra had to be made to see reason, or . . . *or else.* Something had to break and this time it wouldn't be him. He couldn't go into exile again; that would kill him, fast or slow.

Somehow, I have to make her see that this empire needs me in control.

He looked up as a door opened behind the vestry and Grand Prelate Wurther's heavy, slow tread broke the silence, his passing making the dust motes swirl. 'Good afternoon, Solon,' the old hog greeted him. 'A frustrating meeting, yes? Symptomatic of the straits we find ourselves in.'

'Aye: symptomatic of weak leadership,' Solon growled.

Wurther settled beside him on the front pew, making the wooden joints creak in distress. 'I agree: it's weak leadership that's making our enemies bold. In a few days, the mob will be barricading parts of the city from us and we'll face open revolt. And come spring, Garod Sacrecour will march again. You're vital to us all, Solon.'

'I don't feel so vital some days,' Solon confessed.

'That's because you need a certain woman to make you whole.'

Yes, he thought, *it's her fault. Everything is.*

'I've tried to intercede, but she won't speak of you,' Wurther told him. 'But women are always saying this and meaning that, Solon. They're physically and intellectually weaker than us, so they seek to compensate by manipulations and deceits. Lyra is no different: she refuses to subordinate herself to a man, even one she loves. But put her in her place and she'll come to realise it was what she wanted all along.'

'What do you know of women?' Solon sniffed, although it all sounded right and true.

'A lifetime of observation, years spent dealing with nuns and the secrets of the Unburdening. If there was no code of silence around Unburdening, I could tell you so much of women. The tragedy is that the worst deceits are those they tell themselves. They're even capable of denying a love their whole being yearns for.'

Solon swallowed. 'What are you saying?'

'That Lyra loves you, even if she refuses to say so, and she will thank you in time for what must be done.' Wurther said grimly, 'We must make her see reason. We have a way.'

Solon bowed his head. 'Then let it be done,' he growled.

'Excellent – but I would ask that you visit her one last time, Solon, and plead your case. If she acquiesces, then we're all spared an unnecessary ordeal. Be gentlemanly if she refuses – and for Kore's sake, *don't* press the matter – but give her the chance to come round.'

Wurther offered his signet to kiss as he rose and added, 'In tabula, taking the queen wins the game. Make the decisive move, Solon.'

Calan Dubrayle made his way tentatively into the Royal Chapel, the small stone church that stood between the residential and administrative wings of the Bastion. As a resolute unbeliever, he seldom came here. The repaired building was austere, but no doubt decorations would be added once craftsmen could be engaged in spring. Although right now, he'd have happily watched it tumble down again.

How dare the Church threaten me?

'Lord Treasurer, thank you for coming,' a cool, resonant voice called and the new chaplain, Father Germane, an austere man with the certainty of the faithful, emerged from a side chapel. Dubrayle didn't respond to the man's greeting or offered handshake; pleasantries had no place in an encounter he'd been blackmailed into attending.

'I'm a busy man,' he snapped. 'What do you want?'

Germane had the arrogance to simper at his temper. He walked past him to look up at the icon of Corineus above the new altar. 'You know, of course, what happened here,' he observed mildly. 'An out-of-control heretic wreaked havoc and could have killed dozens of people, perhaps thousands, if she'd lost *all* control. Since then she's become more erratic, and more deadly. She must be contained, perhaps eliminated entirely.'

'You'd perhaps rather the Pontifex ruled?' Dubrayle replied. He tried not to grit his teeth.

'Ostevan Pontifex is a daemon-possessed heretic and he'll burn in Hel for eternity,' Germane pronounced, like Kore on his throne. 'No, Lord Treasurer, the Church wishes only a restoration of its rightful status and the elimination of heresy. To this end we will go to all lengths, as our enemies are.'

He turned upon Dubrayle. 'That includes dealing with godless, venal men like you. We've been watching you for a long time, looking behind the façade of the dedicated Imperocrat, married but never blessed with children, steeped in financial opacity and double-dealings.' He jabbed a finger. 'We were most interested by the testimony of Pavius Prelatus, who was once called to witness the birthing of an illegitimate child in Silacia, the offspring of a *forced* liaison.'

'It was *not* forced,' Dubrayle blurted, going cold.

'She was thirteen—'

'—and I did not know. And it wasn't rape.' Dubrayle clenched a small fist. 'I wasn't so much older myself—'

'So you say. It would be interesting to see how that stood up in court. Perhaps that day will come.'

Dubrayle swallowed, then lifted his head defiantly. 'Try it.'

'Perhaps we shall.' Germane sniffed. 'But we have more pressing matters: a heretic woman who must be reined in. There's a vote coming, Lord Treasurer. *Vote as my master does.*'

'This is treason—'

'No, not at all. We're merely going to help Her Majesty reach a conclusion that she should have reached on her own. Oh, and if you feel inclined to do anything to warn her, I'd like you to think about the safety of your son, Ramon Sensini, and his delightfully precocious daughter *Julia*, before you open your mouth.'

Dubrayle's legs almost gave way, but he rallied. 'I've never even met them.'

'But you've spoken to both, through the gnosis – you do so frequently, and you send money. Setallius isn't the only one with spies, Lord Dubrayle. They're your only progeny, the only true legacy you have, and your only hope of not seeing your family name extinguished.'

'I'm already resigned to that,' Dubrayle lied.

'No, you're not,' Germane replied. 'You've written to Sensini, offering him formal acknowledgment.'

He remembered all those hopelessly awkward conversations with Ramon through relay-staves, and occasionally he'd even talked with lovely little Julia. *My precious little imp.* The thought of her in the hands of some renegade Volsai made his stomach turn. But he sat up defiantly. 'If you know so much, bring me down.'

'Oh no, Lord Dubrayle, you misunderstand. The grand prelate enjoys sparring with you, and he knows that if you found a similar secret about him, you'd exploit it just as ruthlessly. That's the nature of tabula. He'd rather tame you. Where would be the gain in simply replacing you with another, and losing time and influence while seeking their weaknesses?'

True enough, it's exactly what I'd do . . .

To surrender went against his very soul, but for now he saw no choice. 'Very well. What must I do?'

Spending a week virtually sightless was a kind of Hel, but it did allow Lyra some respite from duties. Basia and Exilium were recovering, though neither could work for long, but Rhune and Sarunia, the Ventian hunters Dirklan favoured, took up some of the slack.

Once more, we survived – somehow. That gave her the wherewithal to face the dread of permanent blindness with a kind of fatalistic calm. What would be, would be. She was healing, and she'd learned a way to destroy one of the Masked Cabal. *Somehow I have to channel that light without blinding myself.*

She'd also discovered something weirdly freeing about being incapacitated: it forced her to strip back her life to what really mattered: holding her son and feeding him, or being with her inner circle and realising that despite frequent disagreements, she enjoyed being with them. Dirklan, Dominius and even dusty Calan Dubrayle could make her laugh, and Relantine was proving to be perceptive and clear-thinking.

But not Solon. Those interviews were awkward, and she never conducted them alone.

She missed Ril, of course. Although her views on Kore and His Paradise were no longer firm, she liked to hope he was there, and that one day Basia would find him.

With her eyes covered, her other senses improved to fill the void. She could often tell who a visitor was by their smell, and hear nuances in their voices she'd likely missed before. Time would play tricks, though: she could be sitting thinking it was night-time, then hear the time-bell chime and realise it was mid-morning. Meal times invariably happened at different times to hunger. Without light, the patterns from her day vanished.

Which was how she found herself awake listening to the churches sound the eighth night bell, which in winter meant the darkest, coldest hours before dawn. Her eyes were slowly recovering, but the room was almost pitch-black now, giving her just outlines, and the crimson smear of embers in the fireplace.

Then the floor creaked, someone sat on her bed and she squawked, 'Who's there?'

But she already knew by the smells, of red wine fumes and sweat. Her heart slammed against her ribs and she clutched her blanket.

'It's me,' Solon replied in a gruff voice.

'Solon? What is it?' A thousand panics flashed through her mind.

'I just needed to talk to you.'

Relief flooded her, and then anger. 'You can't just creep into my room – Kore's sake, Solon–'

She went to call out, but he grabbed her arm. 'Please, Lyra. We *have* to talk.'

She strove against his arm, but she might as well have tried to push the Bastion over. 'I'll listen,' she conceded, 'but if you touch me again, I will scream.'

She heard him swallow. 'Lyra, I'm not that type of man.'

She could hear that he believed that – but she no longer did. On one occasion he'd pulled her into a curtained alcove in the Sculpture Gallery and 'given her what she needed', despite her protests. It had been a little exciting, but it had left a queasy feeling as well. What if her protests hadn't been quite so half-hearted?

Perhaps if we do talk, he'll finally understand? Cautiously, she let out her breath. 'All right then, speak.'

'Lyra, we need to reconcile. Losing you is driving me mad – I can't sleep, I'm drinking too much and I can't think any more. I'm fifty-one, Lyra, but I feel like a lost child.' He leaned over her, his wine-laced breath unpleasant. 'I fell in love, for the first time in my life.'

But I didn't, she thought sadly. *I just wanted to explore, and have someone to fill the darkest part of night.*

'We *need* each other, Lyra,' he told her. 'I'm falling apart and you need me intact – I command your legions.'

The desperation in his voice scared her; the scent of violence or self-harm was as redolent as the foul wine fumes. She felt her guts aching, both for him and because of him.

Play with hearts and you break them, Basia had warned her, and so had Dominius.

'Solon,' she began.

He pulled her sheet aside and put his hand on her breast. His touch burned through the nightdress. 'Lyra, please.'

Heat rose in her face. 'Get your hand off me,' she hissed, then she tried to call out and he clamped his other hand over her mouth and suddenly she was *terrified*.

'This is why adultery really is a *sin*, Lyra,' he told her miserably, ignoring her squirming and her hands as she tried to prise his away. 'Not because of the stolen pleasure: what loving god could condemn that? It's for the damage that comes after: it eats our insides until we're just yearning husks.' He gripped her breast tighter, painfully. 'You feel it too, don't you – the need to be together?'

He bent over her, his stinking wine-breath on her face, his weight bearing down on her. He pressed his mouth to hers and his remembered taste made her skin break out in wet heat.

Oh Kore, he's going to—

'I thought you "weren't that type of man", Solon,' she managed to get out, turning her face aside while her heart hammered beneath his hot, sweaty touch. She tried to cry out, but he smothered her shout with another kiss. He was terrifyingly strong and she groaned with pain as he bared her left breast and squeezed it hard, the way she'd once found so exciting. She gripped her courage to fight, but fear gibbered at her to just *submit* so he wouldn't hurt her . . .

Then the door opened and Exilium Excelsior's voice called, 'Milady?'

Solon left his hand on her breast. 'What is it?' he demanded.

'I heard unexpected voices,' the Estellan replied. 'Milady, is all well?'

Exilium was repairing swiftly, but he was still some way from active duty. Even blind, Lyra could sense the tension crackling between the two men. Solon rose and she could smell the impending violence.

He could kill Exilium with a punch right now . . .

She sat up, pulling up her dress, flushed and frightened. 'Lord Takwyth brought me urgent tidings from the south,' she lied. 'He used the back stairs – but he's leaving, *now*.'

She waited in her personal darkness, in dread, but when he spoke, Solon's voice had a sullen, resigned air. 'Goodnight, my Queen.'

He stamped away, sucking half the air with him. She sagged into her mattress, shaking like a leaf. *He would have done it . . . He would have . . . Dear Kore . . .*

She felt Exilium approach. His voice uncertain, he stammered, 'Milady? I apologise if I interrupted anything. I've been told you and the Knight-Commander have . . . um, a special relationship.'

'There's no such relationship,' she told him. 'Please, make sure the back-stairs door is locked – put your own warding on it, so you'll be aware if anyone tries it.'

In the morning I'll have the lock changed.

When he left, she almost broke down, but that felt like weakness and she could not afford to be weak, so she just breathed instead, and gradually calm prevailed. But her anger didn't go away.

The arrogant presumption of the man, that the whole damned world needs him . . . That I still want him . . . Never! No one is irreplaceable. No one . . .

But it wasn't until hours later, when Rildan woke, that she was able to let go all her dread and fury and relax again into the one pure part of her life.

'Little one,' she told him, 'I would spare you this throne if I could. I think it's cursed. But it's yours by right and I'll give everything to make sure you live to sit on it.' She kissed his little nose and rosebud mouth, his dark eyes and smooth forehead. 'I love you,' she whispered. 'Only you.'

Dupenium, Rondelmar

The giant in the leather head-mask raised his axe and brought it whistling down. The blade cleaved through neck-bones and tissue and a man's head rolled into the basket while the body toppled sideways, fountaining blood.

Cordan Sacrecour flinched and looked away.

A long-fingered, ring-encrusted hand gripped his shoulder. 'Eyes forward, my Prince,' Ostevan Pontifex told him. 'An emperor must be seen to have the stomach for hard justice.'

Cordan shuddered at his touch, but couldn't pull away. 'What did he do?'

'Not enough,' drawled Ostevan.

'I don't understand. Jasper Vendroot was Uncle Garod's most trusted man.'

Ostevan smirked. 'Your uncle doesn't trust his own shadow. And Vendroot let him down: he failed to foresee these riots and his "measures" drove the rioters to greater extremes.'

'Is failure a capital crime?' Cordan asked weakly.

'Failure is High Treason when the man you fail is a duke . . . or a king and emperor, my Prince.' Ostevan's eyes flickered over the icy courtyard, swept of snow, although more was sure to fall, the nobles of Dupenium staring down at the executioner's block, some looking queasy, others pleased. Vendroot hadn't been popular – spymasters never were, according to Uncle Garod. 'It's why they're expendable,' he'd chuckled while passing sentence.

There were another forty men and women lined up, ready to be beheaded: ringleaders of the 'suffragium' riots. Cordan wasn't even sure what *suffragium* was.

'People say these riots are everywhere,' he said, not really wanting to talk with the Pontifex, but he needed to understand this. And the man at his other shoulder was Brylion Fasterius, who terrified him.

'Yes, a refreshingly idealistic change from the dreariness of bread riots,' Ostevan sniffed. 'It'll be swiftly suppressed in most places . . . but not, I suspect, in Pallas. With luck, the Corani and the Pallas mob will rip each other apart, weakening each other fatally.'

'Must there be war?' Cordan asked. 'If I married Lyra we could settle this peacefully.'

Ostevan snorted softly at the very thought, but Uncle Brylion leaned in and growled, 'Say that again and I'll break your face. That heretic bitch *murdered* my men.'

After that Cordan was too petrified to speak again, but he closed his eyes as often as he could as the axe swung, over and over and over, and the baskets of heads were carried off to be spiked on the walls. The torsos would be burned. It was the most utterly wretched afternoon of his life, but at least he managed not to vomit.

Uncle Garod patted his cheek after, and told him he was becoming a man.

Finally it was done and he could escape, gratefully dashing along the damp, dingy back corridors of the old grey castle, looking for his sister. Coramore had taken to escaping the nursery suites for the Cryptorium gardens, where she went nosing around the tombstones.

Gives me the shivers, he thought, but sure enough, when he clambered through a tumbledown section of wall, there she was in her grey cloak, peering up at an icy burnt-out tree. Her face was almost blue with cold but her red hair was bright against the snow.

'Cora, what are you doing?'

She turned furtively, then straightened. 'Nothing.'

'You'll catch your death,' he told her, holding up a hand and radiating warmth from it; he'd learned how to do this just recently. It was wasteful of gnostic energy, he'd been told, but it felt good. 'Come inside.'

'But look,' she said, pointing.

There was an owl in the lower branches, he realised, a dun-coloured bird only eight inches tall. It swivelled its head and looked back at him.

'It's her,' Cora whispered excitedly. '*It's Aradea.*'

35

An Offer

Diversity Among the Blessed Three Hundred

The empire likes to claim all magi as their own: Rondian, through and through. But an examination of the Blessed Three Hundred, those original followers of Corineus who survived gaining the gnosis and became magi, reveals Argundians, Estellani, Noromen, Bricians and every other race of western Yuros were numbered among them. If one thing unites Corineus' flock, it is in fact diversity.

HENEK GRAABE, ARGUNDIAN MAGE-SCHOLAR, DELPH 652

Freihaafen, Mollachia
Janune 936

Tarita woke to bright light shafting through the windows. She was lying face-down under a blanket on a table, in a wooden cabin. There was a fire crackling nearby and outside, the wind was howling.

She went to move and found that under her blanket she was clad in some kind of knee-length Yurosi under-shift. Her midriff was heavily strapped, stiff as a board. She tried to speak, but managed nothing more than a mangled, 'Huh?'

'Tarita,' Waqar said. He was sitting on a wide seat beside her, Jehana beside him. 'You collapsed, just after you kept Jehana from the winged man.' He squeezed her hand. 'Shukran, my friend. Once more, I owe you.'

She looked up and found an array of faces staring at her. Four of them weren't human. The bull-men had big, curious eyes, and they felt too large for the room. There were three Yurosi men: one a big-framed warrior with long pale hair and a blunt, open face; the other two looked like brothers, one with blond hair and a thick beard, the other brown-haired and moustached. There was also a composed, brown-skinned young woman in leather in the corner; she had rather narrow eyes and a moon tattoo on her face.

'Where are we?' she asked in Rondian, rolling over and pulling the blanket around her.

'We're in a hunting lodge northwest of Banezust,' the blond man replied. 'I'm Kyrik Sarkany, King of Mollachia – or I would be if a Keshi mage whose bite can possess ordinary people with daemons hadn't driven me and my comrades into the wilds.'

It all sounded worryingly familiar. 'I'm Tarita—'

'Tarita Alhani of the Merozain Bhaicara,' Kyrik interrupted. 'Can it still be a "brotherhood" when it has sisters?' he asked with a tired smile. 'Waqar and Jehana have explained who you are.' He pointed around the room. 'My brother Valdyr; Fridryk Kippenegger of Schlessen, call him Kip; Maegogh, Burzo, Brun and Maum of the Mantauri. And the lady with the lovely moon-tattoo is Korznici of Clan Vlpa, a Sydian tribe, who's just arrived. Her men are outside with Rothgar Baredge, my head scout, seeing to their horses. I think that's everyone.' Then he paused and added, 'Oh, and we have Sezkia Zhagy. Your Chain-rune is holding, but she's still possessed.'

'Sezkia'? He must mean 'Red Dress'. And he knows about Chain-runes. Tarita focused, and caught his gnostic aura. He wore a periapt at his throat too. 'You're a mage.'

'Indeed. Thank you for coming to our aid. We owe you, all of us.'

Tarita looked around for her clothing and found it washed and folded at the end of the bed. 'How long have I been unconscious?'

'Not long,' said the darker brother, Valdyr. 'Maegogh tended your wounds.'

Tarita felt her eyebrows shoot up as she looked back at the bull-men.

'I am Maegogh, of the Mantauri,' the largest stated. Intriguingly, he too had a gnostic aura and wore a periapt.

'You're a construct?' she asked him.

'Yar,' Maegogh rumbled. 'Is that a problem?'

'No,' she said firmly, 'absolutely not. My friend Ogre is a construct.' She gathered the blanket around her shoulders and managed to sit up, which *hurt*. 'He was taken by that winged man.' *Dear Ahm, protect him!*

'Did you know the winged man?' asked Valdyr. 'You're the only one who saw him.'

Tarita hesitated, then said, 'He was a powerful mage – growing wings like that requires strong morphic gnosis – and his eyes were dark, completely black. I've been trailing such people all the way from Ahmedhassa.'

The Sarkany brothers exchanged a look, then Kyrik said, 'Do you have a name for him?'

Tarita glanced at Waqar, who nodded. 'Asiv Fariddan.'

Valdyr sucked in his breath and the others grunted: confirmation, not surprise.

'I think we all have much to discuss,' Kyrik said, 'but we must first let this young lady wash and dress and confer with her friends. When you are ready, we will eat.'

Kyrik led Korznici, the men and Mantauri out of the room and once they'd gone, Tarita rose and dressed, uncaring that the siblings saw her naked. Right now her only concern was Ogre. She wasn't sure what to do or say around these new people.

'What's happened?' she asked. 'Do we trust them?'

'I trust Valdyr,' Jehana said instantly. 'He's a dwymancer and so am I.'

'Huh. I wouldn't trust another mage just because we share the gnosis.'

'Dwymancy is different,' Jehana said. 'It only accepts those it finds worthy.'

'Of course, O Worthy Princess,' Tarita replied, and turned to Waqar. 'What do you think?'

'What my sister thinks, of course,' he replied. 'You notice these Sarkany princes both speak Keshi?'

'Are they Crusaders?'

'I think they were prisoners in the East.'

She took that in . . . *They were breeding-house prisoners.* 'Oh . . .'

'Indeed,' Waqar responded. 'There were crimes on both sides.'

True enough, Tarita reflected. 'All right, but what do they want? I have to get Ogre back.'

'He's probably dead by now,' Waqar said. He sounded sympathetic, but resigned.

'Asiv wouldn't have taken Ogre away just to kill him. Remember, he could have taken Jehana instead,' Tarita replied. She looked at the princess. 'Although I'm not sure he even knew who you were.'

'Luckily for me,' Jehana replied. 'But remember that these Masks can possess other people: if he took Ogre, it was probably to make him a daemon-host too.'

Tarita put a hand to her heart. *Oh Ogre, no . . .*

Waqar laid a hand on hers, then pulled it away when his sister scowled. 'Anyway,' he said, 'I think there are things to be gained here. Jehana can learn from this Valdyr' – he frowned – 'as long as you're chaperoned and nothing untoward happens.'

'I will ensure everything is proper,' Jehana told him.

'Good. These people have been fighting Asiv Fariddan for some time: they have learned things about the Masked Cabal, so let's find out what. Then once you've mastered the dwyma, we can leave. Maybe I can convince Rashid that the Shihad has achieved enough, and we can all go home?'

'He conspired with the Masks to launch this war,' Tarita reminded him. 'He won't stop now.'

'But if we can destroy the Masks, perhaps we can end it and even find justice for Mother?'

Tarita snorted. 'I had no idea the royalty of Kesh were so damned naïve.'

They all gathered in the main room of the hunting lodge. Tarita had found the building so skilfully concealed that it was virtually invisible. The walls were timber and the roof covered in turf, but inside it was warm, and the table was laden with meat, as well as lentils, vegetables and berries, apparently the Mautauri's favoured foods.

Tarita had also taken the time to check on Sezkia, who was roped to a chair in a back room. They'd had to gag her to stem the tide of taunts and abuse that poured from her lips. She might not be able to reach the gnosis, but her bite was still infectious and she was filled with malice. Tarita's primary concern was the Chain-rune: the daemon was fighting it, and he was strong. She reckoned they had a few days at best. If they hadn't cured her by then, they'd have to kill her.

She was aware of a degree of watchfulness in the air as walking painfully, she followed Jehana and Waqar into the main lodge. They were ushered to chairs at the head of the table, to the left of Kyrik Sarkany.

'Sal'Ahm, Prince Waqar Mubarak,' the Mollach king said, speaking Keshi, offering exactly the right gestures of respect that a host ruler would give a guest of superior rank – he'd very clearly lived long in Kesh to know not just the harbadab, but also the correct rank of his guest. 'My house is honoured to host such illustrious guests as you and your sister, the exalted Jehana. And welcome too, Tarita of Ja'afar. The renown of the Merozain order transcends distance. You too honour my house.'

Impressive, Tarita thought as she curtsied. *Multilingual, cultured and knowledgeable*. He wore a Yurosi wedding ring and she wondered about his wife. *This Korznici, perhaps?*

Kyrik welcomed the others, each in their own tongue, then switched to Rondian to say, 'The only tongue we all share is Rondian so I trust that will be acceptable?' When all murmured assent, he raised a hand over the food. 'We have no priest here, but it is said that a king is ordained by the gods. So in the name of Kore, of Ahm, of Minaus the Bullhead and Amazar the Sky Stallion, I bid you welcome.'

Again, all murmured assent and thanks, then Kyrik picked up his goblet and gestured for everyone else to do the same. 'We are of course, all *enemies* here,' he said bluntly, to Tarita's surprise. 'Mollachia is of the Rondian Empire and obedient to Kore. Our honoured guests, the prince and princess, are of Kesh and revere Ahm. My wife's people are represented at this table by Korznici of the Sydian Plains, worshippers of the Celestial Horses. Friend Kip and his men and Mantauri give sacrifice to Minaus. We number magi, dwymancers, constructs, Easterners and Westerners. This room, most would say, should now descend into a bloodbath.'

He paused before adding, 'But we're not enemies here. *We are friends.* Some of us have married outside our culture. We share common perils and common enemies. But more than that, I believe all here to be good of heart. We have it in us to be an example to others, to show that people who think and feel can find common cause. Our similarities are many more than our differences. So this is my cup-wish tonight: for peace, my friends, peace to us all.' He raised his goblet to them all and drank, and everyone else did the same.

Not just impressive, Tarita thought. *Inspiring.*

Waqar was clearly impressed. He immediately fell into earnest conversation with Kyrik, while Jehana and Valdyr shared a shy, muted but intense exchange. Tarita found herself speaking across the table with the giant Schlessen, Kip, who knew less of table manners than she did, but ate enthusiastically. He reminded her of Ogre, especially when he smiled, and was almost as broad and tall.

'You are of Javon, yar?' he noted.

'Do you know it?' she asked, wary of men who'd been on Crusade.

'Ney, but I have been told of it. My wife is from Dhassa.'

Tarita was surprised, and prepared to be suspicious of a man who stole an Eastern wife and brought her to this cold wilderness, but Kip was speaking with such affection for her and their children, and he'd clearly learned her tongue, so she found herself warming to him.

Once they'd eased their hunger, Kyrik spoke again. 'Friends, we've all come here by different paths and driven by different needs. You find Mollachia at war – a small struggle compared to the mighty clash of Shihad and Empire, but of great moment to us. I do not ask you to take up arms on our behalf – well, actually I do, but I won't be offended if other needs take precedence – but what I do ask is that you share your story and purpose, so that we might perhaps aid each other.'

Tarita had never expected such a forum, given this place appeared to be rife with secret cabals and heretical magic, but she thought Kyrik Sarkany a genuinely open and frank man. She wondered how Waqar, a Mubarak prince despite himself, would respond.

To set the example, Kyrik started, telling them of returning from exile to find a struggle against Imperial tax-farmers; of his trek across half of Yuros to unite Mollachs and Sydians; of dwymancer ghosts on mountain peaks and a Keshi mage whose blood ran black.

'Asiv Fariddan,' Waqar said, when Kyrik finished. 'His name was found when Tarita and I investigated the Masked Cabal who murdered Sultan Salim and launched the Shihad. They murdered my mother and tried to capture my sister, who has the dwyma-gift.' Waqar went on to describe his investigation, omitting his suspicions about Sultan Rashid, but he did bring up the spear, scimitar and book recovered from Midpoint Tower. Tarita fetched the scimitar and book and read them the title: *Daemonicon di Naxius*.

'Naxius,' growled Valdyr Sarkany. 'He's the man behind the Masked Cabal. The dwymancer in Pallas, Nara of Misencourt, found this out.'

Tarita glanced at Jehana, who made a strangled noise, echoing her own thoughts. *No wonder Asiv took Ogre alive – he's going to return him to Naxius . . . Dear Ahm, his webs are all round us!*

'What are these artefacts for?' Kyrik wondered.

'We don't know,' Tarita admitted. 'I'm not a scholar.'

'I am,' Jehana said suddenly. 'May I look at the book?'

Tarita hesitated. 'It's encrypted, in no known language.'

Jehana's face fell. 'Then it's of no use to us.'

'But we've got it and Naxius wanted it: the Mask we killed at Midpoint Tower went to specific trouble to recover that book and scimitar. That means they matter.'

Kip took the scimitar and tried the edge, drawing blood. 'Looks like argenstael, but it's properly sharp.'

'It can break steel,' Tarita told him.

He raised his eyebrows. 'Does it destroy these possessed men?'

Tarita shook her head. 'This blade doesn't poison them.' But she was fascinated by this revelation, that the daemon-progeny could be fatally wounded by a silver alloy.

Next, they heard how Kip's people had joined Kyrik's, and of the Sydian tribe stranded far away, as well the current status of Mollachia, with Asiv and his daemon-possessed Reekers in control of the towns.

Once all had been told, Kyrik spoke again. 'So, now we know. For my part, Asiv Fariddan holds Hegikaro, my home. In all likelihood he has murdered my wife and he's infected men of Mollachia with this daemon-sickness, probably the Imperial legion in Lapisz too. My purpose is to destroy him, then save those we can.'

Valdyr immediately added, 'I fight with my brother. But there is a thing I must do, concerning the dwyma and I must depart on that task soon . . . but I hope to do so holding an argenstael blade, I confess.'

'You'll have one,' Kyrik promised. 'We all will.'

'My purpose,' Kip said, 'is to make my new homeland safe for my new king. I fight with him, as do all my Bullheads.' Maegogh and the other Mantauri all growled agreement.

They all turned to the Sydian girl. 'Kirol,' Korznici said, in her unhurried monotone, 'Clan Vlpa are trapped in the Tuzvolg, culling our herds and living day to day in hostile lands. Many blame you for our losses and say we should never have come, but I have told them that none could have foreseen this turn of events. I remind them of your true love for Hajya, and that this land is now also theirs. They will fight for you when the time comes.'

They will all fight for him, Tarita noted. *He's a unifying figure.*

She was next around the table. She'd seldom spoken to large groups before, but she raised her chin boldly. 'I'm far from home and Javon, my own country, has not joined the Shihad. I rightly shouldn't be here, but Asiv Fariddan has captured my friend, Ogre. He'll probably be sent to Naxius. I must prevent that.'

It wasn't a complete commitment to Kyrik's 'common cause', as everyone realised, but those listening made approving sounds.

Jehana spoke before her brother, to Tarita's surprise. 'I must learn from Valdyr. Where he goes, I go.'

Waqar didn't look best pleased by that, but he said smoothly, 'I must protect my sister, so I suppose that places me with Prince Valdyr as well.'

Where he too might learn of the dwyma, Tarita thought, noting how careful he'd been not to mention his own potential. *Clearly a Mubarak doesn't give trust as readily as lesser men.*

If Kyrik was concerned that two Easterners were going with his brother, he gave no sign. 'Then I think we have common cause, at least for a time. Let us rest; we must depart at first light for Freihaafen.'

'What's Freihaafen?' Tarita asked Kip, as everyone rose.

He gave her a broad grin. 'Freihaafen is Paradise.'

It was an intriguing and pleasant thought, but as she went to find a cot to lie down, still feeling woozy from her wound, her thoughts returned to her kidnapped friend. *I'm coming for you, Ogre. Just hold on.*

Hegikaro, Mollachia

The rocking, jolting motion jerked Ogre awake and yet again sent him sliding into the caged wall. Visions flashed before his eyes: lying bound across a giant bird's back, high in freezing air, a naked Keshi man riding behind him, laughing triumphantly; landing in a snowy field beside a desolate farm. And now . . .

The wagon struck cobbled stones and Ogre sat up, testing his bindings. Through the wooden and steel bars, he could see the backs of a driver and four horses. When the man at the reins turned, he could see his jet-black eyes, and the six horsemen riding alongside had the same dark gaze. Then one lowered his cowl and peered in at him, and Ogre saw a mask of lacquered copper, a birdlike visage with a long beak and leering eyes. The mouth, uncovered, was wreathed in a well-manicured black beard.

'Sal'Ahm, Ogre,' the man said, in a thick Keshi accent.

Ogre had read the Lantric tales at his Master's lair. 'Beak,' he croaked.

'Indeed, I am Beak: notorious for putting my nose into places it shouldn't go. Like this place, perhaps: a snowbound kingdom no one cares about. So why are the dwymancers here? Why is a Merozain here? What do you think, Ogre? What does pretty little Tarita think?'

He's been rummaging in my mind . . . He looked away, fearing gnostic knives stabbing into his brain, but Beak only laughed.

'We'll have plenty of time to talk, Ogre,' he snickered.

They entered a mossy, grey-slate town beside an iced-over lake. A tall castle stood on a rocky outcrop above. There weren't many people about, but he saw a boy watching him, held on the shoulder of a grey-haired young-old woman. Neither had the black eyes of his captors, but they stared at him as if he were just another monstrosity in a world of horror.

'This is Hegikaro, Ogre,' Beak called. 'It's the capital of this wretched place. I cast out the king and now rule here, for what it's worth. It's a model for what all of Yuros will become in the next year or two.' The claim was made with utter certainty.

'What will you do with me?' Ogre asked.

'You? You'll be dangled as bait for your little Merozain moxie,' Beak said lightly. 'But I have good news for you too: the Master has already dispatched a windship to take you home. Won't that be nice for you?'

Then he roared with laughter and spurred away.

Freihaafen, Mollachia

Kip might be right, Tarita thought. *This place might just be Paradise.* Although if it was, the Godspeakers and Kore priests had been wildly wrong over who would be admitted. *None of them, for a start*, she noted, smiling to herself. There were Yurosi and Ahmedhassans here, magi and constructs too – all bathing naked in the warm waters that bubbled through the bottom of the lake, close to shore. But no clergymen, and she didn't miss them at all.

They'd only want us to put our clothes back on and pray, she mused, as she peeled her tunic slowly over her head and let her best assets jiggle. Then with some added hip-sway and sass, she waded into the warm lake, steam swirling around her thighs, noting that Waqar was among the men eyeing her with interest.

Let's see if that changes your mind about me, she thought, not that she was sure exactly how she felt about Waqar now. She'd vowed never to crawl, and never to look back if someone rejected her . . . but it still rankled, especially as company would be welcome tonight, when she was in such dread for Ogre.

Her injuries were almost healed now, although the scar wasn't going to be pretty: the puncture-crater was still scabbed and painful. But her back was a mess of scars anyway, from her previous fights, and she'd recovered from her paralysis ... She waded out to a trio of Dhassan women, one of whom was Sabina, Fridryk Kippenegger's gorgeous wife, the unofficial head-woman around here. They were sitting around a hot vent in the lake-floor.

'So,' she asked, looking around, 'are any of the men here unwed?' The bathers were dotted here and there, mostly among their own gender, but not entirely. Nothing lewd was going on, but she'd spotted some smouldering looks being exchanged. She hoped Waqar's eyes were still fixed on her, but wouldn't give him the satisfaction of looking back.

The Dhassans exchanged amused glances and Sabina pointed at Waqar. 'That one.'

'And Rothgar,' her friend Pani added, wistfully. 'But I think he fancies the young Sydian mage, though he denies it.'

'And the prince, Valdyr,' the third lady added, a plump woman called Faleesa.

'Damaged,' Sabina murmured, 'poor man. So many scars.' Her eyes ran down Tarita's back. 'Worse than you, dearie. Flogged half to death he was, but the worst scars are on the inside.'

Tarita looked around, but Valdyr wasn't here, and nor was Jehana. *So everyone else is taken ... I guess I'm in for a quiet night.* 'And unwed women?'

'Not many, really. Kimali's eldest daughter is almost of age,' Pani said. 'And some new widows. So sad.'

Two men died at the mines, Tarita recalled. Her thoughts returned to Ogre. She'd tried scrying, but predictably, he was strongly warded, and the mountains around them made the effort unsustainable.

Since they'd arrived, the smith of this small community had begun forging argenstael weapons from the metal ingots they'd recovered from Banezust. Sezkia Zhagy had been blindfolded and gagged and imprisoned in a small hut inside the palisade; they dared not allow her out, for fear the daemon-link would enable Abraxas to find this refuge. Tarita pitied her, but she'd been unable to expel the daemon, so the precautions were necessary.

At some point we'll have to either free her or kill her ...

Her eyes were drawn unwillingly to Waqar, who'd just risen from the water and was heading for the shore, water running down his muscular back and taut, shapely buttocks. Her throat went a little dry.

'So he's a Mubarak,' Faleesa murmured. 'No wonder they're royal and all.'

'Blessed by Ahm with a godlike face and body,' Pani added, with an earthy sigh.

The three Dhassan women trailed their eyes from Waqar's behind to Tarita's face and back. 'Have you got to know him, friend Tarita?'

'A lady would never tell,' Tarita told them loftily.

The three women snorted. 'You're no more a lady than we are,' Sabina judged, rightly.

The talk turned to life here while they enjoyed the vista of the woods and peaks reflected on the steaming lake surface. It was truly a beautiful place, and Tarita was intrigued by the mix of peoples. *This is a place where differences are celebrated*, she thought. *Ogre would love it. It's perfect for him – and his Semakha.*

She asked the three women how they came here, enjoying talking about something other than cabals and conspiracies. They were all former prostitutes and some were still dealing with the scars of that life, but they'd been taken in by soldiers who'd honoured their promises to love and protect them.

'Not everyone's happy all of the time,' Sabina admitted, 'but if a man steps out of line, Kip has a word. And if a woman starts letting more than her eyes wander, we three sort it out.'

'Do we ever!' Faleesa and Pani giggled.

'What about the Mantauri?' Tarita asked.

'Maegogh keeps them in line,' Sabina replied.

'They're very calm,' Faleesa added. 'All that strength, but very gentle.'

'When they first joined us, we were all worried,' Pani admitted, 'but they're honestly no trouble. I say it's because they aren't carnivores. There's no predator in them. But when they're roused for battle, watch out!'

Ogre's a carnivore, but he's also gentle, Tarita reflected, wishing she could just magic him free.

Then she heard the pulse of a gnostic contact, someone she didn't know, calling her name into the aether. She threw up her hand apologetically to the three Dhassan women, stood and headed away into the deeper, colder water, calling heat as she did and listening hard.

<Tarita Alhani . . . Tarita Alhani . . . > a masculine Keshi voice called, his voice echoing in the distinctive way that told her he was using a relay-stave to amplify his call. But she didn't know him.

She didn't snatch at the call; that risked betraying her position. Instead she let her awareness drift into the aether before answering in Keshi, *<I am Tarita.>*

A hooded shape wearing a bird-like mask appeared in her inner vision. *<And I'm Beak.>*

<Would you prefer I just called you Asiv?> she replied tartly.

The masked man chuckled slyly. *<I just wanted to assure you that Ogre is in good hands. Would you like to see? Just scry him: I've removed the wards and opened a trace in his Chain-rune so that you can find him.>*

I probably shouldn't rise to the bait . . . But she engaged clairvoyance and found Ogre, chained to an 'X' of wooden beams, just as she'd been bound by Alyssa. She suspected that was deliberate, which meant that Asiv had already been ripping through Ogre's mind.

<Bastido,> she breathed, opting for Rimoni oaths. *<If you've hurt him . . . >*

<Oh, don't worry. The Master wouldn't want his old pet irrevocably damaged,> Asiv replied. *<But as for a little pain . . . the beast is robust. The men are fascinated to see how much he can take.>*

<You dried-up turd of pig excrement,> she rasped. *<What do you want?>*

<Nothing of value to you,> Asiv replied. *<Just a pair of heretics: Jehana Mebarak and Valdyr Sarkany.>*

<No chance – but how about Sezkia Zhagy for Ogre?>

It was Asiv's turn to sneer. *<She's nothing. Kill her, whatever you wish. We have thousands of suitable hosts.>*

So he only wants dwymancers, Tarita thought. *<I rather imagine your precious Master will be a little upset to learn you had Jehana at your mercy and chose a construct instead,>* she told him.

That barb struck home: Asiv visibly flinched, mask and all. But he recovered swiftly. <*I rather got the impression there's little love lost between you and the Mubarak siblings,*> he observed. <*One treats you like dirt-caste scum and the other scorns your advances.*>

<*I am dirt-caste scum,*> she retorted.

The Gatti mage laughed. <*And proud of it, I see. My birth was no higher. Don't these nobles set your teeth on edge? You and I fought for all we have. Why shouldn't we trade them like market produce? They would.*>

<*Ah, but I'm a Merozain,*> she replied. <*The Brothers don't just teach the gnosis, they teach the value of life. I don't sell people out to the likes of you.*>

<*But you've not even heard all my offer. We control Ahmedhassa, Tarita, and soon we'll also control Yuros. How will Javon fare when the sultan returns victorious and remembers the old feuds? I can prevent that. Surely that's worth a couple of lives?*>

<*No.*>

<*We could even arrange an advantageous marriage for you. I could force Waqar to take you to his bed. What a pair you'd make – the Keshi prince and his Merozain wife.*>

<*What, just after I sell out his sister?*> she replied sceptically.

<*Handle it right and he'd never know. Anyway, he's not the only prince you could set your sights on: how about Attam or Xoredh? Or Teileman? You're Ascendant . . . you're worth it for the bloodline alone . . . *>

It was a crumb of comfort that Ogre must have kept the secret of her barren womb from Asiv . . . especially as she explored the opportunities a hostage exchange might present.

<*Why should I believe you?*> she demanded, because it would be expected. <*You're just a pawn in another man's tabula game. I know about your Puppet-master Naxius.*>

<*Then obviously you know I speak with his voice when I make the offer. The Master's war is against the magi of Yuros, not Ahmedhassa. He brought the Shihad here to crush his foes. Who rules Ahmedhassa doesn't concern him.*>

Tarita wished she knew enough about Naxius to say whether that were true.

<*Think about it, girl. There's not long – the Master is sending a ship to collect Ogre. Then we'll come for your dwymancer friends anyway. Wouldn't it be better to get something out of the transaction?*>

<*I'll not countenance anything while you're treating Ogre like that,*> she snapped.

Asiv chuckled. <*Then I shall humour you and give him some creature comforts – as a token of trust, hmm?*>

<*Trust?*> she echoed derisively. <*How long do I have?*>

<*Not long.*>

His image faded. She hugged her chest, barely aware that she was standing in freezing water with her skin turning blue. *He knows I can't surrender the dwymancers for Ogre . . . that would be madness. If I tell him I'm doing it, he'll know I'm lying . . . And therefore he'll betray me . . .*

She smiled slowly. Given those parameters, this wasn't a hostage exchange, but an invitation to a duel . . .

Hegikaro, Mollachia

Ogre was almost powerless to move, his muscles frozen by hours kneeling in the mud, but the men who unlocked his manacles dragged him to a large iron tub and shoved him in. Warm water soaked into his aching body, soothing yet painful on his broken skin.

Then the tall, inhumanly beautiful Asiv Fariddan walked into the courtyard, robed in white, his copper skin oiled and his hair and beard intricately braided. The black-eyed servants went motionless.

'Ah, Ogre – or *Masakh*, we would say in Gatti. How do you fare?'

Ogre glared under lowered brows at the flawless being before him. 'What do you want?'

'Nothing but your comfort, effendi,' Asiv purred. 'You have your little friend Tarita to thank: she and I have come to an arrangement for your well-being. Isn't that marvellous?'

Ogre's nostrils flared. 'What arrangement?'

Asiv's hooded eyes twinkled. 'Everyone has a price, Ogre. You should be flattered she was willing to include you in the arrangement. I think she and I will have a profitable relationship.'

Ogre wouldn't look at his gloating captor, certain Tarita wouldn't do deals with this man. Asiv had been using mystic gnosis to go through his mind, a foul experience that told him exactly what sort of person he was: an abuser, a torturer and a user of others, everything Tarita wasn't.

'You're not going to free me,' he rumbled.

Asiv tilted his head, interested. 'The Master was right: he did breed intelligence into you – and you're correct. We're going to lure the little slut in, then pollute her and use her as a weapon to destroy the dwymancers.'

'*Nooo!*' Ogre roared, erupting from the tub and swinging his immense fist at the Gatti mage's face, with all his power and fury . . .

Asiv swayed aside like a serpent, then slammed a kinesis blow into Ogre's chest and hurled him backwards. He struck the stone wall, cracking mortar and flopping stunned to the floor.

'Do any such thing again, Masakh, and you'll go back to the courtyard,' Asiv said. 'I can make even you scream until your lungs burst.'

Asiv said nothing more of Tarita. Ogre was still in a Chain-rune bound to manacles and he imagined that would be the case for the rest of his life, however long that was. But he did gain some freedoms: he could move between certain rooms, and eat when he wanted, so he had been making up for the recent months of privation. He could drink, too, but after a first despairing night when he'd drunk himself to oblivion, he'd avoided that pitfall.

As he traversed one gloomy chamber, Ogre realised it was the throne hall. He looked around and saw a crowned man sitting alone, holding court over no one. *Dragan, the new king.* He had iron-grey hair and a granite face. His closed-in, morose expression suggested he wasn't happy with his realm.

The king heard his footsteps and glanced up. His eyes went ichor-black and Ogre realised the man was a prisoner, just as he was. They both looked away.

The windship arrived the next day.

Ogre was lying on the big bed in his chamber, staring into the dark recesses of the high-beamed stone ceiling, unable to summon the energy to move. This tiny window of adventure was about to slam shut, ending these few months of freedom. It was back to pain and drudgery, low ceilings and locked doors. And the Master . . .

I've seen life and death. I've seen the open skies and the sea. I've travelled with a princess. And most of all, I've shared laughter with a real friend. It was terrifying and wonderful, to be so alive . . .

How long would it be, he wondered, until he forgot what that felt like?

Then Asiv spoke in his head: <*Ogre, come to the western battlements. Your ship has arrived.*>

He didn't want to greet it, but he knew better than to refuse. So he rose, wrapped a cloak around the rough leather tunic he'd been given and shuffled his way through the almost deserted castle. The narrow stone steps made it an awkward climb, but when he reached the top he found Asiv already there, wearing his Beak mask and clearly delighted with himself.

Ogre looked over the wall to a drop of a hundred feet or more and wondered, if he jumped, would anyone catch him?

I was saved from Naxius once, by the Ordo Costruo. I will not despair.

His thoughts were interrupted by the appearance of the windship, a square-rigged two-masted Yurosi transport ship with a single ballista in the prow, flying Imperial banners. It dropped into the courtyard. The moment it had settled on its landing stanchions, a portal opened in the side of the hull, steps dropped to the ground and a pair of bulky shapes emerged, robed and cloaked, with deep cowls that concealed their faces. But when they stepped into the light, the afternoon sun glittered on copper masks: not images from the Lantric plays this time, but figures from old woodcut illustrations to the *Book of Kore*. Both were skull-masks; the first was bronze, dappled like sand, with no teeth and the illusion of no eye sockets: Cadearvo, Angel of Famine. The other was livid green with a scarlet serpent instead of a tongue: Scaramu, Angel of Plague.

It was only when the newcomers passed through their honour guard that Ogre realised how big they were: eight foot tall, at least, with a build to match his own, although they were straighter of stance and walked with an easier grace. They went straight to Asiv and the three Masks bowed to each other in a self-satisfied way.

'Have you found the dwymancers?' Cadearvo asked in a distorted, desolate rumble.

'Only an old lair, at Watcher's Peak,' Asiv replied. 'It's been desecrated, but Sarkany hasn't returned there.'

'Why are they not found?' the other, Scaramu said in an oily lilt, the voice also distorted.

Asiv's voice took on a haughty defensiveness. 'You have no idea what the land is like here. Sheer cliffs and hidden valleys, thick forests and constant wind and rain. Visibility is impossible, the snow—'

'I'm hearing excuses,' Cadearvo replied. 'The Master wants Sarkany captured or dead, and the Mubarak girl, *alive*. We're here to ensure his desires are met.'

Asiv's arrogance visibly wavered and he swiftly capitulated. 'All my resources are at your disposal. Plans are already afoot. Traps have been set and we stand ready—'

Scaramu raised a hand to silence the Gatti mage. 'Enough, Beak. Brief us within.' Then with ponderous menace, the two newcomers turned to Ogre, placed hands on their masks and removed them. The faces beneath would have horrified most people: both had skin of a greenish-dun colour, slitted amber eyes, flat noses and huge jaws. Rope-like hair hung in thick cords.

For Ogre, it was like looking in a distorted mirror, except that *his* was the distortion, because their faces were more regular and more commanding. They were a long way from human concepts of beauty, but both had a striking quality. Cadearvo was male, with a domineering visage, thick dark hair and a dark allure.

But it was to Scaramu that Ogre's eyes were drawn, to a face he'd carried in his heart for more than fifteen years. She'd been vulnerable then, but now her full-lipped, sultry-eyed features were confident, commanding.

'Hello, Ogre,' said Semakha. 'It's been a long time.'

'I always wondered if I'd ever see you again,' Ogre said. 'I thought about you every day.'

Asiv had taken Cadearvo below, but Semakha had bade Ogre stay.

'Really?' She yawned, gazing out over Lake Drozst. 'I had too many other things to think about. The Master kept me very busy.'

She forgot me. That hurt, and so did her thoughtless tone. Ogre remembered the scared female who'd been placed with him, and how they'd spent every moment they could together, talking and holding hands as he told her everything he knew, to give her a chance of survival. He'd been lonely and desperate to befriend and nurture her, to love her.

I've carried my love of you for fifteen years . . . He didn't say the words. It was becoming clear that she couldn't have cared less.

'You were a proto-breed, Ogre: an earlier, *weaker* version of me,' Semakha remarked, shredding his heart. 'The Master made me stronger and smarter, and with more gnostic capacity. With *my* generation, he perfected the mix of man and beast. Compared to us, you're little more than an animal.'

He looked away, wishing he were dead.

'When the Masked Cabal was formed, the Master elevated me and my kind, his *greater* servants, for even though he himself is human, mankind are *not* the pinnacle. To prove this, he implanted a daemon-spawn next to my heart – not Abraxas, but a greater daemon: Lucian Himself, the lord of Hel. I have become one of the most powerful beings on Urte.' She put her big, clawed hand under his chin and made Ogre look at her.

'The Lord of Hel is real, Ogre. He is the first and greatest daemon. And soon, He will leave the aether and make Urte his own.' She studied him coldly. 'The Master says you can still play a part, Ogre. You're a useful specimen.'

He tried to glimpse the real Semakha inside this complacently sadistic *monster* before him, but that timid innocent was long gone. 'I'd rather die,' he growled.

Her face changed from mock-tenderness to contempt. 'That's not your choice,' she jeered.

He reacted on gut instinct, a sudden rush of loathing, lunging for her . . .

But even as he moved, she caught his arms and slammed her forehead into his nose. He was sent reeling, a moment later her fist struck his jaw and he was thrown onto his back on the walkway. She tinkled with laughter above him. 'Too slow, too weak, Ogre. Have a care, lest I tell the Master that we can easily do without you.'

To complete his humiliation, she dragged him, still stunned, down the stairs to the 'X' cross-beam and chained him up again. 'You can rot here,' she told him. 'Cadearvo and I will use your bed.'

36

Fuel for Fire

Dwymancy and Madness

Lest we forget, these dwymancers succumbed to madness and became destructive menaces to us and even the natural world they claimed to serve. Heresy is not a label the Church uses lightly.

HEREDIUS COMFATERI, IMPERIAL CONFESSOR, PALLAS 703

Norostein, Noros
Janune 936

Seth and Ramon climbed to Ringwald, the highest of the three city tiers, using a postern gate and taking the backstreets through the blizzard to the Royal Keep, which sat above the inner city. It was so coated in snow it could barely be picked out from the mountains above. The old-fashioned castle was centuries old, cold and draughty and in poor repair since the empire annexed Noros after the Revolt, but there were Royal Guardsmen at the gates: men who'd been with King Phyllios when he died and who had seen Seth exact revenge on his killer. That she was a woman didn't trouble them; she'd been a mage with a deadly spear that had wrecked fortified gates. To them, Seth was a hero, and their salutes were reverent.

Guard Captain Era Hyson came to meet them. 'I was appointed by King Phyllios himself, in 928, after the death of my predecessor,' Hyson said, as he led them inside. 'Appointing the Guard Captain was one of the few prerogatives he retained. As well as protecting him, we patrol the city, preventing crime and apprehending wrongdoers.'

So a real King's Man, not a sycophant of the governor, Seth noted. *And with an uncertain future now the king's dead.* 'We may have some wrongdoers for you, Captain, but we'll need to move carefully. Where can we talk?'

Hyson took them to a meeting room. 'No one took council with the king after 910 – it was illegal for him to meet with anyone except with the governor's representative present.' He opened the doors and they found two men already waiting: the Justiciar, Vorn Detabrey, and a man Ramon clearly knew, because he flew to him, hugged him and pounded his back, before introducing him as Vannaton Mercer.

'Alaron's father?' Seth asked.

'Aye, and I remember you, Master Korion,' Mercer replied. 'Or as I should say, Your Grace.'

'Seth to you, sir,' Seth exclaimed, gladly shaking his hand, and they spent a brief time catching up on news.

Vann Mercer told them Alaron and his Merozains were labouring day and night at Midpoint Tower to save the Leviathan Bridge. 'Without my son, the Bridge would have been lost already,' he declared proudly, 'although he regrets not being here to defend his home.'

'We'll do it for him,' Ramon vowed. 'It's good to see you, sir, but are you here in an official capacity?'

'I am – I'm on the Noros Roundtable,' Vann replied. 'It's a citizens' group. We petition the governor for clean wells, better roads, more guardsmen and the like.'

'I've dealt with Roundtables in Bricia,' Seth replied; most had been reasonable people, but there were always a few . . . 'How're your dealings with Governor Myron?'

Vann's expression answered that question for him. 'Well, we're the ones distributing those rations the governor deigns to release, to make sure it's divided fairly,' he said. 'His negligence endangers us all – and Justiciar Detabrey says there are legal precedents for a Roundtable protesting to Pallas and bringing down a governor.'

Seth perked up at that. 'Who would you protest to?'

'The Imperocrator, Rael Relantine,' Detabrey replied. 'He's newly appointed from the Justiciary, where all the best men come from,' he added wryly. 'If we can highlight Governor Myron's deficiencies, we might have him removed, or at least, instructed to act responsibly.'

'It sounds like something that would take a long time,' Seth commented, 'and we need action now. Can we persuade Pallas to move quickly?' He glanced at Ramon, knowing that trying to crank the wheels of governance in Pallas endangered his daughter. Ramon had so far been unable to find where Julia was being held.

The Silacian frowned, but said, 'It's possible we can do something. I have some connections – from the Third Crusade – with the Treasurer, Calan Dubrayle. He might be able to influence Relantine.'

Detabrey whistled. 'That's an impressive connection, Capitano Sensini.'

'Maybe. We're not close. No promises, but I can try.'

Seth put a hand on his friend's shoulder, knowing fully what was being risked.

'Thank you,' Detabrey said, unaware of the deeper game. 'Because the other options aren't so peaceful.'

'The mood among the burghers and refugees is becoming very dark against the governor,' Vann told them. 'They're crammed dozens to a house in Copperleaf, fearing the Shihad will break the walls any day and knowing slaughter will follow, while the favoured few inside Ringwald are untouched. It's no secret that Myron has dozens of transporter vessels loaded with their wealth, ready to run if worst comes to worst.'

'It wouldn't take much for that anger to turn to violence,' Detabrey added.

'It could spark a new Noros Revolt,' Hyson warned, 'and in the middle of an invasion, with half of Noros displaced, that's a recipe for disaster. But people need to eat – and see Myron sharing their hardship.'

Seth nodded soberly. The idea of the citizenry hurling themselves at the inner walls while his men defended the outer was terrifying. 'We must persuade Myron to open his stores and distribute them in an equitable manner.'

'I'll speak to Dubrayle,' Ramon said. 'If you have a relay-stave, I can do it now.'

Hyson produced one and handed it over. 'The King had a small number stashed away, from a time when he still hoped other vassal-states might rise to support his cause. None did, and they went unused.'

'What happens to the Royal Guard now?' Seth asked.

'We don't know. Myron is speaking of disbanding us and sending us into Lowertown – without our weapons and armour. He's already emptied the king's treasury and taken anything of value he could find from his rooms.'

'Did King Phyllios have any kin?'

'No. After the Revolt of 908 failed, the Sacrecours dealt harshly with Noros,' Detabrey answered. 'Anyone with a serious claim to the throne was executed as a traitor or imprisoned and died without issue. There are rumours of hidden heirs, but for obvious reasons no one has come forward. Phyllios was kept alive in a show of clemency to reassure fellow ruling magi families that they were *special.*'

'So if there was a Revolt, in whose name would it be?' Ramon wondered.

'In the People's name,' Detabrey said, 'a *Res Publica*: a state run for the people, by the people, like in Lantris long ago. I recently met a bright young fellow who was quite the evangelist upon the subject.'

Seth decided this conversation was quite treasonous enough without exploring that. 'Let's talk to Calan Dubrayle and hope this can be resolved *within* the law.'

Ramon asked for privacy and when he was alone, he took a moment to compose his thoughts before sending his call winging into the aether, seeking a private sigil he seldom used. <*Father,*> he whispered.

The response was slow, and cautious. <*Ramon?*> Then Calan Dubrayle's face appeared: the narrow head, dapper features, receding hairline and tired eyes. Ramon was struck by the similarities to his own reflection he'd never noticed before; it was as if he were growing into his father's face as he aged. Dubrayle was in a well-lit and tidy office, stacked with papers and ledgers. <*To what do I owe this privilege?*>

He wasn't sure if Dubrayle even knew that Julia was missing, so he kept that up his sleeve for now. <*I'm your wayward son – so obviously I'm only going to contact you if I need something.*>

The Lord Treasurer smiled momentarily. *<There was always the hope it was social.>*

Ramon doubted Calan Dubrayle did anything 'social'. *<Father,>* he began. It felt strange calling him that. *<There's something going on here you might want to know about.>* He quickly explained the situation, which didn't take long as Dubrayle was well-briefed on the state of the city's defence. When he got to Governor Myron, the Treasurer looked thoughtful.

<Myron tells us he's defending the city with utmost vigour,> he told Ramon. *<Noros is a difficult province, but under Myron it's up-to-date with tax and levies and dissent is quickly quelled. He's well regarded here.>*

<Right now, he's endangering the entire city,> Ramon replied. *<He's using others as a shield, failing to support the defences, starving his own people and preparing to run with ships laden down with plunder. He needs to be told that he's on a battlefield now and subordinate to the military commander – Seth Korion.>*

<Korion's under warrant for deserting his post.>

<Seth has saved Noros from the Shihad.>

<Perhaps, but his orders were to stay in the North. Lord Sulpeter commands the Imperial Army, not Korion.>

<Would you rather there were still Noromen in Noros to pay those Imperial taxes and levies, Father? Or Amteh-worshippers giving their largesse to Sultan Rashid?>

<Sulpeter will defeat the Shihad in the spring,> Dubrayle said firmly. Then he dropped his voice. *<Then there's the matter of Julia.>*

So he does know. Ramon wasn't surprised; it made sense that Pavius or Myron would threaten Dubrayle as well. *<You've never met Julia . . . or me.>*

Dubrayle winced. *<I wish I had. You're probably wondering whether I care enough to modify my behaviour for a girl I've never met. I don't know how to answer that. It depends on what they want me to do.>*

Ramon realised that he'd have said the same thing in his father's position, but picturing Julia in the hands of strangers was ripping him up. *<I'm going to get her back, Father. Don't doubt that.>*

Dubrayle drummed his fingers on his desk, then said, *<Here in Pallas, people are more worried about Seth Korion than Rhys Myron. They see the insurrections in Rimoni – this 'Lord of Rym' – and speculate that Noros and Bricia will join him, under Korion's banner. Is that possible?>*

<It's preposterous,> Ramon snorted. <Seth believes in the empire more than you do! And as for the 'Lord of Rym', I've spent the best part of three years battling him – I'm in the Mercenary Guild of Becchio – and frankly, we've been losing. Word is, he's advancing north, capitalising on the Shihad disrupting the empire to seize more land.> Ramon stopped as a thought struck him. <Perhaps he's intending to join forces with the Shihad?>

<Why would a Yurosi do that?>

<A Yurosi who hated the empire might well do such a thing,> Ramon replied. <He's a butcher, Father. And we think he's some kind of necromancer, because his core legions are like draugs: they're mindlessly ferocious – we've seen them pluck arrows from their own guts. Some believe they can't be killed.>

Dubrayle leaned back in his chair, his face thoughtful. Ramon tsked impatiently – this discussion was supposed to be about a corrupt governor, not a Rimoni warlord – but he knew better than to interrupt his father's thoughts.

<Dear Kore . . . > the Treasurer breathed. <Reeker Night . . . Tear and Jest . . . Ryburn . . . and now this Lord of Rym.> He looked Ramon intently. <Very well, I will bring up Governor Myron, but I must tell you: I doubt I'll get anywhere. My enemies know about Julia and that can only be through Pavius Prelatus. They're squeezing me as well. I'm sorry, Ramon, but it looks very much as if both of our futures hinge on finding your daughter.>

They shared an intent look and Ramon felt an odd stirring, because they understood each other. He really is my father, and we're not so unalike. Running the Imperial Treasury must be like being a familioso or running a mercenary legion: you'd have to be smart and ruthless.

But neither liked emotional moments, so they rattled off perfunctory goodbyes.

Once his father's face had dissipated and he was alone, Ramon sat pondering the brief conversation. He's been threatened as well . . . and something about the Lord of Rym rang a bell. What was Reeker Night? I'll have to ask him about it, he thought, and realised that he was already looking forward to their next conversation.

When he re-joined the others, they were sharing hot tea and talking quietly about troop dispositions. They looked up anxiously and Seth asked, 'How did it go?'

'He'll do what he can, but turns out, Myron's got friends in *very* high places, so his hands are probably tied.'

'Then we're on our own?' Seth asked.

'Difficult to say,' Ramon answered, before silently adding, for Seth alone: *<There's only so far a man will go for kin he's never met, so it's not a lever Dubrayle's enemies can pull too hard upon.>* 'I think we'll need alternate plans,' he added, out loud.

Hysen's face fell. 'If we don't resolve this, the city will fall, or revolt.' He looked at Seth anxiously, clearly wondering which way he'd jump under such circumstances, but Seth gave no indication.

They had to part with the matter unresolved

Seth and Ramon made their way back to Lowertown, flitting like ghosts through frozen streets, the snow still thick on the icy gale. 'Our lads are going to freeze their arses off tonight,' Ramon commented.

'I know,' Seth replied, 'but think of those poor bastards in Rashid's army: they must be going through Hel – and all thanks to their own weather-magi, not that they'll know it.'

Latif had felt such utter misery in all his life only once before, the night he'd somehow escaped the slaughter of Sultan Salim's entire household, including his fellow impersonators and their families. Still raw from the murders of his wife and son and his sultan – his friend – he'd fled into the filthy, dangerous slums of Sagostabad, prey for any who saw him and with nothing to live for – until he'd been rescued by the touch of an elephant's trunk: Rani, looming out of the darkness to gently stroke his tear-stained face. That, and Sanjeep's kindness, to take in a battered stranger, had saved his life. Now, buried beneath blizzards exhaled from the mouth of Shaitan and yet burning up with a fever, it was Rani and Sanjeep standing by him once again.

His burned left arm had become infected, swelling up and oozing noisome pus, while his body temperature fluctuated wildly, first so hot he tried to bury himself in snow, then shivering with a cold so bone-deep, he had to be restrained from crawling into the firepit.

Piru-Satabam III no longer existed. The fourteen surviving elephants of the forty had been sent to join another elephant unit to make up the numbers. Selmir was still their commander, though: the only one of the three to have survived the fighting.

'By not going near it,' Ashmak had noted, in a whisper.

The days after the failed storming of the city blurred into one. Near-constant blizzards, winds so strong you could barely stand, snowfalls deeper than three men lying head to toe, and a biting cold that got *everywhere*. Tents were blown away, fire-pits were buried, sentries froze to death at their posts and everyone huddled together or died alone.

Before he fell ill, Latif persuaded Ashmak and Sanjeep that they needed to sleep with Rani, covering her with their tent-canvas, placing the how-dah in the lee of her body and tending a fire beside her head. Even in these Hel-ish conditions, she radiated heat. They grew accustomed to her occasional bowel movements and together they weathered the worst of the storm. Ashmak's pregnant Vereloni woman slept with him and Latif ignored their occasional coupling – it was one way to stay warm, after all – until the infection took him into his own delirious world.

In his dreams Salim died over and again, hanging in chains while the Masked Cabal blasted him with gnostic fire. When he cut Salim down, the sultan turned into Latif's dead son, and he cried blood . . .

He woke finally to find himself wrapped in an unpleasantly stinking blanket, with the taste of warm spiced mash on his tongue. He choked and spluttered, and realised Sanjeep was feeding him.

'Namaste,' the old Lakh said, his sand-and-honey voice a welcome sound.

'Thank Ahm!' Latif panted.

'God is great,' Sanjeep replied. 'Look, Rani, our friend is returned to us.'

The elephant's trunk snaked out and caressed Latif's face with what felt like fond curiosity. Latif noticed his arm was freshly bandaged and no longer agony.

'Ashmak persuaded a healer-mage to see you. He said restoring an archer to fighting capacity was better use of her time than helping men who would never fight again, even if they recovered.' Sanjeep's voice held no judgement on that, but Latif cringed a little.

'Other men suffered for my little burn.'

'Not just a "little burn", my friend. The infection was spreading. You were dying as surely as they are.'

Latif decided that maybe it was okay in that case. It was a good thought to carry back down into sleep.

The following days brought recovery, both in his body and in the weather. Even as a non-mage he could feel the supernatural elements of the storm receding hour by hour.

Unfortunately for the Shihad, however, normal weather in late Janune in high-country Noros was not a great deal more hospitable, especially in a Sunsurge year. By the time Latif was able to get about again, the skies were slate-grey cloud and the winds were gentler, but the thick snow was impossibly deep and the roads were impassable. Now the skies were once again flyable, every surviving windship had been sent to seek supplies.

Latif ventured out to empty their piss-bucket into the trench, then sought the feed tents to get straw for Rani. With so many dead, at least the rationing had been eased a little. He was standing in line, chatting mindlessly with a Gatti spearman with braided hair and frostbitten feet, when they heard a thudding sound: a column of mounted men, who came cantering into the midst of the camp.

'Who're they?' the Gatti wondered.

'Attam's heavy cavalry?' someone suggested.

'No, they got slashed up at Venderon,' Latif reminded them. 'These men look like—' He stopped suddenly. *Chod, those are* Yurosi *warhorses* . . .

'Watch out!' he yelped as the column of riders turned, spurs were rammed into flanks and suddenly their lances dipped and they were plunging through the snow towards the feed-line.

'Run!' someone yelled, and they scattered blindly, but Latif saw a rider bearing down on him and dived aside an instant before a lance-head skewered him. The rider impaled the Gatti man instead. All round them, Shihadi had been ridden or cut down and the Yurosi were wheeling about for another attack.

Latif came to his feet and almost without thinking, leaped for one of the Yurosi knights, crashing into the warhorse's flank and clinging on as his weight dragged them down, horse and all. They crashed into a snowdrift, Latif on top, holding onto the man's back and pressing his face into the snow. The horse was thrashing madly, huge hooves only just missing him, but he clung onto the fallen rider, silently begging him to give up and die.

The man pinned beneath Latif expired, suffocated in the snowdrift, as the feed-stores burst into flame–

–and just as suddenly, the attackers were gone.

Slowly the survivors got to their feet, cursing the Yurosi and praising Ahm, but Latif was too drained to do more than kneel over his enemy, shaking like a leaf, as heat from the burning straw washed over him.

'You there,' shouted a voice, one Latif knew. 'Is he dead?'

'Ai, Hazarapati Selmir,' Latif said, keeping his head down.

His commander loomed above him. 'And you killed him?' Selmir demanded.

'Ai, Hazarapati.' Latif kept his gaze on the ground, wishing he could just bolt. He'd met Selmir when he was Salim's impersonator and had made an enemy.

'Stand, hero,' Selmir said grandly.

Reluctantly, Latif stood, averting his face. 'I'm just a humble soldier, Hazarapati.'

He felt Selmir's' eyes searching him, then Selmir grabbed his arm and raised it, turning to face those watching. 'A Piru-Satabam man,' he proclaimed, as if he himself had taught Latif how to slay Yurosi raiders. 'The infidel shall not prevail – Ahm is Great!'

Then he strode away while Latif struggled not to faint in relief.

He didn't know me . . . Great Ahm, you are mighty indeed.

To escape this pavilion, Sultan Rashid Mubarak thought gloomily, *would be a profound relief.*

But the pavilion was the only thing that allowed him to avoid the eyes of his poor, suffering men, those he'd let down by failing to storm Norostein.

I gambled all on getting in on the first day . . . and Fate threw that wager back in my face. My weather-magi were outmatched and the backlash is destroying us . . . Mine the decision, mine the fault . . .

He knew he should be walking among his men, sharing their

hardship, but that first morning, he'd come across so many dead, frozen where they lay sleeping beneath inadequate blankets, wrapped in inadequate clothing, that he couldn't bear it. *Some of those men were wearing sandals, for Ahm's sake!*

Since then he'd retreated here, with the sycophants and the blame-avoiders, the parroting Godspeakers and the endless cycle of commanders reporting that their unit had been foremost in the battle and robbed of glory only by ill-chance. Finally he'd cleared them out too and pondered the débâcle alone.

Where is your 'genius' now? he berated himself. *How many have we lost to this storm? A hundred thousand? Two?* There *had* to be a way to get inside, some better way than just flinging men at the walls, but everything he could think of – the fire-ships, the aerial landings inside the walls – had failed him, and now he was short of windships too, needing those remaining to keep supply lines open.

It was painful to recognise a weakness in his personal armoury. His greatest triumphs had always been at a strategic level, but this siege had turned tactical. He needed his senapatis and hazarapatis to show their mettle now, to outwit the defenders, but he'd purged many of the best when he took control, in case they became a threat.

This is my *failure . . .*

A voice stole across his consciousness, saying, 'It's how we recover from defeat that reveals our mettle.' Ironhelm, cloaked and cowled, stood at the tent flap.

'Spare me the platitudes,' Rashid replied. 'I've said it many a time myself.'

'But you've not lived it.' The masked man strode to the map-table. 'The situation is now perilous, Sultan, but not hopeless. The Master stands with you.'

'Then have him send aid,' Rashid snapped. 'I've lost more than a hundred thousand men in just a week: half to the battle, and half to the cold thereafter. Illness is breaking out. Raiders are targeting our stores and food-dumps.' He pummelled the table despairingly. 'We tried *everything* – mass assaults, ram-ships, fire-ships, that accursed spear – and still they held. A fifteenth of our numbers, and *they held.*'

'Do not despair,' Ironhelm replied, his metallic mask distorting his humanity. 'The Master can help you.'

'I've already purchased his aid: I let your Master place one hand around my soul! His promise was revenge upon Yuros and a Throne of Thrones, ruling two continents: tell him to deliver.'

Ironhelm's mask moved, the expression changing to a taut smile. 'He will, if you let him. He can make your men hardier, to endure any conditions. You need only let him work his magic.'

Rashid felt his face go pale. 'I know what you offer and I will not have it. I want to rule men, not daemons.'

'Then I have naught else to say,' Ironhelm replied coldly. He strode for the flap, then turned and added, 'Best you take the city, Great Sultan. The Master does not tolerate failure, even in one as lofty as you.'

37

Mutual Treachery

Race and Love

The Book of Kore *and the Kalistham both identify a 'chosen race' – Frandian and Ahmedhassan respectively – for whom Paradise is exclusively reserved. Both preach racial exclusivity. Yet a five-minute stroll in any city in the land will tell you that love doesn't recognise these constraints. The heart leads and we follow. Racial purity is a lie.*

JOVAN TYR, HEALER, AQUILLEA 787

Freihaafen, Mollachia
Late Janune 936

Tarita woke on a frigid morning, huddled in her little tent with the cold paralysing her limbs and the enormity of the oncoming day freezing her mind. Her plan was so risky she'd doubted anyone would help her, but Kyrik Sarkany had been surprisingly receptive, as long as his wife Hajya was part of the exchange. That had required a further conversation with Asiv, who made a show of reluctance, but agreed. It was strange to negotiate a transaction both knew they would renege on, but she and the Gatti mage played along, maintaining the pretence.

Asiv thinks I'll bring men vital to the resistance into his reach . . . and he's right. I think he'll dangle Ogre and Hajya enough that we'll get a shot at snatching them . . . But am I deluding myself?

Valdyr and his wolf had already left for Cuz Sarkan, apparently a place significant to the dwyma, taking Jehana and Waqar. Rothgar Baredge was guiding them. She'd had an awkward farewell with Waqar, who'd told her plainly that her hopes of freeing an illegal construct were a waste of her skills.

'As an Ahmedhassan, it's your duty to come with us,' he'd said.

'As a Javonesi, you're lucky I've lifted a finger in your aid,' she'd retorted, hating his arrogant assumption that Mubaraks outweighed anyone else in the world and burning the last hope of romance ever blooming between them. 'But I still expect the reward you promised.'

It hadn't been an amicable parting and she did half-wonder if he was right: was she putting friendship ahead of rationality? In what world would anyone put poor Ogre before a dwyma-wielding princess?

But no: if she distracted Asiv, she'd still be helping them . . . And Ogre had rescued her at Epineo. *I owe him this.*

Freihaafen came alive as the sun rose, crimson and gold light blooming in the sky and turning the steam to magical pink clouds speared by shafts of light. Tarita joined the other residents at the lake, horned Mantauri and human silhouettes dark against the illuminated mists. It was otherworldly and beautiful.

Right now I'm free, she thought, immersing her cold limbs into the warm water. That felt good, and so did freedom . . . perhaps as good as her dream of being a prince's concubine. Then Kyrik Sarkany hailed her from the water's edge and she rose. It was time to begin.

She joined those who'd be risking their lives for her plan at the smithy, where several men and Mantauri were labouring under the direction of a burly, heavily bearded Rondian smith named Corley. Molten liquid was being poured into moulds for a variety of blades – zweihandles, shortswords, daggers and axe-heads. These needed a few more days of tempering, but Corley led them to his previous batch, which were being affixed to hilts or shafts while a leatherworker and his wife finished the scabbards. The weapons had a shimmery finish, the edges were brittle and the weight was lighter than Tarita was used to.

'I hate this argenstael,' Corley growled. 'It's too fragile, it's a bugger to sharpen and there's not enough heft.'

'But it'll slay the Possessed in one blow,' Kyrik replied, clapping his shoulder. 'Well done, my friend.'

Tarita made a practise lunge with a shortsword, then shook her head.

'I'll use the scimitar from Midpoint. I've never used a straight blade before and now's not the time to try something new. But I'll take an argenstael dagger.'

Once they'd all tried out various lengths and weights and made their choices, they wolfed down a hearty breakfast. Kyrik told them, 'Keep your regular blades too. If the argenstael breaks, you'll need a back-up. And if that's the case, remember to go for the head.' He turned to Tarita and yet again asked, 'Are you sure they won't deal honourably?'

'Absolutely certain.'

'It's my wife's life we're risking.'

'We'll retrieve her,' she said, with a confidence she didn't feel. *And you too, Ogre . . . I'll see you soon . . . or I'll see you in the Hereafter.*

Szajver River, East Mollachia

Jehana trudged along the path, her feet in heavy boots over woollen Yurosi bags called 'socks', with her face wrapped in scarves to protect her skin and shield her eyes. She was carrying what felt like her body-weight in heavy fur clothing, and a pack as well. Without the gnosis to lighten the load and strengthen her limbs, she would have collapsed.

'Are you bearing up?' Valdyr Sarkany asked, dropping back to her side. He was even more heavily laden, and his weathered face was strained. His eyes were narrowed against the glare off the snow.

'This is the most miserable place in the world,' she replied. 'Why would anyone choose to live in such a cold place when you've got a whole continent?'

Valdyr looked a little hurt at that. 'It is the land of my fathers – it is beautiful in summer.'

'Then holiday here in summer,' Jehana snapped back.

Valdyr looked at her with bleak amusement. 'The people of Mollachia do not "holiday", Princess. We struggle, we strive and we endure. And we enjoy nature's bounty.'

She glanced ahead at Rothgar Baredge, leading the way. The wolf Gricoama was padding along somewhere in the trees, keeping watch.

Waqar was bringing up the rear and keeping an eye on their back-trail. She'd spent time with Valdyr these past days as they made for this mysterious mountain, although the Mollach was difficult company. He was nervous of her, clearly because she was Ahmedhassan. She'd been offended, until he'd very awkwardly confessed what she'd suspected, that he'd been a breeding-house prisoner.

'Women of dark skin make me nervous,' he'd admitted. 'It's not personal.'

Jehana had never thought about what the breeding-houses must be like for Rondian prisoners; her sympathies had always been for the Ahmedhassans who had to endure coupling with slugskins. But a glimpse of what Valdyr had endured – and surely the women captives had suffered even worse – made her feel such places should be all shut down.

Don't we have enough magi by now?

At Freihaafen they'd spent some time communing with the dwyma, listening to it, sharing visions of it – he saw it as a Tree of Life, she as a Sea of Stars – but that was all either of them could currently do. She needed to gain full use of it and he to regain it. But Valdyr had revealed some of what he already knew: calling storms, freezing lakes and summoning lightning. Perhaps this mountain was where she could come into her full power?

'Cuz Sarkan,' she said, trying out the awkward Mollach word. 'It's like your name.'

'Ysh, "Sarkan" in my tongue means "Draken". My ancestors took the name to intimidate their foes,' Valdyr said with a grim smile. 'Cuz Sarkan is a volcano, a fire mountain. In our lore, draken breathe fire.'

'Is such a place safe?'

'The volcano hasn't erupted for many generations. People don't go there often, though: there's no drinkable water, no life, because of the toxic fumes.'

'Then what will we find?' Jehana wondered. 'Dwyma is the energy of life. If nothing lives there . . . ?'

'I don't know – it's just what I've been told to do,' Valdyr replied.

'By ghosts?' she clarified.

'Ysh, by ghosts.'

'I hope your ghosts know what they're doing,' she commented, making him smile. 'Is it much further?' She really had no idea where they were. Maps were all very well, but these frozen mountains were bewildering. They'd been travelling for three days now and how Rothgar found them a path, she had no idea.

'Not far now,' Valdyr told her. He paused and pointed down the valley to a reddish ribbon winding through the snow. 'See, that river is flowing, despite the cold: it's the Szajver River, the Bloodmouth. It emerges from beneath Cuz Sarkan and never freezes. We'll be at the mountain mid-afternoon.' The heartening news re-energised her tired muscles.

When Valdyr went to join Rothgar, Waqar caught her up. She still wasn't used to seeing his beard so unkempt. He was eying their companions suspiciously. 'Are you sure you trust this Valdyr?' he murmured. 'If you succeed in this place, you'll gain full use of the dwyma – but he'll *regain* it. He'll know how to use it and you won't. You'll be in his power.'

'Brother,' she replied, 'you *have* to put aside the Shihad. These Yurosi are not enemies.'

'Sister, you're naïve. The power you wield could be turned on our people. I doubt this Mollach prince has forgotten his time in Kesh.'

Jehana felt compelled to defend the younger Sarkany. 'I believe his heart is good.'

'We'll see,' Waqar said in a low voice. 'You told me he's called storms. He's exactly what we most fear: someone who could destroy our army.'

'He hates the empire more than he hates us,' Jehana replied.

Waqar studied her face intently, then sighed. 'I hope you're right.'

Osiapa River, Mollachia

Tarita scowled as the scrying spell she'd woven into the steam rising from their cooking pot failed to give her the images she sought. She'd been trying to use clairvoyance to find Jehana and Waqar, but the mountains and snow were too effective a barrier.

'No luck?' Kyrik asked, who'd been focusing on Valdyr, but with no better fortune.

'None,' she admitted. 'We could use your blood to trace your brother, but it's a slow and difficult spell.'

The Mollach king grimaced, then shook his head. 'We can't help them, or them us. Let's press on. We're already cutting it fine.' He rose to his feet. 'We need to be there in three hours and there's still a good few miles to go.'

He doused the fire and in minutes they were once again trudging through snow in temperatures barely above freezing. Tarita found the clothing: thick fur coats with deep hoods, gloves and socks and boots, heavy and uncomfortable, but they had a pleasing anonymity as well, useful in case Asiv's scouts had spotted them. But their own scouts reported no one on the trail, nor any sign that Asiv knew from which direction they'd appear.

There were only four in the immediate party: herself, Kyrik and Korznici, and the bound prisoner, Sezkia Zhagy. For appearances, Kyrik and Korznici were wearing wrist-bindings as well: at the exchange, they'd be pretending to be Valdyr and Jehana.

But on a different, less open trail, Kip and Maegogh had a war-party on the move. No one believed that Asiv would be fooled by the 'exchange' – the point was to get their surprise extra warriors as close to the site as possible when violence broke out.

I can take down Asiv, Tarita had told them, praying she was right. *You handle the rest.*

Fearing Sezkia would give them trouble, she was still gagged and blindfolded, which meant she had to be walked, an awkward hindrance. Remembering the demure, kindly girl she'd been, Kyrik was still hoped for some way to exorcise the daemon. The three of them were loosely roped together, to give the semblance of captivity, but he and Korznici could unloop their hands easily, while Sezkia was properly bound.

Valdyr said his friend Nara knows ways to cure the infected. I really hope that's true.

He caught up with Korznici, distracting himself by musing that for all the time the Sydian girl and Rothgar had been spending together, precious little romance was apparent. Taking a chance, he asked, 'All is well?'

'Ysh,' Korznici replied. He'd met few young people as self-possessed and unemotional as her, but as a Sfera mage, he guessed she'd had to grow up fast.

'Rothgar cares about you,' he said. 'You know that, don't you?'

She gave him a quizzical look. 'I know.' *Mind your own business*, her expression warned.

'I didn't think you Sydian women were shy about these things?'

'I care about him also,' she replied. 'But I am now head of the Sfera. I must strengthen the mage-blood in our tribe and your friend is not mage.'

'Ah.'

'I would sleep with him if he asked, even so; but he wishes marriage or nothing.'

That sounded like Rothgar. 'He's an honourable man.'

'He's a stupid man,' she sniffed. 'But a good man, also.' She made a cutting gesture with her hand, ending the subject. 'Is it far?'

Kyrik looked around, getting his bearings. The rendezvous, confirmed only that morning to minimise each party's preparations, was a ruined keep on the north shore of Lake Droszt. Kip and his party should already be near the site; doubtless Asiv's men were also close.

'Next rise, we'll see the lake,' he said, then he called to Tarita, 'We should prepare here.'

Tarita joined them and re-affirmed her hold on Sezkia's gnosis while Kyrik and Korznici got to work. Hajya had been the nearest thing to a mother the young Sfera had; she wanted her back as much as he did.

He and Korznici had similar gnostic affinities, primarily Theurgy, and particularly illusion. He set about building a robust deception, one that would survive close examination, which took time and concentration. First he altered his face, then wove a concealing illusion around his magical aura. Then they pulled out the ropes Tarita had prepared, which gave the appearance of being enchanted with a Chain-rune of her casting. Korznici did the same.

When they were done, anyone looking at them would see Valdyr and Jehana. It wasn't a disguise they could maintain for long, or under stress, but for most men and magi, it would suffice.

But will it fool a daemon-possessed Mask long enough for us to cut him down? Kyrik wondered.

Hegikaro Castle, Mollachia

Dragan Zhagy gazed out over his empty throne hall, wondering why any of this had happened. He hadn't spoken in days, when he'd once been the nexus of the community. *I was Gazda. I had the respect of all.*

But Kyrik Sarkany was turning this kingdom into a pigsty, Abraxas reminded him, and it was almost a relief to hear that hideous voice. Since the bloody coronation, both Abraxas and Asiv had been excluding him from the shared intellect, leaving him like a piece of fruit at the end of the harvest, rotting on the branch.

The rebels have my daughter, Dragan snarled back.

Then he thought: *Niy, you have my daughter, daemon: my beautiful, innocent daughter.*

Innocent? Abraxas cackled slyly. *Yes, she was innocent . . . But at least you're king, eh? Rejoice.*

It was true – he was king, the thing a gazda was meant to protect the people against. A King of Nobody, because no one came any more, for dread of his once-respected Vitezai Sarkanum. Ordinary people locked themselves away in cellars, eating their stores and praying for a miracle to free them.

I agreed to take you into myself to depose Kyrik, not to destroy Mollachia, you filth!

In retaliation, Abraxas *lashed* him, raking mental claws through his head, shredding his awareness until he sagged weakly on the throne, gasping for breath and his tiny rebellion ended unmarked. *You don't matter any more,* the daemon taunted him. Somewhere in the towers above him, Asiv was deciding the fate of Mollachia with his sinister new allies.

The Angels of the Last Day are here . . .

Then he sat up at the sound of boots in the courtyard outside the western window, the first noise he'd heard all day. So many had fled the castle and those left were silent in all they did, haunting the keep like wraiths.

He got up slowly and walked to the barred window. Below him, a pair of black-eyed guards were unhooking the manacles and chains binding Ogre to the wooden cross-piece where he'd been bound, kneeling in his own piss and shit. The creature lurched to his feet, weak and unsteady. They led him to a trough, let him drink and wash, then fed him slops.

Another pair led Hajya, Kyrik Sarkany's barbarian wife, up from the dungeons. She was clad only in a ragged, bloody shift and she howled at the sunlight, throwing up hands to protect her black orbs. Abraxas dwelt in her too, but they'd anointed her purely for torment. She was possessed, not a shepherd with some self-determination. Her emaciated, shaking body was covered in sores, her once-black curls were tangled and grey. Broken . . . *almost*.

She still fights, Dragan noted with grudging admiration. Few of his men had fought so long.

He spun as the double doors at the end of the hall crashed open and Asiv Fariddan strode in, flanked by the immense masked figures of Scaramu and Cadearvo. He'd caught glimpses of their real faces; they were monsters, like the Ogre-creature, but Asiv tiptoed around them as if they were royalty.

'So, Dragan, there's been a change of plan,' Asiv drawled.

Dragan's heart thudded. 'What change?'

He knew Asiv had decided upon some kind of hostage-exchange with the rebels: Ogre and Hajya for his Sezkia and some others, but he hadn't shared the details, or even permitted Dragan to be involved.

'I'm needed elsewhere,' Asiv said, to Dragan's surprise. 'One of my scouts spied Valdyr on the move and I must ensure whatever he's doing comes to an unhappy ending. You'll take my place on the hostage recovery.'

Dragan blinked in surprise – and hope. 'To recover my Sezkia?'

'Among other things,' Scaramu growled. 'But I'm in control.'

He'd have agreed to anything, just to be there. 'Of course.'

'Then come,' Asiv said, turning and marching to the door. 'Our vessels await.'

Dragan trailed the three Masks like an after-thought to the battlements, where two windships, a Keshi skiff and an empire sloop, were moored to the walls. Ogre and Hajya were pushed into the hold of the sloop. The Sydian was still mewling piteously against the sunlight, but the construct complied stoically. Dragan followed Scaramu aboard, while Cadearvo followed Asiv to the skiff. The moment they were on board, the small craft rose swiftly into the air, wind rushed to their sail and they surged away.

'Where are they going?' Dragan wondered.

Scaramu regarded him coldly from behind her inhuman mask. 'That's of no matter. Our business is to slaughter these rebel fools and capture the Merozain, if we can.'

'But I thought we were exchanging prisoners?' *If this turns to blood, Sezkia will be helpless.* 'Sezkia–'

'If she survives, well and good. If not . . .' Scaramu faced him and said, 'Some advice: there's no room for sentiment in the Master's service. Think only of yourself. All else is weakness.'

I have no desire to be in his service at all, he thought miserably. Abraxas just laughed.

There had to be some way to keep the daemon out of his mind, he was sure, but Asiv had never shown him how. A mage would know, but he'd never been that. Nor had Sezkia. They'd been lambs fed to lions.

Getting the sloop underway took time, but there was no hurry: the rendezvous was still an hour away. As Abraxas gradually opened him up to the full shared mind, he realised that his Vitezai were converging on a ruined fort on the north shore of Lake Droszt.

Then Scaramu glided up. 'It's time.'

38

Without Hope

The Battle of Jusse, 791

The First Argundian War, 790-792, was the first open fracturing of the Rondian Empire. The Battle of Jusse, in which Martius Magnus' Rondian legions were lured into a trap and defeated, remains the pinnacle of Argundian military history. The Argundians claim inspiration from the voorvul, a native fox which, when cornered, will react with extraordinary ferocity; it has been known to slay creatures many times its size.

GLASSYN BYNE, RONDIAN MAGE-HISTORIAN, 908

Cuz Sarkan, Mollachia
Late Janune 936

The thick clouds clinging to the stony path swallowed the travellers and in moments they'd moved from brightness to twilit gloom. Valdyr thought the air was warmer, though, and it had a sulphuric reek. Rothgar was somewhere ahead; Gricoama prowled the back-trail.

Waqar joined him, his sister a few paces behind. 'Tell me about the volcano,' the Keshi prince said.

'I've never been there,' Valdyr replied, 'but it's spoken of in our tales. There's a crater with a ring-shaped lake around a central spire of granite – the old core, people say. In the tales, draken dwell there: the Stonefolk, the first-folk of Mollachia, used to sacrifice to the drakenlord for a good harvest.'

'Sacrifice what?' Jehana asked, wrinkling her nose.

'Maidens,' Valdyr admitted. 'It was long ago.'

Barbarian, her eyes said. 'Why does no one ever sacrifice virgin boys?' she sniffed.

'Who'd want one?' Valdyr asked, only realising he'd made a joke when Jehana snorted.

'But these are just fairy tales, ai?' Waqar said.

'Of course. There are no such things as draken – or there wasn't, until the Pallas Animagi bred them.'

They were climbing steadily. First the vegetation vanished, then the snow, so now they were traversing stone and gravel and small tarns of tainted water. But the mist clung to the slopes, never affording them more than a few hundred feet of visibility.

'Whereabouts do we need to go to find what you're looking for?' Jehana asked.

'All I was told was "inside the mountain",' Valdyr replied.

'By a ghost,' Waqar said sceptically.

'Yes, by a dead woman who was once Luhti, or Lanthea.' He glanced at Jehana, who knew the name. 'Before she died, she told me the seed of the Elétfa is here at Cuz Sarkan.'

'Why would anyone put such a precious thing in such a dangerous place?' Waqar wondered.

'I don't know. Maybe to ensure that only one capable of using it could find it? We need to hurry,' he added tersely, an oppressive feeling building inside him.

Someone's trying to find me, he thought, worried. He couldn't create wards to block scrying, but the dwyma cloaked him. He hurried on, stroking the wolf's neck when Gricoama gave him a worried stare. *Ysh, I know*, he thought. *The hunt is on.*

Asiv Fariddan took his skiff right to the edge of the cloudbank that enveloped the slopes of Cuz Sarkan, then set it down on a flat expanse of rough gravel and pumice. He took the time to lash down the sails, while Cadearvo waited impatiently.

The enormous construct-magus, a foot taller than Ogre, thanks to his straighter spine, had removed his mask, revealing his brutally handsome features. He looked impassively confident. After flexing his shoulders and fingers, he drew his massive falchion and shifted into an elaborate, deadly routine. Asiv, no swordsman himself, could recognise real skill and power when he saw it.

For the past few nights, Cadearvo and Scaramu had shared the guest room at Hegikaro Castle below Asiv's royal suite. He'd heard them pounding at each other until they'd actually broken the bed.

'We're the superior breed,' Cadearvo had boasted next morning. 'One day our kind will rule yours.'

Having him so near, with that big blade in hand, was not a comforting sensation.

That there was a rank above him in Naxius' order was also troubling, especially since Asiv had regarded himself as the Master's right hand. And Cadearvo had a different daemon inside him: Shaitan himself, he claimed, which was even more frightening.

I must place my faith in the Master. He has never let me down . . .

With that thought to steel him, Asiv finished his task, loosened his own scimitar, then pointed northeast, where a track could be discerned. 'That way, I believe.'

Inside a few minutes Asiv found footprints in the gravel – and wolf-prints too, which gave him pause. Waqar didn't overly worry him; by reputation he was more concerned with honour than winning, but the wolf was a menace, his bite deadly as argenstael. Jehana, both a mage and a dwymancer, was an unknown, but she was the true prize here, the Master had said. He wondered why.

But the greatest threat might be the brute behind him.

I'm loyal, he reminded himself. *The Master won't turn his back on me for these monsters.*

'We'll have to run,' he told Cadearvo. 'Night-sight won't work in these clouds and I don't intend to fly face-first into a cliff.' He turned and broke into a jog and Cadearvo followed suit, his weight shaking the ground as they closed in on their prey . . .

Lake Droszt, Mollachia

Tarita Alhani crouched at the edge of the pines, looking down from the ridge to the old ruin at the edge of the lake where the exchange would take place. The sky was grey, but it was dry. Beyond the crumbling grey mound of stone, the frozen Lake Droszt spread before her, gleaming in the stark white landscape. Smoke drifted from chimneys in Hegikaro, a few miles south across the ice, and from villages and farmsteads to the south and west.

Concealed in the pines behind her, about a minute from the fortress if they sprinted, were a dozen Mantauri, Fridryk Kippenegger's best fighters. At her side were Kyrik and Korznici, disguised as Valdyr and Jehana – even she'd had a difficult time penetrating their disguise. They were taking care to use the false names too, for Sezkia was still aware, despite being blindfolded and her gnosis Chained. Tarita was not alone in being convinced there would be hidden enemies. Treachery here was a given.

Then someone called her name in the aether, a throaty male voice with a heavy Mollach accent. <*Yes?*> she answered, choosing Rondian.

The man responded in kind. <*We come: you should be able to see our ship.*>

A square-sailed vessel was approaching from the direction of Hegikaro. <*Who are you?*> she demanded. <*Where's Asiv?*>

<*I am Dragan Zhagy,*> he responded. <*Asiv is not here.*>

Instantly, her hackles rose. <*Where is he?*>

<*In Hegikaro,*> he replied.

She studied him through the link: a grey-haired Mollach with grizzled, lupine features.

<*He sent me. Sezkia is my daughter.*>

It was *almost* plausible. <*If this goes wrong, your daughter dies first,*> she warned.

<*If she dies, you'll scream for all eternity,*> Dragan told her with flat certainty. <*I'll see to it myself.*>

She didn't respond but prepared for the agreed fly-past. Kyrik and Korznici removed their hats, showing Valdyr and Jehana's faces, and she pulled Sezkia's hood from her head. The possessed woman glared at her, but she was unable to do more than grunt. Tarita checked the Chain-rune, which still held, then signalled to Dragan. <*You may approach.*>

The sloop circled the keep, then skimmed past their position, some sixty yards overhead. Dragan Zhagy was in the prow and she counted a skeleton crew of six to fly the vessel, as agreed. Her heart thudded as she saw Ogre, chained to the rail, his head bowed, looking at her miserably. He wasn't physically gagged, and he was trying to shout, although no words came. *He wants to warn me . . . but I already know this is going to be a bloodbath . . .*

Beside her friend was a wretched-looking woman, cringing in the light. Tarita heard Kyrik's despairing groan as he saw his wife. 'Silence, *Valdyr*,' she reminded him.

The vessel swung away, back towards the lake, and Dragan called, <*We are satisfied: go to the north wall of the keep. The roof is flat. We will dock against the south wall.*>

Also as agreed. She signalled agreement, then tugged on the ropes. Sezkia was still worryingly compliant as Tarita escorted the three 'prisoners' down the slope, through a broken postern gate and into a chamber almost overgrown with dead ivy. Engaging sylvan gnosis, she opened a path to a curved stairway and led the way upwards.

The ruined keep was just a blockhouse, no inner courtyards or bailey, and a flat roof that doubled as a fighting platform. There was a large hole on the east side where the roof had partially collapsed.

She put Sezkia beside her, with Korznici on her left and Kyrik on her right, shielding hard in case someone decided the easiest way to solve this was to mow them all down, but the sloop came gliding in and gently kissed the far wall. Dragan was in the prow, his glacial eyes on his daughter.

Then someone emerged from the hold and Tarita caught her breath, because they had Ogre's bulk and power, but whoever it was stood straighter and moved with predatory grace. The figure was armoured, with a female breastplate, and a skull-mask of emerald hues had a red snake emerging like a tongue.

Tarita had heard of Scaramu, the Angel of Plague, but her eyes flashed to Ogre as a sickening thought struck her. 'Who are you?' she called.

The giant woman pulled her mask from her face. She was clearly akin to Ogre, but she had lustrous dark hair and a more regular, narrow face, smoother skin, with high cheekbones and a heavy jaw.

'I think you know,' she replied in a deep, sensuous voice. 'I am Semakha.' Then her eyes flashed black. 'Give us your prisoners and we'll give you this' – she glanced at Ogre contemptuously – '*thing*.'

Oh no, Ogre! For a moment Tarita could barely think past her grief for her friend. *You must be devastated . . .*

Ogre, gazing at her with a despairing expression, made a warning gesture with his head.

I know, Ogre . . . My poor man, I know . . .

Tarita straightened and took on the persona of a cold-hearted wheeler-dealer, cashing in some dupes for those who mattered to her. 'Well,' she said, 'here are my prisoners.'

'Did you have any trouble with them?' Semakha asked.

'They never knew what hit them,' she replied, placing her new argenstael dagger against Sezkia's cheek, which made Dragan Zhagy hiss. 'Swapping two for three isn't very fair though: perhaps I should keep one back?'

The Mollach king growled like a beast, but Semakha guffawed. 'I thought we'd be the heartless bastards here, Merozain. Take what was agreed and be thankful they're intact.'

Tarita pushed the argenstael knife-tip right up against Sezkia's eyeball. 'There are two of you, one of me. So here's how this will play out: Ogre and Hajya may approach, and I'll send the two pandaemancers. I'll keep this one here, for surety. Then once we've both inspected, I'll release this one.'

She watched Dragan and Semakha confer: the big ogress appeared willing to comply, but Dragan, clearly anxious for his daughter, looked hostile. Semakha overruled him and called, 'One at a time.'

Tarita hesitated. *They don't know Jehana . . . although Abraxas might . . .*

But sending Korznici forward would put her in the most danger and she wanted Kyrik and Korznici to be able to protect each other. 'No,' she called back, 'my way: both at once.'

Semakha opened her cloak, revealing a diamond-tipped iron rod, two feet long, in her belt. 'Very well. On the count of three . . .'

Tarita gripped Korznici's shoulder, whispering, 'The moment this goes bad, get to Kyrik.'

And in her mind, she heard Maegogh's rumble: *<Merozain girl, there are men coming out of the frozen lake . . . >*

Cuz Sarkan, Mollachia

As it became steeper, Jehana found herself having to dig deeper into her reservoir of gnostic energy. The trek to Epineo had hardened her a little, but not enough. And now the air was becoming warmer, the borrowed furs she was forced to wear made her sweat profusely.

Finally, *thankfully*, Rothgar bade them stop and they took off the heavy coats, rolled them into bundles and concealed them off the path. Gricoama came padding up from behind. Valdyr stroked the beast's head. 'He's worried.'

'You can speak with him?' Waqar asked, in Rondian.

'Not with words.' Valdyr indicated their back-trail. 'He thinks we're being followed, and so do I.'

Jehana's throat went dry. If they were being pursued, it was likely to be Asiv Fariddan himself. Alyssa Dulayne had been terrifying enough, and Waqar had told her that when he'd tried to save Sultan Salim, the cabal members had just toyed with him.

I'll not be so useless this time, he'd vowed this morning. She dreaded that he'd have the chance to make good on that promise. And Valdyr was increasingly brittle. The mere mention of Asiv's name made him flinch and he was getting jumpier moment by moment.

As they set out, Waqar murmured in her ear, 'Is there some history between Valdyr and this Asiv?'

She gave him an uncomfortable look, not wanting to betray Valdyr's privacy . . . but this was *Waqar.* 'The dwyma keeps few secrets. He was nine years old when he went on Crusade – the Second Crusade, seventeen years ago. He was captured and sent to a breeding-house run by Asiv.'

Waqar stared. 'Dear Ahm,' he murmured. He clutched her arm. 'If we're cornered, we've got to look out for each other, Sister. Neither Rothgar or Valdyr will stand a chance against someone like Asiv.'

She swallowed and nodded to show she understood.

They reached a rubble-strewn slope where a broken piece of statuary lay, the huge head of a stern, bearded man. Gazing up the slope, they saw the headless shape of a seated figure.

'It's my ancestor, Melgren Sarkany,' Valdyr said. 'They say he actually learned how to breathe fire, by imbibing lamp-oil, then lighting it as he spat it out.'

'People do that in the East for entertainment,' Waqar replied, off-handed.

Valdyr raised an eyebrow. 'Melgren did it to burn an enemy's face off.'

Jehana shuddered. 'How much further? We're losing the light.'

'The statue was set here to mark the way to the crater lake.' He indicated a narrow defile that split the slope behind the broken monument. 'It's that way.'

They looked back, but nothing stirred the mist. Valdyr scowled. 'He's coming, I know he is . . .' He turned to Rothgar. 'My friend, this is no place for you. There are magi coming, and the place we're going is of the dwyma. You're between two fires.'

Rothgar's weathered face closed up. 'Is that a command?' he asked reluctantly.

'It is. Hide, and await us. If someone comes after us, don't try to intervene, *please*. You're too valuable to us to lose in a mage-duel.'

'As you command,' the ranger said, sounding resigned. He stroked Gricoama's head, gave Waqar and Jehana a cursory nod, then trotted away, quickly disappearing amongst the rubble.

Jehana was impressed: an Eastern lord would more likely have instructed a lesser to stay close, ready to be sacrificed in a crisis. Clearly the Sarkany brothers were of a different mettle. But that nobility of spirit didn't allay her fears. *In the East, the naïve die young.*

Entering the cutting, the walls grew steeper, but now they were descending into warm, fuggy air reeking of sulphur. They closed up. Rock-falls all but blocked the way in places, but they clambered over them and continued, listening hard in both directions. The air grew hotter and fouler, until they had to wrap scarves around their noses and mouths to go on.

At last, emerging onto a truly outlandish vista, all three stopped and stared.

They were in the crater, with the rim hundreds of feet above them. The stone looked like slate and jet, all jagged black rocks and gleaming with moisture. A ring of bubbling water filled the crater, sending steam streaming upwards into the gloom. The sun was gone and the shadows were racing in, but clearly visible in the middle of the lake was a spire of stone a hundred feet tall, leaning somewhat like a drunken man.

Her heart thudded as she saw an arched doorway carved into the granite of the central spire. 'Look – that must be the way–' she exclaimed.

Valdyr followed her gaze. 'Yes . . . I think it must be . . .' He stroked Gricoama's fur, then gave a helpless shrug and said, 'So, you're both magi: how do we get across?'

Jehana smiled. 'Leave that to me.' Finally faced with a task she could do, she raised her hands confidently and stepped to the edge of the lake. 'I can walk on water.'

She sent ripples of pale energy into the surface of the water at her feet, then stepped onto the bubbling surface as it congealed around her, into foot-wide circles that held her weight.

'Step where I step,' she called over her shoulder. 'And hurry, they'll only last a minute.'

Valdyr and Waqar glanced sideways at each other. Jehana sensed a little mistrust between Yurosi and Ahmedhassan, but Valdyr stepped onto the first 'pad', wobbling a little, then, wholly borne up by her spell, he took the next step. His arms flailed but aided by a nudge of kinesis from Waqar, he righted himself. A few moments later, Gricoama took a hesitant step, then followed until he too was moving with increasing confidence.

As the light failed, the surface of the water took on a luminescent blue-green glow. Twice the depths flashed scarlet, then faded, hinting at lava breaking the bottom of the lake, then cooling. This was a liminal place, ever-changing, fragile and perilous.

Jehana was first to alight on the tiny central isle. The square-cut opening in the spike of granite loomed over them. Shaping volcanic rock was no mean feat; she wondered whose path they were walking.

When the two men and the wolf arrived, she couldn't resist a smile of triumph as they leaped from the surface of the water to join her.

'Shukran, Sister,' Waqar murmured approvingly, but it was the tiny hint of a smile on Valdyr's face that gave her the greater pride.

See? I am an Eastern woman and I have worth. She hoped her little deed would help him heal.

39

Under the Mountain

Hermetic: Sylvanic Gnosis

Sylvan gnosis is the manipulation of flora: it is therefore perhaps the closest Study to the heretical dwymancy. Sylvan-magi have pried most intently into that heresy, seeking an edge, a foolish search . . . for if they were ever to succeed, the magi would turn on them as they turned on Eloy and his flock.

RUE BALADYNE, GNOSTIC HISTORIAN, CANOSSI 643

Cuz Sarkan, Mollachia
Late Janune 936

Valdyr Sarkany had expected the passage in the spire of volcanic rock to lead up and away from where stones melted and flowed like treacle, but instead, it revealed steps going down into heat so intense they all reeled, their skin instantly dripping wet. There was no other light than a faint red glow emanating from the stairs, which spoke of greater heat to come. Waqar removed his helm, holding it in his left hand, with his drawn scimitar in his right. Valdyr kept his zweihandle on his back; the space was too confined for such a weapon. But he rested his hand on the grip of his argenstael dagger.

'I'll go first,' Waqar offered and Valdyr nodded agreement. Looking upwards he saw no ceiling, but the smoke and heat were clearly escaping somehow, through fissures in the jagged, broken roof.

Waqar took the stairs, moving cautiously, Jehana behind him and Valdyr bringing up the rear. It was like climbing down a spiral-shaped chimney. The hot breeze whipping them, drying skin and eyes, was foul with sulphur and barely breathable, but Valdyr found that if he opened to the dwyma, it sustained him, feeding him enough air to breathe. He sensed Jehana doing the same, but when Waqar stopped to tie a scarf against his nose and mouth, they could see he was breathing hard, visibly fighting panic and suffocation.

Luckily, it wasn't long before the steps opened onto a ring-shaped platform in a circular chamber overlooking a shaft dropping to a lake of molten stone, bubbling red-gold. It might be two hundred or so feet below, but the heat was almost unbearable. Valdyr realised that the rock spire grew wider beneath the lake surface, and that it was hollow, but the polished stone of the steps hinted at years of stability. The smooth black walls gave no clue as to why this place even existed.

They had to shout to be heard over the roaring rush of searing air. Gricoama's fur was plastered to him and the wolf, profoundly distressed, kept growling at the glowing pit below.

'Where now?' Waqar shouted, looking round – there was only this ring of flat stone around the crater lake, and no further steps down.

'We should look around,' Jehana yelled, and Valdyr nodded agreement.

The Mubaraks drifted to the right while Valdyr led Gricoama the other way, seeking some sign of what they should do now. *What is it you expected me to find, Luhti?* He wished she could have told him more.

It occurred to him that the answer might lie in dwymancy, so he rested a hand on Gricoama, closed his eyes, shut out the fiery cavern and the Ahmedhassans on the opposite side and instead sought the dwyma, whispering, '*I am here.*'

Something chimed inside him and he felt an incredible sense of fluid energy streaming through him, like blood in the veins or sap in leaves or rivers flowing, shimmering through him, jolting him awake and alive, a capillary in a vast network of life. His eyes flew open and lit up as he looked up at a tree-shaped sea of stars as if seen from the *inside*: the Elétfa as he'd never seen it before. It was breath-taking, beautiful, and so many things at once: light, water, blood, energy, birth and death. Branches rose and stretched, then flowed down and became roots that fed upwards again, thousands of them.

And there, high in the Tree, he saw what he needed: seeds of life, hanging in the branches, far out of reach. But a spiralling path of light climbed the inside of the Tree towards them. That's where he had to go.

'Do you see it?' he called to Jehana, his voice filled with awe.

Jehana followed the rim of the platform around the shaft, fearfully conscious of the lake of fire below. Although she was sweating profusely, the roaring heat of the volcano was instantly drying her up, desiccating her skin further every second. She had no idea what to do next. At Epineo, she'd been awakened, or so she thought, but although she could sense great power here, she felt estranged from it. She glanced across the chamber and saw Valdyr had stopped examining the walls and was just standing there, his hand on Gricoama's coat, staring into space with joy washing across his face.

'Do you see it?' he called.

She didn't, but she realised she'd been so busy examining the *physical* elements of the chamber, she'd forgotten the *metaphysical*. Closing her eyes, she opened up to the dwyma as Valdyr had shown her when they'd first met. It responded instantly, as if it were only a heartbeat from her fingertips: first as a sensation of energy blazing past, then as water, and finally as stars in the firmament. She sighed in completeness as a Tree of Light lit up all around her . . .

Then something engulfed her, giant hands grasped at her and she shrieked in shock and horror as the Tree vanished and a terrifying visage snarled into her face . . .

Waqar was on the far side of the chamber when Valdyr spoke, examining a symbol etched into the stonework, a Tree whose branches curved around to become roots – as his sister exclaimed exultantly, he turned to see her near the door, hands raised to the roof as if experiencing some kind of religious awakening, mirroring Valdyr's stance. Their faces were entranced.

Then he spotted two dark figures, one slender, the other bulky, emerging from the doorway behind them. He shouted a warning, but he was too late: his sister was trapped by one massive arm against the chest of a giant figure with a dun-coloured skull-mask. He let the mage-bolt he'd prepared dissipate, not wanting to risk striking her, and whipping out the argenstael dagger, he tore around the curved walkway towards them.

'I have the Master's prize,' the giant boomed to his comrade, presumably Asiv Fariddan. 'Kill the Mollach.'

Then Skull-mask turned back to Waqar and a blast of kinesis and flame and energy sent Waqar careering backwards. He struck the curved wall again and spun along it in a whirling ball of sparks that sent all his senses into utter turmoil. He hit the platform, bounced, slid and pitched over the edge of the walkway–

Valdyr was ripped from the beauty of the tree by Jehana's scream. His eyes flew open, although the Tree remained lit before him, and he glimpsed Jehana in the grasp of something too large to be human. Gricoama was turning awkwardly on the narrow platform – until he was suddenly hurled by kinesis into the empty space, yowling as he vanished in a flash of fire into the shaft below. His heart lurching, Valdyr tried to react, but familiar talons wrapped about his mind as a lithe figure strode towards him.

'Little Valdyr,' his enemy gloated, his blade snaking out. 'We're bound to each other, my darling. All of your most important moments were with me. Shall we make more memories?'

Lake Droszt, Mollachia

With every step the hostages took towards each another, Tarita could feel the tension increasing, shrieking in the air around her. The illusory faces were holding up well, concealing Kyrik and Korznici's identities, but they surely only had moments before this all went to Hel. Kyrik's rage at what had been done to his wife was bleeding into the air; any moment might give everything away. Although Ogre was stoic, Hajya looked dreadful, radiating the wrongness of the possessed.

She could be as much a danger to us as anyone else here . . .

Semakha was poised behind Ogre, no weapons drawn but all her potential for destruction evident in the bulge of her biceps and the set of her jaw. The Plague-mask of Scaramu sat on her forehead like a twisted helmet. Dragan Zhagy beside her was fixated on his daughter, and the knife Tarita held to the girl's eye. His teeth bared, he struggled to contain his savagery.

She could sense Kip and his Bullheads clambering up the northern side of the rise; they'd moved when they saw men riding from the lake . . .

. . . then she saw Hajya's eyes flash black and whispered, <Now,> into the aether . . .

. . . Just as Semakha shouted, 'Attack!'

And everybody moved at once.

Kyrik was burningly conscious that when their disguises were inevitably penetrated, Korznici was his responsibility – but so was Hajya. Seeing his worldly-wise, earthy wife in that dreadful state, systematically destroyed before being sent back to taunt him, was ripping at his soul. It was all he could do to keep his veil of illusion intact.

Each step they took felt like the tread of Kore marching towards the Last Day. His nerves stretched taut, he started loosening the bonds on his wrists. A torrent of spells dammed up behind his lips, he awaited the moment.

Then the ogress in the Plague-mask roared, 'Attack!' and Hel burst forth.

Through the hole in the roof at the eastern side of the keep poured a dozen black-eyed men of the Vitezai Sarkanum, climbing each other's shoulders to get to them, while half a dozen more erupted from the windship hold. Dragan began to advance on Tarita while the giantess Semakha grabbed Ogre's collar and with incredible strength, hurled the massive construct backwards onto the vessel's deck, where ropes immediately snaked out, lashing him down.

But Kyrik's immediate peril was before him: Hajya, roaring in grief and torment, her eyes black, leaped at him. His mind shrieked, *She is my wife and I cannot hurt her*—

But terrifying as it was, it was mostly as anticipated, except they were facing Dragan and Semakha instead of Asiv. *My mistress was a Volsai*, Tarita had said. *This is what the enemy will do – and this is how we counter it.*

He pulled a fistful of silver dust from his pocket and hurled it in Hajya's face. She shrieked, clawing at her skin, and collapsed, which tore his heart, but there was no time; he was swept up in the fray. He darted past her and blasted the other handful of dust into the faces of the men charging from the windship. They were Shepherds, with enhanced speed, ferocity and endurance, but they weren't magi and couldn't shield. The cloud of silver struck them and shrieking, they fell back as the powdered metal fizzed in the air about them. Korznici, still beside him, was hurling her own silver-storm into the faces of those emerging from the hole in the roof.

Without pausing, he drew his dagger and buried the argenstael blade in a Vitezai man's chest: the wound erupted in black ash and he went down – and all the possessed men shrieked as one as the pain reverberated through their linked minds.

From the corner of his eye he saw Tarita blasting at Dragan and hope surged as the Gazda reeled: he perhaps had the strength of the Masks, but not the skill. But then a dozen grappling hooks flew over the battlements on both sides.

Their foes were bringing more to bear . . .

Seeing the fighting break out, Kip felt the familiar surge of *Kamfrud* as he led the Mantauri up the rocky slope to the ruins; they too were revelling in the battle-joy. There were flashes of light above and the aether seared with energy. 'Get up there,' he roared, 'up, up–'

They were all magi: some flew, others, like him, were using Earthgnosis and kinesis to grip the walls, landing on the top just as grappling hooks appeared and dozens more attackers came over the sides.

The more the merrier, he exulted. 'Minaus,' he bellowed, 'behold your servants!' His zweihandle swinging, he piled into the fray. A pair of black-eyed men spun with savage speed, clearly the 'Shepherds' he'd been warned of, and they traded blows that would have levelled other men – then his zweihandle caught the first and cleaved him to the spine and down he went; the second followed with his next blow. Around him, his Bullheads and Mantauri were wreaking similar havoc. Reaching Kyrik and Korznici, they fanned out, forming a cordon.

But more of the enemy were arriving, blue-skinned and soaking wet, although they'd taken no other harm from hiding beneath the frozen lake. They were cutting them down, but each kill burned away a little more of the silver and Kip could see they were in danger of being overwhelmed.

'Hold the line,' he roared, as another wave of enemy struck them. 'Minaus is watching us. *Hold on!*'

As the Mantauri swarmed across the rooftop, Tarita found herself momentarily behind them. They were holding their own, so she went after Ogre, launching herself upwards, cartwheeling over the throng and landing gracefully – then immediately spinning to carve down one black-eyed man with argenstael, hurling another over the battlements with kinesis and somersaulting over the next – and Semakha too – to land on the afterdeck of the windship.

'*Ogre?*' she yelled, as without conscious thought she beheaded the olive-skinned black-eyed wind-pilot, almost slipping in the black ichor fountaining from his neck-stump. As his link to the keel was cut, the vessel lurched and dropped a few feet. Tarita glared around until she spotted Ogre, caught in writhing ropes in the bow – but before she could move, Semakha leaped from the battlements and landed between them, her Plague mask lowered over her face.

'*Ogre,*' Tarita shouted again, trying rouse him, and went for Semakha, her blade slashing with all her strength. But Scaramu was viciously fast, especially for a giantess: her iron rod whipped up and blocked the blow, blazing out purple light from the gem on the end: necromantic energy that chilled the air.

But the scimitar, taken from the Ordo Costruo treasury at Midpoint Tower, was made for such battles: the rod snapped, the crystal shattered and the blade slashed open Semakha's forearm, eliciting a startled roar of pain.

But the ogress immediately retaliated, and her left fist slammed so hard into her shields that Tarita was rocked backwards. She staggered, but then swayed aside just in time for the massive battle-axe that had somehow appeared in Semakha's right fist to crunch into the rail where her head had been an instant before.

Then the ship lurched again, tearing the mooring ropes from the battlements, as the keel leached more power. They staggered apart, took new stances and closed once again, totally mismatched in physique, but both blindingly fast.

'We'll feed your body to Ogre on the journey home,' Semakha growled, swinging her two-handed battle-axe easily in one hand. Tarita's argenstael dagger shattered on contact, but her scimitar, belling and vibrating, held every blow.

'That blade belongs to the Master,' Semakha snarled, driving her back into the mainmast, but before she could strike, Tarita had darted around and slashed the taut rope binding the lowest spar. The freed spar swung around, catching Semakha in the chest and hurling her sideways, and Tarita ran at her, blazing mage-fire.

The ogress already had shields up, and the spar, still whipping around, almost took Tarita's own head off. She leaped aside just in time, and finding herself close to the prow, started screaming, 'Ogre, Ogre, *get up! GET UP!*'

Semakha slowed, sending a mental pulse thrumming into the aether, and five of the possessed Mollach men turned and simultaneously launched themselves from the battlements onto the drifting windship. Tarita managed to catch two in mid-air, hurling them back with kinesis, but the other three landed neatly behind Semakha.

Tarita leaped across the hatch to the hold, and glancing down, acted on a sudden impulsive thought, slamming Earth-gnosis, the elemental antithesis of Air-gnosis, into the timber. The keel groaned and cracked open and with translucent energy bleeding from the split, the windship began to slowly fall away from the fort's walls until it was dropping stern-first towards the icy shore of Lake Drozst. Tarita grabbed at the foremast just in time, and everyone except Semakha, who was clinging to the mainmast, started sliding down the deck towards the stern.

Tarita chanced a quick glance into the bow and saw Ogre was jammed behind a hatch, still caught up in the ropes. '*Get up!*' she repeated, but she could see he was too dazed even to understand her.

Semakha pushed off from the mainmast and came storming up the sloping deck. With a gesture, she sent another spar at Tarita, which swept her against the side and almost over it, as the ship tilted further, picking up speed as it plummeted towards the frozen lake. Then the ogress was on her, that great axe smashing down, sending her shields scarlet and almost breaking the silver scimitar – but at last Ogre became aware of his surroundings and wailed in despair as Tarita was overborne by Semakha's crushing weight and power–

They'd known there would be treachery, that their enemy had far greater numbers than they could muster, and that perhaps even argenstael blades wouldn't be enough. They'd already lost a Mantaur, and their thin line was about to collapse.

Under the lake? Kip cursed. *We never thought of that . . . but–*

'Now!' he roared.

They'd been fighting defensively against those overwhelming numbers, locking shields like good legionaries, warding and blocking, even though the enemy had brought in all their reserves . . .

. . . until they were packed together, without shelter . . .

. . . when, from behind the wall of shields, Maegogh rose, a three-foot-wide pottery globe in his massive arms. With a roar, he hurled it up, blazing mage-fire into it as it flew over their shields, over the heads of the possessed . . .

. . . while inside the globe, sloshing argenstael alloy had been kept at boiling-point by rods enchanted with gnostic heat. As the mage-fire struck, a triggered enchantment exploded inside the globe, bursting it open and sending the searing silver alloy spraying over the fifty or more Vitezai encircling Kip's men.

My people can shield. Our foes can't.

The red-hot argenstael struck faces, eyes, bared arms and hands – and knifed through their connection to Abraxas. Screeching as one, their linked minds unable to deal with the simultaneous explosions of agony, they fell to their knees, clutching their heads.

'Now!' Kip roared again, and shoving his way to the fore, he jammed his argenstael dagger into the throat of the nearest Vitezai, whose burned flesh was already smoking. The dagger bit, the man's ichor-blood exploded in his veins, smoke boiled from his eyes and mouth and he collapsed, already dead.

The air quickly filled with smoke and stench of burned ichor as Kip's men waded through the stricken enemy.

Suddenly, the tide had turned . . .

Dragan Zhagy had been directing his possessed men, whilst seeking to reach and cut down Kyrik and the Sydian woman with him, whoever she was – not Jehana Mubarak, for Asiv was tracking Valdyr and the princess to Cuz Sarkan.

Kyrik was born to lie . . .

But foremost in his thoughts was Sezkia, who'd been stunned, but was still alive. Why the Merozain had spared her, he had no idea, but he was grateful for a fool's misstep. He sent a searing current of energy to crack the Chain-rune, but as he reached her, her beautiful face was already alive with fury as she begged Abraxas for vengeance. He barely recognised the Hel-beast at his feet, in truth, but she was still his, his only lifeline–

–then liquid argenstael exploded over his men, who went down like skittles, and for the first time *real* fear, not just for Sezkia but for them all, overwhelmed him. His shields preserved his daughter and him, but he felt the cursed metal as it burned skin and blinded eyes, and he felt them die, the concussion of each successive death threatening to rip his mind apart.

Rise, he screamed into their minds, *get up – fight!*

Abraxas was gibbering and snarling in the aether, railing *Kill-them-kill-them-kill-them!* but the deaths of too many linked minds was overpowering his senses. He clung to Sezkia's hand, pulling her up and with him, moving backwards, away from the combat, seeking escape for himself and the only person he still cared for in this world . . .

It was a lurch of the windship that saved Tarita. It dropped suddenly, rendering her and Semakha weightless for a moment – and the massive blast of kinesis she'd just sent at the ogress hurled Semakha up into the rigging, like a fly swatted into a net.

Semakha retaliated by unleashing a torrent of mesmeric-gnosis, bypassing Tarita's physical shields and instead locking onto her mind, but this new front in their battle was no fair contest, because suddenly the ogress was reinforced a thousand-fold.

<*You're a novice,*> she snarled, <*but I contain Lucian and I have lived ten million lives.*>

She and her daemon gleefully ripped through Tarita's defences and swiftly found her weakness: the sickening instant in the middle of that desperate mêlée in the siege of Forensa, when her neck broke and she lost all feeling. It replayed in her mind, again, and again, and again, while everything else shut down . . .

Her shields vanished and her body went limp on the tilting deck as the paralysis dragged her back down again into her most terrifying nightmare. She found herself lying prone on the sloped deck, unable to move a muscle, as the ogress descended from the rigging, booming with laughter as she planted her feet and raised her axe . . .

40

Towards the Light

The Concept of Sacrifice

It is possible that the oldest religious act is sacrifice: a man giving a morsel of badly
needed food to an unseen power, to placate it or to beg aid. Was it an act of nobility,
or selfishness, foolishness or virtue? And did anything at all notice?

MALONTEES, PHILOSOPHER, LANTRIS 295

Cuz Sarkan, Mollachia
Late Janune 936

The weight of every bitter memory came crashing down on Valdyr, the
claustrophobic oppression of one powerful, perverse and untrammelled
man. The physical humiliations had been horrifying enough, but Asiv
had tormented his mind as well, using Valdyr as the receptacle for the
souls of daemons. The feral hate-beasts had been loathsome, but some
daemons had been far worse: monsters of utter malice, craving life and
unable to distinguish pleasure from pain, wanting only to wreak their
sordid desires on whatever they could reach.

Eventually he'd been taken from Asiv and returned to the breeding-
house to produce more magi children for the sultan. The Hadishah
mystic-healers didn't care what had been done to him, but to limit his
self-harm and keep him alive they cauterised his memories, dulling the
agony and leaving just a dim remembrance of those Hel-ish experi-
ments. But Valdyr's overwhelming fear of Asiv Faridden was bone- and
sinew-deep, seared into every pore of his body. His mind might not

remember everything that was done to him, but his body would never forget . . .

Now Asiv's kinesis locked around him, freezing his limbs, while tendrils of gnosis prised at his mind, seeking to burrow into those cauterised memories and drag them out again. He fought with all his strength. If he could, he would have hurled himself into the volcano, but even that escape was denied him.

'*What is this?*' Asiv breathed as he reached out and stroked Valdyr's cheek. His face filled Valdyr's sight, his eyes burrowing into his skull, staring at the small coil of green inside Valdyr's heart. '*Is it the dwyma?*'

Asiv reached and Valdyr shrieked to the only person he'd let inside his guard, '*Nara – NARA!*'

Pallas, Rondelmar

Lyra's sight was returning, to her unutterable relief, and she was filled with a renewed wonder at the beauty of light. Right now the waning sun was glinting off a diadem in her hands as she played with the reflection, sending refracted rays onto the mirror over her image, while the maid, Nita, braided her hair. The merchant's daughter had a calm manner and a pleasant voice; she was singing a folk-song as she worked.

Then Valdyr of Mollachia bellowed, '*Nara – NARA!*' into her skull. His face appeared in the mirror as his voice came crackling through the air.

Nita shrieked, dropped her brush and staggered backwards, falling over a chair and sprawling on the rug while Lyra gaped, taking in the Mollach's red-lit face . . . and then her perspective in the mirror-image swung and she was staring through Valdyr's eyes at the dark face of an impossibly beautiful Eastern man, whose eyes were boring into his skull . . . and hers . . . and whose dark hand grasped Valdyr's soul – and touched hers–

There was no time to act or react, only to *be*. She shouted protectively and lit up, making the dwyma flare between them like a bolt of lightning . . .

Cuz Sarkan, Mollachia

Within the chamber of the volcano, the verdant flame inside Valdyr's chest billowed and burst out, making Asiv recoil in agony as his right hand burst into green flame. The Gatti mage let out a hideous shriek like a tortured animal, and suddenly the Elétfa was not just a vision inside Valdyr's head but an actual *physical* presence. Time seemed first to slow, then almost stop as Valdyr's feet took him from the walkway and onto a vein of the Tree.

He heard a cry of shock and turned slowly to see Waqar Mubarak spinning slowly into the void. He *reached*, and veins of the Tree twisted into a net, catching the Keshi prince, who thrashed in its grip, no longer falling but still terrified.

Valdyr turned back to face Asiv, but the dark mage was staggering away, screaming. Nara of Misencourt's radiant face hung above them. He looked up and mouthed *'Thank you!'* then sundered the link to concentrate on the here and now. A spiral path wound upwards into the Tree. The flames of the fire-pit roared below . . .

Asiv was only a few feet away, but he might as well have been on a different star. He was weeping in agony, cradling his right hand, which had been burned to a twisted talon. Beyond him was the giant in the skull mask, blazing mage-bolts at him and Waqar, but they just burst impotently against the Tree.

Feeling like a Lantric god, Valdyr seized a strand of the Elétfa and willed lightning into his grasp, moving with ponderous surety as he turned to face Asiv. He loosed his lightning-bolt, which arced through space with weird slowness. Asiv, seeing it coming, shot like a blowfly along the wall and out through the arch after Skull-mask, who was carrying Jehana. The lightning-bolt finally struck in a coruscating burst of sparks, but it hit where they'd been a moment before.

'Jehana,' Waqar roared, *'Jehana!'* He went after them, churning through the air with glacial slowness, but Valdyr shouted, 'Waqar, they're gone – *she's gone* – stay with me!'

He can gain the dwyma here: he has to stay—

But the Keshi prince blindly clawed his way through the miracle of the Elétfa, his face nothing but grief and rage. He reached for the walkway platform, then suddenly he too was gone in a blur . . .

Valdyr swallowed, wavering . . . *Should I go after her too?* . . . But he looked up and saw the seed pods, hanging like suns in the upper branches, and a moment later Gricoama formed in the air like a wraith made of ash, yowling and staring upwards. Valdyr stroked the wolf's fur and followed his gaze: the stairway spiralling towards the light was calling them. He knew what he had to do . . .

Waqar couldn't think of anything except his beloved sister in the hands of his enemies, the murderers of his mother and his sovereign. He flailed through the air, bounding unseeing through veins and rivers of stars, bursting like a comet above the lava lake and pelting up the stairs, half-mad with fury and dread. He burst from the archway in the stone into the open air, almost hurtling right off the edge of the platform and into the lake of boiling water before he caught himself, staggered back and stared. The night was far advanced, the moon westering and the pre-dawn light glowed in the east . . .

He'd been inside the Elétfa all night, although it had felt like just a few moments. There was no sign of his enemies, for all he'd been less than a minute behind them.

Waqar screamed Jehana's name, but got no response. He scryed her face and got nothing. Engaging Earth-gnosis, he found the last boots to tread this platform had departed several hours ago. Drained of all hope, his strength also dissipated. He sat on the edge of the platform, looking down at the pallid glow of the crater lake, and wept. He'd failed, and worse than failed: his enemies had his sister, and they were long gone.

Finally, he roused himself to go back down into the circular chamber beneath the granite spire. He prayed he would find the Mollach prince there, perhaps with some token of success, but the fiery chamber was empty, the miraculous star-tree vanished. He was alone, and none of his attempts could make that vision re-appear.

Finally, he trudged back upstairs and watched the sun rise. When he could see what he was doing, he mimicked his sister's earlier spell, hardening the water so he could walk back to the shore. He found giant boot-prints in the gravel, but he knew it would be futile chasing her. All he could do was pray that they wouldn't harm her, though that felt like a forlorn hope. He reached out with his mind and felt a response: Ajniha, hearkening to his call and winging to find him . . .

What else have we lost? he wondered. *What happened beside the lake? Is anyone else still alive?*

Lake Droszt, Mollachia

Ogre's thoughts finally unscrambled, but his gnosis was still bound by the physical chains confining his wrists. The snake-like ropes entangled his limbs. He tried to wrench them apart, and at last the rope-spells ran out of energy and he thrashed free. He heard Semakha laughing derisively and looking down the plummeting ship, he saw she was standing over someone on the sloped deck, lifting the axe in her big hand.

She was menacing Tarita, who wasn't moving.

Ogre let gravity do the work, but he roared to distract the giantess as he plummeted towards her. She was about to bring the axe down on Tarita's neck, but his bellowing made her look up and she twisted lithely to meet him, just as he slammed into her, his arms thrust out either side of her head – and before she'd realised his intention, he brought his hands together so that the chain still attached to his wrists bit into her neck. His weight and momentum ripped her off her feet and they rolled down the deck, thrashing and kicking, and through the open hatch into the hold.

She tried to propel him away, but the Chain-rune embedded in the manacles was wrapped around her now and her spell failed. Knowing he had only moments before she regained enough grip on the gnosis to free herself, he screamed her name, *willing* her to remember that once she'd been another kind of being.

'Semakha – please, *remember*, Semakha,' he cried, desperate for some sign that he'd reached her . . .

But before she could respond, the ship crashed into the ice stern-first, shattering timbers – then the keel burst apart, releasing a blast of raw energy which flash-heated the water bursting into the hold. He had time for one great breath before he and Semakha plummeted through the wreckage into the green depths, still ripping at each other.

Semakha was struggling madly, her eyes bulging, but the impact had pushed the chain deeper into the folds of her powerful neck, choking off her windpipe. Her frantic attempts to reach the gnosis failed and the flow of air from her mouth and nostrils was faltering.

'*Ogre*,' she pleaded, the sound coming in bubbles, '*I'm still . . . your . . . Semakha.*'

At the sign he'd so craved, he loosened his grip, relief surging through him – and felt a dreadful, icy blaze of pain as they hit the bottom. He looked down to see a hilt plunged into his midriff – then Semakha pulled the knife out and stabbed him again, and again . . . somehow, she'd managed to free a hand.

Bucking in agony, his entire body convulsed into one immense wrenching motion–

–and Semakha's neck snapped.

The ogress went instantly limp in his grasp, and although part of him was howling in grief, he was struck with revulsion at the thought of being chained to something containing a daemon. Pulling free, he turned his eyes upwards to the light . . .

. . . and realised he wasn't going to make it. His lungs were almost empty, the manacles and chains were weighing him down, the freezing water was numbing his limbs, and blood was billowing out of his torso in a dark cloud.

He groaned in defeat, losing the last of his air. His eyes rolled back in his skull as he let the weight of the chains take him back to the bottom, to lie beside his broken, lost love.

Tarita felt her head sliding along the shattered deck, then she got tangled in debris. Unable to move to free herself, all she could see was sky. But her mind was scarcely present; most of her awareness was lost in repeating flashes of the moment her neck broke.

She could feel nothing at all below her chin and despite the chaos around her, all she heard were voices from the past:

'*Paralysed . . . she'll never move again . . . never even twitch a finger by herself . . .*'

'*We'll be cleaning her piss and shit until she dies . . .*'

'*It's better if we just let her perish . . .*'

Even when Semakha's spell was suddenly broken, it made no difference, for Tarita was trapped in the memory, oblivious to external sensations. The ship was coming apart around her while she lay there unable to move, because her body had forgotten how.

But at last another memory surfaced: her mistress, Elena, telling her, 'Our worst moments are the gaps in our armour, but we have to remember that we pulled through them – and that's how we're alive.'

And with those words, she found her way back.

I did recover – I did learn to walk again!

At last the fighting spirit that had carried Tarita through paralysis and out the other side returned and she convulsed into motion as nerves remembered connections and muscles recalled how to move – just as the mainmast fell sideways, breaking the ship in half. Her body was tossed upwards, then she and the shattered timbers rained back down and plunged into the churning depths.

Water-gnosis, kinesis, breathe and move! she ordered herself – then she saw a face she knew going slack as it lost the battle for life and screaming inside, she started thrashing downwards . . .

Dragan gripped Sezkia's hand, shouted, 'Fly!' and sought Air-gnosis – but another swathe of deaths among his men ripped apart his awareness and shattered the spell. His sword broke when a giant zweihandle came crashing down on it; reeling around, he saw Kyrik Sarkany standing over his spitting, snarling daughter.

'Nooo!' she howled, launching herself at Kyrik – who buried an argenstael dagger in her heart. Her lovely face contorted in agony as the ichor immolated inside her and she fell onto her face.

Dragan went berserk, shrieking as he sought to reach her, but as three more Vitezai succumbed to the argenstael, the shared agony overcame him again and he staggered and fell to his knees. He pulled himself up, thrashing about with gnosis-fire – but more deaths sent more pain stabbing through his chest and the spells spluttered. Bellowing in dread and rage, he leaped at Kyrik – As *a spear of silver to the back, then argenstael to the side* – and his last warrior went down. He reeled again, momentarily blind.

There was no one left but him, and when he opened his eyes, it was at a fence of blades. Kyrik pushed through and his argenstael dagger gouged into his neck . . .

Dragan froze.

In the aether, Abraxas paused from gobbling up the souls of his men and turned his attention on Dragan. A thousand gibbering mouths were waiting to devour him: the inevitable fate for those who took a daemon to their breast . . .

He looked up at Kyrik. 'You killed my daughter.'

'No, Dragan, *you* killed her,' Kyrik – his kirol, his *king* – answered.

'Niy, Niy, you were going to destroy Mollachia,' Dragan panted. 'We were *pure*, and you brought that Sydian filth here. You were *destroying* us.'

'We *are* Sydian, Dragan,' Kyrik retorted. 'We're the people of Zlateyr of the Sydian Plains. What *you* let inside us – that was *far* worse. You let a *daemon* take your body and soul, Dragan, and you fed your own daughter to it too. You tricked good men who trusted you into doing the same – and now they're all dead. *You* are the one destroying us.'

Dragan's mind went numb as what was left of his humanity acknowledged this was true.

'But Asiv–' He gulped down a sudden sob. 'I thought I could preserve us from within–'

Rise and fight, Abraxas snarled. *Or die and come to me . . .*

He dropped his sword. 'Kyrik, *please*,' he begged, praying Kyrik understood.

Kyrik's eyes narrowed, then the argenstael dagger punched downwards, past his collarbone and into his heart. His veins ignited, the spawn inside his chest shrivelled and his heart thudded to a stop, the air sucked from him. His eyes flew open . . .

A wall of faces loomed over him, screaming condemnation and scorn, mouths opening to engulf him for ever – until Kyrik's face flashed in the sky and he came apart in a blaze of blue fire.

Kyrik stared down at the body of the man he'd once revered, hoping he'd burned the gazda's soul away in time. Kip and the Mantauri were watching, knowing what he'd done; he saw understanding and was grateful for that. *I wish the others could have received the same mercy.* Dragan Zhagy had been like a father to him. *Is it a victory, when it costs so much?*

Then he looked around him, his eyes seeking the one who mattered above all, and found Hajya stretched out on the ground, motionless, with Korznici bending over her.

He hurried to her side. 'Is she–?'

'She lives,' Korznici told him. 'I had to knock her unconscious, then I kept her safe.'

Kyrik pulled the young woman's forehead to him and kissed it fervently. 'You are a miracle,' he told the blushing Sfera, then he bent over his wife and begged Ahm and Kore and whatever other god might exist to keep her with him and find a way to make her clean.

Ogre's consciousness, swimming through murky waters, focused on a bright light blooming in the distance. He clawed towards it until suddenly he was awake and lying on cold gravel at the edge of an iced-over lake, in shocking pain from a dozen stab wounds. Someone was kneeling over him: Tarita, he realised at last, her hair a wet tangle and tears in her eyes. The cold was as frightening as the sharp throbbing. He could feel his soul's grip on his body slipping with every second.

I'm dying, he thought. *These are my last moments.*

He managed to murmur, 'Tarita–' through bubbles of fluid.

'Ogre,' she squealed, 'don't try to talk – I'm here–'

'Tarita,' he managed again, 'I'm dying . . .'

'No' – her eyes were wide with panic – 'it's–'

He squeezed her hand to quieten her, to let him say what had to be said before he was torn from this terrible world. 'Tarita, I wish I could have told you sooner . . .' He closed his eyes, gritting his teeth against the agonising pain. 'I should have told you . . . *I love you, Tarita*. Not Semakha, *you*. You are light and air to me. The greatest bliss was to cradle you as you slept. These last months have made all the past worthwhile.'

His mind drifted; the wall of darkness was coming closer, so he spoke over her, adding, 'I am so glad to have known . . . you . . . my love . . .'

Whatever she was saying in return, he couldn't catch. The roaring in his head was too loud, a wave of deafening silence that bore him down into the darkness.

41

After the Ordeal

Death

Even before the gnosis revealed that we do indeed have a soul that can, for a time at least, exist beyond the death of our bodies, religion had enshrined the notion that there is something after this life. What is more natural, having been given a taste of the possibilities of Life, than that we would crave the chance to return and get it right?

HUEL GALBREA, HEALER-MAGE, JASTENBERG 709

Freihaafen, Mollachia
Late Janune 936

It was morning, the day after the bloody evening at the ruin beside Lake Droszt. Kyrik sat stony-eyed, gazing silently across the lake. Seven pyres were still guttering on the icy beach. He wondered if they could see them at Hegikaro – and if they knew what the flames meant.

Dragan is dead, people of Mollachia. I'll come to Hegikaro soon and set you free from this evil.

Because *Evil* was what they faced. He only had to look at Hajya beside him, pawing at the chains tethering her. There was daemon's ichor in her blood, so he couldn't even comfort her with his touch. Her thick cloud of curling hair was matted and bloody, her once-solid body little more than skin and bone, her nails ragged and her skin pocked with sores and welts. When she'd woken last night, she'd shrieked and howled at the loss of her daemonic masters, until Korznici had done something with the gnosis that helped her sleep. As the dawn glimmered, she'd lapsed into a torpor deeper than sleep.

Kip came and sat beside him, producing a flask of a fiery liquor. 'My cup-wish is for the head of Asiv Fariddan to roll,' the Schlessen growled, 'and for those who died today to find peace.'

They shared swallows, murmuring over the fallen. 'You're a good man,' Kip told him. 'A worthy thane. Burning away Dragan's soul was a mercy.' He indicated the last three pyres, for Dragan and Sezkia and the immense ogress. 'It's a shame we couldn't do the same for his daughter.'

They'd immolated the bodies of all the fallen, in case the ichor was somehow still potent; they'd had to add three of their own to the pyres as well: a grievous loss, although it had still been an almost unbeliev-able victory. But until he could do something for Hajya, it wouldn't feel that way.

'What next?' Kip asked.

Kyrik sighed. 'Back to Freihaafen. We can't risk Hegikaro by our-selves and until we hear from Valdyr's party, we won't know our strength. Asiv Fariddan wasn't here so my guess is he followed Valdyr to the mountain.'

They mulled over that grim thought as the sunlight lit the chilly landscape, turning the icy lake to rose-gold glass.

Hajya suddenly woke and gave a wretched cry as the sunlight struck her, writhing away from it in pain. The sight of her pulling her rags around her face and huddling away from the light tore at Kyrik's heart and he rose to drape a blanket over her, allowing her to rest again. His reward was a half-hearted lunge and an attempt to bite him, which he quelled with kinesis, weeping silently. *Hajya my love, I want you back, as you were.*

Ogre woke to a distant throbbing inside his belly and the smell of tea. His mouth filling with saliva, first he realised that somehow – beyond all expectation – he wasn't dead after all, and almost immediately, that thought was followed by the memory of all the idiocy he'd blathered when he thought he was dying. As Tarita's spicy fragrance washed over him, he closed his eyes and wished he really had died.

Reluctantly, he opened his eyes again. He was lying on the roof of the ruined keep, near a small fire blazing cheerily with a pan of tea bubbling in the middle. Mist hung heavily about them. Under the blanket covering his body he could feel a bulky bandage around his middle. He looked at Tarita, sitting on her haunches and sipping from a steaming mug. She'd acquired a Schlessen smock-dress from somewhere; it had probably been made for a child because the bodice was too small and exposed far too much flesh.

He turned to stare at the dawn-streaked sky instead, mortified to still be breathing.

'Sal'Ahm, Ogre,' Tarita said, in a perky voice. 'How are you this beautiful morning?'

Her tone told him she hadn't forgotten what he'd said either.

Kore's Balls, I'm an idiot. 'I'm . . . um . . . alive.'

'That's wonderful.' She slurped her tea. 'It wasn't a forgone conclusion, but I got you out just in time, staunched the blood and filled you with healing-gnosis. When you managed to give that lovely speech, I knew you'd make it.'

He pulled a face. 'You should have said so.'

'I *tried*,' she pointed out, 'but *someone* wasn't listening.'

He felt himself go crimson. Cringing, he muttered, 'I thought I was dying.'

'I know,' she smirked. 'It was rather charming. Fortunately, there was only me to hear it.' She patted his arm. 'Your secret's safe with me.'

But it's not a secret any more, he thought miserably. *She'll not want me around now.* He looked away again, torn between the visceral relief of surviving and the horror of having killed the woman he'd spent so many years aching to see again.

'Semakha?' he groaned. 'I think I broke her neck – was that enough . . . ?'

'To kill her?' And at his faint nod, she carried on, 'It was. Even daemons can't manage when the spinal cord goes. I can relate to that.' She looked at him sympathetically. 'So Naxius sent her to collect you? What a cruel thing to do.' She placed her small hand on his larger one. 'I'm very sorry, Ogre. She should have had a better life.'

Ogre thought about Semakha's callous self-satisfaction. 'I don't think she thought that,' he said mournfully. 'She gloated about how wonderful she was. But Naxius was all she knew. I was more fortunate.'

'And you still are.' She sipped her tea. 'Kyrik's people killed Dragan and Sezkia and all the rest of the possessed men are dead. And we have you back.' She gave him a warm smile. 'Best of all.'

This was far better than he'd dared hope, but there was suddenly a huge hole in his future. 'What happens next?' he asked fearfully.

'Well, it's not all good news. Asiv has kidnapped Jehana and Valdyr's disappeared into some mystical Tree of Light. Once Waqar gets back here, we'll all go back to Freihaafen – that's Kyrik's hidden camp – and work out what to do next. You're not out of danger, you know: you've been stabbed in the stomach and suffered a lot of internal damage. I've sealed everything and drained the toxins, but any exertion could tear it open, so that means bed-rest, Ogre, for at least a month.' She looked away. 'And I need to decide whether I'm going south.'

'With Waqar?' he blurted, unable to stop himself.

'Ai, with Waqar.'

His familiar isolation swept back in. 'Have you slept with him?' he asked, wincing at himself.

She gave him an arch look. 'Not for want of trying. I warned you, Ogre: I'm not a good girl. The problem is that he's a good man ... I mean, far too good for the likes of me. But I'm working on it.'

'Then I wish you luck,' he mumbled, trying to mean it. 'Sorry about my babbling yesterday. I spoke a lot of stupid words I don't remember. Whatever they were, forget them. Now I need to sleep.'

Tarita felt a strange turmoil in her gut. *Poor Ogre*, she thought. *You've gone through so much, but this world would never allow seven-foot-tall illegal constructs to have a normal life.* Her heart went out to him, lying there weak and wounded, but holding the worst hurts inside. *You deserve better, my friend.*

She'd been so terrified that she'd lost him, seeing those awful rents in his flesh, even after she got him breathing again. But he'd rescued her from Alyssa's Hadishah, so she refused to give up. She drew the water from his lungs and pumped in air, all the while trying to re-spark his heart – and when it had finally thudded back to life, she'd wept like a child.

Impulsively, she bent and whispered in his ear, 'I love you too, Ogre, my *friend*, but you want the impossible.'

He heard her, but didn't respond.

She was already regretting being so cruel, offering hope, then snatching it away in the next breath, but it felt necessary. *Well done, Merozain*, she thought sarcastically: *All that power and no idea how to think before you speak*. Jehana had been right when she warned her not to joke and flirt with Ogre as she would any other male. *I should have listened*.

How she'd disentangle herself from this mess, she didn't yet know, but right now, they had to move. Kyrik wanted them all gone inside the hour, so she headed for the wrecked ship to find materials for a stretcher for Ogre. She'd have to use kinesis to carry her giant friend home, which was going to be exhausting. But it was the least she could do. And the most.

Freihaafen, Mollachia

Returning to Freihaafen was a strange feeling for Waqar. The steam-wreathed lake and forested hills of the hidden valley could have been lifted straight from the *Kalistham*, in particular the verses describing the Great Prophet's ascent to Paradise. But he'd allowed Asiv and the skull-masked giant, another illegal construct like Ogre, to snatch Jehana from him, which was tearing his soul. Despite the beauty of this place, he just wanted to leave.

It was galling, but he needed Tarita. He didn't have the right affinities to use shared familial blood to trace Jehana the way they had when they'd hunted his mother. But first, he had to deal with a barrage of questions from Kyrik about what had befallen Valdyr, although there was little he could tell him. What he'd seen was confusing, and in any case, he'd been entirely focused on trying to get to Jehana.

'He's in the skies,' was all he could really say. 'He's climbing the Tree of Light.' When he said the words out loud, they sounded like a metaphor for death; part of him wondered whether he'd imagined it all.

Finally, he was able to go in search of Tarita, finding her on a hillock above the lake, her arms wrapped round her knees against the chill, staring vacantly into space. He sat silently next her, waiting until she noticed him – but when she did, she acted like she'd been aware of him the whole time. Perhaps she had.

'I need your help,' he told her, thrusting a borrowed copper bowl at her. 'The blood-scrying? You have clairvoyance-gnosis and I don't. You need to cast it for me.'

She looked up at him wearily, as if she had the weight of the world on her back. 'Of course, Great Prince.'

He gave her an irritated look. 'We've been through too much together for you to play that game.'

'Only a prince would think it a game,' she told him quietly.

He fumed quietly, but drew his dagger and laid it against his wrist. 'How much blood?'

'A quarter-measure,' she sighed. She helped him nick a vein and managed the spell, having to battle tight wardings and exert her considerable gnostic strength, but at last the blood ran across the bowl, defying gravity. 'She's due south of us . . . in Hegikaro, maybe, or even further away – the spell doesn't indicate distance.'

Waqar unrolled a map and grimaced. 'Norostein is also due south of us, which is where the Shihad is encamped. We'll need to triangulate the reading, then fly south. We can go anytime. Whatever you want, it's yours.'

Her eyes narrowed. 'I'm not even sure I wish to go south.'

'You promised me you'd find Jehana. Well, she's still lost.'

'*You* lost her.'

'If you'd been at Cuz Sarkan she'd never have been taken!' He sailed on, riding a wave of righteous fury, 'My sister has been kidnapped by this Masked Cabal – she is the only mage-dwymancer in the world! She is also a Princess of Kesh and niece of the Sultan of all Ahmedhassa, so it is your *clear duty* to Ahm and to your conscience to help get her back!'

She responded with the most surly curtsey the harbadab could conceive, one that should have earned her a slap at the very least. 'Shukran, Great Prince. I am honoured to serve.' She turned and stomped away.

He caught her up and grabbed her arm. 'What's *wrong* with you? Is this because I wouldn't sleep with you?'

She snorted, and wrenched her arm free. 'No, *Great Prince*, it damned well isn't! I am a free woman and I do *not* like being told what to do.' She set her hands to her hips. 'You heard me at Kyrik's little "common cause" discussion: I told you then my priority was to rescue Ogre, then go home. I've done that and it almost killed me. The ogress unpicked my defences like they were *nothing*: I was an *eye-blink* from being cut in half. I'm out of my depth and I have no allegiance to anyone here. I just want to go home.'

'So you're scared.' That was utterly clear to him.

But she was also proud. 'Fuck you, "Great One",' she retorted, eyes blazing. She spun on her heel and stormed off.

Damn my stupid tongue . . . Waqar slapped his own forehead and ran after her again, babbling, 'I'm sorry, I didn't mean that – dear Ahm, you've been heroic beyond belief, and I've no right to ask this of you, I know that . . . I'm the one – it's me who's scared! My sister is in the hands of those freaks and it's driving me insane.' He seized her hand again and fell to one knee. 'Please, Tarita, I'm begging you to help me. *Anything* you want, it's yours.'

And suddenly, there it was: *Anything you want, it's yours.*

Men who wanted something had lied to her before, often. But Waqar's sincerity was blazingly obvious. He'd do *anything* for his beloved sister. Which also meant that anything he gave her was meaningless to him: gold, jewels, silks, a title, a place in his bed – from which she'd be ousted by a *real* princess in good time . . . none of it would matter.

People will always need something from a mage, Mistress Alhana had once told her. *Some work only for reward, but others give everything they have for free. You'll find your own balance, Tarita – but never forget, even magi need coin, and you can't help anyone if you burn yourself out.*

She groaned inwardly. She was going to have to decide, which meant someone would be hurt, no matter which option she took.

'I don't have a price,' she told him. 'My mistress told me to do things because I need to do them.' She looked away, her heart torn. *Everyone needs me, but I can be in only one place at a time.* Ogre needed her. Kyrik needed her – without Valdyr, his people were defenceless against Asiv. But without her, Waqar had no chance at all. She ground her teeth, thinking furiously, then sighed. 'Ai, ai . . . I'll help you in this.'

He kissed her hand. 'Shukran, Tarita, Shukran. I don't know what to make of you, but I am for ever grateful, this I swear.'

Her heart pounded a little, to have a prince – *this prince* – kneel to her so, despite everything. 'Well then,' she said heavily, 'if you've already told Kyrik I'm leaving . . .' She scanned the shoreline, wondering if it was cruel or kind to Ogre to leave without a word. But that would be cowardice. 'I need to say my goodbyes,' she told him, and strode back to the longhouse.

She found Ogre under a towering tree, huddled in a blanket and peering intently at the *Daemonicon di Naxius*. He looked up at her sadly. 'Ogre knows Master; so perhaps he knows these signs. It is slow to translate and Kyrik has neither paper nor ink, but I try.'

Her eyes widened in appreciation. 'You really are a miracle,' she told him.

'Yet Ogre is impossible to love.'

'That's *not* what I said,' she replied. 'I said, what you want between us is impossible. I do love you, like a brother. Like a best friend. But I'm not your Lady Ogre; she is still out there.'

He looked at her sadly. 'Ogre doesn't like it when friend Tarita lies.' He looked at the lakeshore, where Waqar was readying Ajniha. 'Go. Your prince awaits.' He returned his attention to the book.

The hurt in his voice cut her, but maybe the pain was necessary. 'I'm still your friend, Ogre,' she insisted, but when he didn't respond, she turned to leave, feeling wretched.

Waqar took Ajniha soaring upwards and out of the hidden valley; Tarita rode behind, her arms around his waist. South of a village called Ujtabor, on the road that led to Banezust, they stopped to recast the spell. This time when Tarita pushed her search through the veils of the aether, she sensed a counter-spell and quelled it only with difficulty. *They know we're searching . . .*

573

When the blood ran from the middle of the bowl to the edge, Waqar swore and buried his head in his hand. Tarita let the scrying lapse. 'Still south,' she breathed.

Hegikaro was west of where they were.

'They're taking her to Rashid, at Norostein,' Waqar groaned. 'We'll need to clear Collistein Pass before dusk.'

The clouds were already closing in as they took to the air again.

42

Delusional Ambition

Cold and the Human Body

Extreme cold causes blood vessels to constrict, restricting blood flow to preserve inner heat. As you freeze, your extremities become damaged until eventually it's permanent, then as the cold reaches your core, you begin to die. Your faculties will become so addled that you may think you are burning up and in removing clothing, seal your own fate. As you die, the cold will colonise you completely, mummifying your body.

GEMMA TYR, HEALER-NUN, CORAINE 792

Norostein, Noros
Janune 936

Latif woke to cold steel across his throat. He went rigid, trying to blink his eyes free of grit, to find a young woman he didn't know kneeling over him. She was wrapped in a bekira-shroud, with a periapt dangling from her neck, a small ruby that glittered like a red star. There was no pity in her eyes, just obedience and ambition.

Selmir was standing over them, looking down with cold glee. The improvised tent was as it always was: blankets lying around the fire-pit, weapons and Rani's trunk-spikes piled in one corner, weighing down the flap. It was some time before dawn, Latif estimated.

'Ai, I'm sure of it now,' Selmir purred, studying his face. 'And you're even using your real name.'

'Wha–?' Latif began, but Selmir snorted derisively.

'Don't even try, Impersonator.' He nudged Latif's ribs with his boot.

'I spent more than a year in some desert Hel-hole because of what you said about me at Riverdown. You destroyed my career.'

Latif looked around blearily and found Sanjeep and Fara kneeling, both terrified. Ashmak was standing beside the howdah, his face unreadable. Rani was watching in distress, her trunk flicking about anxiously.

So he did *recognise me* ... The game was up, further pretence was useless. He bared his throat more fully to the knife the young woman held and said, 'I remember you ruining your own career with your imbecilic tactics and utter disregard for the lives of the men you led.'

'Who is this man, Hazarapati?' Ashmak asked Selmir.

'Well, isn't that a question? Why don't you tell him, Impersonator?'

'I was one of Sultan Salim's impersonators,' Latif said calmly. 'I was chosen for my facial and physical resemblance to him and became one of his household. We impersonators would appear as him in public if his life appeared threatened. We were trained not just to mimic him, but to know who and what he knew. At times we even fulfilled his roles: for that reason, we were anointed with his authority.'

'A slave given sultan's rank,' Selmir snarled. 'Sultan Rashid would never stoop so low.'

'Rashid is a mage,' Latif retorted. 'Salim had only human solutions and impersonators are an old and time-honoured ploy.' He paused, mourning his dearest friend. 'I became Salim's favoured impersonator, the one given the most serious responsibility. During the Third Crusade, he had to be in the north, so I assumed his role overseeing the siege of Riverdown.'

'Riverdown,' Selmir echoed, his voice haunted.

'Hazarapati Selmir was a military advisor who, with more than one hundred thousand men, failed to overcome twelve thousand. His failings exposed, he was sent north to account for himself, but evidently he had sufficient powerful friends to protect him and insufficient honour to do the rightful thing and take his own life.'

'You dare criticise me? I was a military man with years of experience, you jumped-up slave–'

'Years of incompetence, more likely,' Latif replied. He looked up at the young woman holding the knife to his throat. 'You've tied yourself to a falling star, girl.'

'Shut your mouth, pig,' she hissed back.

'You're just a fraud, Latif,' Selmir jeered, 'nothing but a professional liar – and my Hatimuk cannot be swayed.' He put his hands on his hips and made a great show of pondering something he'd clearly already decided. 'Listen . . . Ashmak, isn't it? There's a reward for this one, more than ten thousand racheems, if you know the right people. Certain people have made it known that the last impersonator is a loose end they want severed. Are you with me? I offer you a one-fifth share.'

So that's why he's doing this in the early hours of the morning and not in front of the army . . . Latif's eyes went to Ashmak's face, but he couldn't read his inscrutable, acne-ravaged features.

'One-fifth?' Ashmak sniffed. 'Rashid might give me the whole lot.'

'Rashid might have sanctioned Salim's death but he won't acknowledge involvement. You'll get nothing but trinkets from him. But I know who to speak to for full recompense.'

'One-third.'

'One-quarter.'

Ashmak's eyes narrowed, then he shrugged. 'Done.' He spat on his hand and offered it. Selmir clasped his hand, meeting his eye with a satisfied smile, Sanjeep and Fara blanched, but Ashmak relinquished his grip and turning to Latif, smiled sadly. 'I'm sorry, my friend, but it's a wicked world.'

'It surely is,' Selmir said nonchalantly. 'Hatimuk, bring him.'

Hatimuk gripped Latif under the shoulder, kinesis powering her grip as she hauled him upright, too quickly for his weakened limbs. He staggered, she sought to get her balance and Latif jerked out the knife he kept beneath his headrest and buried it in her breast, right above the heart. Her eyes popped out in shock as her legs gave way.

Selmir raised his hand, gnosis-fire leaping to his finger-tips – as Ashmak slammed his wide-bladed knife into the hazarapati's back and sent a mage-bolt pulsing down the blade. It burst inside his chest. Selmir staggered forward, pitched onto his face, shuddered and went still.

Fara hid her face, her shoulders shaking, while Sanjeep ran to Rani and grasped her trunk, murmuring comfort. Latif shared a pregnant look with Ashmak, then bent over Hatimuk in time to see her death shudder.

'Nice work, Effendi. She was likely more dangerous than he was,' Ashmak drawled. 'But is it true? You really were Salim's impersonator? What the Hel are you doing here?'

Latif gave a weak laugh. 'I was minding my own business until some prick came along and drafted me into the Shihad. And branded me as his slave, too.'

'What a prick!' grinned Ashmak. 'But no, I remember that day: I had come only for Rani. You could have walked away, but you showed off your prowess with the bow and begged to join us. Why would you do that?'

Latif hung his head. He could have lied – should have, probably, but he was frightened and tired and they still had two bodies to dispose of. He wasn't thinking straight. 'You heard Selmir: Rashid sanctioned Salim's death.'

'He "might have sanctioned",' Ashmak replied. 'Selmir was guessing.'

'It's not a hard equation, Ashmak. Salim died and Rashid became sultan. The whole of Salim's household died that night: his wives and children and all his impersonators and their wives and children. My wife and son died, and I should have. So why am I here? To kill Rashid and spit on his grave.'

Ashmak, Sanjeep and Fara gaped at him. Even Rani stared.

Then Ashmak shrugged and said, 'Fair enough. Let's toss these pieces of offal into the shitting-ditch while it's still snowing. We can worry about your delusional ambition later.'

After two weeks of searing cold, the attacks on Norostein began again, launched without fanfare, but the city was ready. This time, there was no weather-gnosis and no smashing windships into towers – evidently the expendable vessels had been used up.

The assault did begin with a new type of barrage, though: the sultan's mage-engineers had fashioned giant catapults that were hauled into place by the elephants, along with wagons laden with boulders. The battering was concentrated on the damaged walls near the main gatehouse, but once again, the real assault was at Gash Lane.

Seth was already awake when Delton hammered on his door, just after dawn. He'd been speaking by relay-stave to Carmina and his daughters at Fanford Castle. <*Governor Myron sent men who demanded to be allowed in to seize papers,*> Carmina was saying, her soft face taut with anxiety. <*We denied him, of course.*>

Myron, you piece of turd, Seth thought angrily, but he calmed himself and sent soothingly, <*You did right, dearest. He's after you and the girls.*>

Carmina put her hand to her mouth. <*Oh Kore, what have you done now?*>

<*It's political,*> Seth sent back. <*I've done nothing wrong.*>

She didn't look terribly reassured, especially when she heard Delton calling, 'Sir, the enemy are attacking the lane!'

Seth bit his lip, then forced a reassuring smile. <*I have to go, dearest. Love to you all.*>

<*Be careful, Husband.*> She touched her fingertips to her lips.

He broke the connection, armoured himself, with Delton's aid, then hurried downstairs. There were plenty of loyal battle-magi around the Lowertown tavern where he was staying, just in case Myron tried to arrest him there.

Seth took the main gates and left Ramon to Gash Lane. The waves of Shihadi attacks were designed primarily to wear down the defence, but by mid-morning, although the phalanxes of Keshi archers were running out of arrows, the men were still slogging through the trampled slush, planting ladders and climbing, only to be pushed back by defenders armed with long poles to dislodge the ladders and jagged stones and flaming oil to rain down upon the attackers. Wind-vessels hovered above, exchanging ballistae shafts with the towers. Every so often a dhou would take a hit, sending it plummeting to the ground and causing more deaths amongst the Shihadi, but the ballista crews were being steadily destroyed as well.

'Are you holding?' flashed from aide to aide via relay-staves. Delton brought Seth constant updates as he helped Pilus Lukaz and his men defend the walls east of the gatehouse. Frozen corpses piled up in the moat as the Easterners charged, planted their ladders, were beaten back and charged again.

There's a desperate courage to them, Seth reflected with admiration. *They know what's going to happen, but they attack anyway. It's as if their own lives mean nothing to them.*

But when they lost the light, just three bells after midday, the walls were still holding.

'True Believers,' Ramon sniffed, when Seth voiced his thought in the taproom of the tavern that evening. 'They think we're Shaitan's progeny.'

'But isn't that our fault?' Seth asked, waving for another beer. 'Three Crusades and all that's gone between?'

'Probably,' Ramon yawned, 'but that doesn't mean we lay down and die, *amici*.'

'But it does mean we do better afterwards.'

'Sure – just have a word with your dear friend Lyra Vereinen when you're next in Pallas.'

Seth chuckled. 'You know, I did meet her, in a way. After the generals were selected for the five armies, there was a banquet. I got to bow to her, but we never spoke. Mind you, she gave quite a good speech.'

'Is she as fair of face as the Rondian coins have her?'

Seth laughed, then mused on that. 'Wearier. Unhappy, I thought.'

Ramon rolled his eyes. 'Give a filly a crown, unlimited wealth and a dashing husband and they'll still contrive to be miserable. Although you and Carmina are content.'

'Content?' Seth echoed. 'Yes, that about sums it up. But there's not a lot of passion.'

'Passion's hard to keep up. I think that's why I've never married myself. I get bored too easily.'

'But there never was passion,' Seth confessed, 'not even at the start. I think she'd already fallen in love with someone else during the Crusade, but they must have been unattainable. I was definitely second choice. Carmina and I just sort of slumped against each other in the final days of the Crusade.'

'You're *Seth Korion*,' Ramon snorted. 'War hero, Earl of Bres and rich as Gildenhands. And a good, decent man besides. You're no woman's second choice, *amici*.'

'Maybe . . . but the love the balladeers sing of sounds so much better than I've experienced. All that passion.'

'Songs?' Ramon looked scornful. 'Passion's overrated, Seth. It makes you do stupid things and leaves a horrible mess – I know this all too well.'

'Carmina once said . . .' Seth hesitated. 'I shouldn't really say . . . No, I will: she once told me, we were talking about you and Lanna, whom you were energetically bedding at the time, you may recall, and she told me, "It hurts to see someone you love with another".'

'*Carmina?*' He pulled a face. 'Well, she gave me no clues, *amici*, and really, she isn't my type. Lanna, though . . . I liked her a lot, but the life I was about to return to – you know, the whole *familioso* thing? – it wasn't for her. Leaving little Julia with her was the hardest thing I've ever done.'

'Do you see your daughter often?' Seth asked, relieved at the change of subject.

'About thrice a year. She's six now, a tiny dot, but so composed. Precocious, wise-hearted. Lanna's good with her.' Ramon's face closed up. 'So will the Noories keep attacking tomorrow, d'you think?'

Seth was just as happy to leave personal talk behind. 'I don't see they have a choice. Do you think you could use weather-magery to conjure another storm yourself?'

Ramon frowned. 'Not really, *amici*. Breaking is far easier than making. Weather-gnosis is a specialist thing; we'd've needed another three years in the Arcanum and I don't think I'd have been welcomed, do you? And anyway, the Crusade was calling. There're a few with the Noros magi, but they're in a stand-off against the remaining Shihadi weather-mages, so at the moment we're all at nature's mercy.'

The Shihad's assaults didn't stop the next day, or the next, and the weather worsened. Seth hated watching the attackers below, some clearly so numb with cold and sick with foreign illnesses that they could barely stand – grinding their lives against the walls. Some died in the press without a wound, only falling when the retreat was sounded.

Sickness struck the defenders too, in Copperleaf and Lowertown. A suspicious fire in a Copperleaf granary destroyed tons of badly needed food, immediately putting the defenders onto reduced rations, and still

Governor Myron refused to help. The general populace were now being barred from the higher tier of the city and every day the protesting crowds outside the Ringwald gates grew larger and more unruly.

Neither Lord Sulpeter nor Prince Elvero were riding to their relief and Pallas was still silent on Governor Myron's status, leaving the city's leadership in doubt and increasing their sense of abandonment. The mage-engineers were repairing as best they could, but the walls were crumbling more every day and a major breach was inevitable. The relentless battering and desperate rushes left thousands dead after each sally and there were no pauses for truce, no attempts to clear the bodies. Only the bitter cold was preventing a full-blown epidemic.

Each evening, Seth and Ramon gathered everyone at their tavern-base for debriefing. As well as their aides, the legion commanders and the specialist magi – healers, weather-magi and engineers like Tanderaum – they included Justiciar Detabrey and other valued advisors.

'On paper we're eight legions, but the roll-calls are closer to half that now,' Pelk of the Waystars was growling to Yarronis of the Silver Hawks as Seth entered.

'The last of the attackers have retreated,' Seth told the room. 'It's a deluge out there, so it should be quiet tonight. We've held again.'

There was a drawn-out exhalation of relief from everyone present, then a barrage of questions about casualties and the state of the walls, which were grim, but manageable.

Seth turned to Ramon, who'd had his people run a stock-take.

'Not sure why he always leaves the bad news to me,' Ramon remarked. 'The fact is, where food is concerned, we're not doing so well. Governor Myron's doling out niggardly rations, while the windships coming and going from his palace lead us to believe he's already stripped the Royal Treasury and sent it to his summer retreat in Bricia – to "protect" it, of course. We're nigh out of grain, meat, drink and fuel to burn, and don't even mention bandages.'

'We should march in and take what we need,' Tribune Pelk growled.

'He's got two Imperial Legions protecting Ringwald,' Seth reminded them, 'not to mention the best walls in Norostein, with that narrow front, lots of towers and ballistae. We can't fight Rashid on the outer walls and Myron on the inner ones.'

'What about the petition to Pallas?' Yarronis asked.

'It's been buried,' Ramon reported. 'I spoke to my contact there again today. As far as our darling empress is concerned, Myron is doing an exemplary job.'

'What's Myron's next move?' Gedyn Drapheim, one of Seth's Bricians, wondered.

'He'll sit tight: he's secured the treasury and at the first lull in the fighting – the next big storm, I reckon – he'll push for full control of the city and arrest as many of us as he can.'

They all looked at Justiciar Detabrey, who nodded. 'It's only the siege preventing him from exerting his full authority, but once the emergency has passed, he'll have to assert himself, to show Pallas he can control the province.'

The room, largely filled with Noromen, took that badly. 'Our men are giving our lives to further the career of a Pallacian noble, is what you're saying?' Pelk summarised angrily.

'And to protect their wives, children and countrymen,' Seth reminded them.

'Aye,' Yarronis scowled, 'but after this, even assuming Rashid doesn't just fly in another army, it'll be us labouring to rebuild while those bastards in Ringwald just lap up the cream. We've had the Pallas boot on our jugular a long time. We're choking.'

'That won't be changing,' Detabrey noted. 'The Imperial Treasury is broke, everyone knows that. The Church seizures were a salve, not a solution to the problem. Whoever emerges triumphant, Sacrecour, Corani or whoever, they'll need to extract all the tax, tributes and levies they can. Wars cost millions and we'll be saddled with more than our share, as usual.'

The bleak summation caused heads to drop further. Seth exchanged a look with Ramon, knowing they were both thinking, *We need to get them out of this defeatist attitude.* 'What would victory look like, right now?' he asked.

'Is that a serious question?' Pelk asked.

'Of course.'

'Victory,' the sour-faced legate answered, 'would deliver us the keys to Ringwald and see the governor sent packing, or better yet, see him locked up. It would see sovereignty restored, some lost kin of Phyllios, I suppose, and no rukking governor from Pallas to tell us what to do.' He looked at Seth coolly. 'But another Noros generation has been lost to this Shihad: we can't fight the empire again – we might not even exist in a year's time.'

The room fell back into gloomy silence.

Seth looked at his Brician legates, Drapheim and Jacopus Dune, carefully. He'd already sounded them out. 'Gentlemen, Legate Pelk is quite correct, Noros is in dire straits, but her plight isn't unique. All the vassal-states have been bled dry these past five years, ever since the Third Crusade destroyed our economy. I'm Earl of Bres and I can tell you that we're facing tax demands well beyond our means; so too Midrea, Andressea and Brevis. Even Aquillea's staggering. In its desperation to recover, the Imperial Treasury is driving us all into penury. They've already lost Rimoni to this "Lord of Rym" – there are no governors or Imperial legions in the south any more. Do they have the ability to hold onto the rest?'

'What are you actually saying?' Pelk demanded.

'I'm saying that I'm the most powerful man in Bricia, in terms of wealth and personal military resource, and I know that I would have the numbers there to oust the Imperial governor and declare an emergency ruling council in the name of a Brician "res publica". Legates Drapheim and Dune are well-connected in Kerno and Laben, where there are half a dozen powerful men ready to support such a move, and with the Imperial legions in Bricia stationed in the Knebb Valley, there would be little resistance. Bricia is fed up with feathering the nests of Pallacian nobles.'

If Myron has spies here, he's got enough to have us all arrested, Seth thought. He wondered if the Noros Revolt had begun in a similar way. His father had helped crush that revolt; he'd be turning in his grave if he could hear his son now.

The taproom fell silent again and they could hear the evening sounds – the rain on the windows and roof-tops, the lower ranks drinking below, but mostly the rumble of casualty carts trundling past. Around them, forty thousand men were settling into whatever housing they could find for another bleak night, with little food and virtually no wood or coal to burn. It was change-of-watch time: men were marching to the walls to relieve those who'd been manning them since late afternoon. Distant shrieks from the wounded hung in the air.

'A "res publica"?' one of the aides asked at last. 'What's that?'

'A *suffragium*,' said Seth, 'with temporary leaders voted into and out of office. In the short term, it would be an emergency council of those leading the rebellion. Longer-term, it would mean men of property voting representatives onto a Ruling Council: isn't that right, Justiciar?' he said, turning to Detabrey.

'That's it, in a nutshell,' the justiciar replied.

'Why not a king?' Pelk asked.

'At least four ducal families in Bricia claim to be descendants of the last Brician monarch,' Seth said, 'Give them a sniff of a crown and they'll tear Bricia apart. No doubt Noros has similar issues. It's vital there's unity against the empire, and Justiciar Detabrey believes suffragium is the best way to achieve that.'

'I do,' Detabrey agreed, 'but we're getting ahead of ourselves. If we can force Pallas to expel Myron, we're still acting legally. It's only the next step, refusing to permit a new governor to take authority, that would be an act of rebellion.'

Another brooding silence fell, then Drapheim said, 'Nothing can happen while Myron holds Ringwald. If we can't oust Myron, no one's going to rebel against anything.'

'Then we've come full circle,' Pelk groaned. 'We've already agreed that the Ringwald is impregnable, at least during this siege. We just don't have the manpower.'

They fell silent, until Ramon asked, 'What about *woman* power? Would the defenders actually hurl women from the walls?'

The soldiers gave a shudder. 'We can't ask *women* to fight our battles,' Pelk snorted. 'Dear Kore, it's them we're fighting for – our men would go mad if we put them in danger.'

'Have you heard of the Sisters' Crusade?' Ramon asked. 'It's even spread to Lantris now. I saw *nuns* rioting in Pernepolis, and young women – *wealthy* young women – standing right beside them. Point them at Myron and watch him squirm.'

'What if that's a mare we can't tame?' Yarronis asked.

'So you're more afraid of your wife than Myron?'

'Have you met my wife?' the legate replied drily. 'She'd be in the front line if I let her.'

'Then let her,' Vaal Soren, of the Noros Alpenfleur Legion, normally a quiet, studious man, put in forcibly. 'We're all married to mages and mine's not short of opinions. I'd tremble for any ranker who got in her way.'

Seth took a deep breath. 'Then let's speak to the women.'

'How do I look?' Vania di Aelno asked, primping in her rather low-cut habit.

'Like a very slutty nun,' Ramon replied, fiddling with his own uncomfortable labourer's guise. 'My dreams won't be the same for months.'

'That's what I was aiming for,' Vania smirked. 'How're the walls holding?'

'Well enough. Those poor Noorie bastards can barely climb the ladders now, they're so cold and tired and sick. Their archers have run out of arrows and their magi are too scared to use their gnosis for fear of attracting a response. But the walls are almost down in a dozen places, especially around the gatehouse. We've only got a matter of days now.'

'Then best we break into Ringwald,' Vania said confidently. 'Let's go.'

The clamour outside had been growing all morning and as they went down to the street, a new chant rang out: '*MYRON, MYRON, COME ON OUT, MYRON!*' They were swiftly swept into a river of people, mostly women and old men, all making their way from Lowertown and the other tiers to the gates of Ringwald.

'*MYRON, MYRON, COME ON OUT, MYRON!*'

When they reached the main square in front of the gates, Ramon propelled Vania through the press, then found an awning and clambered up, careful not to reveal his gnosis. He sucked in his breath: he'd asked for ten thousand women, thinking he'd get nowhere near that . . . but there were easily three times as many here, pressing in on every side: a siege within a siege. Mothers, daughters, sisters and sweethearts were screaming for their men, the soldiers guarding the top tier, to come down and support their own, and the men above were glancing about fearfully while their officers barked orders. There was a thunderous hammering on the gates, and when at last Pavius Prelatus appeared in his full regalia, he couldn't get out a word before being howled down by his own priests and nuns, who'd been forbidden entry to Ringwald along with the masses.

Vania leaped onto a conveniently upturned wagon and silently drew a thumb across her own throat. After a moment, everyone else did the same, making the prelate visibly blanche.

'Bring out Myron!' someone shouted, and the cry went up everywhere: 'BRING OUT MYRON!'

Ladders began to go up and women made way for a big battering ram that had appeared in the square as the protest became a full-out assault on the walls. The nuns were leading the way, augmented by Vania and some of the female battle-magi from Ramon's legion. Those climbing the ladders went slowly, waiting on each step for shouted support, drawing the crowds with them.

<How's it going?> Seth called.

<Peaceful so far, but it's warming up,> Ramon replied. <There's a lot of genuine anger here. And you?> The only thing he could hear of the battle, two miles south of the walls, was the rhythmic booming of catapulted boulders striking stone.

<The siege-engines have settled on the three weakest points. The best we can do is rush men to what's left of the walls as soon as they give up the bombardment and attack.>

<Then best we resolve this, before we're fighting on two fronts,> Ramon replied, closing the connection.

Moments later, there was an immense roar: the first of the nuns reaching the top of the ladders had found themselves confronted by a wall of locked shields. They made a show of hammering on them.

<LET US IN – MYRON, LET US IN!>

Newcomers scrambled up behind the sisters, a mix of nuns, wild-haired young women and stout matrons, all of them waving their fists and shrieking at the defenders on the battlements.

'Tomi?' one mother shrieked at a soldier above, 'Our Tomi? You let us in, boy!'

'Go 'ome, Ma!' a plaintive voice shouted, making the crowd roar with laughter.

'*Come on, our Tomi, let us in,*' those nearest the woman cried at the hapless soldier.

But tempers were rising too, on both sides. There was a booming crash as the battering ram hit, but wards flashed and the big gates barely moved. As the ram crew took it back for a second go, Ramon heard the buzzing in his ear of someone trying to reach him.

He climbed the awning and jumped through the window, greeting the clothier he'd earlier befriended, then shut himself in the hall and answered the gnostic contact.

Calan Dubrayle's anxious, exhausted face appeared. His words were barely audible above the din outside.

<*Father,*> Ramon said cheerily, <*I thought I'd hear from you.*>

<*What are you doing? I've got Governor Myron telling me that Noros is rebelling—*>

<*Not true – this is a spontaneous civilians' protest.*>

Dubrayle scowled. <*I told you to let me resolve this.*>

<*You're taking too long, Father.*>

<*And I need longer – you have to call this off. Myron's frightened – he's about to sanction violent counter-measures.*>

<*Myron's robbing the state's treasury and starving his own people!*>

<*You don't understand. The Royal Council are united behind Myron. They're determined to give him whatever support he needs—*>

<*Kore's Blood – but why? He's a damned liability.*>

He rubbed his face. <*Because when Seth Korion deserted and went to Norostein, he made rebellion throughout the south a very real possibility. So Lyra's council now think it's vital to prop up the governor. Lyra's barely hanging on anyway, so if a general revolt is sparked, the empire will disintegrate. Better the Shihad takes Norostein than Noros rebels.*>

That sounded likely, to Ramon, but it wasn't his concern. <Why should I care?>

<Because I'm tied too tightly to the Corani to survive if the Sacrecours regain power.>

<Again, why should I care?>

Dubrayle sighed heavily. <Because there's one reason I'm holding on here and that is for you, my son. I see myself in you, and much more. I was never a battle-mage, but you're an emerging force as a military man, and you're smart enough to survive Pallacian politics. I can imagine you, with my backing, in this place.>

Ramon was astounded. His father, who'd never even publicly acknowledged him before, was now speaking of taking him to the heart of the empire! Although his first reaction was to wonder if this was a sop to make him obey Dubrayle, the notion was dazzling. Imagine wielding all that influence . . .

<Can't the Royal Council be brought to see that Myron's a liability?> Ramon asked.

Dubrayle shook his head. <Not when Myron is tied to Pavius, who has Julia.>

Ramon bit his lip. It all came back to Julia . . . <Then these riots do have a use, Father. Use your connections: tell them if they want the civil riots to stop, I need to meet Myron and Pavius to discuss how.>

<What are you planning?>

<Me?> Ramon winked. <Nothing at all.>

They broke the contact, then Ramon sent to Vania, <Vee, keep this simmering, but don't let it boil over. I want pressure, pressure, pressure.>

He sensed her smirk of mischief. <Sounds good to me, Boss. Who knew being a nun could be such fun?>

He left her to it and was just leaving the clothier's when Seth's voice blared into his skull. <Ramon, Ramon – where are you? We have a full breach: they're breaking in!>

43

Death and the Necromancer

Thaumaturgy: Earth

From the earth we came, and to the earth we return when all is done. Our bones will become stone and our flesh the dirt in which flowers grow. Our bodies truly never die.

ZAIN TEACHING, C. 600

Norostein, Noros
Janune 936

All morning, Seth had watched the rocks from the siege-engines raining down on them. By midday the walls east of the main gates were teetering, so he pulled his defenders back to a cordon facing the imminent collapse, and when a great stretch of wall came crashing down soon after, the Shihad attacked all along the front, trying to prevent him from reinforcing the breach, while a hundred windships rose in unison and swung towards the city.

The enemy stormed over the frozen moat, pushing up the boulder- and corpse-strewn slope, while Seth hurled men into the gap to hold it. Javelins met spears, mage-bolts flashed and fireballs burst, but it was like trying to hold back the high tide and sheer weight of numbers forced him back in the bloodiest fighting of the war so far. Then the neighbouring section of wall went down, undermined by the enemy's Earth-gnosis, and a great mass of attackers burst into the square behind the main gates where King Phyllios had died.

Seth managed to set ranks at the edge of the square. Thin lines of heavily armoured legionaries locked their shields and hacked at the half-starved, frozen desert-dwellers who'd been brought thousands of miles into conditions they could barely endure. It was more murder than melee, but for every man who fell, the Shihad had ten times more.

Overhead, soaring eagle-riders hurled spears, some impaling two men at once, then a ballista shaft struck a bird and when it slammed into the ground, the rider's body whiplashed in the saddle, his neck snapping. Windships landing on rooftops disgorged men inside the walls, but it was another suicidal deployment, for the ships were in easy range of fire-arrows and the ballistae Seth had deployed throughout Lowertown. Although many burst into flames before they could land their troops, crashing inside the city, still hundreds of men were landed safely. Seth thanked Kore he'd had the civilians and refugees pulled back to the second tier, otherwise it would have been a massacre. Instead, the attackers ran straight into battle with Seth's reserves, positioned in the lanes and alleys.

As the pressure on the square intensified, Seth took his command group into the lines, to counter the Keshi magi trying to force a breakthrough. They rallied on a barricade of broken wagons. 'Up, up,' Pilus Lukaz shouted, bringing his cohort forward to relieve an exhausted unit. 'Shields high!'

'There!' Seth shouted, blazing gnosis-fire into a shielded knot of mounted Keshi behind the front lines. His pure-blood power effortlessly shattered their wards just before his aides unleashed their own fire, which raged through the knot of Shihadi magi. Fireballs flew back at them, while Keshi archers on the broken ramparts used their last arrows indiscriminately, seeking only to clear a gap so their soldiers could pour through.

They blasted apart another attack, then Delton hauled Seth back, begging him to listen. 'They're hitting the main gates now, sir – they'll take them any moment.'

We can't hold, was what he clearly wished he could say.

But we have to.

'Hold this line,' Seth told the frightened aide. 'There's nothing behind us right now.'

He backed off and pulsed a signal into the aether, an intimate sign that only Ramon would detect, then brought in his last reserves to engineer some kind of disengagement so he could pull his men back to the second tier. Lowertown was lost and now he had to prevent the enemy sweeping right through to the upper tier.

'We're inside,' Attam growled, and Rashid felt his heart finally lift from its dark pit.

The sultan clipped his heels to the flanks of his white warhorse and walked him forward, his eyes on the breach east of the main gates. The jagged gap now reached the ground and thousands of men were pushing through into the chaos beyond.

'How do the windships fare?' he asked.

Xoredh, his relay-stave crackling with energy, replied, 'The first wave has been isolated and cut down, but they've tied up the enemy reserves. The second wave's going in now.'

'Deny them a controlled retreat: we must take the second tier, and the third.' The weather-magi had warned that another storm was coming; his army couldn't survive that. They *had* to get in. 'Bring up the elephants. We must break the lines behind the breach and flood the lower tiers.' He turned to Attam. 'See it done, my son.'

Attam bowed in the saddle, then raised a hand and his severely depleted retinue went cantering forward. Trumpets blared and the few dozen surviving elephants lurched into motion, plodding forward as spearman scattered before them.

'Sweep the Crusaders away,' Attam roared. 'Open up the city for us.'

If you weren't a mage, Latif thought bitterly, *I could put an arrow in your throat from here.*

But such a shot would be futile, so all he could do was keep his face averted as Rani plodded past Sultan Rashid Mubarak, astride his beautiful white horse and speaking to his sinister younger son.

It was almost a full six-day since Selmir had 'disappeared', but no one had even voiced the possibility of murder, let alone actively investigated. After all, desertions were not unknown, even among the magi, and Selmir had had a reputation for hanging back . . .

Their new hazarapati, Ghoshin, led the combined force, bellowing about victory, but Latif's crew were all convinced that no one who went through that breach was getting out alive. 'Vishnarayan, protect us!' Sanjeep cried aloud, with even more passion than usual.

'For an Amteh worshipper, Sanjeep is mighty friendly with the Lakh gods during a fight,' Ashmak noted ironically. 'Mind, I'll take whatever help we can get.'

'Just keep us alive, my friend,' Latif said fervently. 'I don't want to die with the deed undone.'

They'd reached a strange kind of understanding since Selmir's death. Over the months of deprivation, slaughter and terror, Latif had stopped being Ashmak's slave and become a comrade, even a kind of brother. Ashmak now treated Sanjeep as a kind of uncle, and in his mind Rani was his *luck*. They were his family now and Ashmak was fiercely loyal to his own, a deep desert trait. They mattered more to him than the how and whys of Latif's desire for vengeance on Sultan Salim's murderers.

'You'll get your chance,' he growled. 'This is battle, and backs can't be watched for ever. But it's on you,' he reminded Latif. 'Don't involve us.'

'I won't,' Latif said. 'It's my fight, not yours.'

But first they had to survive the next few minutes. The last of the karkadann were going in first. Their low-slung bodies and giant horns made them unsuitable for bearing bowmen, but they made useful battering rams. They carried long howdahs bearing teams of magi and pikemen, ploughing pitilessly through their own men as they charged the barricades in the square. Ranks of Yurosi legionaries supported by magi stood behind the barriers of entangled wood and metal, hurling javelins and fire at the beasts and their riders.

Latif readied his arrows as Rani waded closer, ready to support the karkadann if they broke through. He saw the thrashing beasts taking pikes and spears in the face and sides as they battered at the piles of debris. Three went down, one after the other, then one managed to plough through a weak point, impaling a battle-mage on that impressive horn. Another of the beasts pushed in behind, and another, and the breach began to look like a breakthrough.

Sanjeep guided Rani to join the elephants advancing on the break in the lines. With spearmen singing victoriously, the Shihad swept forward. Latif exchanged shafts with archers on the walls above while Ashmak shielded them. For now personal vengeance didn't matter; what mattered was that tonight they'd sleep under a roof.

We're inside, his heart sang. *We're inside . . .*

The secondary line was about one thing only: buying time.

Seth felt his entire defence teetering. Ramon's cavalry were dealing with the windships landing behind them, but he needed a legion to hold this square while the other legions disengaged and retreated to the Copperleaf walls, like a hand applied to a bleeding wound.

Fifteen minutes, he'd told his commanders. *You'll have fifteen minutes to get your units from the outer walls to Copperleaf.* How to extricate them without them being cut down from behind was the difficulty; they all knew that some unlucky souls in the rearguard were going to die for the rest.

Delton found their horses and followed his Bricians as they tried to stop the oversized rynosaurs from sweeping them away. His battle-magi blazed at them; some dropped, but others ploughed on, often with dead crews and running blind, but they hit the Noromen lines like avalanches and tore through, tossing men aside or trampling obliviously over them. And behind them came the elephants, great towers of armoured flesh with mage-bolts and arrows flying from the wicker cabins on top.

'Throw them back!' Seth shouted, launching himself into a gap and blasting fire into the eyes of one of the horned beasts; two men darted beneath it and stabbed upwards – only to be crushed when the creature collapsed on top of them. More and more enemy were pouring into the break, tearing his lines open.

<*Jelaska, counter-charge!*> he called into the aether.

There was no reply, just a sudden and horrific outpouring of necromantic gnosis that caught a section of Keshi and ripped their souls away – then the Argundian pikemen went forward in a thick, bristling line, wading into the masses of Shihadi. Seth glimpsed Jelaska, her grey hair a banner: she blasted one elephant team apart, then panicked their beast and sent it careening back into the oncoming Easterners. But almost everyone else in the square was losing ground and the conical helms of the Argundians were getting drawn deeper in.

Seth swallowed, feeling sick as he realised he'd unthinkingly decided which legion's sacrifice would cover the retreat . . .

<Hold here!> he shouted to Jelaska, through the aether. *<Anchor us – and don't you damned well die!>*

<We all die, Seth Korion,> she responded, breaking the link.

The Argundians planted their shields in a line across the path of the multitudes pouring through as Seth found his secundus and shouted, 'All legions fall back to Copperleaf!'

'Fifteen minutes, sir,' Delton was calling, 'and quarter of a mile. We have to get out or we'll be too late.'

Some said you could feel your end coming, but if that was the case, premonitions were imprecise, because Jelaska Lyndrethuse, Argundian necromancer, had been contemplating death actively for the past five years.

But it was likely imminent now. The shame of it was, she was going to be taking most of her brave boys with her. The Lyndrethuse family legion, recruited from the valley her kin had ruled for centuries, had been with her on two Crusades, one dull, the other harrowing and glorious. She knew all their names, past and present; she'd got drunk with them, been laid by a few, seen deserts and mountains, mighty sea-cliffs and gleaming palaces. Her only regret was that she'd never brought life into this world, but too much necromancy tended to destroy that capacity.

But I'm tired of it all now. I just want to stop.

She certainly hadn't planned to be the rearguard here, but chance and split-second decisions had decided for her. She saw tidal waves of Ahmedhassans – she refused to think of them as *Noories* now, the derisory word felt uncomfortable when she'd seen so much courage among them – slam into her lines, and although her boys hurled them back time and again, they just kept coming.

'We can't hold them, Lady,' burly Moltus told her, his voice cracking just a little. There was grey in his beard now, she realised with a start. *Poor lad . . . I remember his father . . .*

'No backwards steps,' she shouted as the next charge began, led by a knot of horsemen under the Mubarak Lion banner. 'Kore sees your death-wounds, boys: you make sure there's none in your backs!'

She stalked behind the central maniple, listening to the aether: Seth's men were using the time she was purchasing to get to the inner walls, but they needed longer.

'See those *smeerlappen*?' she bawled, pointing at the Mubarak flag. 'We're going to change the rukking succession in Kesh, my brudas! They're going to need a new prince!'

The brazen trumpets howled and amidst the din they hit her again with horned karkadann and towering elephants, cavalry and footmen striking her thin lines, which bent, rallied, buckled and clung on. The sheer weight of men piled up, scrambling onto the shoulders of those in front and hurling themselves bodily over the shield-wall, crushing *her boys* to the ground.

She sent a violet blaze, ripping souls from bodies and feeding on them, becoming the monster that had lurked inside her since near-death on the Leviathan Bridge in 930. She barely saw her dearest go down, battle-magi veterans like Moltus and Sanni, Grondeth and Falsko – she didn't want to. There was a seething mess of bloodlust and hunger inside her now and the more she killed, the stronger she grew, tearing apart men without even touching them. Shafts thudded into her flesh as she forgot how to shield, but nothing could stop her any more.

'Come on, you rukking scum,' she howled. 'I'm Glamortha: I am the Angel of Death!'

Attam Mubarak threw a backwards glance at the haunted face of his father. *He wants to keep me from the fray, but it's only in battle that I'm really alive* . . . Borne along on that thought, he turned back to ride the irresistible tide pouring across the square as they finally cracked the Argundian pikemen and freed the river of men to flow.

There was only one knot of resistance now: a rock in the flood, and there at the heart of it was the prize bitch they would take down: for Riverdown and for glory.

'Remember,' he told his men, 'she's a death-eater. She'll die hard – and she'll have a scarab to preserve her. Kill her, and destroy whatever emerges from her mouth.' He glared about him, ensuring his comrades understood. Then he slammed his fist against his breastplate and roared, 'Forward!'

In seconds, the Argundian jadugara had sent most of his retinue to oblivion.

One moment they were powering through the few remaining Yurosi, then purple light blazed, his friends began to scream, clutching at their chests and throats, their horses reared, whinnying most horribly – and they all collapsed . . .

Attam's mount stumbled over a body and fell. Feeling bones crunch, his inner hymn of glory stuttered to a halt . . . as a wraith-like figure stalked towards him, a desiccated corpse with a cloud of grey hair and shredded black robes. Arrows jutted from her front and side, even her left breast, but she was singing some barbarous song as purple bolts blasted from her hands into the press of men who were now tumbling over themselves to get away.

As Attam struggled to free himself, his broken leg grating agonisingly, the necromancer woman tore the head off his cousin Fedhi and burned his friend Salabas to the bone. Then she was looming over him, a leaf-blade dagger in her hand. The blade was shimmering.

He stopped struggling and instead, wrenched his scimitar free and in one savage motion, twisted and lunged at her, sending gnosis-fire streaming along the blade, even as she bent over him and her dagger plunged down.

His scimitar slashed through her skeletal neck and her head spun and landed in his lap. Her body fell sideways, her dagger only scraping his breastplate, but he barely saw that through the white blaze of agony that burned his awareness away.

A few moments later, a creature with many legs and a bloody carapace crawled out of the Argundian jadugara's mouth, up his breastplate and into his own mouth.

Rashid had never acknowledged to himself how much he loved his hulking, brutish elder son until the moment a nimbus of purplish light enveloped Attam and his horsemen and all the beasts went crashing down.

'Attam!' he shouted, spurring his white stallion out of the crowd of men surrounding him – magi with shields, advisors and clergy, aides and runners, hangers-on . . . and Xoredh. He pushed through the retreating men and into the square, which was mostly full of the dying. Fires were breaking out in the buildings around the square, wreathing it in smoke so that suddenly, he could barely see more than ten yards.

So many bodies. Rashid dismounted to wade through the carnage. Blood was running everywhere. Discarded weapons and body parts were piled indiscriminately together. Where the Argundian rearguard had held the line, the corpses were three- or four-deep.

'Attam!' he shouted again, pushing aside dazed survivors, wandering about like men awaking from a nightmare. His protectors were somewhere behind him, scrambling to catch up. There was an elephant nearby, the men in the howdah just outlines in the murk.

'*ATTAM!*'

His heart leaped into his mouth as a familiar frame rose from the dead and dying: his indestructible son, tossing a skeletal figure aside and grinning savagely.

Rashid uttered a shuddering sigh of relief. *Dear Ahm, thank you!* 'Attam,' he called, 'I trust you've had your fill of blood?' Then he saw how his son was staggering and noticed the crooked right leg. He went to his son and seized his shoulder.

He met Attam's blank gaze – and then froze as his son's eyes flashed purple and a gnosis-lit dagger whipped around and punched through his wondrously inscribed, bejewelled armour, straight between his ribs. Cold heat exploded in his chest.

His legs turned to jelly as he slid down his son's body.

Latif held the nocked arrow, his fingers pinched about the shaft and the bowstring, ready to pull and shoot, but the sultan was shielded by the body of his wounded son. He cursed, wondering if he should have taken the shot a moment earlier, when the sultan was, for once in his life, alone.

Beside him, Ashmak fretted, but Sanjeep held Rani's reins and kept her still.

They all know why I hate him; they even sympathise . . . but it's my revenge.

—which was snatched away as he watched in wide-eyed disbelief. Crown Prince Attam drove a dagger into his father's chest and purple light exploded inside the wound. Rashid slumped and fell, but Attam was already pulling out the dagger before whirling to face Rashid's retinue, who'd finally caught up with their sultan.

'*Who else dies today, smeerlappen?*' Attam snarled. Latif, shocked, had just recognised the *Argundian* words when the crown prince pulled a Yurosi greatsword from the body of one of the fallen and hacked the nearest man almost in two. The guardsmen recoiled in shock, but three more died in as many blows before they finally realised that something was dreadfully wrong with their young prince and tried to fight back.

Howling with laughter, Attam waded into them, purple light streaming from his blade, leaving the sultan's body alone in the midst of the carnage.

Latif dropped his bow and leaped from the howdah, barely noticing the sickening crunch as he landed on a heap of dead spearmen. He scrambled to Rashid's side and cupped his head. 'Rashid,' he said, tearing off his helmet and pitching his voice *just so.*

The sultan looked up at him with glazed eyes. '*Salim? Am I dead already?*'

'Dying,' Latif told him, holding his dagger out of sight. '*Rashid, what have you done?*'

Rashid Mubarak flinched. 'My son . . . I lost my son, Salim. Shaitan's bargain . . .'

'*What happened? Tell me.*'

'The old tales are true . . . you can bargain with the Evil One. His agent on Urte is Ervyn Naxius . . . he offered me revenge on Yuros . . . to punish the infidel for their crimes . . . But I had to take your throne . . .'

Naxius: the Ordo Costruo renegade. 'Is Naxius behind the Masked Cabal?'

'Ai,' Rashid panted, visibly clinging to life. 'Salim, I'm so sorry . . . I loved you, truly, but you chose *peace* . . . Life is struggle: we're only ever hunters or prey . . .' His face was suddenly fearful. 'Naxius promised aid . . . but he made me accept one of his *daemons* into my *family* . . .'

'*What do you mean, "daemons"?*' Latif was beginning to feel very afraid.

'My son was given a mask . . . and a daemon inside his breast . . . He is a Mask: *Ironhelm*, all-powerful, all-seeing . . . with all the knowledge needed to launch an assault on Yuros.'

Latif tore his gaze from the stricken sultan to Attam Mubarak, who was now surrounded by battle-magi who were trying to keep him from his brother. More of them were dying every moment, but Attam could barely stand now. Arrows jutted from his flesh and blood was pouring from wounds all over him.

'Attam is Ironhelm?' Latif gasped. *Ironhelm . . . who killed my wife and son . . .*

Rashid pulled Latif's head to his lips and murmured, 'Not . . . not Attam . . . *Xoredh.*'

Then his eyes rolled and his face went slack.

Latif felt an incredible rush of emotions: hate and exultation, vindication, justice . . . and horror, remorse and despair. *Dear Ahm, how can you judge such a man? He saved the East, brought the Crusaders to their knees and sold his soul to a man of evil, for vengeance. Rashid Mubarak is a genius who has brought ruin on a generation.*

He looked up through tear-glazed eyes in time to see Xoredh Mubarak step through the press of men penning his brother Attam. He swung his blade, the huge warrior's head toppled from his tree-trunk body and both parts crashed down. Then he stamped on something near the fallen head. He looked around.

Ironhelm is Xoredh. He killed my family.

And now he's Sultan of Kesh . . .

Latif ducked his head and ran.

Seth Korion reformed his legions on the walls of Copperleaf, placing Pilus Lukaz's men above the gatehouse of the main route that ran from the gates below to Ringwald above. As the men took up positions, peering through the crenelated battlements into the close-packed streets below, Delton relayed reports.

'The Mountain Cats have reached the eastern walls intact, sir,' the aide croaked, 'and the Alpenfleur too.'

'What about Jelaska's men?' Seth asked heavily, although he knew the answer.

'Nothing, sir.'

Seth blinked away tears and made himself focus on the *now*. 'Are our lines set?'

'Almost sir, but—'

Delton stopped speaking as a sudden sound rose, at first in front of them, but then throughout Lowertown, where the Shihad was marching in, out of sight amidst the mile-wide ribbon of houses below. Seth knew that sound . . .

At Ardijah, the people chanted like that when they learned that the caliph was dead. 'Someone important has died,' he told Delton. 'Those are mourning songs.'

'Sounds like a Brevian washer-wraith,' Lukaz muttered.

With every moment, the sound swelled and came closer, but no one appeared. The men around him and the civilians in the squares behind listened fearfully, unsure what it portended.

In Ardijah they mourned for a month . . .

'Tell the commanders to maintain the alert,' he told Delton, 'but I think the fighting's done for the day.' *Maybe for longer.*

He was right, although it wasn't until that evening when they learned why, under a flag of truce. The news was beyond all hope: Sultan Rashid Mubarak was dead and the Shihad, now ensconced in Lowertown, was in mourning.

44

Lamentable but Necessary

Angelus and Daemon

In the Book of Kore, it is said that certain seraphim rejected Kore and were cast from Paradise – these are the daemons wizards and other magi have dealings with. Interestingly, the Kalistham takes the opposite view: that wild daemons or 'afreets' came first, but Ahm the Father raised some to virtue. They became the angels, or 'devas'. The moral implications of both views are instructive.

ODESSA D'ARK, ORDO COSTRUO, HEBUSALIM 862

Pallas, Rondelmar
Janune 936

'Today?' Solon asked Father Germane, who'd summoned him to an old gallery in the North Tower where imperial battle trophies, banners and standards of conquered foes, were stored. Judging by the spiders colonising the corners, it hadn't been cleaned for a long time.

'Today, at the Royal Council meeting,' Germane confirmed. 'Everyone is primed.'

'Setallius?'

'He's been diverted. We can't move against him until legal authority is invested in you.'

'Dubrayle?'

'We own him.'

Solon was surprised to find his hand shaking. He clenched it into a fist. *Too much merlo last night*, he scolded himself. But this close to his goal, he'd needed it. He was as nervous as he'd been on the eve of betraying Medelie's coup. But this would be done *right*. No one would get hurt – and Lyra would finally be brought to heel. *It's for her own good.*

'How quickly can you mobilise?' Germane asked.

'Inside the hour,' Solon growled. 'The moment the power is vested in me, I'll go to the Esdale Barracks and take direct control. All the Corani legions will be with me and the duke in Coraine will bend the knee. The Pallacian imperial troops know me. We'll use the Treasury to buy off any who waver. It's all prepared.'

Germane looked satisfied. 'Then Kore be with you . . . Emperor.' He gave the Imperial salute, then slunk out, leaving Solon alone with the dusty old trophies.

When I'm ruler, I'll clean these and redisplay them. There's too much womanly frippery in this damned palace. The realm needs reminding of our past glories.

It was so close now. The jaws of the trap had been prized open and the mechanism set.

Today, Lyra, you will submit to me, willing or no.

'Milady?' Dirklan said, alarmingly close, and Lyra jumped.

'Dirklan! I didn't hear you!' she gasped. He'd appeared over her shoulder, like the wraith of his nickname, as she sat at the mirror, preparing for the council meeting.

'I'd be a pretty poor spy if everyone could hear me coming,' he quipped. 'Are you well?'

She swallowed the acid in her throat and said, 'I'm fine, truly.'

She felt anything but fine, though – every time a shadow moved she thought it was Solon. Every time a man spoke it was *him*. To have someone even brush against her made her shudder. *He was going to take me, even unwilling. I know it.* But she couldn't speak of that, not even to Dirklan.

She no longer needed the bandages and her vision was returning to normal, to her intense relief; being blind had scared her. What with that and Solon's menacing visit, she'd not been sleeping and felt utterly exhausted as a consequence.

'I've received a tip-off about the street riots,' Dirklan said. 'I'll be late for today's council meeting.'

'Anything I should know of?'

'Too early to say: a sighting of Tad Kaden, I'm told. It may be nothing.'

After her spymaster had departed, Lyra sat staring into the mirror at the pale, sad-looking blonde woman with bags under her eyes, until a gruff female voice interrupted her musing. Brigeda, one of several Volsai woman taking turns filling in as her bodyguard, called, 'Milady, the counsellors say something urgent has arisen and ask that you begin the meeting early – is that to your liking?'

It'll mean Dirklan's not there, but he's got no vote . . . 'Yes, all right. Let's just get it over with,' she said.

She left Brigeda outside the council chamber, then paused, feeling suddenly nauseous. *Solon will be in there.* Her locks had been replaced and new wards set, but she still felt monstrously unready to face him.

She'd gone for a severe, unreachable look today, choosing a prim dress with a high neckline, tying up her hair and setting her coronet firmly in place. She schooled her face into an imperious expression, then nodded to the doormen and entered.

All her counsellors except Dirklan were present. 'Good morning,' she said, carefully not looking at Solon. 'I'm told there's an urgent matter?'

They mumbled greetings as she sat, then Imperocrator Rael Relantine spoke in a grave, courtroom voice. 'There is, Milady. It concerns a case you might remember – Lady Orsa Basham of Siberland?'

Lyra cast her mind back. 'Yes? What's happened? Dear Kore, don't say Argundy have invaded Siberland?'

Relantine shook his head. 'No, Majesty. But we have another similar case. We've identified another titular noble whose actions present a grave risk to the empire.'

Lyra stared. 'Who?' An awful thought struck her as she realised who *wasn't* present. 'You don't mean Lord Setallius, surely?'

Relantine looked at her sadly. 'No, Majesty. The person endangering us all is *you.*'

The door opened and Sir Roland de Farenbrette and Sir Nestor Sulpeter, Lord Rolven's youngest son, took up guard positions beside the door, then Justiciar Relantine raised his voice. 'This is now a hearing of the Regal Court, the highest court of the empire, being the members of the Royal Council. It is invested with supreme power and is charged to adjudicate upon the competency of Empress Lyra Vereinen and her right to rule.'

Norostein, Noros

Ramon Sensini slipped through the narrow postern gate set halfway up the eastern flanks of the Ringwald walls. The only approach was via an exposed path, right under the battlements above, but he'd been signalled to come forward.

If he was going to be betrayed, now was probably the time, but Guard Captain Era Hyson, the man he'd come to see, opened the gate and led him to a tiny, draughty well-square behind the guardhouse.

'Is Pavius going to play this straight, Era?'

'I believe so,' Hyson replied. 'Myron called me in yesterday morning, said you'd asked for me to facilitate a meeting to settle this civil disobedience. He's getting a lot of pressure from his own supporters – they'll be vulnerable if the protests turn violent.'

'Will Pavius come alone?'

'Yes; Myron doesn't want to be actively involved. I don't think Pavius will concede anything, though. With the Shihad in mourning they see a chance. I think Myron intends to move against Lord Korion very soon.'

'I think you're right,' Ramon admitted. 'Where's Pavius now?'

'Waiting for us in the Astradyne Chapel, just a block away. I've got men ready to escort you, but if they are trying to trap you, I can't do much. We've been mostly disbanded – there's only one cohort of us left.'

'Thank you, Captain.' He added sincerely, 'I'll not ask anyone to die for me.'

Followed by the last cohort of Royal Guards, they walked through a picturesque, *very* wealthy neighbourhood: every property in Ringwald was walled, with its own small garden. In a normal year, the residents would be at their rural retreats, but with the Shihad encamped across the countryside, smoke was pouring from every chimney.

The Astradyne Chapel was dedicated to a small order of magi-priests who had worshipped seraphim as higher beings than orthodox Kore doctrine espoused. As they entered, Ramon listened to the aether, then murmured to Hyson, 'I've detected at least a century of men, closing in on us. I meant what I said: don't die for me.' He shook the captain's hand, then slipped into the chapel where he found Pavius Prelatus kneeling before a shrine to the seraphim Barachiel. The prelate looked up as two Kirkegarde knights emerged. 'I'm glad you've come to us,' he said smugly. 'It saves us hunting.'

Ramon showed them empty hands. 'I'm here to talk about ending the riots. They'll only escalate now Lowertown has fallen,' he replied. 'But first, show me my daughter. My father wonders if you are just bluffing.'

'I'll arrange a lock of her hair,' Pavius said. 'Or maybe a finger?'

'Just let me speak to her,' Ramon asked. 'It's her birthday and I want her to see her father.'

'Her birthday?' Pavius looked sceptical. 'Why should I care?'

Ramon met his eyes. 'Because otherwise I'll assume you're bluffing, and then we'll see how brave you are.'

Pavius drew himself up to his full height – which was an inch or so shorter than Ramon – and raised his voice querulously. 'I dictate the terms here . . . *half-blood*.' He turned to his Kirkegarde minders and jabbed a finger at Ramon. 'Take him.'

The two men advanced as Ramon pulsed a signal and Era Hyson stepped into the chapel. At his gesture, the five guards with him fanned out.

'I was asked to broker this meeting as an honourable man,' Captain Hyson said crisply. 'I will enforce the peace here, on my honour.'

'We have a warrant for his arrest,' Pavius snapped.

'This meeting was called under truce and therefore the warrant may not be served.'

Pavius gave him a seething look, then locked gazes with Ramon.

'Seven against three,' Ramon commented. 'Are you going to play fair?'

The prelate's eyes flickered uncertainly, then he signed the Kirkegarde men to step back. He turned to Hyson and snapped, 'Your career is over, fool.' Then he returned his attention to Ramon. 'Very well, Sensini, let's remind ourselves who holds the true power here.' He went to a ritual basin, poured water into it, drew on the gnosis and conjured. Light appeared in his hands and drizzled into the basin. Images rose like steam, becoming a globe of light a foot or more across. 'Secrelius,' he called. 'Secrelius—'

The name brought mixed emotions. *Secrelius is a killer . . . but he works alone . . .* 'Nice company for a prelate,' Ramon commented.

Pavius gave him a superior smile. 'Kore finds uses for us all.' He spread his fingers and an image appeared in the globe: a bald, leering man wearing heavy winter robes. 'Ah, there you are,' Pavius said. 'Sensini wants to see his child.'

Secrelius turned his head and the globe followed his glance.

Ramon saw a middle-aged woman with long brown hair, sitting with a perky-faced little girl with short black hair sprouting in all directions.

'Oi, Healer,' Secrelius called. 'Bring the girl.'

The brown-haired woman turned. Ramon presumed she was seeing a globe of light containing Pavius' image, for her eyes narrowed. She'd aged since he last saw her, her face fuller, with a few wrinkles, but his heart warmed. 'Lanna,' he called, 'it's okay.'

'Ramon?' Lanna Jureigh's eyes widened at the sound of his voice.

'Papa!' the girl exclaimed, bounding from her seat and running to the globe. 'Papa, we're—'

Secrelius swept her up and clamped his hand over her mouth. 'See, Sensini: we've got your daughter.' He smirked. 'So what ezzackly d'ye propose t'do 'bout it?'

Pallas, Rondelmar

At Justiciar Relantine's signal, a priest entered, Father Germane, the new chaplain of the Royal Chapel, who placed the *Book of Kore* before her. Then Relantine asked, 'Are you Lyra Vereinen, daughter of Ainar Borodium and Natia Sacrecour?'

Lyra stared at the justiciar, red-faced and utterly livid – and petrified. 'You know who I am,' she grated.

She looked about her, seeking some sign of support, but Wurther's normally kindly face was sorrowful, as if she'd let him down, Dubrayle was sullenly watchful, and Takwyth ... she couldn't bear to gaze on *him*. The two knights at the door, Sir Roland and Sir Nestor, looked at her without pity.

'Nevertheless,' Relantine said, 'please affirm your identity, under oath.'

You prick, she thought. 'I am Lyra Vereinen, daughter of Natia Sacrecour.'

'And of Ainar Borodium?'

She glared. 'I never met my father, but I presume so,' she snarled. *There, make a lie of that if you can.* 'You cannot do this: I veto it. *I veto!*'

Relantine dropped his voice, sounding mild, conversational. 'Majesty, your veto cannot be used to defend yourself against a competency hearing, or else no one unfit to rule could ever be removed. The court refuses your veto.'

'You *traitor* – I asked you *specifically* about the veto–'

'Did you?' Relantine asked quizzically. 'I don't recall.' He tapped the papers before him. 'For the information of the counsellors, Queen Lyra refers to her own ruling on *Crown versus Lady Orsa Basham*, in which the following was adopted into case law: that where an emergency affecting the security of the realm can be attributed to the competency of a titled feudal lord, they must be made to accept Crown oversight; or if they are an unwed female, be permitted to select a husband to manage their affairs to the satisfaction of the Crown.'

Her eyes flew to Solon Takwyth, who was watching her with a stoic, martyred expression on his *loathsome* face. 'You can't do this to me!'

He didn't meet her gaze, or react.

'Please, Milady,' Relantine put in, 'this is unpleasant enough for us all without your interjections.'

They put Relantine under my nose and he led me by it, she wailed inside. 'I appointed you,' she shouted at him.

'Should that prevent me doing my duty?' Relantine asked smoothly. 'As it is, I must aid my fellow counsellors in seeing us through this crisis.' He looked down at his notes, then his voice reverted to that of a court clerk. 'Under the statutes, in the Regal Court one counsellor must take the role of judge – as Imperocrator, I will serve in that capacity. Our first task is to determine if there is an emergency, and whether that emergency is the result of the queen's unfitness to rule. I throw this open to the counsellors.'

Dominius Wurther coughed, then rumbled, 'Though it pains me to say it, as I admire and respect Queen Lyra, I believe that she is inadequate for her role. In her reign we've seen the bankruptcy of the Treasury, the breakdown of the relationship between Crown and the Church, the loss of the southern provinces, an invasion from the East, civil war break out with Dupenium, an insurrection inside the Celestium and marital infidelity. We now stand on the brink of the disintegration of the empire and the end of the world as we have known it for five centuries. An era of chaos awaits us. If that doesn't constitute an emergency, I don't know what does. She means well, but she is inadequate to deal with these challenges: a woman with no martial, legal or gnostic training, and no political alliances beyond House Corani. I believe her unfit to rule.'

Despite herself, Lyra felt tears streaming down her face: hearing this from someone she trusted – and whose life she'd saved with her *heretical* power.

That thought led to another: *Dear Kore, will this lead in turn to a heresy trial?* But then she realised that Dominius hadn't brought that up when he could have, and they'd no more than hinted that they knew Ainar wasn't her father. *Because they want to undermine my fitness to rule, not my legitimacy...*

'I seldom agree with the Grand Prelate,' Calan Dubrayle said distantly, 'but I must concur on this: we're teetering on the brink and I believe new leadership is required. I don't think ill of the queen, but our survival requires another to take up Imperial authority.' He fell silent, and looked at the table.

'I concur, and have nothing to add,' Solon Takwyth said, not looking up.

You bastard! You pretend you love me and you do this?

'As presiding justiciar I cannot offer opinion or vote,' Relantine said, although his tone suggested he agreed with all they'd said. 'Let me see those in favour of the proposition.' All three men raised their hands.

'Then we have established that an emergency is upon us,' Relantine said. 'But is she truly unfit to rule?'

'She has robbed my Church,' Wurther said instantly. 'Open war between Crown and Church? Never has such a thing been done before – never in history! No other evidence is needed, your honour.'

This is his revenge, Lyra thought furiously. *He will never forgive me for this.*

'She has no fiscal training and consistently ignores my advice,' Dubrayle said tonelessly, as if reciting lines by rote. 'She accepted the need to tax the Church, but she resisted seventeen previous statutes designed to right the Treasury accounts. I believe we would have had balanced books without taxing the Church had she not resisted my advice.'

All those greedy, petty taxes I prevented, to stop good people – poor people – from being driven further into penury . . .

'Our armies have been defeated in the south because the man she wrongly married led them to disaster,' Takwyth contributed, looking at her finally. 'Had she married a better man, victory would have been ours.'

A 'better' man . . . Lyra could feel the coils about her tighten. *He's going to have me by force this time – with legal blessing.* Suddenly her future felt only so long as the end of a rope or the edge of a knife, because she would *not* submit to him.

'I think Her Majesty's inadequacies with the law are amply demonstrated already,' Relantine said lightly, as if point-scoring in a debate. 'Therefore, I think–'

He broke off when a panel opened in the side wall and all eyes shot to it.

Dirklan Setallius stepped through, followed by the towering Mort Singolo. 'Gentlemen, I must have lost track of time – or did you start early?'

Justiciar Relantine sat up. 'As an *advisory* member of the Royal Council, you have no voice or vote here, Spymaster. This is a sitting of the Regal Court and you are not required.' He flicked a finger to Roland de Farenbrette, who strode towards the newcomers, while Lyra stared, her heart thumping.

Mort Singolo stepped in front of Sir Roland. 'Back up.'

'You don't scare me, Axeman.'

Mort blew Roland a kiss. 'Bravo.'

Relantine sighed. 'What do you want, Volsai Master?'

'To see justice done,' Dirklan said. 'I'm well aware of my limited status here, and I'm also aware you're acting within the law. I'm here merely to observe.' He looked meaningfully at Takwyth. 'I've worked long and hard with you all to stabilise Corani rule. I deserve to be here.'

Lyra felt her brief hope wink out. For a moment she'd thought Volsai might pour in and spirit her away, but instead she felt another coil tighten about her as Setallius took his customary seat at the bottom of the table, his curtain of silver hair all but concealing his face.

'Very well, but your man waits outside,' Relantine said.

'I'll leave when they do,' Mort Singolo said, looking at Sir Roland and Sir Nestor, planting his feet and folding his arms across his big chest.

'The Regal Court is entitled to place guards, for security.'

'As the person responsible for security, I endorse your right,' Setallius drawled. 'Wait outside, Mort. If we need armed men in this room, the empire has already fallen.'

Mort obeyed, leaving with a lingering and not very pleasant look at the two knights.

Relantine *tsked*, but turned his face back to Lyra. 'Majesty, do you have anything to say in your defence?'

She took a deep breath, brushing angrily at her tears and fighting for composure. 'I do not deny that we're in danger,' she began, 'but I challenge any of you to say you could have done better. My husband beat all-comers except *Takwyth* at the recent tourney – he was a knight *and* a leader. The army despatches are clear: the Sacrecour and Argundian armies let us down, not him. Yes, I vetoed some of Calan's ludicrously unfair tax proposals, and yes, I sanctioned the Church raids – and even the most devoted parishioners now see why! And if I can be entrapped by a piece of law, then congratulations, Justiciar. Do you rob babies for pleasure as well?'

She glared around the chamber, hating them all but focusing increasingly on Solon. 'Don't think I don't see where this is going: *that man there*, who can't take rejection, has set out systematically to *possess* me, all because he thinks he's above the law – that we need him so badly he can do what he likes!'

Distantly, she felt Aradea wonder at her distress and it occurred to her that maybe she could call upon the dwyma and pull the entire Bastion down on their heads ... which would probably kill Rildan and bring about the end for all the Corani she had fought for.

They've got me, she realised. She glared again at Takwyth, clutching at straws. *If I can ruin him, perhaps I can prevent this. It's all being done for him, after all.*

She spoke before she lost courage. 'You accuse me of being unfit to rule, but what of the man who so clearly wants my crown? Just three nights hence he tried to rape me – he would have, had not Exilium intervened.'

The accusation rang around the chamber and everyone flinched, then looked at Solon.

He looked back, eyes narrowing, then shook his head. 'She's lying.'

His temerity made her blood boil.

'That is a serious counter-allegation,' Relantine said carefully, 'but fortunately, we're in a position to verify it easily enough. We have a character witness waiting outside in case they are needed, who is ideally placed to attest on this matter: the Regal Court calls Domara Ophenine, Royal Midwife.'

Lyra clutched at her breast as another betraying blade slid into her chest.

Nestor Sulpeter opened the door and brought Domara in. She was dressed in sober grey, with her silver hair tied back so tightly her scalp looked about to peel off. She took the vows in a cold bark, then looked at Lyra without a trace of sympathy.

'Domara, have you witnessed Lord Solon Takwyth and Empress Lyra Vereinen together?'

'I have,' she answered, coldly at first but heat rising. 'I've seen them copulating like animals, in every position that Nature and Kore abhors.' She jabbed a finger at Lyra. 'It's *her*, not him. He's a good man, but she's a *slut*.'

Lyra felt her jaw drop, bewildered that someone she'd trusted with the life of her only child could so clearly hate her so much and she had never known.

'Please confine yourself to the facts, Mistress Domara,' Relantine droned. 'When did you last observe them?'

'Three nights hence.'

'Ah, that night. The alleged "incident". Tell us of it.'

Domara's eyes lit up. 'I'd not heard them for several weeks, but that night the familiar noises started up again and I went to see. There's a place in the corridor where you can see into her chamber. There they were talking and embracing.'

'Embracing?' Lyra flared.

'Your Majesty, let the witness speak,' Relantine snapped. 'Lady Domara, pray continue.'

Domara's stony face gave no sign of pity. 'I saw Lord Solon fondling the queen's . . . ahem . . . chest; and they kissed. Then Exilium entered, they spoke in low voices and Lord Solon left. I saw no animosity.'

Lyra felt dizziness come over her. She'd always regarded fainting as contrived, a put-on escape for timid ladies, but she almost collapsed as the trap closed about her. 'What have I *ever* done to you?' she asked the midwife.

'You're unworthy – not like my dear Cordan. Why, you're not even Ainar's–'

'Just answer the court's questions, Midwife,' Relantine interrupted. 'Not hers.'

'But–'

'Thank you. Please wait outside, in case you're called again.'

As Domara left, Lyra's vision swam and the walls closed in. Then Relantine asked, 'Can you substantiate your accusation, Majesty? It's a man's honour you are besmirching.'

His precious honour . . . She bowed her head. 'No, I can't prove it. But he knows.'

'Lord Takwyth?'

The knight mumbled, 'There was no such attempt upon her virtue made. We had quarrelled, but I went to her to make up. She was hostile initially, but when I kissed her, she was willing. We were interrupted, and in propriety I left.'

'Thank you,' Relantine said, in a pained voice. 'Do you have aught else to say, Majesty?'

She shook her head hopelessly.

'Then let us proceed,' the justiciar said, addressing the room again. 'We have established that we are in a state of emergency and that Queen Lyra is unfit to rule. The case law of *Crown versus Basham* offers two choices: she may select a husband, whose appointment is approved by her familial guardian, of which she has none, so this prerogative reverts to her legal guardians, being this august body. Failing that, we may appoint someone to take up her authorities. As those authorities are to be empress, however, this would require an enforced abdication.' He looked up. 'You must choose, Majesty: either to marry a person of our choice or abdicate, annulling your coronation and relinquishing your claim – and your son's claim – to the throne.'

It's over . . .

'I . . . choose . . .' she started, her legs wobbling.

Then the desk crashed into her and swallowed her up.

She must have recovered quickly, judging by the fact that everyone was still seated, except for Calan Dubrayle, who had gone to the corner of the room and was in urgent gnostic communication with someone.

I guess I'm not immune to fainting after all.

She'd been laid on a bench under the windows and the pungent, sinus-crushing aroma of smelling salts filled her nasal passages. When she sat up blearily, she saw that the men were waiting stonily for her to rejoin them.

'Majesty, are you with us again?' Relantine asked coolly.

Sir Roland de Farenbrette went to help her stand and she angrily batted his hand away. She swayed unsteadily until she could make her way back to her throne, where she sat, breathing hard.

When she looked up, everyone was seated again, including Dubrayle.

Dominius Wurther was looking down at the bench in front of him, his usually animated face sour, as if ashamed to have been a part of this;

the way he was looking at Solon said that he'd at least half-believed her allegation. But when he looked up, she saw resolution. He would see this through.

Beside him, Solon Takwyth was sitting with his head in one hand, but when he felt her gaze on him, he looked at her with a kind of angry imploring, as if it were her fault that everything had come to this. And Dubrayle was utterly distracted, not looking at her at all. Not a single one of the three men would support her. And Setallius looked disinterested.

Probably more concerned about his own status going forward, she thought. *I hate you all, every single one of you.*

'Majesty,' Relantine said, 'might we have your decision now?'

Rildan, she thought, swallowing the gorge rising in her throat. *I'm doing this for Rildan.*

'I choose to be married, for the sake of my son.'

She watched the imbecilic look of pleasure on Takwyth's face. His sin had been effectively washed away and his lies would soon to be vindicated at the altar. She wished for a lightning-bolt to strike him down, and wondered if Valdyr could show her how.

One of us won't see out the next few weeks, she vowed silently.

'A wise choice, Majesty,' Relantine said gravely. 'That being the case, a husband will be chosen for you, and there being no familial guardian, that task in fact falls upon this very group, as the–'

'Actually, she does have family,' interrupted Dirklan Setallius, from the foot of the table. 'I'm her father.'

45

Untouchable

Children and Purity

*Some hold that a child is the perfect embodiment of innocence, so any child who dies
is not judged, but ascends directly to Kore's arms in Paradise. When I heard this, I
became frightened my father would suffocate me with my pillow that night, so that
I might go straight to heaven. But Mother told me that I was too old to be considered
an innocent, and that sin had already entered me. I was four years old.*

HYSSARA, MEMOIRS OF AN ABBESS, BRES 769

Norostein, Noros
Janune 936

Ramon watched through the globe of light Pavius had conjured, barely
able to contain himself from lashing out as Secrelius mauled his daughter. The rough-looking mage glanced over his shoulder at Lanna Jureigh,
who was watching worriedly. 'Keep your distance,' he warned the
healer, and Lanna went still.

Ramon guessed she was under a Chain-rune and little threat anyway,
but for now all his attention was on Julia. His palms were sweaty and
his throat constricted, just to see her in the assassin's grasp. '*Ciao bella,
Julia,*' he called, keeping his voice calm. 'How are you on your birthday,
darling girl?'

She's only five years old, he reminded himself. *I never wanted her involved
in the dark side of my life.* But now she was.

Secrelius unclamped the girl's mouth. She exclaimed, 'Yuck!' and wiped
her lips, then beamed through the globe at Ramon. 'Papa, where are you?'

Ramon glanced at Pavius, then said, 'Not far, Fantoche. Have you any-one to play with?'

Pavius and Secrelius sneered at the pet name, but Julia perked up and smiled. 'Just Nana-Lanna.'

Pavius began to interrupt and Ramon hissed, 'Please, just another moment: it's her birthday.' He glared until Pavius relented, then turned back to the image in the globe and called, 'I heard your special friend Scaramillo is going to visit.'

'Scaramillo?' Secrelius said incredulously. It meant 'Little Sick Girl'.

Julia's eyes widened. 'Scaramillo? I don't like Scaramillo, Papa.' She bent down and fiddled with the big ring on her left hand. 'She's not nice.'

Secrelius rolled his eyes. 'Right, you've seen the brat, now – hey! Ow!' Julia had wriggled suddenly in his arms – *and punched his thigh with her left hand*. He raised a fist. 'That's enough . . . of . . .'

With a bewildered look on his face, he flopped sideways, off his chair, while Julia rolled out of his grasp and looked into the globe.

'Papa,' she called anxiously, 'Papa, I think he's sick!'

Pavius glared at Ramon. 'What in Hel?'

From out of sight, they heard a gurgling sound, and a thumping noise, then it subsided. Ramon put a finger to his lips warningly and the prelate went still – and pale. 'Julia?'

His daughter's face appeared in the globe as if she'd pushed her head inside it, distorting the image so that her eyes were huge. 'Papa, the naughty man's been sick, but he's sleeping now. It's Scaramillo's fault.'

'Hush, now. It's no one's fault, Fantoche. He's just tired. *Lanna?*'

'I'm here, Ramon,' Lanna said, scooping Julia up. 'Ramon, there's just us: we're in a cottage near Bres – we were going to visit Carmina when they found us.'

Pavius tried to release the spell, but Ramon had a stiletto at his throat in an eye-blink. 'Leave it open, Priest.' He eyed the two Kirkegarde, but they too were standing stock-still, for Hyson's men had drawn weapons.

'Lanna, Seth's family have gone to their other place, you know the one. Go there now – I'll send people as soon as I can.'

'Papa,' Julia called, 'did Scaramillo do well?'

'She did wonderfully well,' he told her. 'Perfect.' *Birthday*, *Fantoche* and *Scaramillo* were their key words for using the poisoned ring. He'd hated teaching her how to do it, but in his world such things could mean life or death.

'You might have told me,' Lanna scolded. 'What's in that thing?'

'What you don't know can't hurt you. Er, probably. Anyway, you're a healer – and for Kore's sake, make sure she twists that ring so the needle's retracted. Now, go, quick: they might have hidden watchers. Find Carmina and let me know when you're safe.' He waved to Julia. 'See you soon, little Boo.'

'Ciao, Papa!'

Ramon nonchalantly broke Pavius' spell with a show of Ascendant-power that made the prelate quake. 'So, now you no longer have your hostage against my good behaviour, I believe it's time to re-negotiate.'

'You trained your five-year-old daughter to kill?' the priest said in a faltering voice, his future withering before his eyes. 'What kind of monster are you?'

'Says the man who blackmails others by kidnapping children? You've got the count of five to come up with a reason for me not to kill you. One . . .'

Pallas, Rondelmar

Setallius looked up at Lyra with his one good eye and she stared back, open-mouthed. Inside her head though, she was bouncing up and down, screaming with joyous terror and soaring over the world like a runaway eagle. *My father my father – I have a father–*

The spymaster pulled a small metal object from his pocket and slid it along the table to Imperocrator Relantine, who'd gone white as a sheet. 'This is Princess Natia's signet, the unique token that vanished when she was kidnapped by the Sacrecours in 909. She was still wearing it a year later when a young priest was permitted to visit her, to take her final Unburdening, before she was executed. I was that "priest".'

He has Mother's ring . . . He saw her alive . . .

Dominius' lugubrious features had gone slack. Dubrayle looked para-lysed and Solon Takwyth was ashen. Lyra could see that like her, they were hanging on every word.

'You've been agonising over consensual union,' Setallius began, 'so I will assure you that ours was *entirely* consensual. I had been having an adulterous affair with Natia prior to her abduction. Some of you might remember Ainar – he was a braggart and a bully, a foolish choice for her, but Magnus insisted, because of his grand plan to unify Argundy and Rondelmar. Ainar and Natia loathed each other, and those of us assigned to protect her knew it. I was a young Volsai, assigned to her security detail, and I did the foolish thing: I fell in love with her, and she with me.' He sniffed suddenly, and through her own streaming eyes, Lyra could see the normally impassive spymaster was barely containing his emotions.

He's my father . . . mine . . . my father!

She wondered how she hadn't seen it before, in the way his hair crowned, and the shape of his nose and chin – but the truth was, she'd never thought to look. *And he's come to my rescue, as fathers always do in the Fey Tales.* Her heart swelled to bursting.

'I managed to trick the guards into giving us – the soon-to-be exe-cuted princess and the priest – some privacy. We talked, we made love – then I had to leave–' He looked up, visibly composing himself. 'The next day, when I returned with knights of Coraine to break her out, the place was empty. Someone had tipped them off. I thought her dead, until much, much later, when I learned that the Keepers had countermanded the execution order. But she was dead by then. And I had no idea . . .' He looked profoundly sad. 'I never knew Natia had con-ceived until five years ago, when Ril Endarion found Lyra. The moment I saw her I recognised her – but what could I say? To claim her risked invalidating her legitimacy as queen, even though as Natia's daughter her claim is entirely valid.' He glared at the men around the table. 'All I could do was to serve as best I could.' He looked along the table to Lyra and said humbly, 'Forgive me, Daughter, please.'

She wanted to hurl herself across the table and embrace him, but all she could do was nod helplessly.

Relantine visibly gulped, then pushed the ring before him in front of Wurther, whose eyes narrowed as he examined it with the gnosis. 'It's Natia's,' he admitted. 'Her aura clings to it.'

'But that doesn't prove—' Takwyth began.

'Oh, come on,' Dubrayle suddenly snapped, 'look them both! If it's not clear to you, you're blind. We can run the gnostic tests if you insist, but for Kore's sake, it's *obvious*.'

Lyra's head was exploding, but even amidst this emotional turmoil, she knew the matter wasn't yet resolved – and so did Relantine, who slapped the table, trying to reassert control.

'Lord Setallius, we acknowledge your right to claim her as your child, but the charges of this court remain. She's been declared unfit to rule and if you don't concur to our marriage candidate, a guardian must be appointed and—'

'About that,' Dirklan interrupted. 'If you accept me as her father, then you are accepting my right to take up the title of Chancellor, and a permanent seat on the Royal Council, are you not?'

Relantine swallowed, then grudgingly said, 'Yes. But you're not sworn in . . .'

Dirklan smiled wryly. 'Then as this matter is incomplete and the composition of the court must legally change, you are obliged to either allow me to be involved now – and therefore start again, by voting on her fitness to rule – or you must drop the matter.'

He was offering them an honourable way out, but if they were willing to stay their course, they still had the upper hand: three votes to one. They would still be able to declare her unfit, and they could still appoint someone over her head, forcing her to abdicate.

By their expressions, they knew this too.

'You are correct, of course, *Chancellor*,' Relantine conceded, after looking at Wurther. 'But this is an emergency court and we must resolve this matter, *now*. I will grant you a vote. On the matter of Queen Lyra's fitness to rule, raise your hands if you feel her to be unfit.'

Wurther and Takwyth raised their hands defiantly.

Setallius said, 'I'm against, of course. My daughter is a fine queen, as we all well know. I'm proud of her.'

Father, Lyra thought, *I'm proud of you too.*

Then all eyes turned to Calan Dubrayle, who was staring at the table, his eyes far away. Then the Treasurer's lips curled into one of his rare, quiet smiles and he looked at Wurther. 'I've just had some bad news, Dominius. One of your prelates, *Pavius*, I think his name was? I'm afraid he's lost someone . . . a five-year-old girl. But I gather she's been reunited with her family, so that's something, isn't it?' Then he turned to Relantine. 'I've changed my mind. My vote is for Queen Lyra to continue her reign.'

Wurther sat back in his seat, then his lugubrious features twisted into a wry smile. Solon buried his face in his arms on the table before him. Relantine's face went slack, then he intoned, 'The motion has no majority and is thus defeated.'

Silence crashed down on the room.

But Lyra didn't hear that, because her heart was singing a seraphic chorus as she leaped to her feet, ran the length of the room and threw herself into the arms of her father, the most perfect place in the world.

Domara rose stonily, watching the queen as she and that *hideous wraith* left the council chamber hand in hand. She wondered why Kore didn't strike them both down. The other counsellors had already left. The verdict had been obvious by the expressions on their faces. No one even glanced at her as they passed.

She glanced up at the icon of Kore on the wall. *How can you stand idly by, Great Father?* she asked the silent statue. *How can you let sin triumph?*

As if in a waking nightmare, she walked unsteadily to a window and stared down at the city, wondering what this meant for her own future. Her family were still pure-bloods, after all these centuries: original members of the Blessed Three Hundred, part of a shrinking but precious heritage.

We built this empire.

'It's a sad day for justice,' a resonant voice said behind her, and she stiffened because she'd thought herself alone, then breathed easier as she recognised Father Germane.

'Aye, it is,' she said, barely holding herself together. *Dear Kore, I could scream.*

'The tragedy is that none of them had the courage to deal with the real issue,' he said. 'They all fear that revealing the depth of her sin would be to bring down House Corani as well. But the truth is, she's a *heretic*.'

Domara felt her chest constrict. 'What do you mean?'

Germane took her hands in his. 'Do you remember the great storm, how the Aerflus froze and the Celestium was buried in snow and ice? And that "earthquake" that wrecked the Royal Chapel? The queen caused both of those – but not with the gnosis. She's a *pandaemancer*, Domara. She uses heretical magic. She is truly the embodiment of Evil on Urte. But those venal *politicians* in that courtroom were too gutless to confront her sin.'

Domara felt a crushing sense of helplessness. 'She's the daughter of Lucian Himself,' she moaned.

'Aye, or his queen: Corinea Reborn. Evil is *real*, Domara, and it dwells in the heart of this realm.'

She almost fell to her knees, but Germane caught her and whispered, 'The souls of every man and woman alive are at stake: from the oldest burgher to the youngest infant, all of the empire takes its cues from the empress. You've been right about her all along. Your faith gives me hope.'

'But what can I do?'

'You can save a child, Domara. You know it is written in the *Book of Kore* that sin enters us with knowledge. Only the innocent are free from sin. Only an innocent child is guaranteed a place in Paradise.'

She knew exactly what he meant. She might not just save that dear child, but perhaps bring down the Evil Queen as well. She bowed her head. 'Then bless me, dear Father, that I may fulfil Kore's purpose.'

He made the Sign of Kore over her, then kissed her forehead. 'Go, with Kore's Blessing.'

His benevolent smile lit a flame in her breast. She strode out into the light, heavenly choruses swelling in her ears. *Holy, holy, holy, Word of Kore,* she sang in her mind as she passed the unquestioning guardsmen and entered the royal suite.

Holy, holy, holy, each Angelus sings . . .

She glimpsed the crippled Estellan, asleep in the bodyguard's chamber. Basia di Sirou's door opposite was closed. She walked into the nursery to find the duty maid, Nita, cooing over baby Rildan as he gurgled to wakefulness.

'I'll take him,' Domara told Nita. 'Go below and prepare lunch for the queen – she's on her way.'

'But it's my duty . . .' Nita faltered. Caring for the child was her favourite part of the day.

'Who do you think you are?' Domara snapped. 'I am Royal Midwife and this child is my life. I exist to serve him.' *And to save him.* 'Now, let me do my duty, and go and do yours.'

The young woman blanched and left. Domara glared after her until she was gone, then bent down and picked up the infant. *Just three months old,* she thought fondly, looking at his happy-blank face and fine black hair. *He's going to be dark, like his father. Look at that perfect little mouth, those delicate ears and tiny wee nose. Not so handsome as my darling Cordan was, mind . . .*

She hummed another line. *'Holy, holy, holy, sweet child of Kore . . .'* while walking to the window. She peered out at the bright winter's day, then looked at the hundred-foot drop to the courtyard below. With a small gesture she broke the sealing wards, unlocked the casement and pushed it open, humming her hymn to soothe Rildan's sudden anxiety.

Holy, holy, holy, Innocence is thine . . .

'This world is ugly, but Paradise is wonderful,' she told him. 'No one goes without and everything tastes like chocolate and strawberries. The seraphim sing praise to Kore all day and all night. You're so lucky that it's going to be the only world you'll ever know . . .'

She lifted him up as he looked at her with solemn, curious eyes.

Then she dropped him . . .

. . . as a lance of cold steel punching through Domara's ribcage, straight into her heart, hurled her sideways. She struck the floor and saw Rildan still hanging gurgling in the air, held aloft in an unseen kinesis grip, then he was drifted sideways into the arms of a pale Basia di Sirou, floating in mid-air like a ghost, her long nightdress trailing around her.

Exilium Excelsior limped to the boy and gathered him to his chest while Nita screamed from the door and the hymn in Domara's head faded into silence.

Rildan slumbered against Lyra's chest. She doubted she'd ever have the courage to let him go again. 'Did I bring this on myself?' she asked Dirklan as they sat side by side on the old stone bench in her snow-covered garden. 'You told me it was unwise to let Solon in.'

'No, the fault is entirely his. He should have been man enough to take your rejection, without resorting to chicanery or force. He accepted the terms of your relationship, then broke them. Do *not* blame yourself.'

She squirmed under his one-eyed gaze. 'You must have been so ashamed of me.'

'I was worried, but not ashamed. Your mother went through the same phase: she used to jest that I was her quintain, you know? The man-shaped device used to practise tilting? Perhaps at first that's all it was, but it became more. And then she was gone.' He stroked Rildan's hair and added, 'There's a lot of her in you.'

'I came so close to losing my son. I'll never be able to reward Nita enough for realising something was amiss and rousing Exilium.' She blinked back tears. 'If Domara could be turned against me, who else?'

'Domara passed every test I could imagine setting,' Dirklan said. 'She appeared to be the absolute epitome of loyalty. Thank Kore for Exilium and Basia.'

'Indeed,' Lyra agreed fervently. 'What a *dreadful* day.' Then she looked at her *father* and added, 'and a wonderful day too.' For a time they just stared at each other, then she asked, 'What happens now?'

'Well, nothing's greatly changed: you're still queen, and we're still at war. The Regal Court need not disclose that it ever sat, so your true parenthood will remain unknown. Officially, I'm still just an advisor – behind the closed doors of the Royal Council, I can function as Chancellor, but we must keep it secret.'

'What about the other counsellors?'

'Well, you can't unseat Wurther, but you do have him over a barrel: not only does he owe you, but he's burned his bridges. You can wring whatever you like from him now. And Dubrayle's fully committed.' His eye narrowed. 'Relantine can be dismissed, but of course he knows our secret, and so do Sir Roland and Sir Nestor. They're all sworn to secrecy, but will that hold?' He looked at her firmly. 'Shall I deal with it?'

She knew how Volsai dealt with such problems. 'I'll leave that to your discretion, but I'd as soon not have bloodshed.'

Dirklan nodded gravely. 'And . . . Takwyth?'

Dear Kore, it's tempting.

But Solon was her Knight-Commander. He'd saved her life, several times, and the guilt of having shared a bed with him wouldn't go away. 'He always says that he has the loyalty of our legions,' she worried. 'He says we can't stand against our enemies without him. I don't know that we can afford to lose him.' She looked up. 'Where is he?'

Dirklan straightened. 'He left the Bastion immediately after the Regal Court was disbanded and took a carriage down to the Esdale Barracks.'

Lyra felt a chill in her breast. 'Is he raising a rebellion?'

'That remains to be seen,' Dirklan said tersely. 'I have people there and I've fully briefed Oryn Levis. What happens next is down to them, but Takwyth has no legal mandate. And if you will excuse me, that's where I need to be.' He rose, pulled her to her feet and asked, 'The night you spoke of: what happened?'

She shuddered. 'He was going to rape me, I have no doubt of that. But Exilium shamed Solon into departing – which shows that he can still feel dishonour, at least! Dirklan – *Father* – if we need him, we need him. I can bide my time.'

'Let's see what transpires in Esdale.'

She hugged him, then stepped away. 'Kore speed you. And whatever happens, please return to me. Tonight, I want to hear about my mother. I want to know *everything.*'

Esdale, Pallas

Solon entered Legion Square flanked by Roland de Farenbrette and Nestor Sulpeter on Corani pegasi. They walked their steeds onto the parade ground, where the ranks were lined up, Corani green and red in great blocks, awaiting the promised address by their commander. He signed to the trumpeters to signal his arrival, the Knight-Commander come to speak to his men.

My lads – the sinews of this empire—

But then he paused. The trumpets were silent and the men were already being addressed. Oryn Levis, his big, bearish body hunched and his voice a drone, was reading from a parchment, his voice being carried by the gnosis to every corner. Behind him, the tribunes who commanded each maniple were surrounded by a crowd of Volsai, led by Patcheart.

'Although not obliged to go on record,' Levis read, 'the Regal Court has chosen to make the following statement: on this day, a group of peers of the realm sought to depose Queen Lyra Vereinen by legal means. *Their motion failed.* A subsequent and related attempt on the life of the new-born Crown Prince Rildan *failed.*' Oryn Levis paused, then added, 'The Regal Court upholds the legitimate reign of Queen Lyra Vereinen. The peers withdrew their motion and therefore any attempt to renew that claim will be a matter of *High Treason.* If they or any others seek to take by force what they could not by deceit, they will be arrested. All men of the Imperial and Corani legions are urged to report any man who seeks to subvert the reign of Queen Lyra. Long live the Empress!'

'*LONG LIVE THE EMPRESS!*' the rankers thundered.

Solon stared along the parade ground, all certainty gone. He could taste the energy in this field and it wasn't for rebellion. There was anger, clear anger, directed at the unnamed conspirators who would stoop to murdering babies.

My strength here is not just my reputation for prowess – it's also about honour . . . All Levis has to do is name me as one of those conspirators and that's gone. I don't know that even a tenth here would side with me . . .

When Dirklan Setallius appeared on the platform and whispered in Patcheart's ear, he knew his bridges were burning. The Wraith would knife him the moment his guard dropped, with his *bitch* daughter's blessing.

But the Duke of Coraine still expects me . . . The legions up there are primed and the Corani heartland will *rise – then these lads will feel the call of home and they'll flock to my banner.* He yanked his reins and turned his steed abruptly, while the closest rankers watched him – he could see them wondering why the boss wasn't up there.

Because you used me and you spat me out, Lyra! You don't deserve me.

He stabbed his spurs into his mount's flanks, it burst into a gallop and spread its wings, he rose into the air, followed by Roland and Nestor. They went soaring over the city, swinging north to Coraine – and rebellion.

EPILOGUE

A Storm from the North

On Perseverance

To persevere in the face of failure requires more than courage, it requires unswerving faith in your purpose, the willingness to sacrifice yourself for that goal and the conviction that those blows which do not slay you will make you stronger. Defeat is the Mother of Victory, if you learn from it.

ANTONIN MEIROS, 847

Pallas, Rondelmar
Janune 936

Lyra recalled a day three months ago when she'd gazed south across the Bruin, thinking that finally her enemies were out in the open. But now there was nowhere she could turn where there was not a foe. The courtiers buzzing round her throne felt like flies on a corpse, making her want to flee the hall, to run to Rildan, to hold him close and weep.

Domara almost killed my son.

My own counsellors almost dragged me into servitude.

Duke Garod readies war again, with Constant's children as his excuse.

Duke Torun Jandreux and Solon, his new 'champion', claim House Corani for themselves.

In the South, the Lord of Rym ravages unchecked and the Shihad remains undefeated.

And here in Pallas, a third of the city is now barricaded against the City Watch, while people march for this suffragium they think will save them all.

And now this . . .

Her fingers clung to the unpadded wooden armrests of the throne, aching from holding on so tight for so long. She heard the trumpets bray, then the herald proclaimed names and a delegation of self-satisfied men in long velvet cloaks sporting golden chains and plumed hats strode down the aisles: the ambassadors of Argundy, Estellayne, Brevis and Andressea, united for once.

Lyra glanced at the empty throne beside hers, where Ril's crown lay, a token of mourning. She took comfort from her father's shadowy presence behind her, next to Basia and Exilium, both on duty again thanks to the miracles of the healer-magi, although neither were yet wholly recovered. Around her the Pallacian courtiers watched avidly, their mood impossible to read. *Are they with me, or against?*

'Gentlemen,' she greeted the ambassadors as evenly as she could. 'You asked for an audience. Would you like to speak in private?' *Please, spare me this humiliation . . .*

The Ambassador for Argundy stepped forward, taking the lead as the largest of the powers represented. 'It befits us to speak before the Imperial throne and court,' he boomed. 'We are instructed by our lords to announce that on the first of Martrois 936 – in two months' time – we will cede from the empire.'

The bald bluntness of the statement took away her breath. There were no demands for concessions, no this-for-that. *They know there's nothing I can give them, and nothing I can withhold. In their eyes, the empire is doomed.*

Something like acid stung her eyes and her vision blurred. *The Sacrecours reigned for almost six hundred years. I've managed six. My son will inherit nothing . . .*

Her throat seized up, her lips moved, but words failed to emerge, while the ambassadors watched her with their cold, judging eyes. She could see their thoughts crawling across their faces as if she had the gnosis: that here was the true Lyra Vereinen: weak, trembling, powerless and paralysed like a doe before the hunter.

That goaded her to speak. 'Gentlemen, you are heard,' she managed. Her voice might have cracked under the strain, but it didn't break. 'The empire hears. History hears. But we do not accept your right to cede from this union. You know the consequences: millions will suffer. There are imperial legions in every state, and possessions we will not relinquish, so warn your masters: the blood of this action is on their hands.'

They listened silently and had the temerity to sniff dismissively, then with feathery plumes swaying, the ambassadors turned their back on her and strutted confidently away.

So that's it, she thought numbly, as her court stared and murmured. *I'm the last Empress of Rondelmar . . . I really am the Empress of the Fall.*

Ari Frankel heard the news in a taproom in Tockburn, drinking by himself. Cheers and singing rolled down the street outside and the patrons looked up as the doors slammed open and a wild-eyed youth burst in, shouting, 'Argundy is ceding! Estellayne, Brevis, Andressea too! The empire's falling apart!'

There was a moment of silent disbelief, then the entire room erupted into chaos. Complete strangers hugged like life-long friends, the firebrands hollered slogans – many of them Ari's – and musical instruments came out. In seconds there was frenzied dancing, and more casks were being broached.

A few ashen-faced patrons slunk out the back way, shopkeepers and small traders suddenly afraid of looting. The Watch hadn't been permitted into Tockburn for almost two weeks now, and criminal gangs were taking 'protection money' to keep the peace. Now, it appeared, everything was up for grabs . . .

Ari and Neif stared at the ceiling, fighting tears, remembering old comrades who had bled and died for this moment. His mind raced on, envisaging the new era–

Then a cold-eyed man appeared beside him and pulled him to his feet. 'Frankel,' Lazar said, his eyes glittering as he shook Ari's hand. 'Well done. You're no small part of this.'

Even now he doesn't smile. But Ari felt his own heart pumping. 'We must seize the moment,' he said, the words tumbling out. 'New pamphlets, a constitution must be drafted . . . we must elect a ruling council, place an ultimatum before the queen–'

'In time,' Lazar interrupted, 'but right now there are higher priorities.

The empire has sympathisers, even in the poor quarters. We have to purge. Come, Tad Kaden wants to speak with you.' He plucked at Ari's sleeve. 'This way.'

They shouldered through the revellers and left by the back door, just in time to see Gorn and a dozen of Lazar's most brutal men driving daggers into the chests of those who'd left the tavern earlier.

Dear Kore, Ari thought, as his gorge rose. *What are we doing?*

Norostein, Noros

Ajniha circled the tiered city of grey stone piled against the Alps like a rock-fall, groaning in relief to have finally arrived. Norostein was unconquered – he could clearly see the red-cloaked Yurosi legionaries on the inner walls – but in the lowest ring of the city, smoke rose from thousands of chimneys and the place was teeming with white- and dun-robed men, stacking bodies, clearing debris, hauling in supplies and shovelling snow. The two armies were mere feet from each other, but doing everything except fighting. The mourning period had created a truce, which so far was holding.

In a few days' time, they'll be slaughtering each other again.

The journey from Mollachia had been relatively uneventful, until he'd been intercepted by a patrol of roc-riders south of Jastenberg and heard the dreadful news: *Rashid is dead. Attam too.* That put just Xoredh and Teileman before him in the succession, but he feared Xoredh would never see him as an ally.

However, to fail to present himself before the new sultan would be taken as rebellion. *Sultan Salim was murdered by the Masked Cabal and Rashid benefited: does that imply Xoredh was also involved?* He still didn't know if Rashid had been one of the Cabal, working with them, or their puppet. He'd probably never know now.

All the things he'd learned about the Masks – the daemonic possession, the vulnerability to argenstael and silver, the identity of their leader, Naxius – could he risk telling Xoredh?

And that they've captured Jehana?

Explaining Tarita as one of his roc-riders, he'd secured her a 'replacement' bird, but she couldn't come into the city, for her face was known to the Masked Cabal. Right now she was setting up camp some thirty miles away deep in the wilderness.

I still don't know what to make of you, Tarita Alhani . . . But I'm grateful you're with me. At times he felt the barriers between them, between her rags and his riches, slowly eroding, some kind of energy building, but that was for another day.

Now he sent Ajniha soaring into the city. He'd been told the Shihad held the lower tier, so he selected the largest square, landed behind the main gates – and was immediately engulfed by reverential soldiers, all trying to express their sorrow at his loss. 'The sultan died just over there,' one said, pointing to a massive pile of offerings, personal effects looted from houses here or perhaps brought all the way from Ahmedhassa and laid on the blood-soaked ground in a giant pile. He went to it, knelt and prayed – more because it was expected – while the throng watched avidly.

Then he saw someone he knew: a gentle-looking young kalfas called Chanadhan, who looked to be waiting dutifully for him. He politely raised a hand. 'Thank you, all, but I am summoned,' he said, indicating the young scribe he'd met in Pontus and again at the fall of Thantis.

He asked Chanadhan, who was beaming in pleasure at being remembered, 'Are you here to take me to the sultan?'

'I've been asked to show you to your quarters. Sultan Xoredh will see you at the first opportunity, Great One.'

'But I have urgent tidings–'

'Sultan Xoredh is in solemn preparation for his coronation, Great Prince.'

'Of course he is. I can't interrupt the sacred rituals.' Waqar hesitated, then asked, 'Is Fatima al'Johsia quartered near?'

Chanadhan ducked his head. 'She's dead, Great Prince.'

Oh no . . . Waqar felt himself close up. 'How?'

'She led an attack, but she was cut off and slain. The spear she bore was recovered, but it had been destroyed.' He looked at him cautiously and added, 'I am sorry for your loss.'

Waqar had a sudden vision of his friends: Tamir, Baneet, Fatima and

Lukadin, singing together from the Godsingers' cupola in Sagostabad, before this nightmare began. Inseparable and happy, the best people he knew. *Now there's just me.* It was scarcely bearable.

The kalfas led him to a manor that had been largely stripped except for a mattress and a few bits of furniture. The blankets looked as if they had once been curtains. But there was food, and heated Yurosi wine, which tasted bitter but was pleasantly warming. The alcohol helped the tears flow as he mourned Fatima.

He wished Tarita had come; he needed someone right now – then he heard banging on a back door. There was a hurried conversation, then Chanadhan knocked and said shyly, 'There is a man asking to see you, Great Prince.'

Waqar looked up guardedly. 'Who is it?'

'He gave the name Latif,' Chanadhan said with a frown.

Waqar tried to think of anyone he knew called Latif. It wasn't an uncommon name, but it belonged to lower castes than his . . .

With a shock, he realised who it might be. 'Show him in.'

Chanadhan admitted a man in archer's garb but unarmed, middling in height and lean of build. As he instantly dropped straight to the floor in a full obeisance, Waqar hurriedly told Chanadhan, 'Shukran. You may go.' Then he closed every curtain, warded the doors and turned to the prostrated archer. 'You're the impersonator,' he exclaimed. 'But the sultan's household were all killed – how can you be here?'

Latif raised his head tentatively. 'It's a long story, but worth hearing, Great Prince.'

'Dear Ahm, I'm sure it is. But my cousin Xoredh is expecting me presently.'

Latif rose fluidly and dared to approach and clutch his arm, but his status was so nebulous – the harbadab had nothing to say about impersonators of dead sultans – that Waqar let him.

'Prince Waqar,' Latif said urgently, 'the one man you *must not see* is Xoredh.'

Xoredh Mubarak sat in the upper hall of the manor he'd chosen in Norostein's lowest tier, examining the royal accoutrements, the crowns and rings, the hordes of gems, the elaborate turbans, and thought about how much he'd longed for them all his life. He'd always known that the sultan's throne was his destiny.

We all knew you'd be sultan one day, Father, and I was always your greatest son: the natural heir. There was no law of primogeniture in Kesh: the tradition was that the dying sultan dictated the order of succession, but the reality was that the strongest man would take whatever he could. *Attam was never going to be a match for me.*

But when Rashid accepted Naxius' terms, dictating that one son became a Mask, of course his father had chosen him. '*On the most worthy must fall the greatest burden,*' his father had said. '*Attam is not capable of surviving daemonic possession – he would lose himself. But you, my brilliant son, you are strong enough to bear this burden.*'

The price for ultimate gnostic power was a daemon-spawn in his breast and to be removed from the succession; not officially, but it was made clear that Attam would be the heir. Certain prominent men were given warded boxes to be opened if Rashid died, revealing exactly what Xoredh had become.

Those men's heads had been delivered to him an hour after Rashid died, along with the unopened boxes. He'd known who they were within a day of accepting the daemon-spawn. *After all, you did put me in charge of intelligence, Father.*

And now he had it all: the throne, the riches and the daemon.

A messenger rang the bell and at his mental summons, entered: a human aide, oblivious to what it was he served. 'My Lord, a herald from–'

'Our new allies,' Xoredh interrupted. 'Show him in, then leave us.'

The man who entered was armed and armoured, but Xoredh felt no threat, for once the aide was gone, the herald's eyes turned oily black and his voice was the thousand-fold hiss of a daemon – but *not* Abraxas. The man's olive skin and black hair wouldn't have looked out of place in Dhassa, but he was Rimoni.

'Great Sultan,' the herald said, 'my Master, the Lord of Rym, greets thee.'

'I return his greetings. Where is he now?'

'On his way here, Great Sultan,' the herald replied. 'In one week, he will stand before the walls, at the rising of the first moon of Febreux. He brings one hundred thousand men, united under one mind. An army that has driven the empire from the South and broken the Mercenary Guild comes to your aid.'

'Norostein will fall, with or without them,' Xoredh snapped.

The herald bowed, not at all put out by his show of temper. 'The Lord of Rym places his resources entirely at your disposal, Great Sultan. The Master requires that our forces unite.'

'Unite . . . In Abraxas?'

The herald smiled. 'No, Great Sultan.' He drew a vial from his pocket: it contained a daemon-spawn, a wriggling millipede with faceted eyes and a lamprey-mouth. 'The Abraxas phase is over; that was only ever a means of testing the possession and proving to a greater daemon that the arrangement could function. The Master now desires that you join us in communion with Lucian – your Shaitan, the Lord of Hel.'

Rym, Rimoni

Cadearvo walked straight at an apparently solid wall and vanished through it. The wooden platform floating through the air behind him bore a body under a blanket. Before him was a tunnel lit by occasional gnostic lights leading to a subterranean palace.

This place had been invisible from above, just another pile of crumbling, sun-bleached stone in a sea of ruin. When the magi destroyed the Rimoni Empire, they'd used earthquakes and fire to level the entire imperial capital, then salted the ground for miles around. Those former citizens who had escaped into the countryside were beset by poverty and feuding. Pallas suffered no rivals and wished to erase the former masters of Yuros, so for centuries this place had been empty.

But Imperial Hill contained a subterranean maze that had become the Master's lair. Even when he was still able to dwell among the Ordo Costruo, he'd been conducting his secret research in this place.

Cadearvo knew it well; he'd been created here as the male

counterpart to Semakha. That she was dead didn't trouble him overly. The Master would create more like her. What *was* troubling was that she'd been bested at all. *We should have killed Ogre outright.*

But done was done, and the Master always knew best.

He entered an austere marble room with a great stone slab facing the setting sun. He floated the body onto the slab and settled it, then drew the blanket aside and checked the comatose woman beneath. She was rather lovely in her nakedness, with soft honey skin, dark nipples and hair.

He stroked Jehana Mubarak's cheek with his taloned hand.

'Cadearvo.' The clear male voice came from the doorway.

The giant immediately knelt. 'Master,' he growled reverently.

Ervyn Naxius entered. He was clad in black silk robes, in his youthful guise, with wavy copper hair and timeless amber eyes. 'Rise, rise my friend,' he said airily. His voice had an eagerness, a hunger even Cadearvo hadn't heard before. 'So, finally, we have an uninitiated dwymancer to play with,' the old magus purred. 'A gift from Lucian Himself.'

They prowled around the girl, admiring the curve of breast and hip, then Naxius stroked her hair and turned it pure white. 'There,' he said. 'That's much better.' He reached inside his robes and unhooked a mask from his belt, a skull mask of bone, and carefully placed it over Jehana's face. In seconds it had bonded with her skin, rising and falling as she breathed.

'Glamortha?' Cadearvo breathed. '*She* is to be Glamortha?'

'Yes, my friend. She is to be our Angel of Death.' Naxius prowled around her, sighing in pleasure. 'Do you know the legend of Glamortha? She remains a virgin until the Last Days, when she mates with Shaitan and becomes the Mother of Daemons.'

ACKNOWLEDGEMENTS

Writing is a team sport. I write some words. My test readers (Kerry Greig, Heather Adams, Paul Linton and Cath Mayo) tell me what does and doesn't work, and generally help knock me and the story into shape. Kerry has the added burden of putting up with me talking about imaginary people all the time – if karma is real, she did something *really bad* in a previous life, to be punished so. My gratitude to each of them is limitless.

Then the wonderful Jo Fletcher takes the submitted manuscript, corrects my wayward grammar and works with me to separate the wheat from the chaff. I could not ask to be in more experienced, skilled and empathetic hands. It's Jo's team at JFB/Quercus (especially Molly Powell), who take the product to market. My thanks go especially once more to Emily Faccini for the fresh maps, Leo Nickolls and Patrick Carpenter for the cover, and all others involved.

None of that would have happened if my agent, the aforementioned Heather, hadn't brought me to Jo's attention and maintained the ongoing relationship. I'm eternally grateful to her and her husband Mike Bryan, for their promotion of my work.

Thanks also to all you book-loving readers, without whom none of us would be employed. Stories connect us.

Finally, I couldn't do all this without the emotional support of family: my children, Brendan and Melissa, my parents Cliff and Biddy, my sister Robyn, and my friends – you know who you are.

Hello to Jason Isaacs.

David Hair, 2018
Bangkok and New Zealand

The Sunsurge Quartet will conclude in

Mother of Daemons

ALSO AVAILABLE FROM

JO FLETCHER BOOKS

Jo Fletcher
BOOKS

MAGE'S BLOOD

THE MOONTIDE QUARTET

DAVID HAIR

The Moontide is coming. Urte stands on the brink of war. Now three seemingly ordinary people will decide the fate of the world.

Urte is divided, its two continents separated by impassable seas. But once every twelve years, the Moontide sees the waters sink to their lowest point and the Leviathan Bridge is revealed, linking east to west for twenty-four short months.

The Rondian emperor, overlord of the west, is hell-bent on ruling both continents, and for the last two Moontides he has led armies of battle-magi across the bridge on crusades of conquest, pillaging his way across Antiopa.

But the people of the east have been preparing – and, this time, they are ready for a fight.

Jo Fletcher
BOOKS

DAVID HAIR

The Pyre

THE RETURN OF RAVANA
Book I

Mandore, Rajasthan, 769 AD: the evil sorcerer-king, Ravindra-Raj, has devised a deadly ritual. He and his seven queens will burn on his funeral pyre, and he will rise again with the powers of Ravana, Demon-King of the epic Ramayana. But things go wrong when a court poet rescues the beautiful, spirited Queen Darya, ruining the ritual – and Ravindra's plans.

Jodhpur, Rajasthan, 2010: At the site of ancient Mandore, Vikram, Amanjit, Deepika and Rasita meet – and are forced to accept that this is not the first time they have come together to fight the deathless king. Now Ravindra and his ghostly brides are hunting them down.

As vicious forces from the past come alive, Vikram needs to unlock truths that have been hidden for centuries, if they are to win this ancient battle . . . for the first and last time.

Jo Fletcher
BOOKS

DAVID HAIR
The
Adversaries

THE RETURN OF RAVANA
Book I I

Mumbai, 2010: Everyone's talking about Swayamvara Live!, the TV reality show recreating the ages-old custom where young men compete for the hand of a noble bride. In this case, the bride is Bollywood stunner Sunita Ashoka, who is pledged to marry the man who wins the on-screen contest. For Vikram Khandavani, it's a chance to draw out his nemesis Ravindra, the reincarnated sorcerer-king – but he's taking a deadly gamble.

Delhi, 1175: King Prithviraj Chauhan is about to storm the swayamvara of the beautiful Sanyogita – but he's not the only one fixated on the bride-to-be: Ravindra-Raj is coming too, and he's riding at the side of a fierce invader. Only Chand Bardai, in another life known as Aram Dhoop, the Poet of Mandore, stands between Ravindra and all the thrones of India.

Jo Fletcher
BOOKS